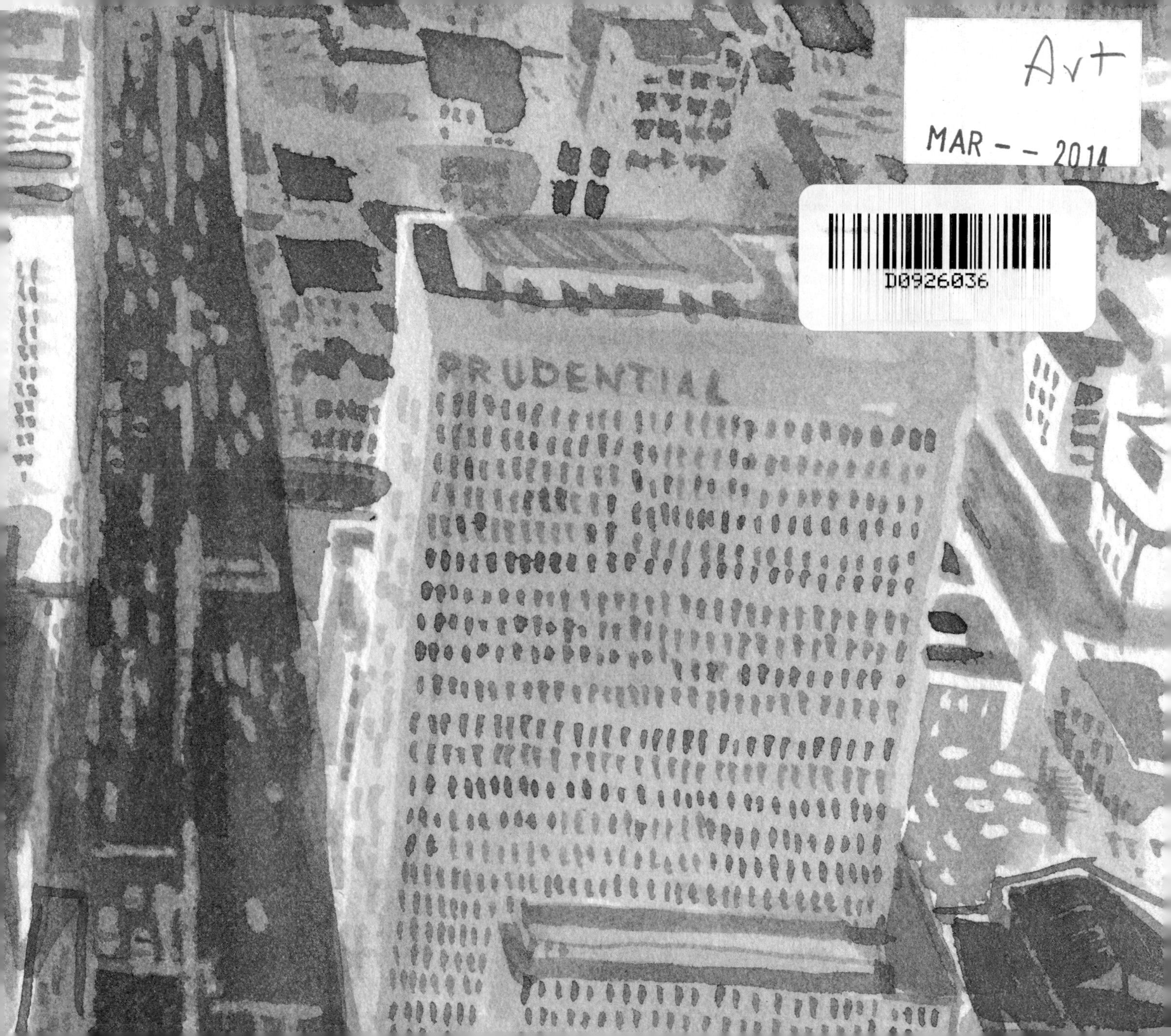
PRUDENTIAL

PUBLISHED BY SECRET ACRES
DESIGNED BY BRENDAN LEACH

SECRET ACRES
237 FLATBUSH AVE #331
BROOKLYN, NY 11217

PRINTED IN USA

LIBRARY OF CONGRESS CONTROL NUMBER: 2013939582
ISBN-13: 978-0-9888149-2-9
ISBN-10: 0-9888149-2-7

SAB023

IRON BOUND

BY
BRENDAN LEACH

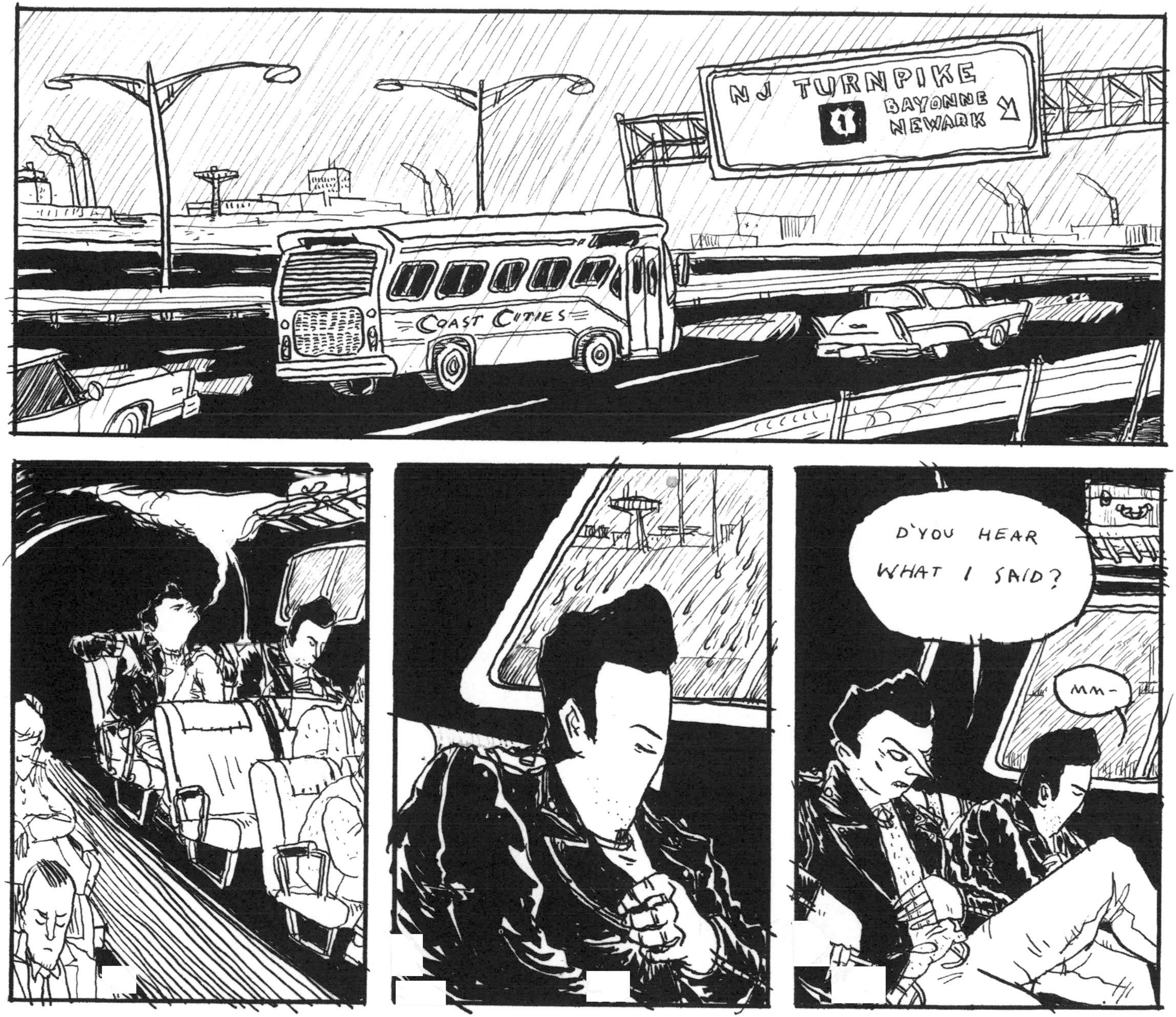
NJ TURNPIKE
1
BAYONNE
NEWARK
COAST CITIES
D'YOU HEAR WHAT I SAID?
MM-

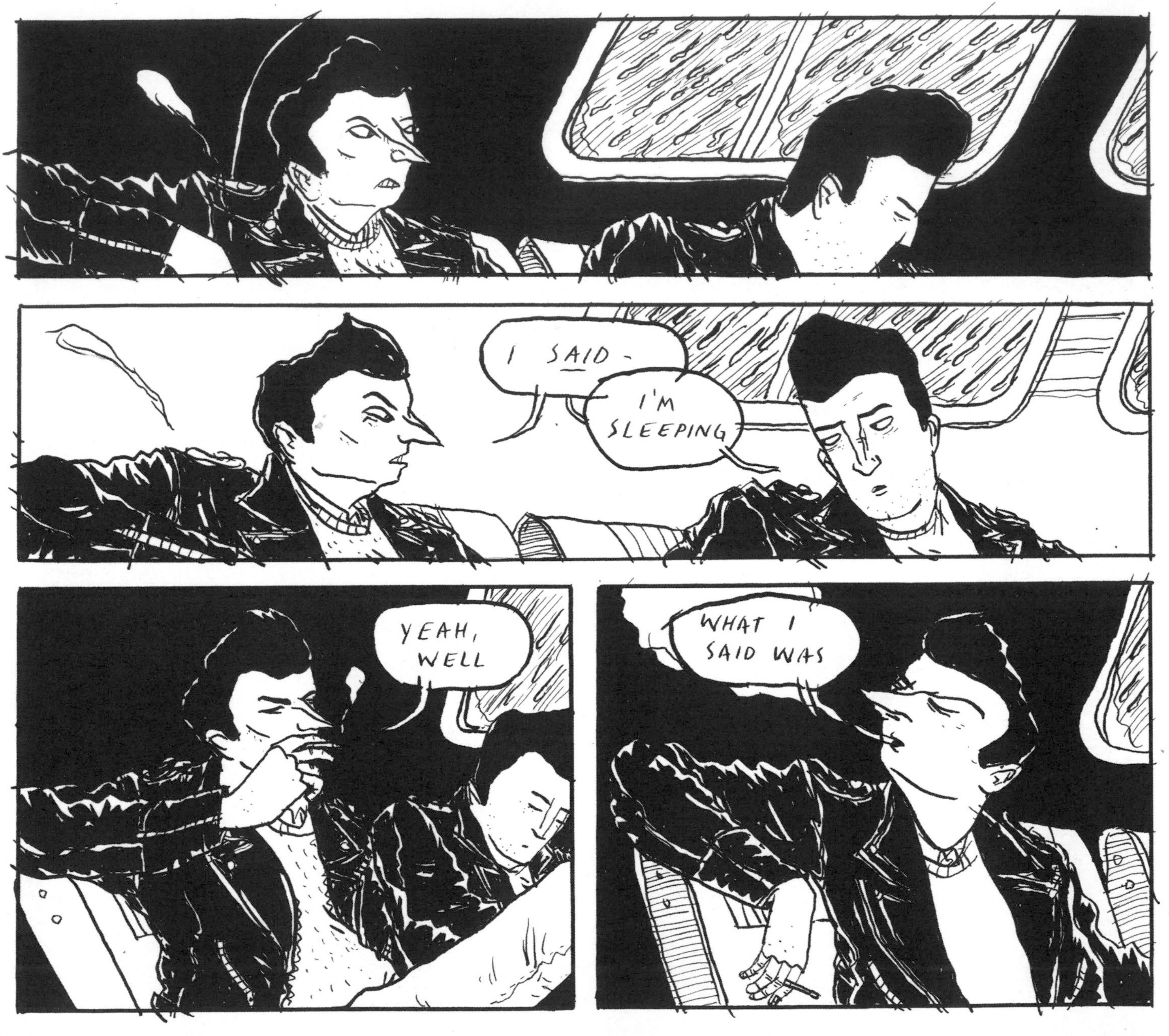

I SAID -
I'M SLEEPING
YEAH, WELL
WHAT I SAID WAS

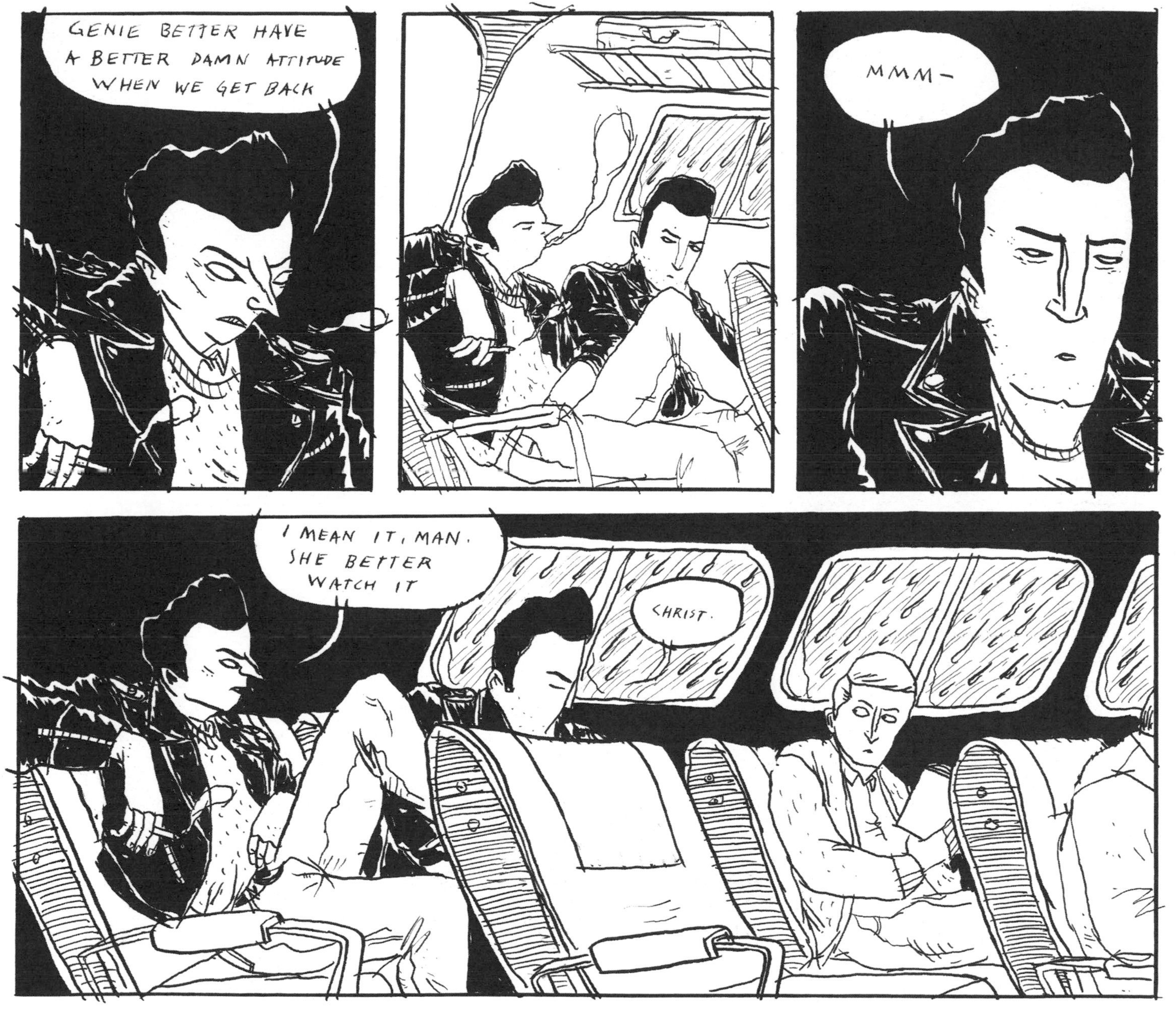
GENIE BETTER HAVE A BETTER DAMN ATTITUDE WHEN WE GET BACK
MMM-
I MEAN IT, MAN. SHE BETTER WATCH IT
CHRIST.

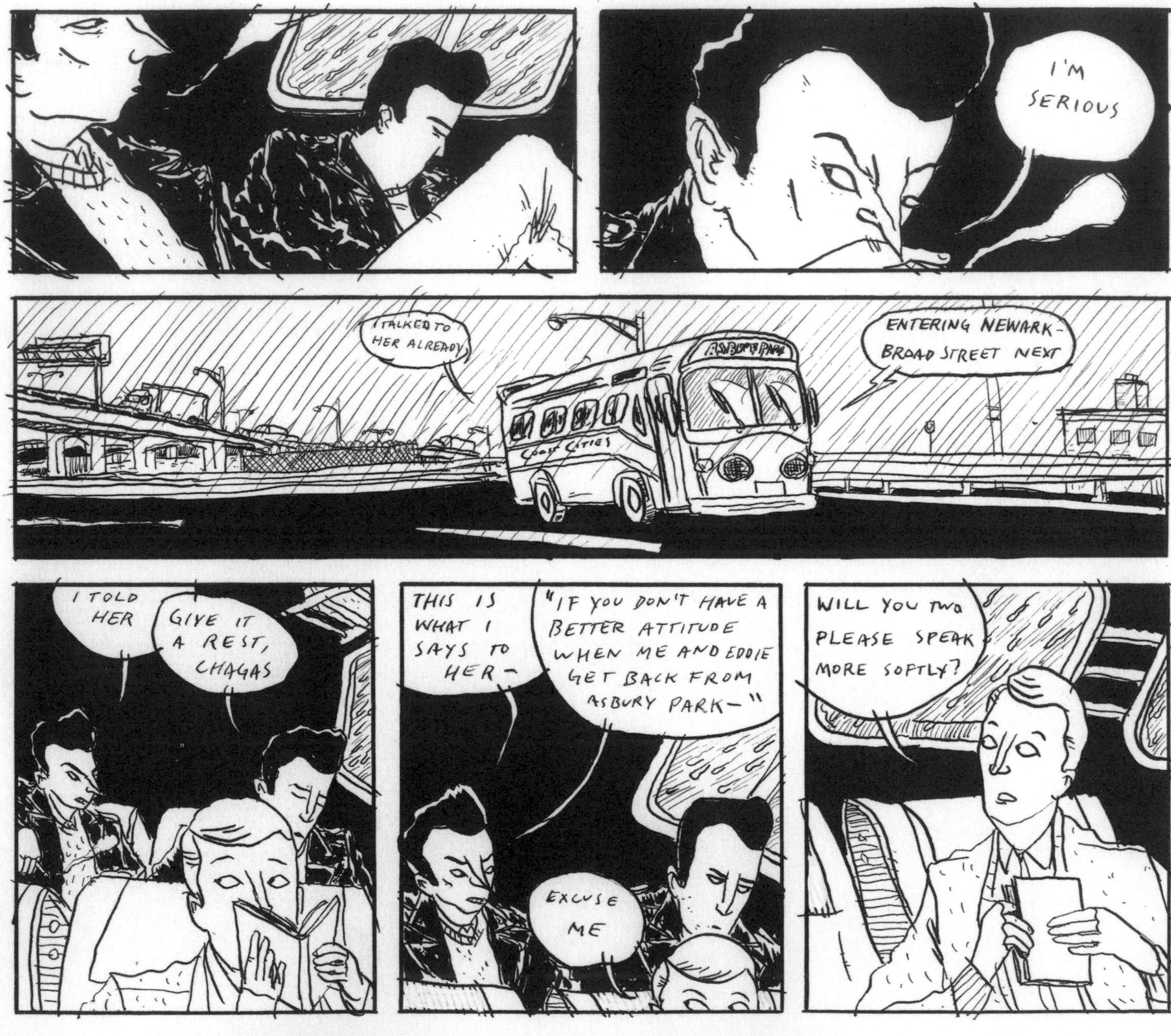
I'M SERIOUS
I TALKED TO HER ALREADY
ENTERING NEWARK- BROAD STREET NEXT
I TOLD HER
GIVE IT A REST, CHAGAS
THIS IS WHAT I SAYS TO HER-
"IF YOU DON'T HAVE A BETTER ATTITUDE WHEN ME AND EDDIE GET BACK FROM ASBURY PARK-"
EXCUSE ME
WILL YOU TWO PLEASE SPEAK MORE SOFTLY?

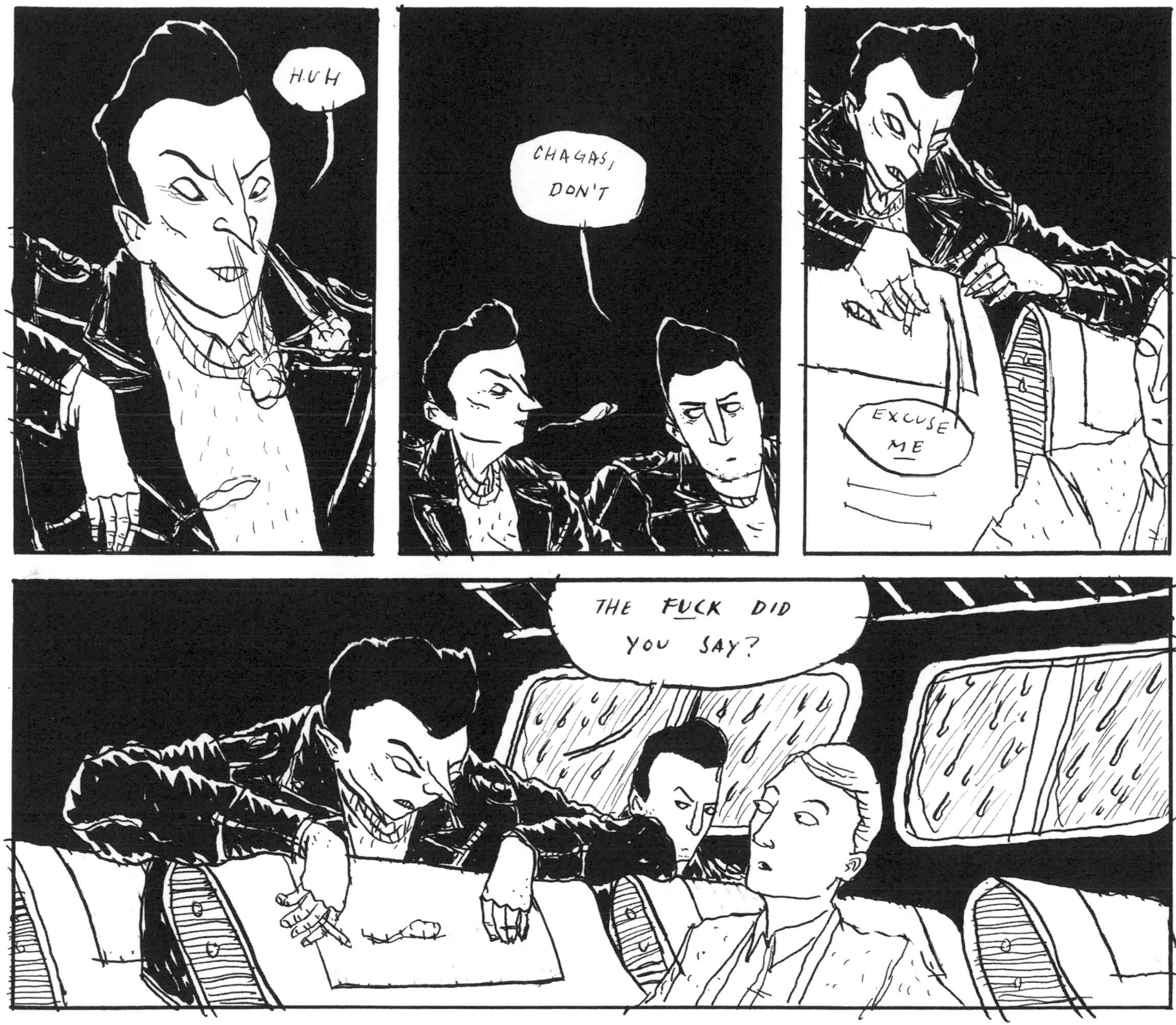
HUH
CHAGAS, DON'T
EXCUSE ME
THE FUCK DID YOU SAY?

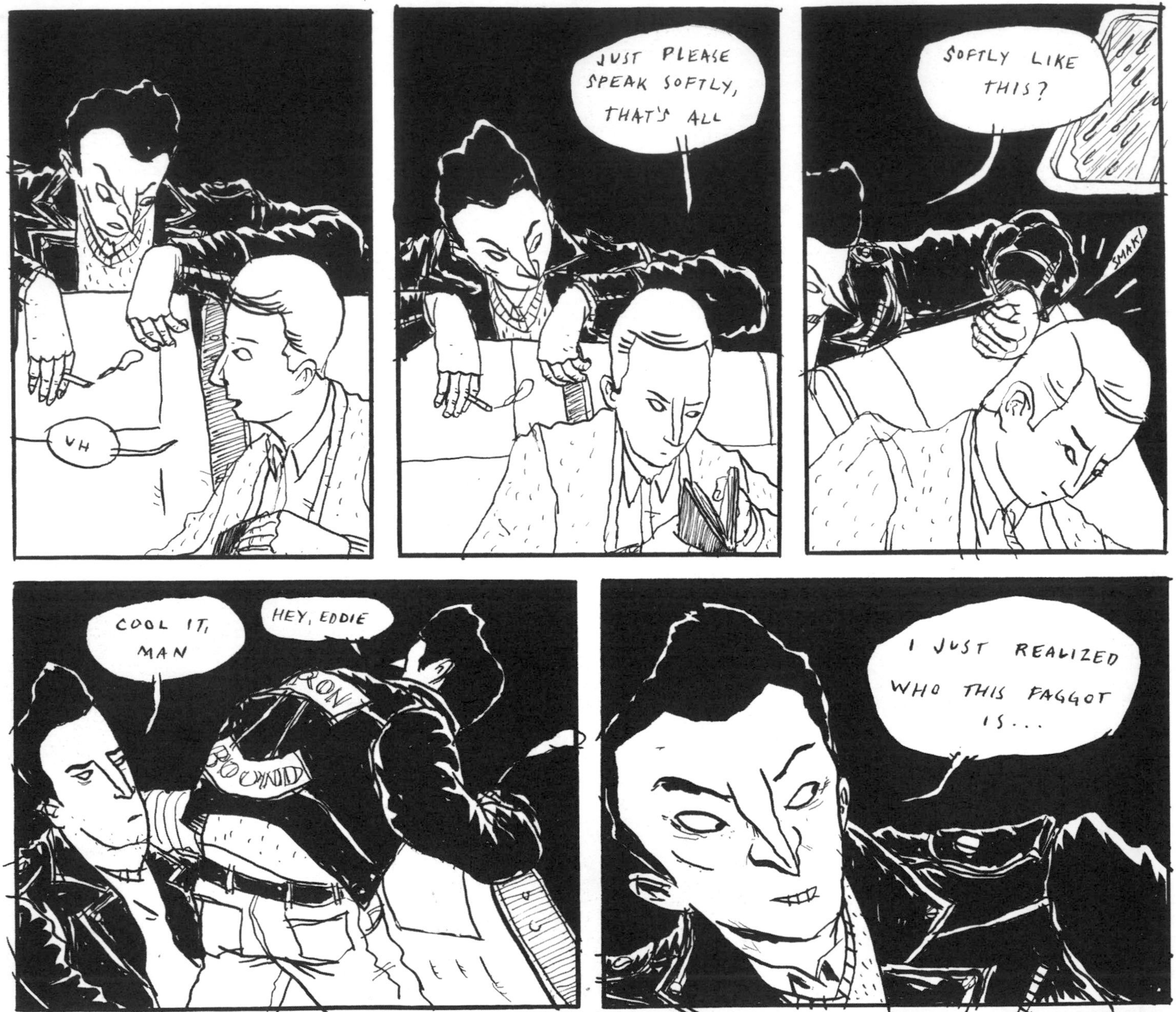
UH
JUST PLEASE SPEAK SOFTLY, THAT'S ALL
SOFTLY LIKE THIS?
SMAK!
COOL IT, MAN
HEY, EDDIE
RON
BOUND
I JUST REALIZED WHO THIS FAGGOT IS...

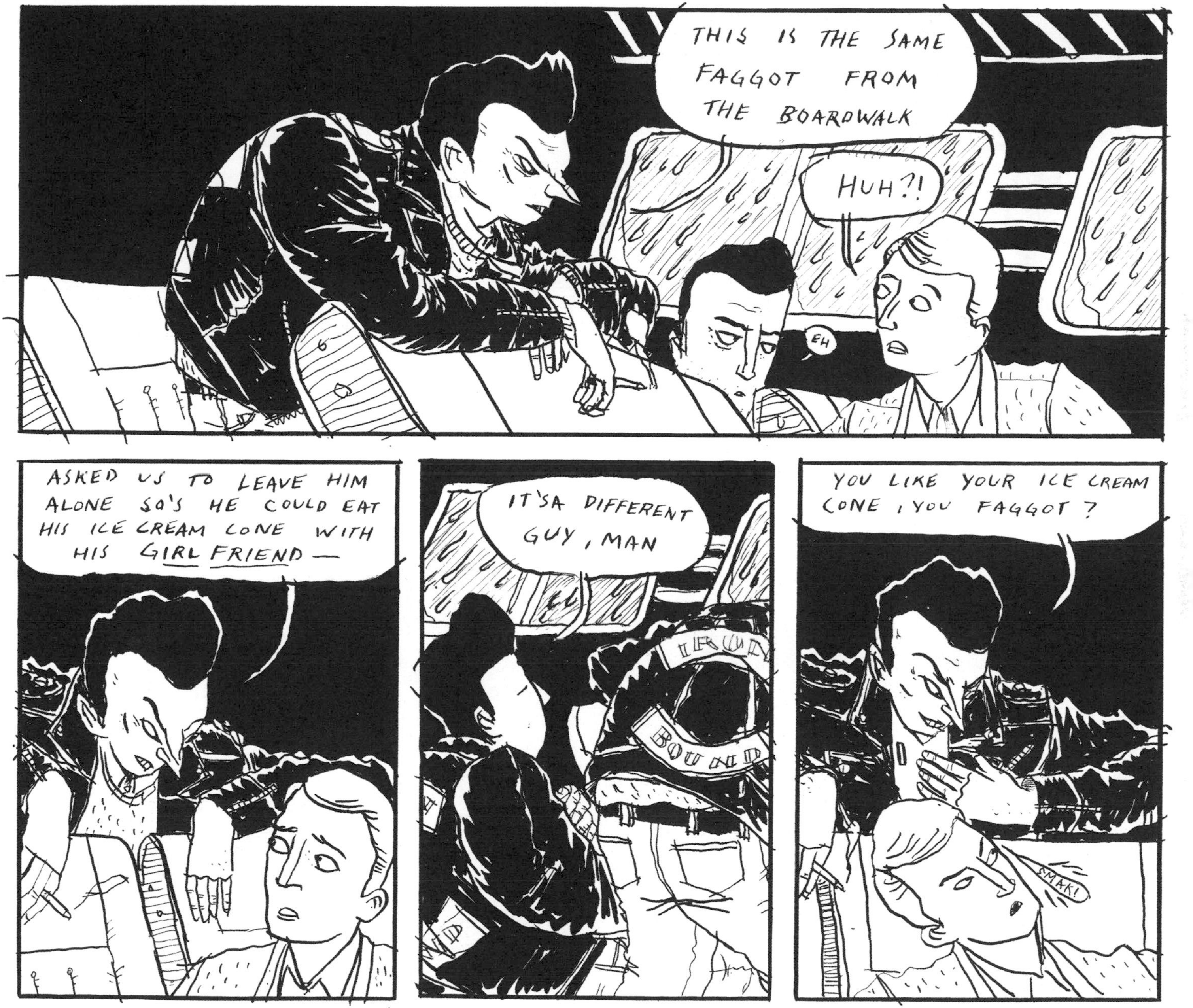
THIS IS THE SAME FAGGOT FROM THE BOARDWALK
HUH?!
EH
ASKED US TO LEAVE HIM ALONE SO'S HE COULD EAT HIS ICE CREAM CONE WITH HIS GIRL FRIEND —
IT'SA DIFFERENT GUY, MAN
BOUND
YOU LIKE YOUR ICE CREAM CONE, YOU FAGGOT?
SMAK!

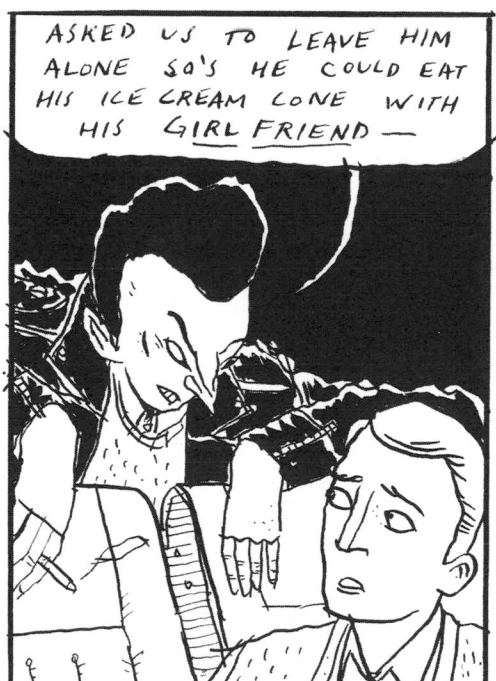

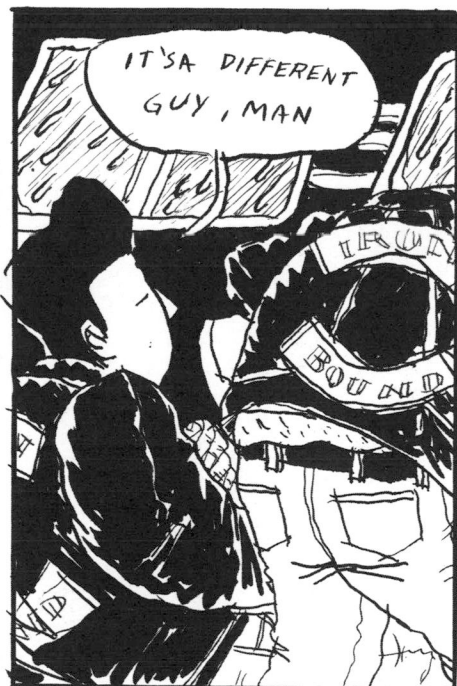

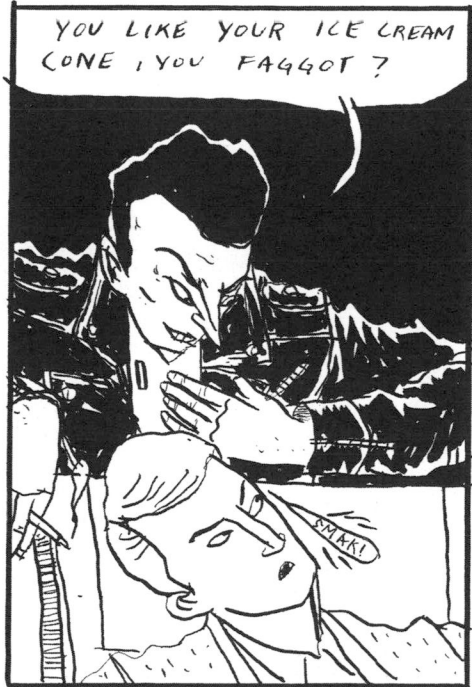

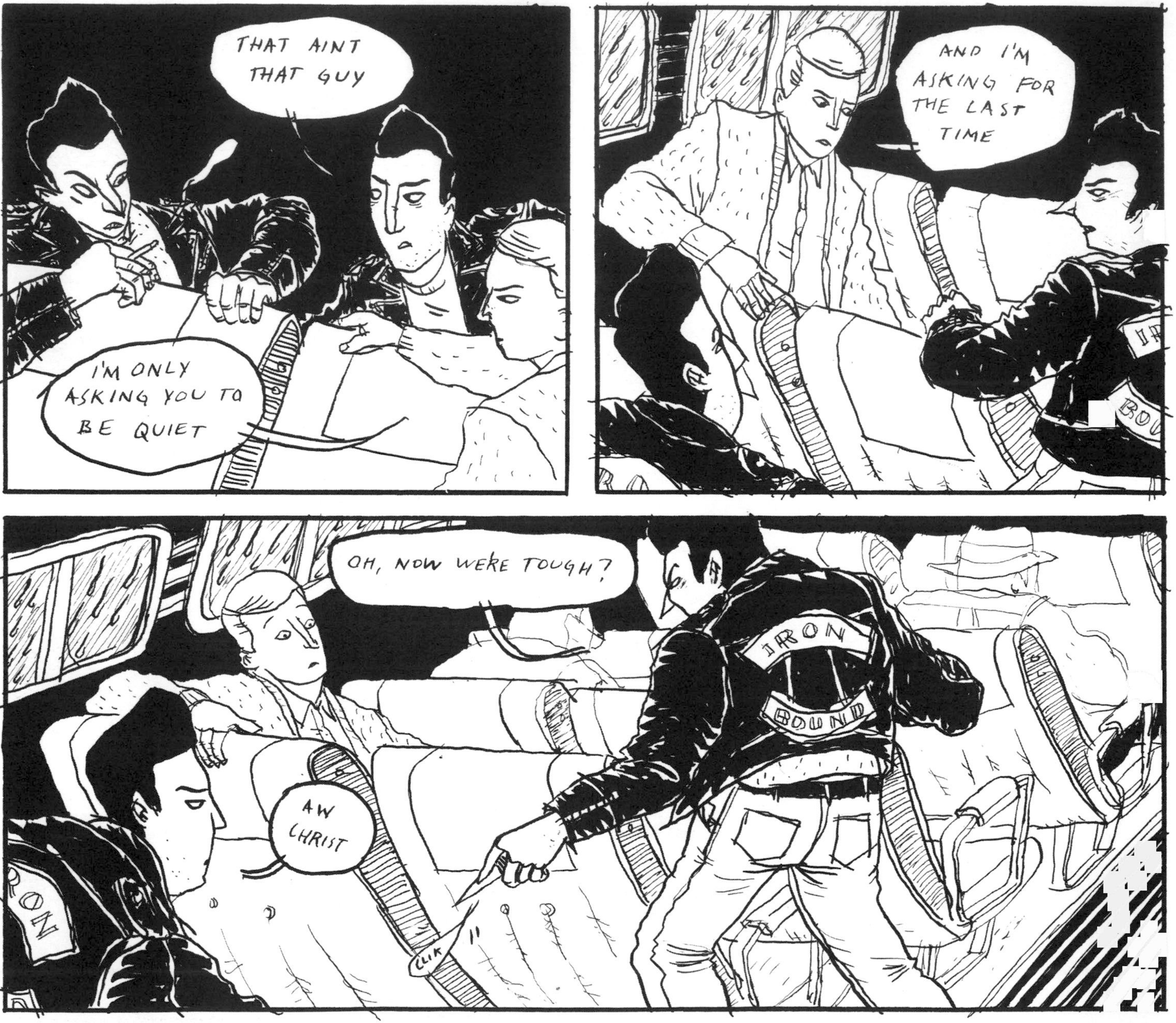
THAT AINT THAT GUY
I'M ONLY ASKING YOU TO BE QUIET
AND I'M ASKING FOR THE LAST TIME
OH, NOW WERE TOUGH?
IRON
BOUND
AW CHRIST
CLIK

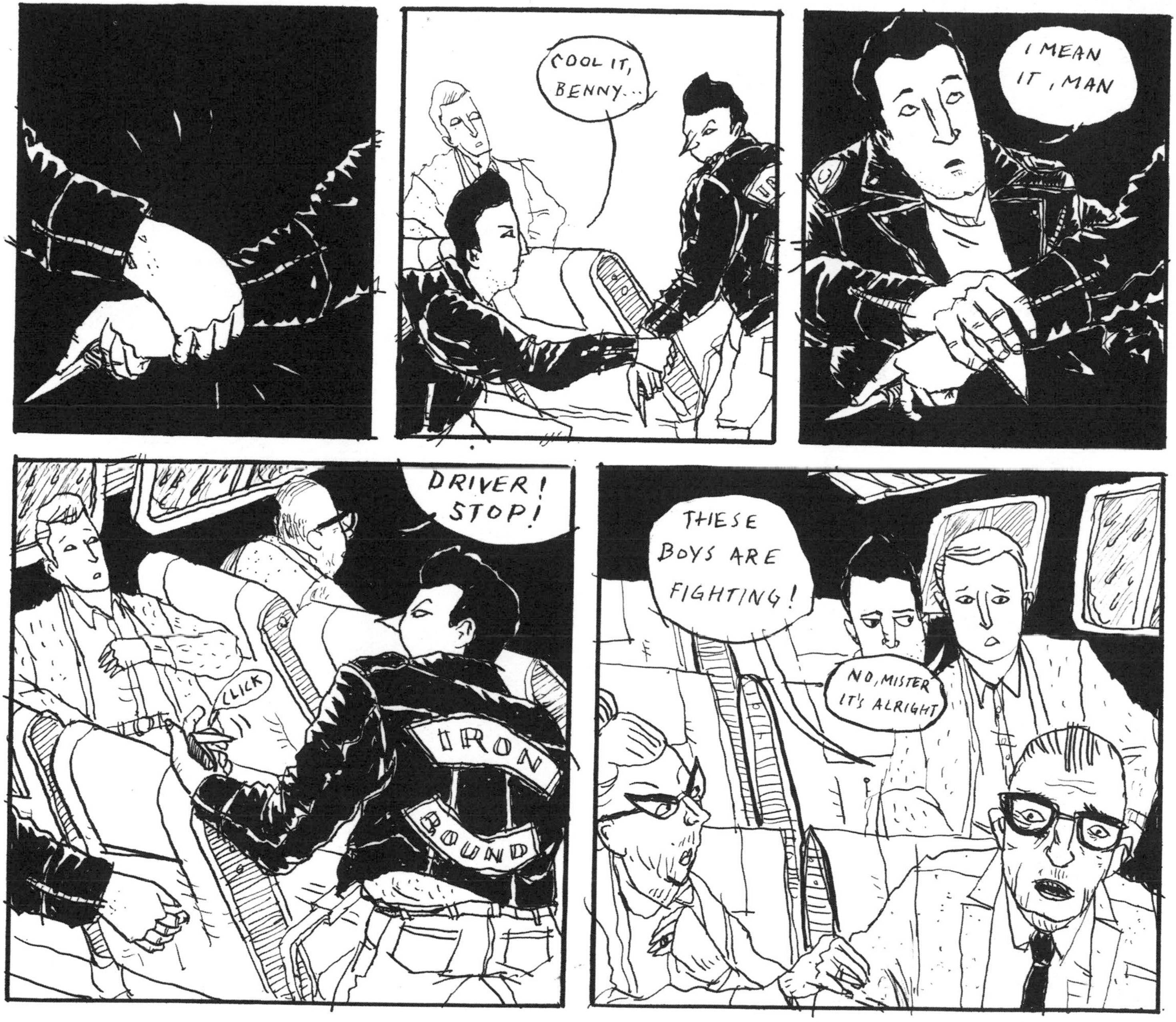

COOL IT, BENNY...
I MEAN IT, MAN
DRIVER! STOP!
CLICK
IRON
BOUND
THESE BOYS ARE FIGHTING!
NO, MISTER IT'S ALRIGHT

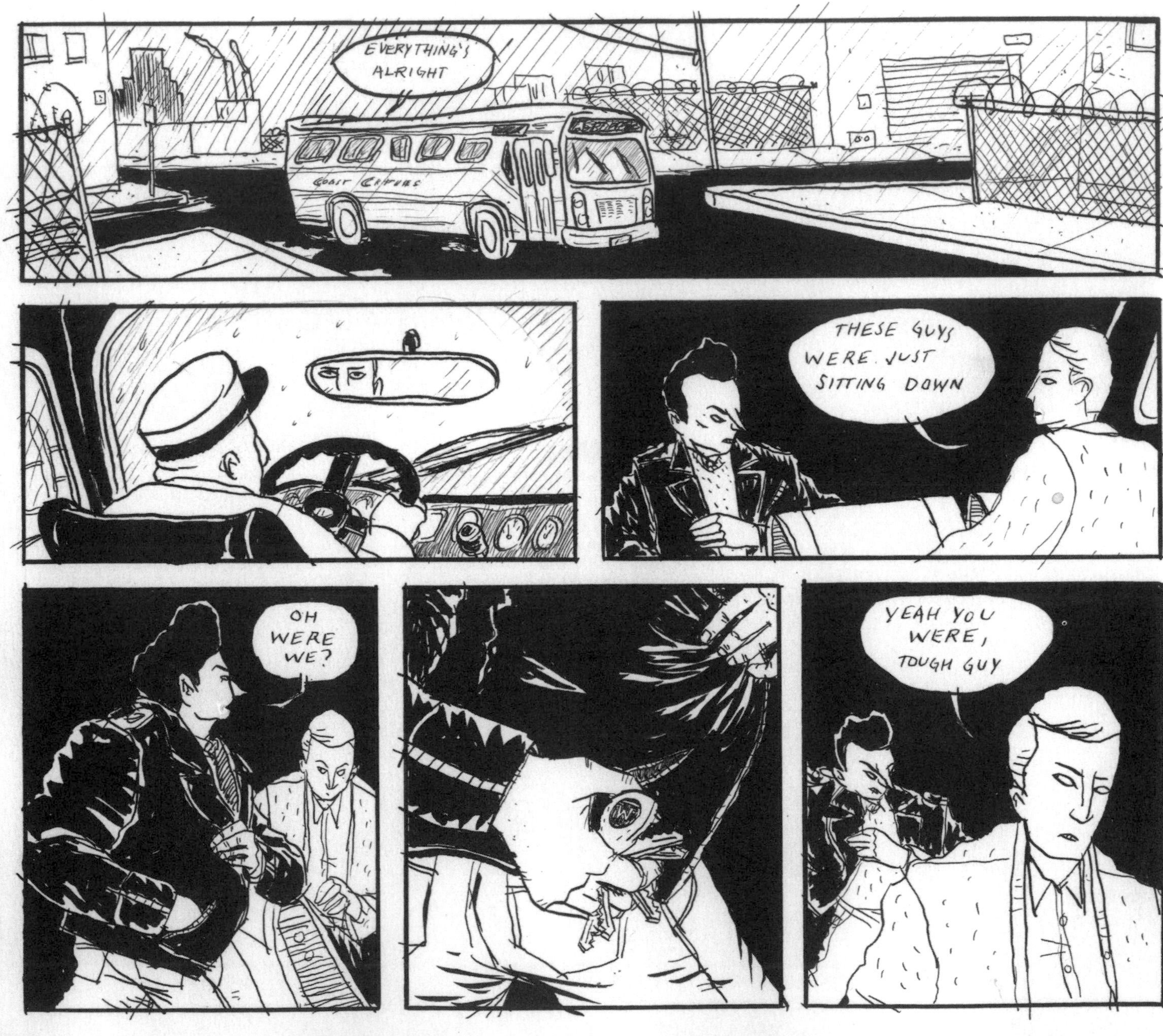
EVERYTHING'S ALRIGHT
THESE GUYS WERE JUST SITTING DOWN
OH WERE WE?
YEAH YOU WERE, TOUGH GUY

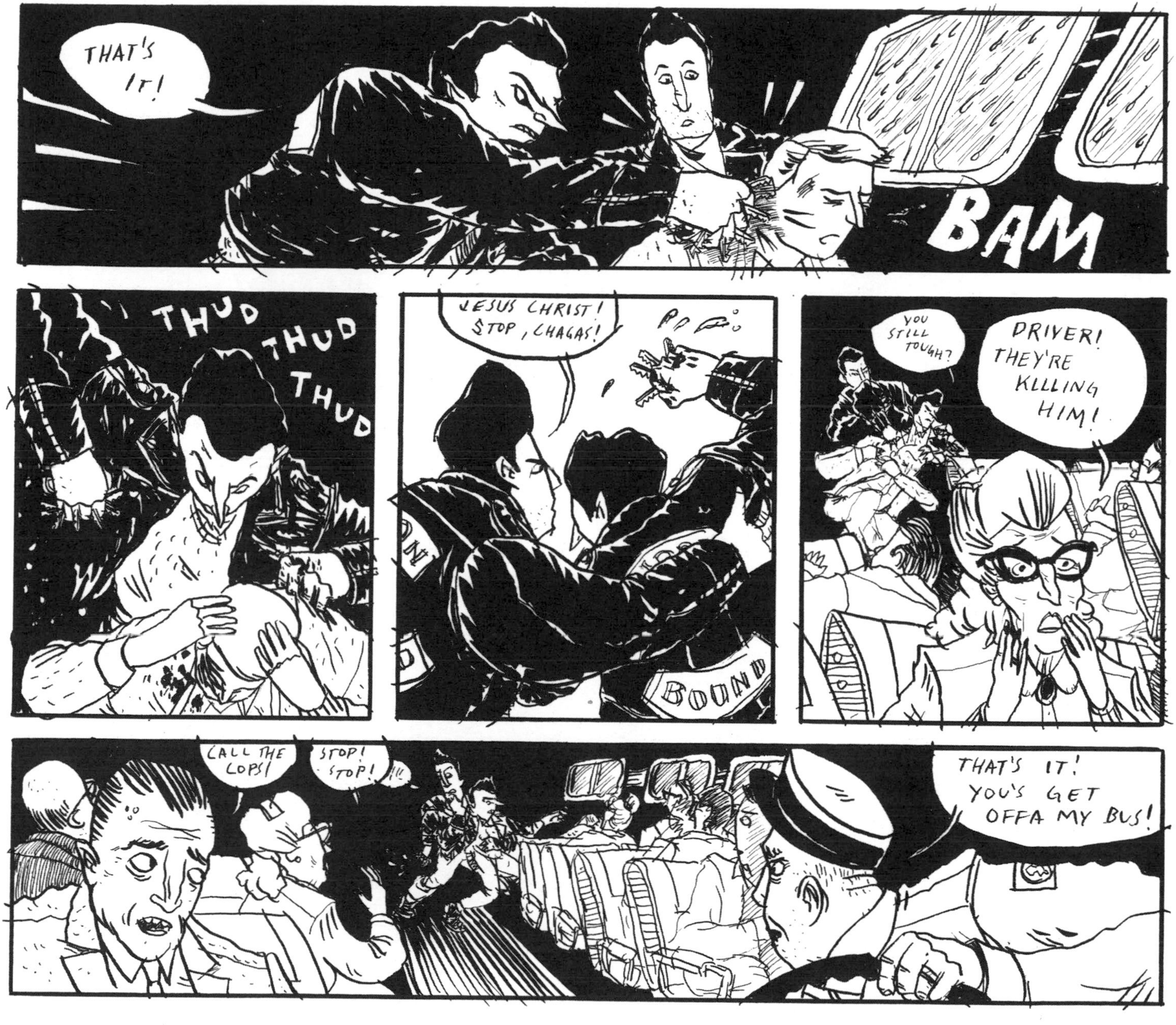
THAT'S IT!
BAM
THUD THUD THUD
JESUS CHRIST! STOP, CHAGAS!
BOUND
YOU STILL TOUGH?
DRIVER! THEY'RE KILLING HIM!
CALL THE COPS!
STOP! STOP!
THAT'S IT! YOU'S GET OFFA MY BUS!

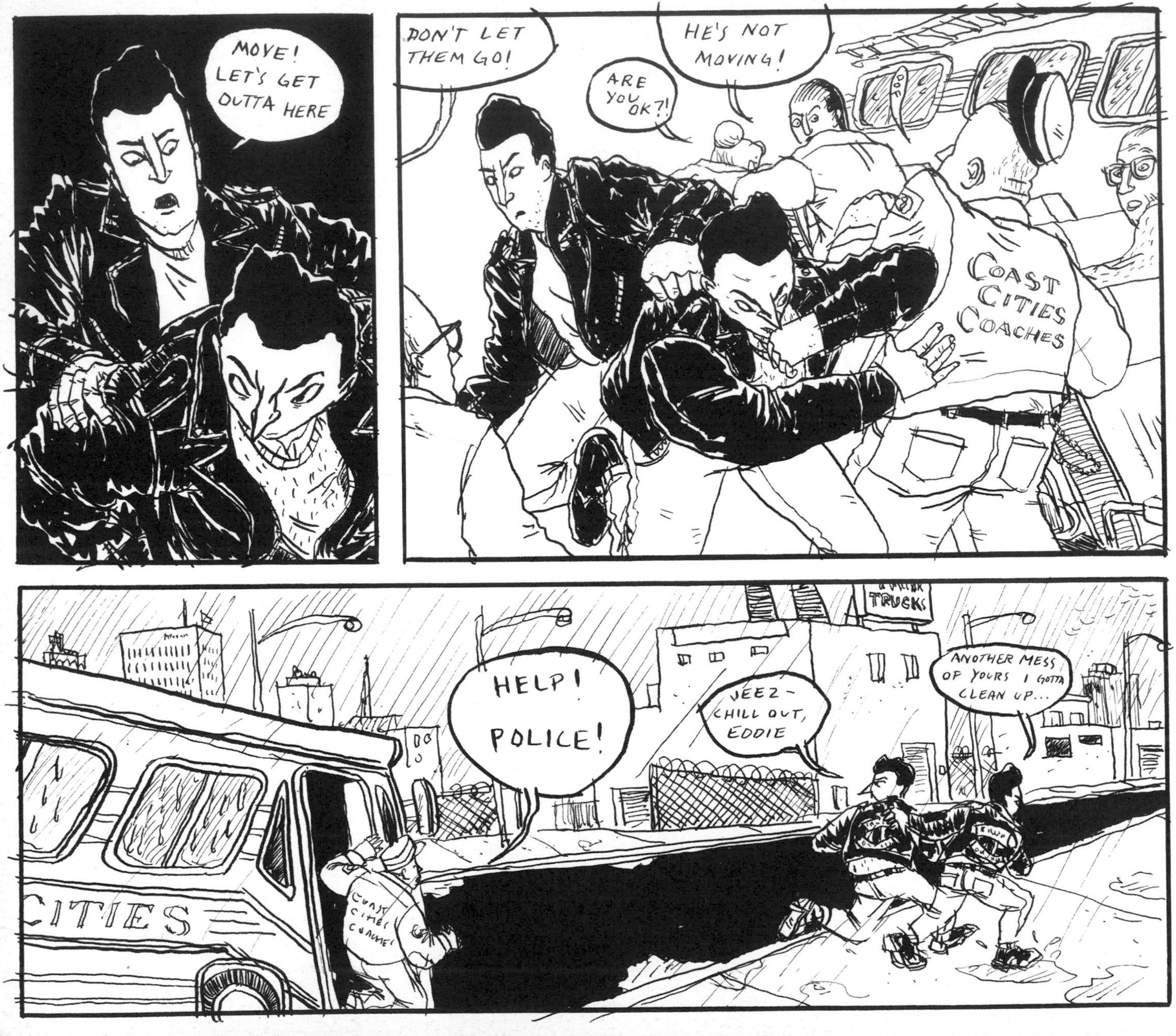
MOVE! LET'S GET OUTTA HERE
DON'T LET THEM GO!
ARE YOU OK?!
HE'S NOT MOVING!
COAST CITIES COACHES
TRUCKS
CITIES
COAST CITIES COACHES
HELP! POLICE!
JEEZ- CHILL OUT, EDDIE
ANOTHER MESS OF YOURS I GOTTA CLEAN UP...

IRON BOUND

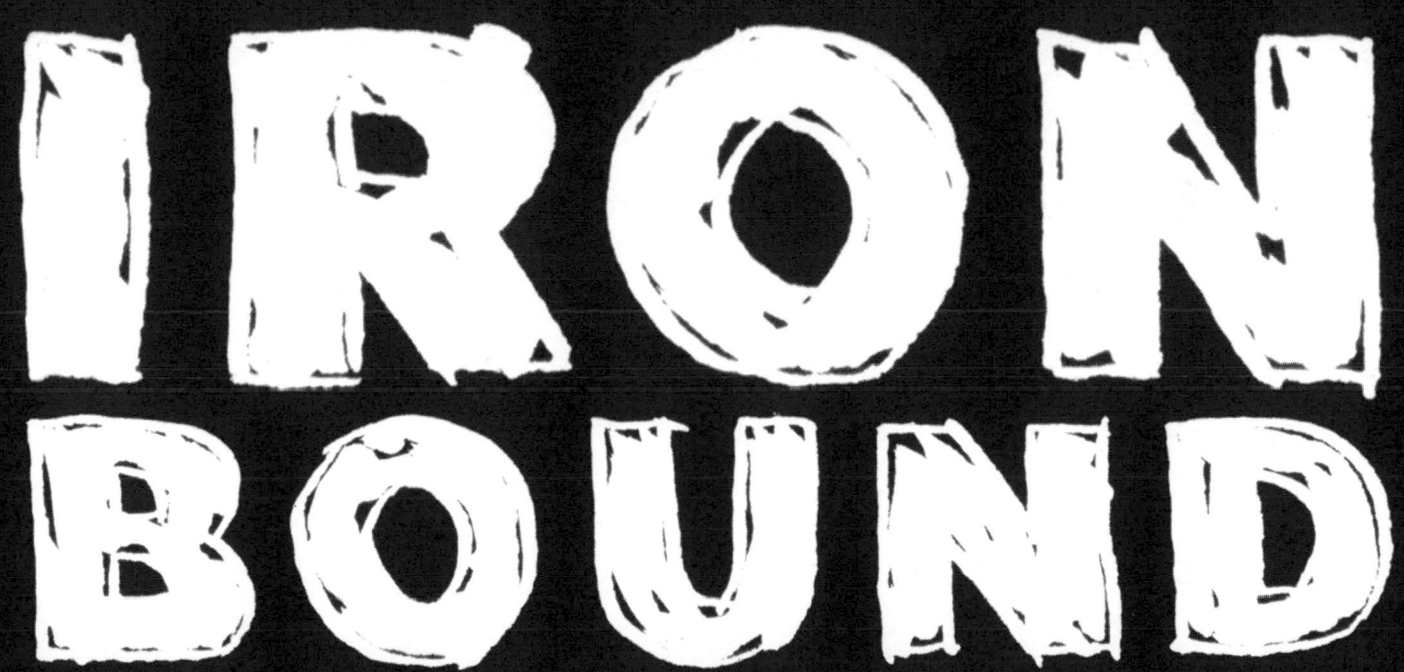

NEWARK, NJ 1961

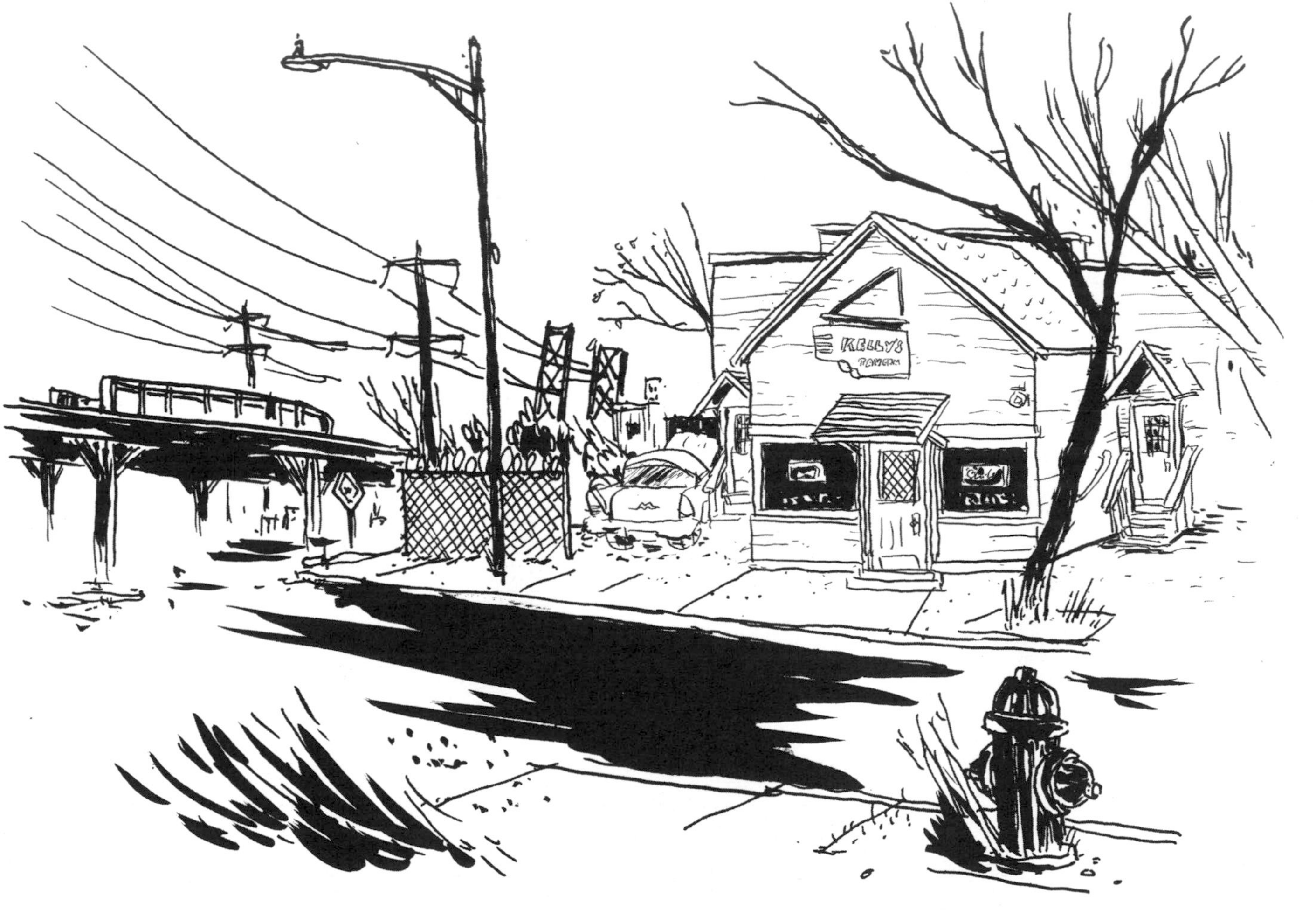
KELLY'S

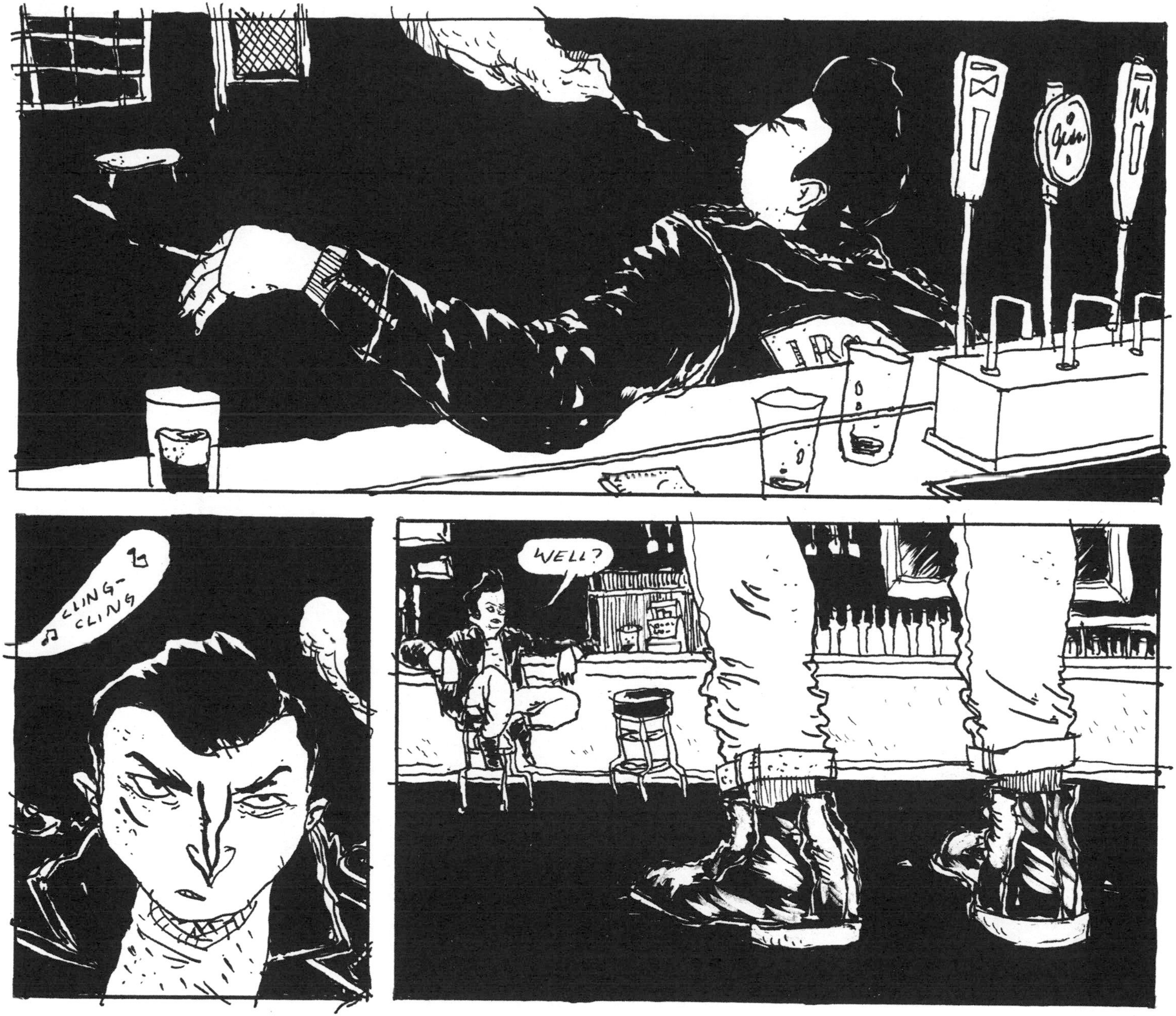
CLING-CLING
WELL?

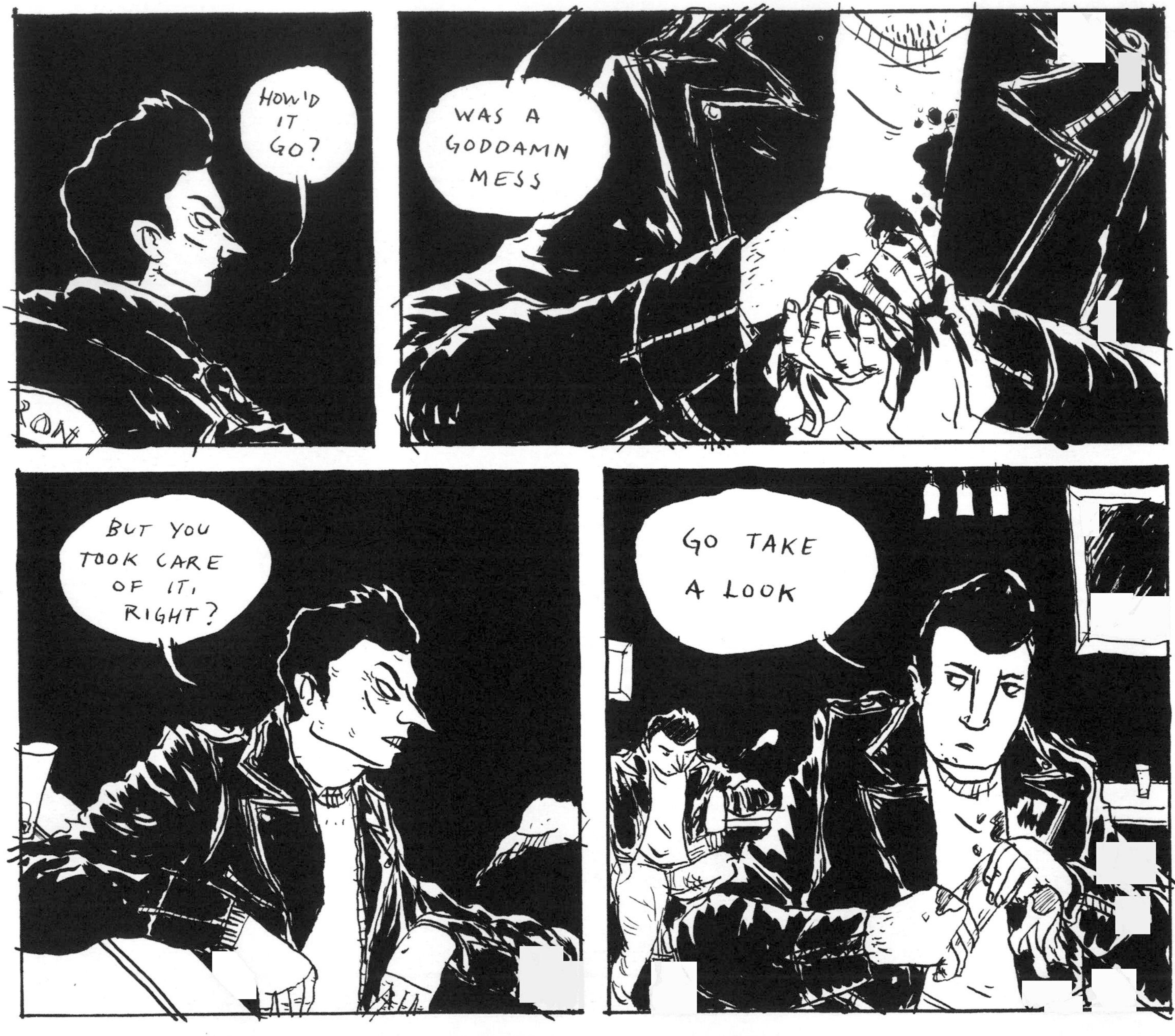
HOW'D IT GO?
WAS A GODDAMN MESS
BUT YOU TOOK CARE OF IT, RIGHT?
GO TAKE A LOOK

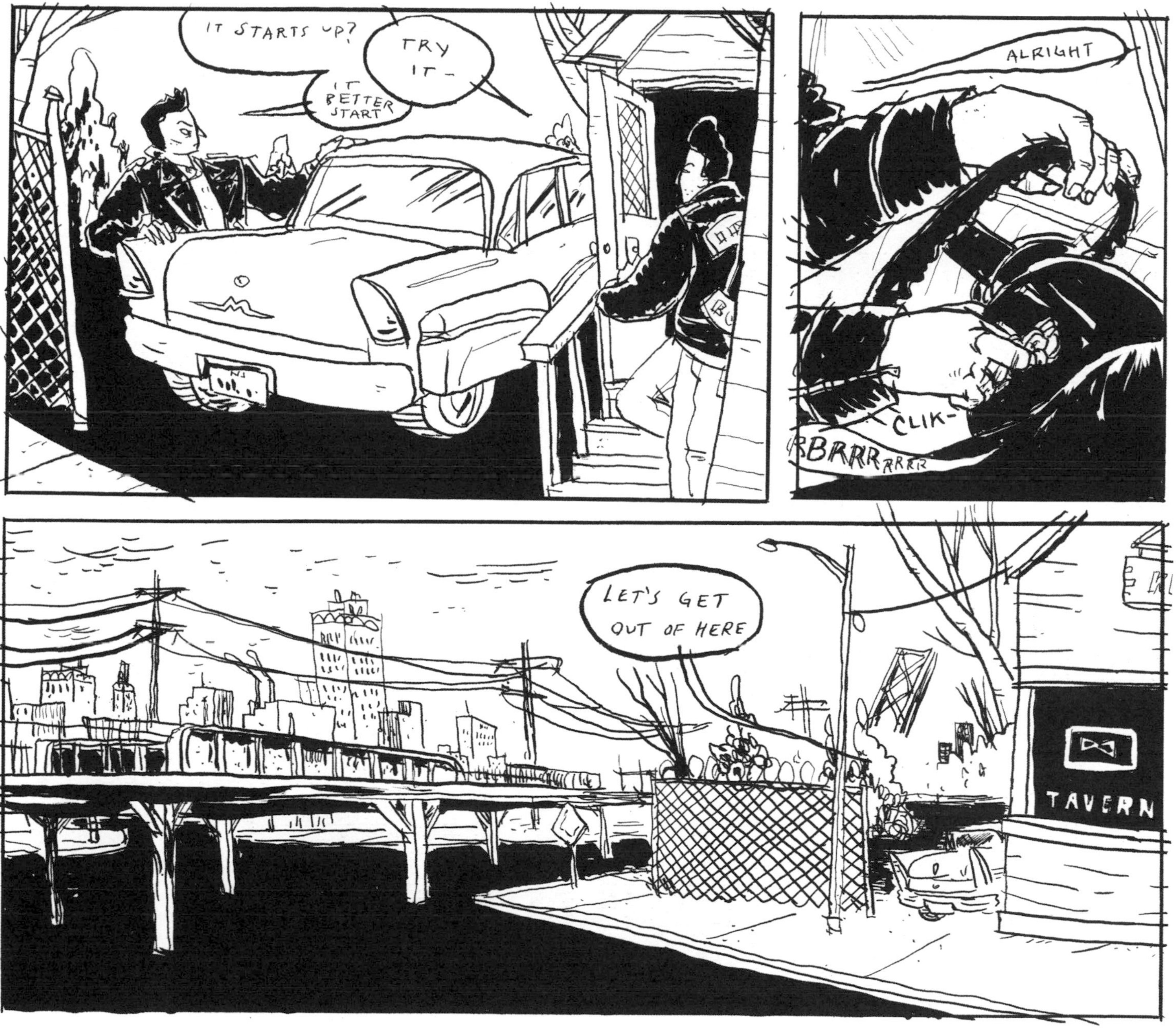
IT STARTS UP?
TRY IT -
IT BETTER START
ALRIGHT
CLIK-
BRRRRRRRR
LET'S GET OUT OF HERE
TAVERN

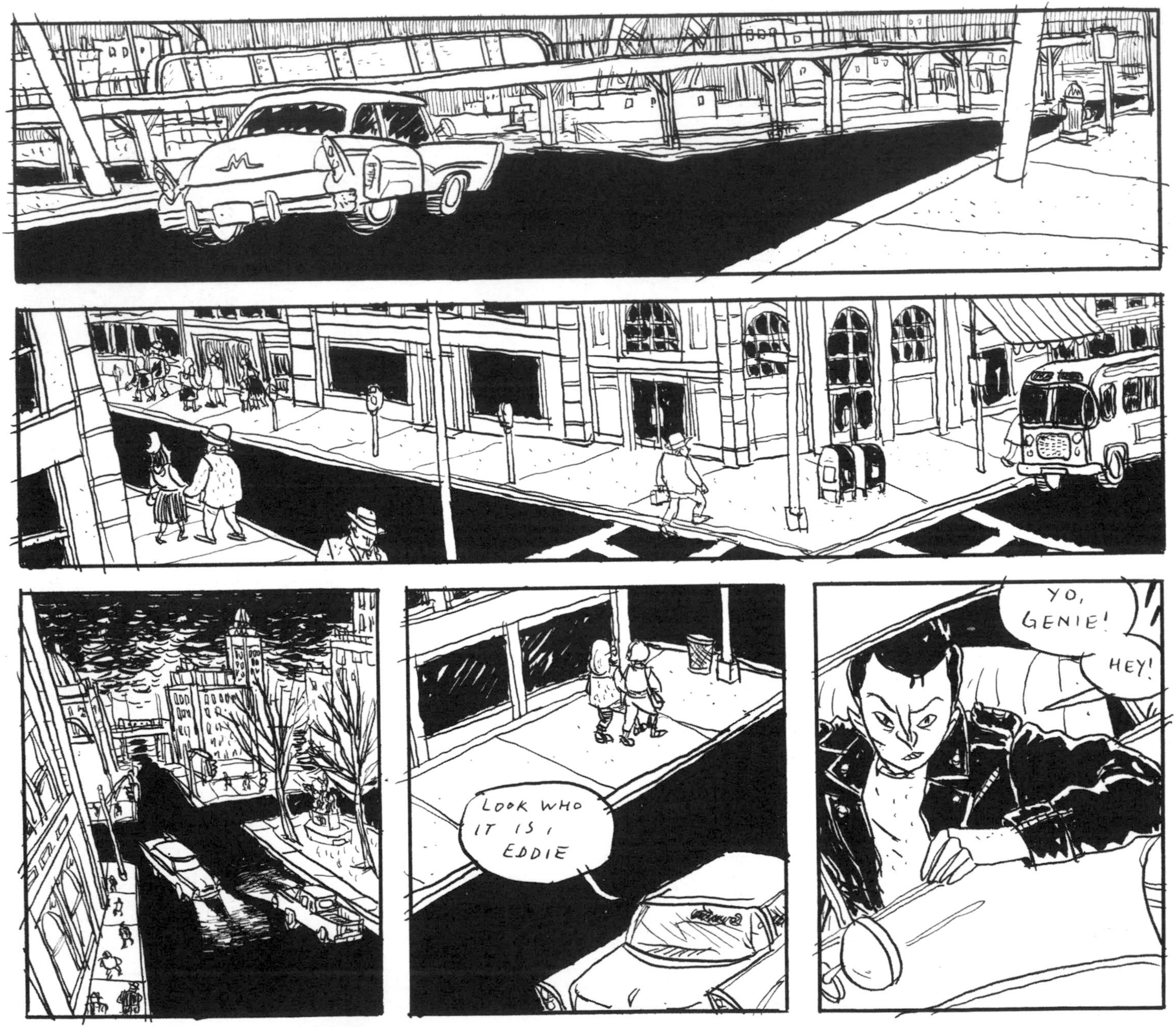
LOOK WHO IT IS, EDDIE
YO, GENIE!
HEY!

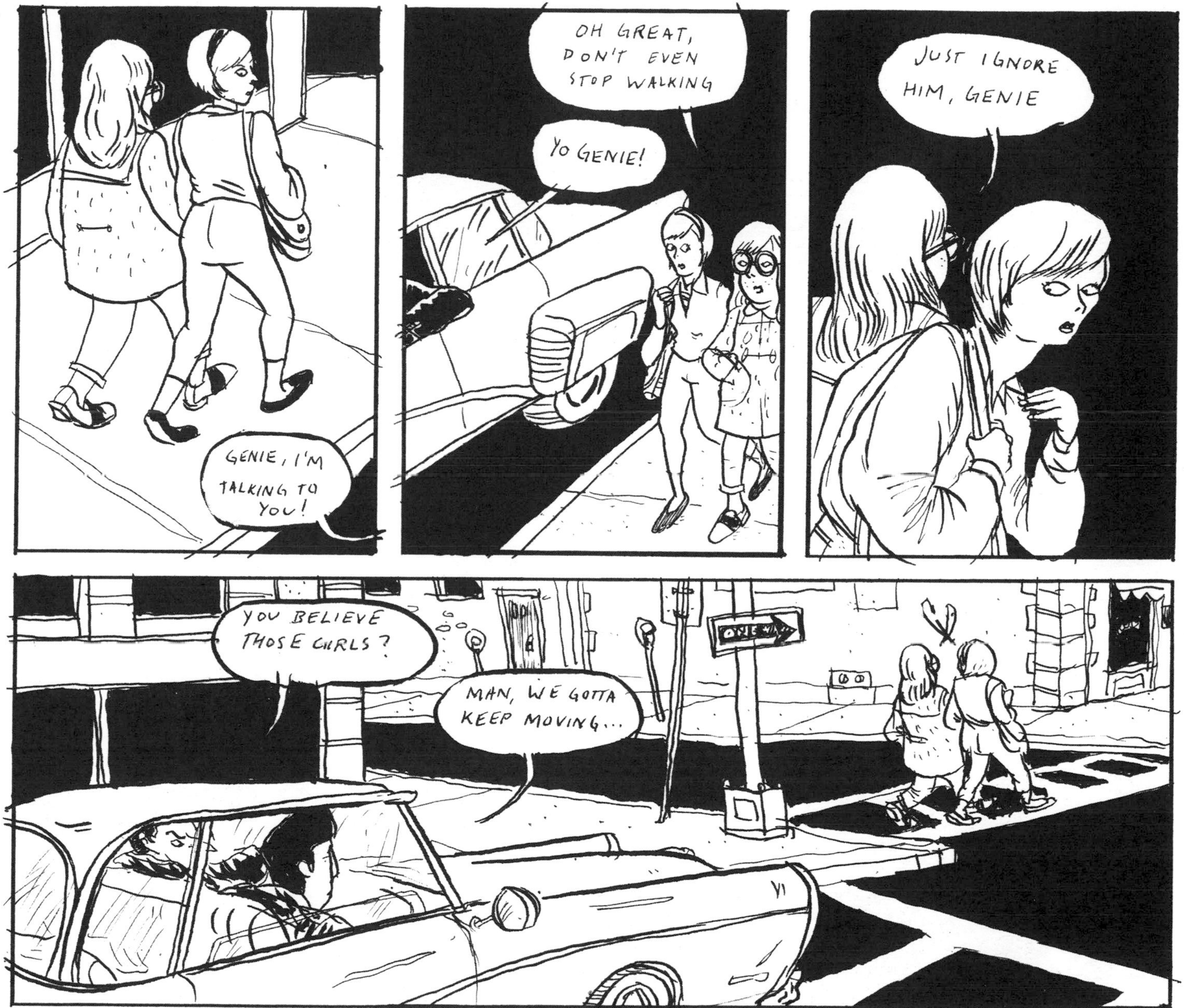
GENIE, I'M TALKING TO YOU!
Yo GENIE!
OH GREAT, DON'T EVEN STOP WALKING
JUST IGNORE HIM, GENIE
YOU BELIEVE THOSE GIRLS?
MAN, WE GOTTA KEEP MOVING...
ONE WAY

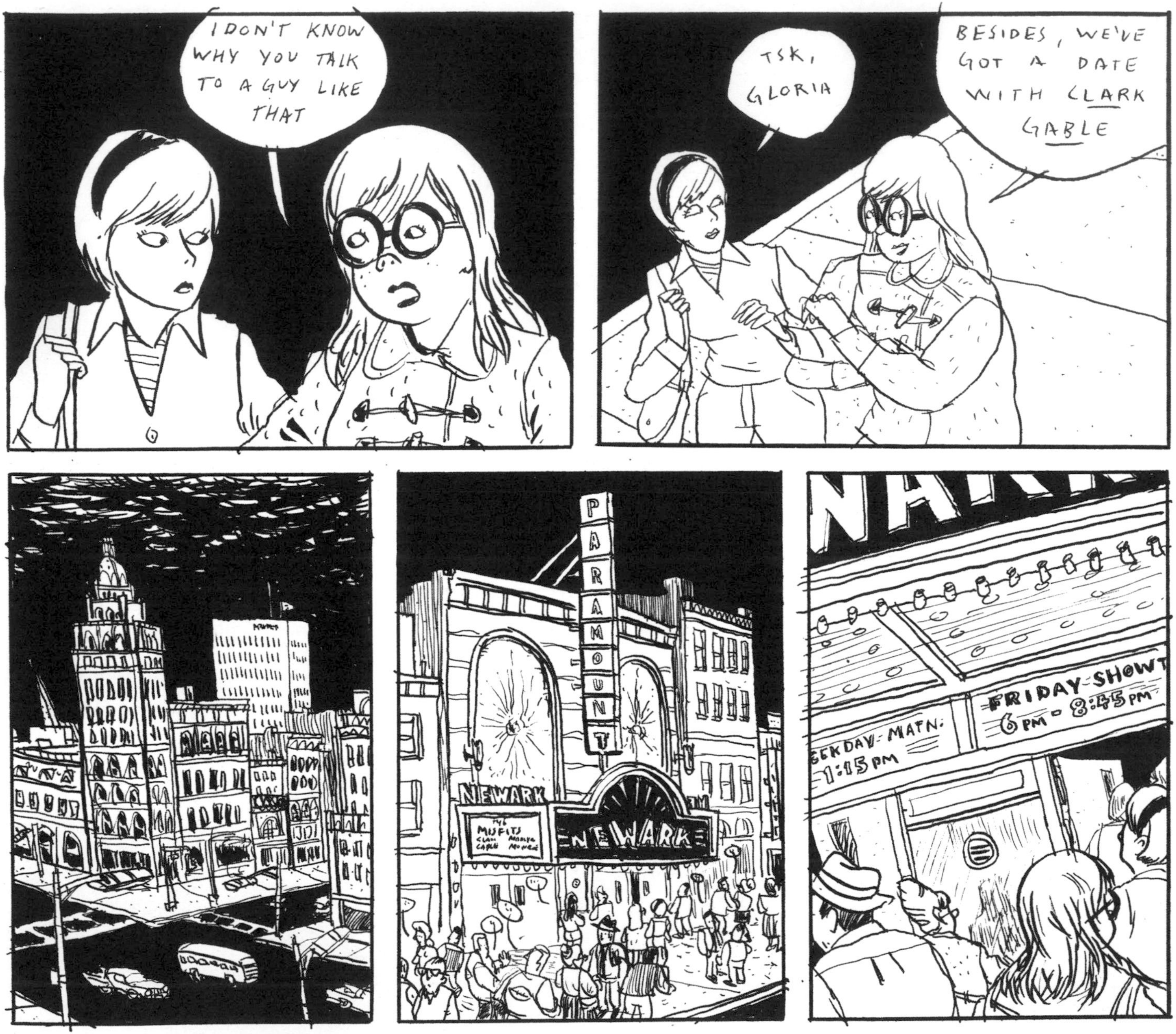
I DON'T KNOW WHY YOU TALK TO A GUY LIKE THAT
TSK, GLORIA
BESIDES, WE'VE GOT A DATE WITH CLARK GABLE
PARAMOUNT
NEWARK
NEWARK
EKDAY-MATN. 1:15 PM
FRIDAY-SHOWT
6 PM - 8:45 PM

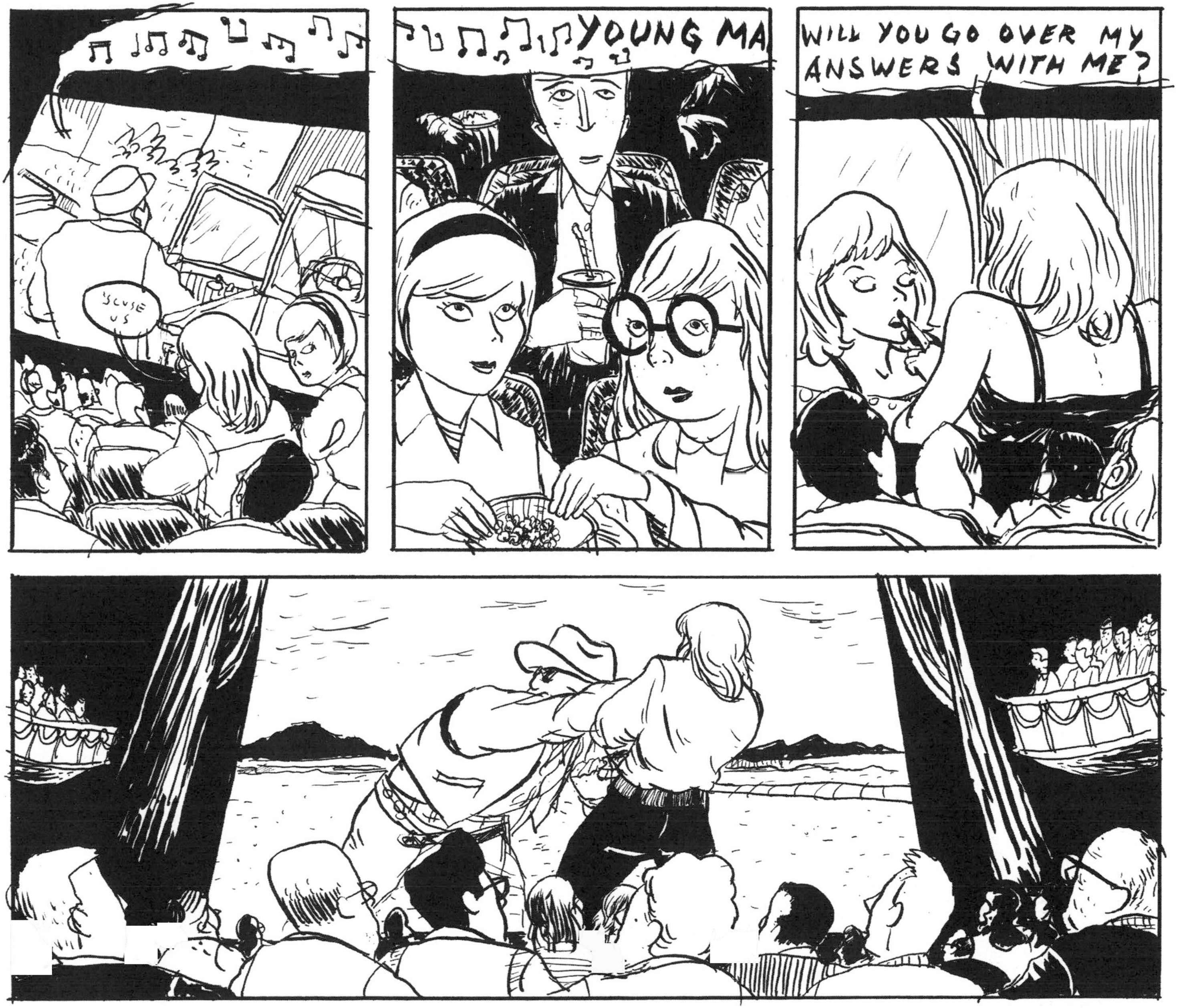

'SCUSE US
YOUNG MA
WILL YOU GO OVER MY ANSWERS WITH ME?

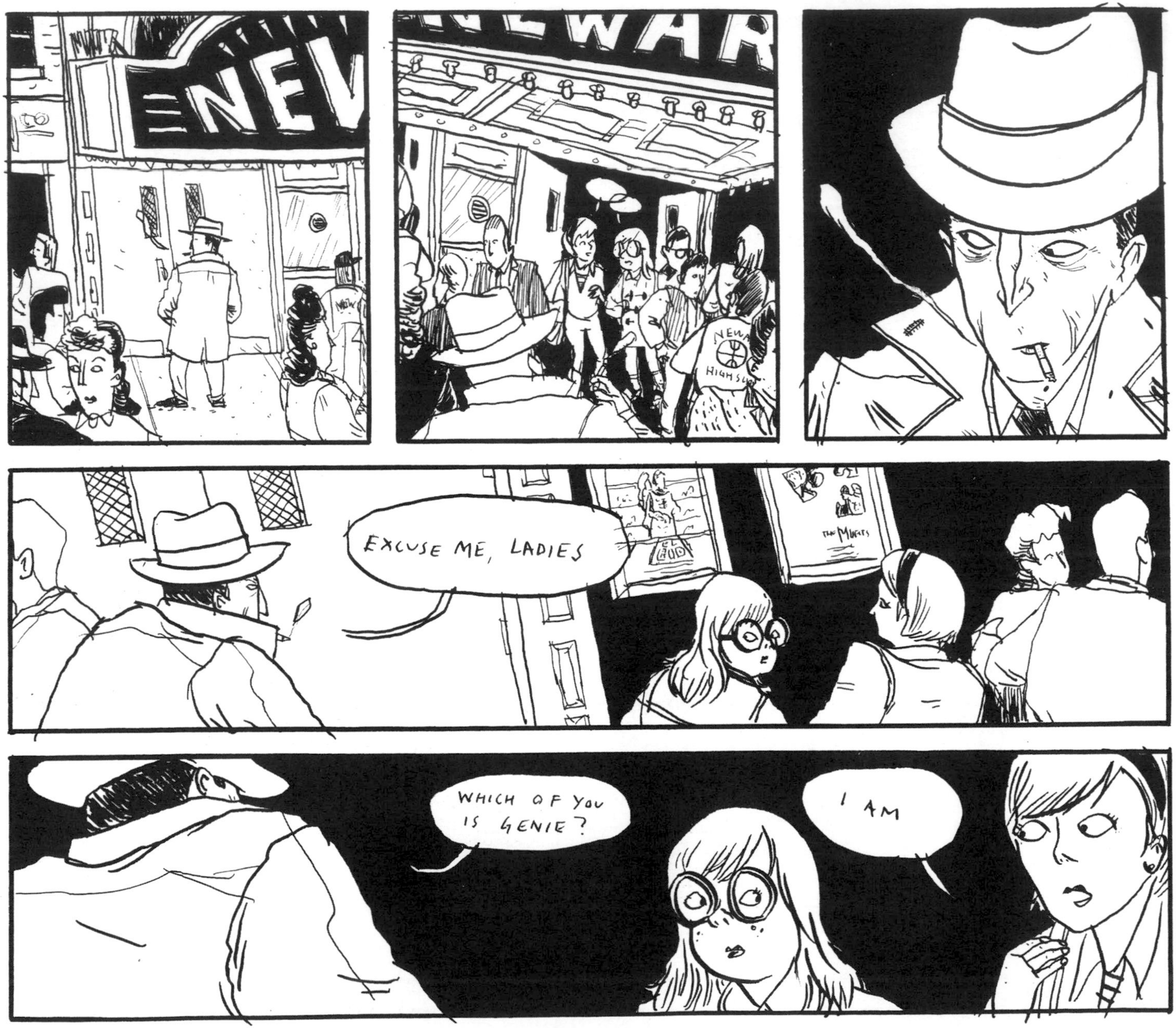
EXCUSE ME, LADIES
WHICH OF YOU IS GENIE?
I AM

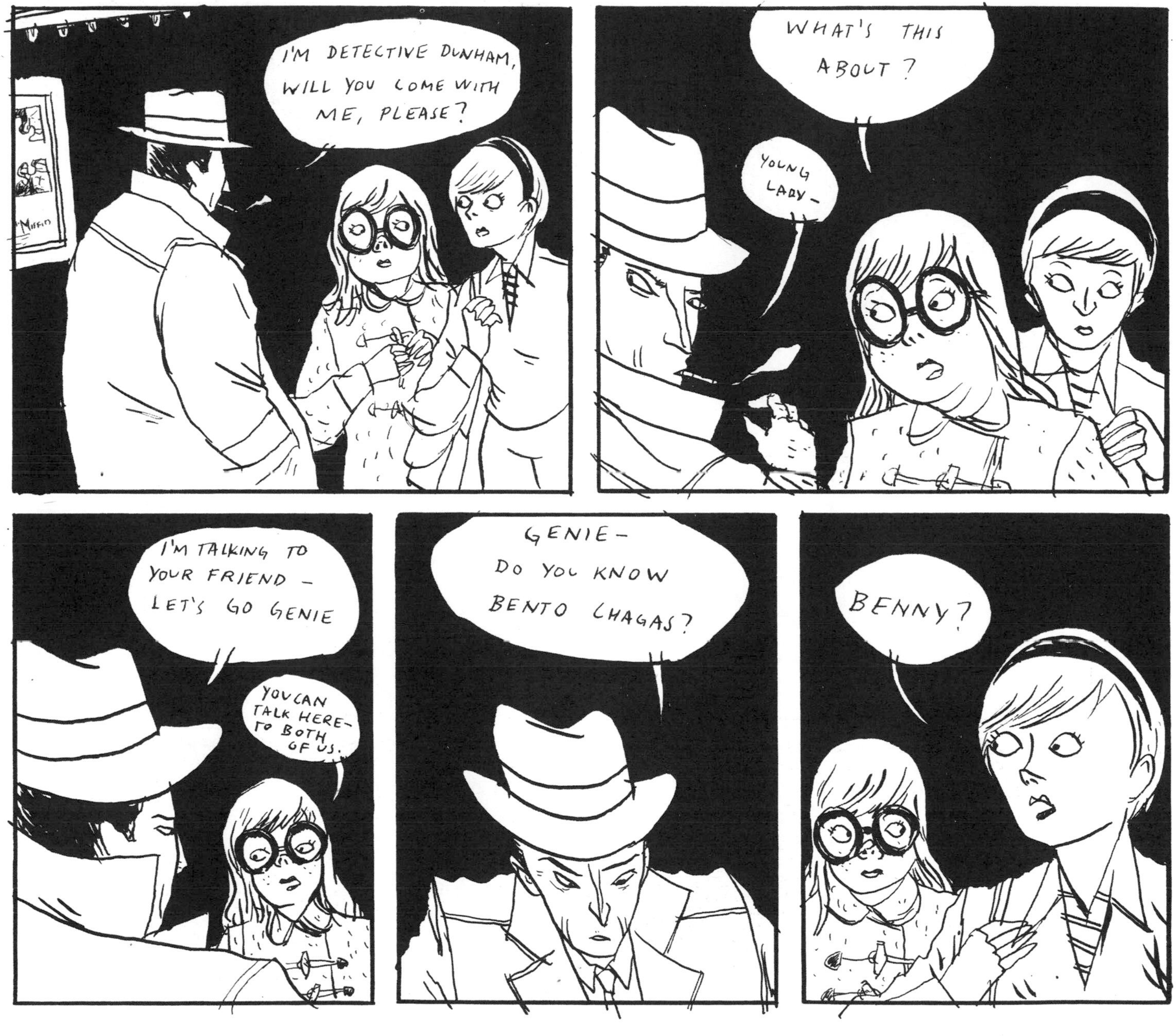
I'M DETECTIVE DUNHAM, WILL YOU COME WITH ME, PLEASE?
WHAT'S THIS ABOUT?
YOUNG LADY-
I'M TALKING TO YOUR FRIEND - LET'S GO GENIE
YOU CAN TALK HERE- TO BOTH OF US.
GENIE- DO YOU KNOW BENTO CHAGAS?
BENNY?

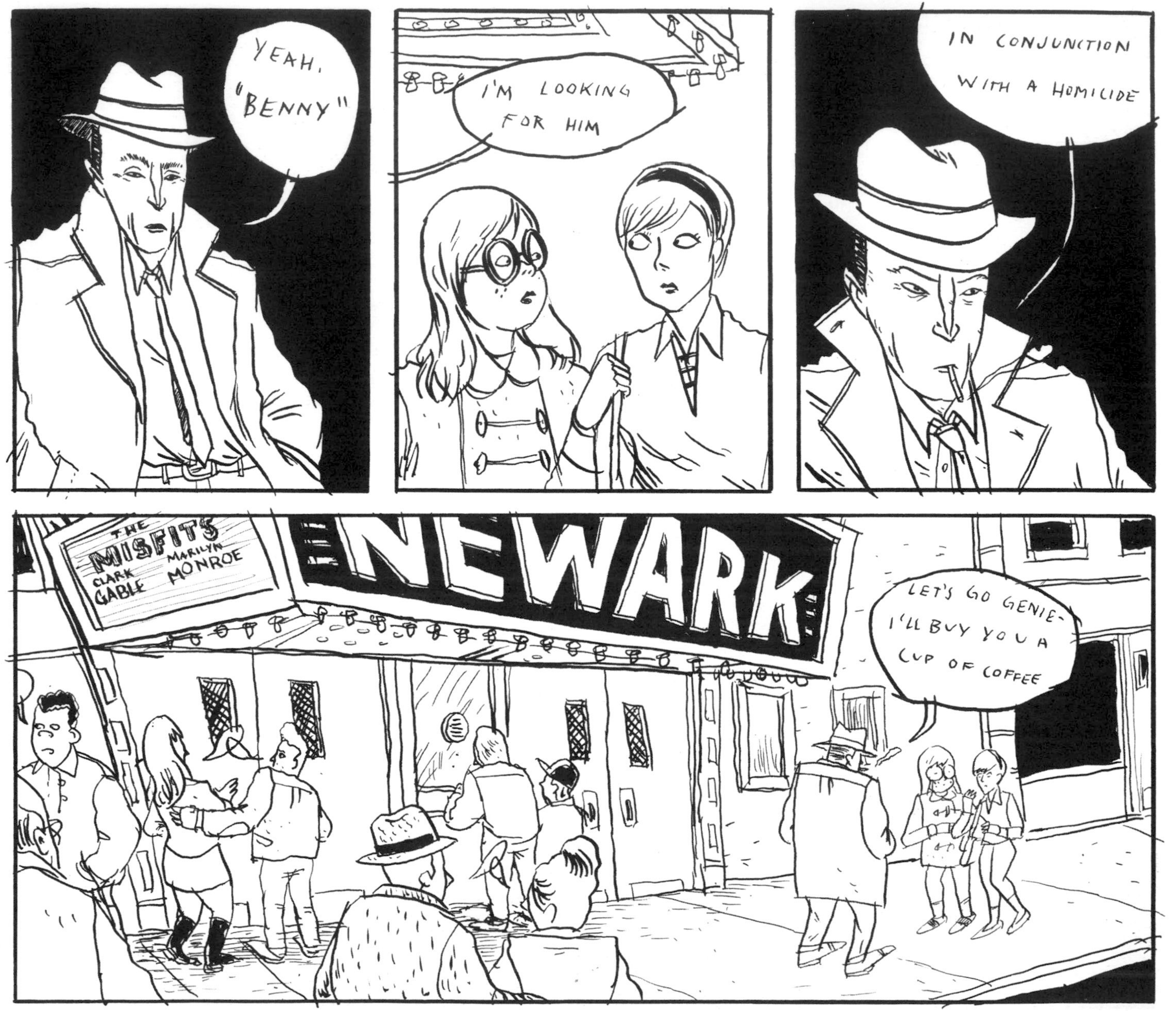
YEAH. "BENNY"
I'M LOOKING FOR HIM
IN CONJUNCTION WITH A HOMICIDE
THE MISFITS CLARK GABLE MARILYN MONROE
NEWARK
LET'S GO GENIE- I'LL BUY YOU A CUP OF COFFEE

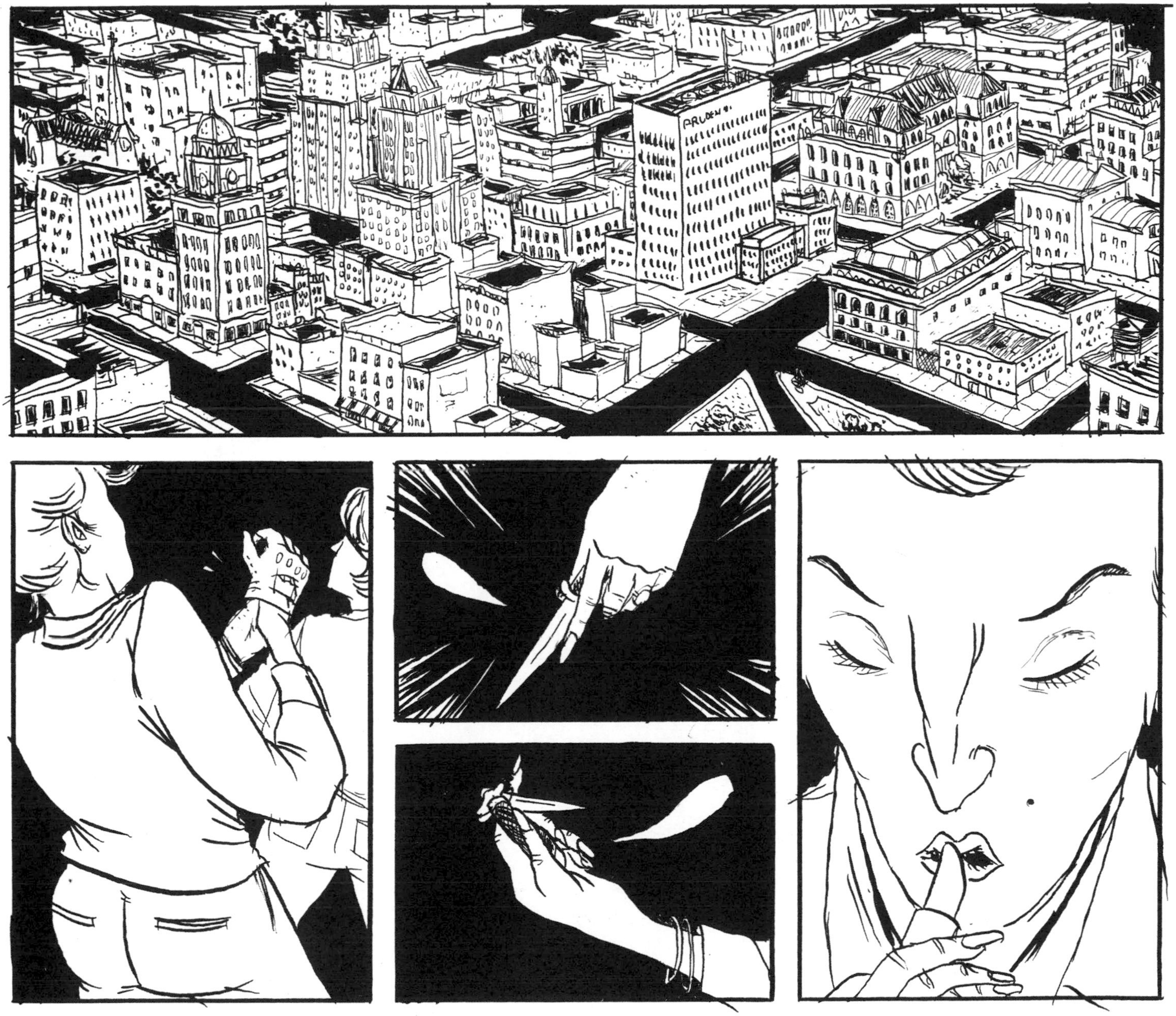
ARLDEN

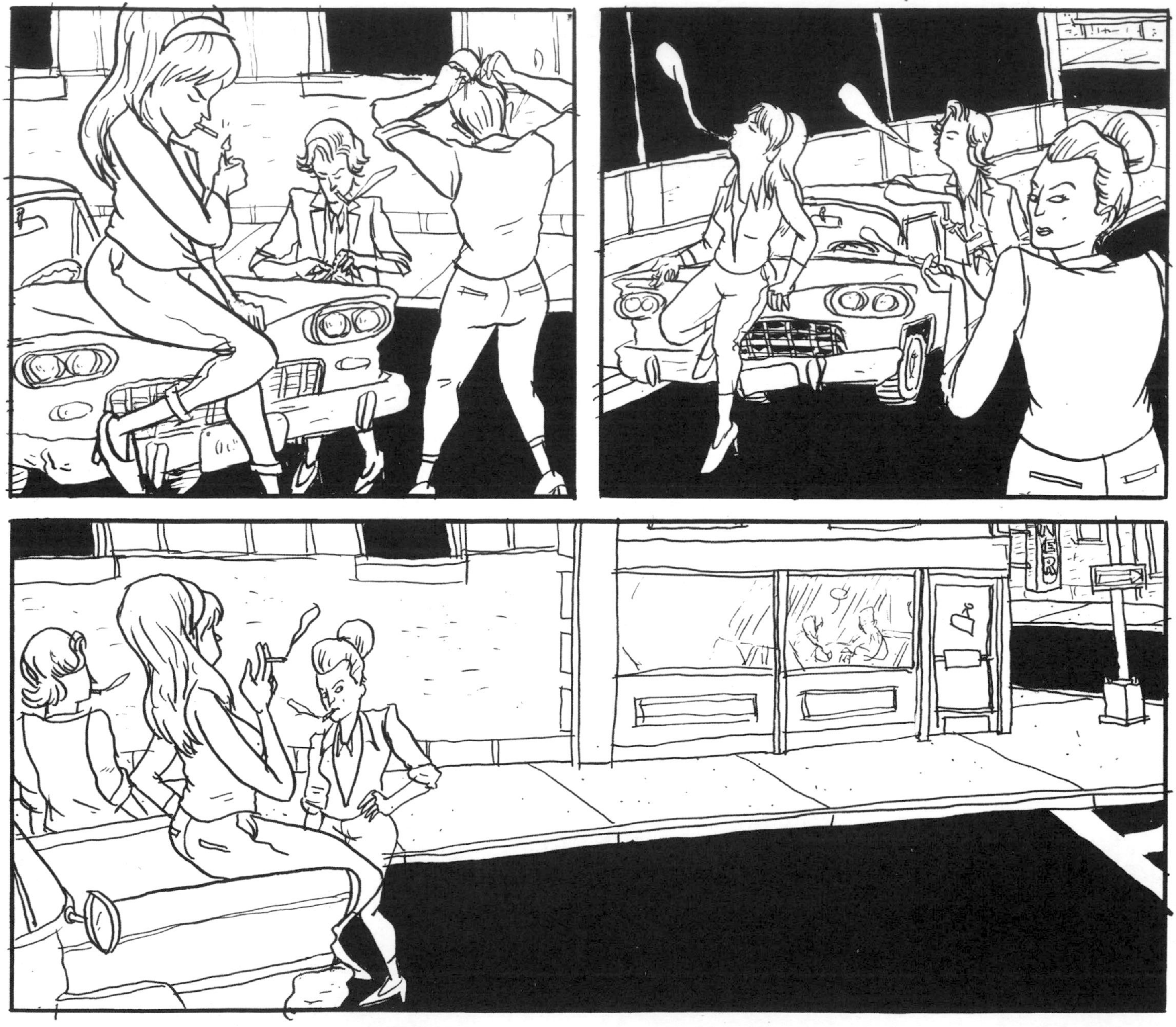

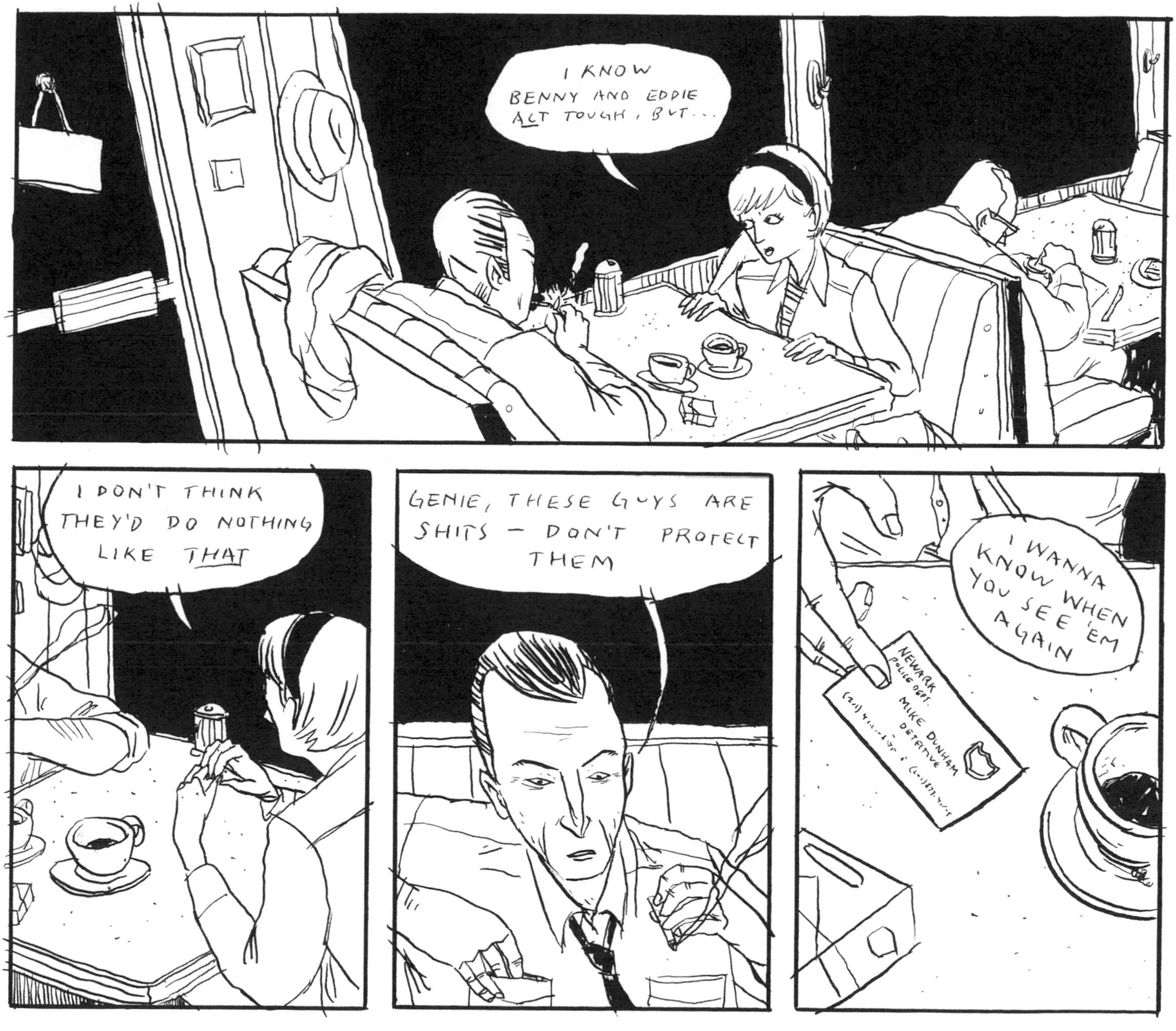
I KNOW BENNY AND EDDIE ACT TOUGH, BUT...
I DON'T THINK THEY'D DO NOTHING LIKE THAT
GENIE, THESE GUYS ARE SHITS - DON'T PROTECT THEM
I WANNA KNOW WHEN YOU SEE 'EM AGAIN
NEWARK POLICE DEPT.
MIKE DUNHAM
DETECTIVE

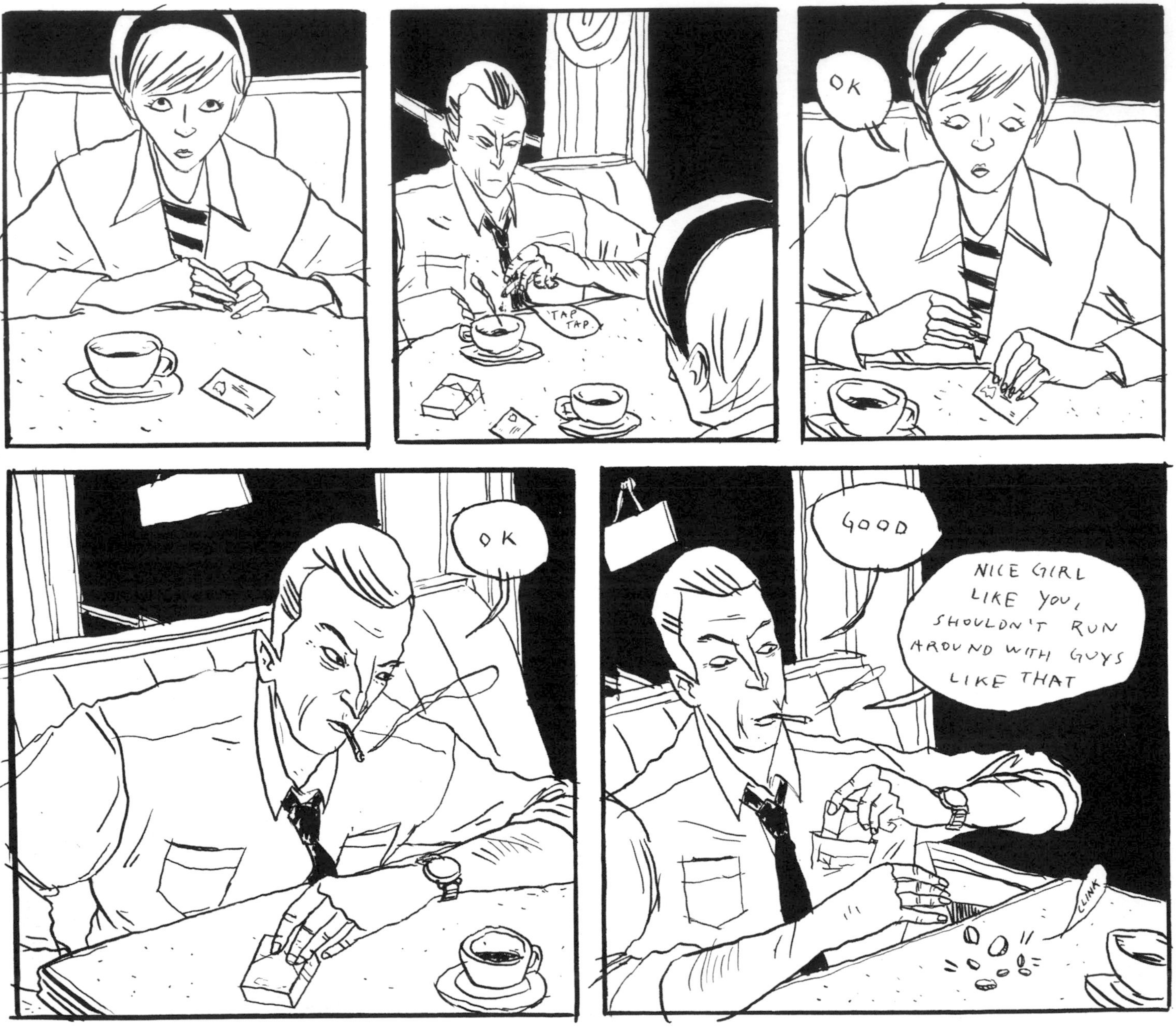
TAP TAP.
OK
OK
GOOD
NICE GIRL LIKE YOU, SHOULDN'T RUN AROUND WITH GUYS LIKE THAT
CLINK

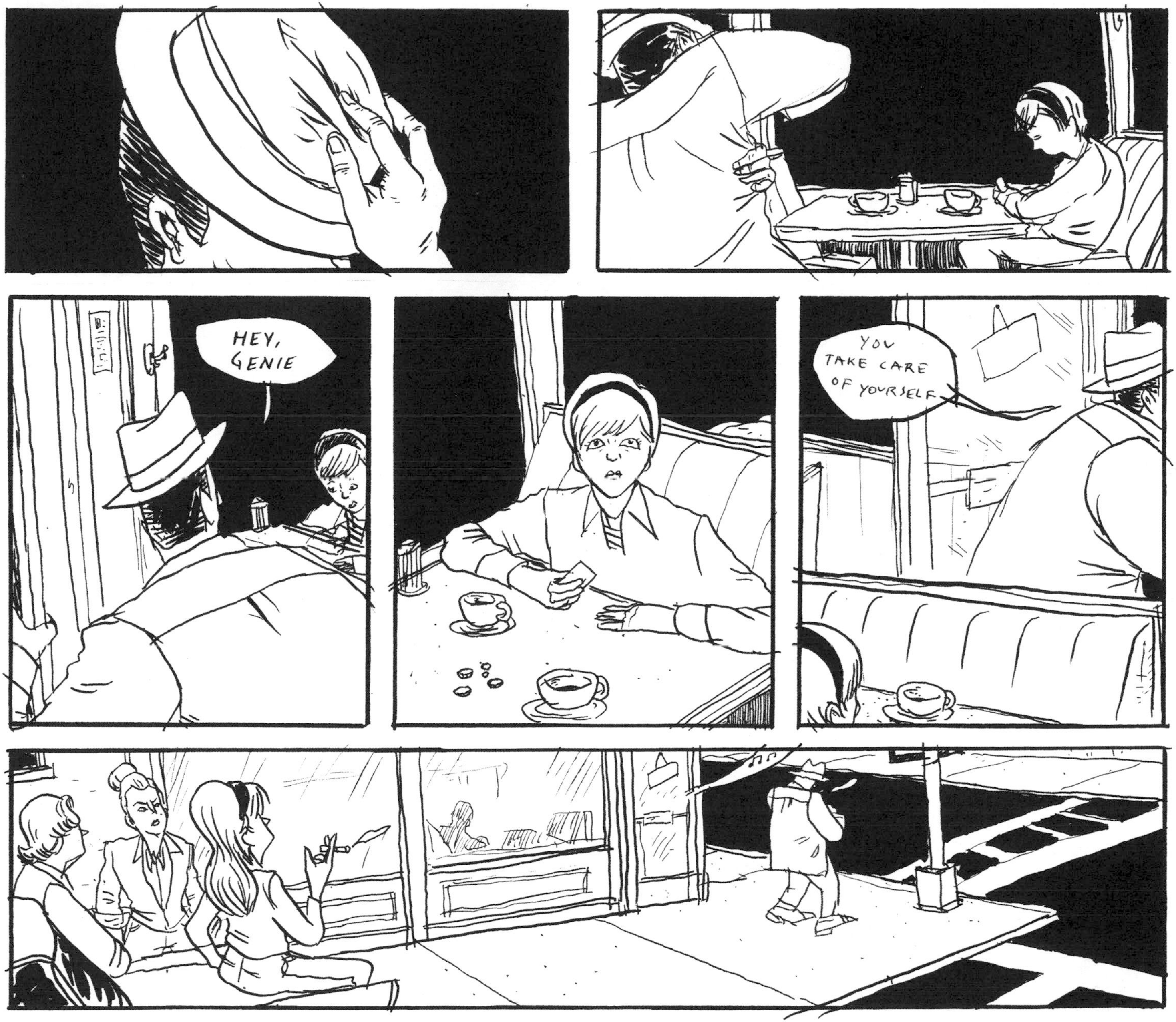
HEY, GENIE
YOU TAKE CARE OF YOURSELF

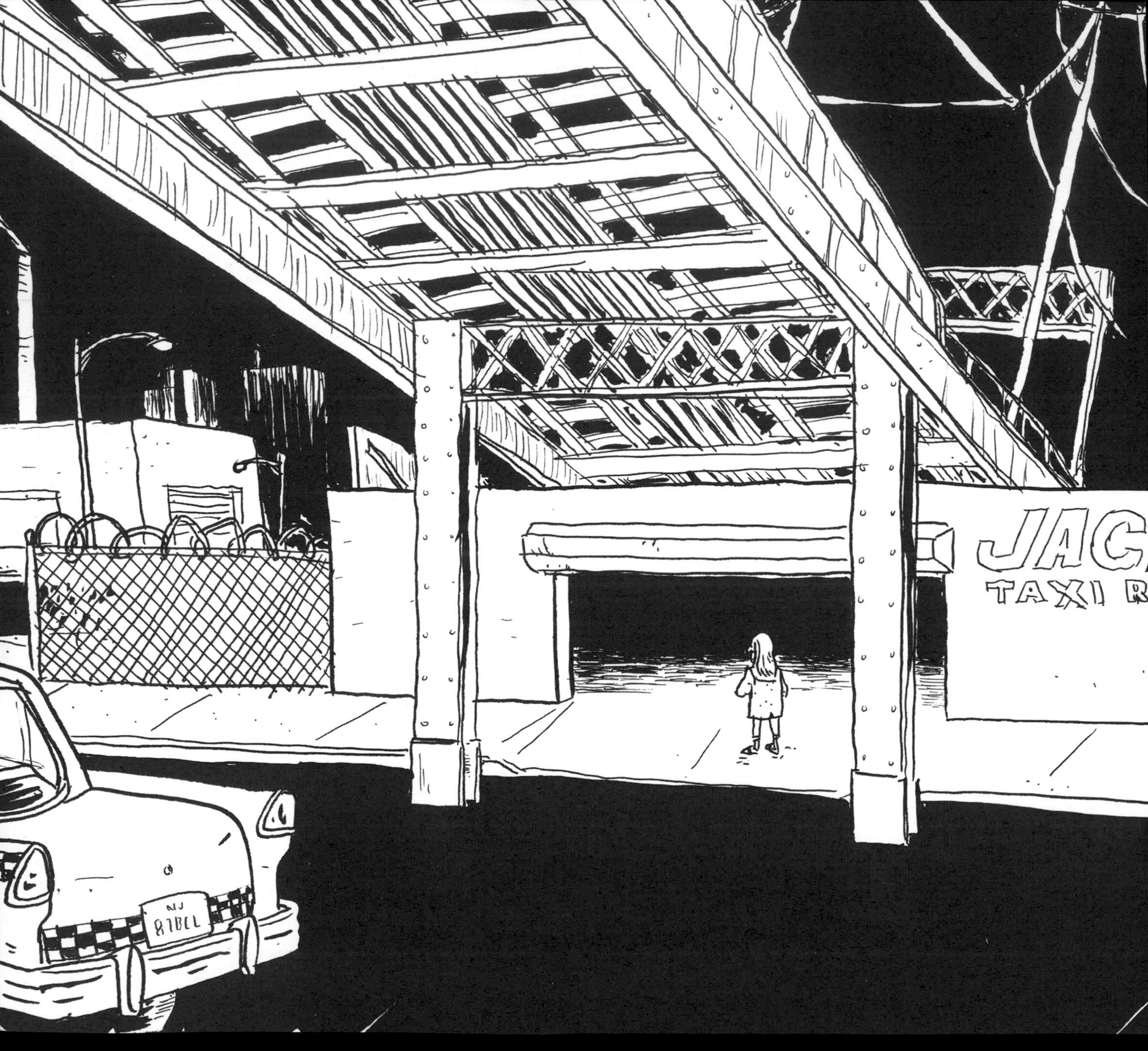
JAC
TAXI R
NJ
87BCL

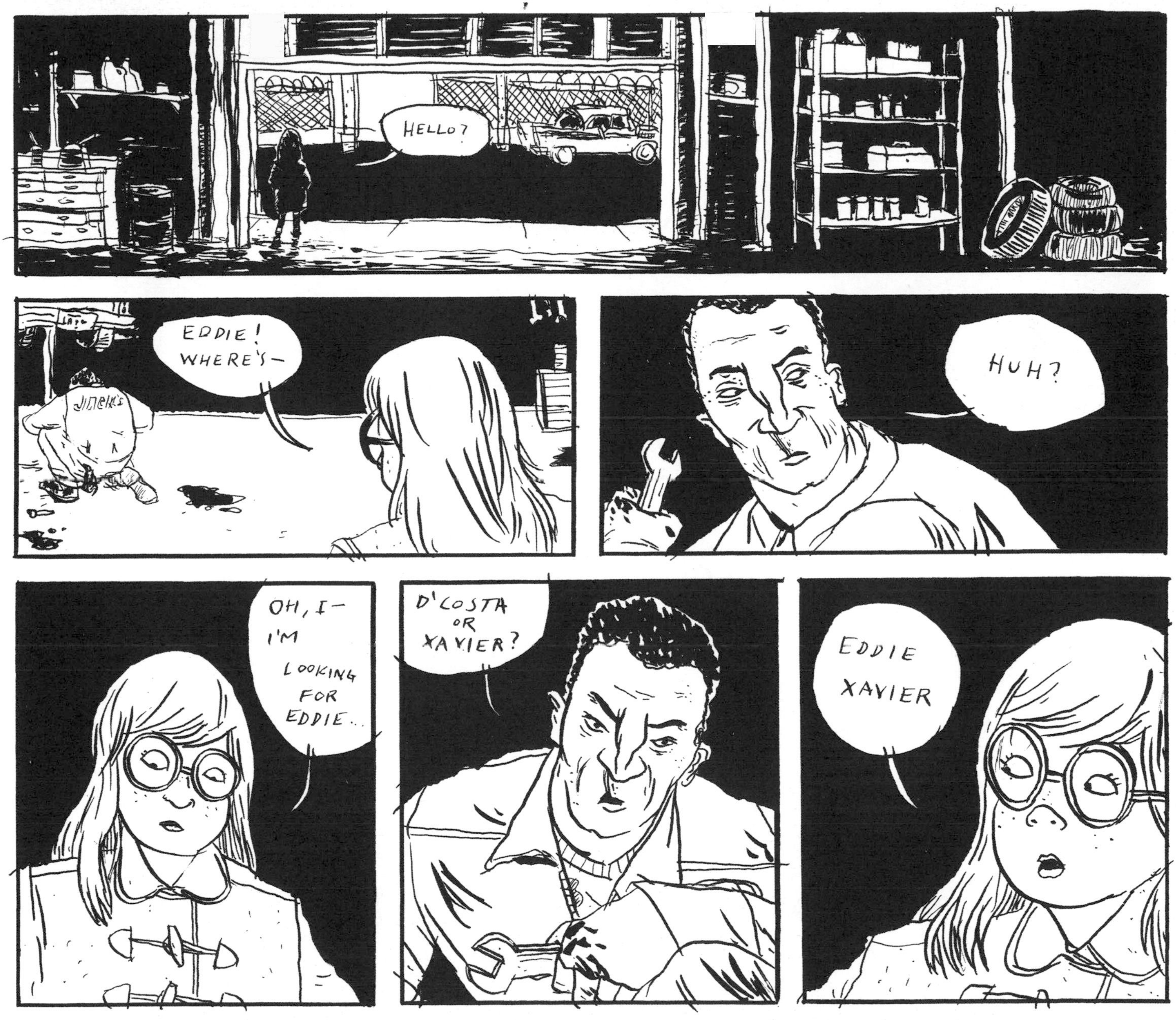
HELLO?
EDDIE! WHERE'S—
HUH?
OH, I— I'M LOOKING FOR EDDIE...
D'COSTA OR XAVIER?
EDDIE XAVIER

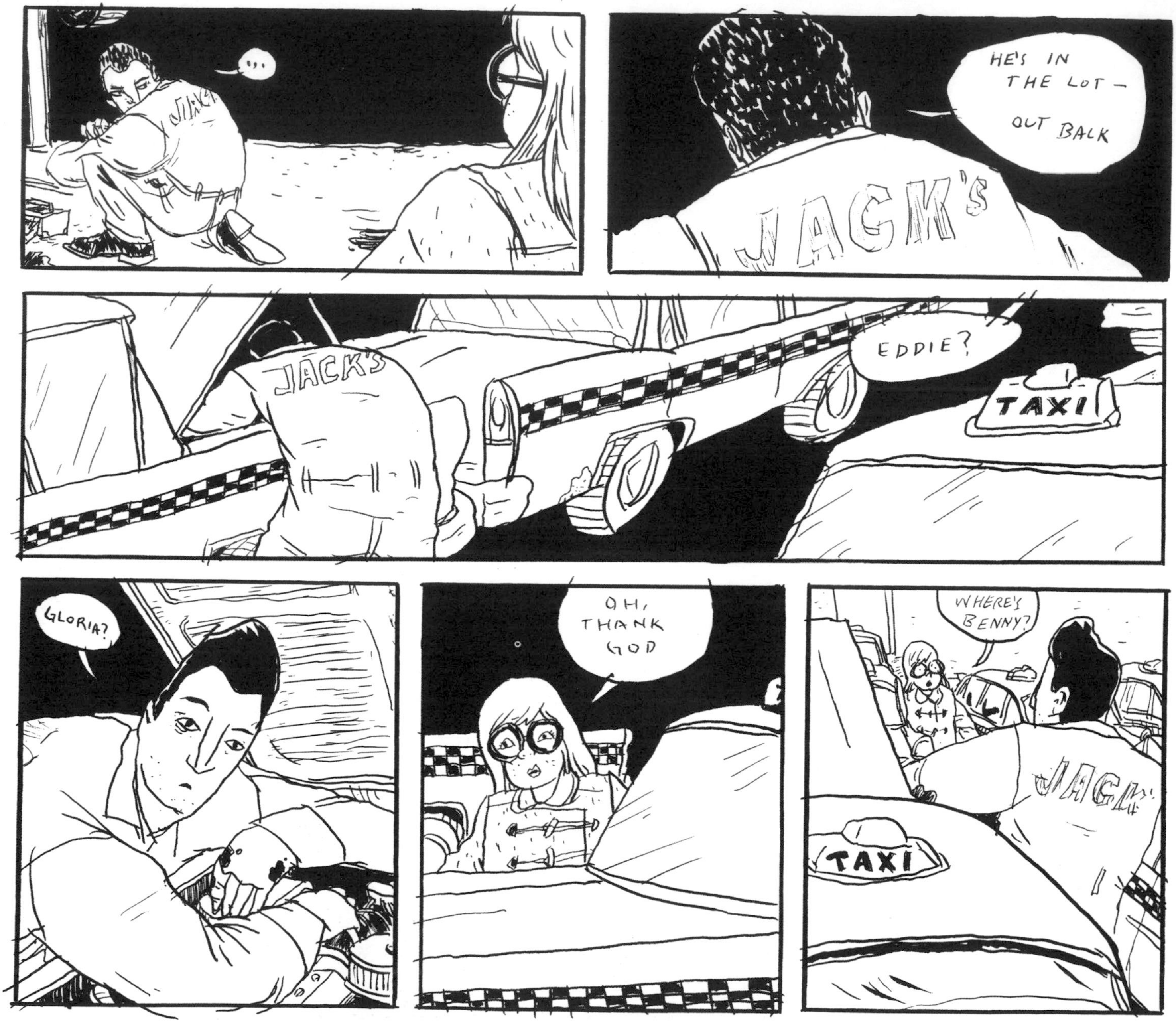
...
HE'S IN THE LOT — OUT BACK
JACK'S
JACK'S
EDDIE?
TAXI
GLORIA?
OH, THANK GOD
WHERE'S BENNY?
TAXI

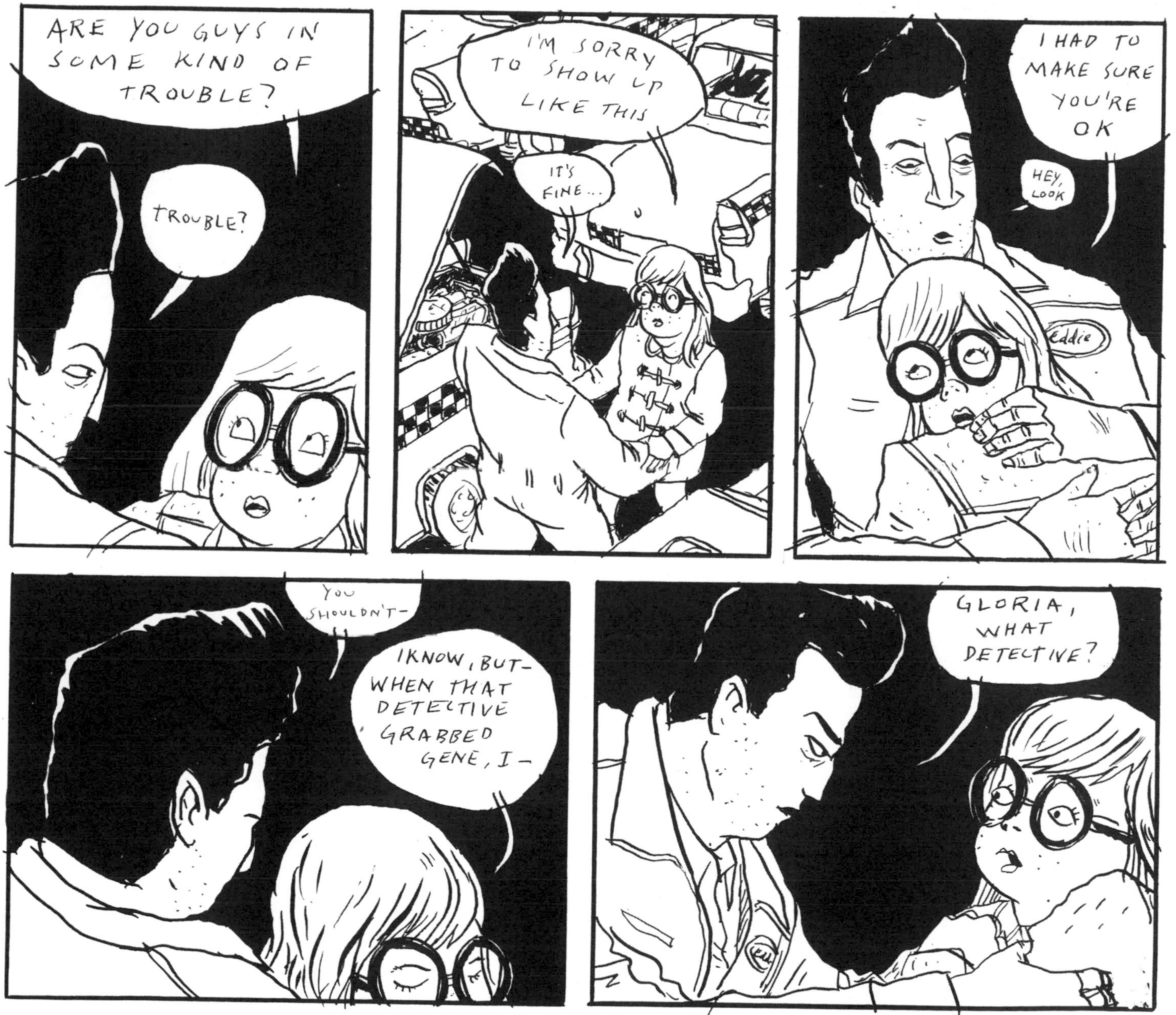
ARE YOU GUYS IN SOME KIND OF TROUBLE?
TROUBLE?
I'M SORRY TO SHOW UP LIKE THIS
IT'S FINE...
I HAD TO MAKE SURE YOU'RE OK
HEY, LOOK
Eddie
YOU SHOULDN'T-
I KNOW, BUT- WHEN THAT DETECTIVE GRABBED GENE, I-
GLORIA, WHAT DETECTIVE?

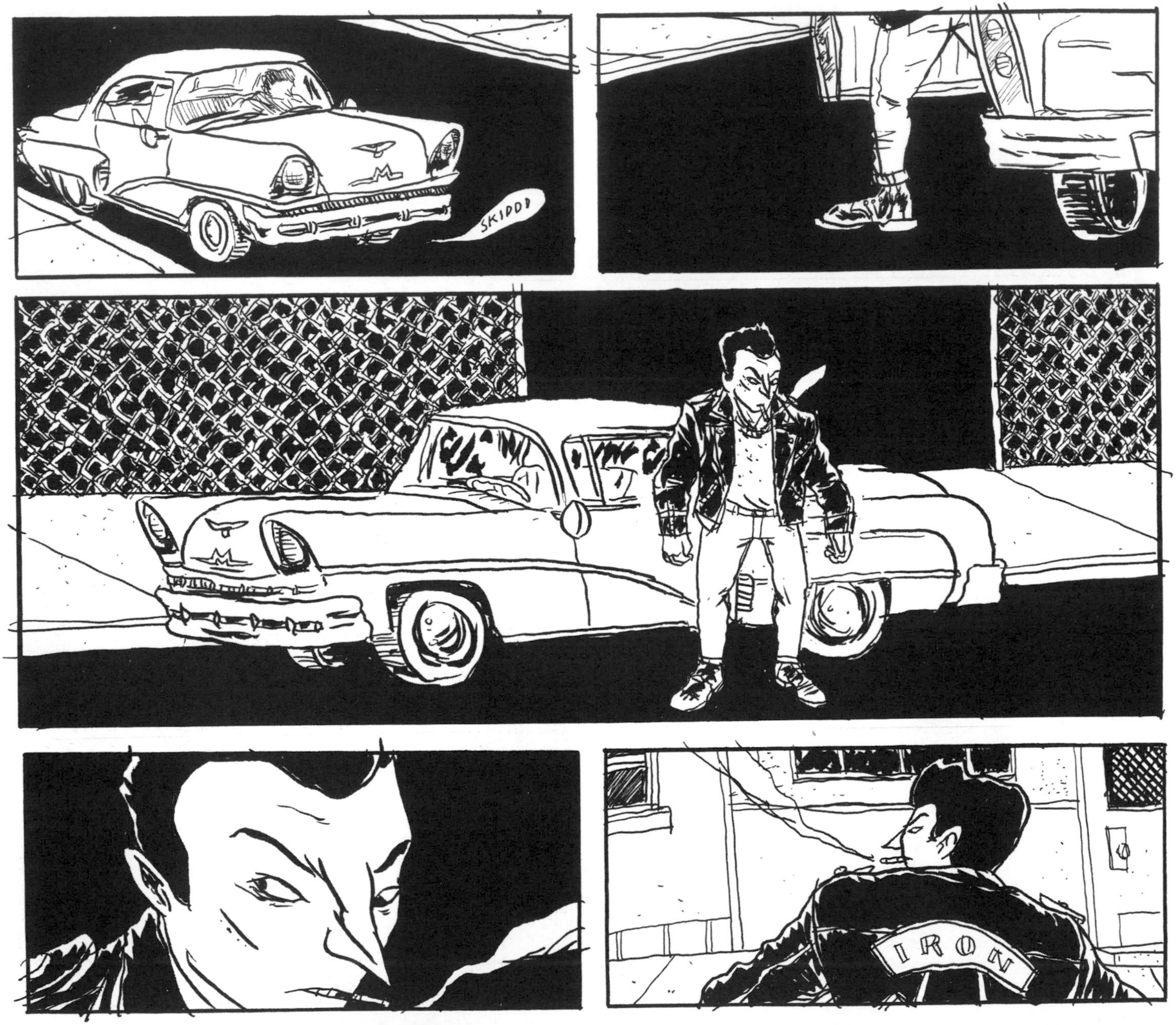
SKIDDD
IRON

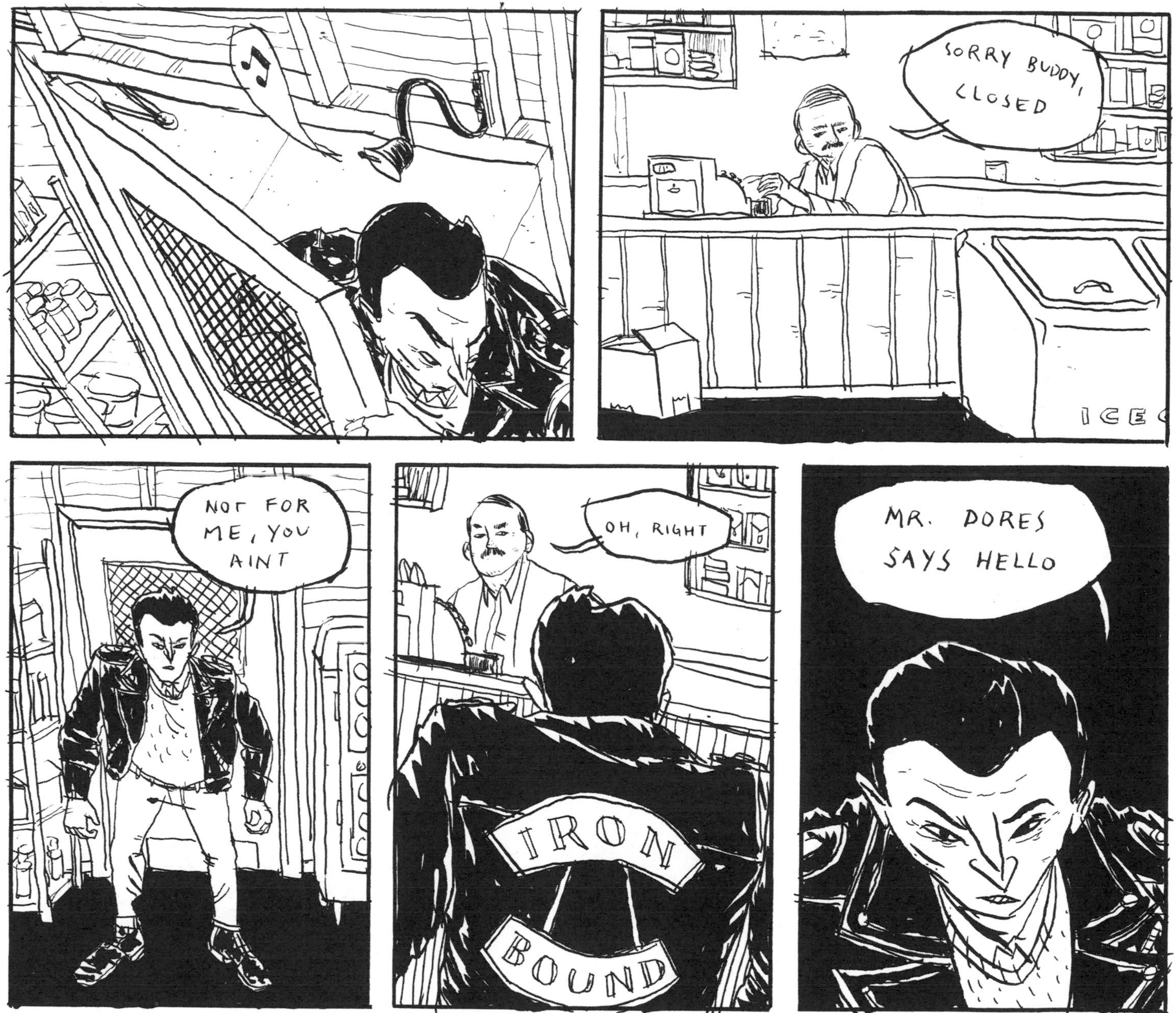
SORRY BUDDY, CLOSED
ICE
NOT FOR ME, YOU AINT
OH, RIGHT
IRON
BOUND
MR. DORES SAYS HELLO

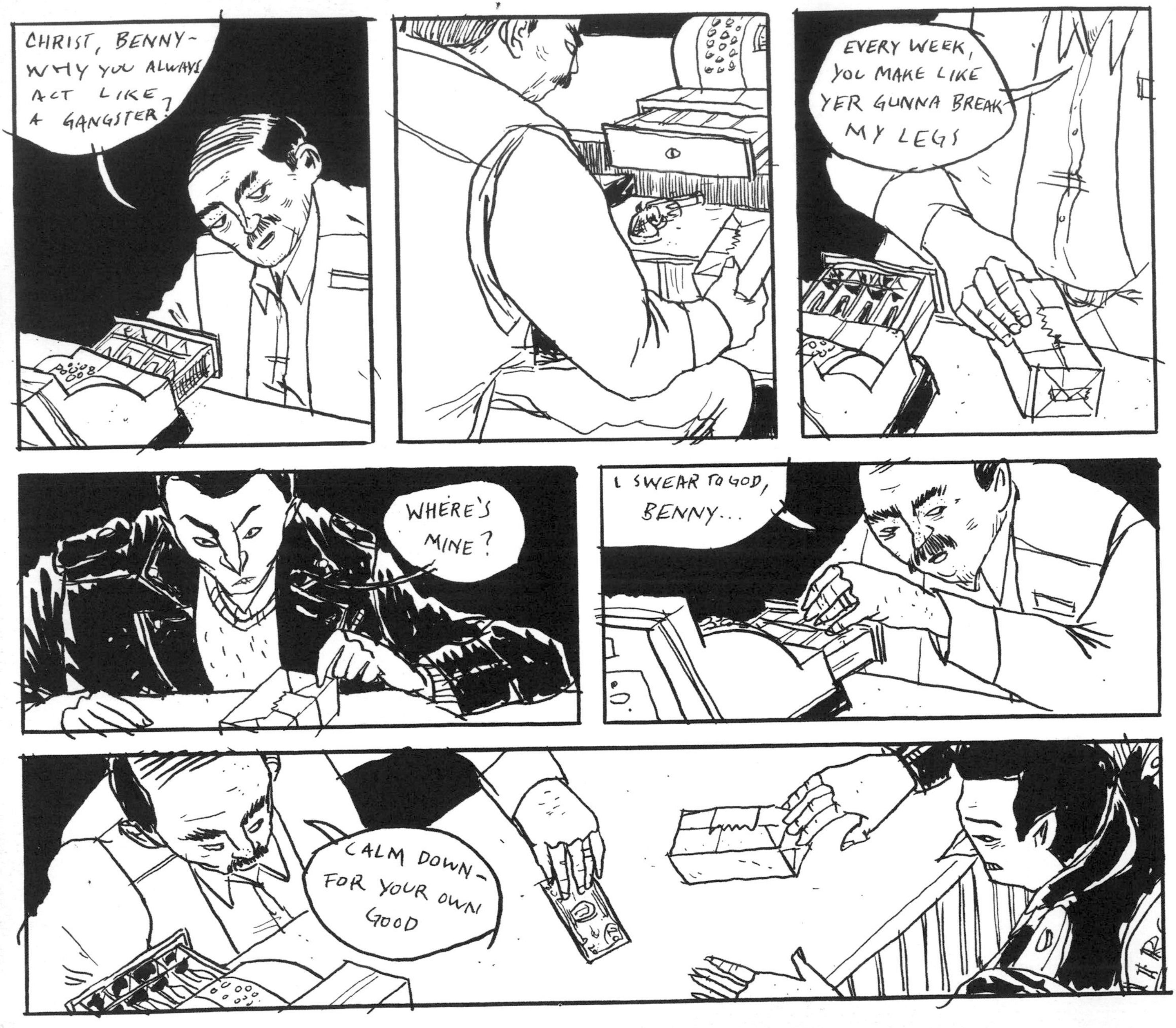
CHRIST, BENNY- WHY YOU ALWAYS ACT LIKE A GANGSTER?
EVERY WEEK, YOU MAKE LIKE YER GUNNA BREAK MY LEGS
WHERE'S MINE?
I SWEAR TO GOD, BENNY...
CALM DOWN- FOR YOUR OWN GOOD

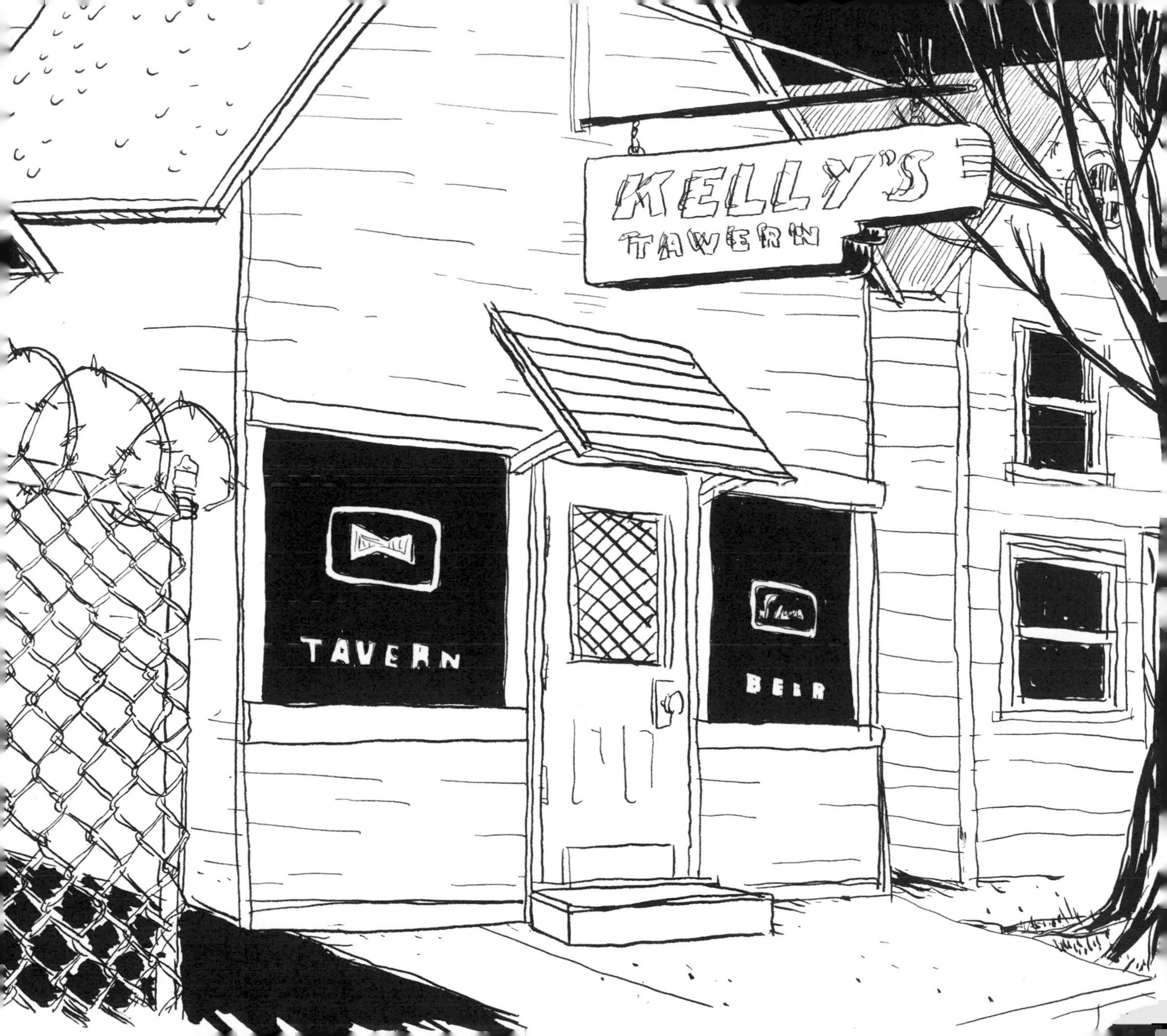
KELLY'S
TAVERN
TAVERN
BEIR

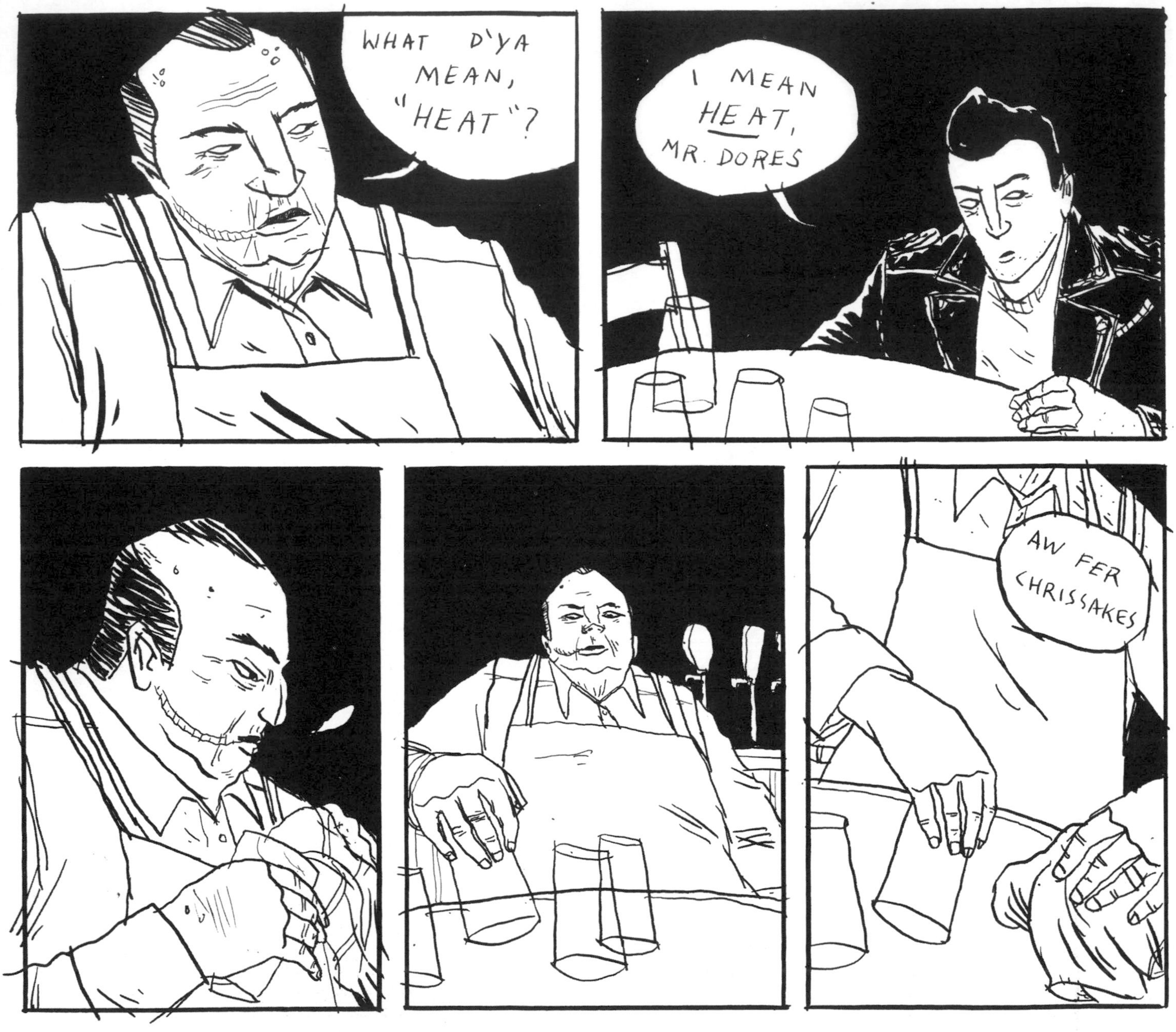
WHAT D'YA MEAN, "HEAT"?
I MEAN HEAT, MR. DORES
AW FER CHRISSAKES

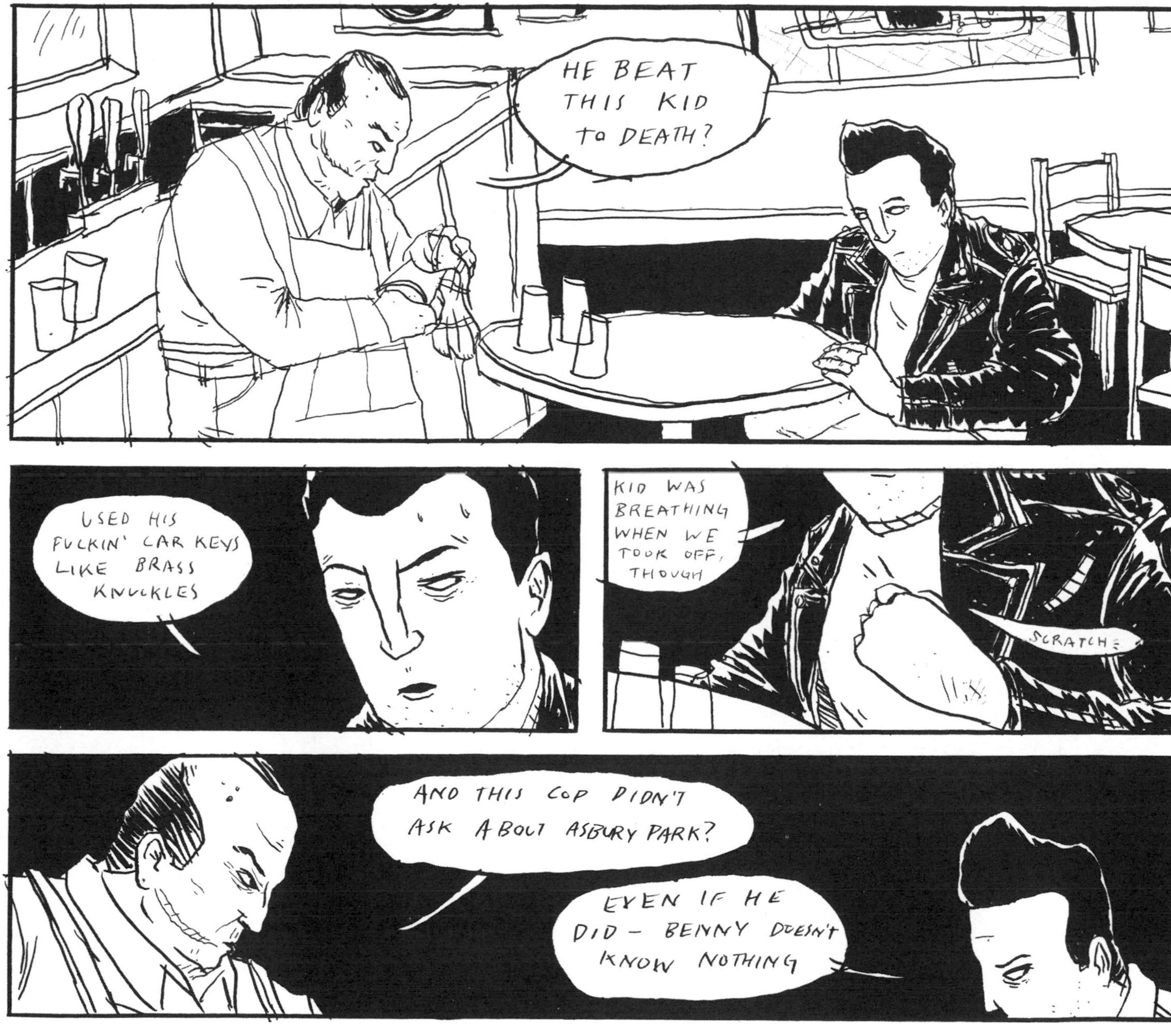
HE BEAT THIS KID TO DEATH?
USED HIS FUCKIN' CAR KEYS LIKE BRASS KNUCKLES
KID WAS BREATHING WHEN WE TOOK OFF, THOUGH
SCRATCH
AND THIS COP DIDN'T ASK ABOUT ASBURY PARK?
EVEN IF HE DID - BENNY DOESN'T KNOW NOTHING

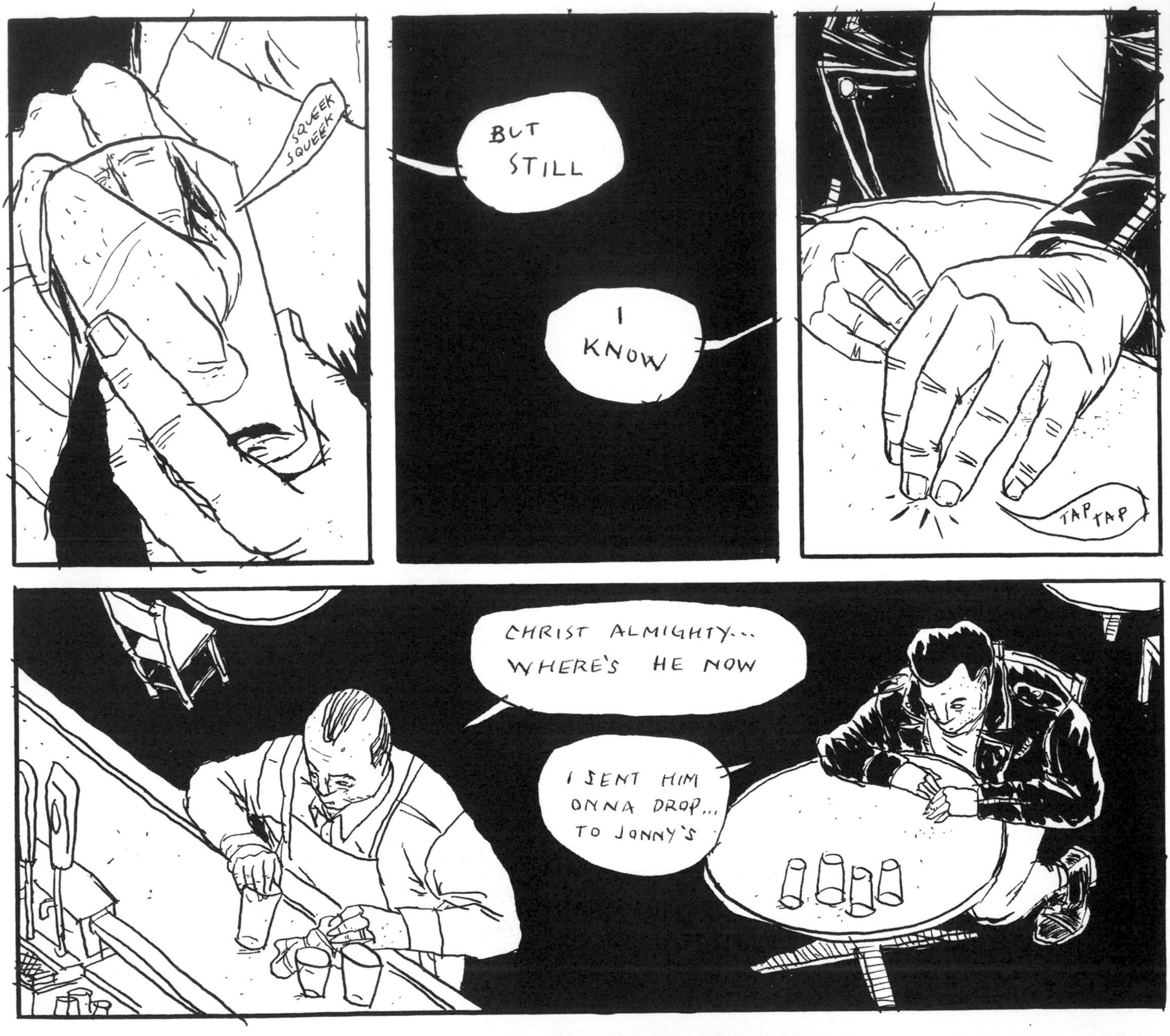
SQUEEK SQUEEK
BUT STILL
I KNOW
TAP TAP
CHRIST ALMIGHTY... WHERE'S HE NOW
I SENT HIM ONNA DROP... TO JONNY'S

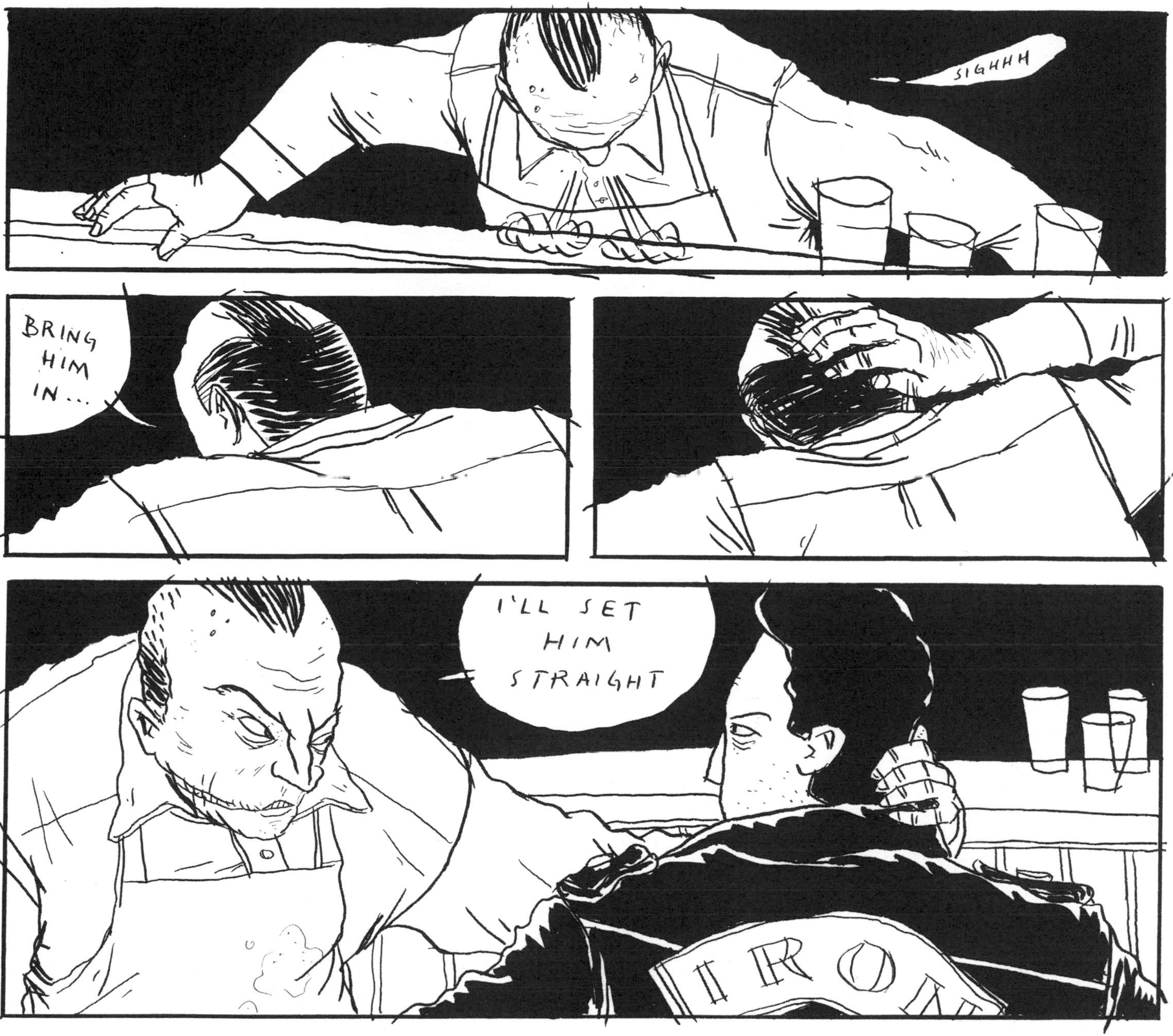
SIGHHH
BRING HIM IN...
I'LL SET HIM STRAIGHT
IRON

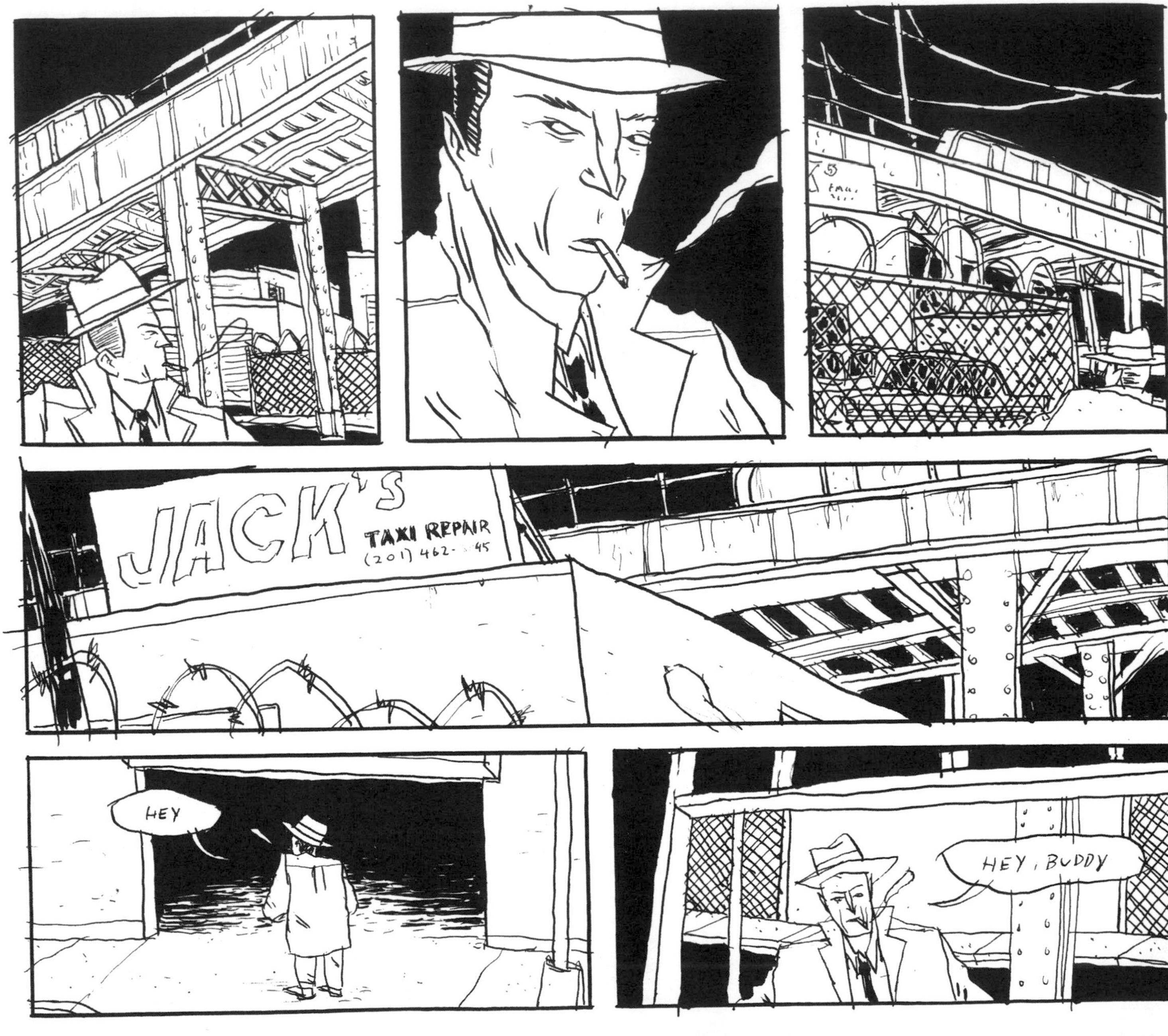
JACK'S
TAXI REPAIR
HEY
HEY, BUDDY

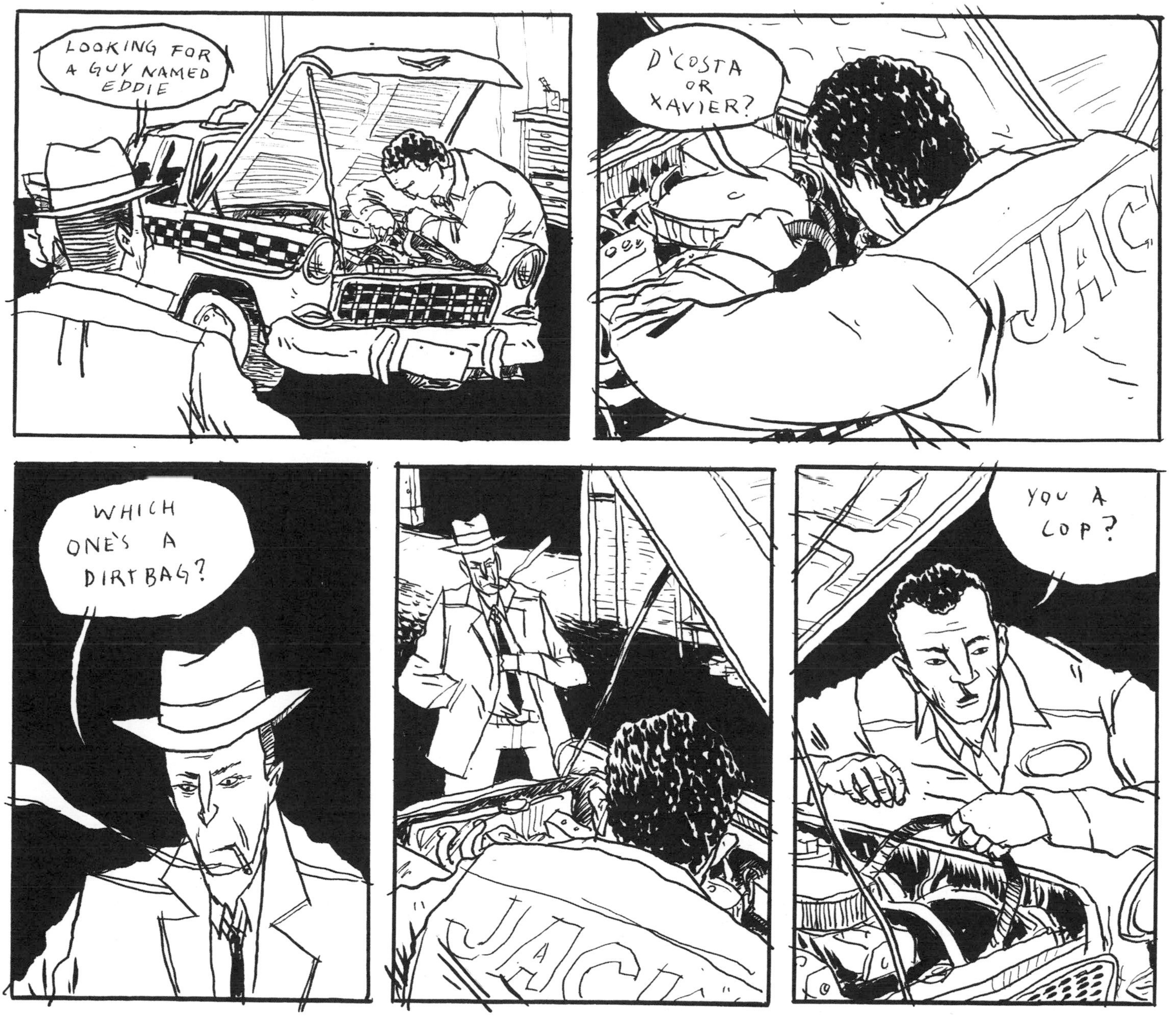
LOOKING FOR A GUY NAMED EDDIE
D'COSTA OR XAVIER?
WHICH ONE'S A DIRTBAG?
YOU A COP?

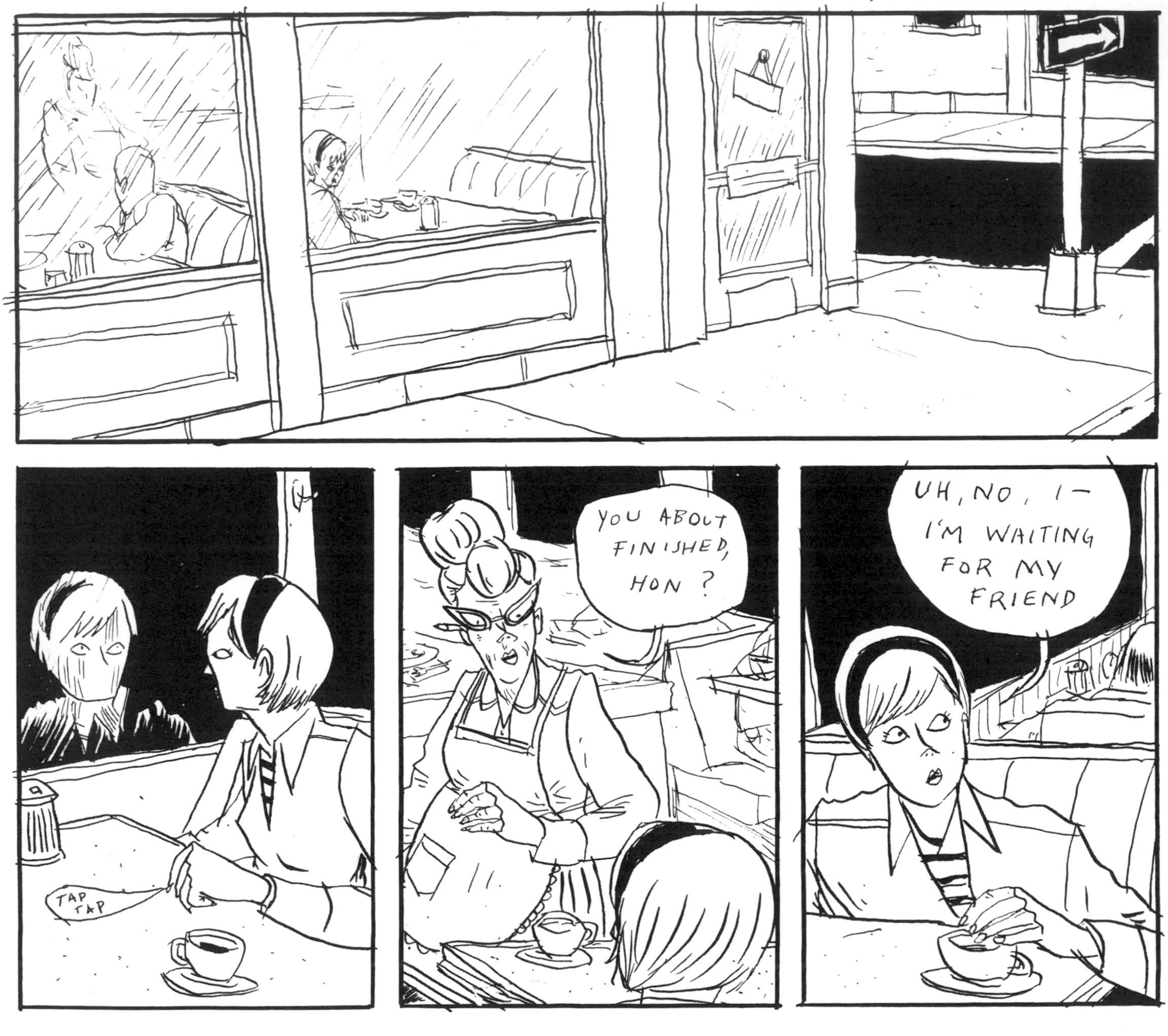
TAP TAP
YOU ABOUT FINISHED, HON ?
UH, NO, I— I'M WAITING FOR MY FRIEND

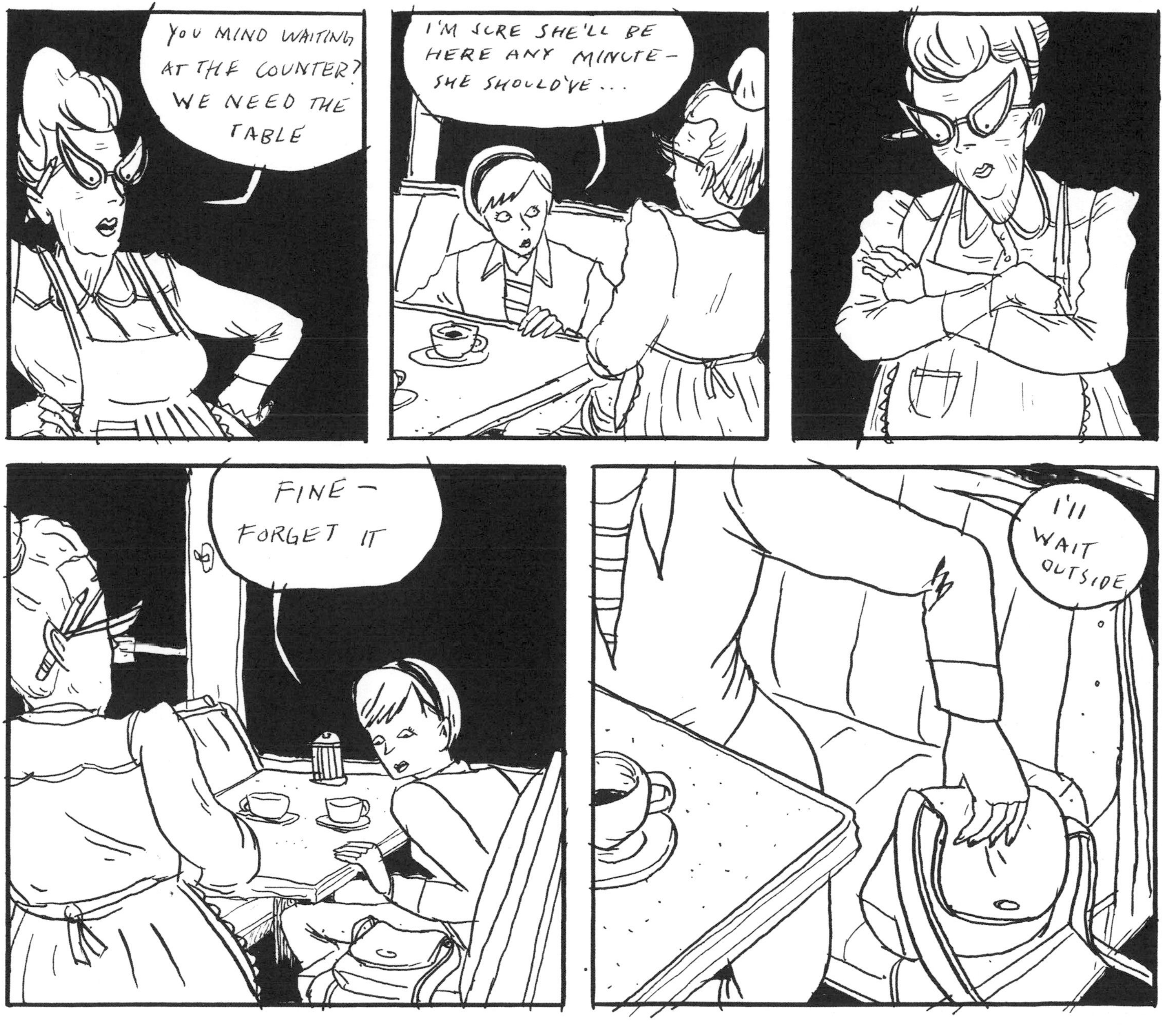
YOU MIND WAITING AT THE COUNTER? WE NEED THE TABLE
I'M SURE SHE'LL BE HERE ANY MINUTE- SHE SHOULD'VE...
FINE- FORGET IT
I'LL WAIT OUTSIDE

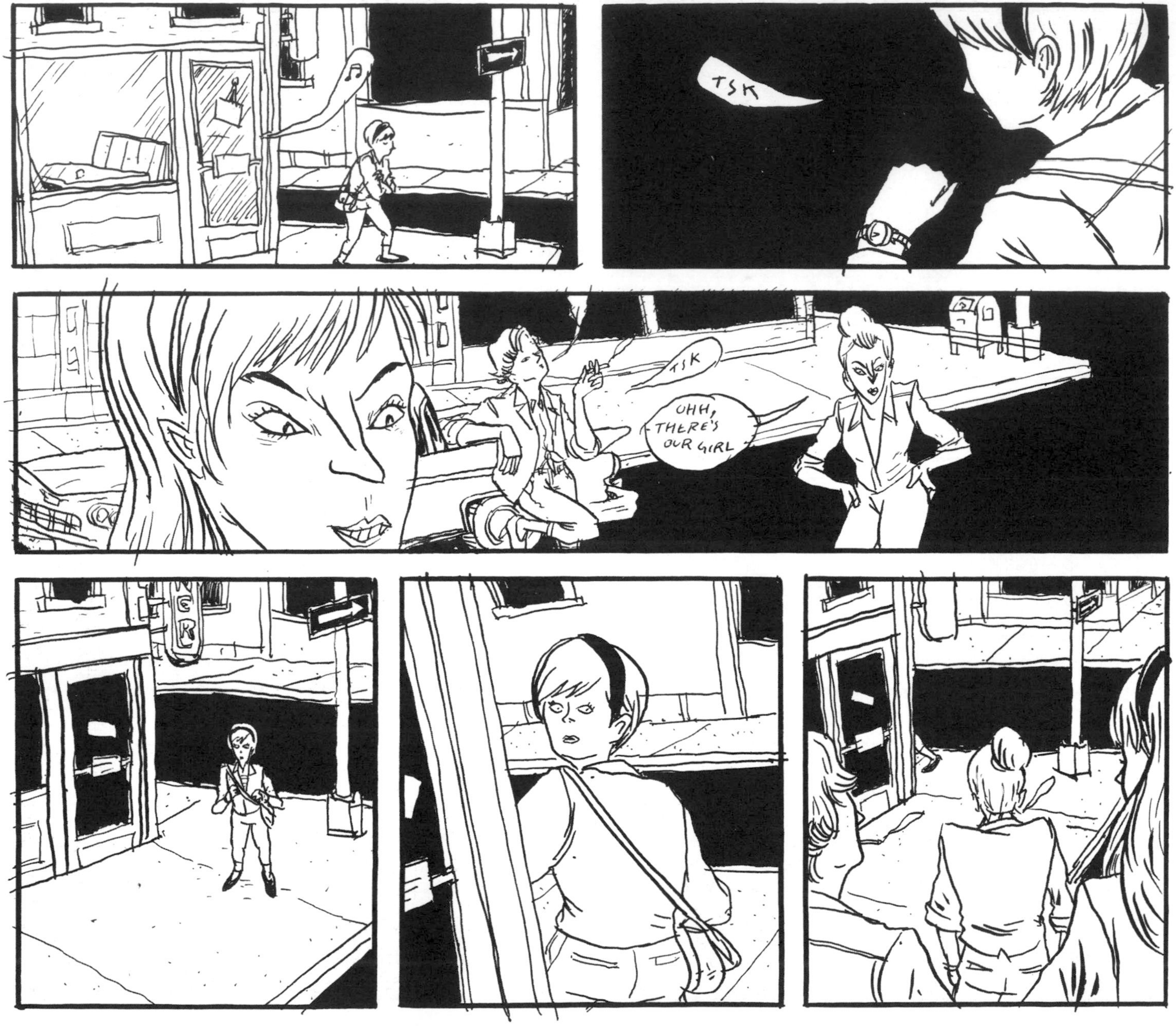
TSK
TSK
UHH, THERE'S OUR GIRL

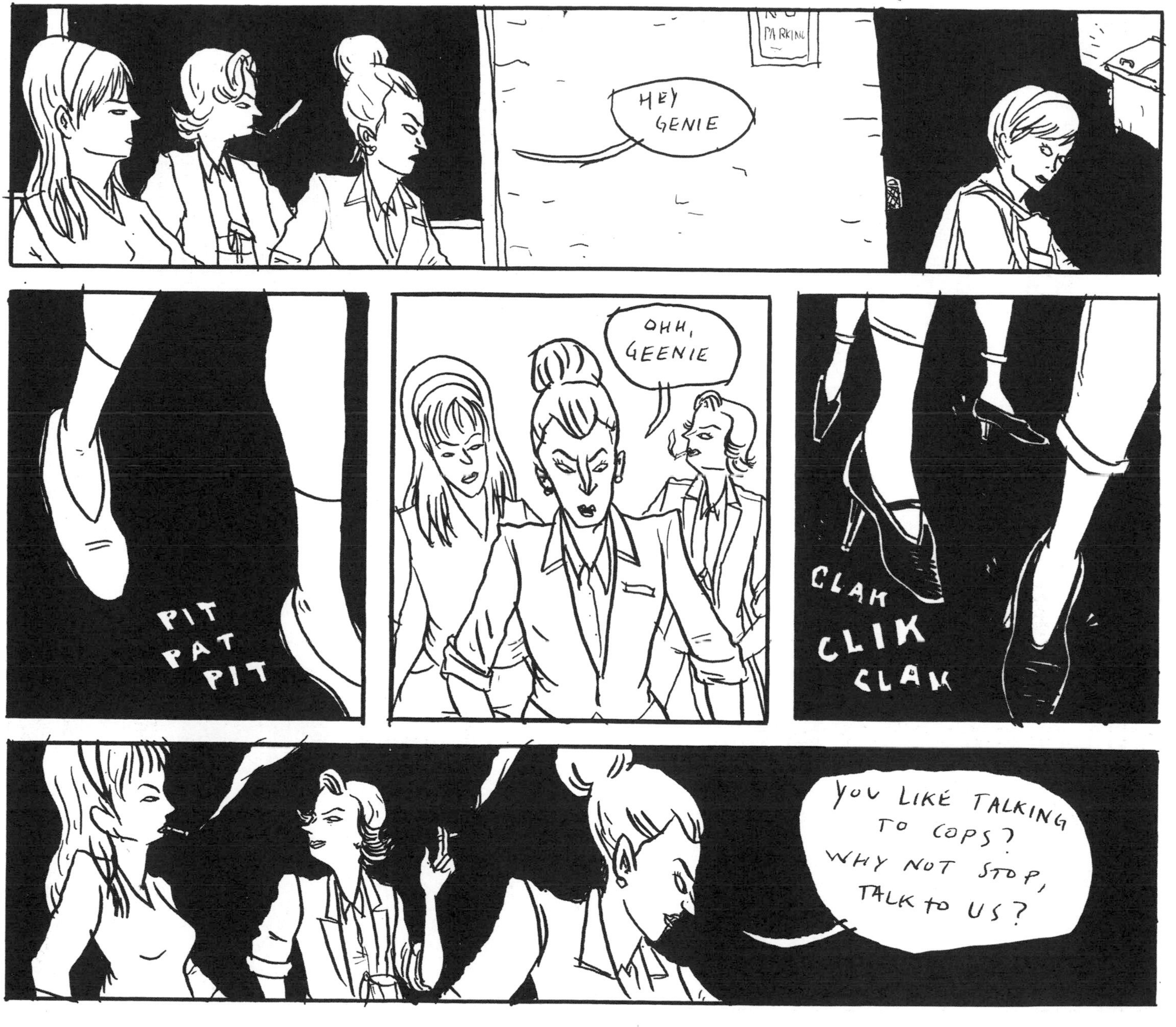
PARKING
HEY GENIE
PIT PAT PIT
OHH, GEENIE
CLAK CLIK CLAK
YOU LIKE TALKING TO COPS? WHY NOT STOP, TALK TO US?

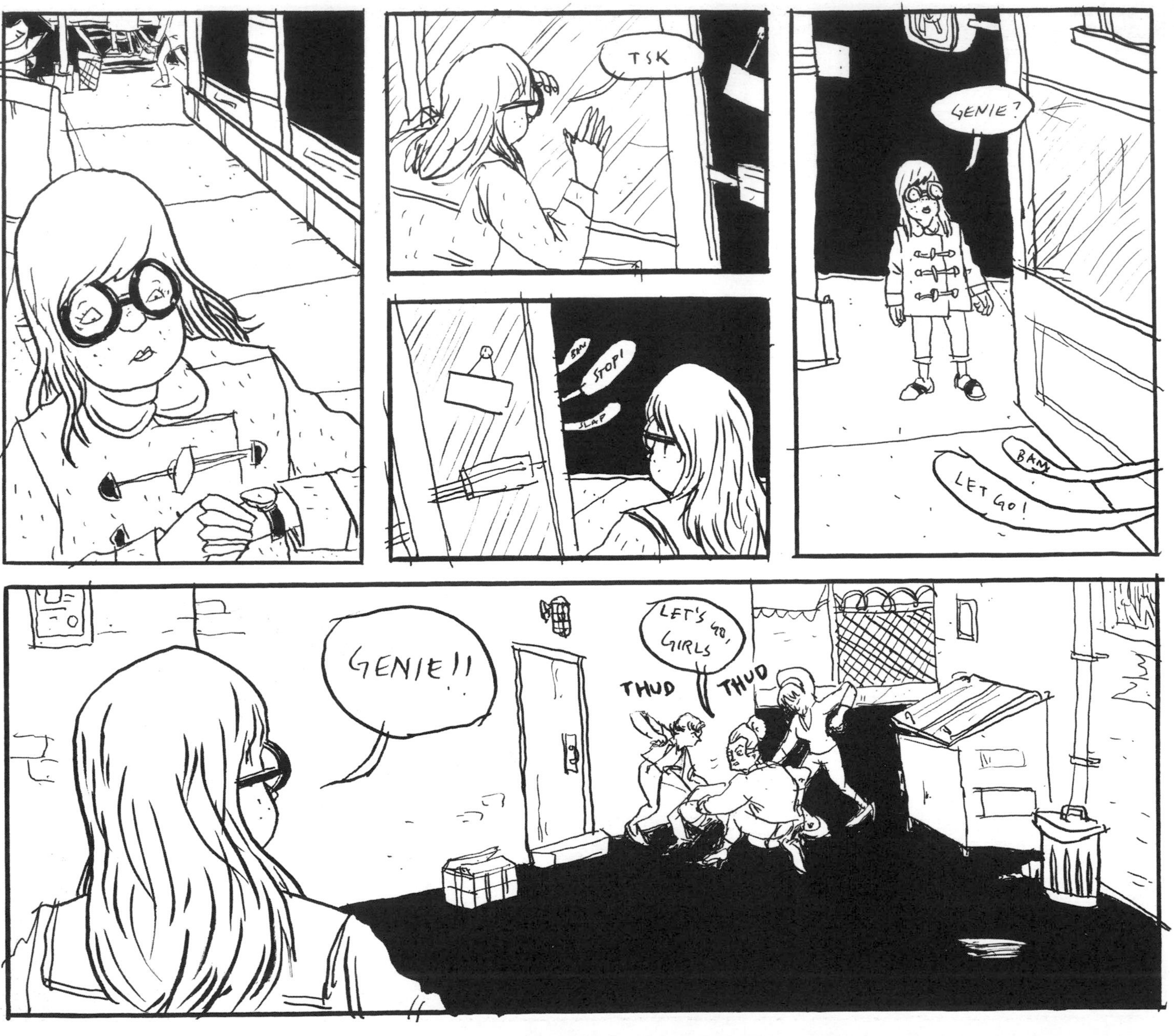
TSK
BAM
STOP!
SLAP
GENIE?
BAM
LET GO!
GENIE!!
THUD
LET'S GO, GIRLS
THUD

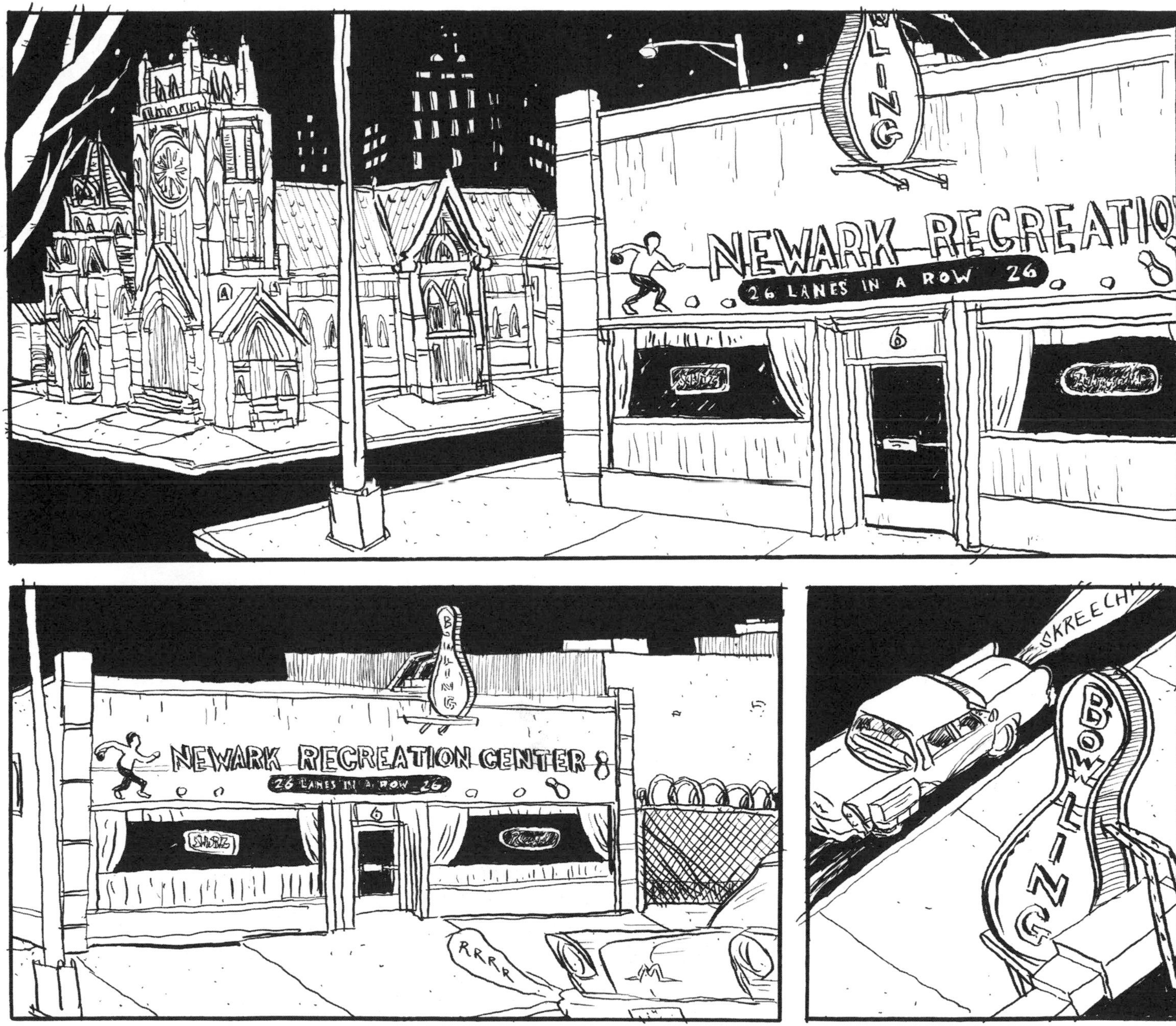
WLING
NEWARK RECREATIO
26 LANES IN A ROW 26
6
NEWARK RECREATION CENTER
26 LANES IN A ROW 26
6
RRRR
SKREECH
BOWLING

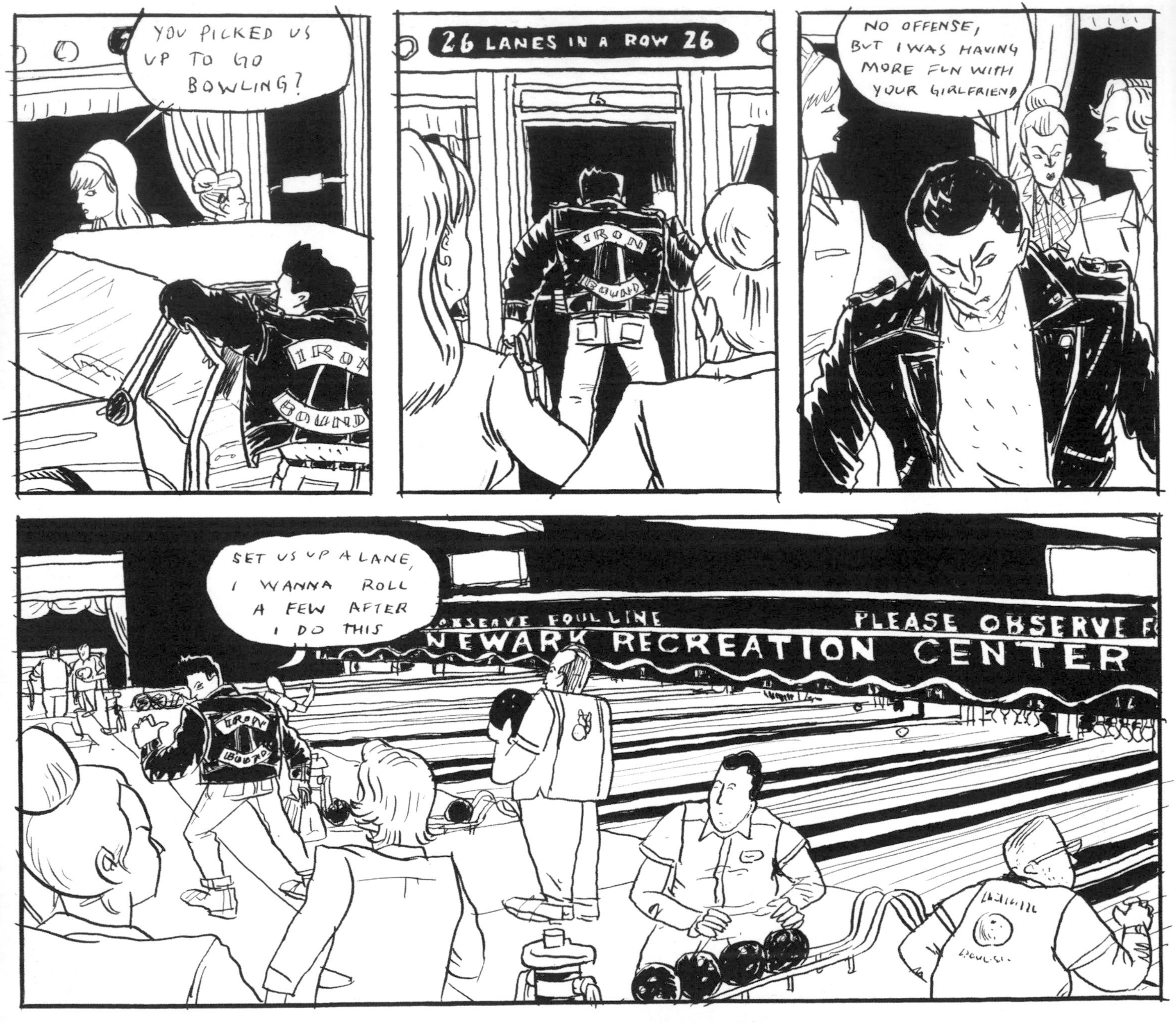
YOU PICKED US UP TO GO BOWLING?
26 LANES IN A ROW 26
IRON BOUND
NO OFFENSE, BUT I WAS HAVING MORE FUN WITH YOUR GIRLFRIEND
SET US UP A LANE, I WANNA ROLL A FEW AFTER I DO THIS
PLEASE OBSERVE
NEWARK RECREATION CENTER

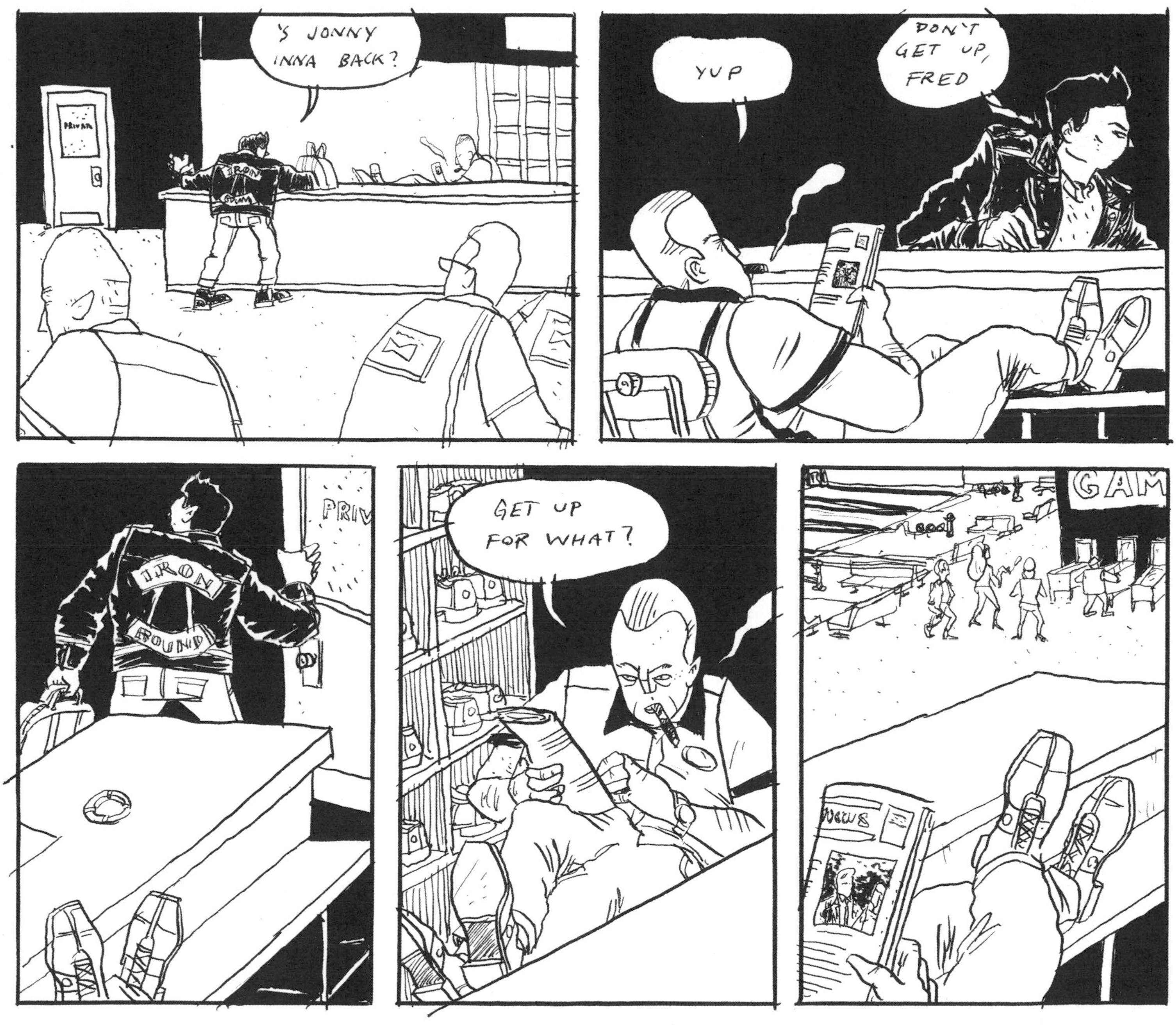
'S JONNY INNA BACK?
PRIVATE
IRON ROUND
YUP
DON'T GET UP, FRED
IRON ROUND
PRIV
GET UP FOR WHAT?
GAM
NEWS

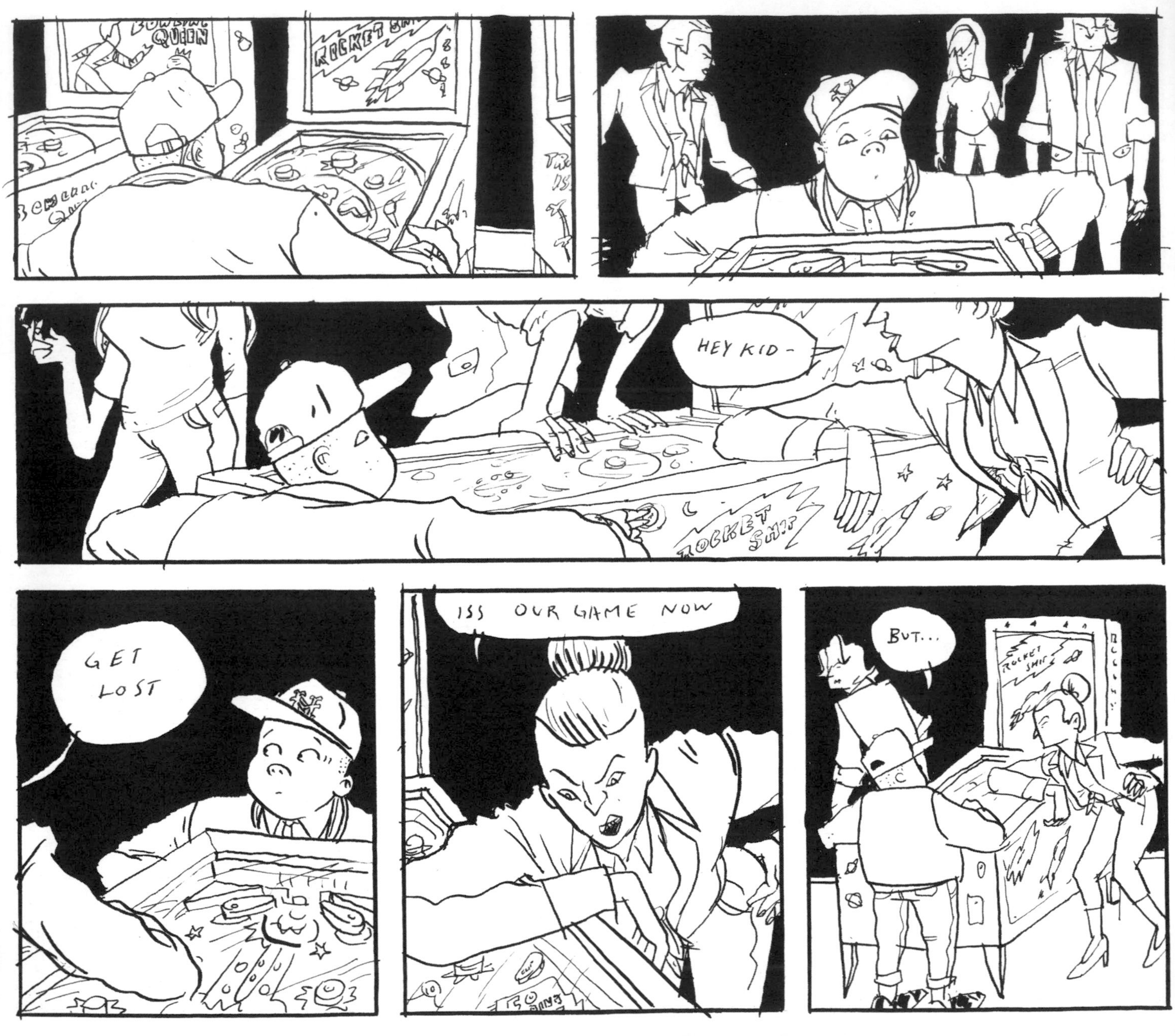
QUEEN
HEY KID-
GET LOST
ISS OUR GAME NOW
BUT...

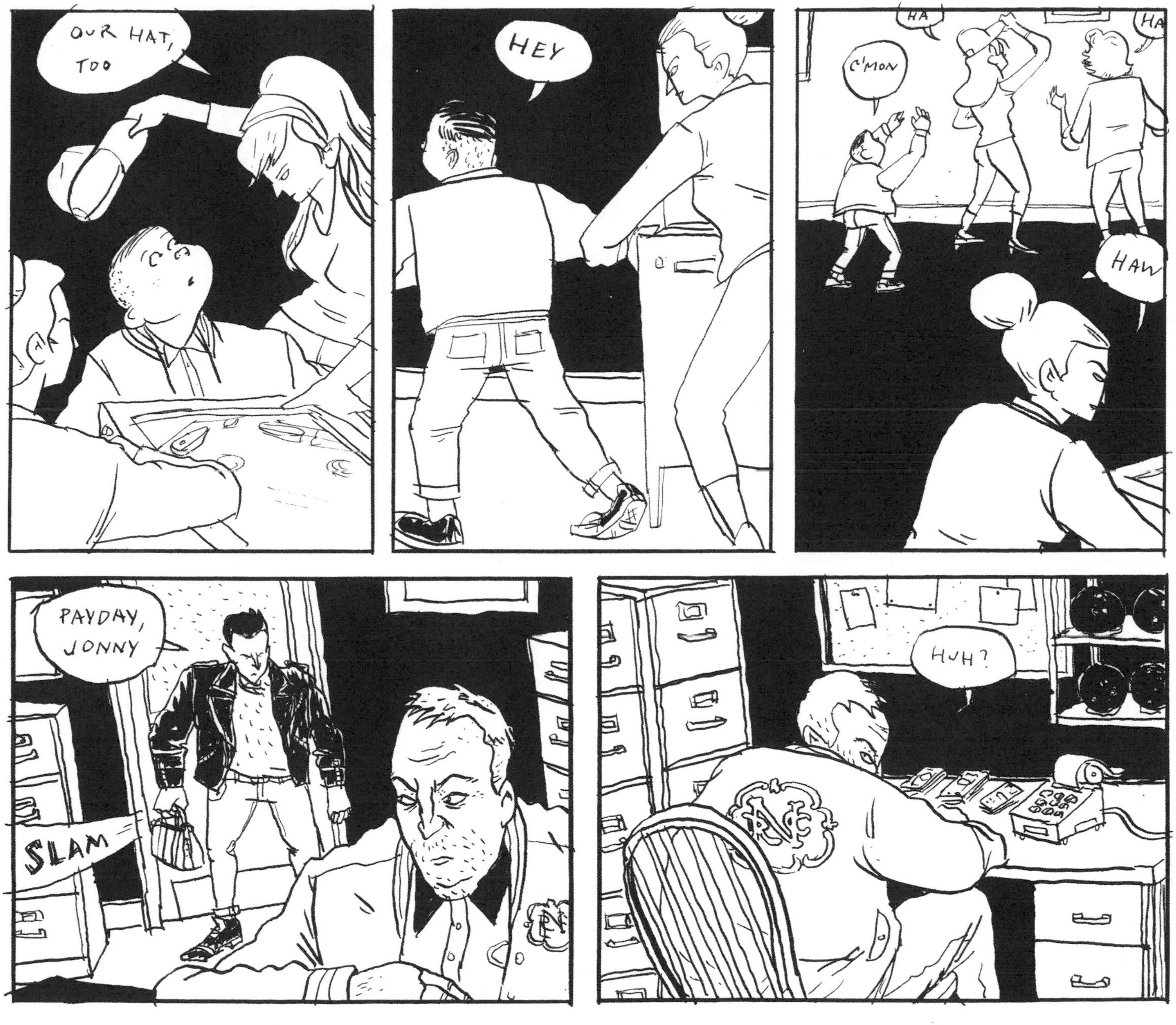
OUR HAT, TOO
HEY
C'MON
HA
HA
HAW
PAYDAY, JONNY
SLAM
HUH?

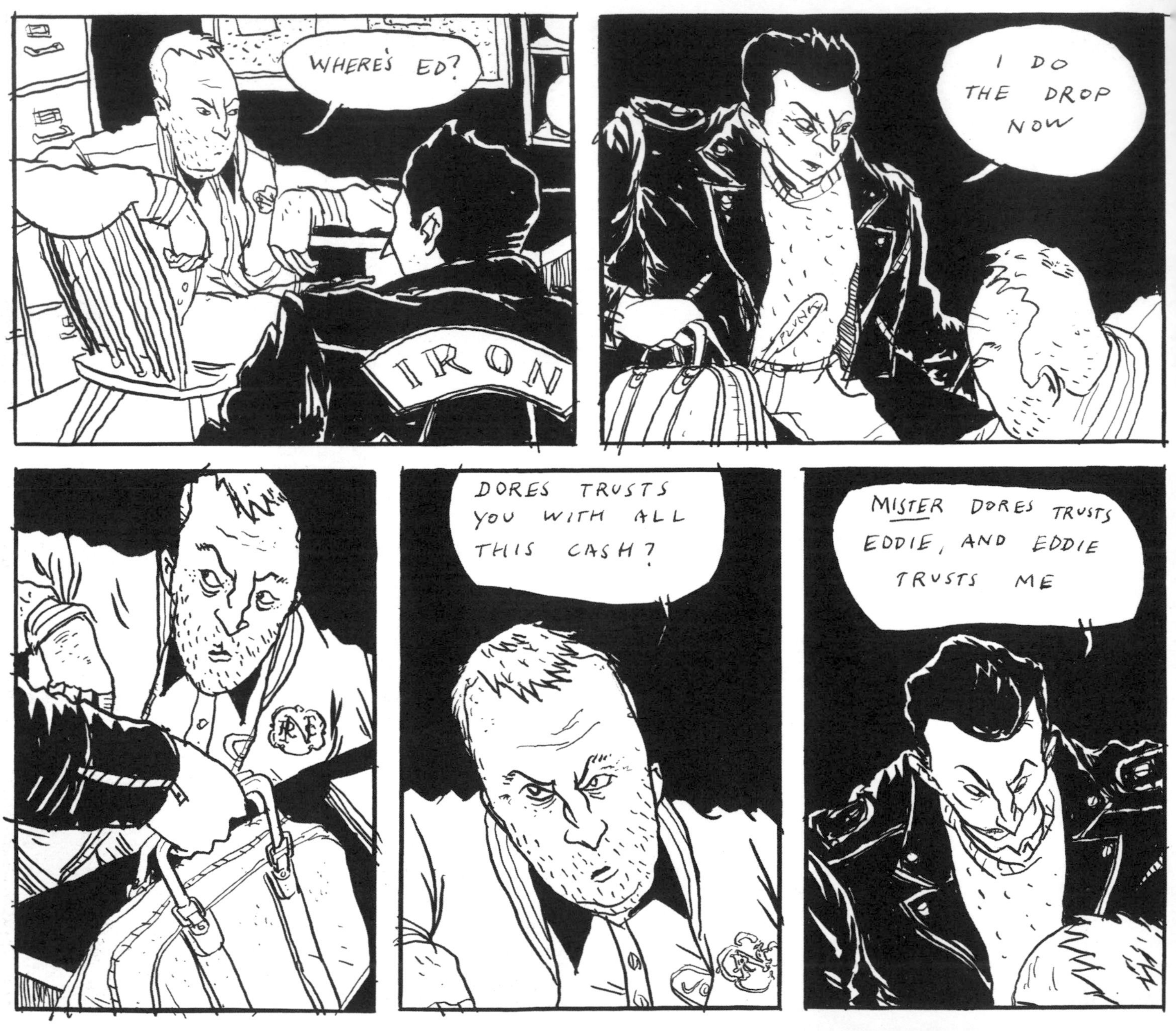
WHERE'S ED?
IRON
I DO THE DROP NOW
PLUNK
DORES TRUSTS YOU WITH ALL THIS CASH?
MISTER DORES TRUSTS EDDIE, AND EDDIE TRUSTS ME

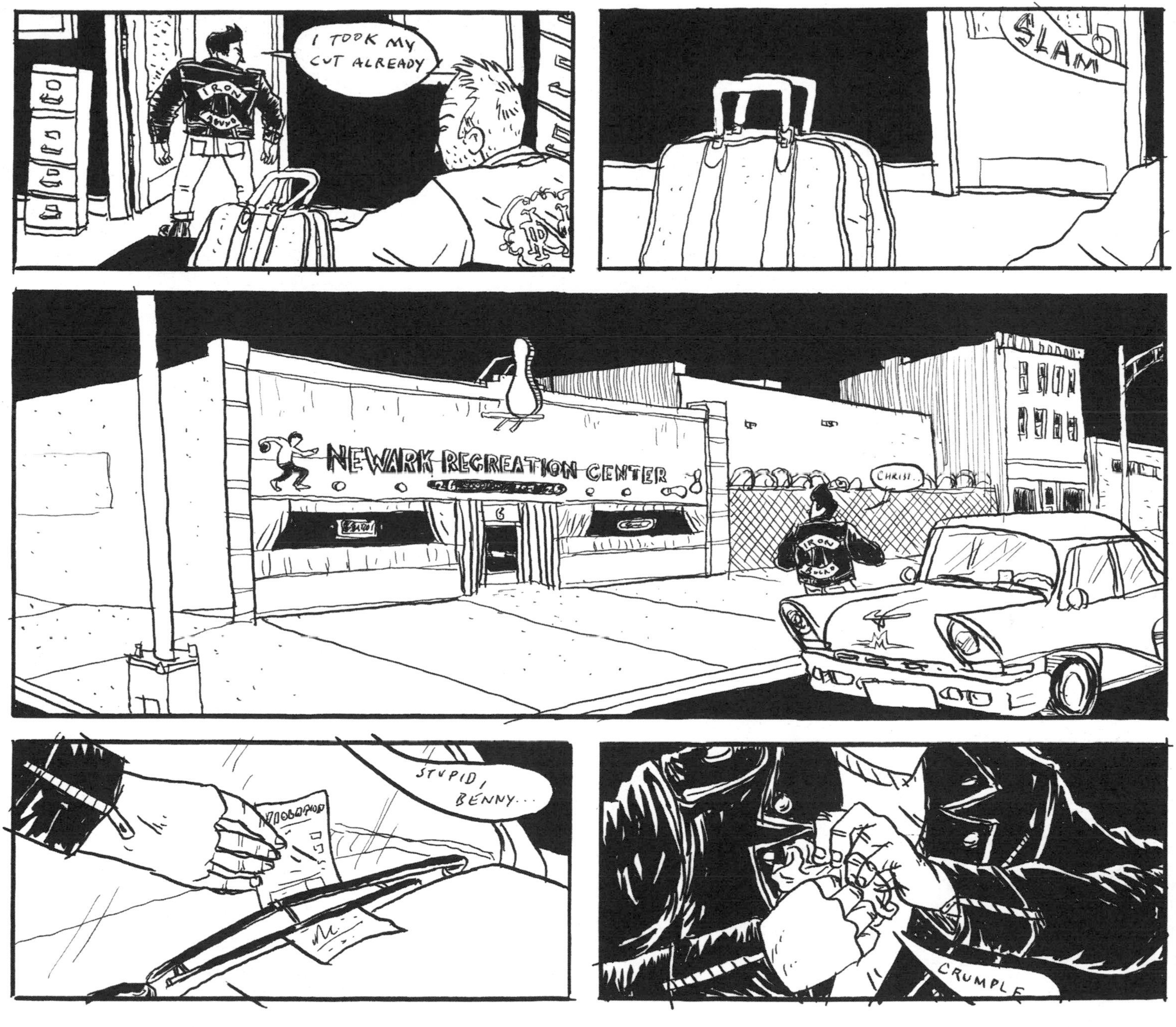
I TOOK MY CUT ALREADY
IRON ROADS
SLAM
NEWARK RECREATION CENTER
CHRIST...
STUPID, BENNY...
CRUMPLE

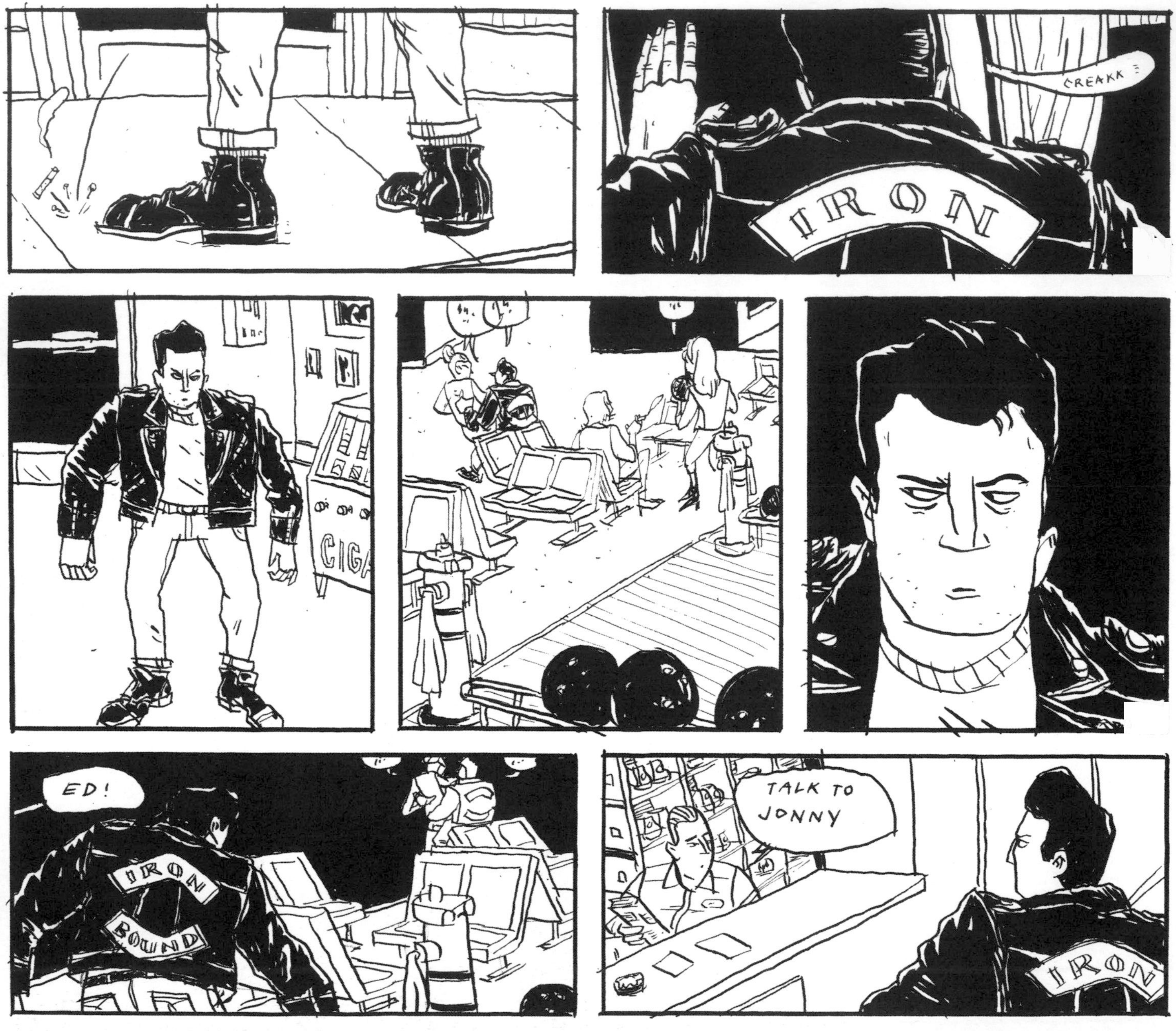
CREAKK
IRON
CIGA
ED!
IRON
BOUND
TALK TO JONNY
IRON

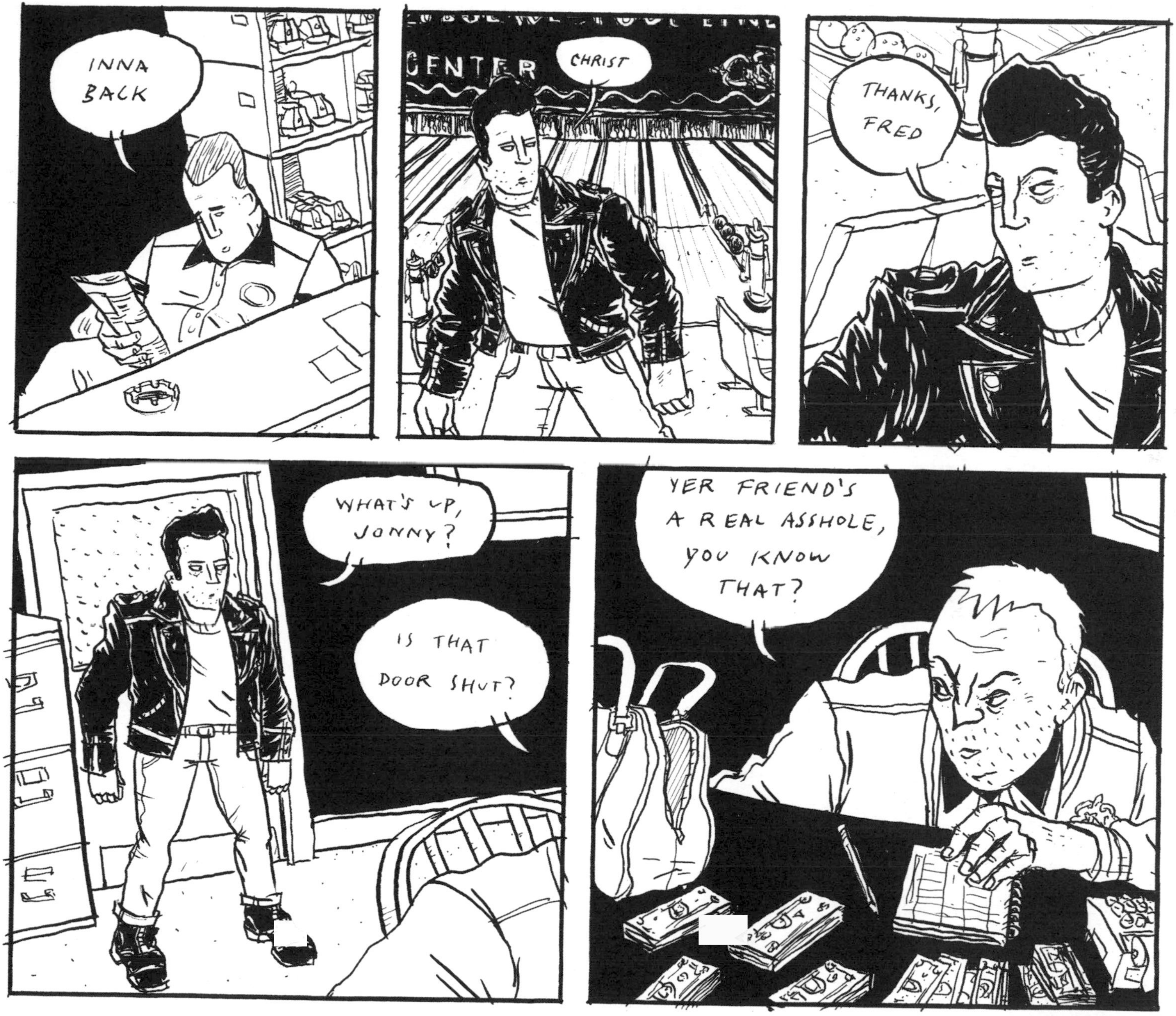
INNA BACK
CENTER
CHRIST
THANKS, FRED
WHAT'S UP, JONNY?
IS THAT DOOR SHUT?
YER FRIEND'S A REAL ASSHOLE, YOU KNOW THAT?

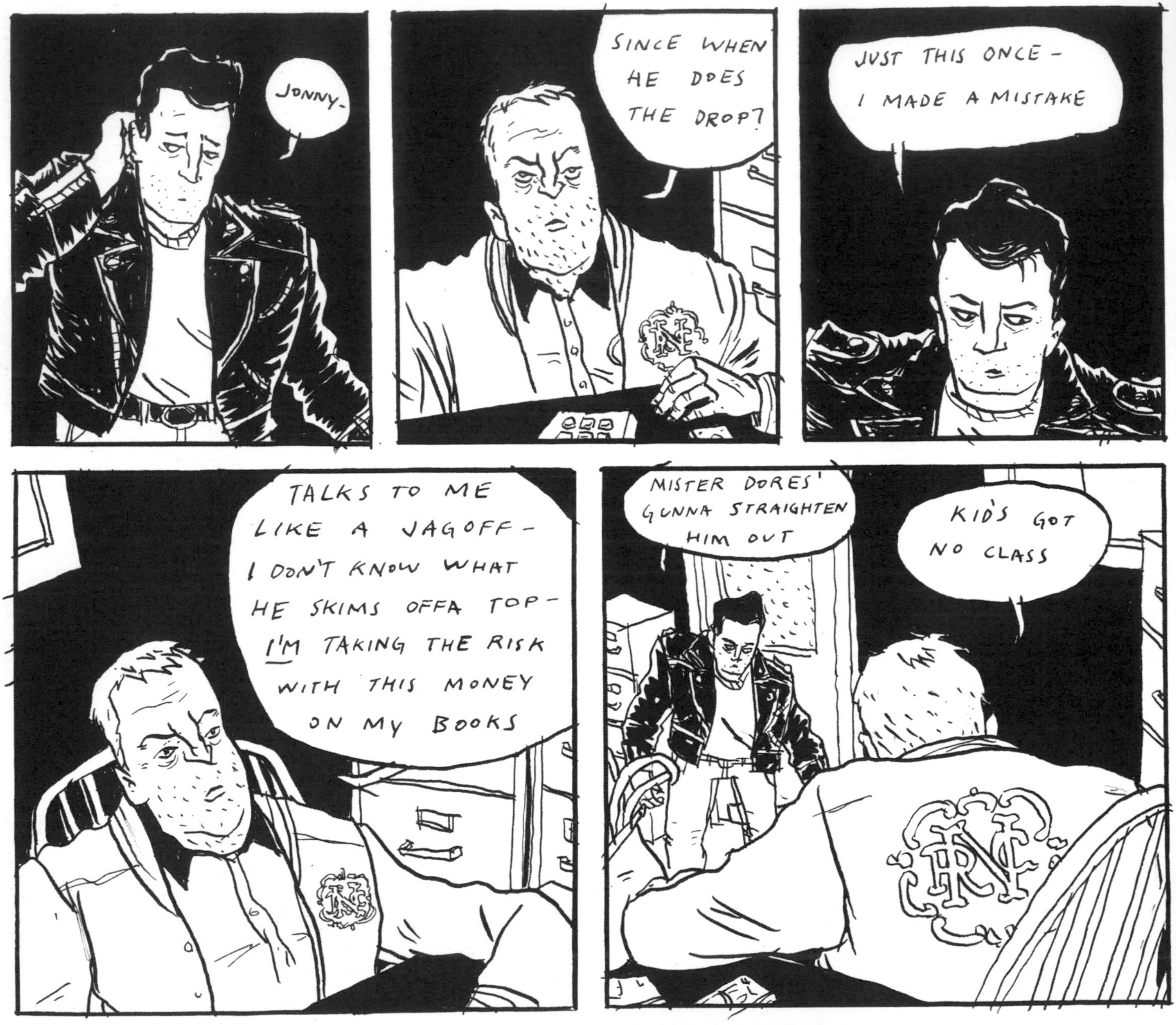
JONNY-
SINCE WHEN HE DOES THE DROP?
JUST THIS ONCE - I MADE A MISTAKE
TALKS TO ME LIKE A JAGOFF - I DON'T KNOW WHAT HE SKIMS OFFA TOP - I'M TAKING THE RISK WITH THIS MONEY ON MY BOOKS
MISTER DORES' GUNNA STRAIGHTEN HIM OUT
KID'S GOT NO CLASS

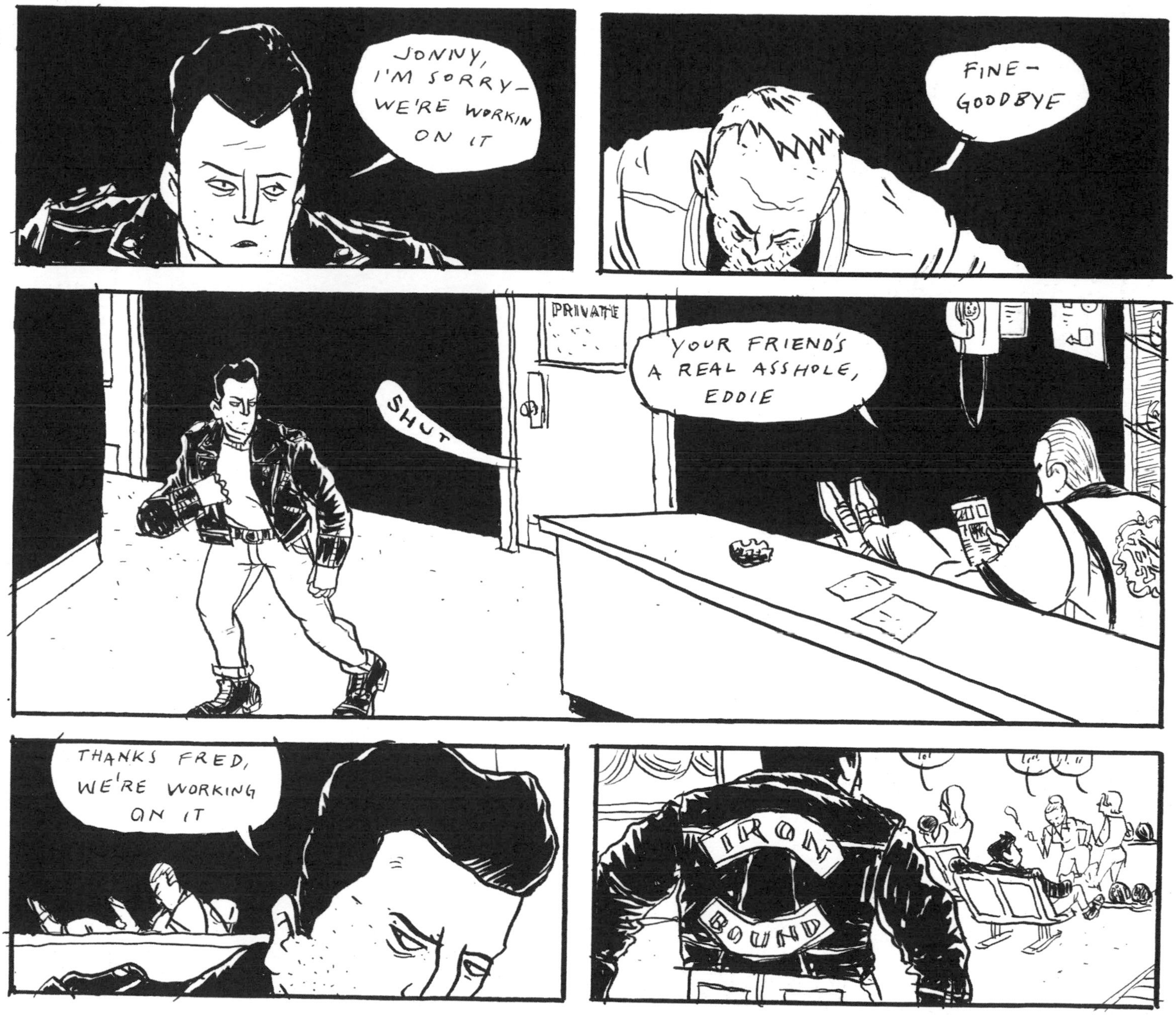
JONNY, I'M SORRY— WE'RE WORKIN ON IT
FINE— GOODBYE
SHUT
PRIVATE
YOUR FRIEND'S A REAL ASSHOLE, EDDIE
THANKS FRED, WE'RE WORKING ON IT
IRON
BOUND

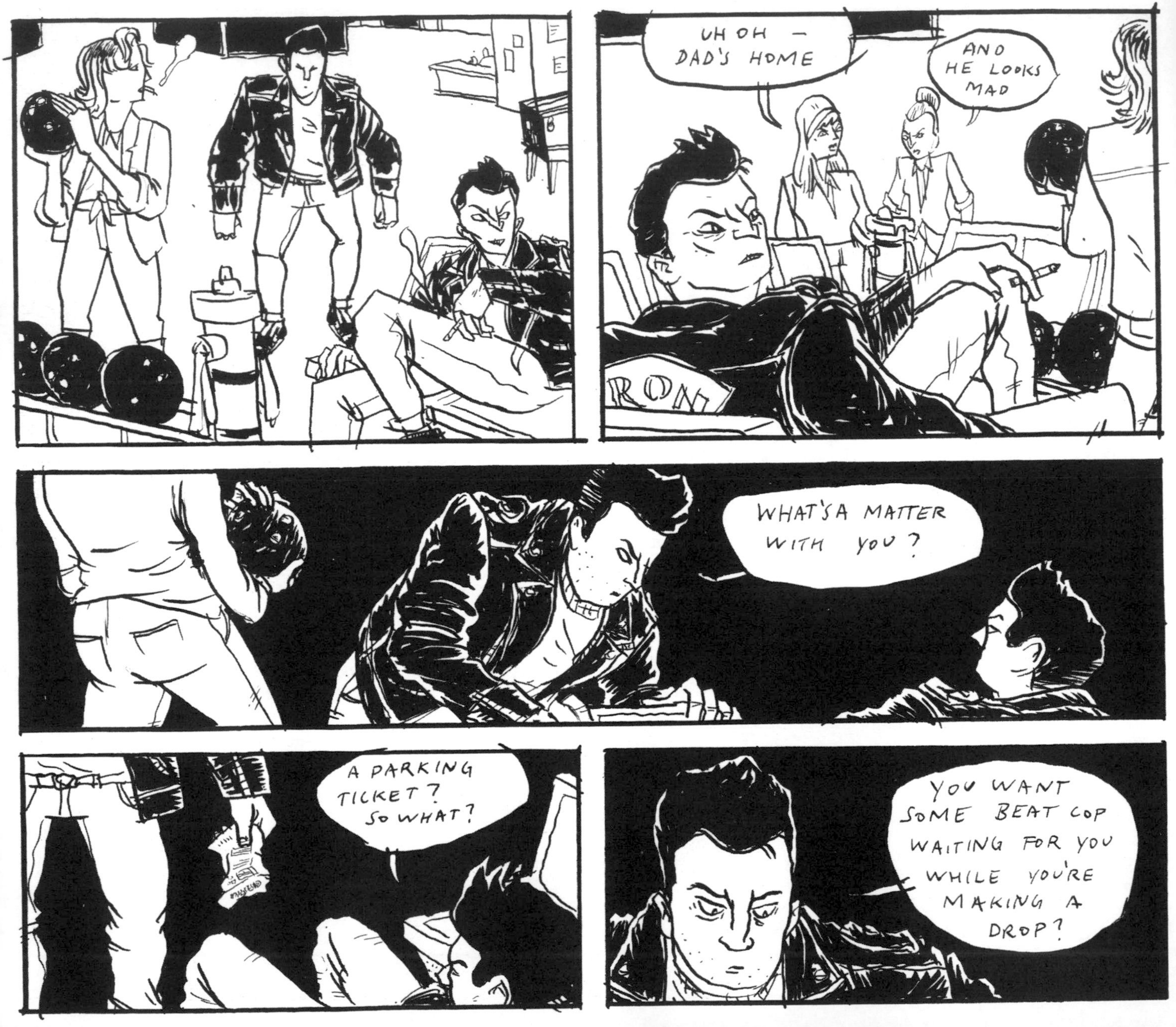
UH OH — DAD'S HOME
AND HE LOOKS MAD
RON
WHAT'SA MATTER WITH YOU?
A PARKING TICKET? SO WHAT?
YOU WANT SOME BEAT COP WAITING FOR YOU WHILE YOU'RE MAKING A DROP?

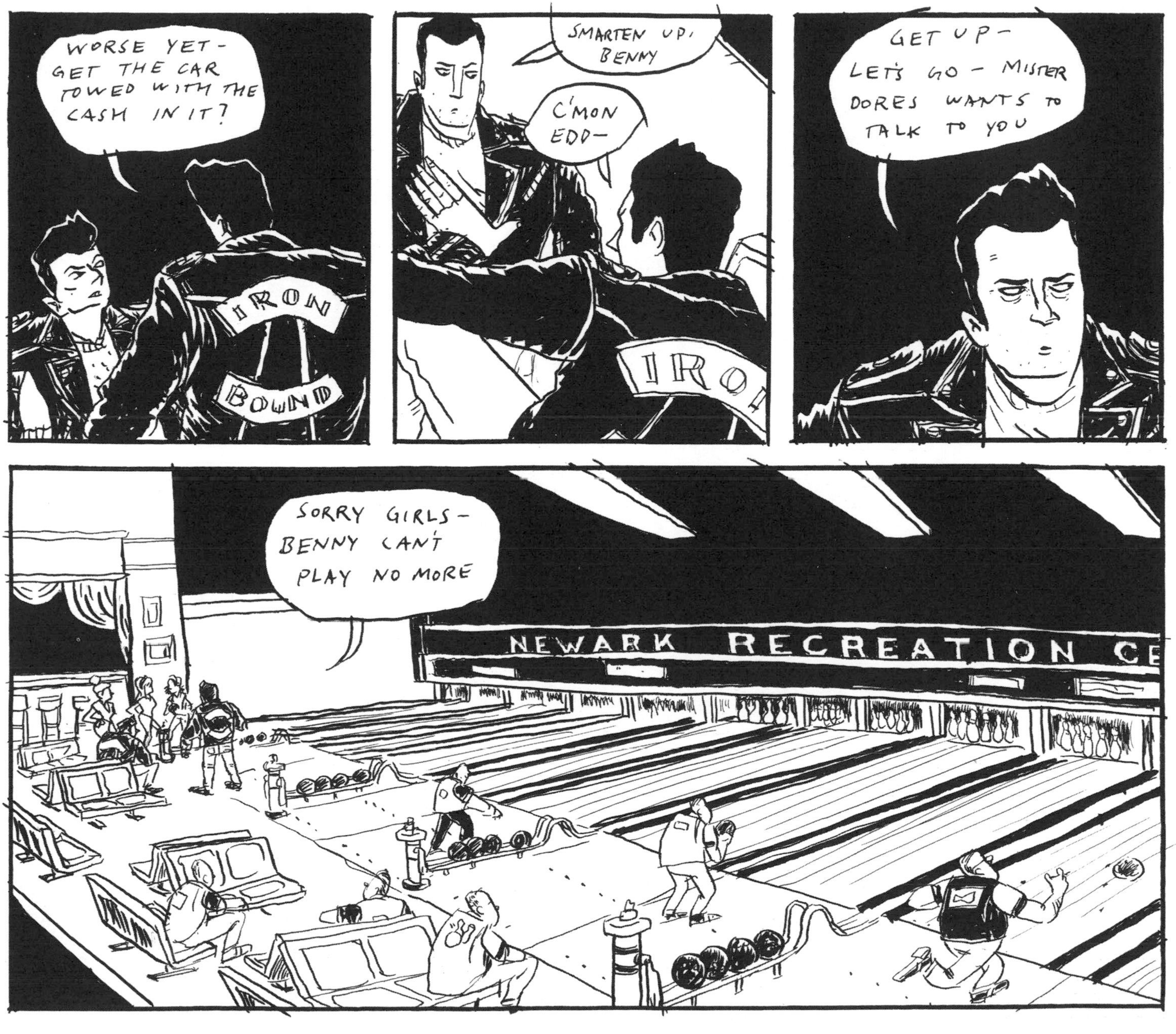
WORSE YET- GET THE CAR TOWED WITH THE CASH IN IT?
IRON
BOUND
SMARTEN UP, BENNY
C'MON EDD-
GET UP- LET'S GO - MISTER DORES WANTS TO TALK TO YOU
SORRY GIRLS- BENNY CAN'T PLAY NO MORE
NEWARK RECREATION CE

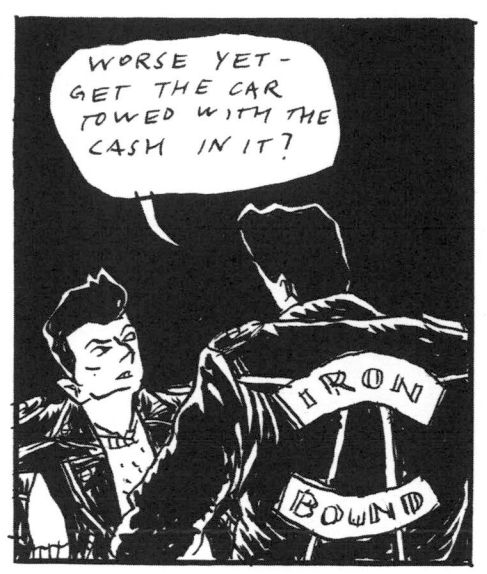

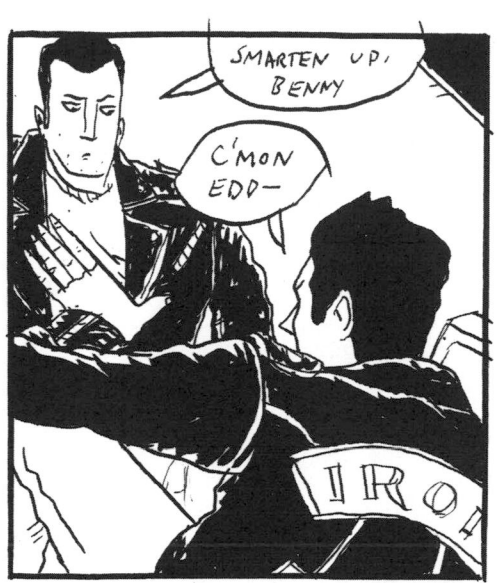

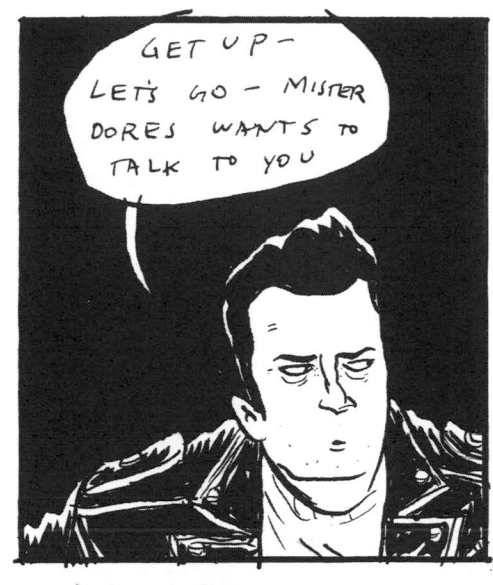

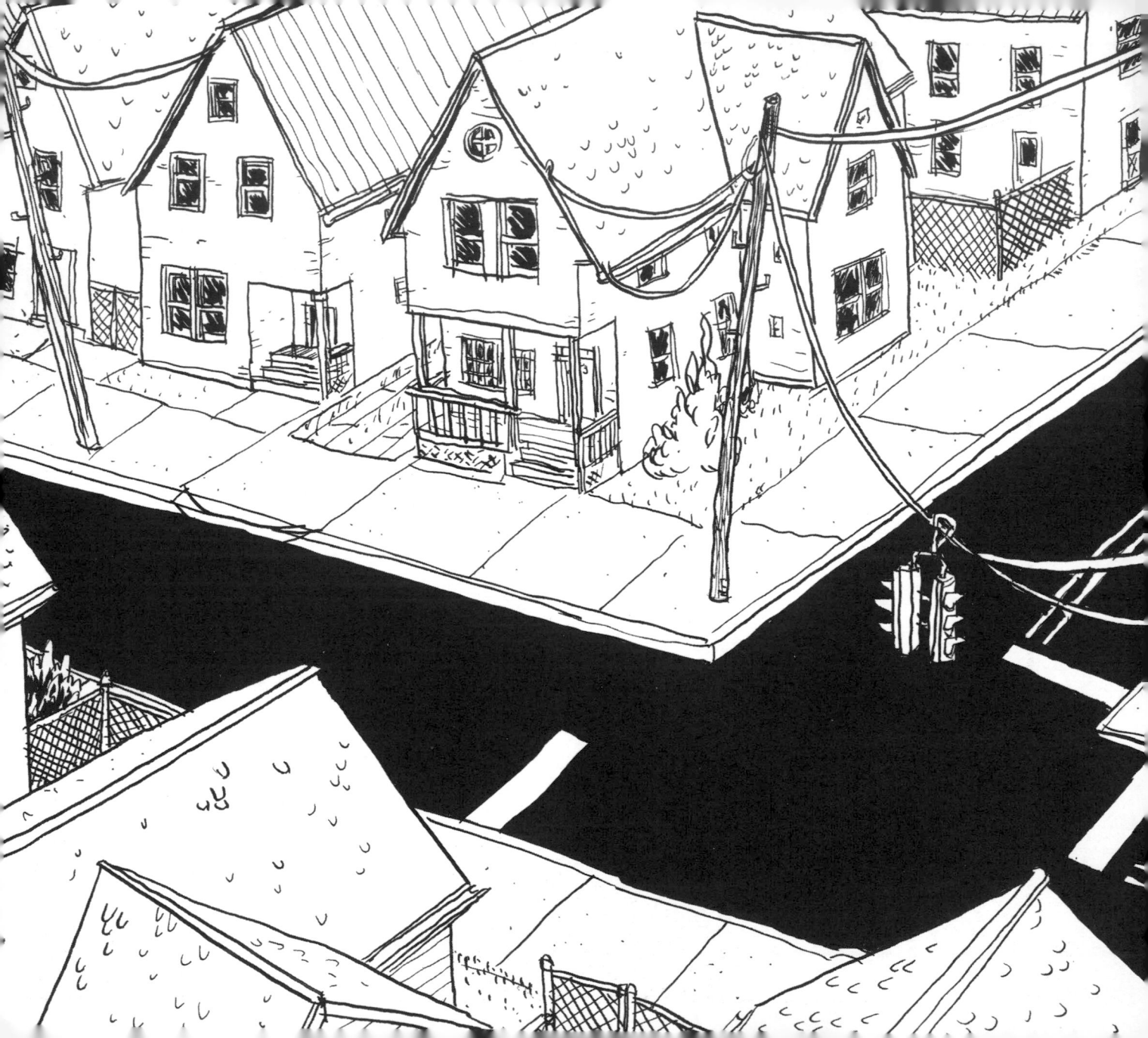

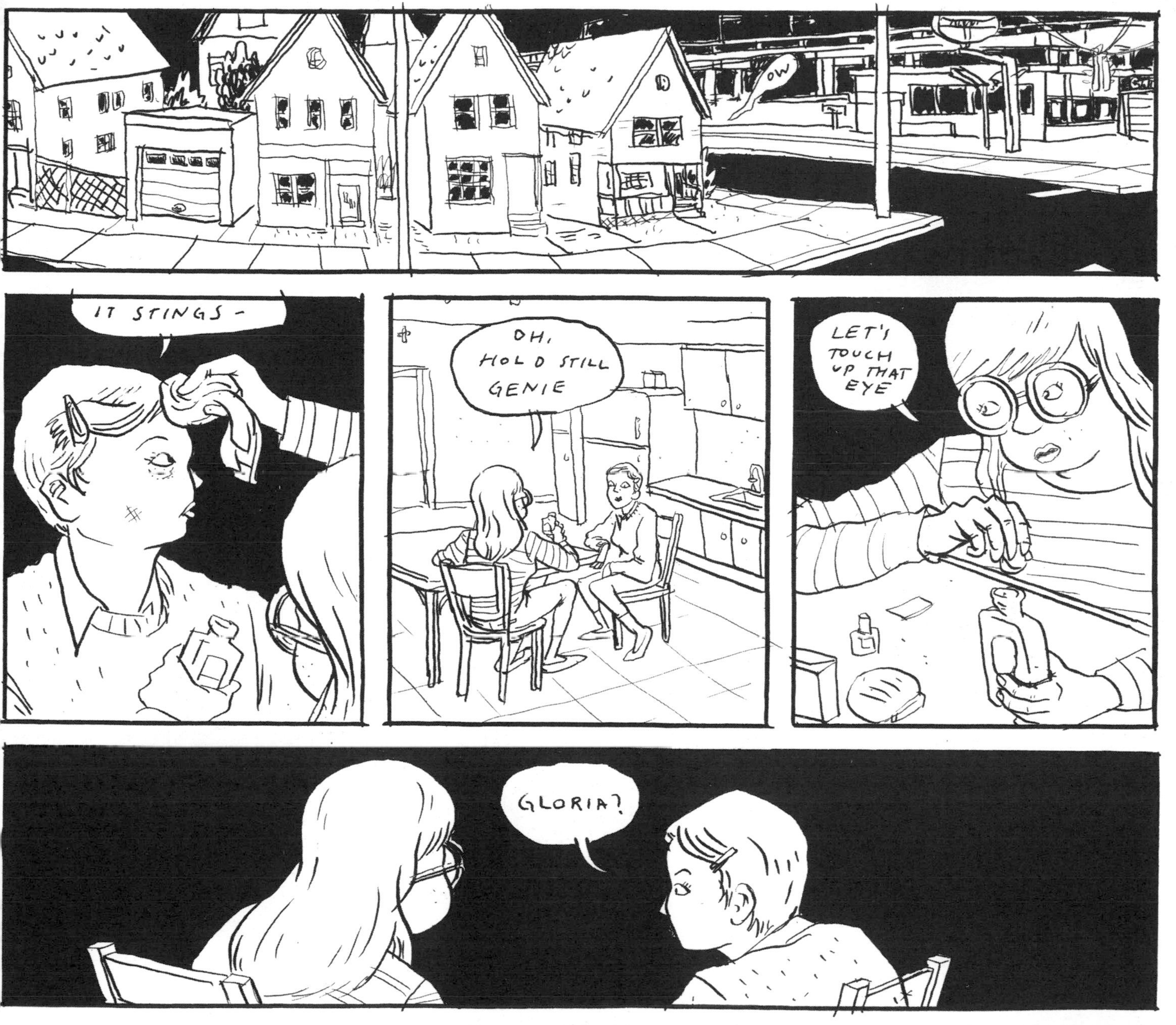
OW
IT STINGS -
OH, HOLD STILL GENIE
LET'S TOUCH UP THAT EYE
GLORIA?

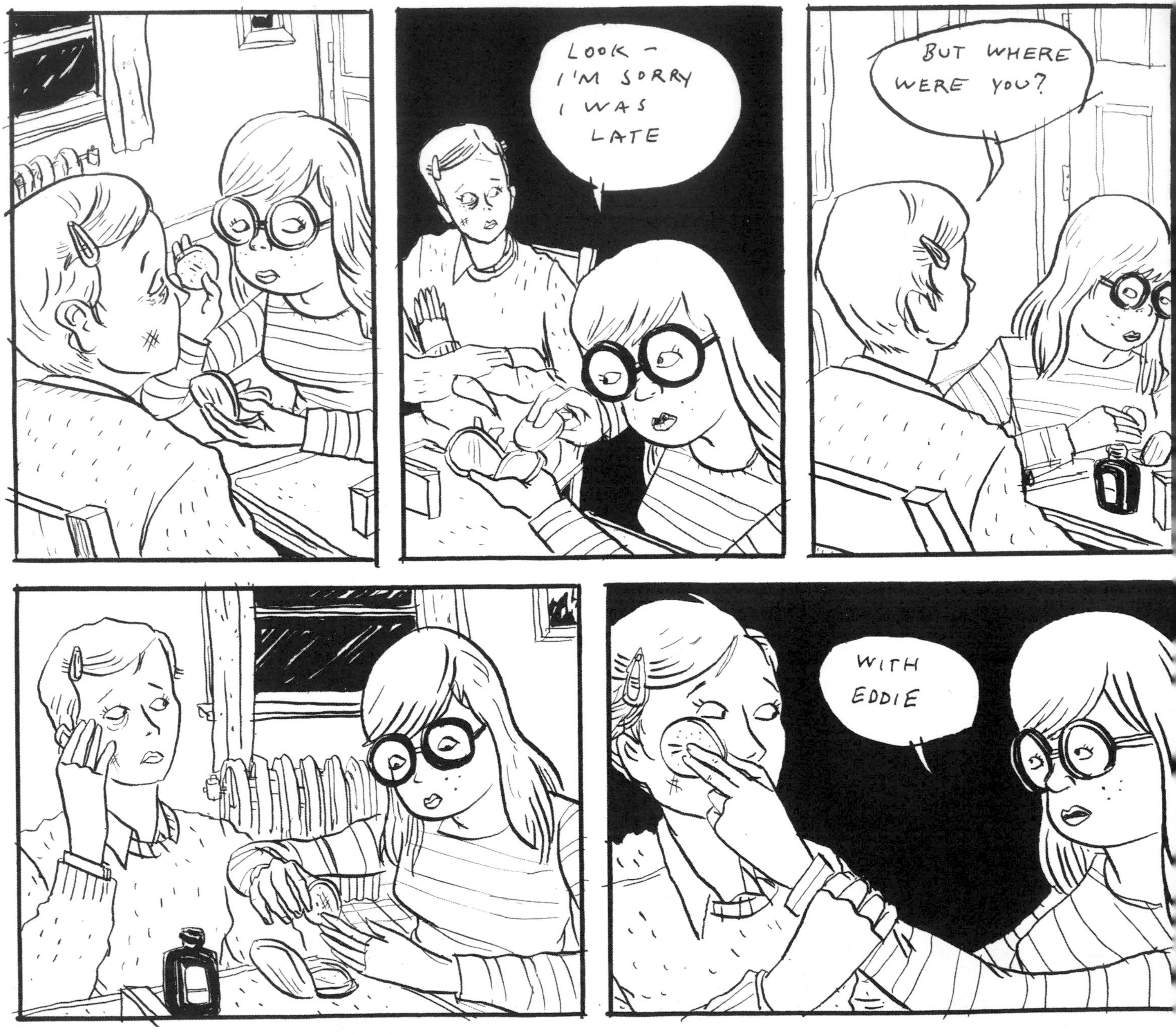
LOOK - I'M SORRY I WAS LATE
BUT WHERE WERE YOU?
WITH EDDIE

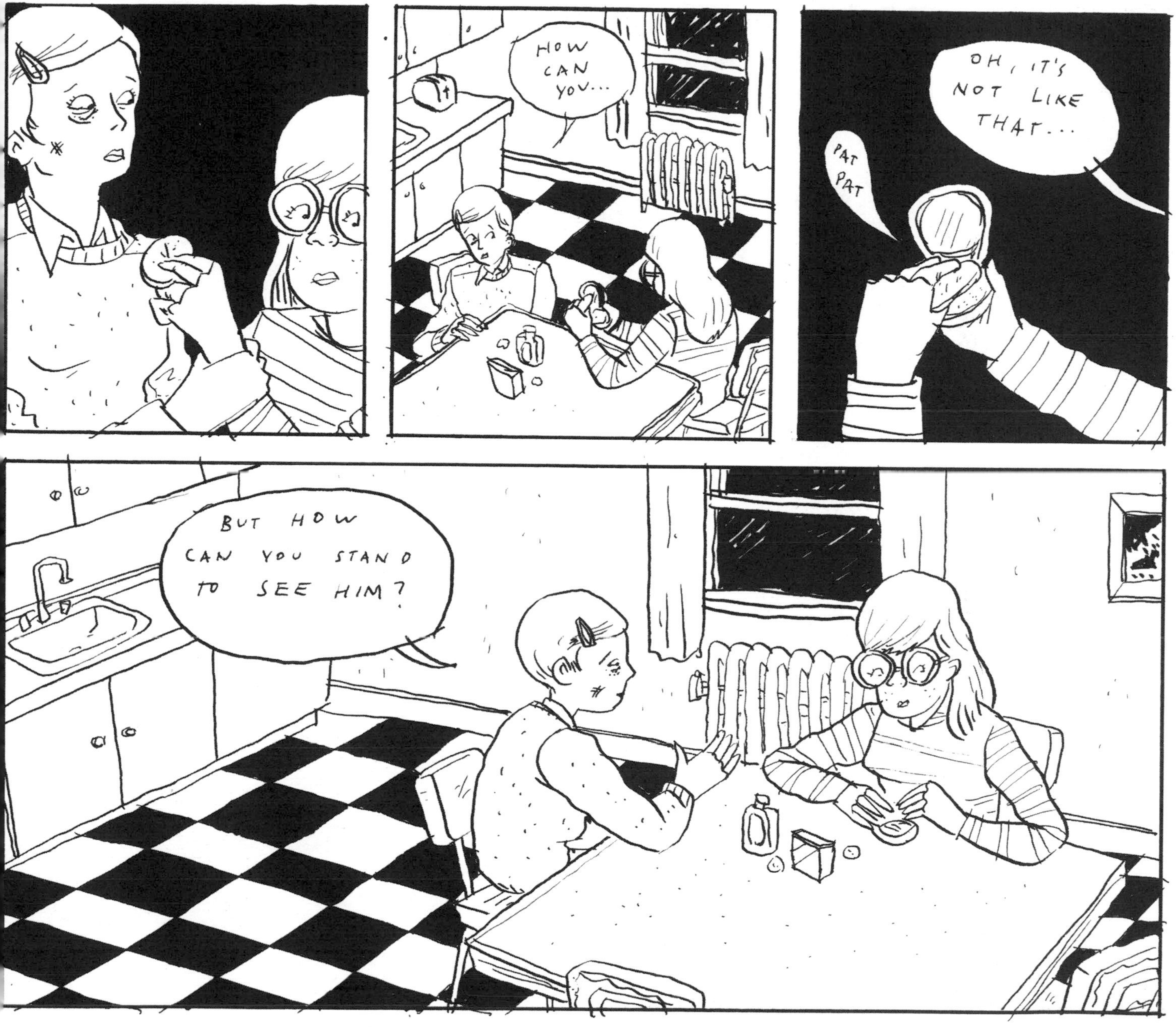
HOW CAN YOU...
PAT PAT
OH, IT'S NOT LIKE THAT...
BUT HOW CAN YOU STAND TO SEE HIM?

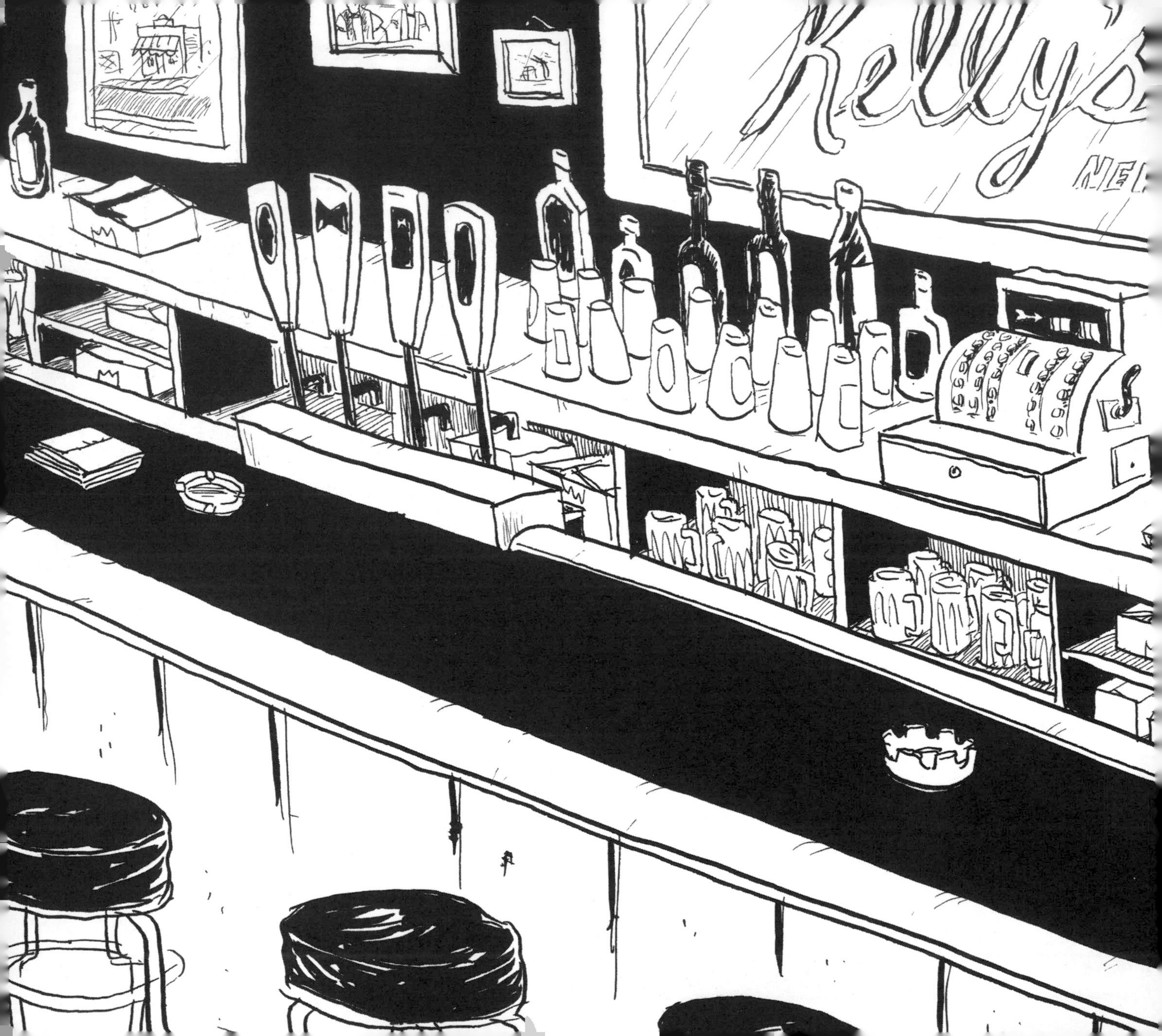
Kelly's

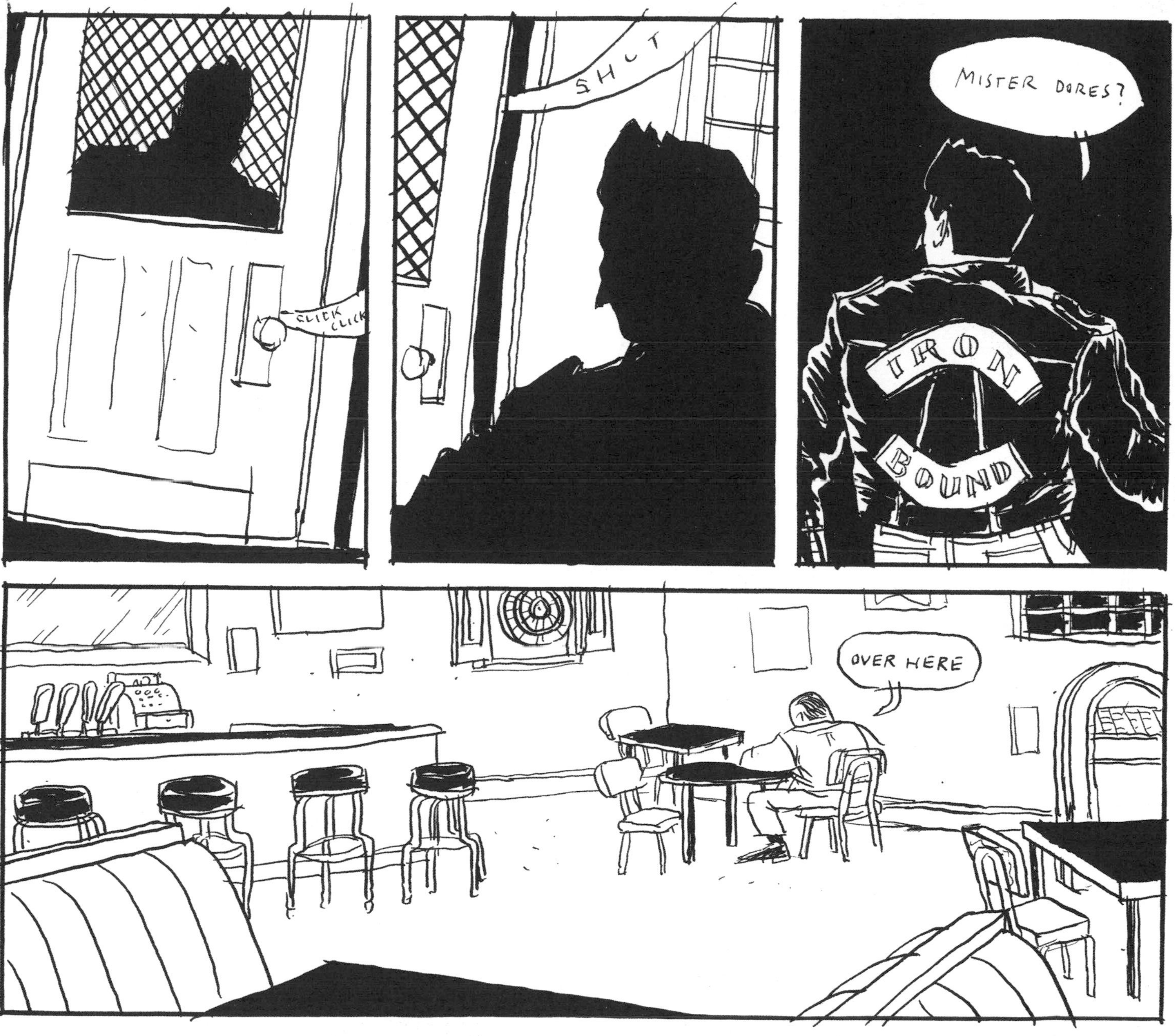
CLICK CLICK
SHUT
MISTER DORES?
IRON
BOUND
OVER HERE

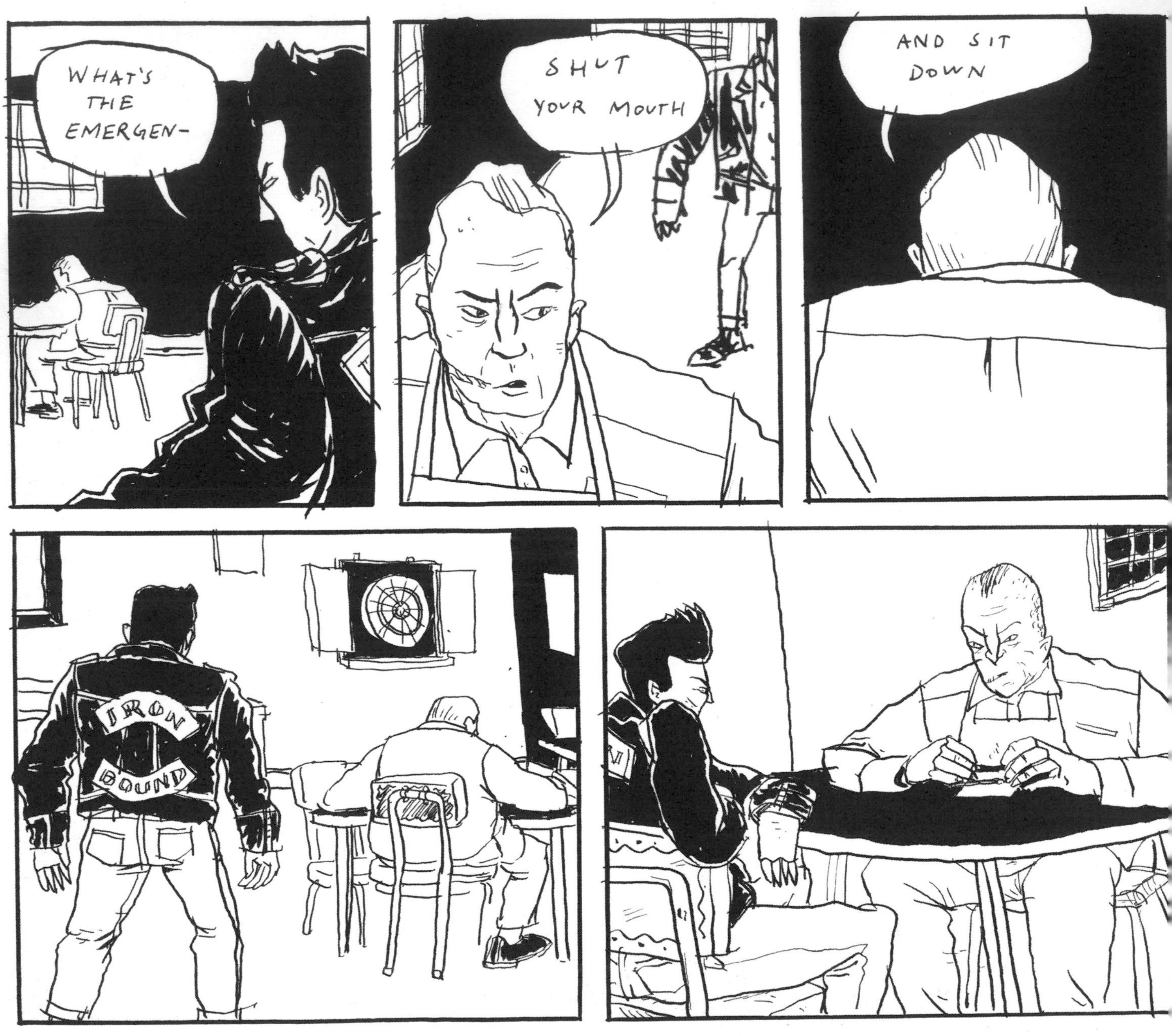
WHAT'S THE EMERGEN-
SHUT YOUR MOUTH
AND SIT DOWN
IRON BOUND

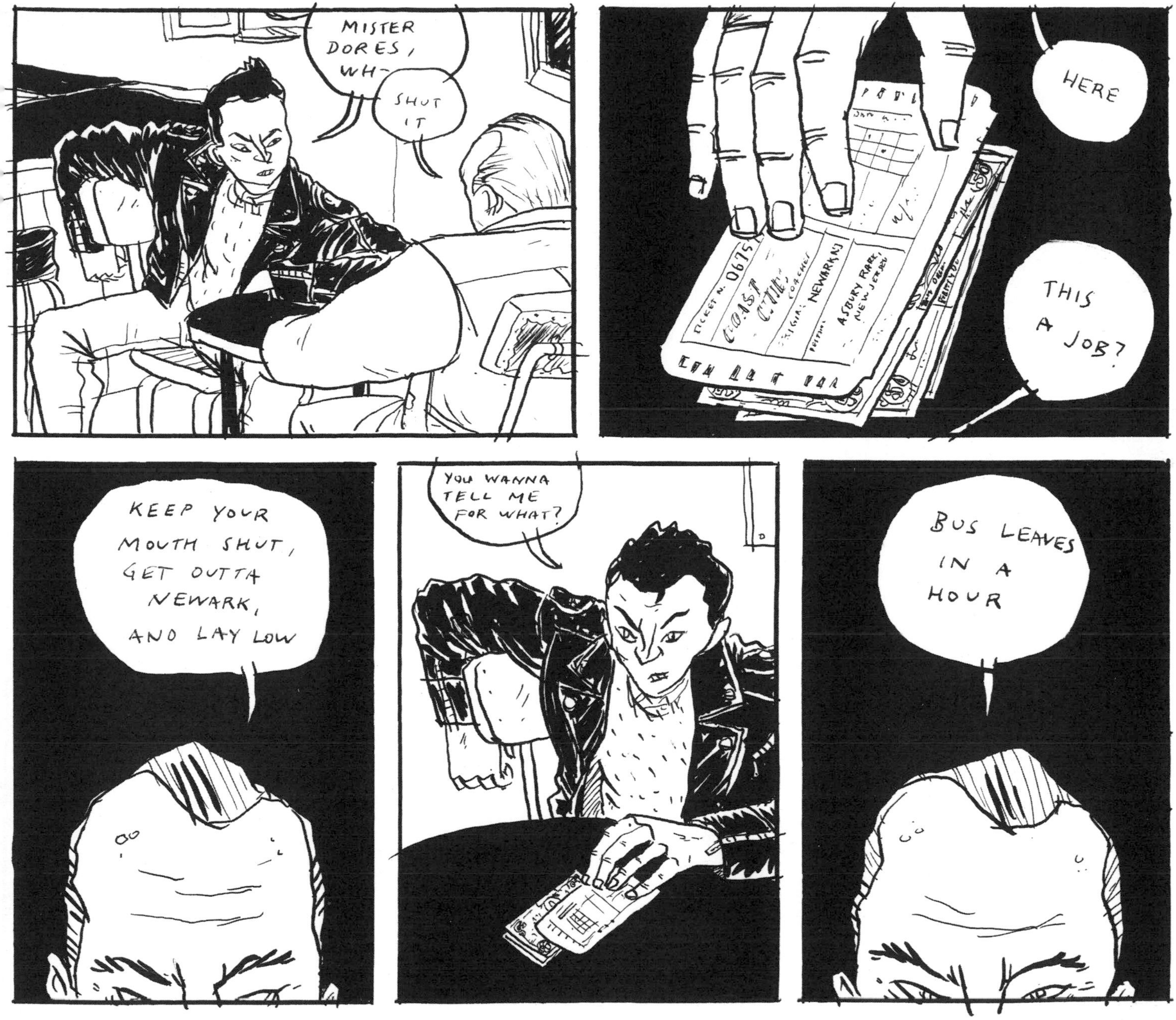
MISTER DORES, WH-
SHUT IT
HERE
THIS A JOB?
KEEP YOUR MOUTH SHUT, GET OUTTA NEWARK, AND LAY LOW
YOU WANNA TELL ME FOR WHAT?
BUS LEAVES IN A HOUR

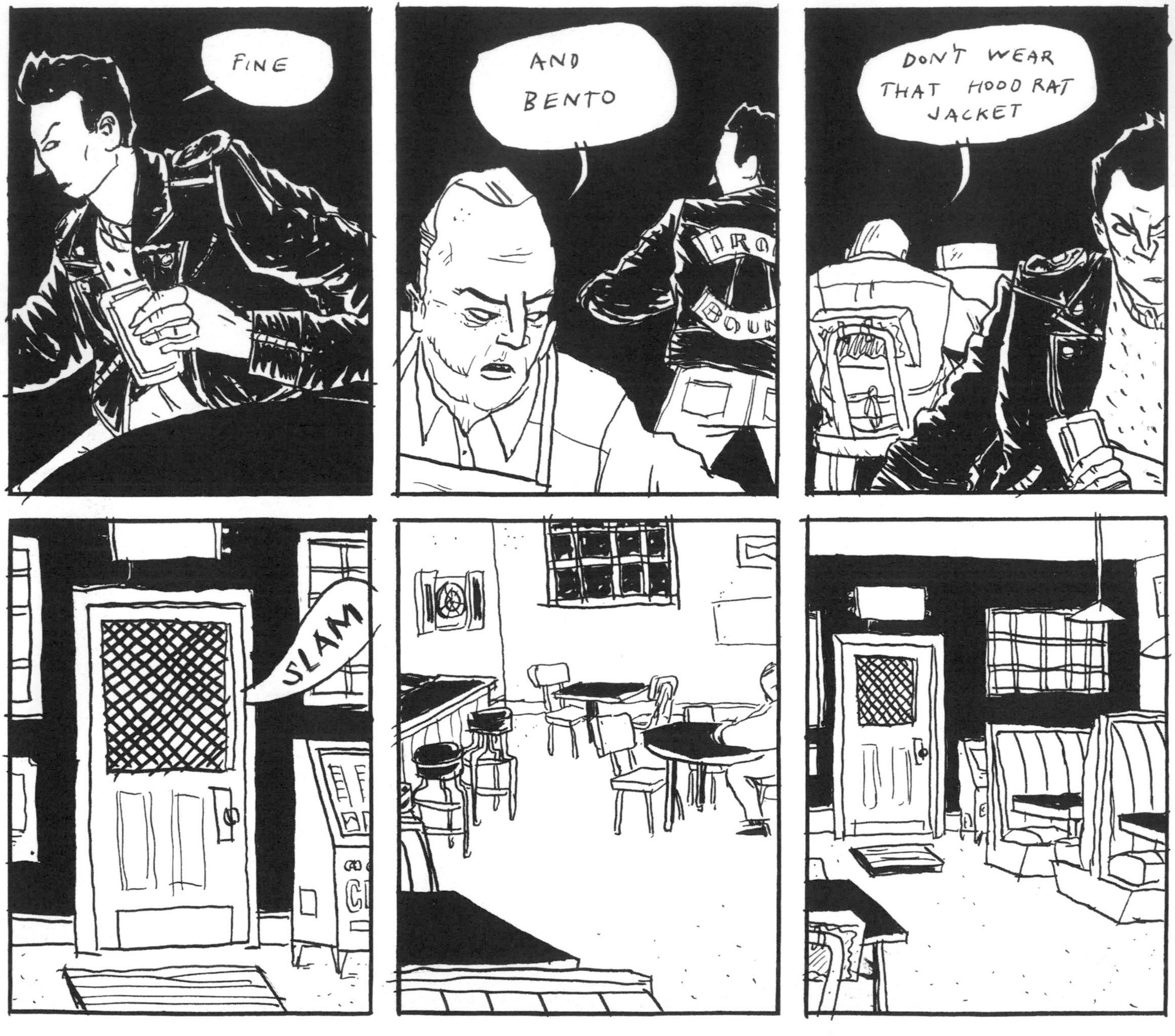
FINE
AND BENTO
DON'T WEAR THAT HOOD RAT JACKET
SLAM

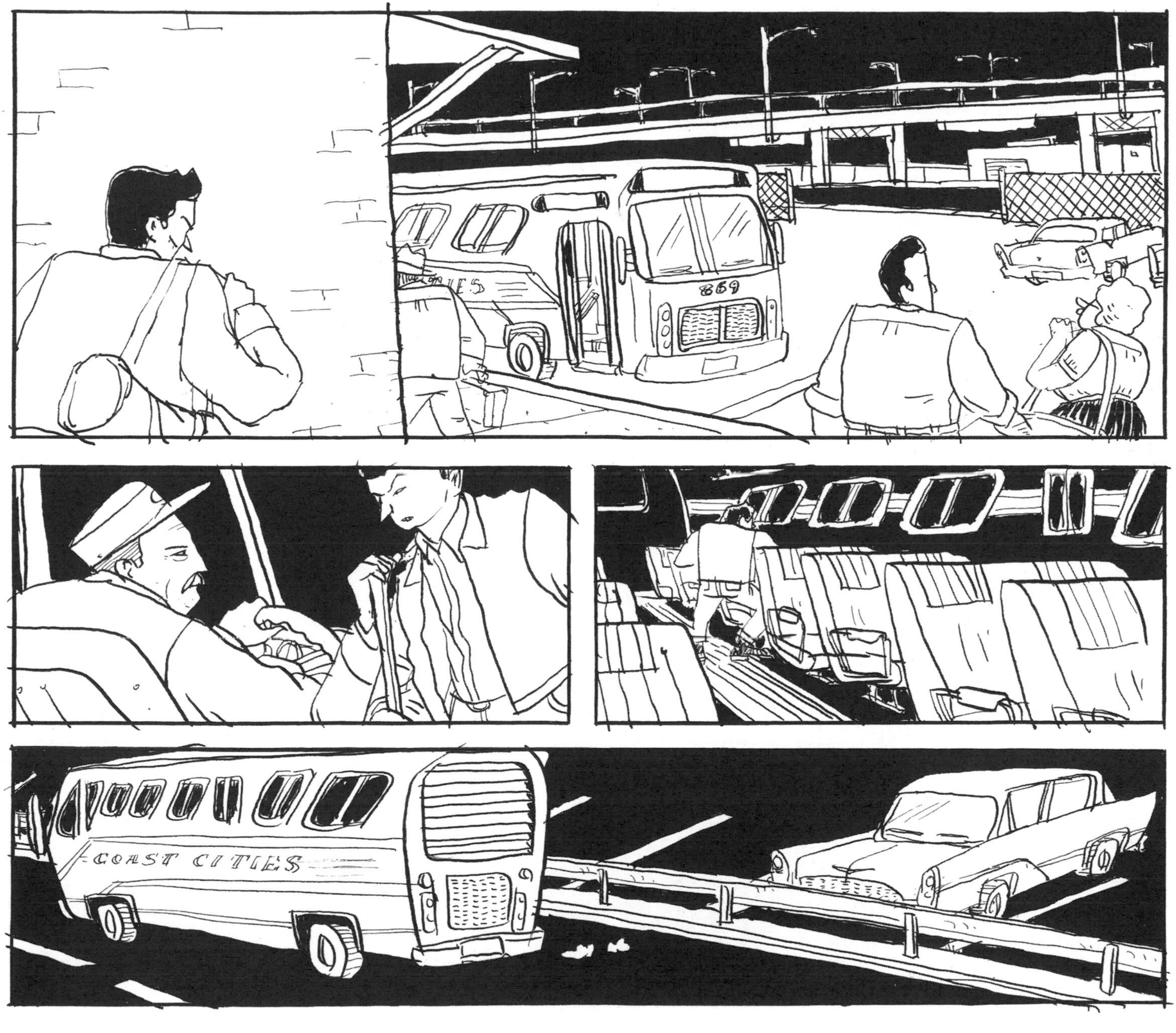
869
COAST CITIES

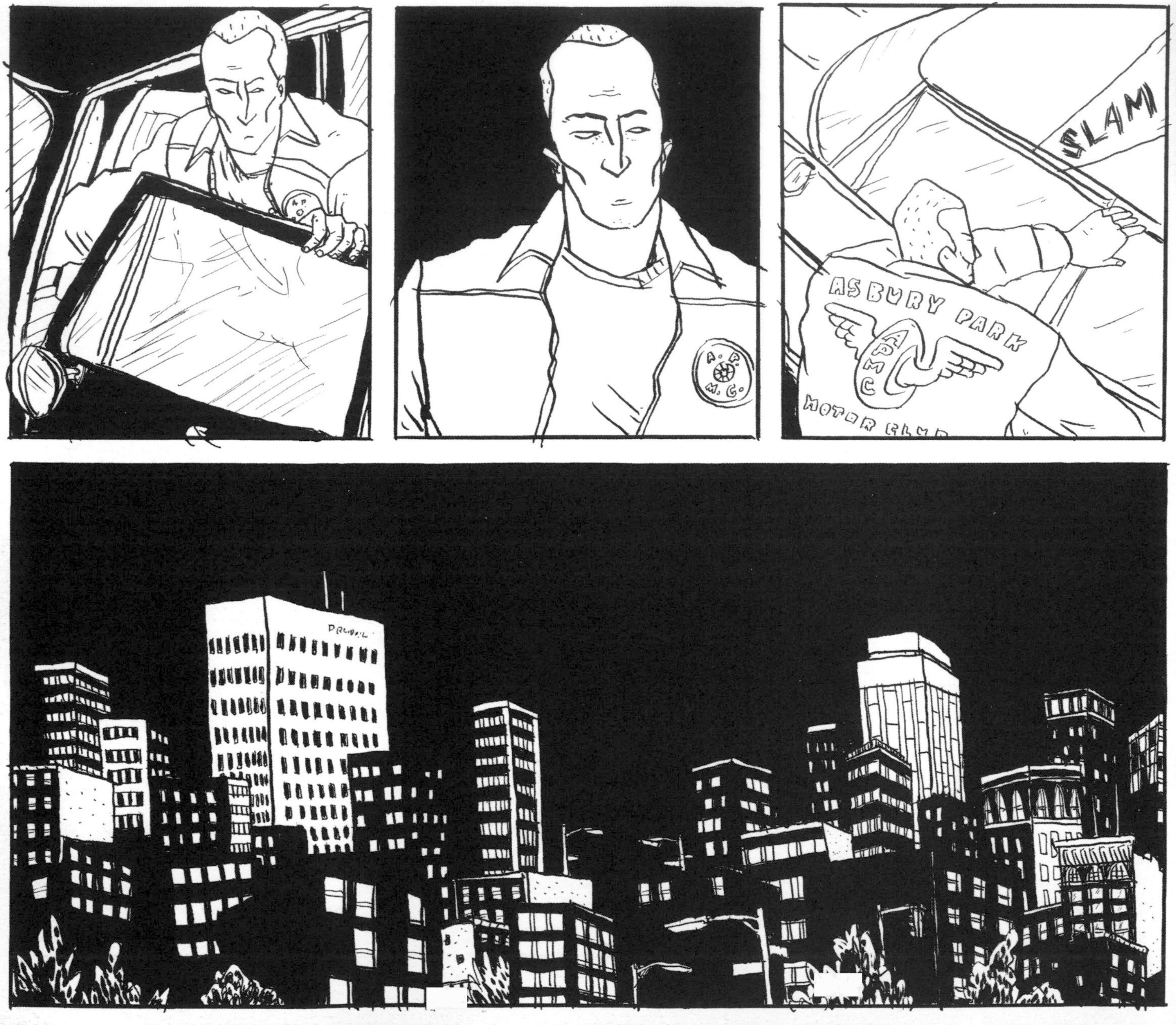
SLAM
ASBURY PARK
APMC

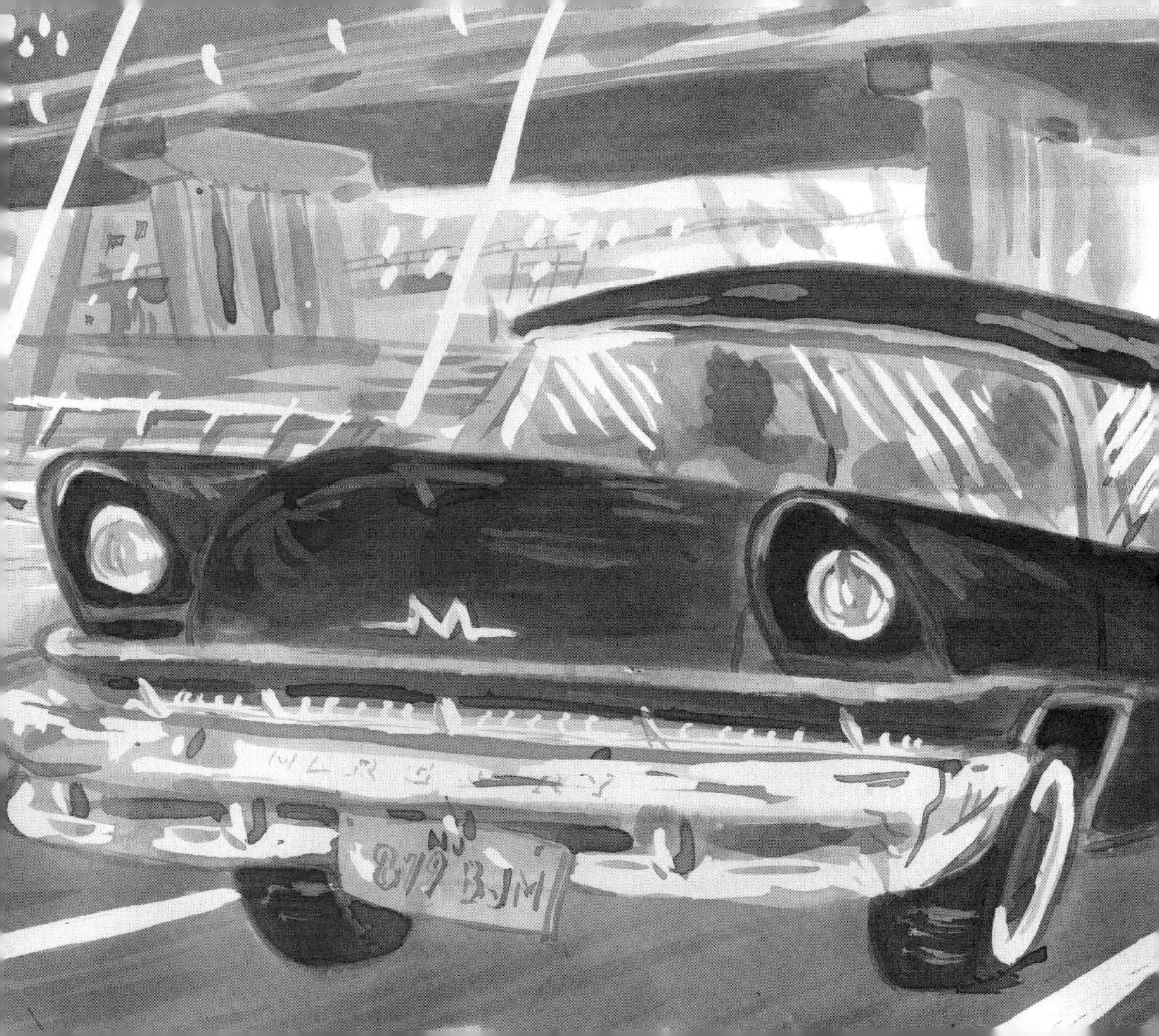
NJ
879 BJM

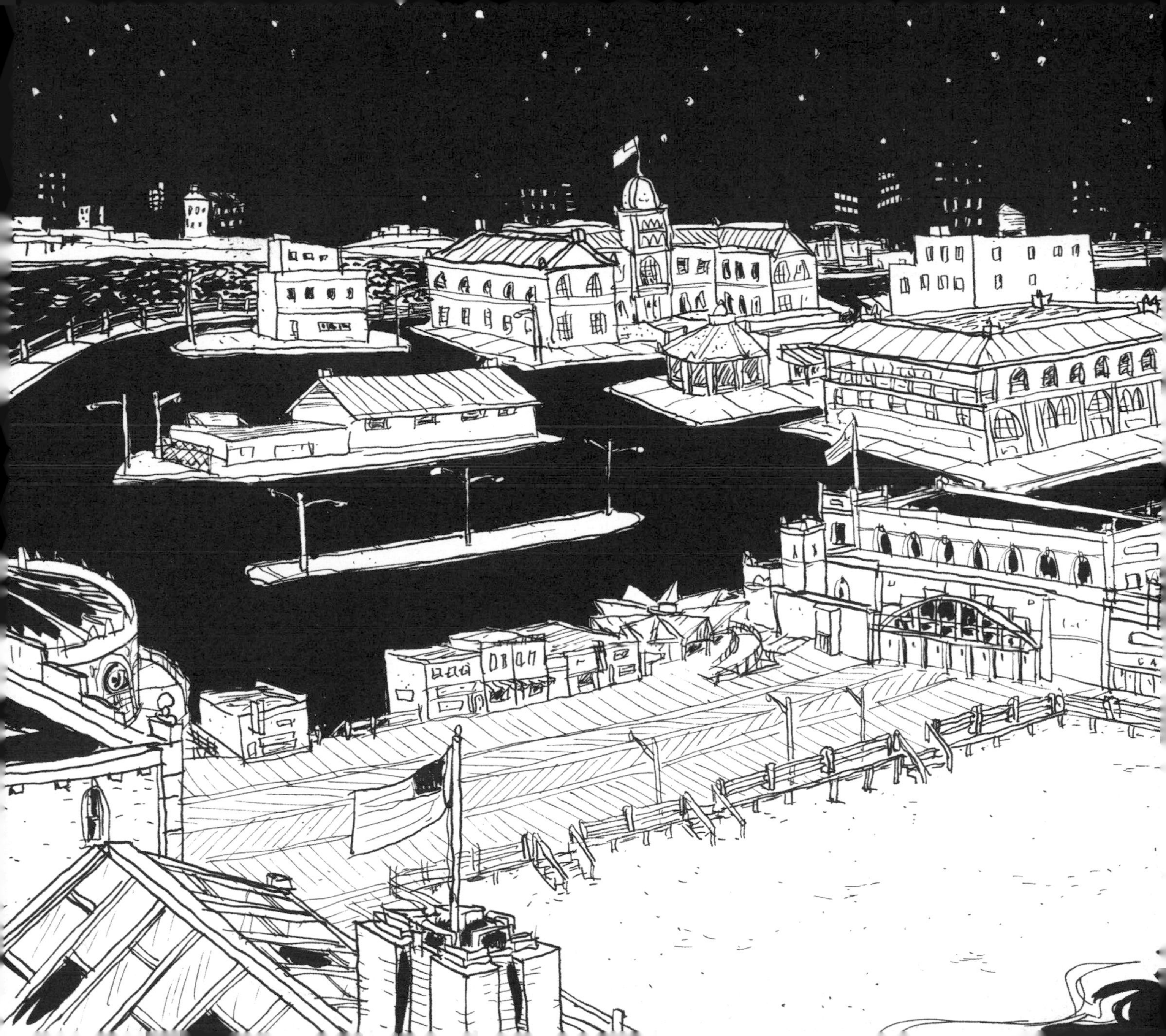

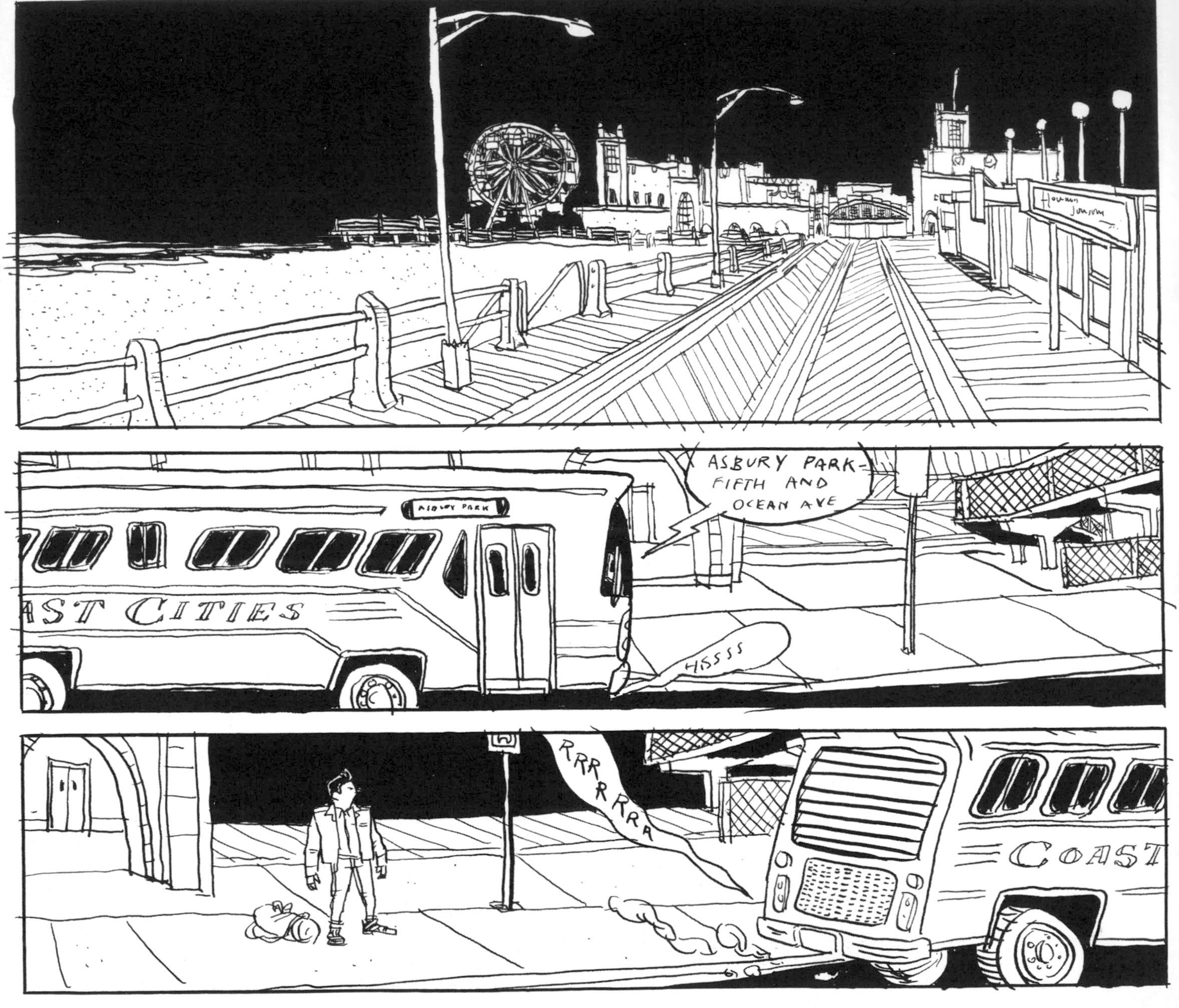
ASBURY PARK-
FIFTH AND
OCEAN AVE
AST CITIES
HISSSS
RRRRRRRA
COAST

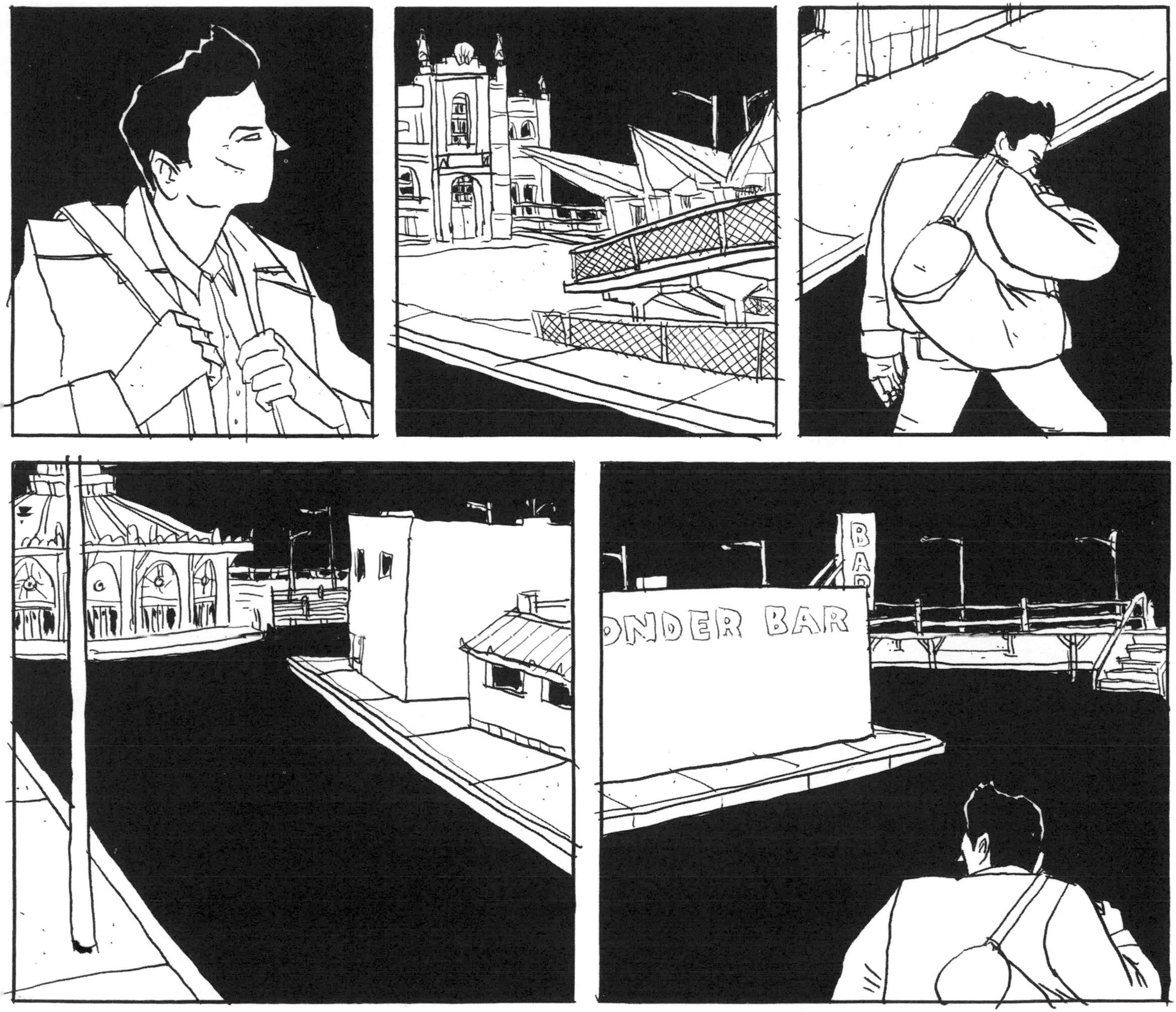
ONDER BAR

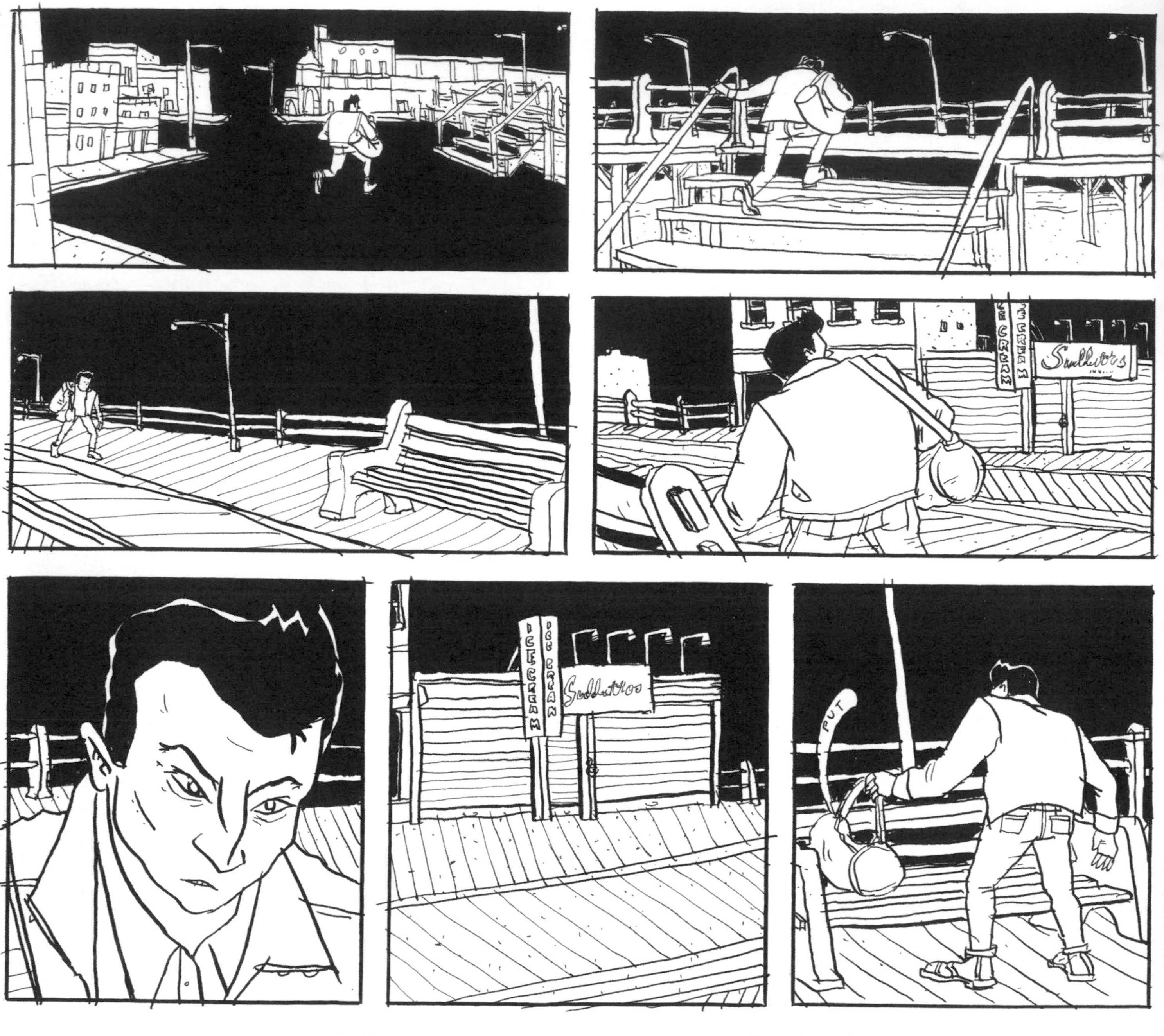
ICE CREAM
ICE CREAM
PUT

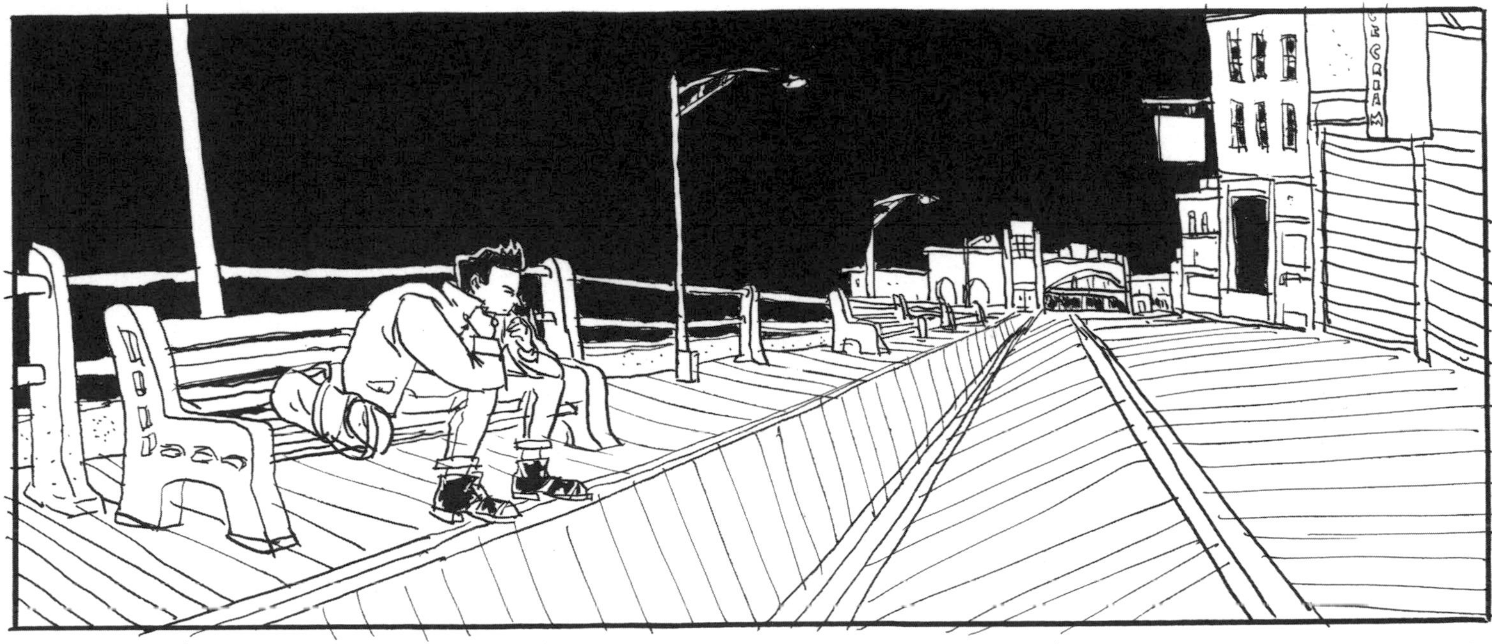
ICE CREAM

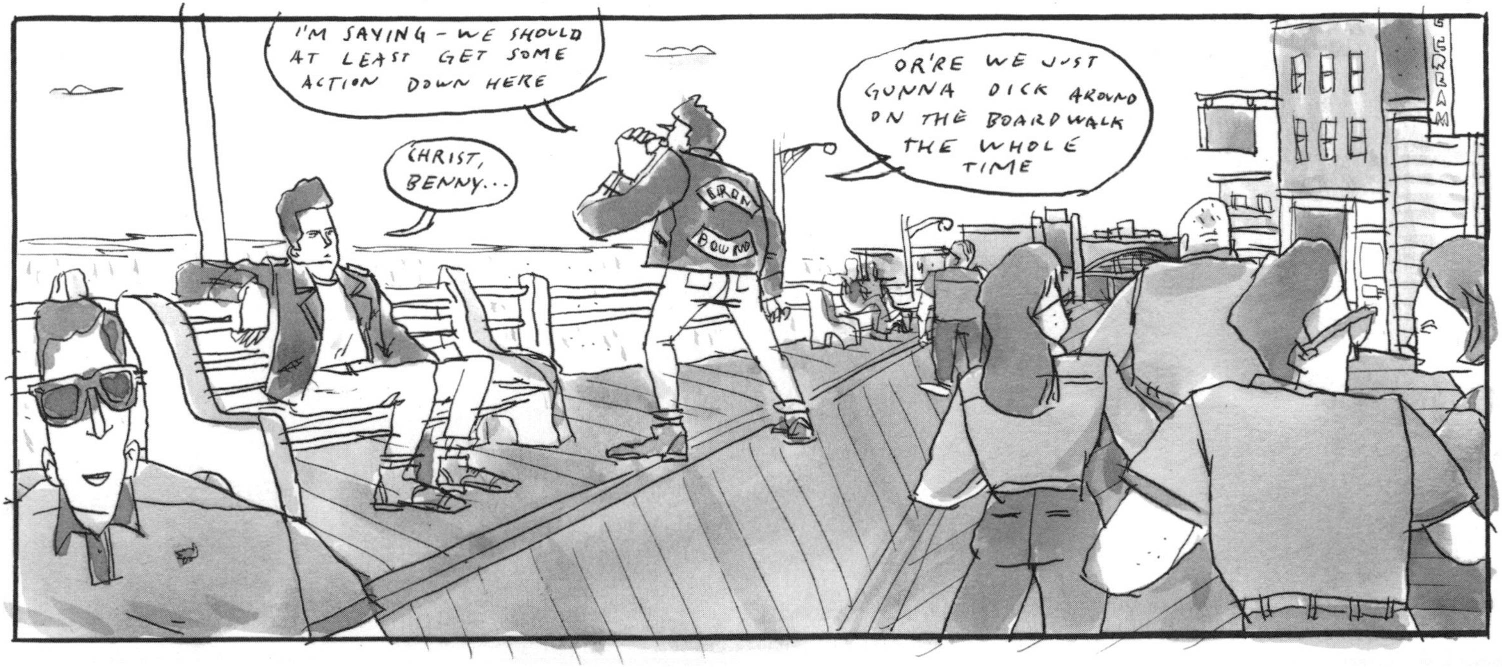
I'M SAYING - WE SHOULD AT LEAST GET SOME ACTION DOWN HERE
CHRIST, BENNY...
OR'RE WE JUST GUNNA DICK AROUND ON THE BOARDWALK THE WHOLE TIME
IRON BOUND
ICE CREAM

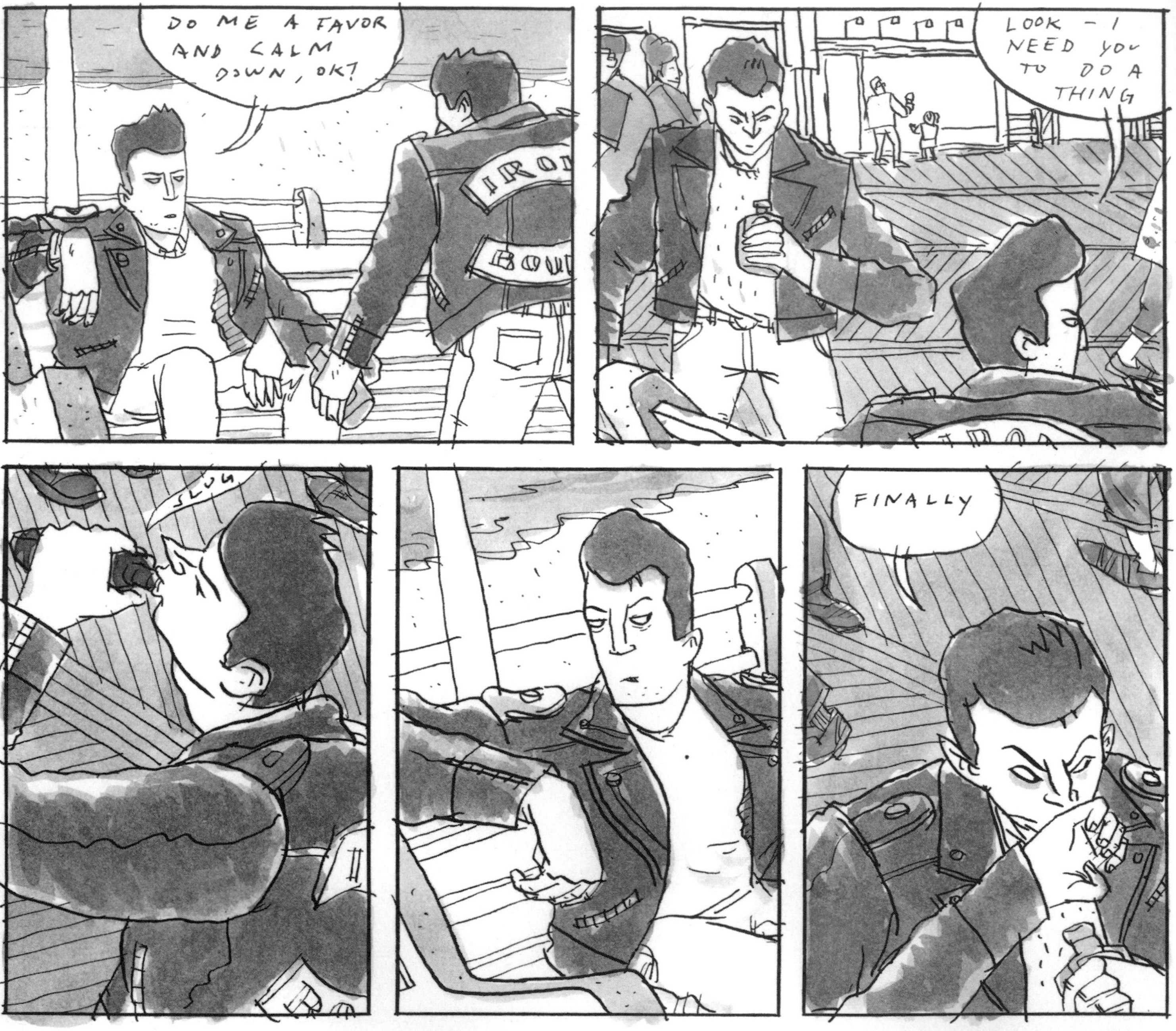
DO ME A FAVOR AND CALM DOWN, OK?
LOOK - I NEED YOU TO DO A THING
SLUG
FINALLY

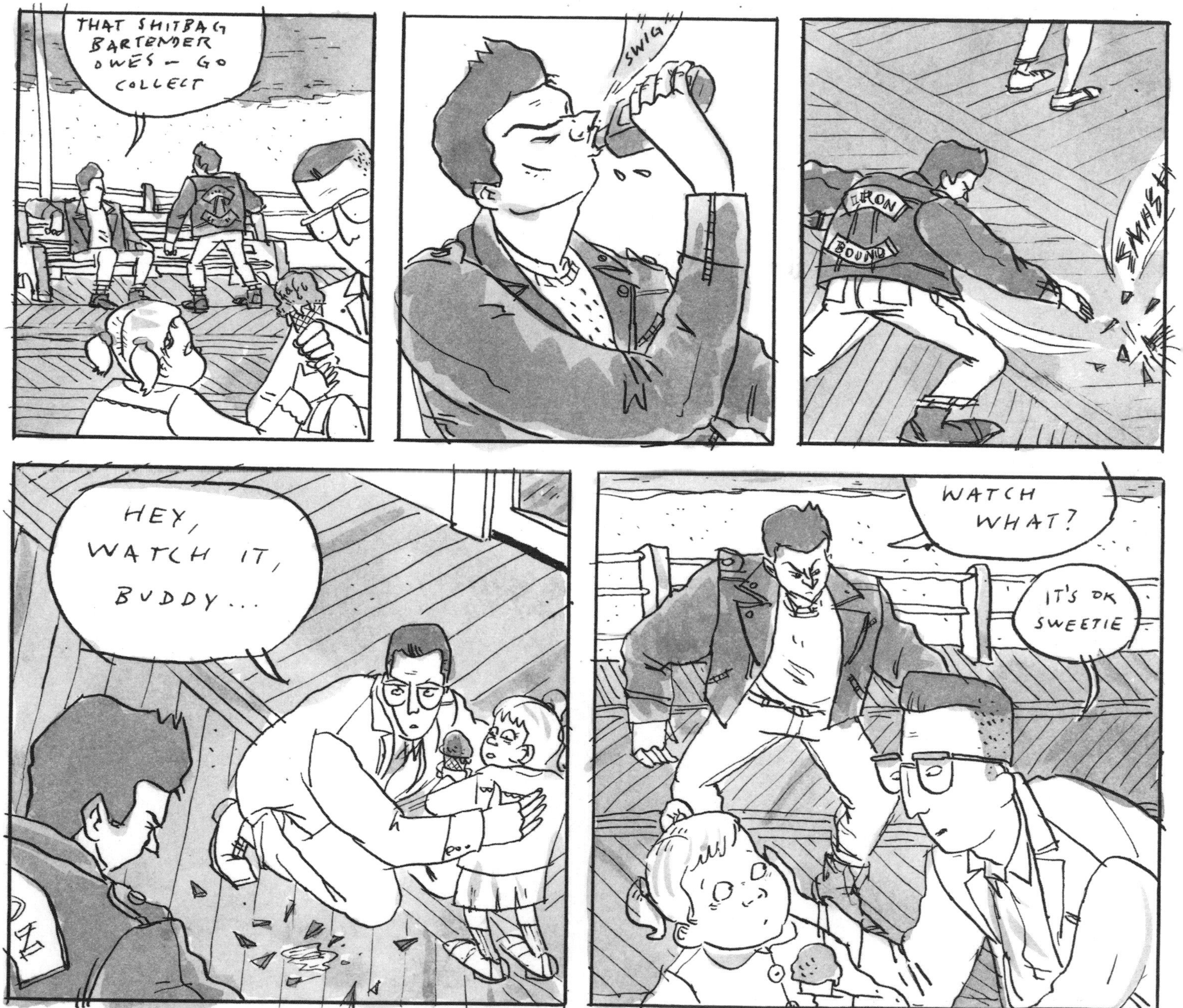
THAT SHITBAG BARTENDER OWES – GO COLLECT
SWIG
IRON
BOUND
SMASH
HEY, WATCH IT, BUDDY...
WATCH WHAT?
IT'S OK SWEETIE

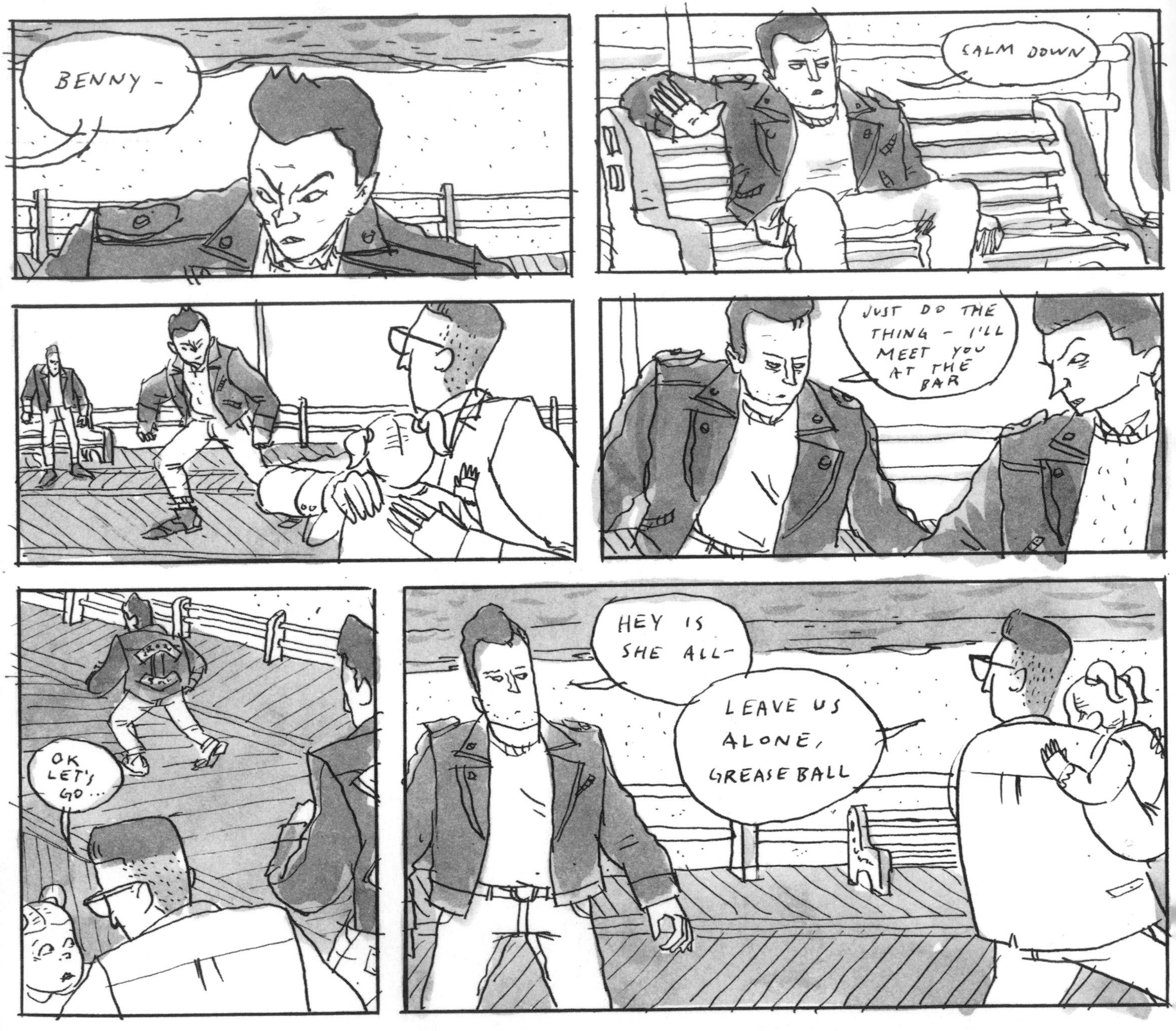
BENNY -
CALM DOWN
JUST DO THE THING - I'LL MEET YOU AT THE BAR
OK LET'S GO...
HEY IS SHE ALL-
LEAVE US ALONE, GREASEBALL

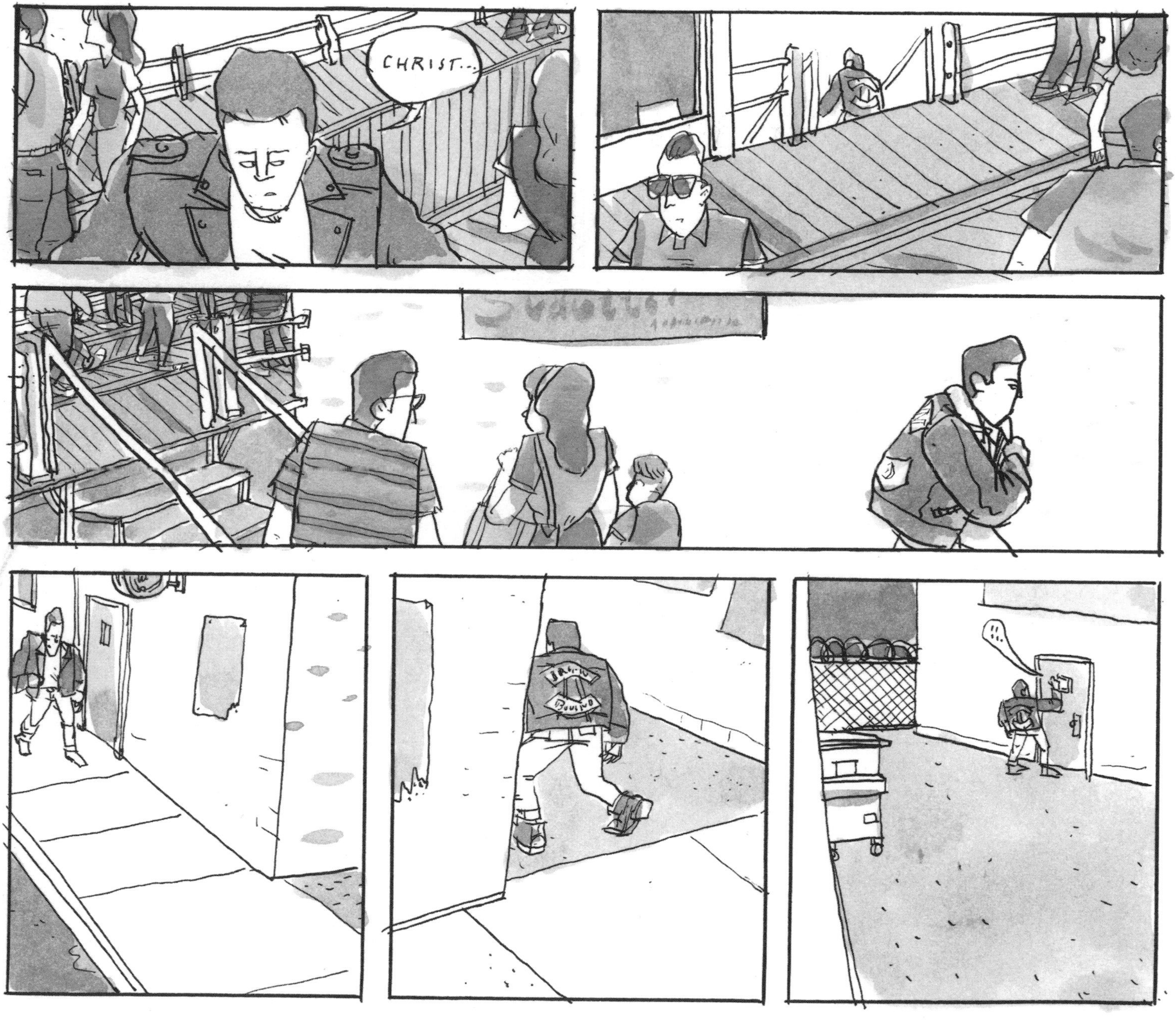
CHRIST...
!!

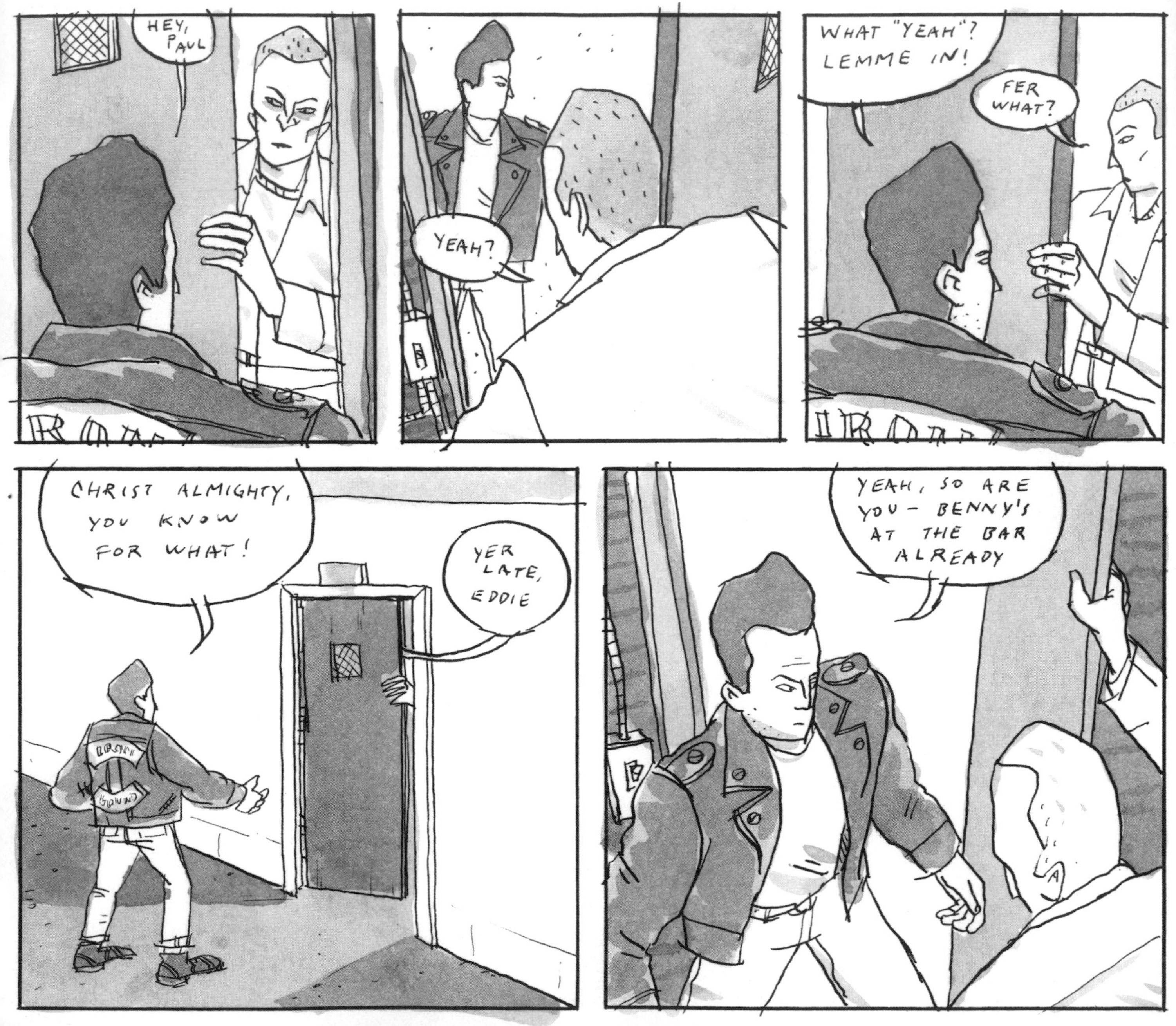
HEY, PAUL
YEAH?
WHAT "YEAH"? LEMME IN!
FER WHAT?
CHRIST ALMIGHTY, YOU KNOW FOR WHAT!
YER LATE, EDDIE
YEAH, SO ARE YOU - BENNY'S AT THE BAR ALREADY

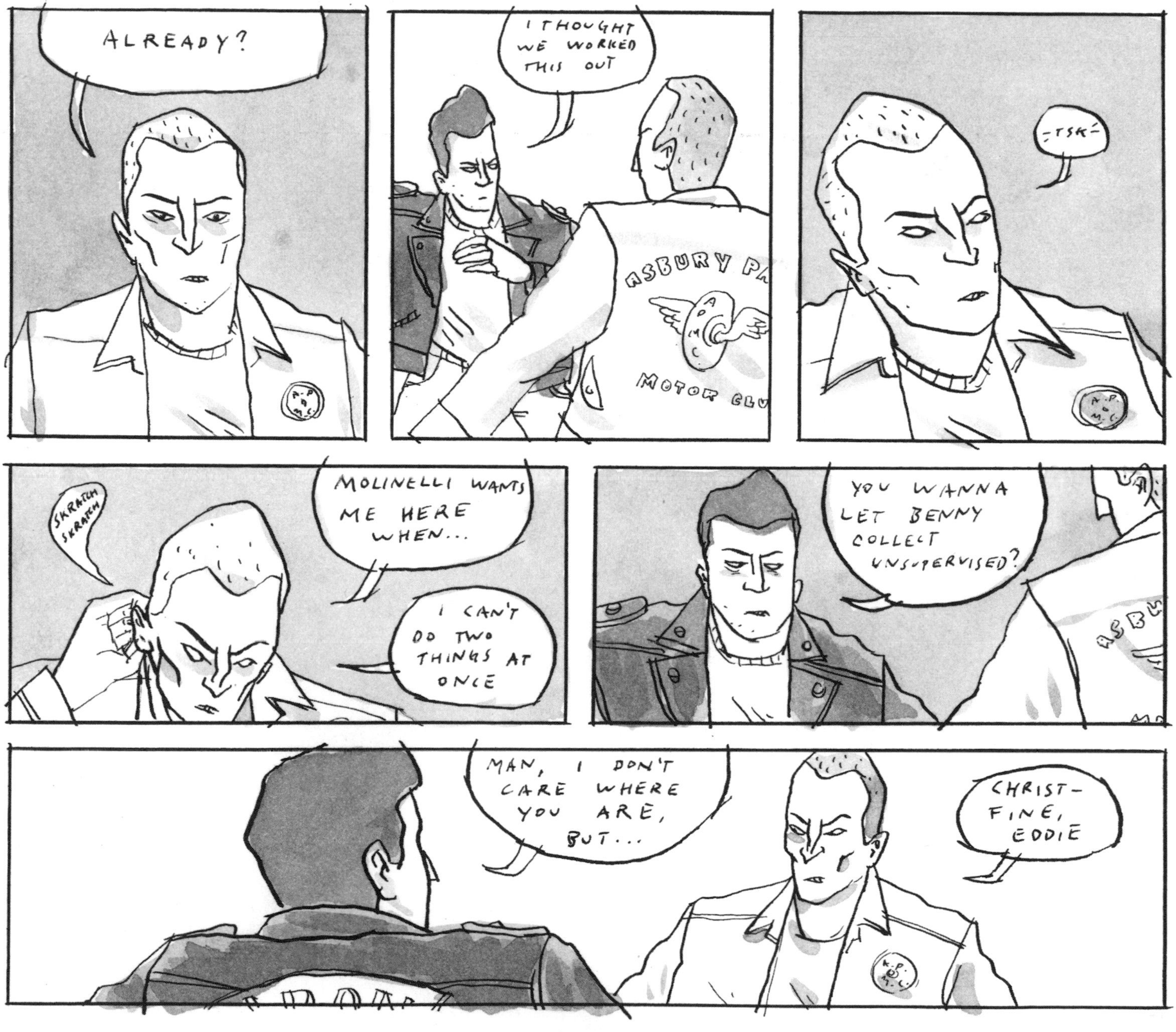
ALREADY?
I THOUGHT WE WORKED THIS OUT
TSK
SKRATCH SKRATCH
MOLINELLI WANTS ME HERE WHEN...
I CAN'T DO TWO THINGS AT ONCE
YOU WANNA LET BENNY COLLECT UNSUPERVISED?
MAN, I DON'T CARE WHERE YOU ARE, BUT...
CHRIST— FINE, EDDIE

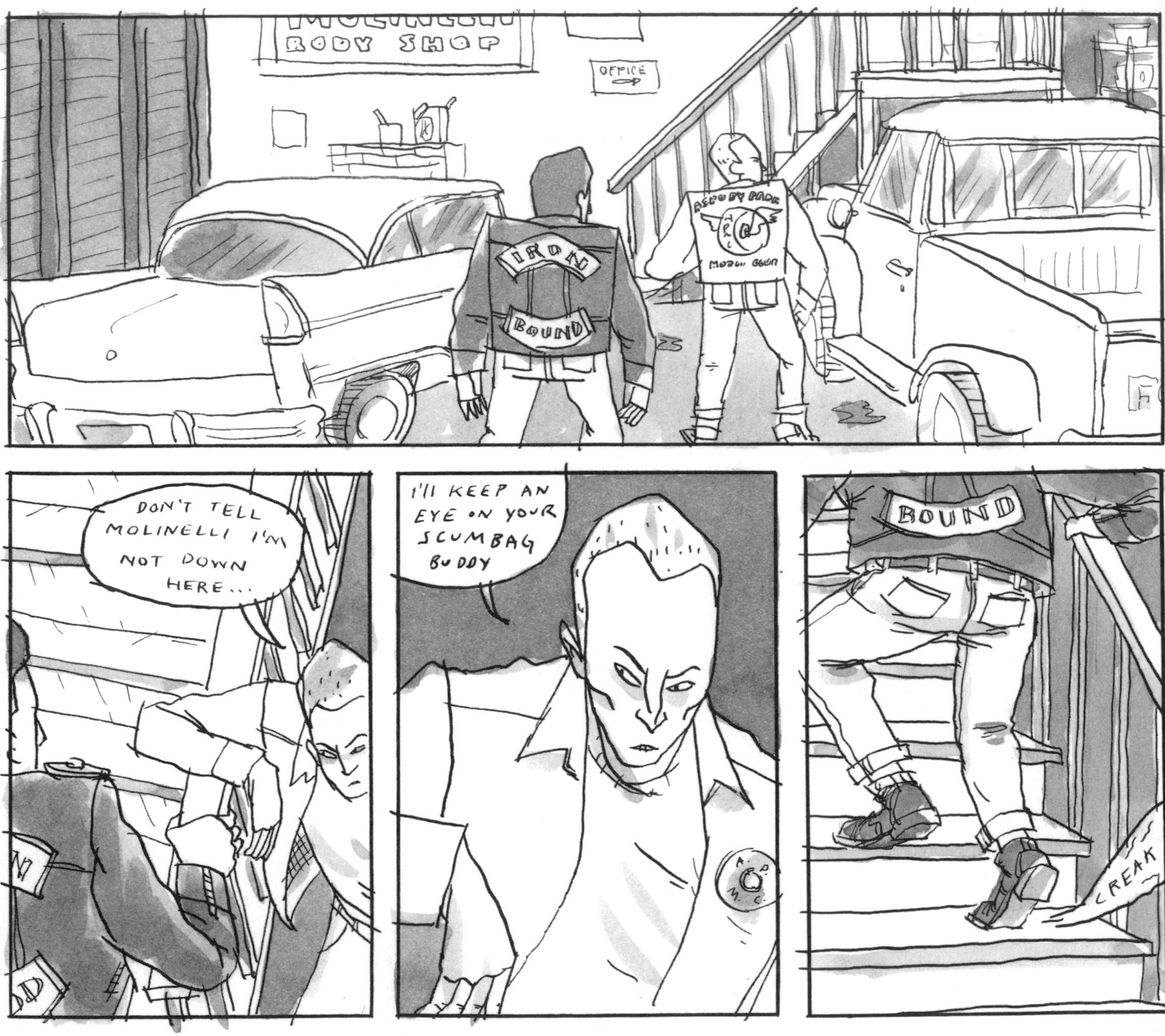

BODY SHOP
OFFICE
IRON
BOUND
DON'T TELL MOLINELLI I'M NOT DOWN HERE...
I'LL KEEP AN EYE ON YOUR SCUMBAG BUDDY
BOUND
CREAK

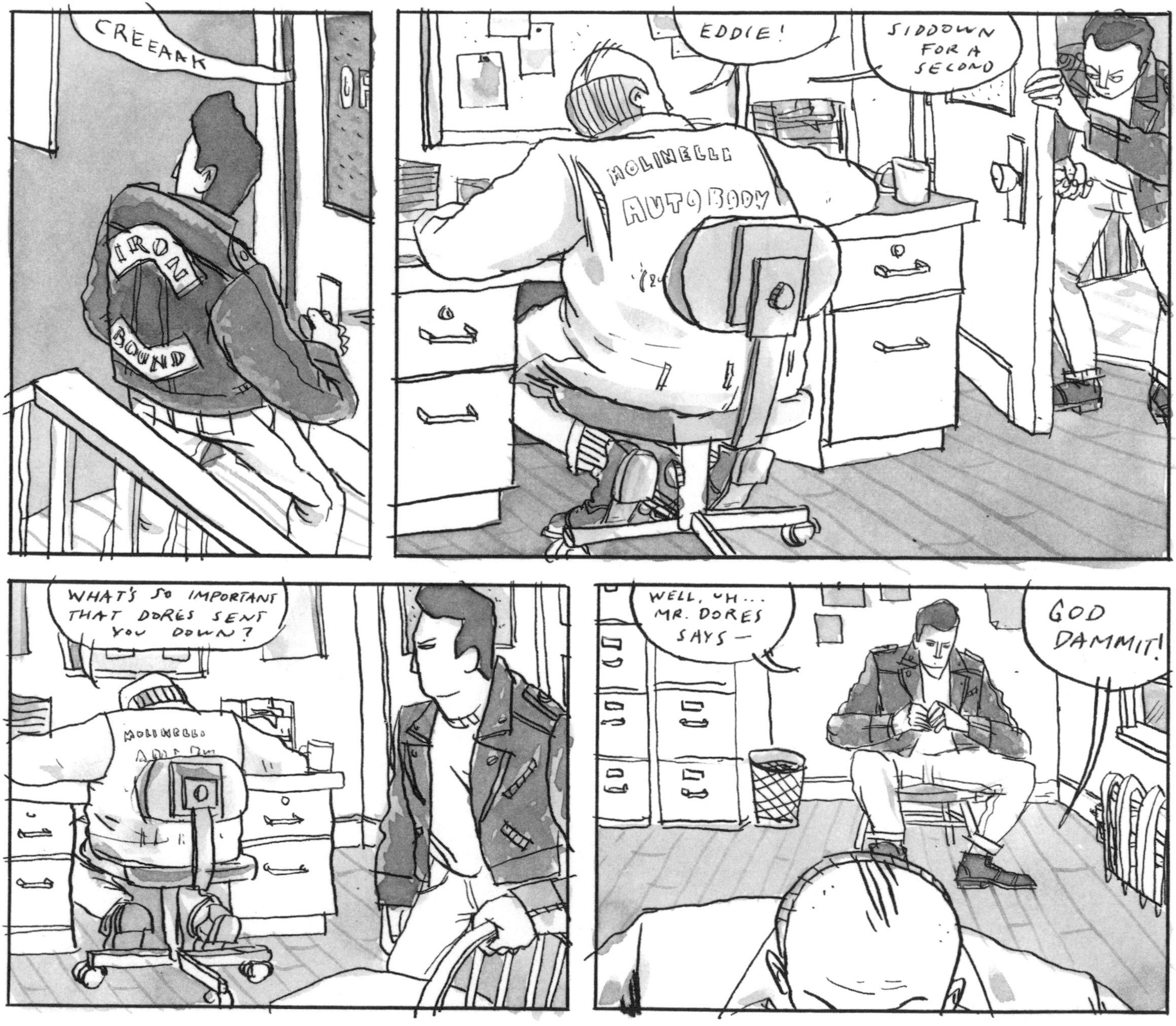
CREEAAK
IRON BOUND
EDDIE!
SIDDOWN FOR A SECOND
MOLINELLI AUTOBODY
WHAT'S SO IMPORTANT THAT DORES SENT YOU DOWN?
WELL, UH... MR. DORES SAYS—
GOD DAMMIT!

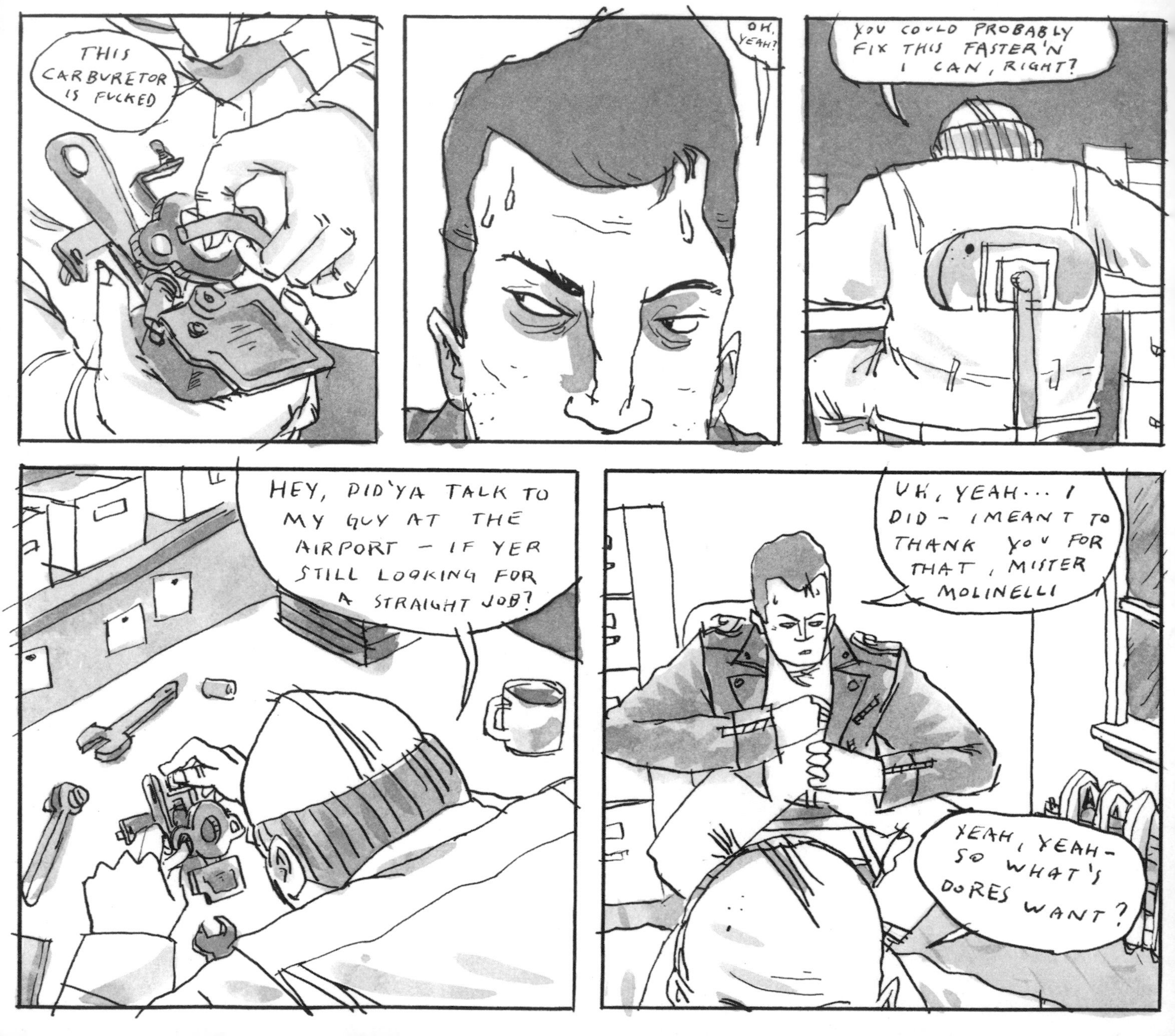
THIS CARBURETOR IS FUCKED
OH, YEAH?
YOU COULD PROBABLY FIX THIS FASTER'N I CAN, RIGHT?
HEY, DID'YA TALK TO MY GUY AT THE AIRPORT - IF YER STILL LOOKING FOR A STRAIGHT JOB?
UH, YEAH... I DID - I MEANT TO THANK YOU FOR THAT, MISTER MOLINELLI
YEAH, YEAH- SO WHAT'S DORES WANT?

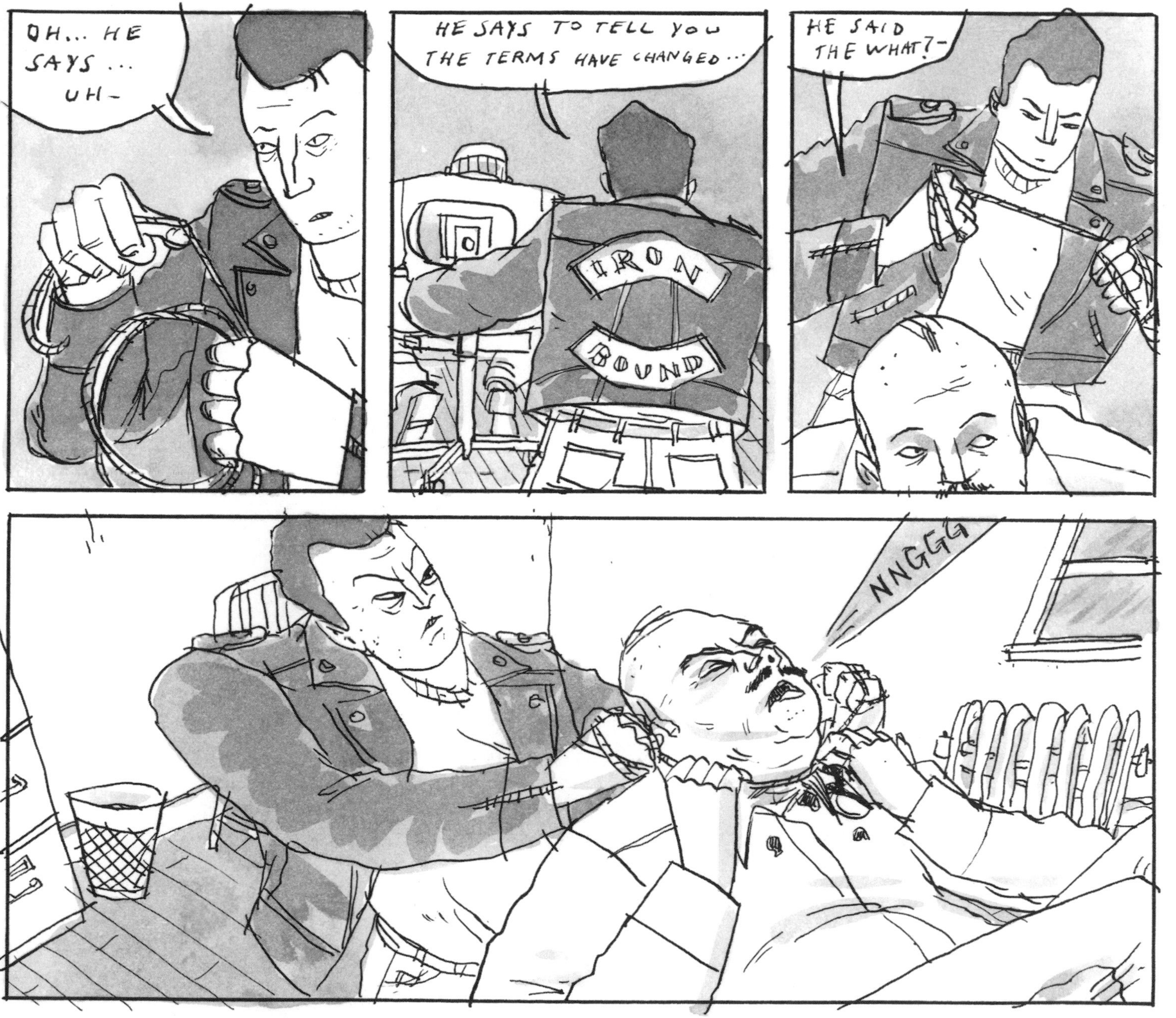
OH... HE SAYS... UH-
HE SAYS TO TELL YOU THE TERMS HAVE CHANGED...
IRON
BOUND
HE SAID THE WHAT?-
NNGGG

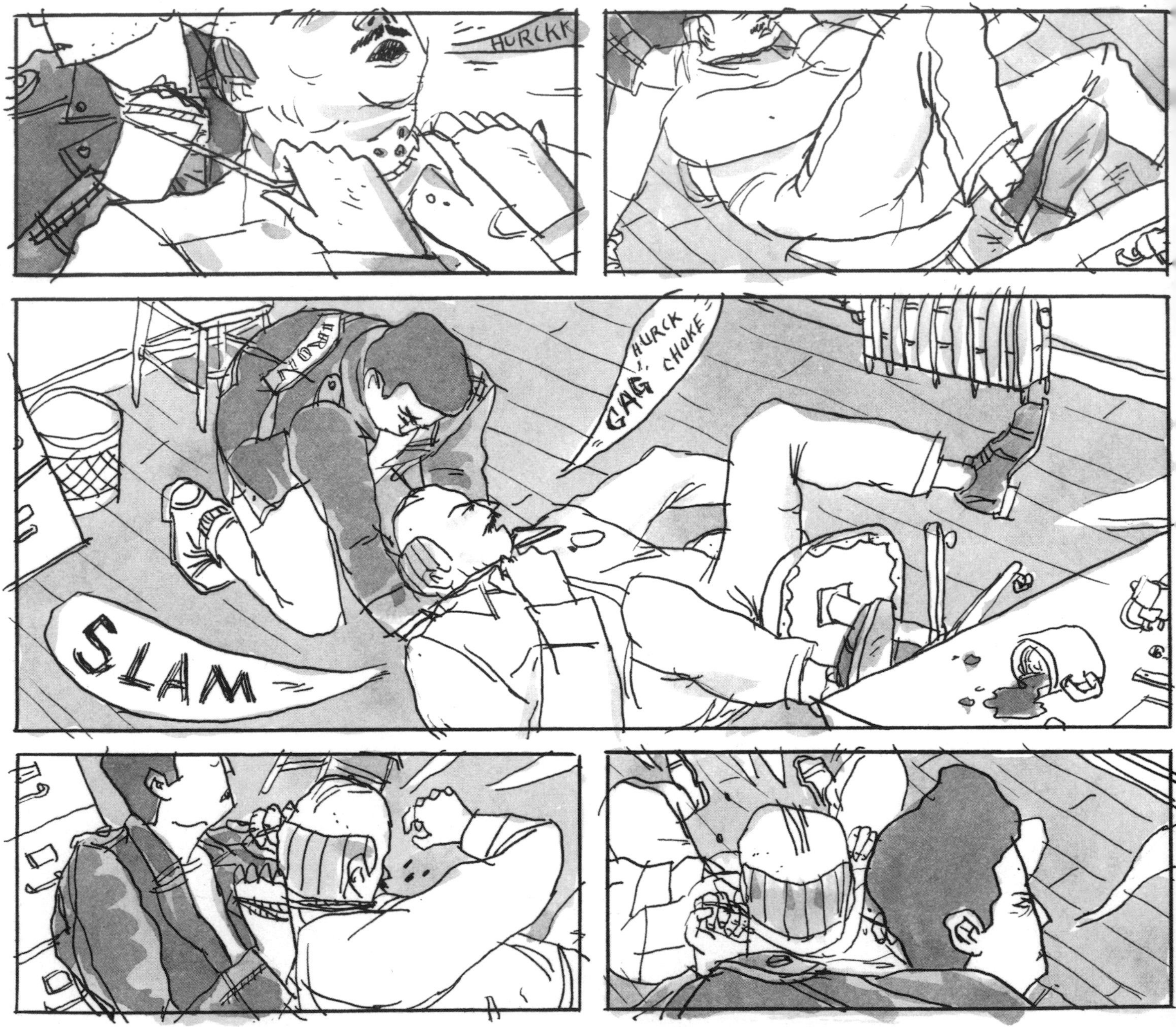
HURCKK
HURCK & CHOKE
GAG
SLAM

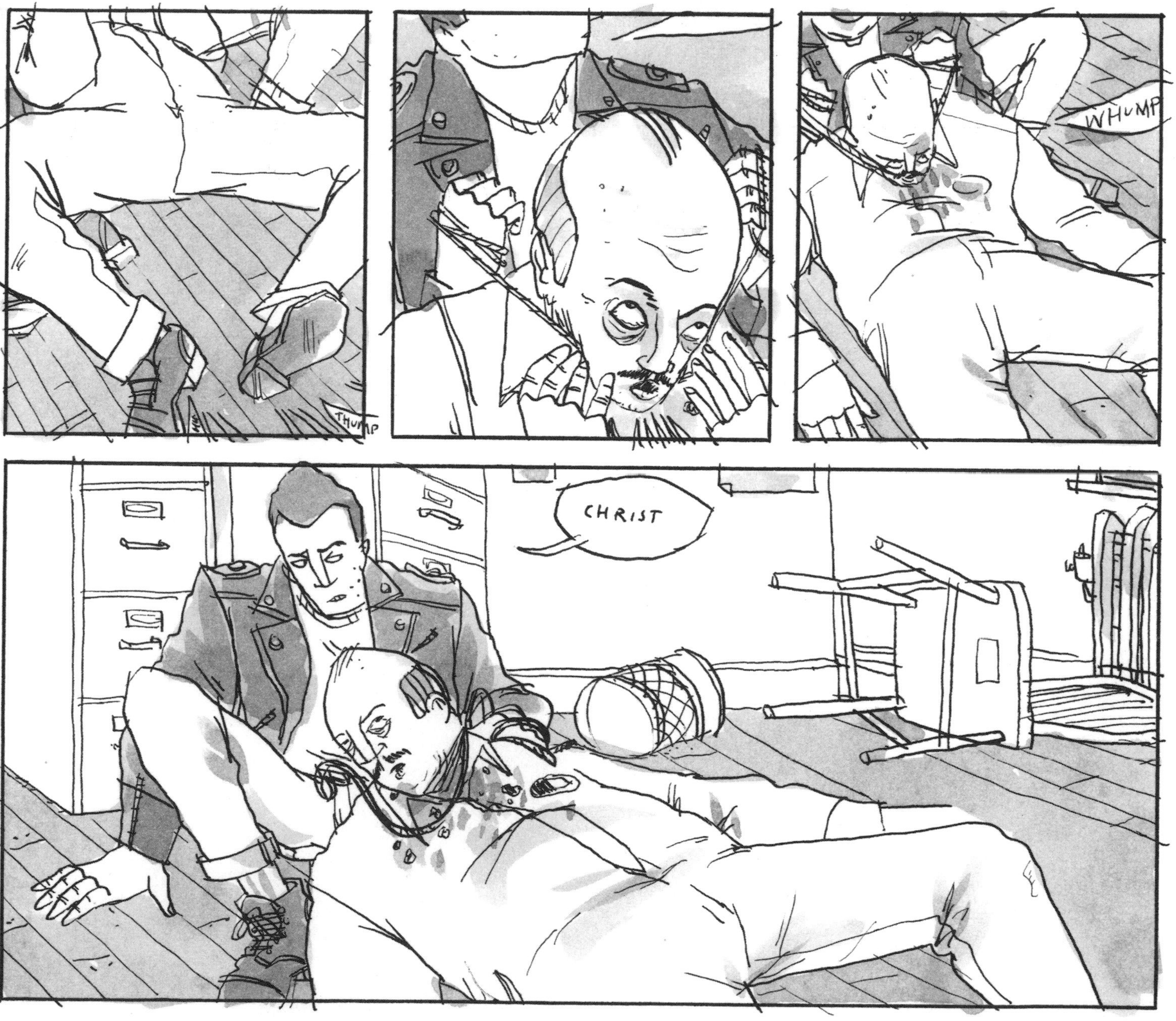
THUMP
WHUMP
CHRIST

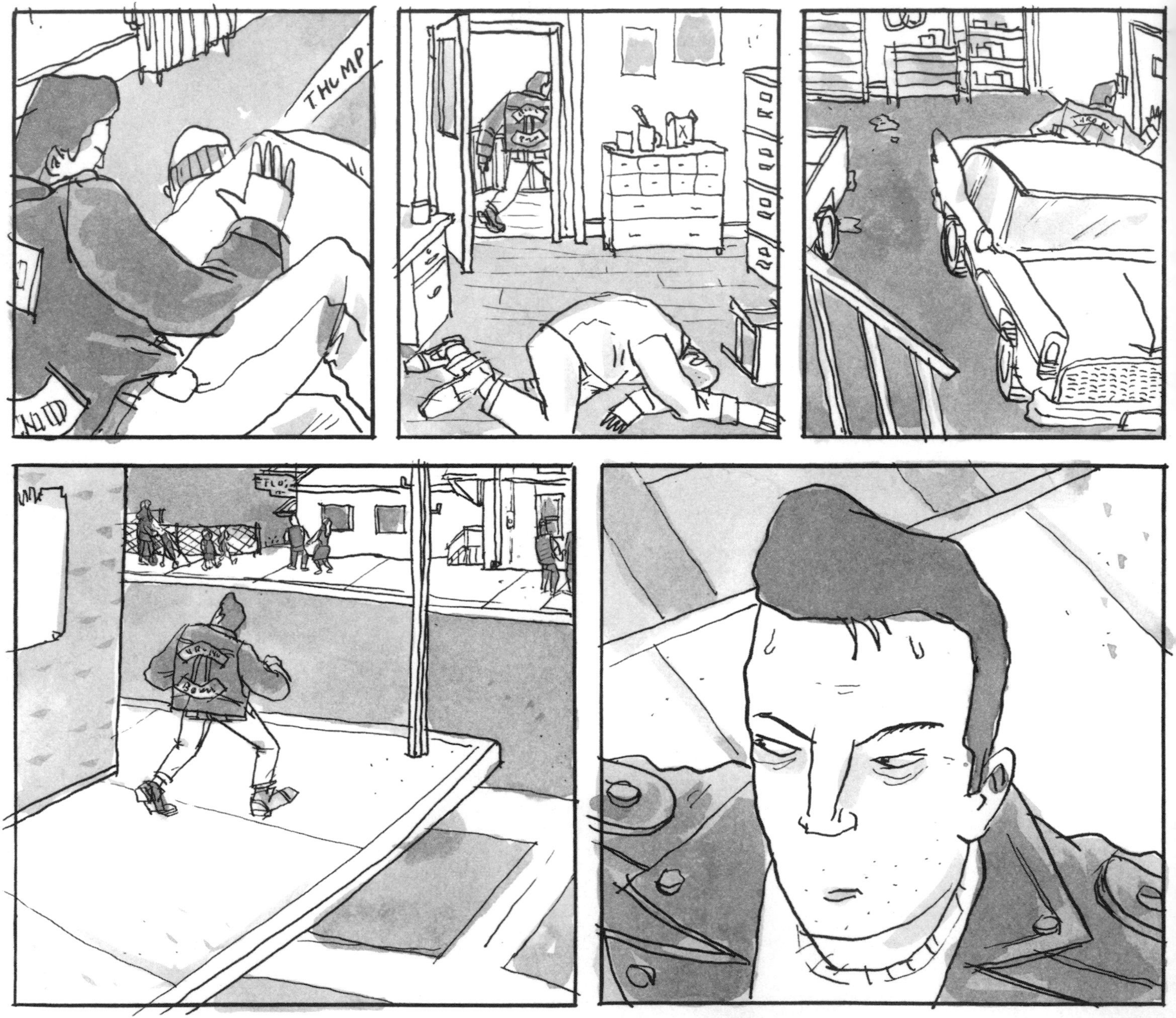
THUMP

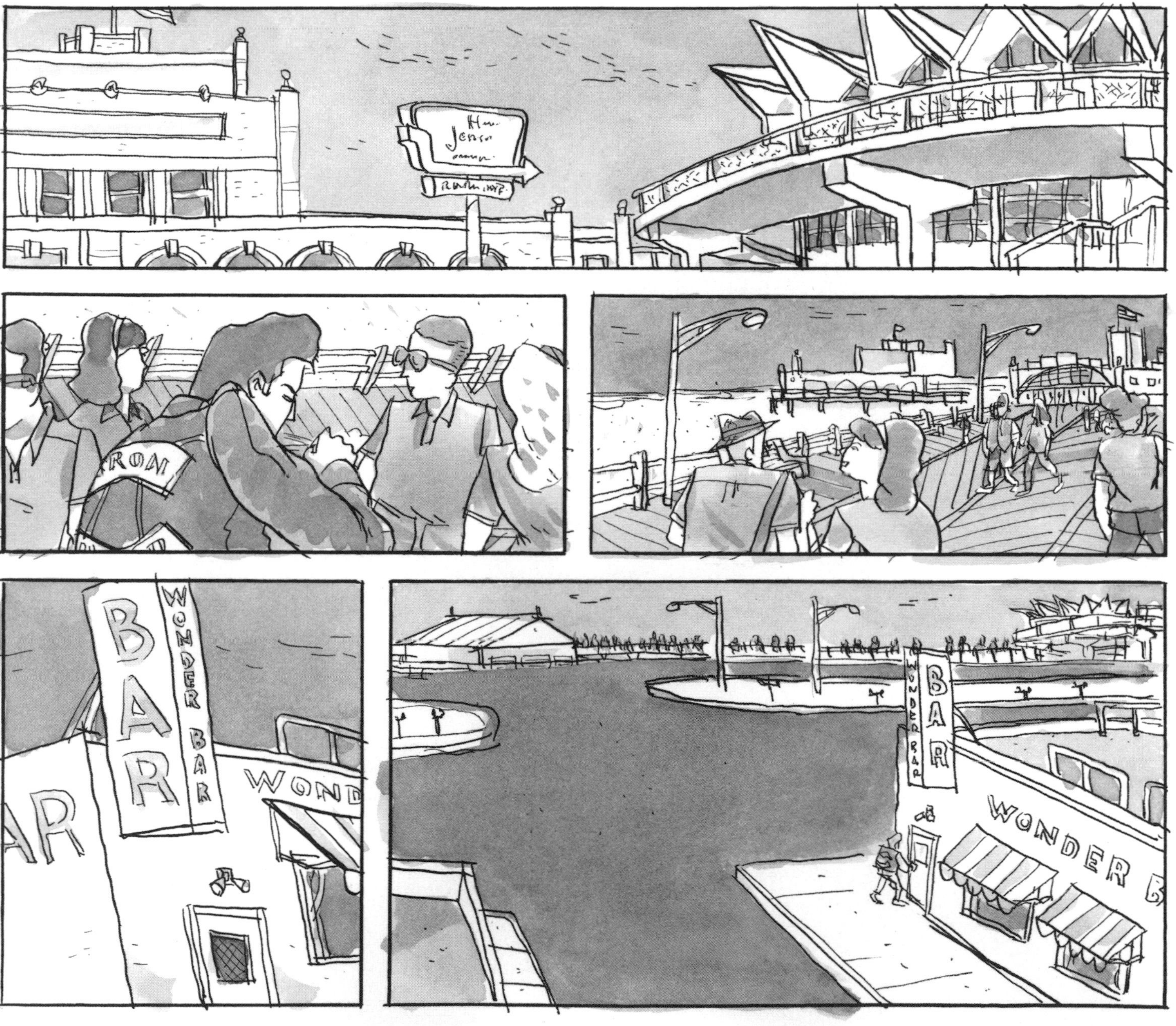
BAR
WONDER BAR
WONDER BAR
BAR
WONDER BAR

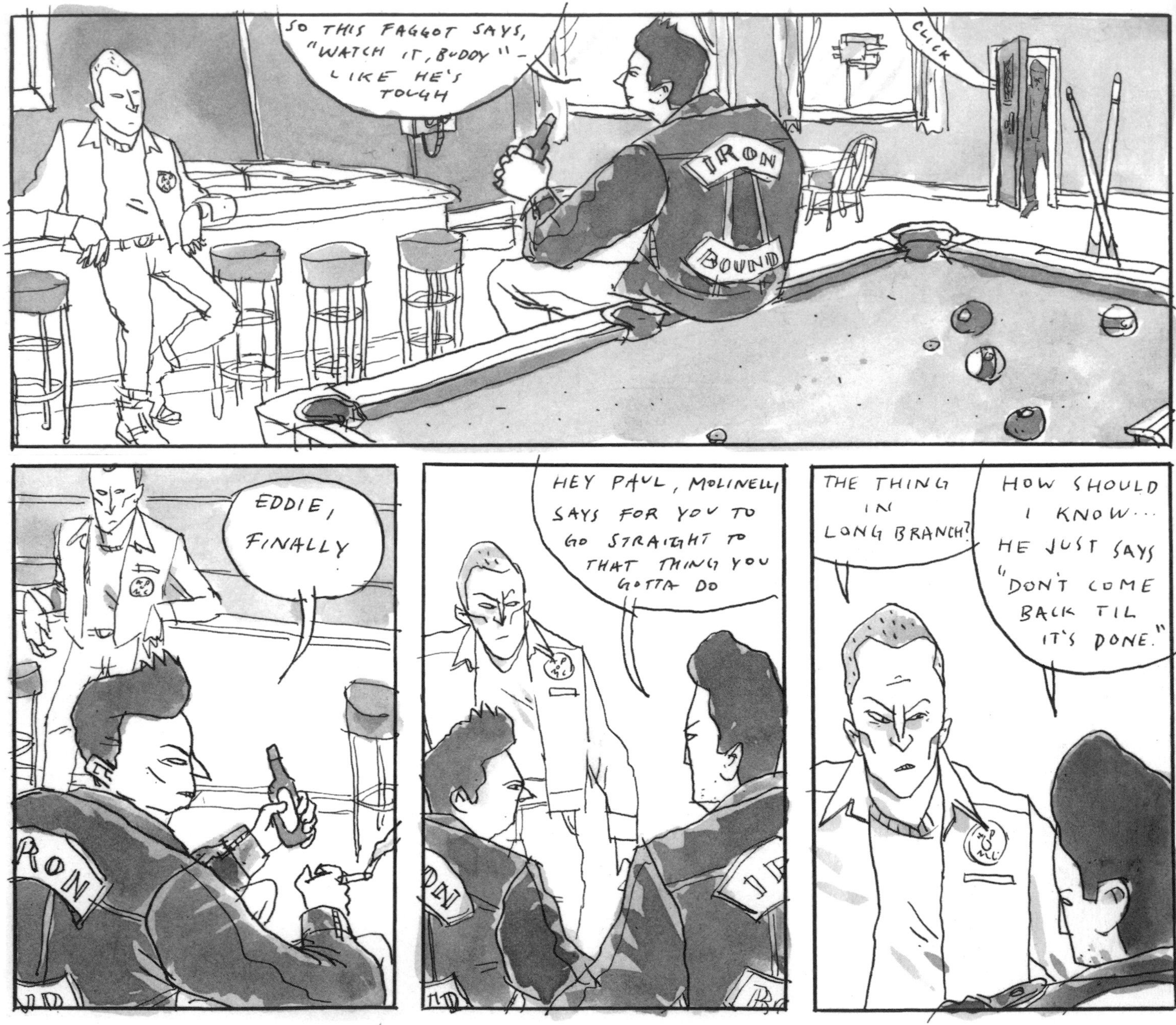
SO THIS FAGGOT SAYS, "WATCH IT, BUDDY" - LIKE HE'S TOUGH
CLICK
IRON BOUND
EDDIE, FINALLY
HEY PAUL, MOLINELLI SAYS FOR YOU TO GO STRAIGHT TO THAT THING YOU GOTTA DO
THE THING IN LONG BRANCH?
HOW SHOULD I KNOW... HE JUST SAYS "DON'T COME BACK TIL IT'S DONE."

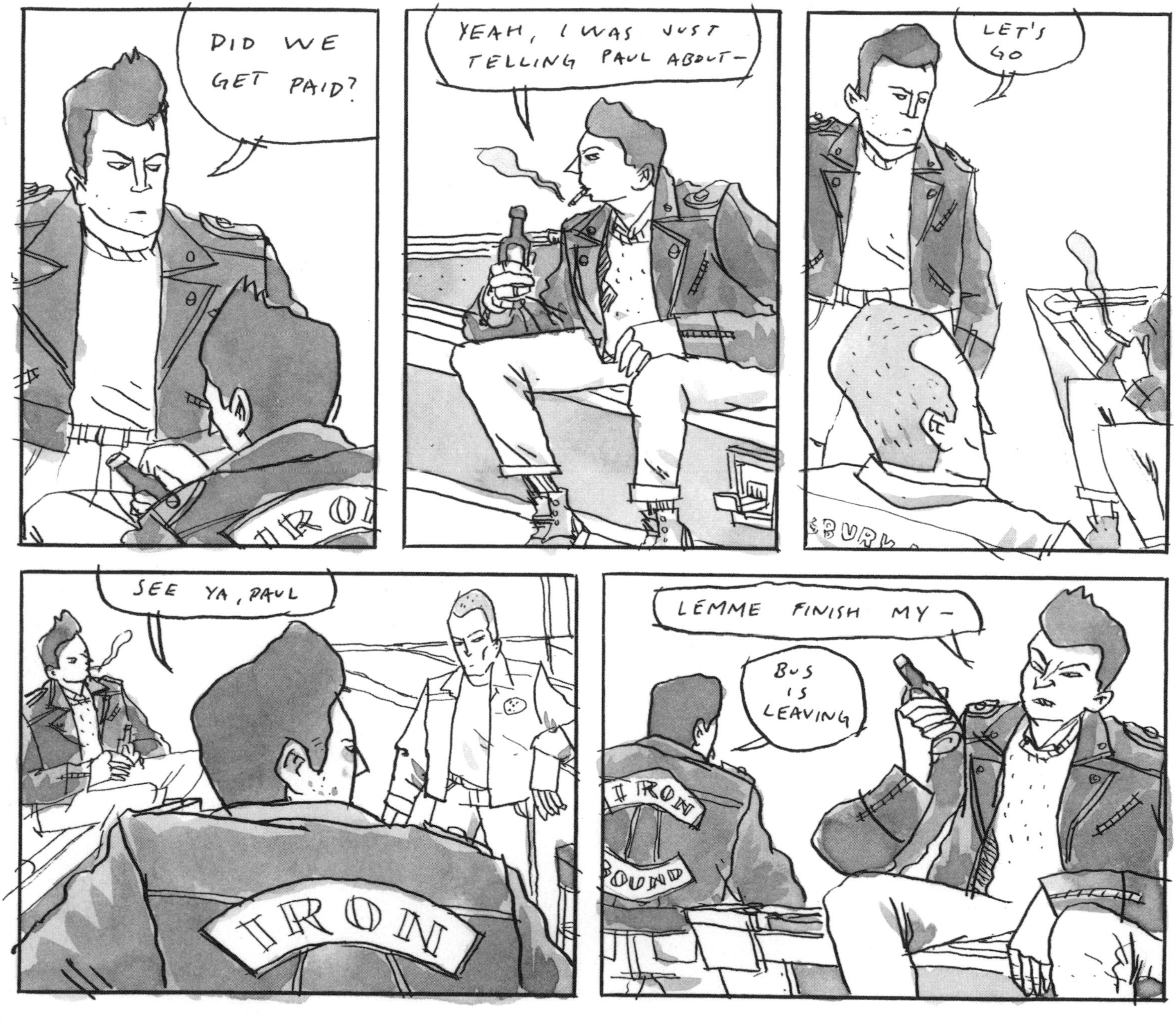
DID WE GET PAID?
YEAH, I WAS JUST TELLING PAUL ABOUT—
LET'S GO
SEE YA, PAUL
IRON
LEMME FINISH MY—
BUS IS LEAVING
IRON

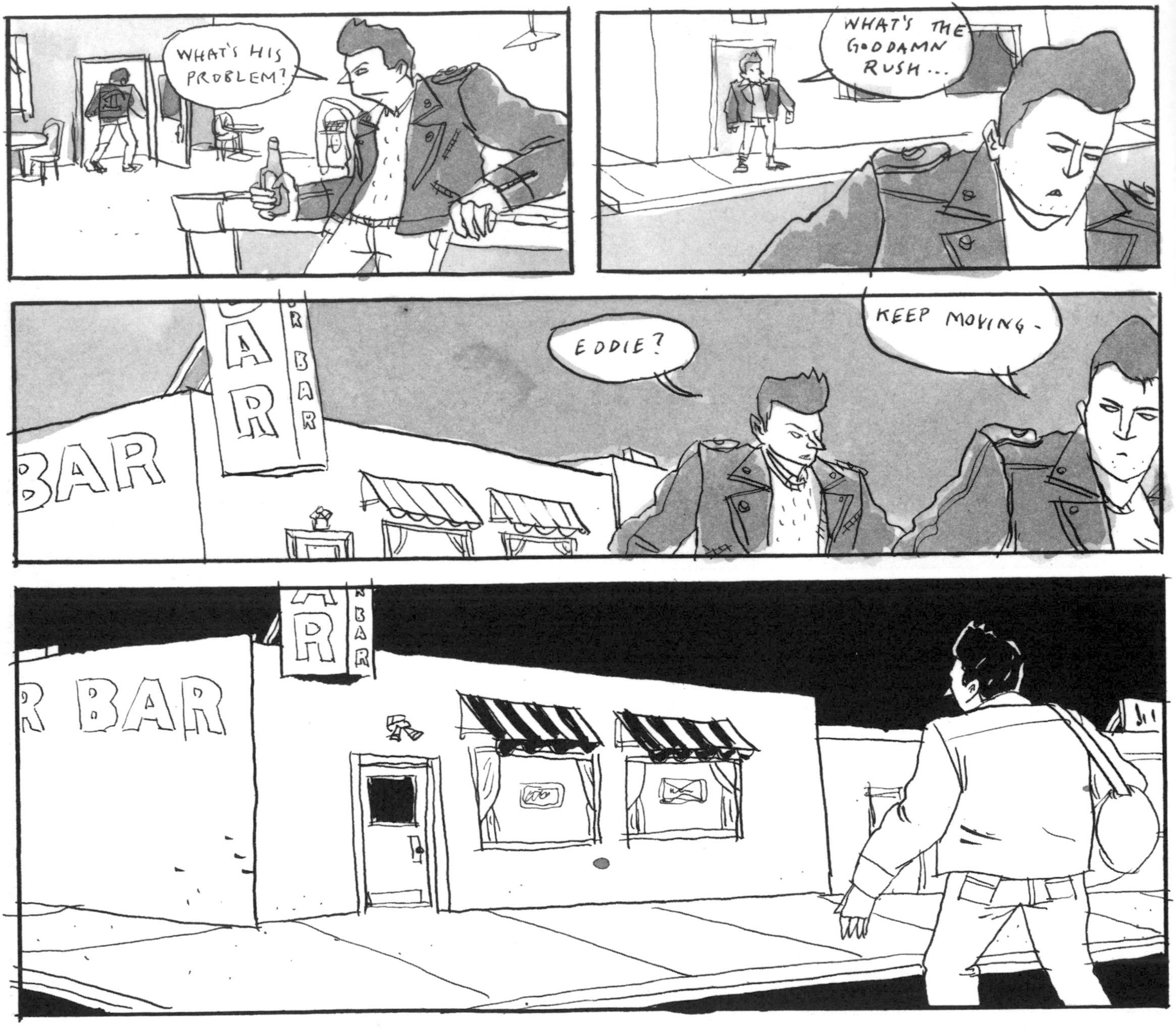
WHAT'S HIS PROBLEM?
WHAT'S THE GODDAMN RUSH...
BAR
BAR
EDDIE?
KEEP MOVING.
BAR
BAR

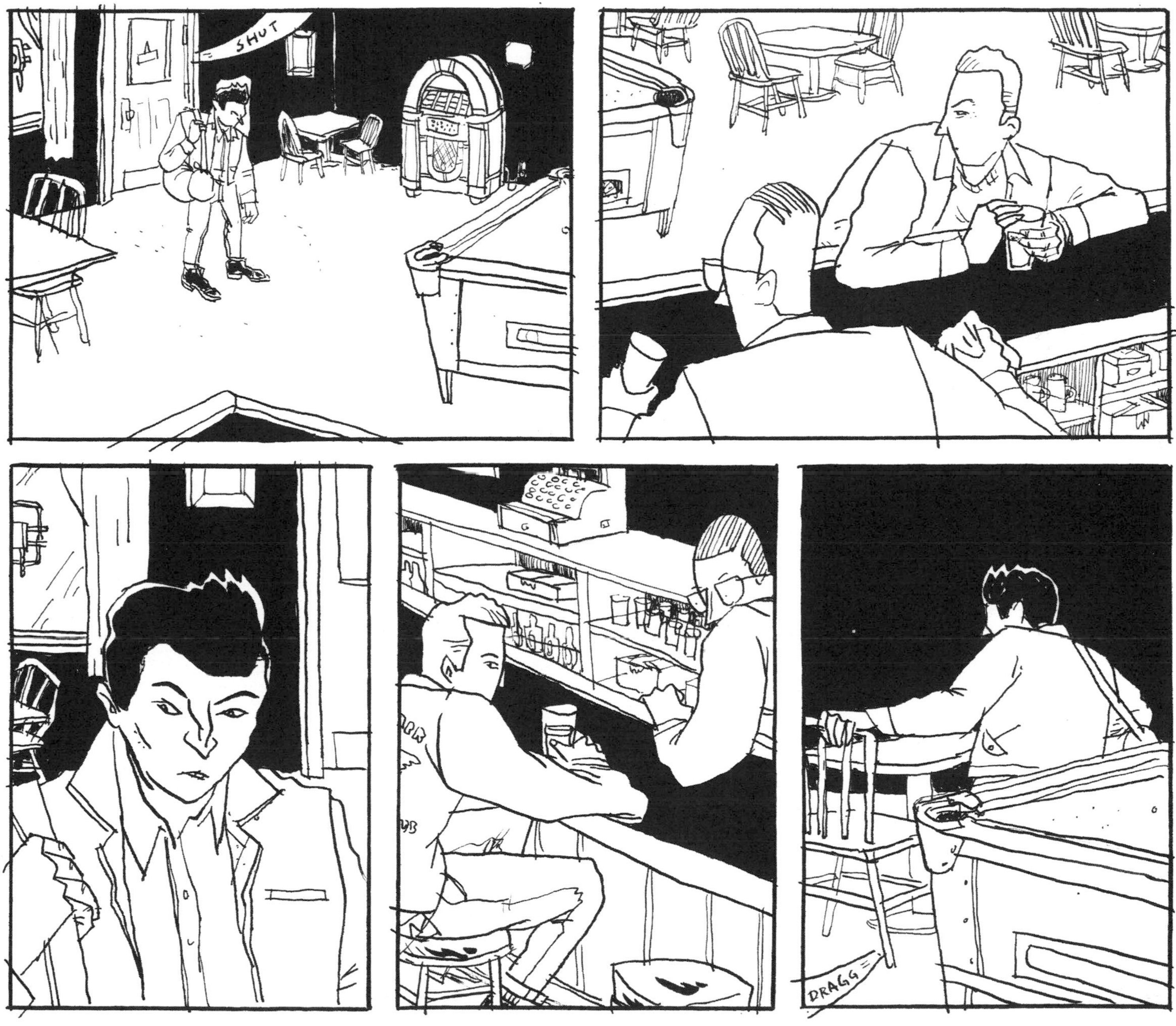
SHUT
DRAGG

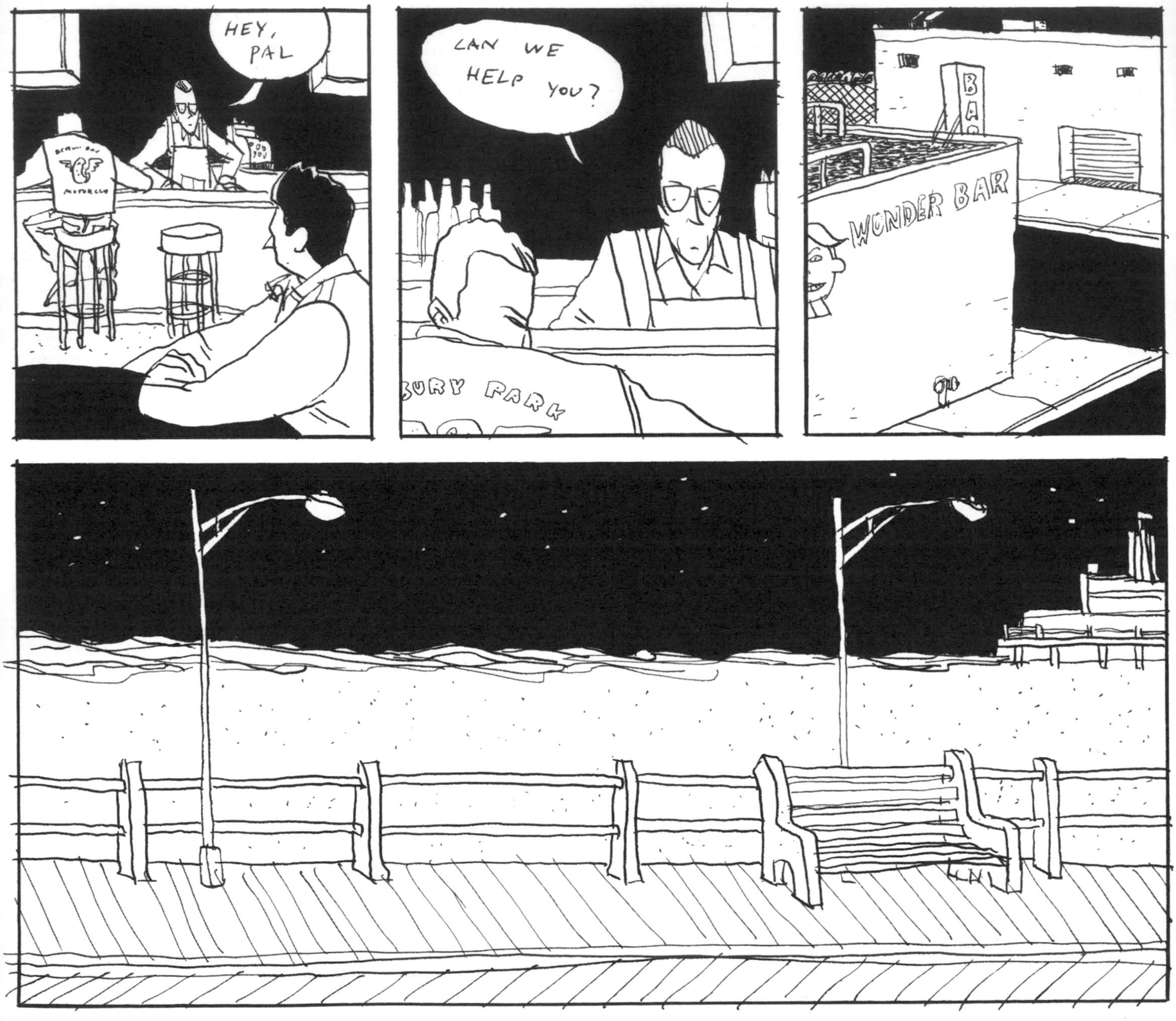
HEY, PAL
CAN WE HELP YOU?
BURY PARK
WONDER BAR

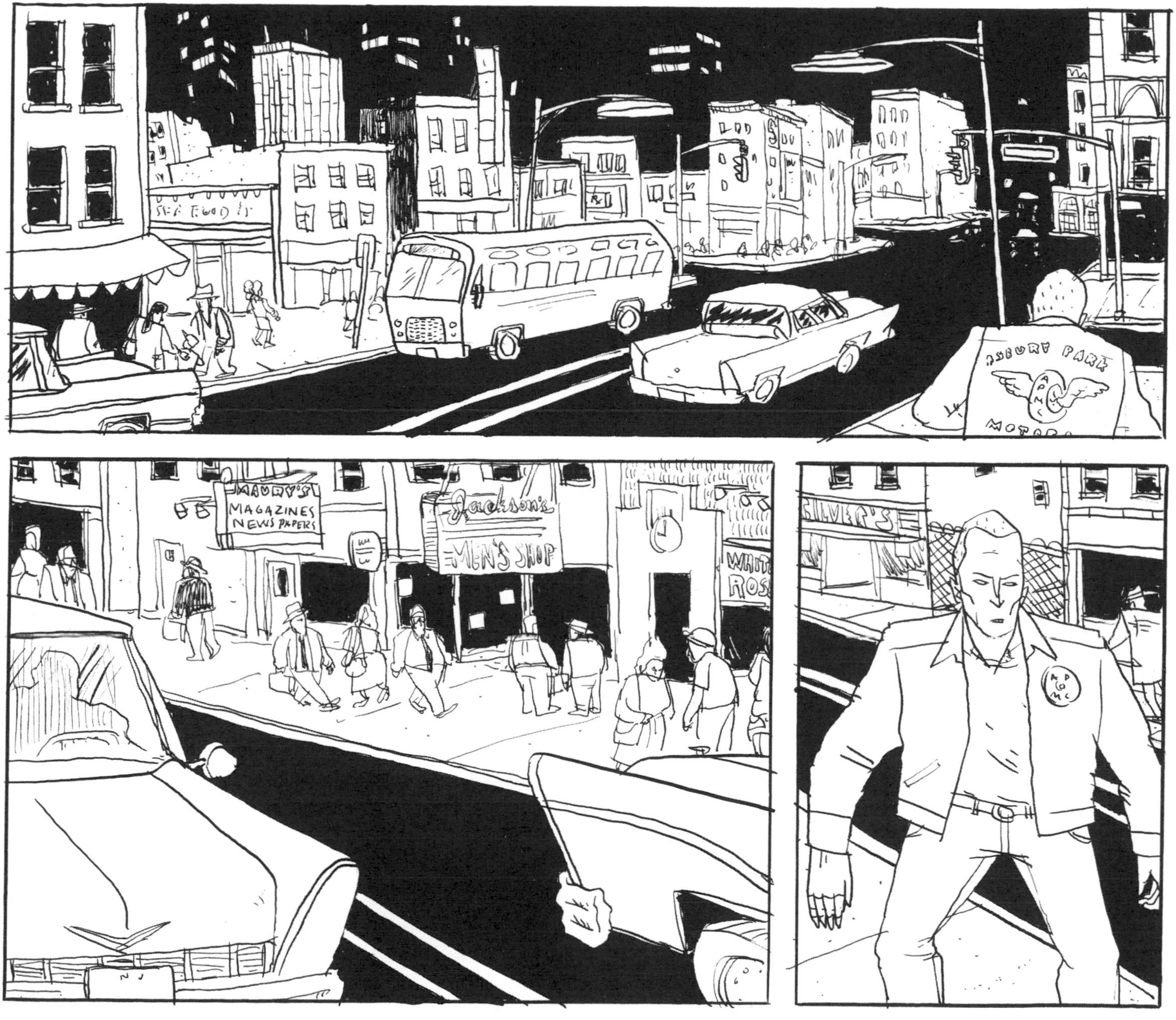
ASBURY PARK
MAURY'S
MAGAZINES
NEWS PAPERS
Jackson's
MEN'S SHOP
SILVER'S

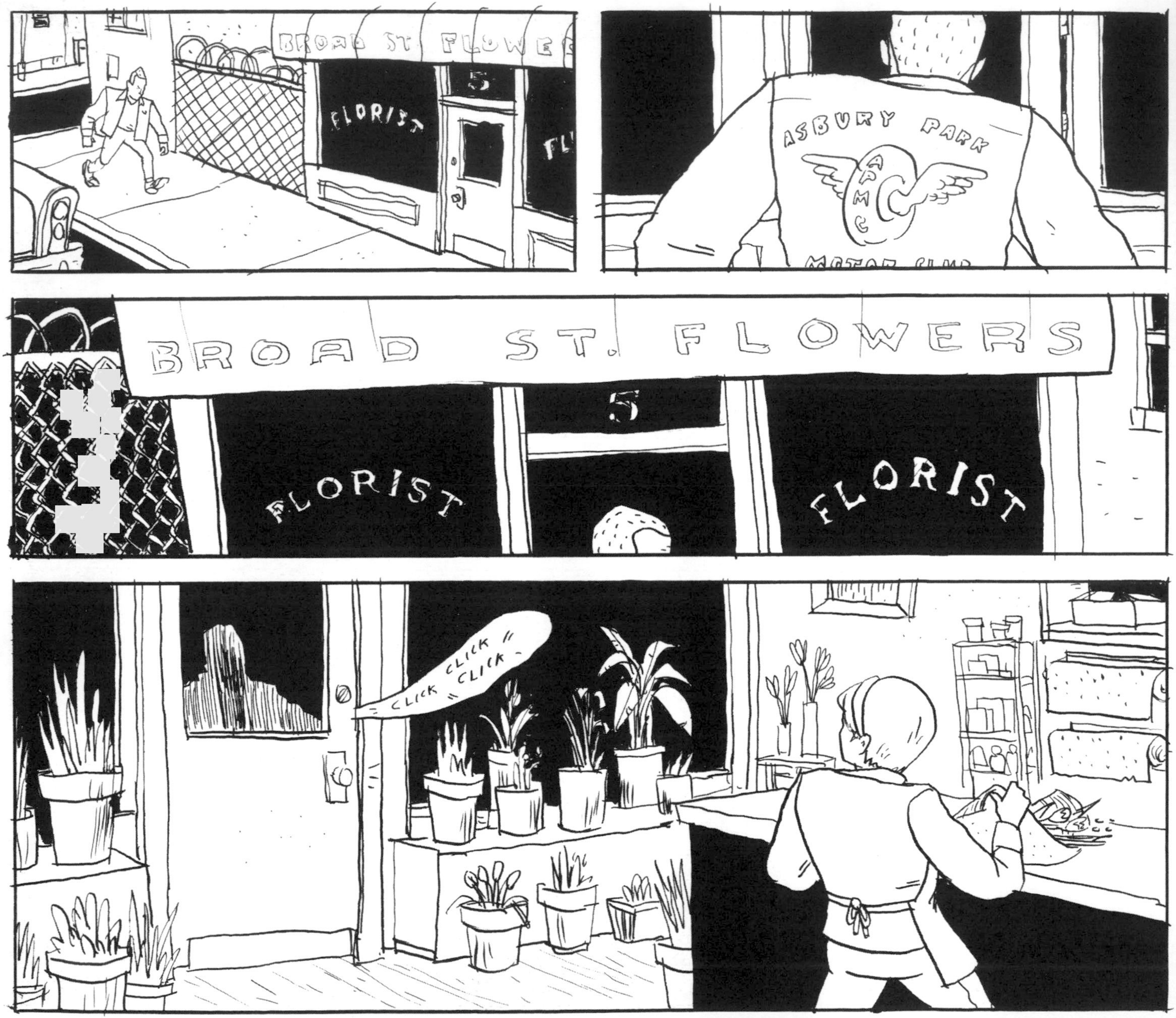
FLORIST
5
ASBURY PARK
BROAD ST. FLOWERS
5
FLORIST
FLORIST
CLICK CLICK CLICK

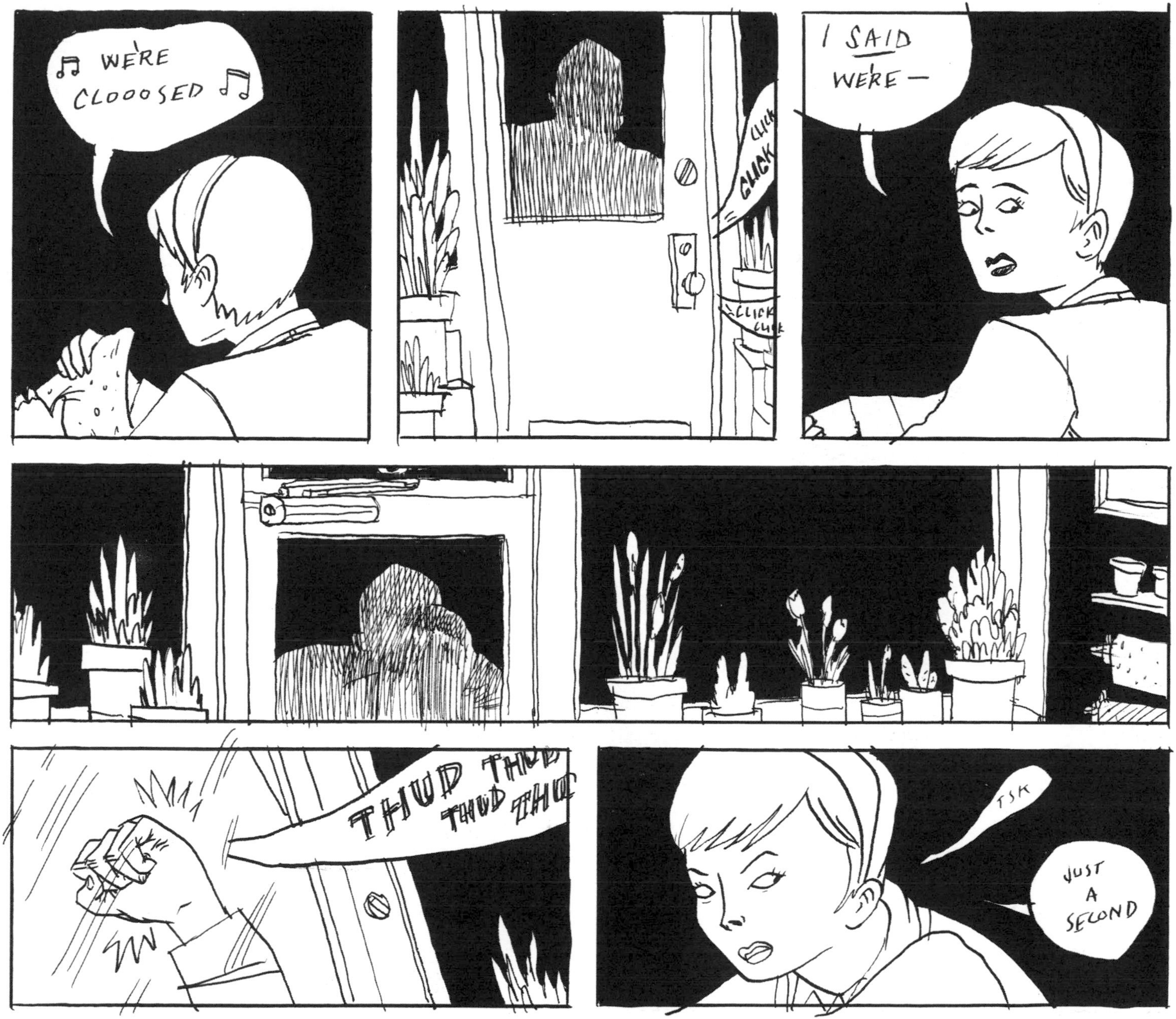
♫ WE'RE CLOOOSED ♫
CLICK CLICK
CLICK CLICK
I SAID WE'RE—
THUD THUD THUD THUD
TSK
JUST A SECOND

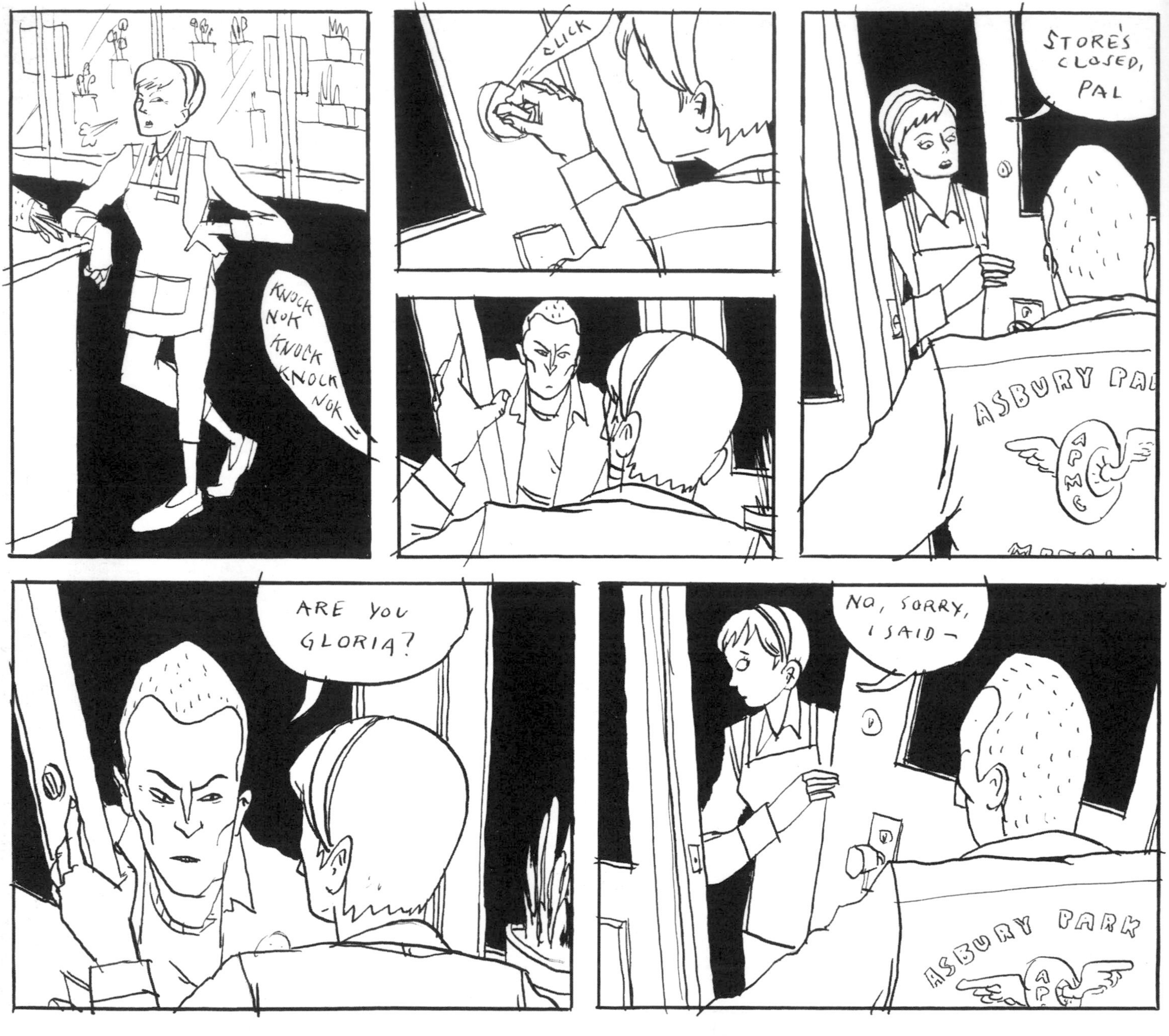
KNOCK
NOK
KNOCK
KNOCK
NOK
CLICK
STORE'S CLOSED, PAL
APMC
ARE YOU GLORIA?
NO, SORRY, I SAID-
ASBURY PARK

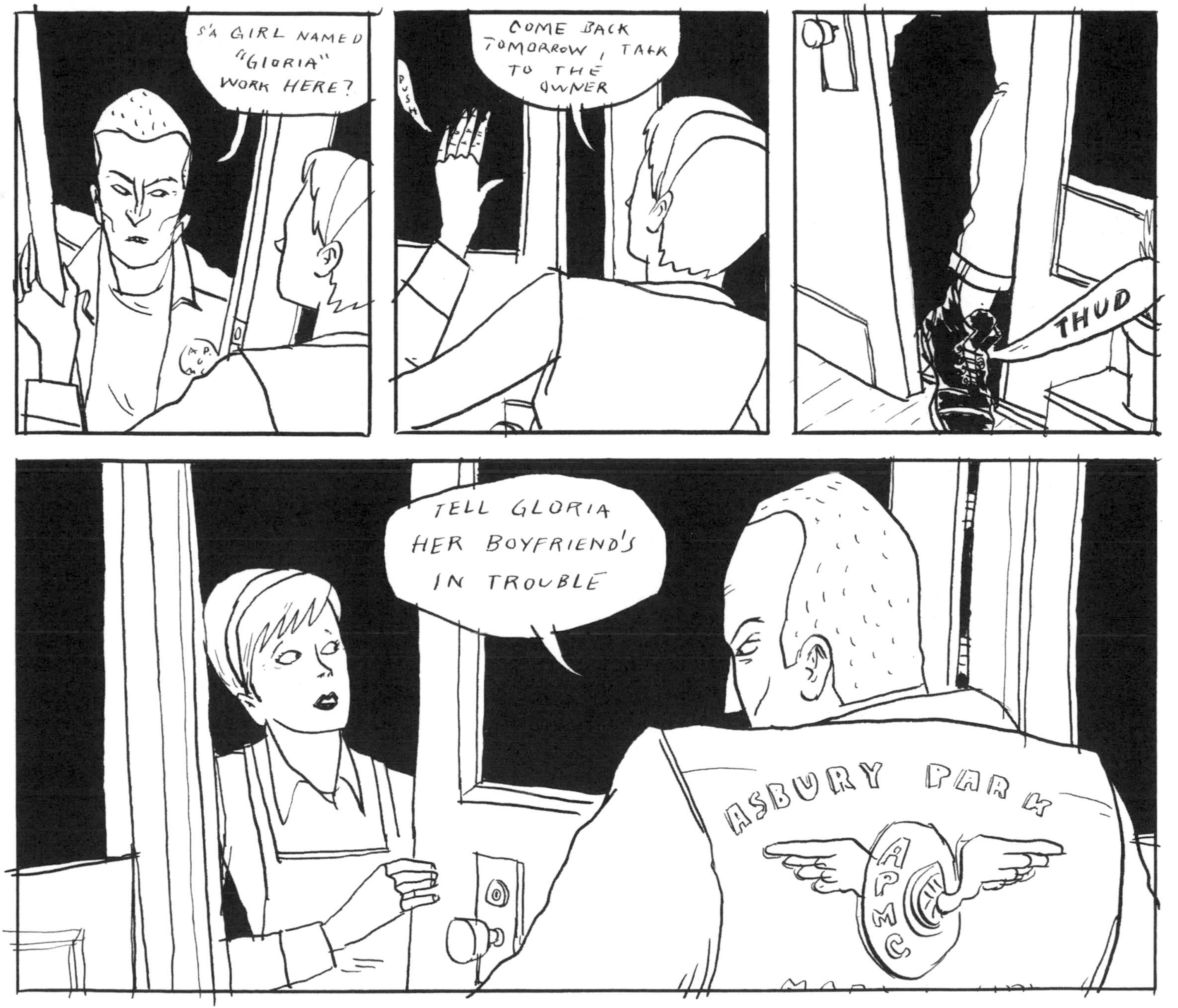
S'A GIRL NAMED "GLORIA" WORK HERE?
COME BACK TOMORROW, TALK TO THE OWNER
PUSH
THUD
TELL GLORIA HER BOYFRIEND'S IN TROUBLE
A.P. M.C.
ASBURY PARK
APMC

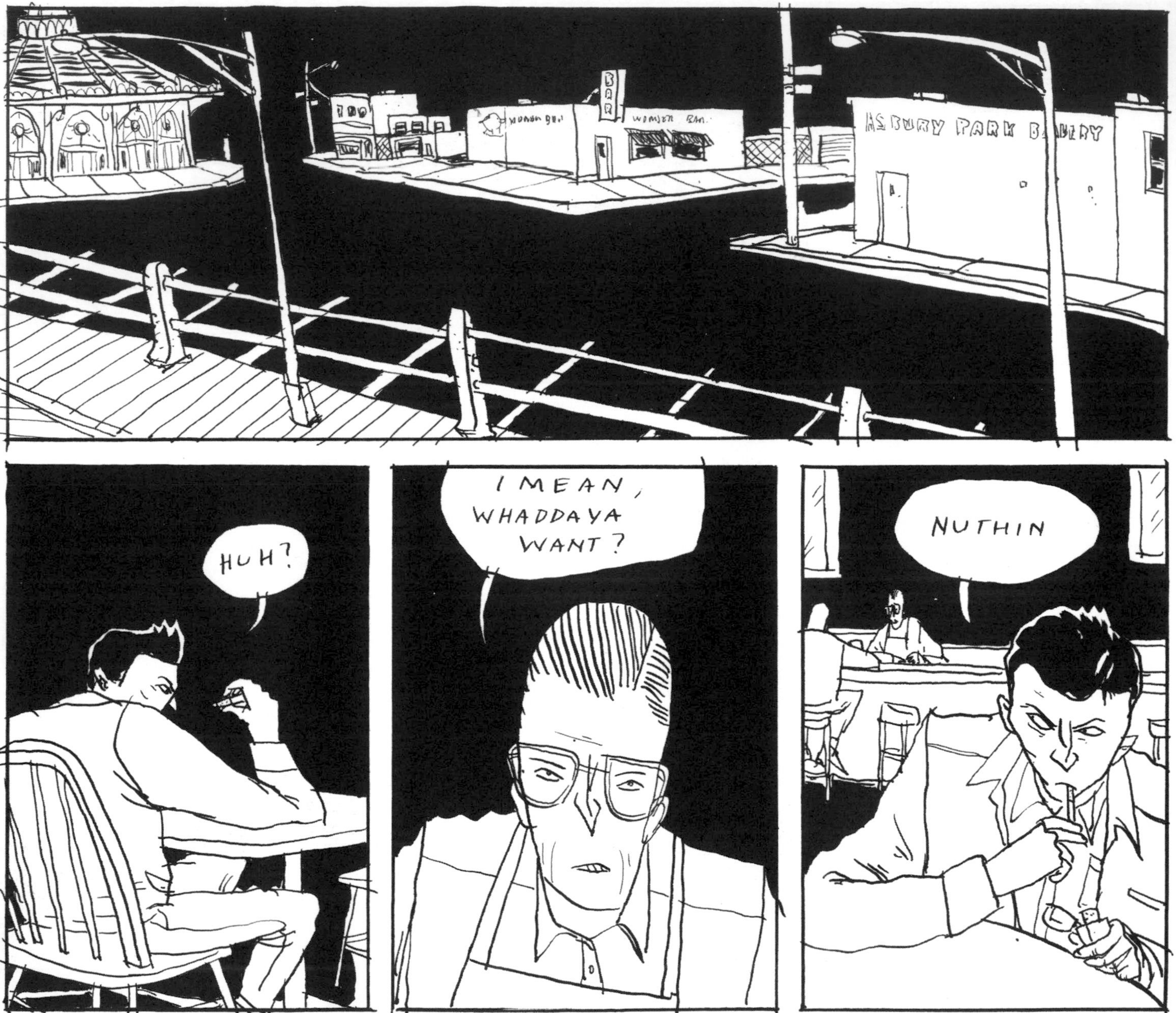
BAR
ASBURY PARK
HUH?
I MEAN, WHADDAYA WANT?
NUTHIN

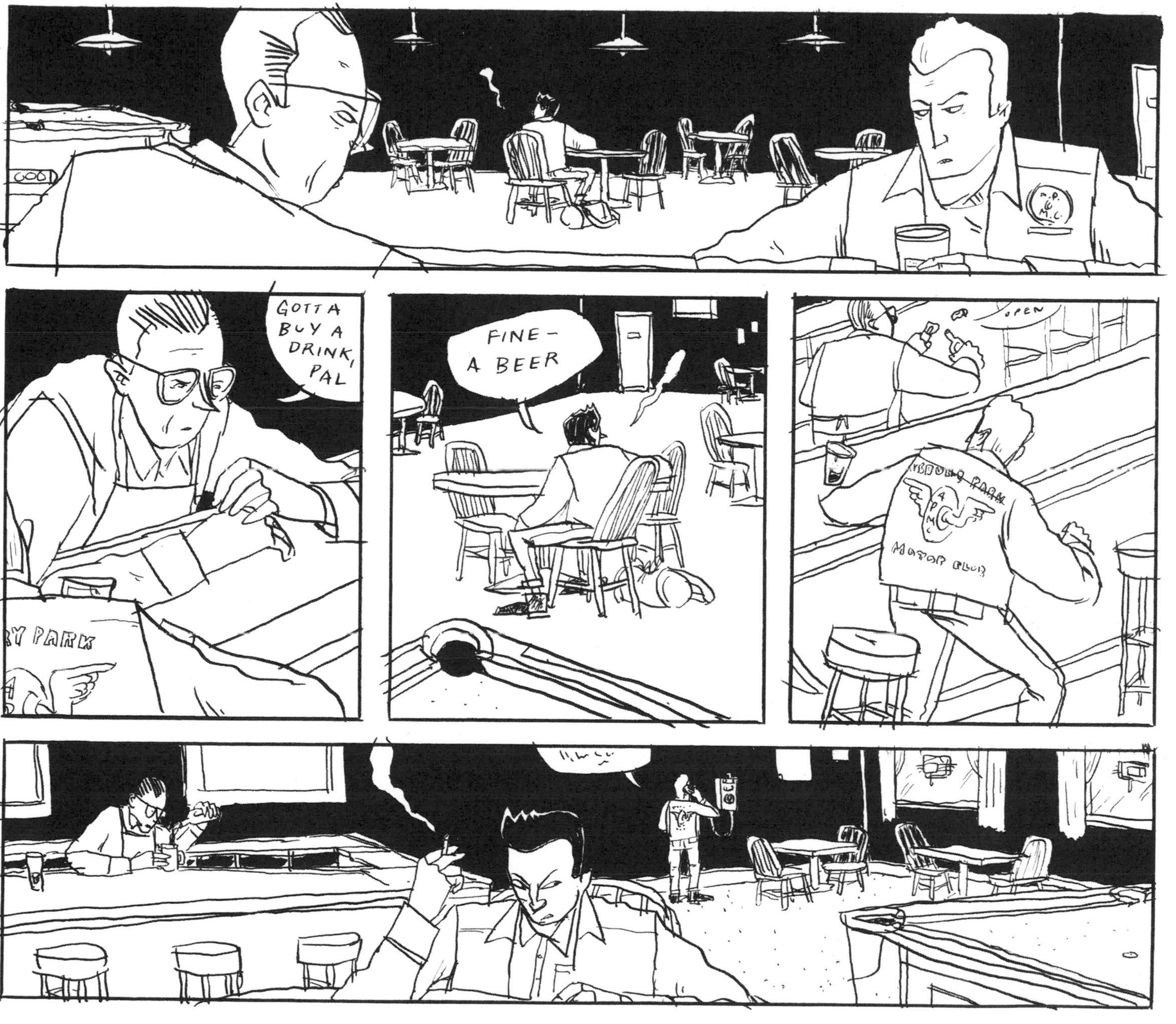
GOTTA BUY A DRINK, PAL
FINE- A BEER
OPEN
MOTOR CLUB

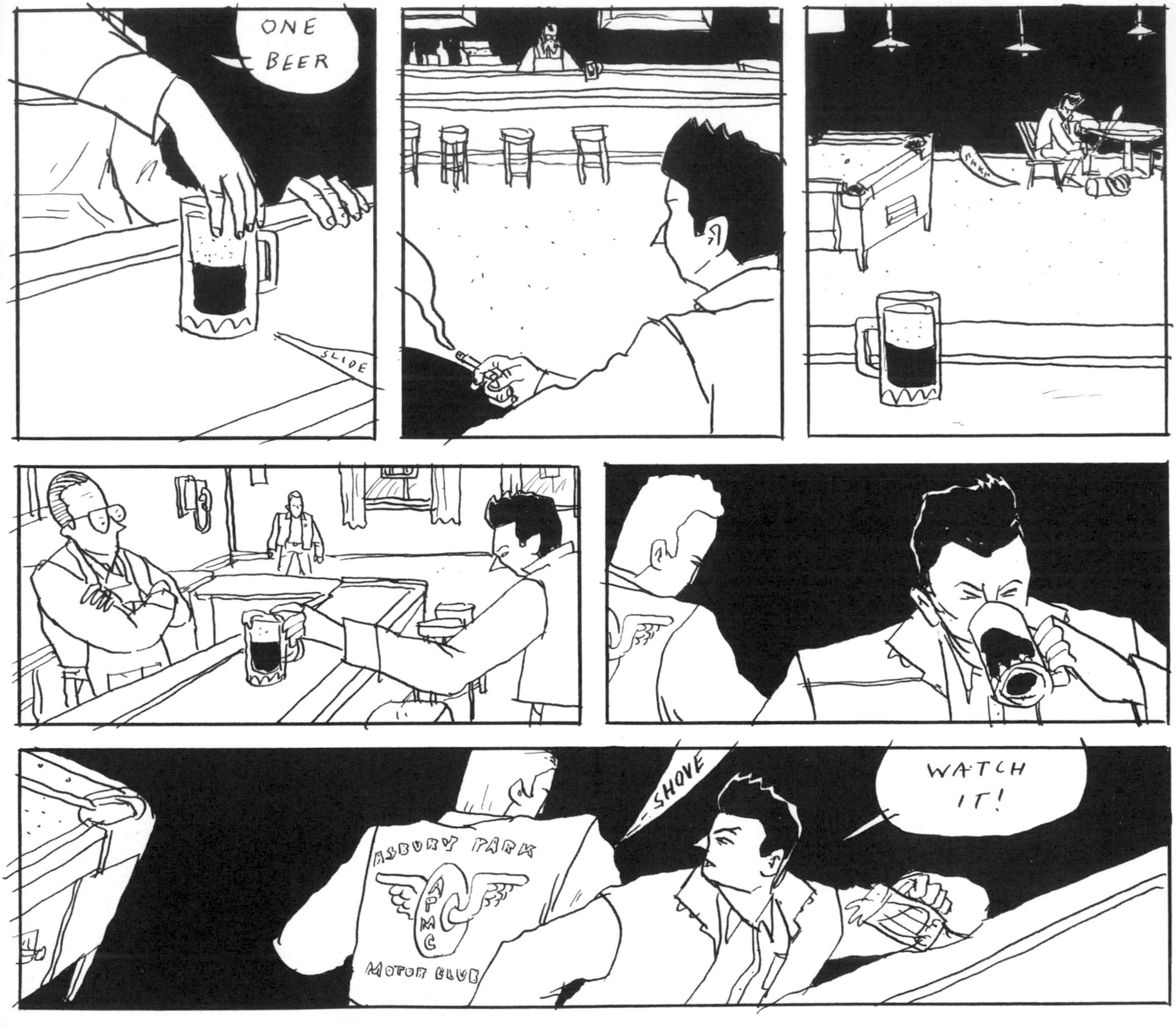
ONE BEER
SLIDE
SHOVE
WATCH IT!
ASBURY PARK
APMC
MOTOR CLUB

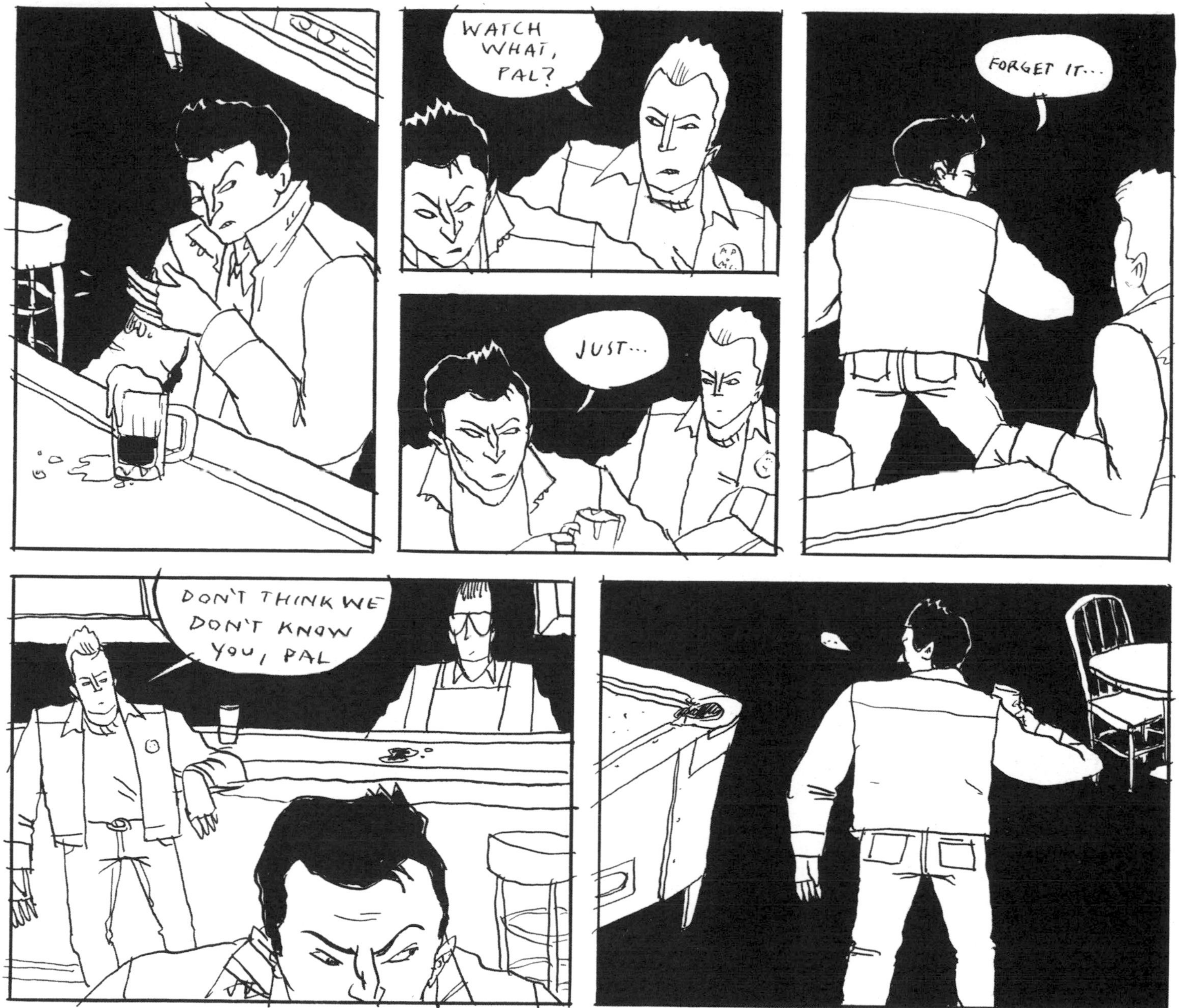
WATCH WHAT, PAL?
JUST...
FORGET IT...
DON'T THINK WE DON'T KNOW YOU, PAL

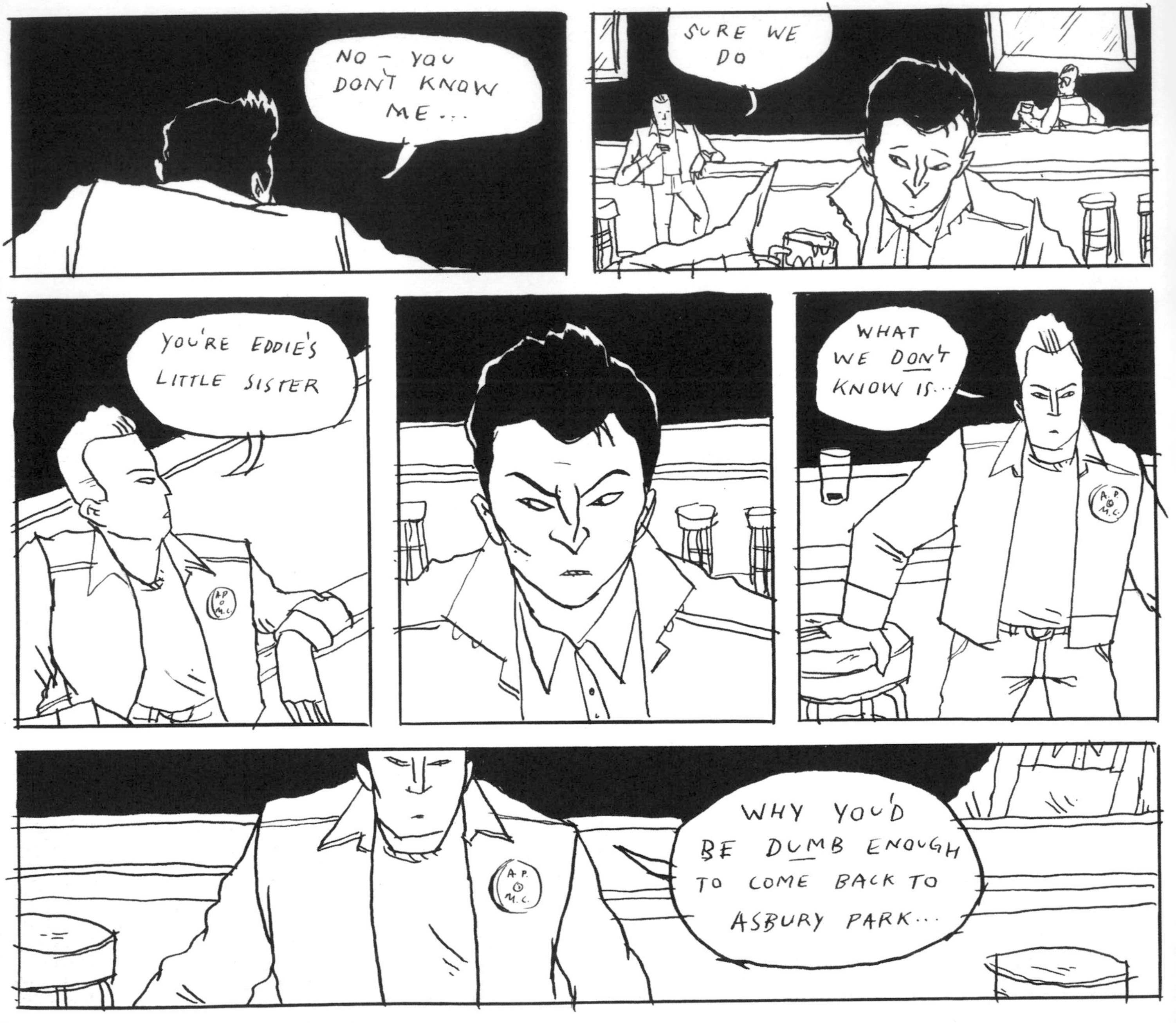
NO - YOU DON'T KNOW ME...
SURE WE DO
YOU'RE EDDIE'S LITTLE SISTER
WHAT WE DON'T KNOW IS...
WHY YOU'D BE DUMB ENOUGH TO COME BACK TO ASBURY PARK...

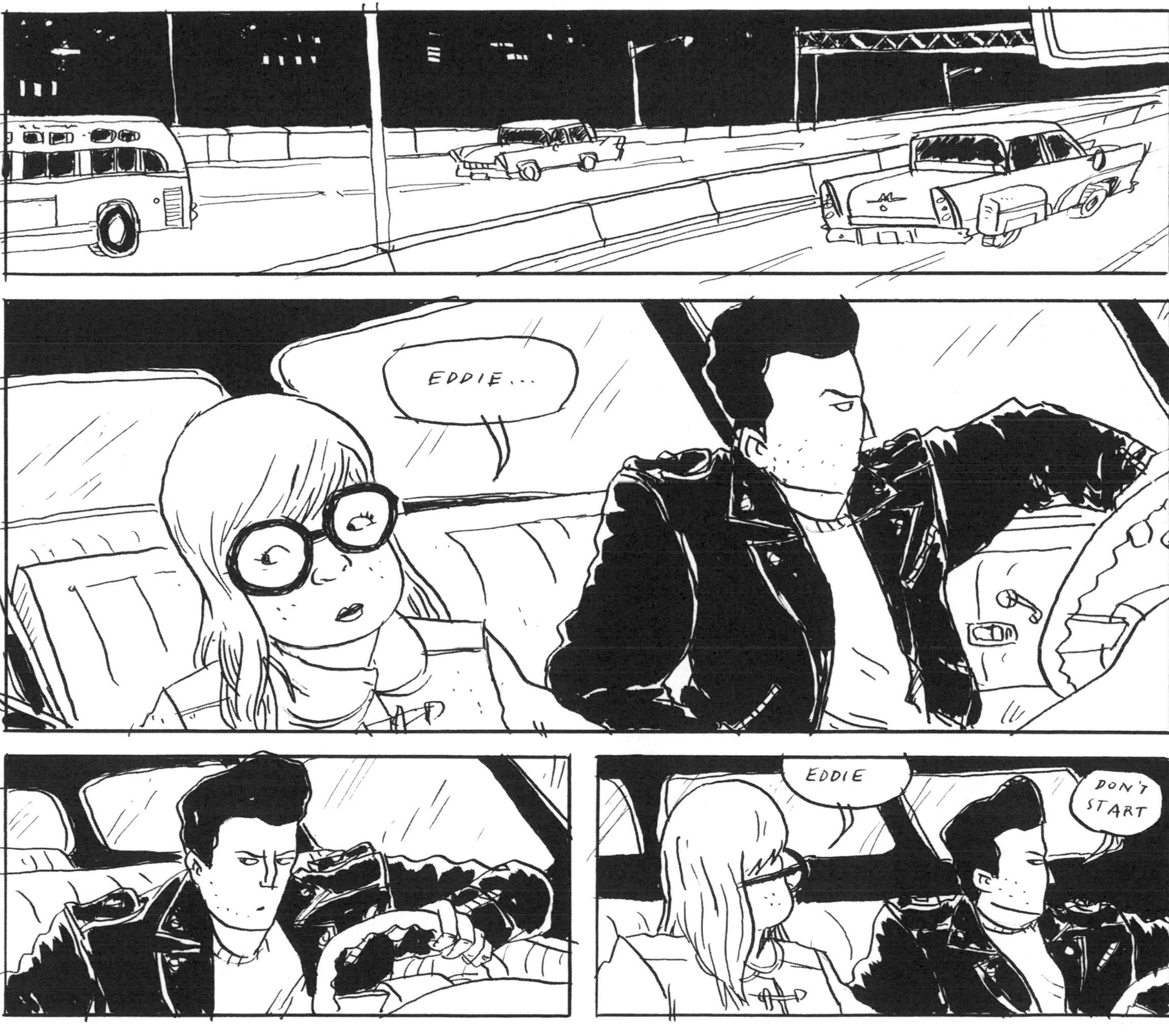
EDDIE...
EDDIE
DON'T START

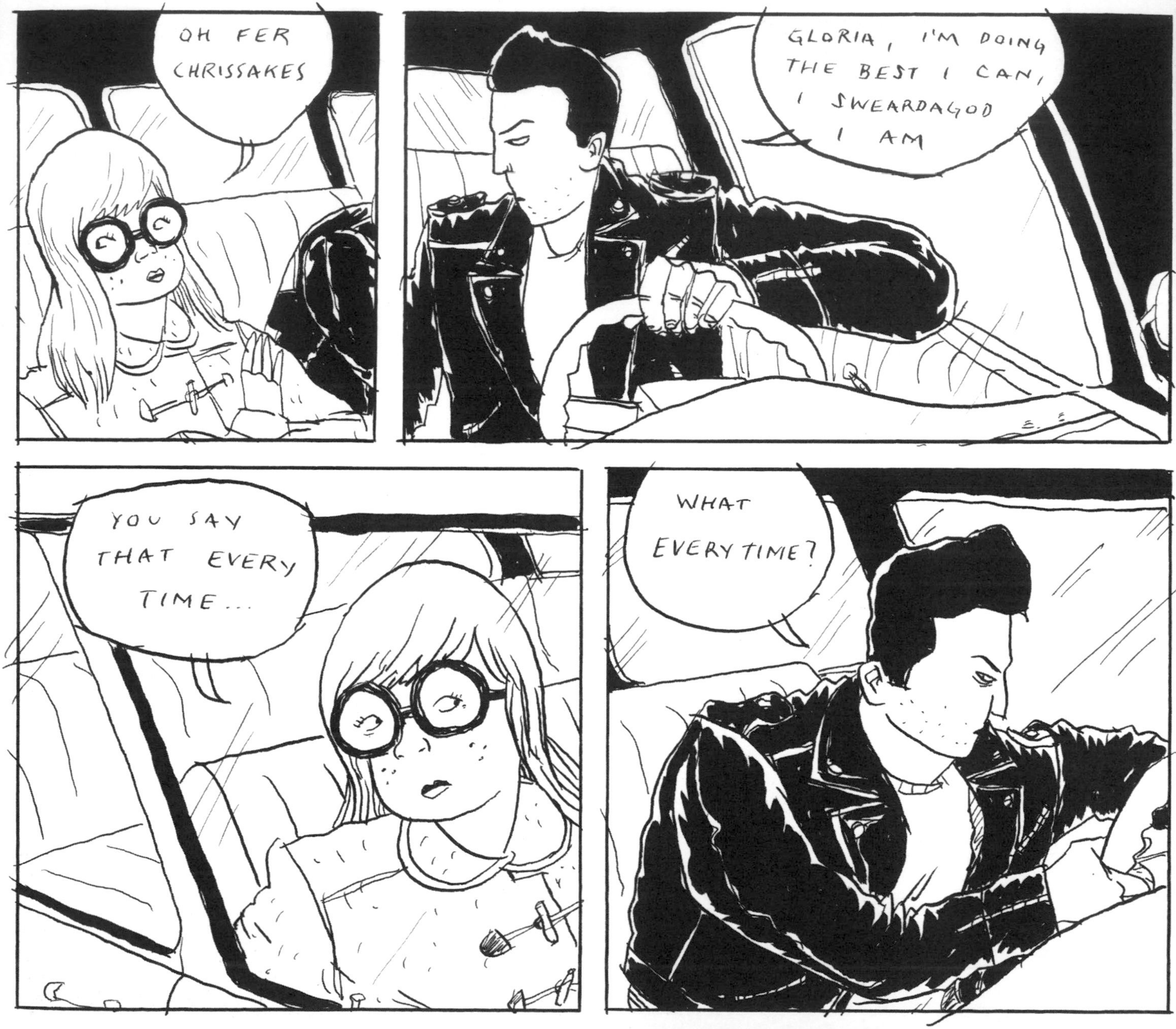
OH FER CHRISSAKES
GLORIA, I'M DOING THE BEST I CAN, I SWEARDAGOD I AM
YOU SAY THAT EVERY TIME...
WHAT EVERY TIME?

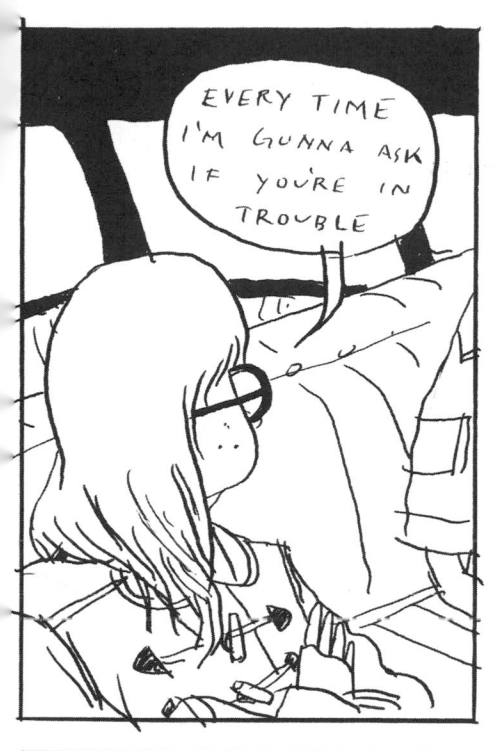

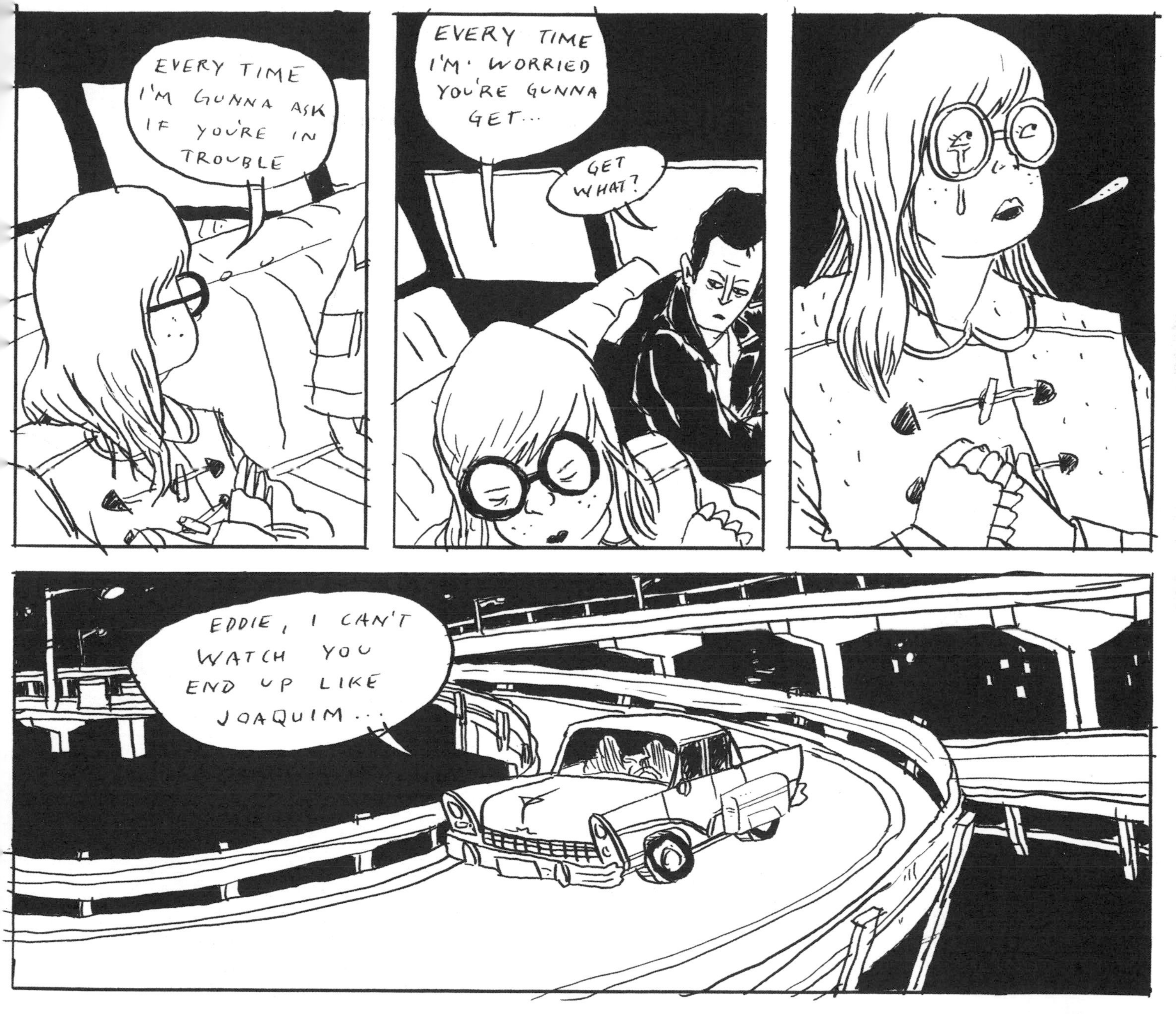
EVERY TIME I'M GUNNA ASK IF YOU'RE IN TROUBLE
EVERY TIME I'M WORRIED YOU'RE GUNNA GET...
GET WHAT?
EDDIE, I CAN'T WATCH YOU END UP LIKE JOAQUIM...

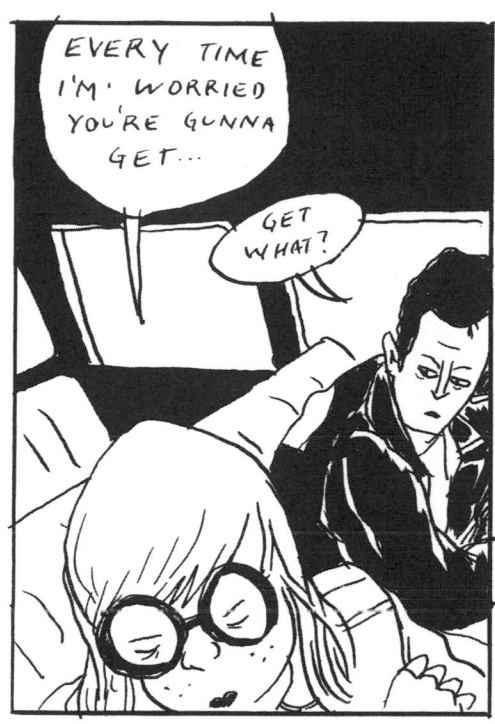

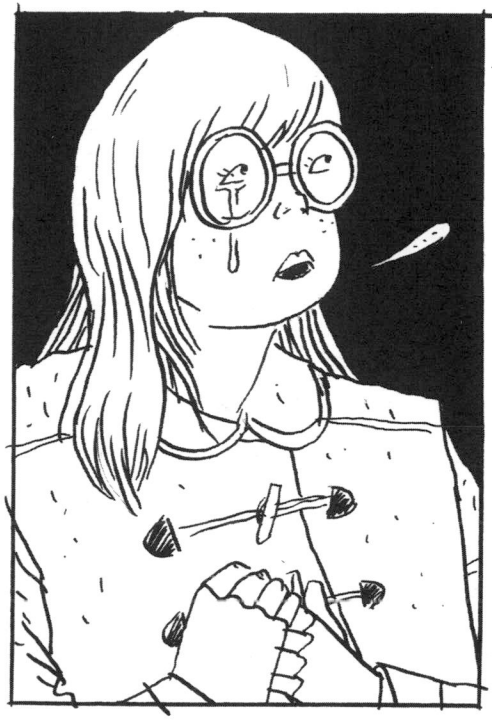

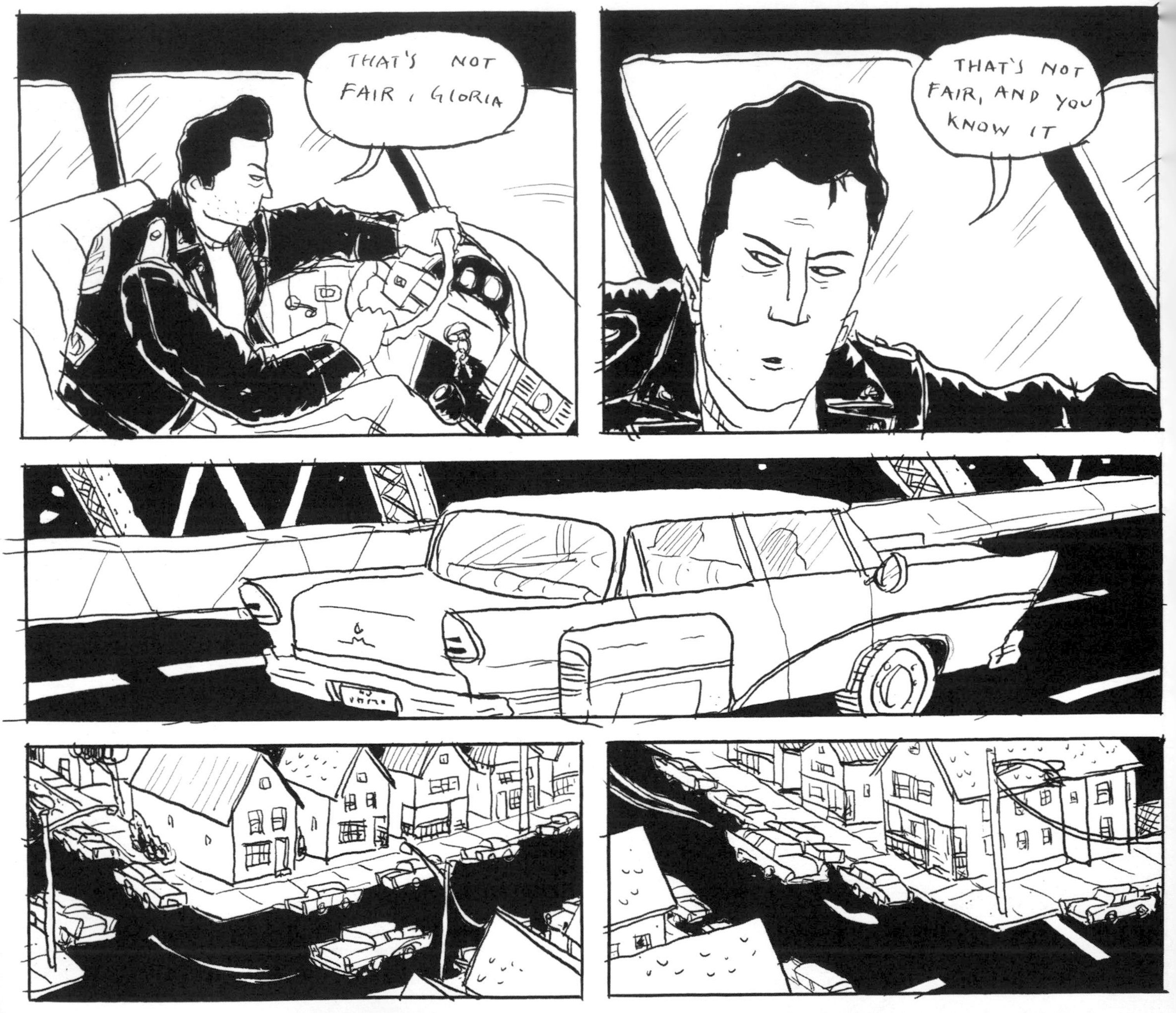
THAT'S NOT FAIR, GLORIA
THAT'S NOT FAIR, AND YOU KNOW IT

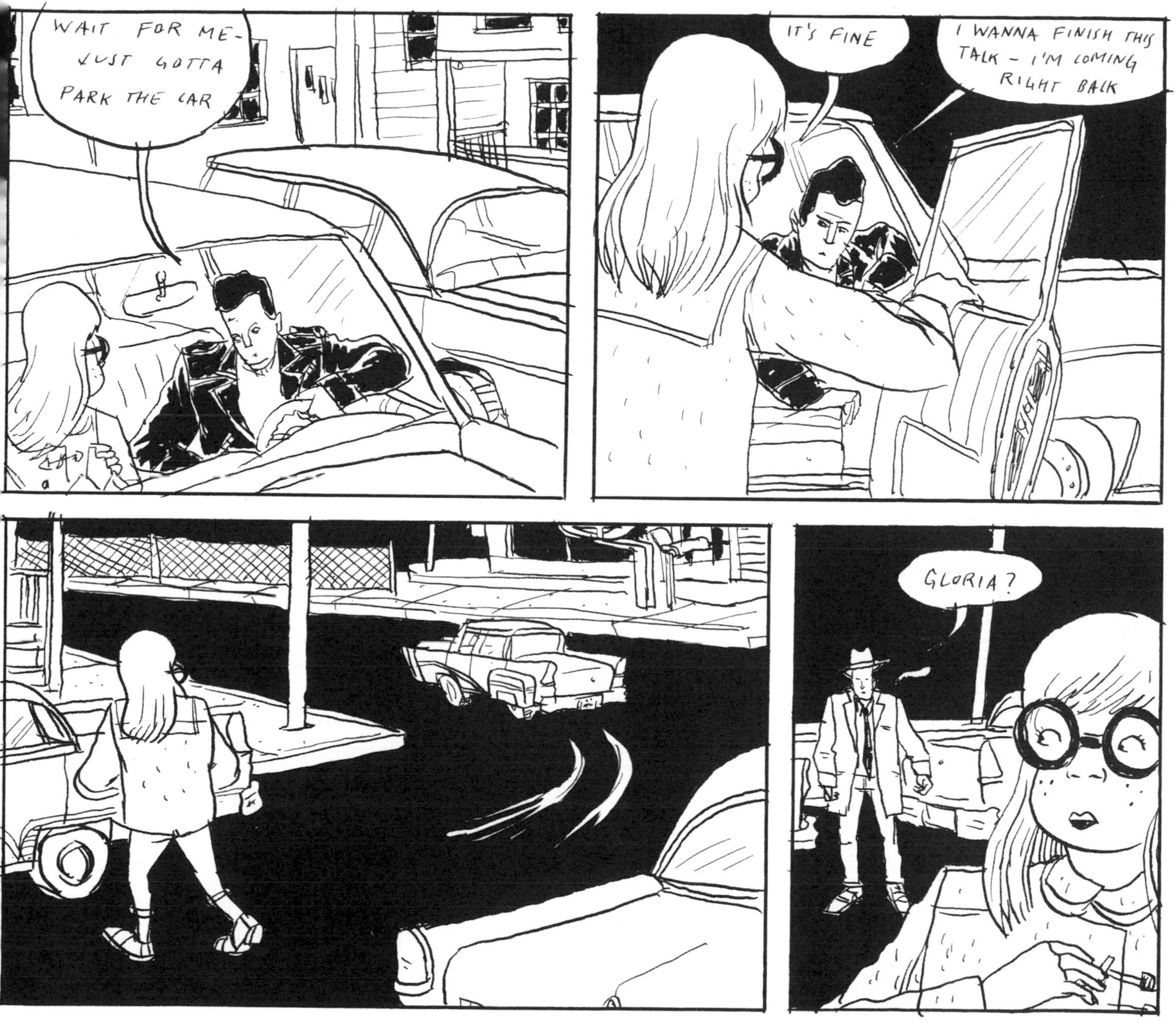
WAIT FOR ME- JUST GOTTA PARK THE CAR
IT'S FINE
I WANNA FINISH THIS TALK - I'M COMING RIGHT BACK
GLORIA?

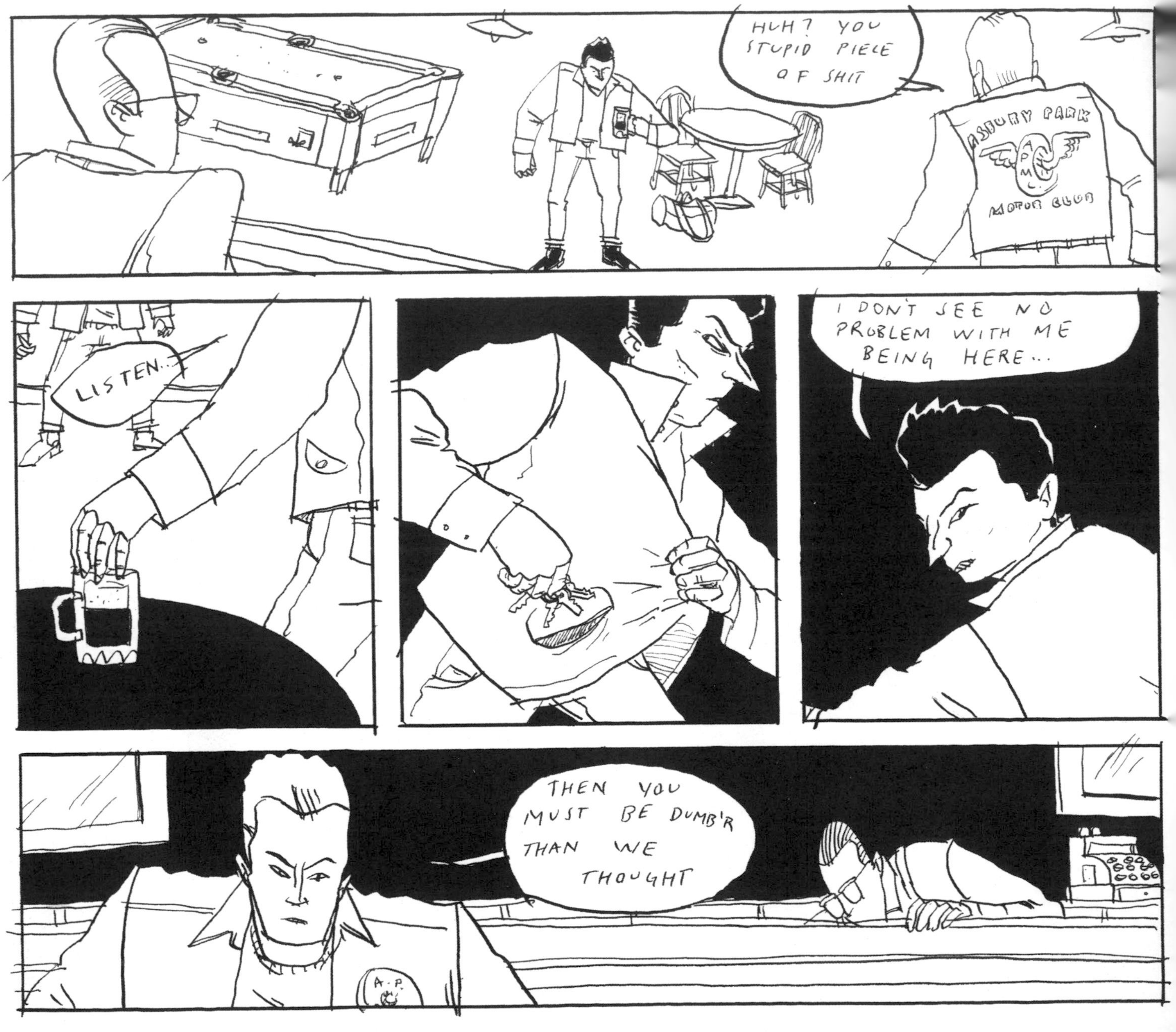
HUH? YOU STUPID PIECE OF SHIT
ASBURY PARK
A P M C
MOTOR CLUB
LISTEN...
I DON'T SEE NO PROBLEM WITH ME BEING HERE...
THEN YOU MUST BE DUMB'R THAN WE THOUGHT
A.P.

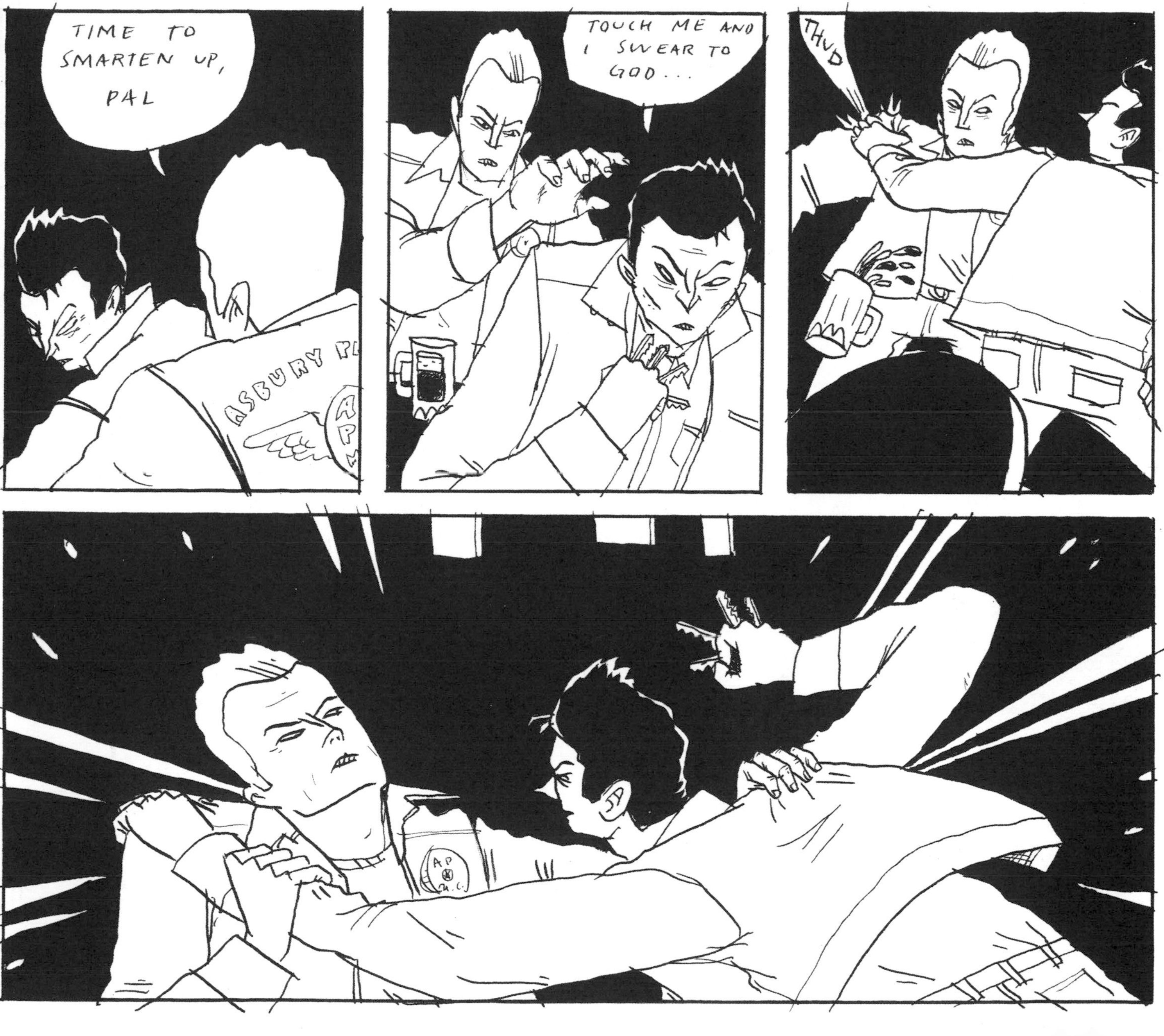
TIME TO SMARTEN UP, PAL
ASBURY P
TOUCH ME AND I SWEAR TO GOD...
THUD

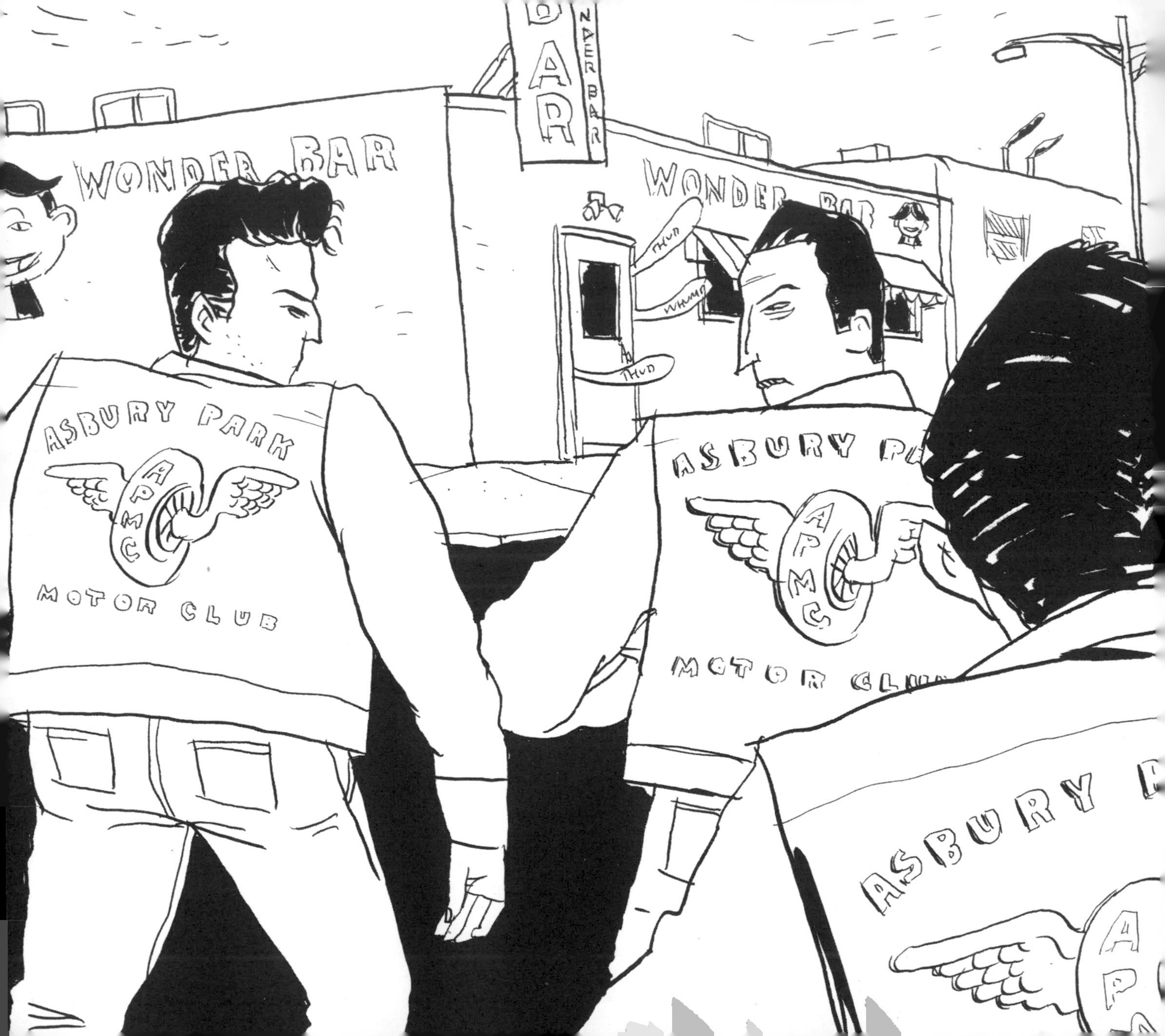

BAR
WONDER BAR
WONDER BAR
WONDER BAR
THUD
WHUMP
THUD
ASBURY PARK
APMC
MOTOR CLUB
ASBURY PARK
APMC
ASBURY

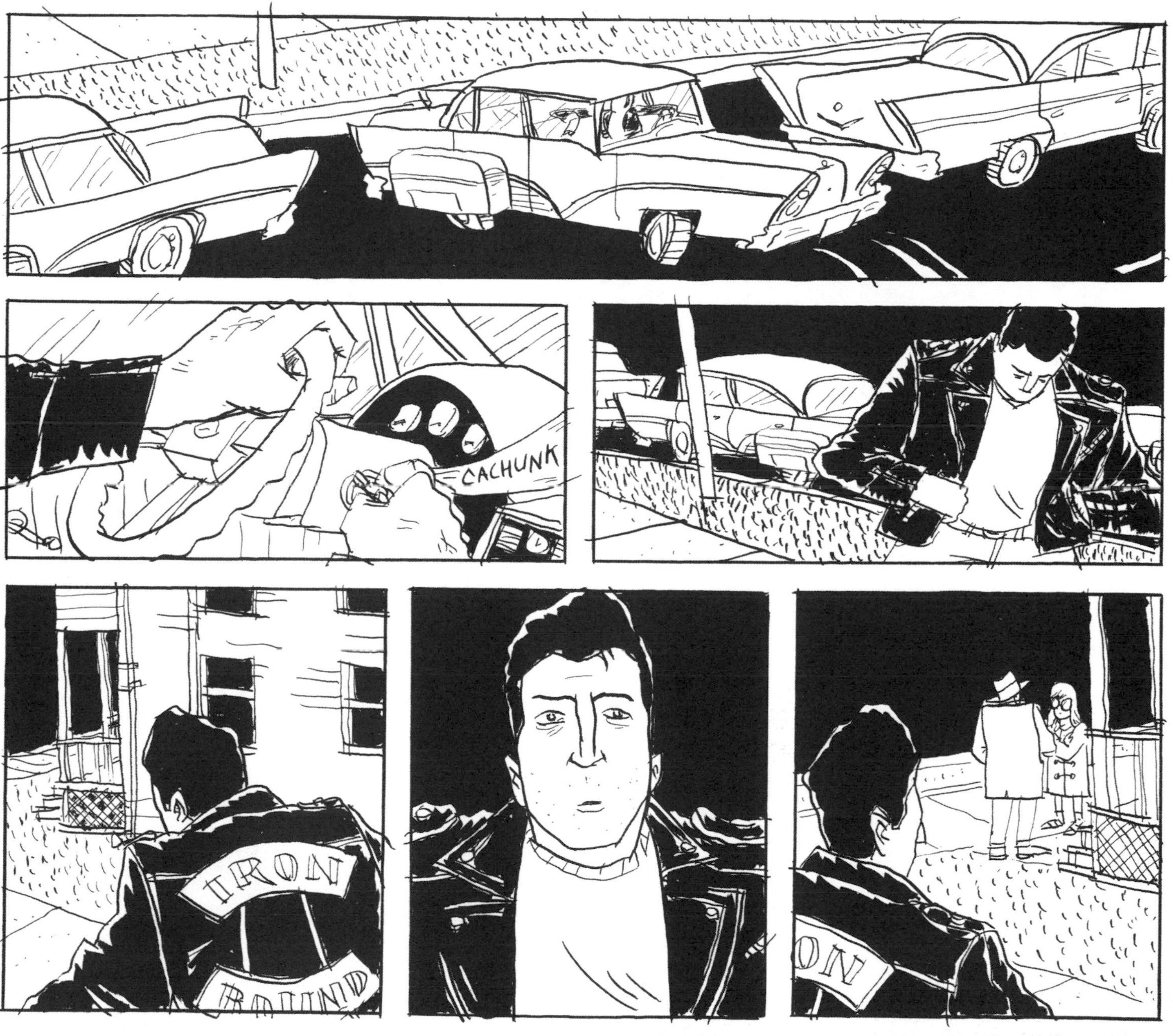
CACHUNK
IRON

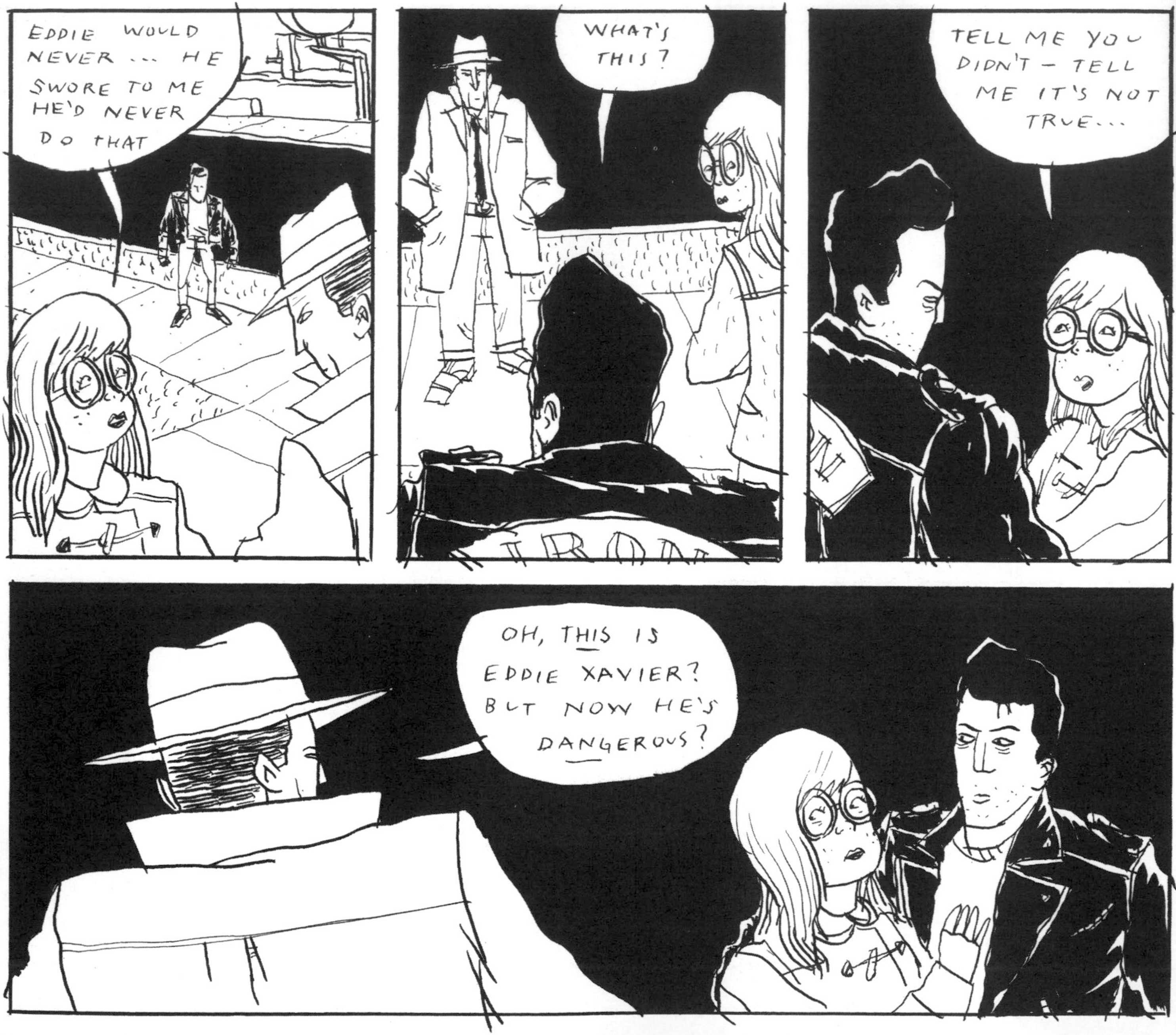
EDDIE WOULD NEVER ... HE SWORE TO ME HE'D NEVER DO THAT
WHAT'S THIS?
TELL ME YOU DIDN'T - TELL ME IT'S NOT TRUE...
OH, THIS IS EDDIE XAVIER? BUT NOW HE'S DANGEROUS?

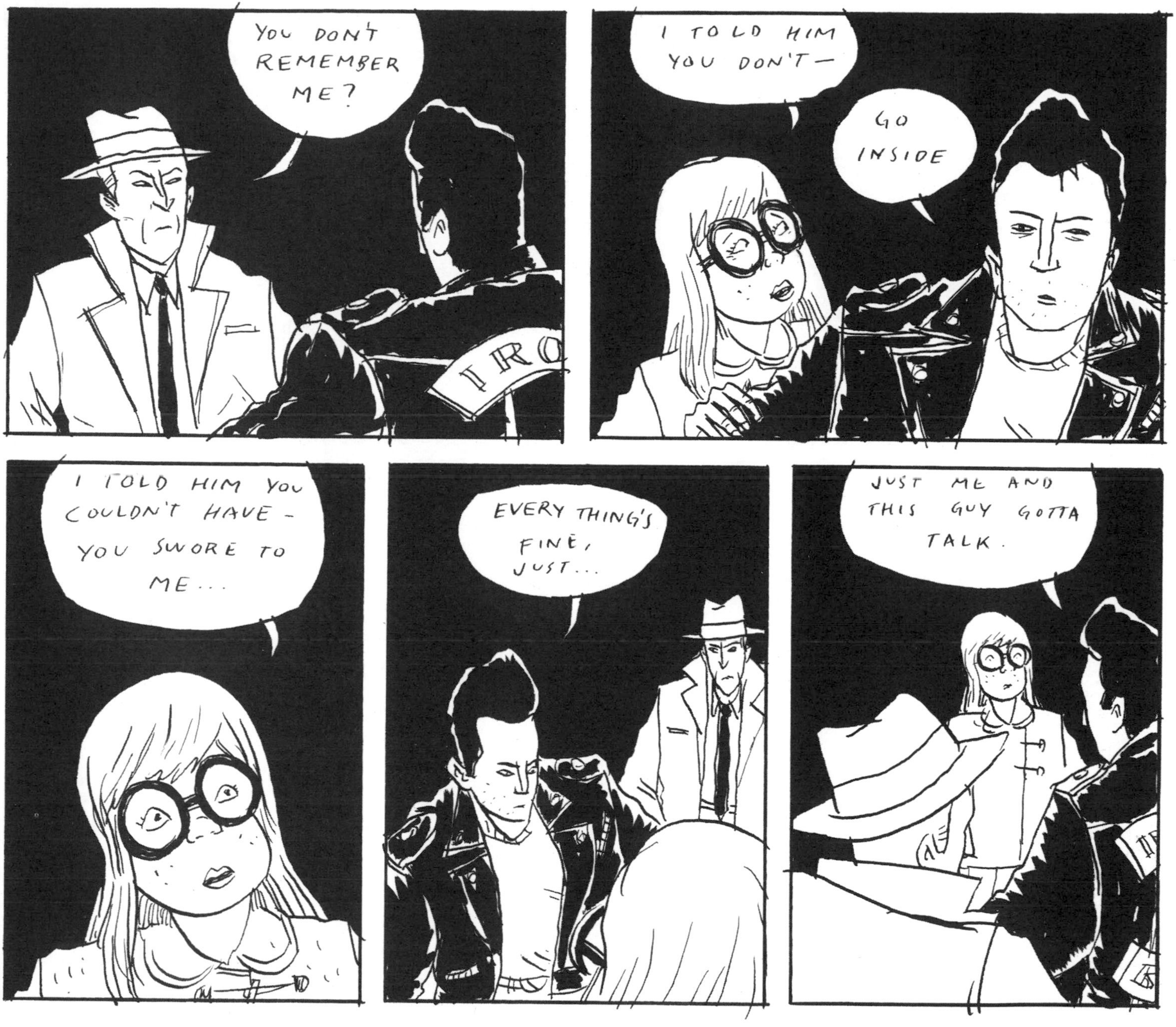
YOU DON'T REMEMBER ME?
I TOLD HIM YOU DON'T—
GO INSIDE
I TOLD HIM YOU COULDN'T HAVE - YOU SWORE TO ME...
EVERY THING'S FINE, JUST...
JUST ME AND THIS GUY GOTTA TALK.

THUD THUD
ASBURY PARK
ASBURY PA
WHUMP

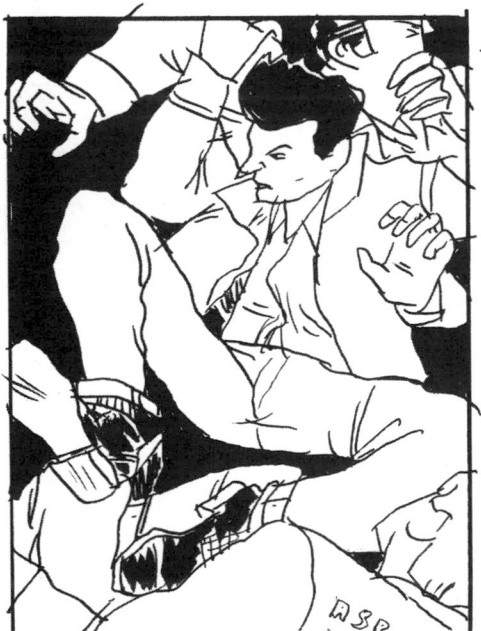

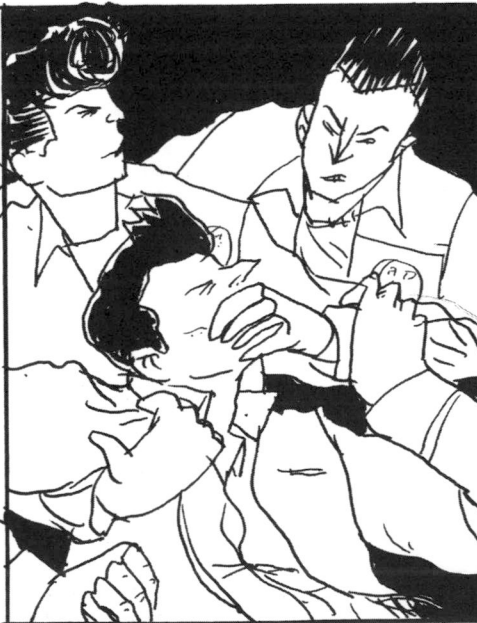

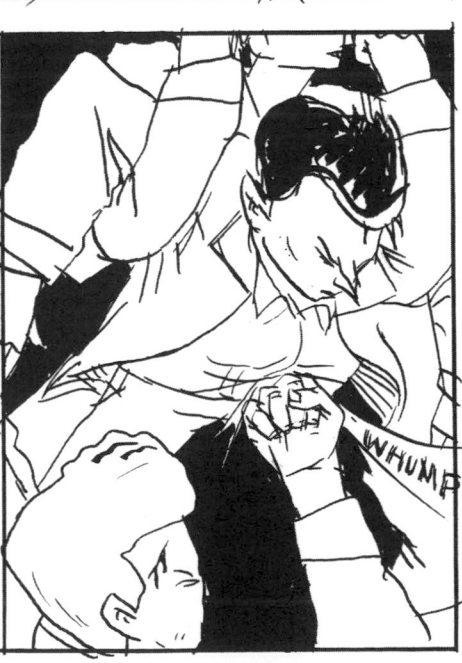

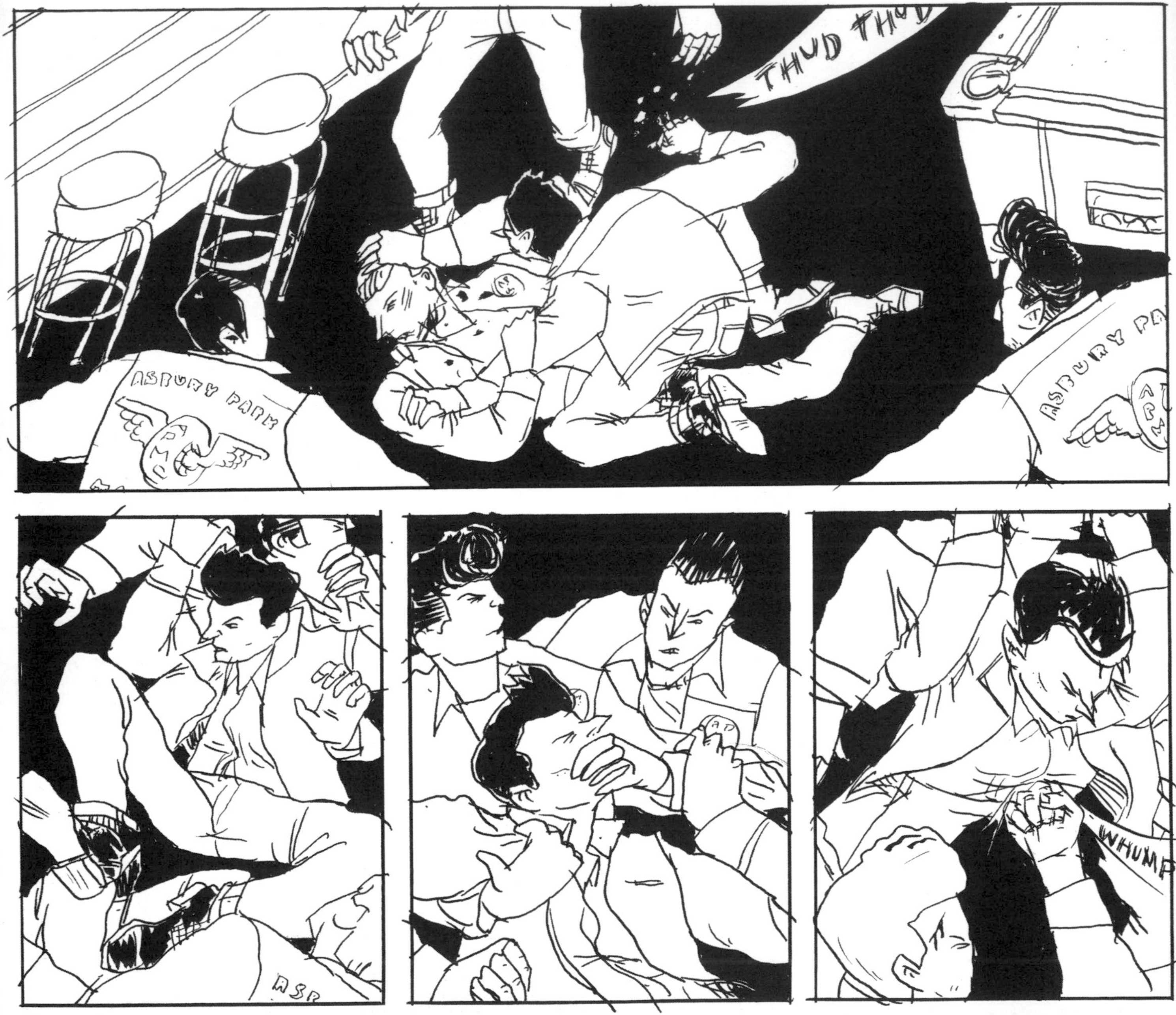

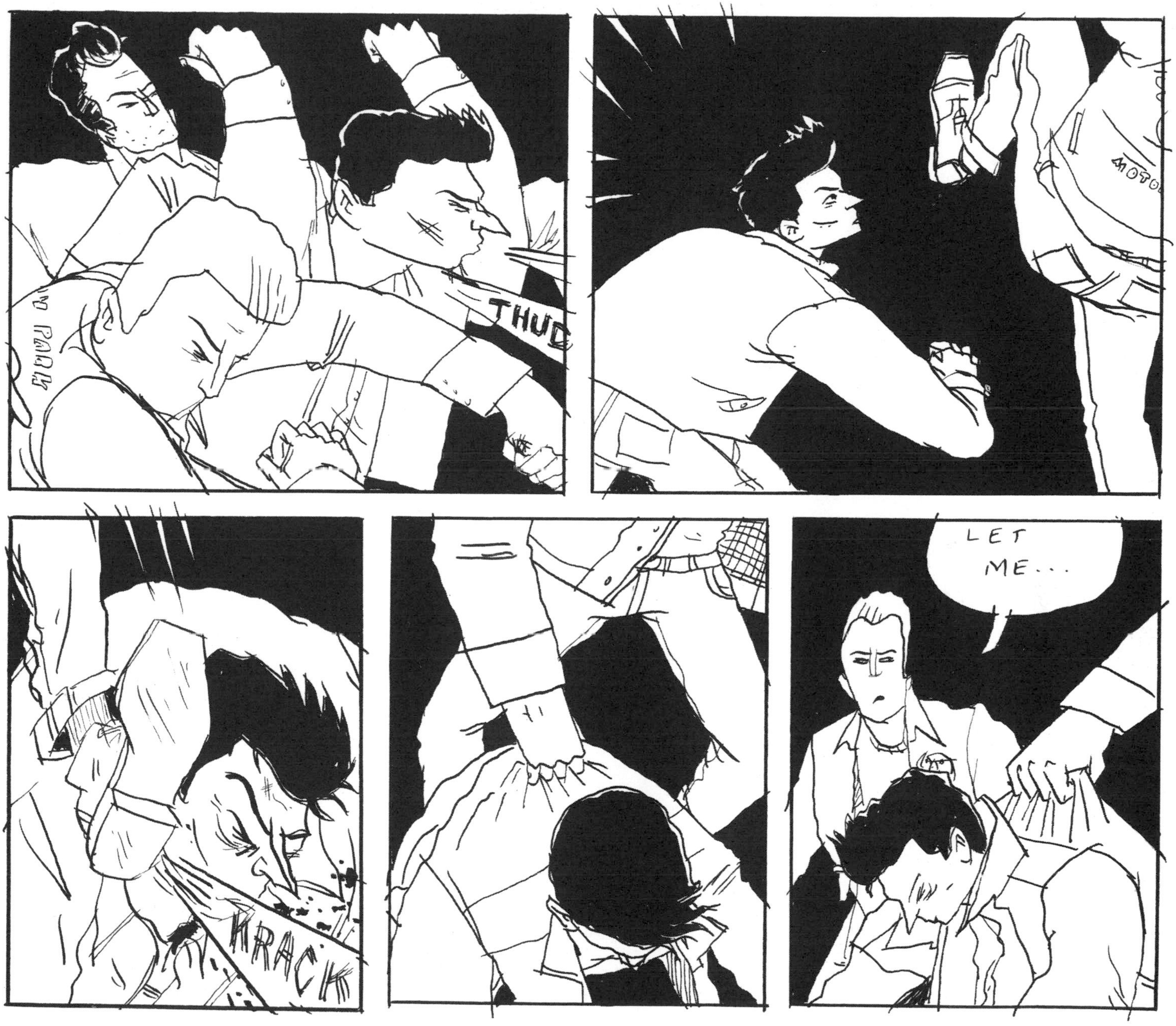
THUD
KRACK
LET ME...

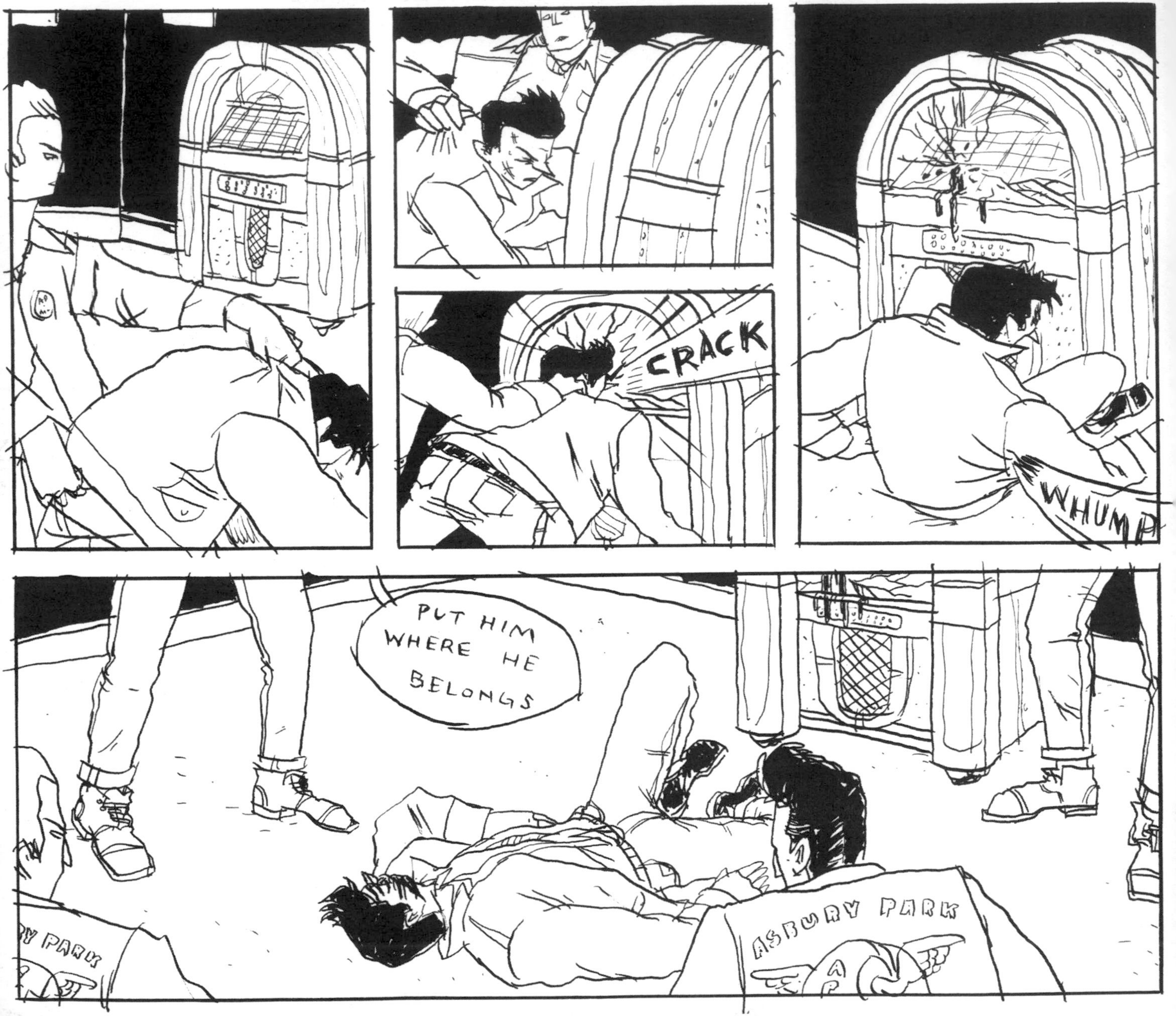
CRACK
WHUMP
PUT HIM WHERE HE BELONGS
ASBURY PARK

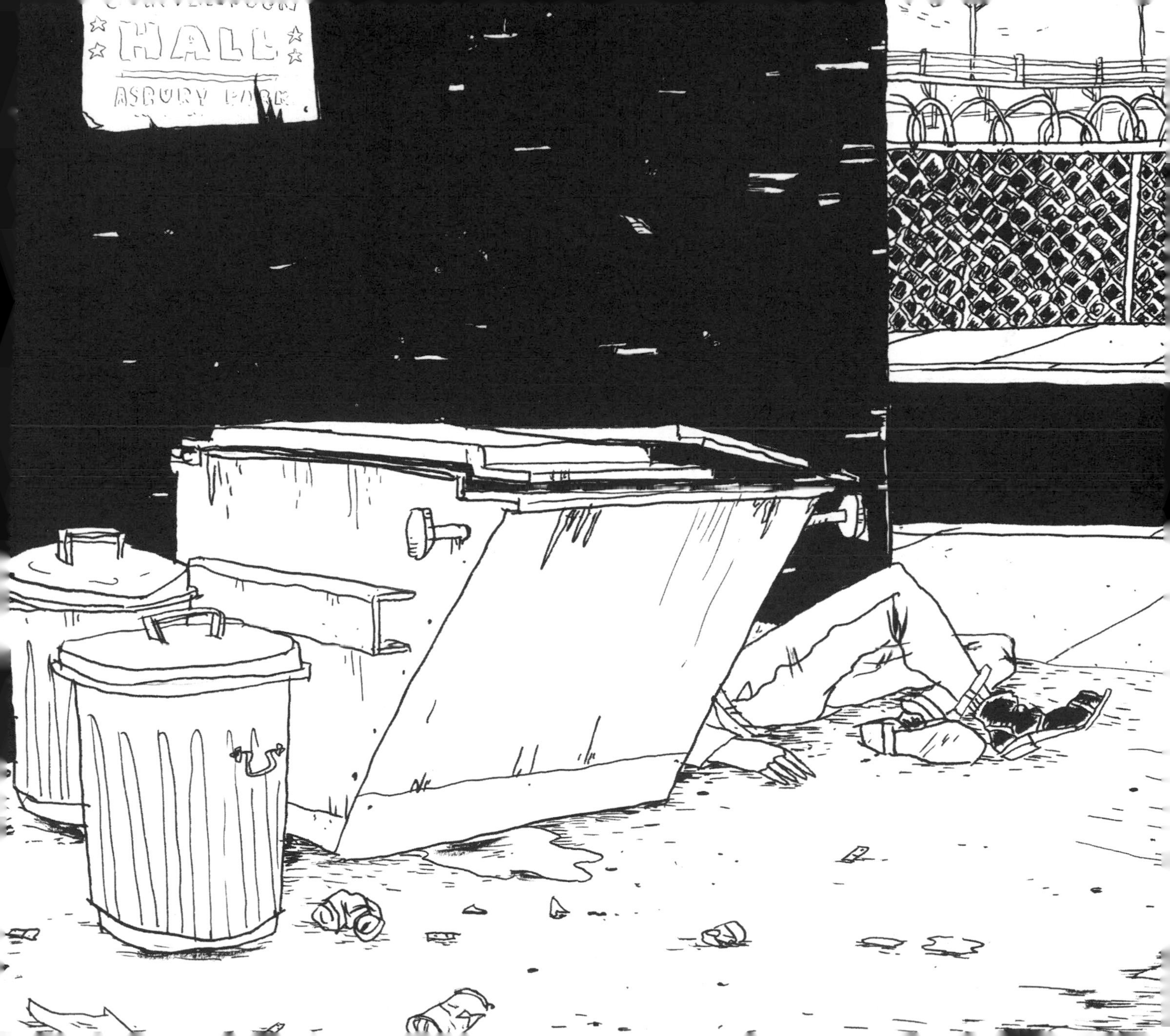
HALL
ASBURY

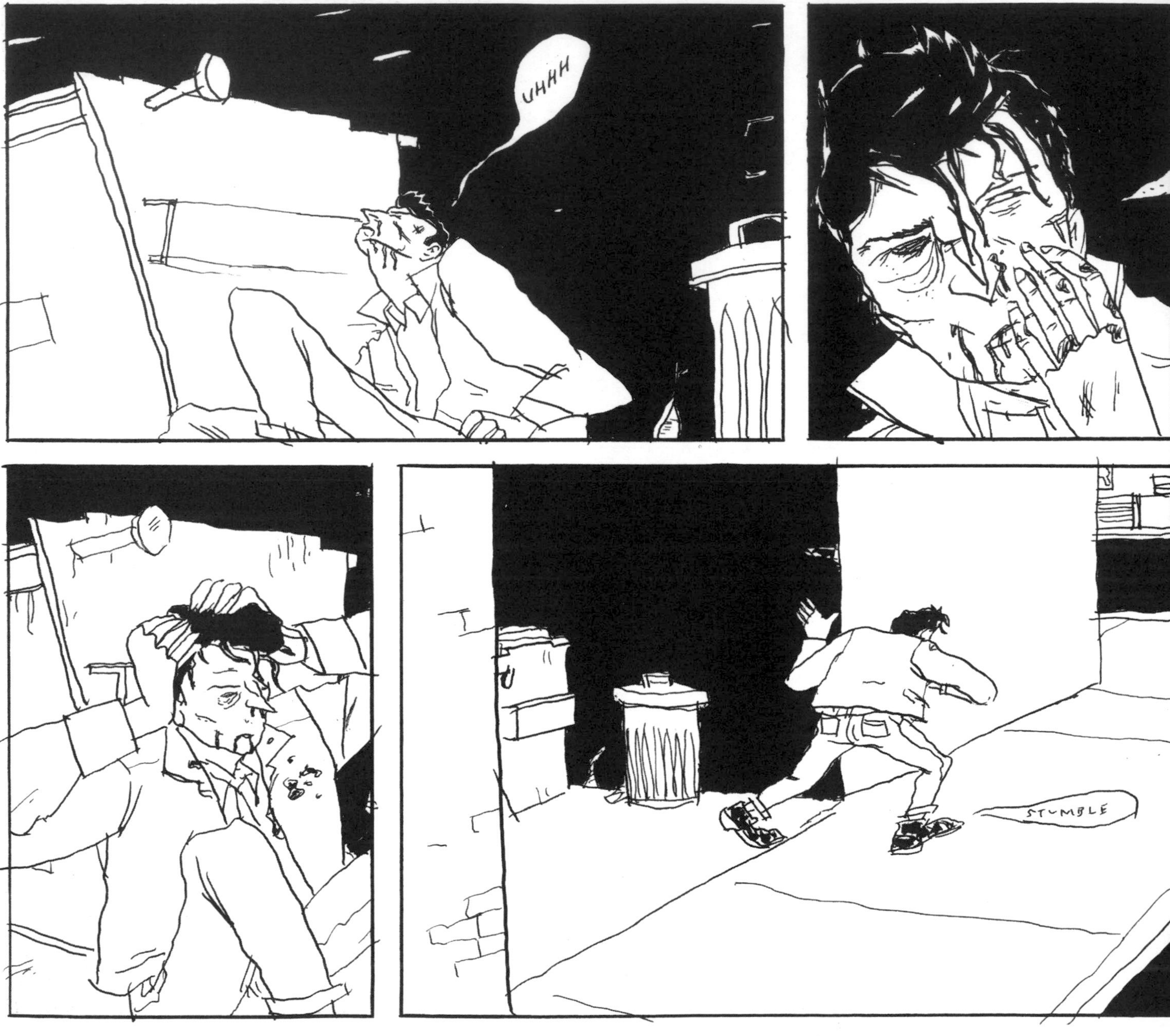
UHHH
STUMBLE

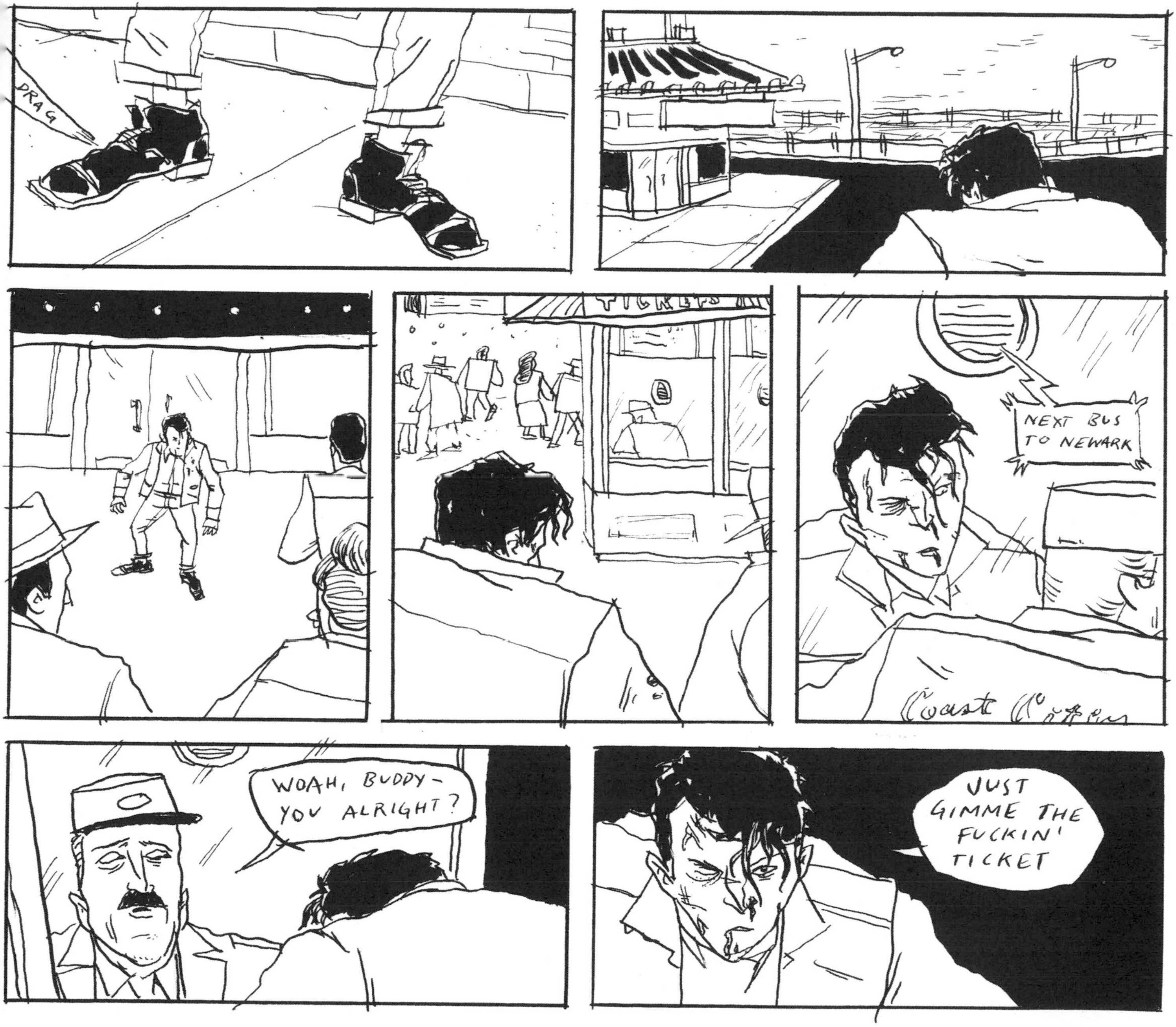
DRAG
NEXT BUS TO NEWARK
WOAH, BUDDY- YOU ALRIGHT?
JUST GIMME THE FUCKIN' TICKET

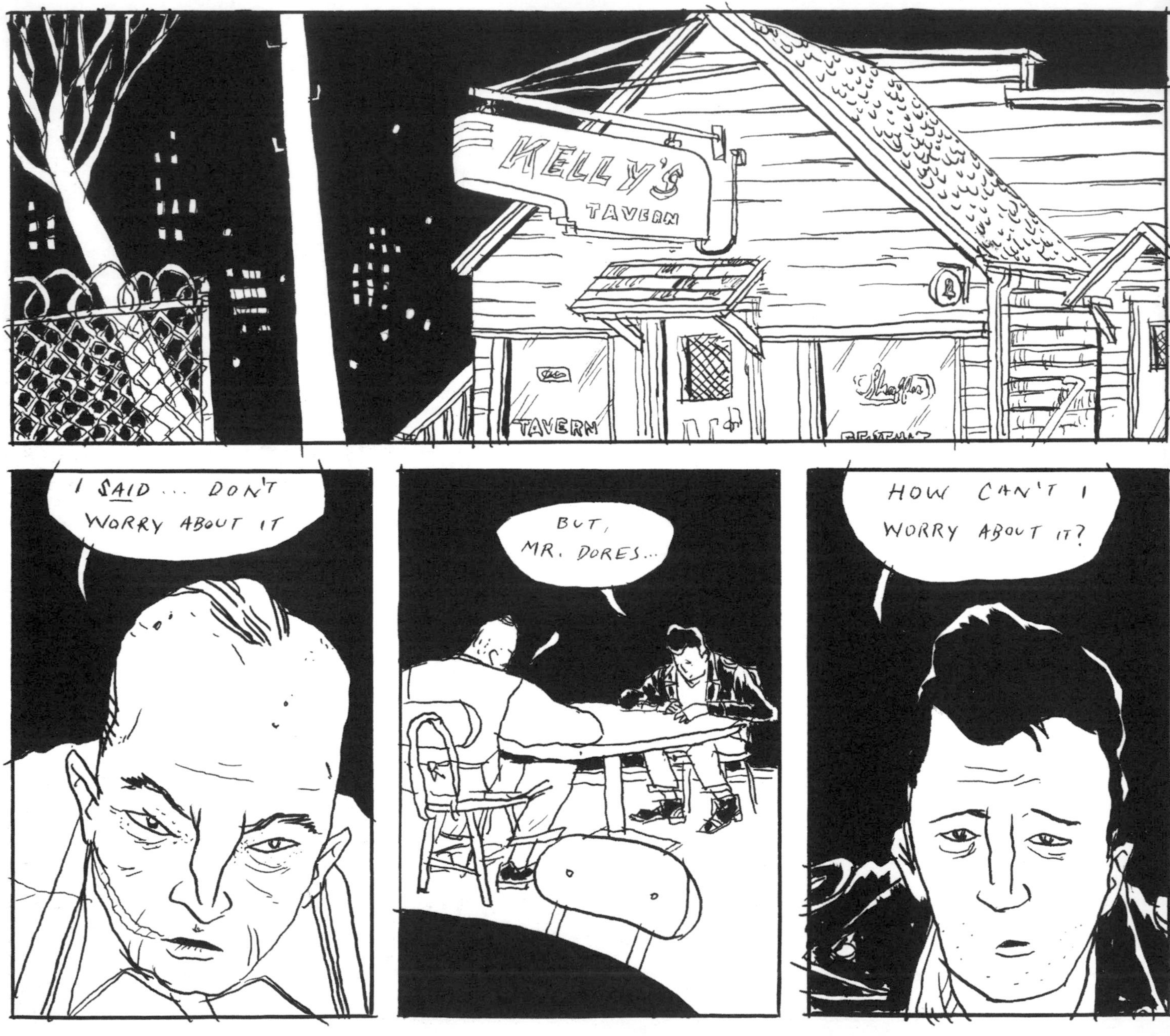
KELLY'S
TAVERN
TAVERN
I SAID... DON'T WORRY ABOUT IT
BUT, MR. DORES...
HOW CAN'T I WORRY ABOUT IT?

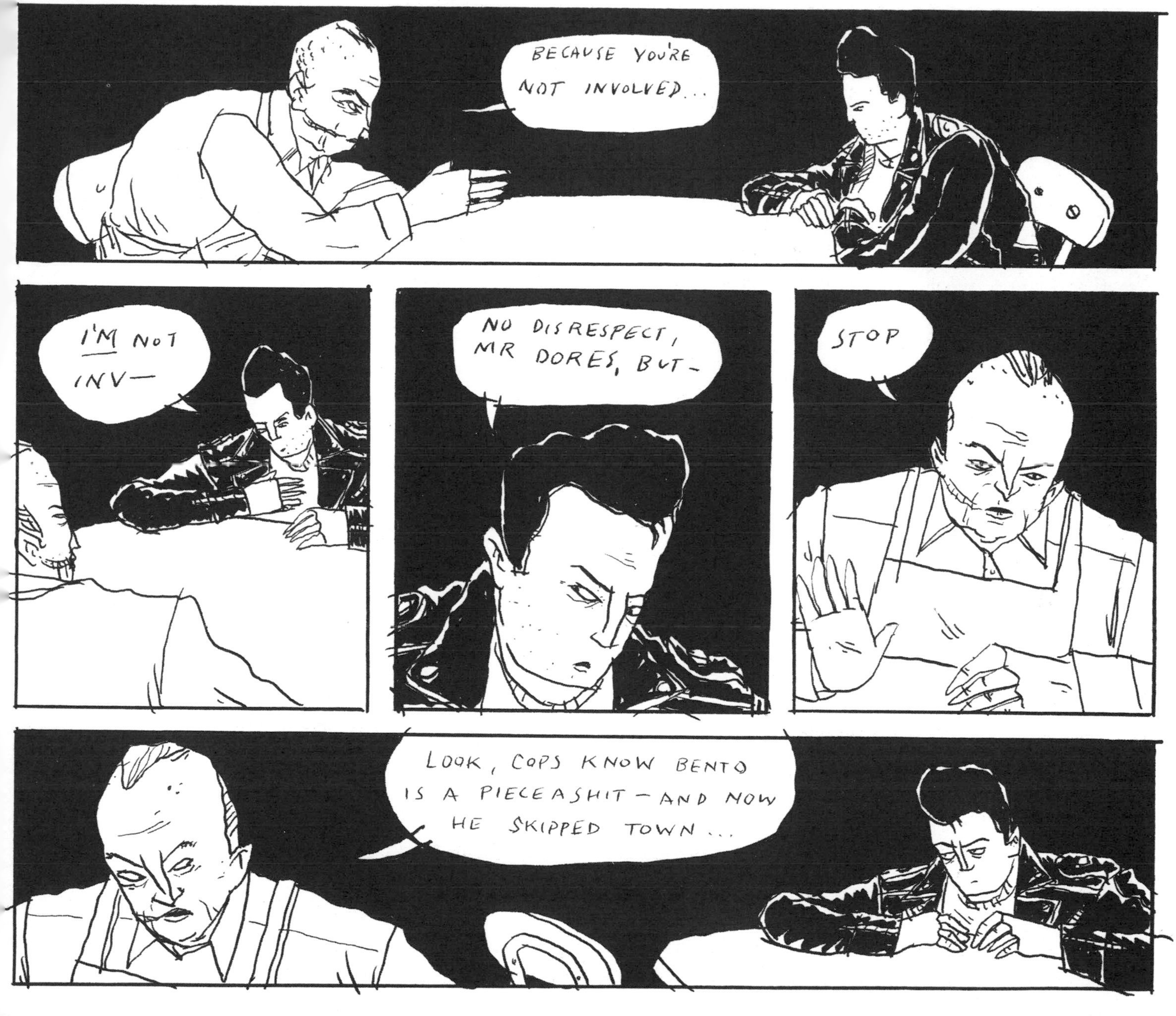
BECAUSE YOU'RE NOT INVOLVED...
I'M NOT INV—
NO DISRESPECT, MR DORES, BUT-
STOP
LOOK, COPS KNOW BENTO IS A PIECEASHIT — AND NOW HE SKIPPED TOWN...

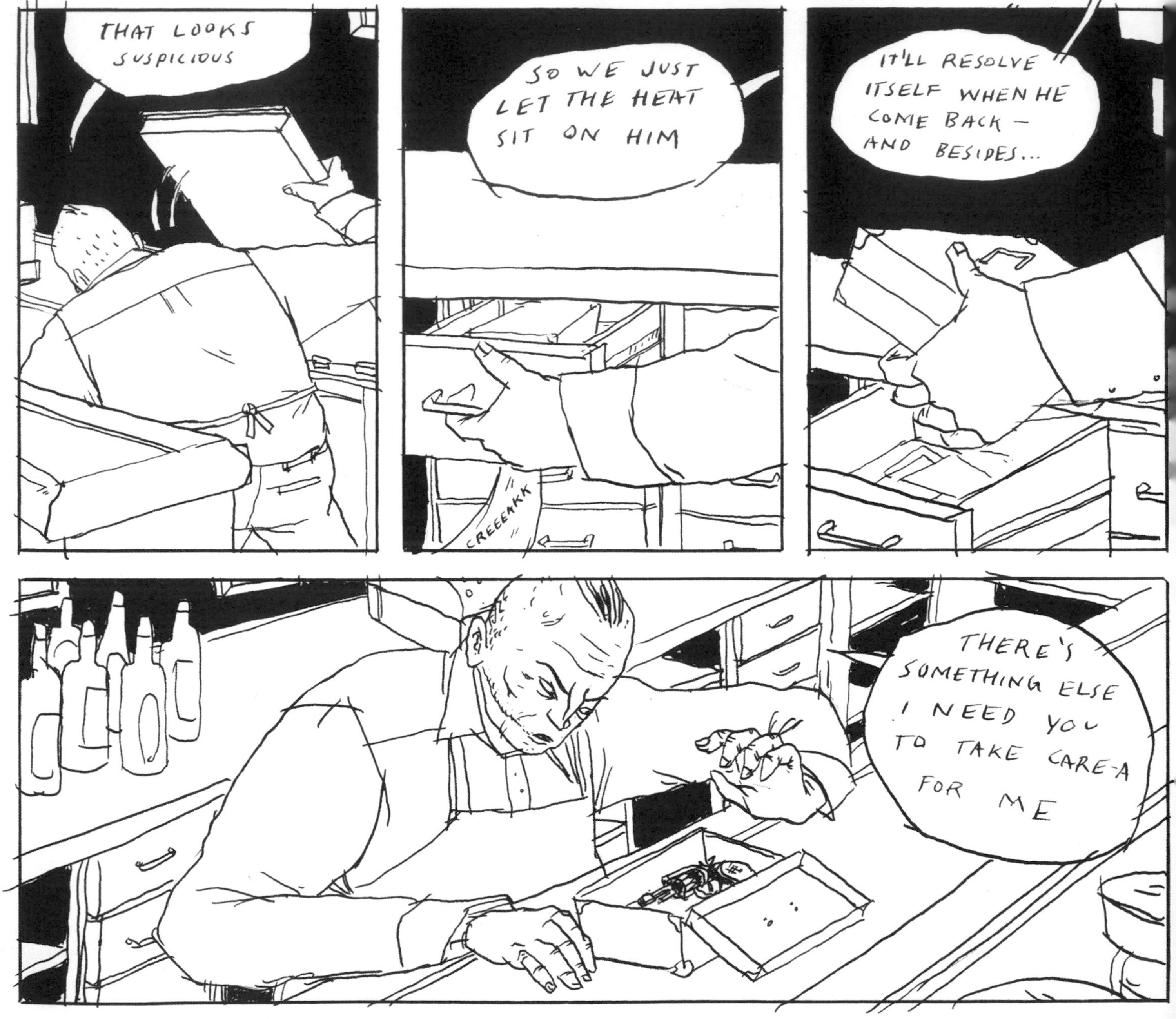
THAT LOOKS SUSPICIOUS
SO WE JUST LET THE HEAT SIT ON HIM
CREEEAKK
IT'LL RESOLVE ITSELF WHEN HE COME BACK — AND BESIDES...
THERE'S SOMETHING ELSE I NEED YOU TO TAKE CARE-A FOR ME

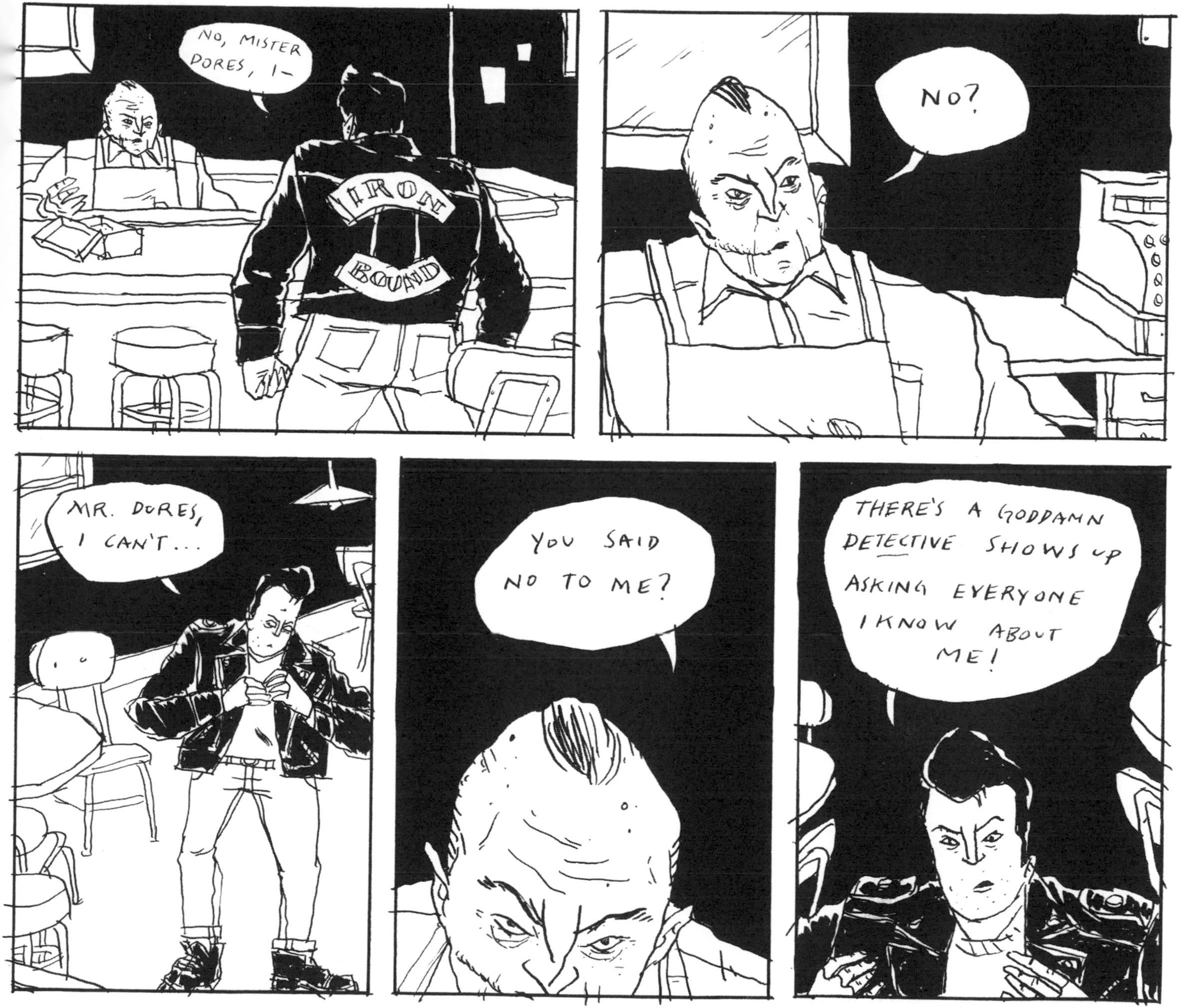
NO, MISTER DORES, I–
IRON BOUND
NO?
MR. DORES, I CAN'T...
YOU SAID NO TO ME?
THERE'S A GODDAMN DETECTIVE SHOWS UP ASKING EVERYONE I KNOW ABOUT ME!

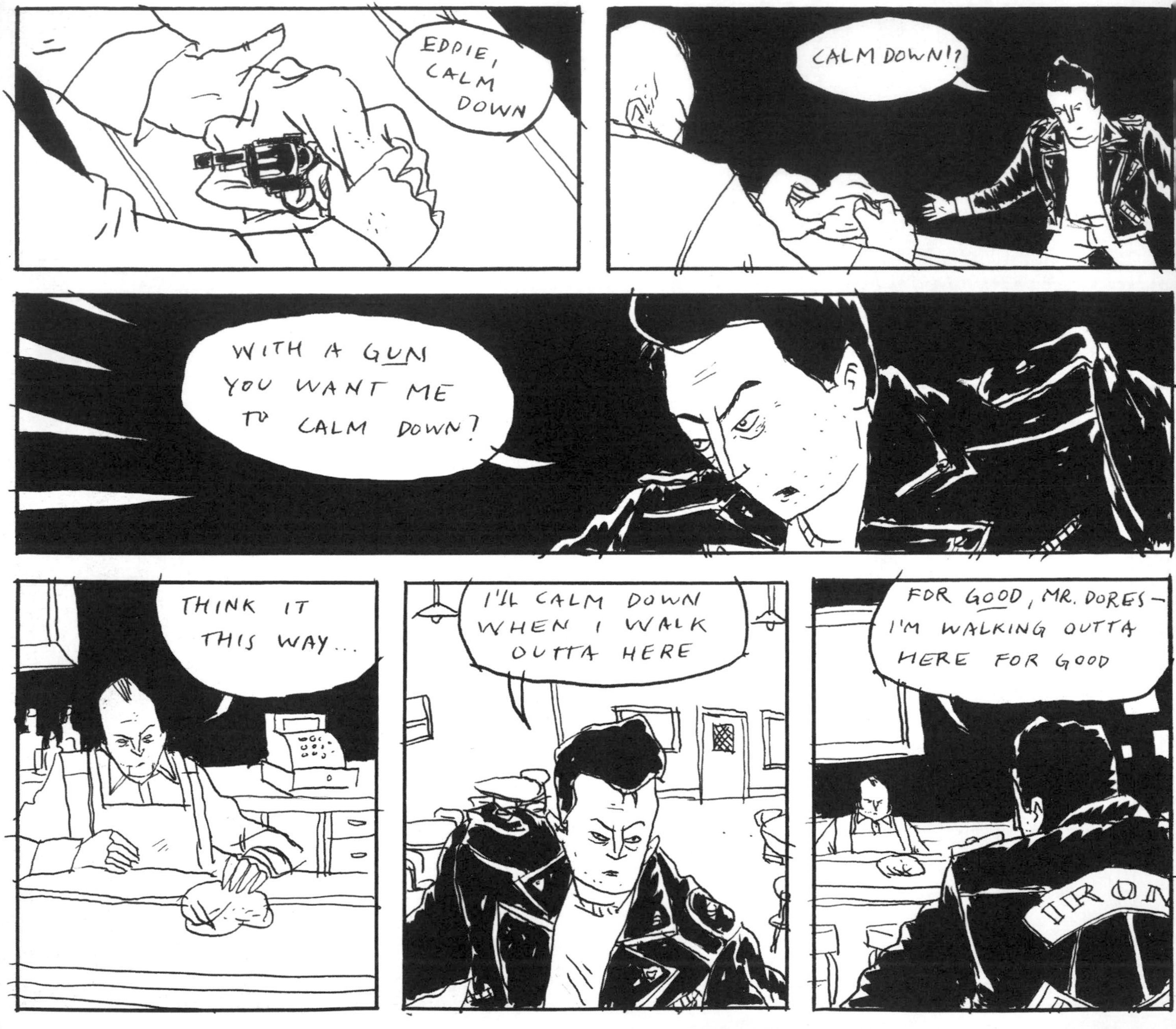
EDDIE, CALM DOWN
CALM DOWN!?
WITH A GUN YOU WANT ME TO CALM DOWN?
THINK IT THIS WAY...
I'LL CALM DOWN WHEN I WALK OUTTA HERE
FOR GOOD, MR. DORES— I'M WALKING OUTTA HERE FOR GOOD
IRON

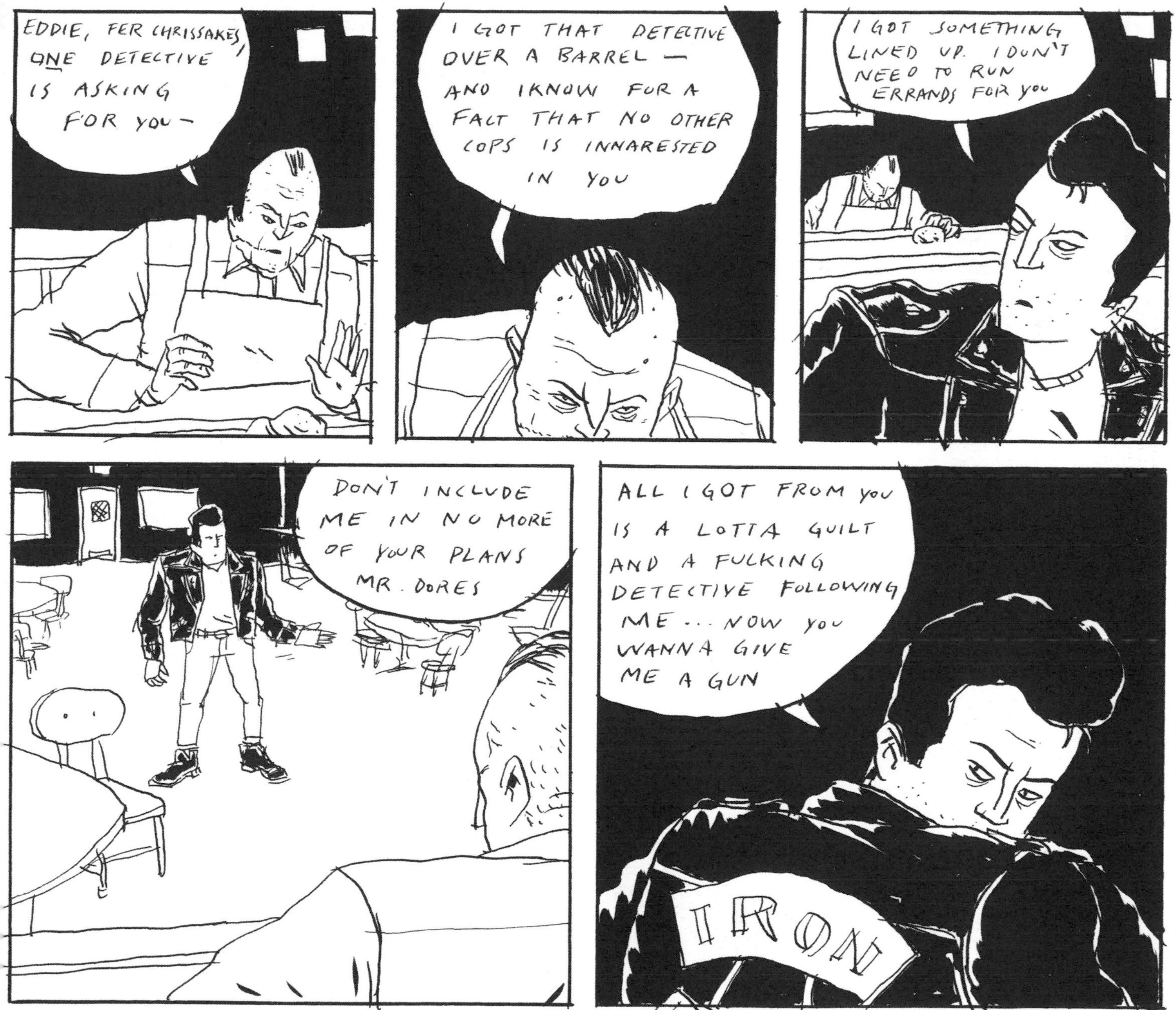
EDDIE, FER CHRISSAKES, ONE DETECTIVE IS ASKING FOR YOU-
I GOT THAT DETECTIVE OVER A BARREL —
AND IKNOW FOR A FACT THAT NO OTHER COPS IS INNARESTED IN YOU
I GOT SOMETHING LINED UP. I DON'T NEED TO RUN ERRANDS FOR YOU
DON'T INCLUDE ME IN NO MORE OF YOUR PLANS MR. DORES
ALL I GOT FROM YOU IS A LOTTA GUILT AND A FUCKING DETECTIVE FOLLOWING ME... NOW YOU WANNA GIVE ME A GUN
IRON

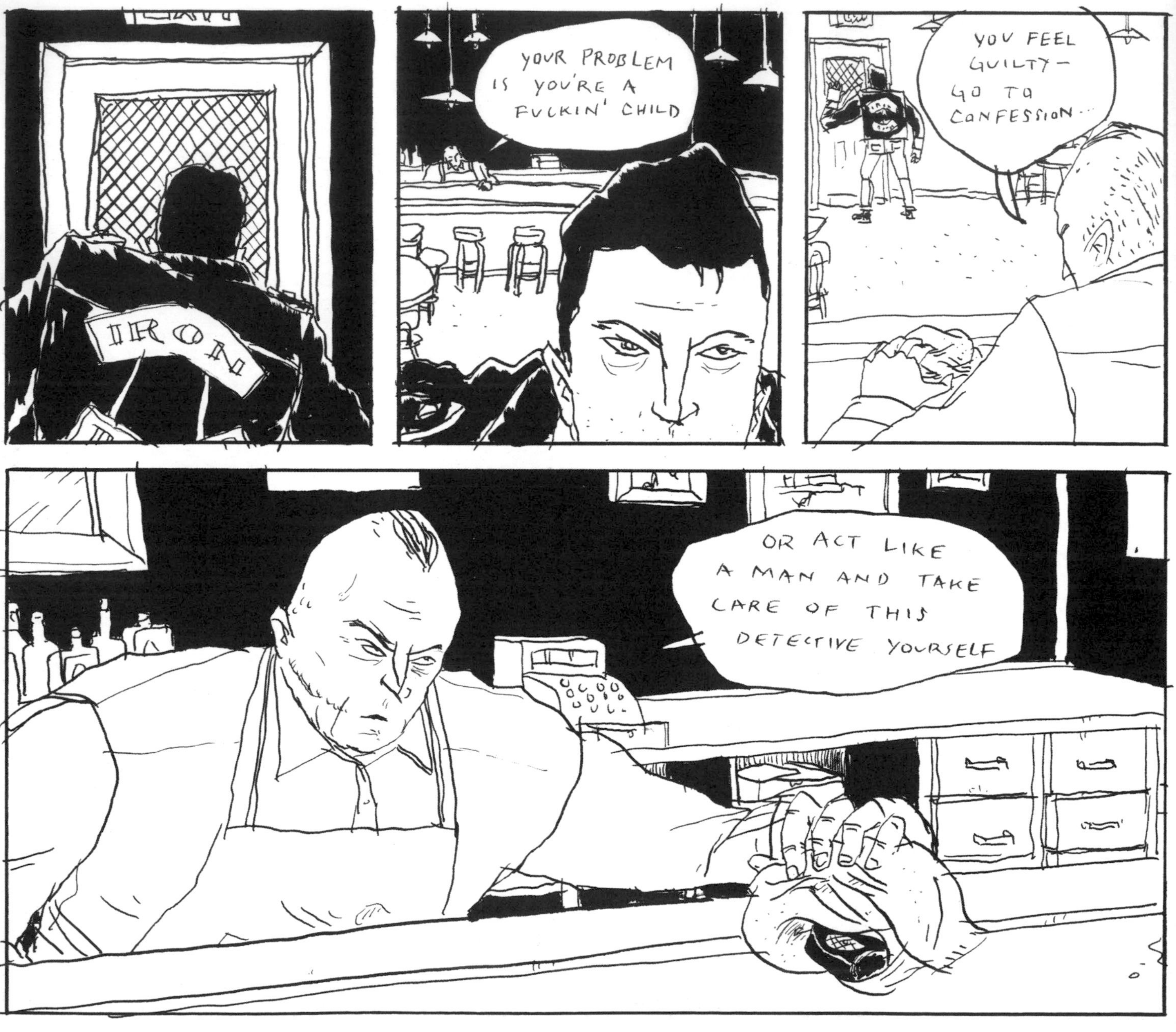
IRON
YOUR PROBLEM IS YOU'RE A FUCKIN' CHILD
YOU FEEL GUILTY— GO TO CONFESSION...
OR ACT LIKE A MAN AND TAKE CARE OF THIS DETECTIVE YOURSELF

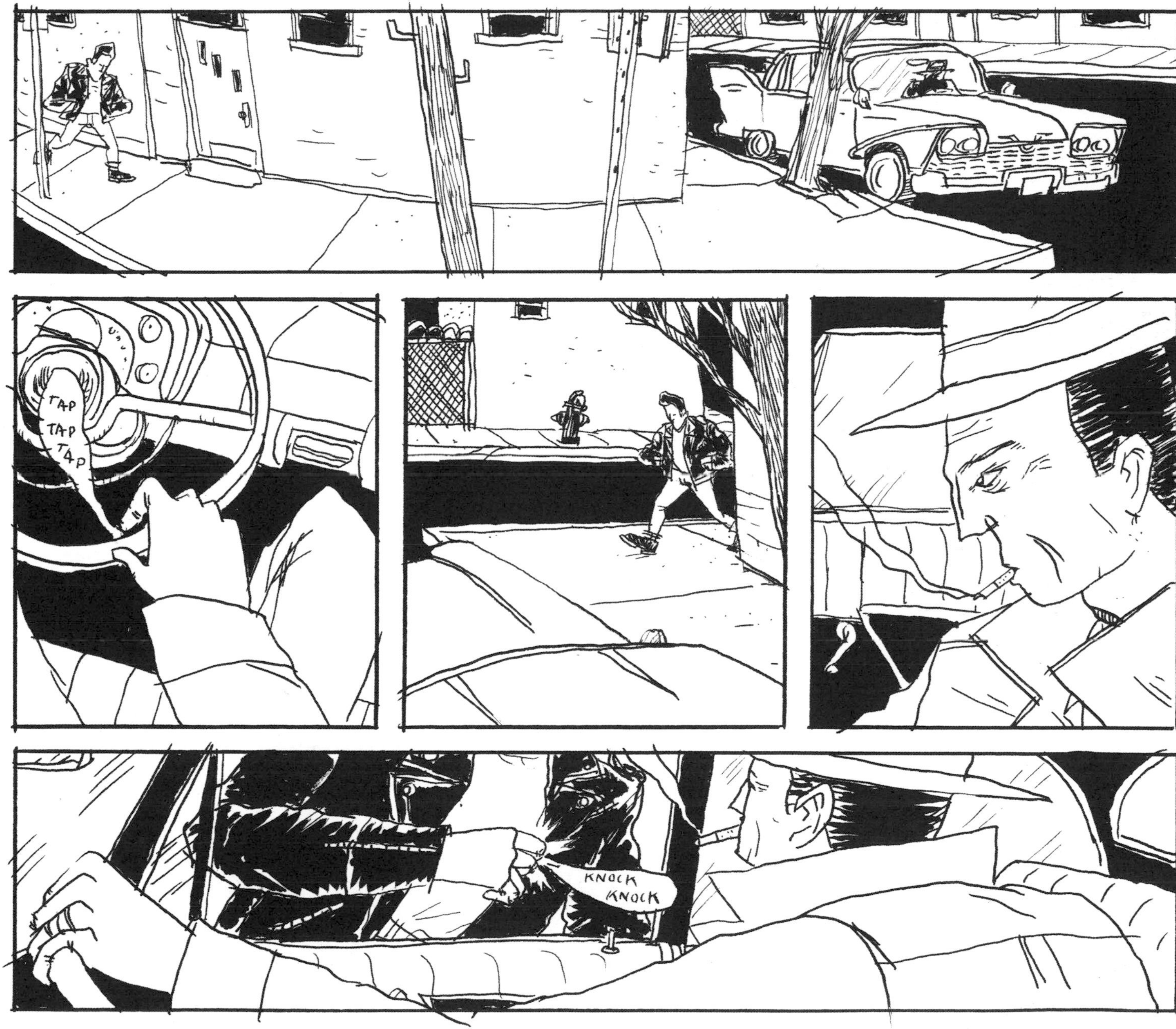
TAP
TAP
TAP
KNOCK
KNOCK

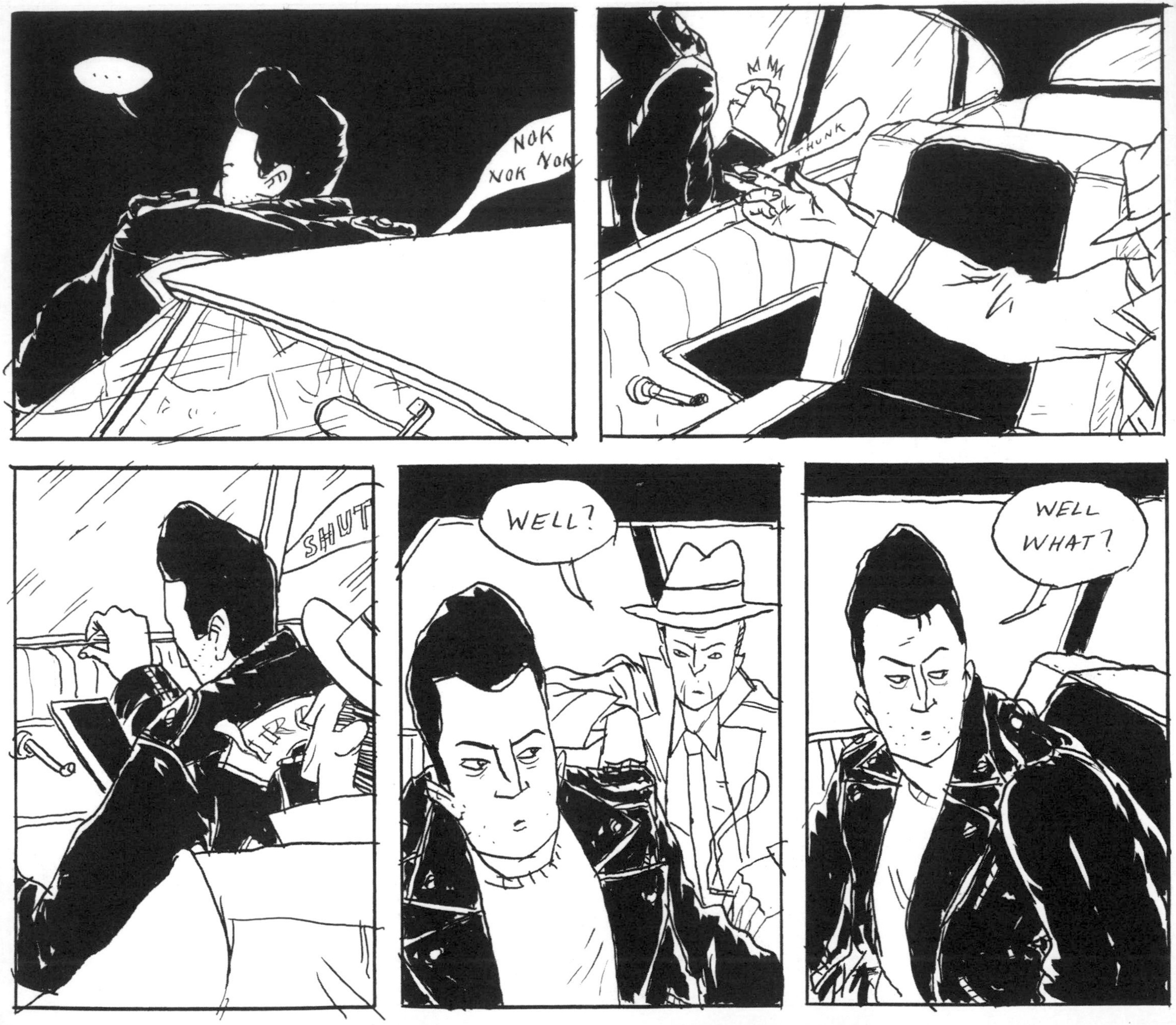
...
NOK NOK NOK
THUNK
SHUT
WELL?
WELL WHAT?

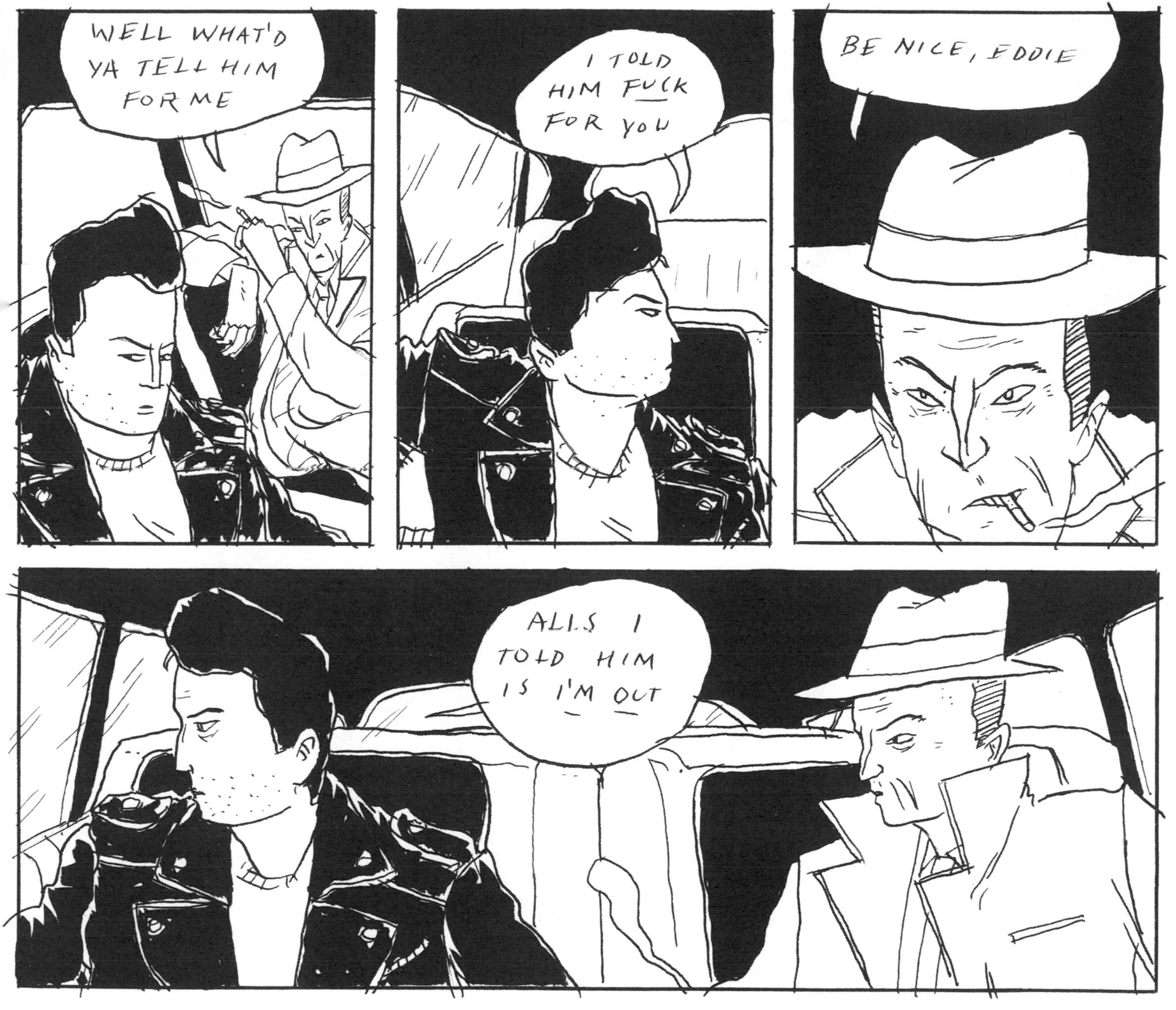
WELL WHAT'D YA TELL HIM FOR ME
I TOLD HIM FUCK FOR YOU
BE NICE, EDDIE
ALLS I TOLD HIM IS I'M OUT

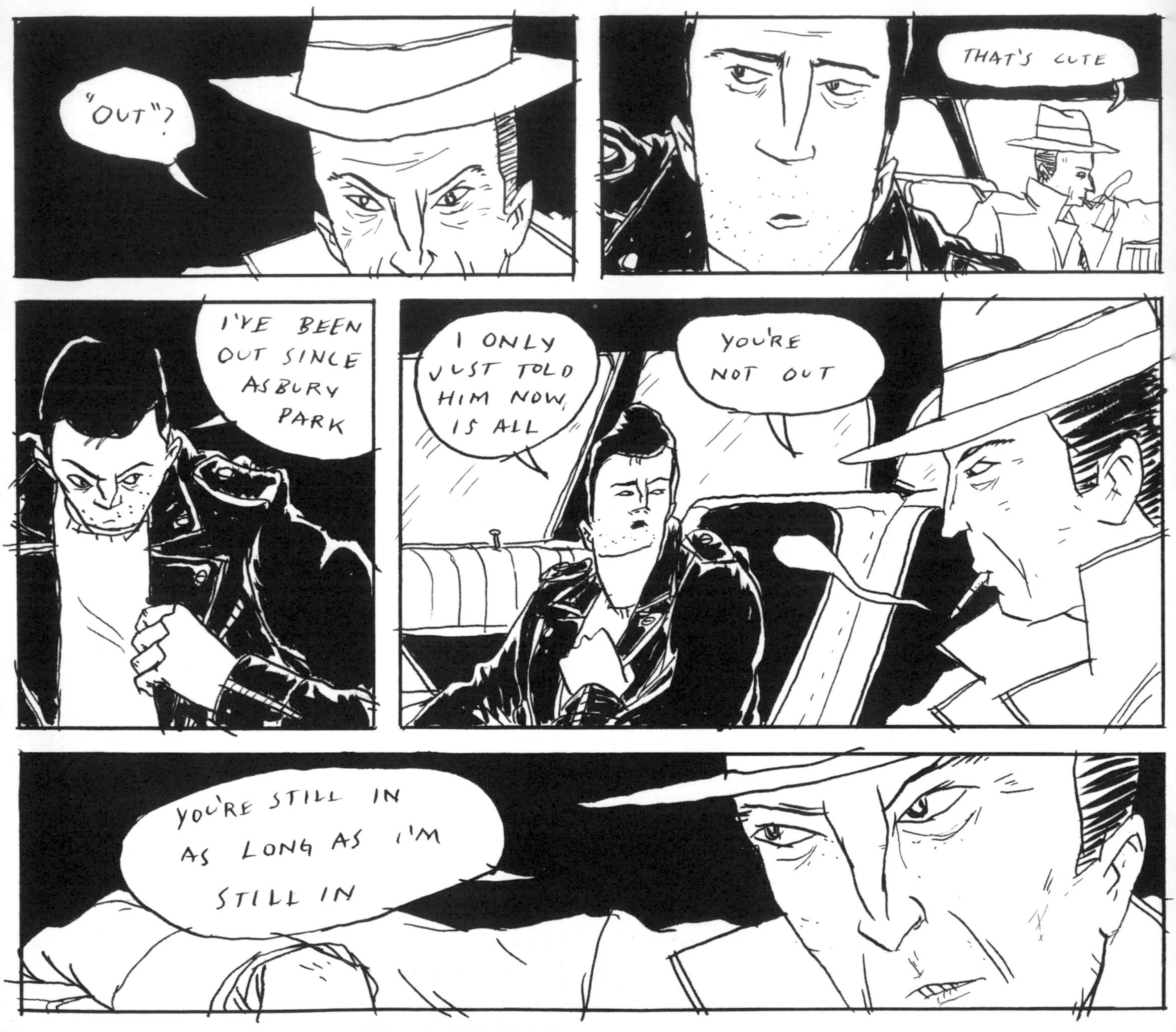
"OUT"?
THAT'S CUTE
I'VE BEEN OUT SINCE ASBURY PARK
I ONLY JUST TOLD HIM NOW, IS ALL
YOU'RE NOT OUT
YOU'RE STILL IN AS LONG AS I'M STILL IN

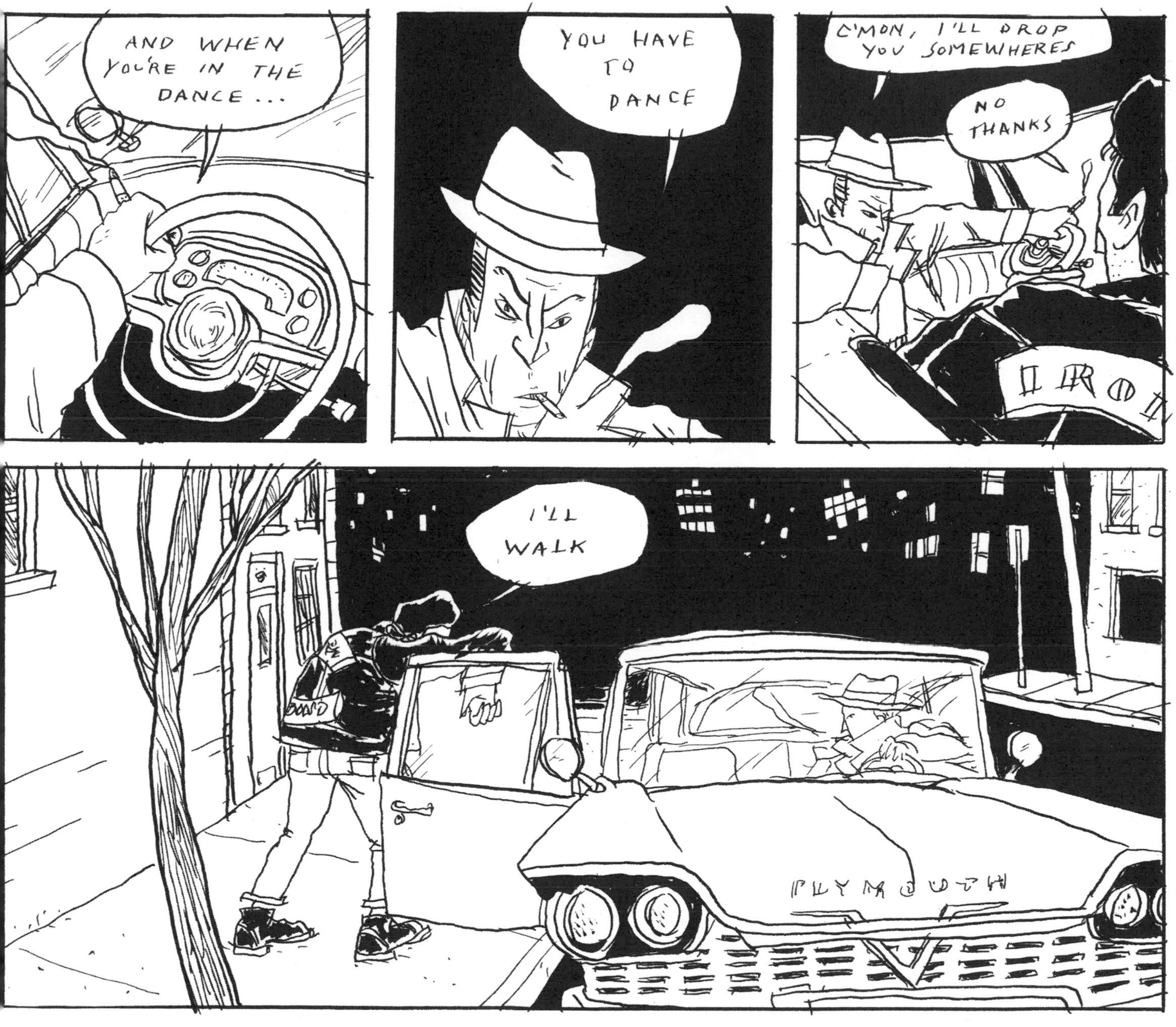
AND WHEN YOU'RE IN THE DANCE...
YOU HAVE TO DANCE
C'MON, I'LL DROP YOU SOMEWHERES
NO THANKS
I'LL WALK
PLYMOUTH

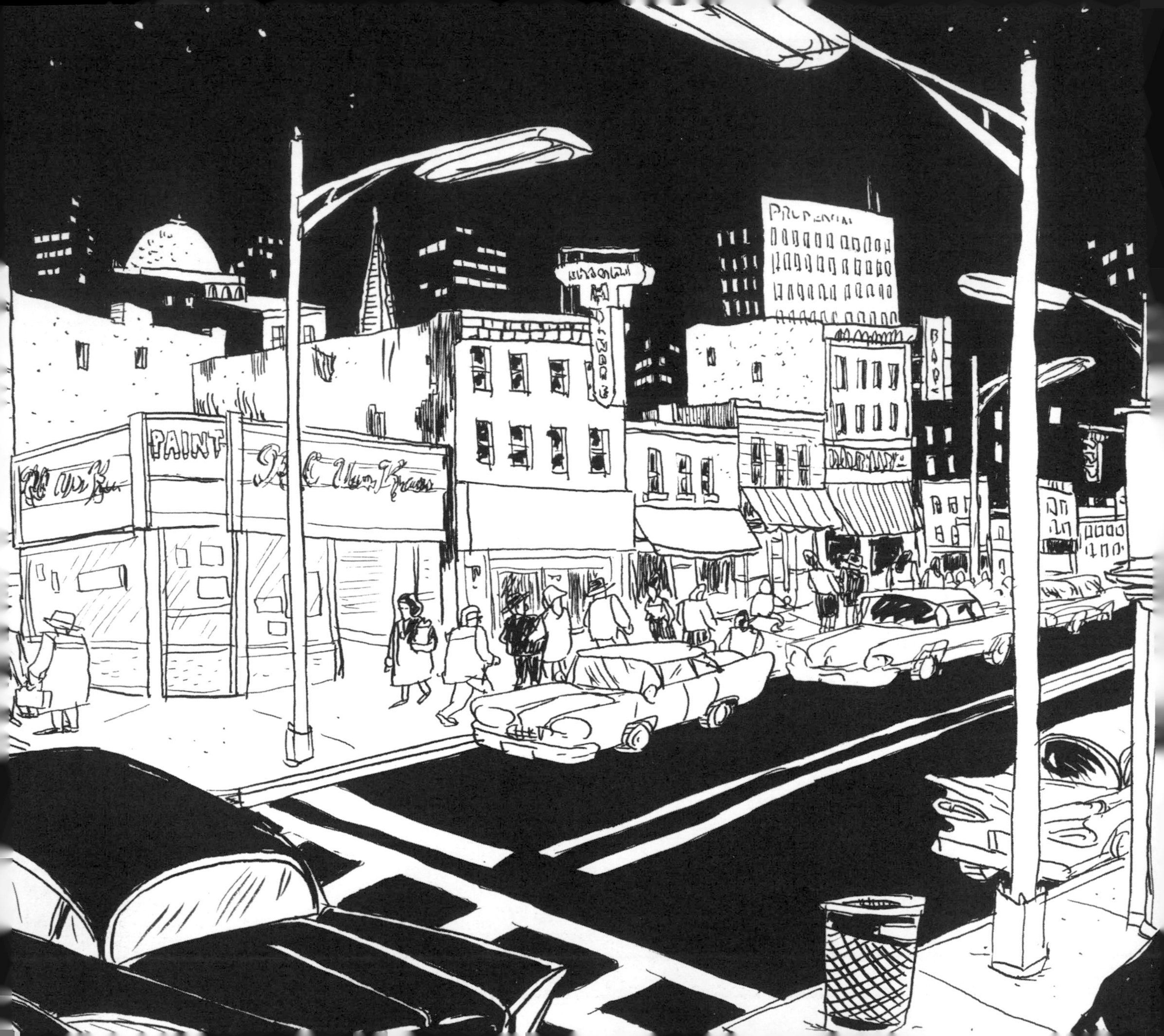
PAINT

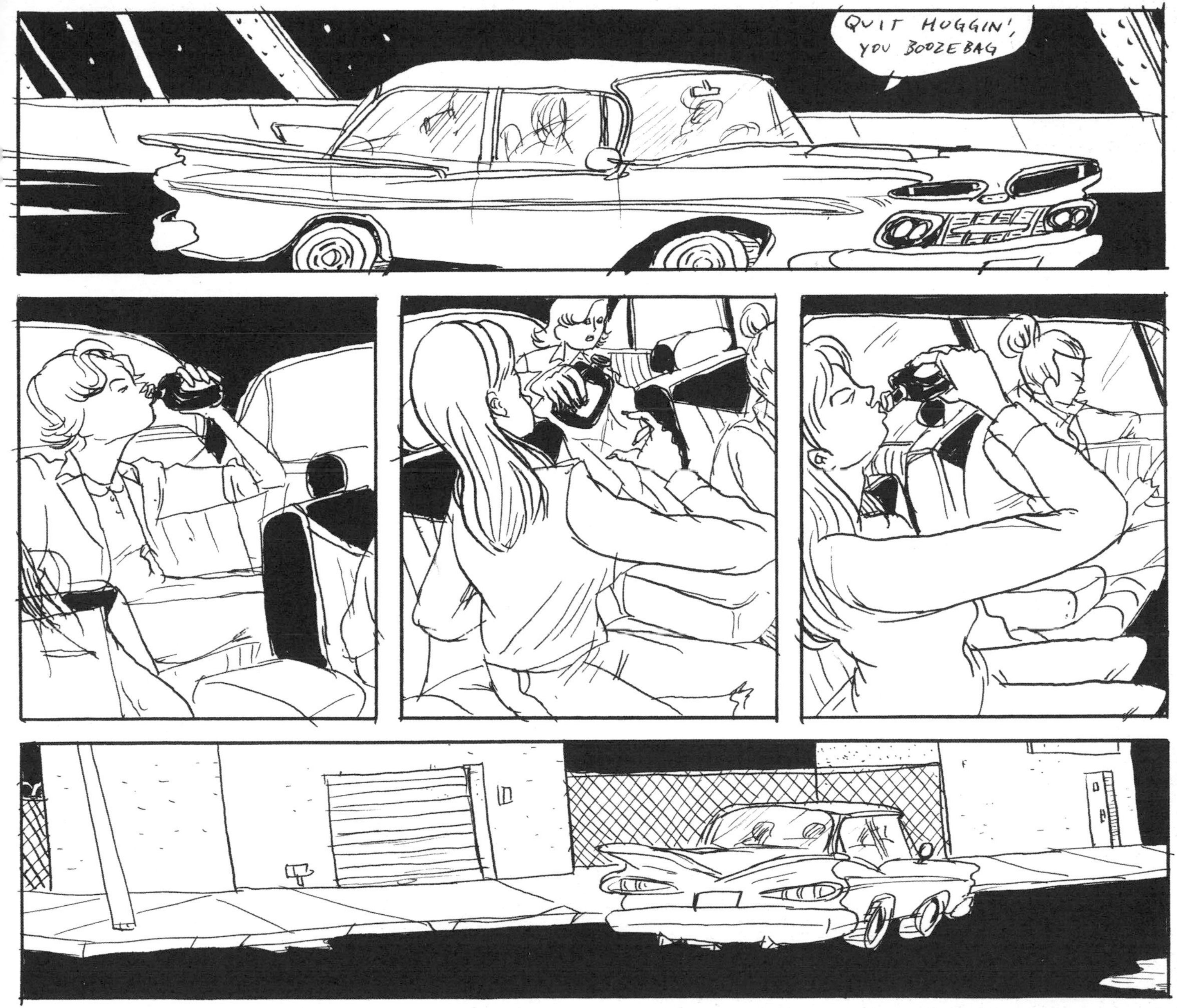
QUIT HOGGIN', YOU BOOZEBAG

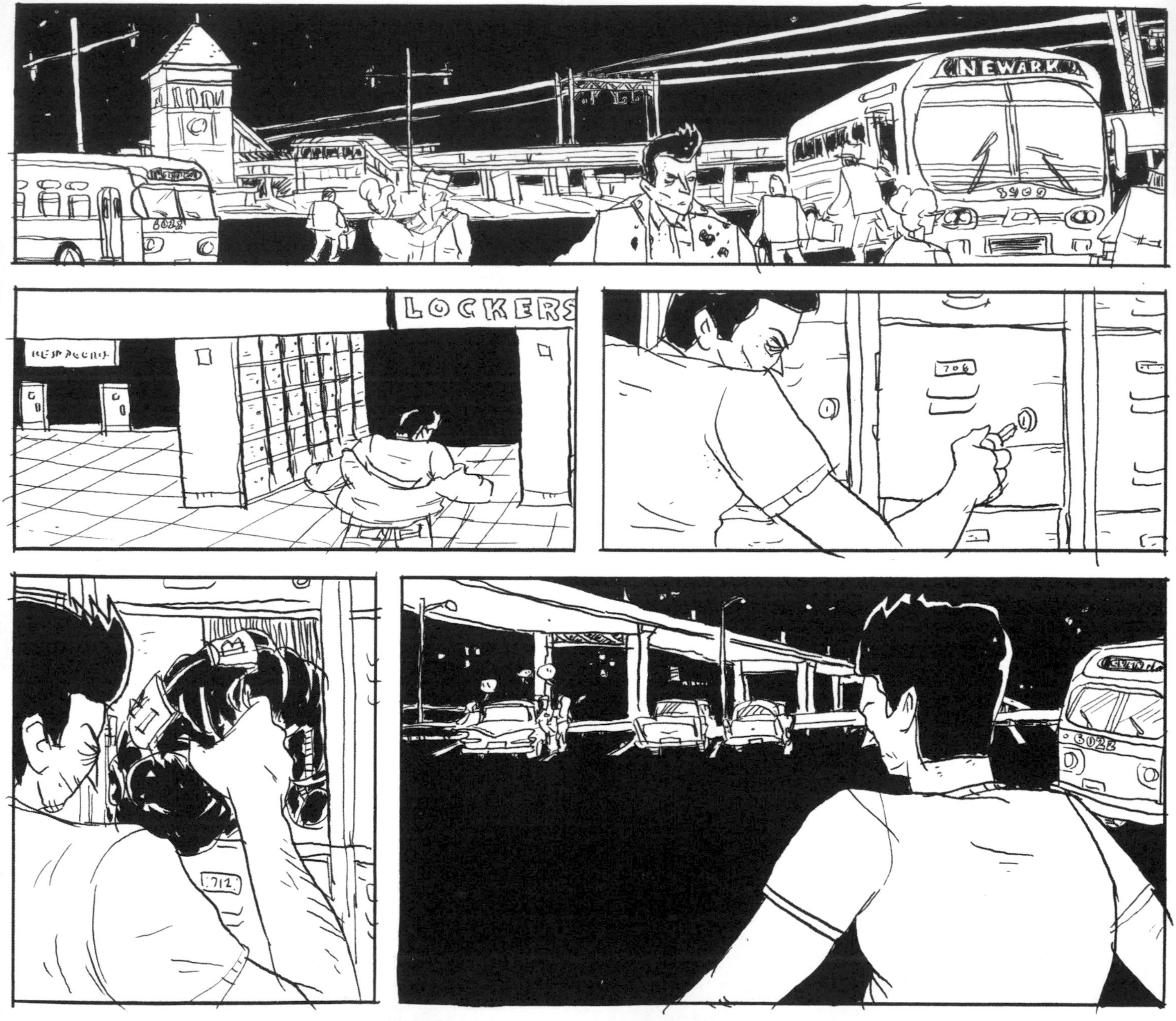
NEWARK
LOCKERS
706
712

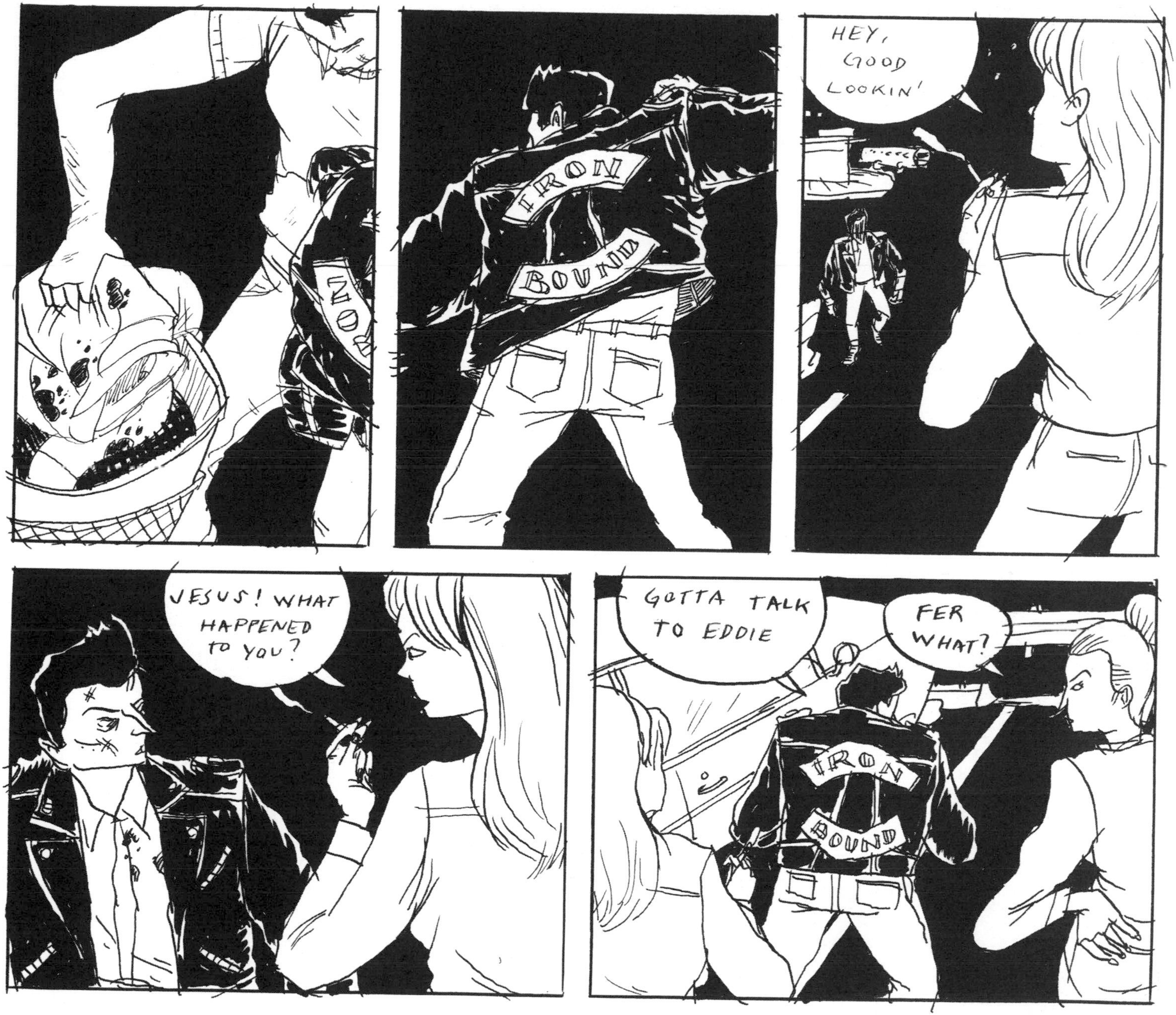
IRON
BOUND
HEY, GOOD LOOKIN'
JESUS! WHAT HAPPENED TO YOU?
GOTTA TALK TO EDDIE
FER WHAT?
IRON
BOUND

BENNY, FERWHAT?
FIND OUT WHAT HAPPENED TO ME
CLIK
CLAK
CLIK

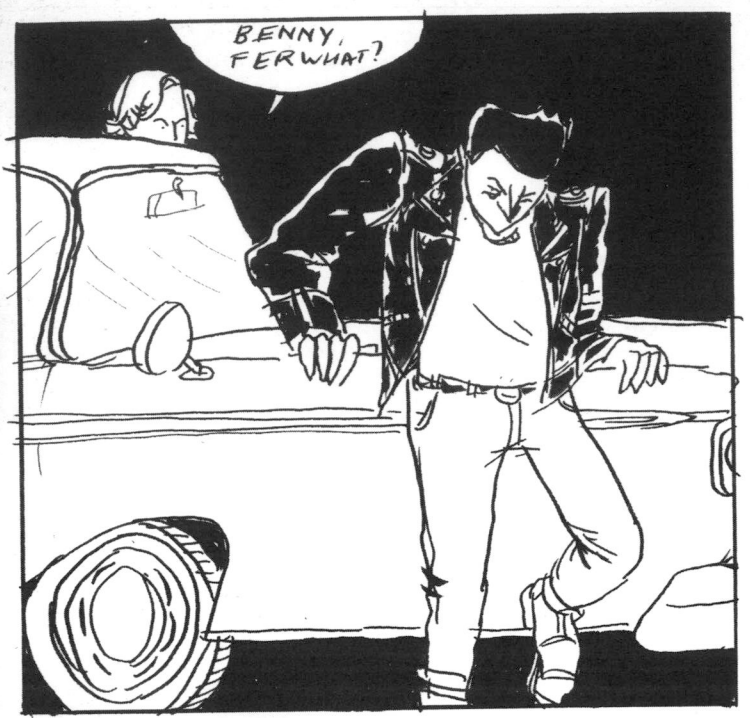

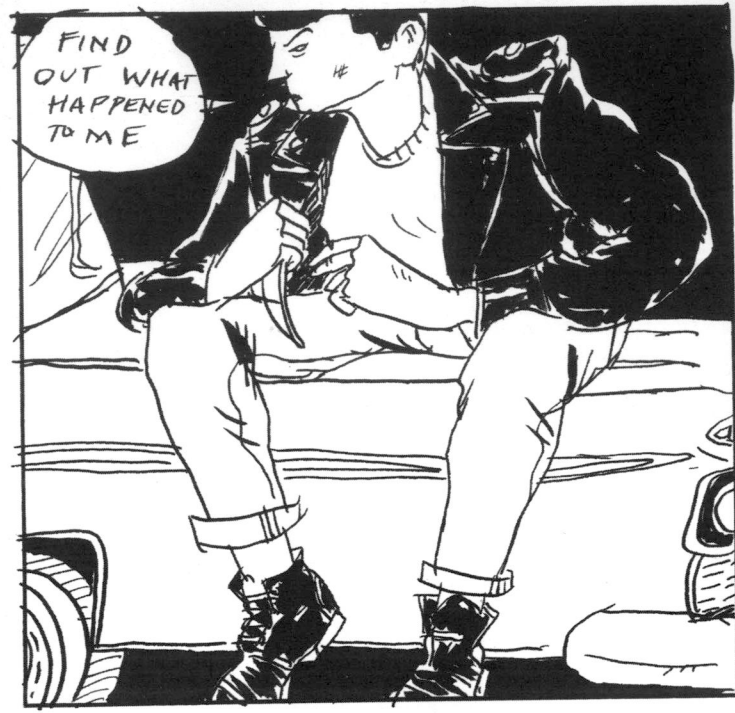

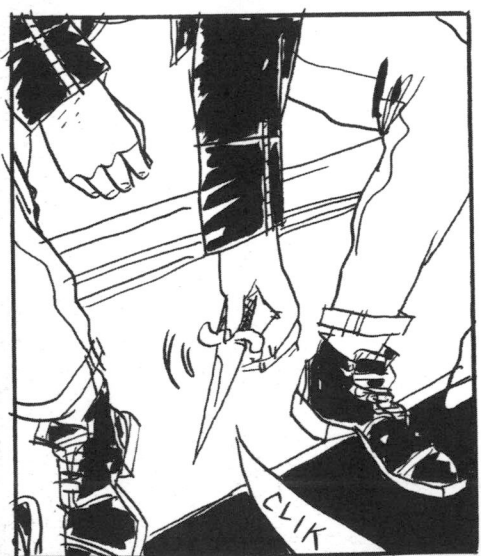

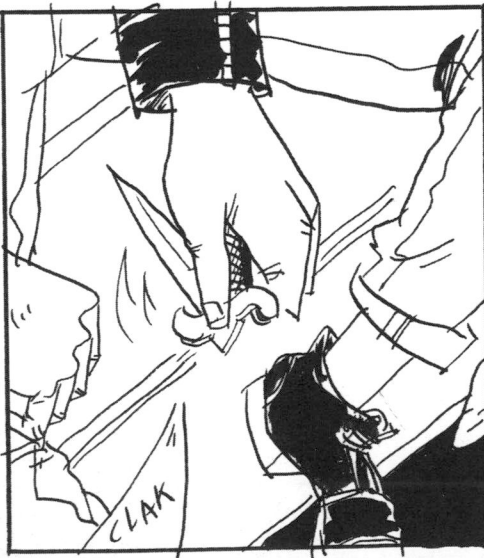

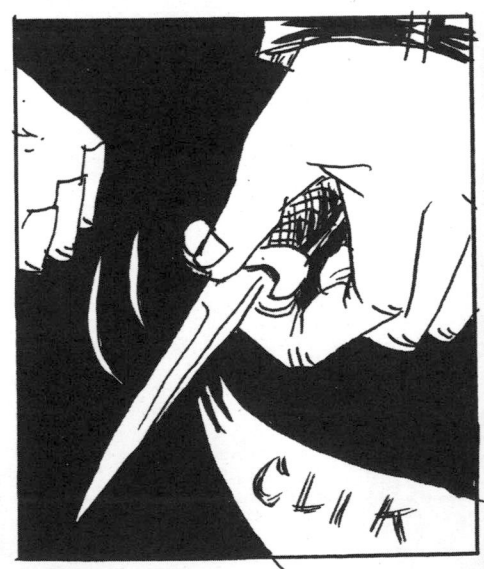

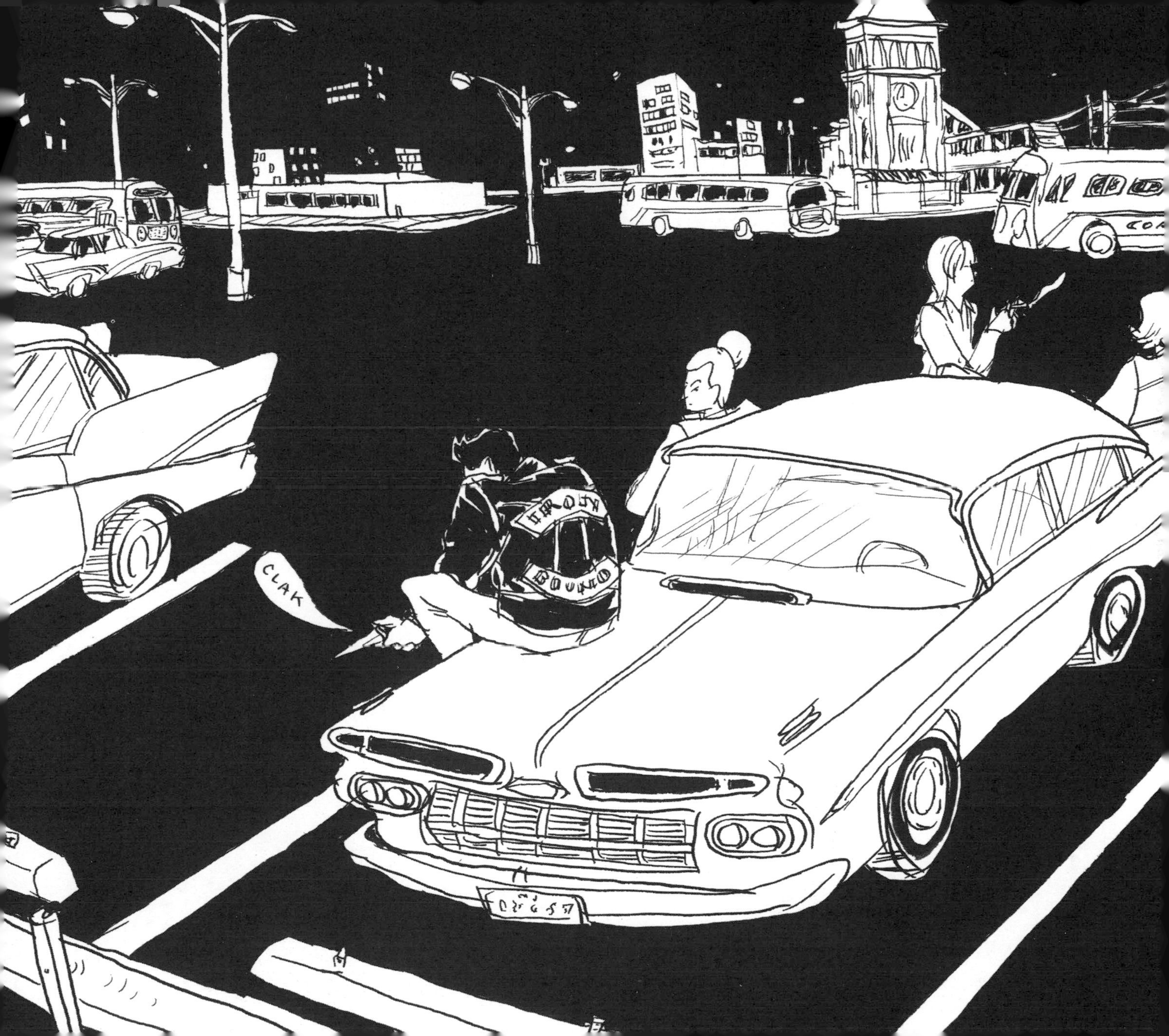
CLAK

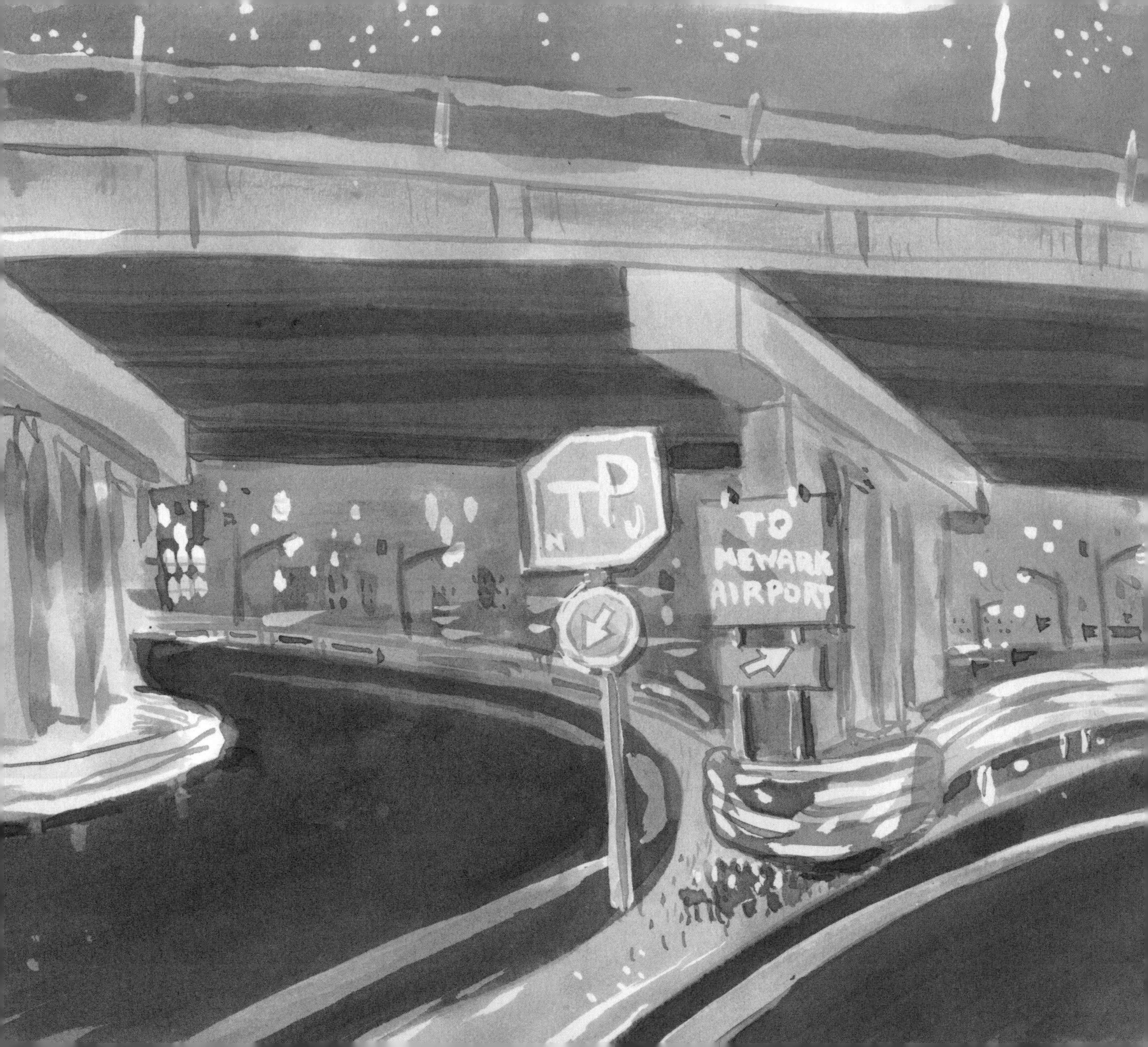
TO
NEWARK
AIRPORT

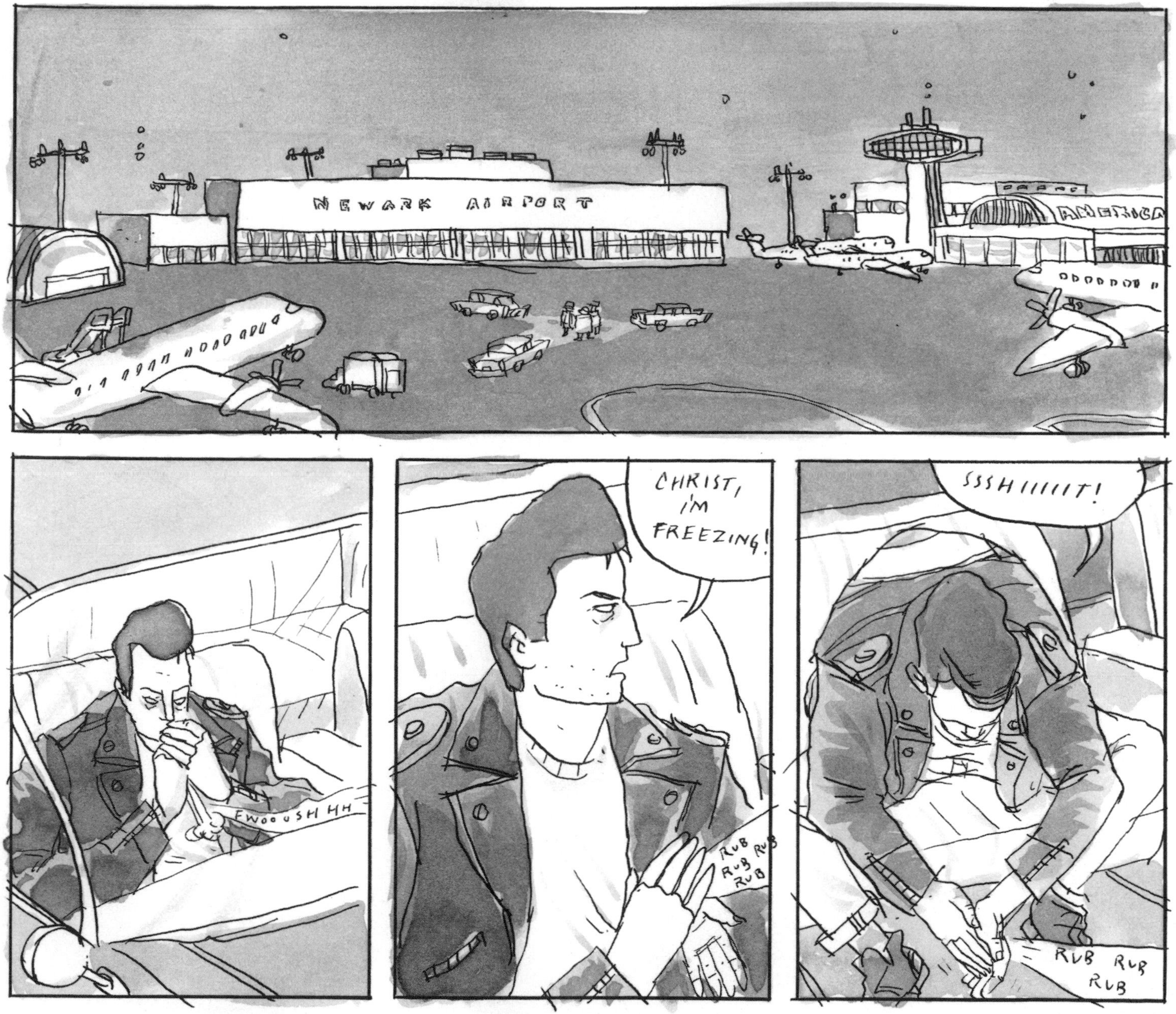
NEWARK AIRPORT
FWOOOUSH HH
CHRIST, I'M FREEZING!
RUB RUB RUB RUB
SSSHIIIIIT!
RUB RUB RUB

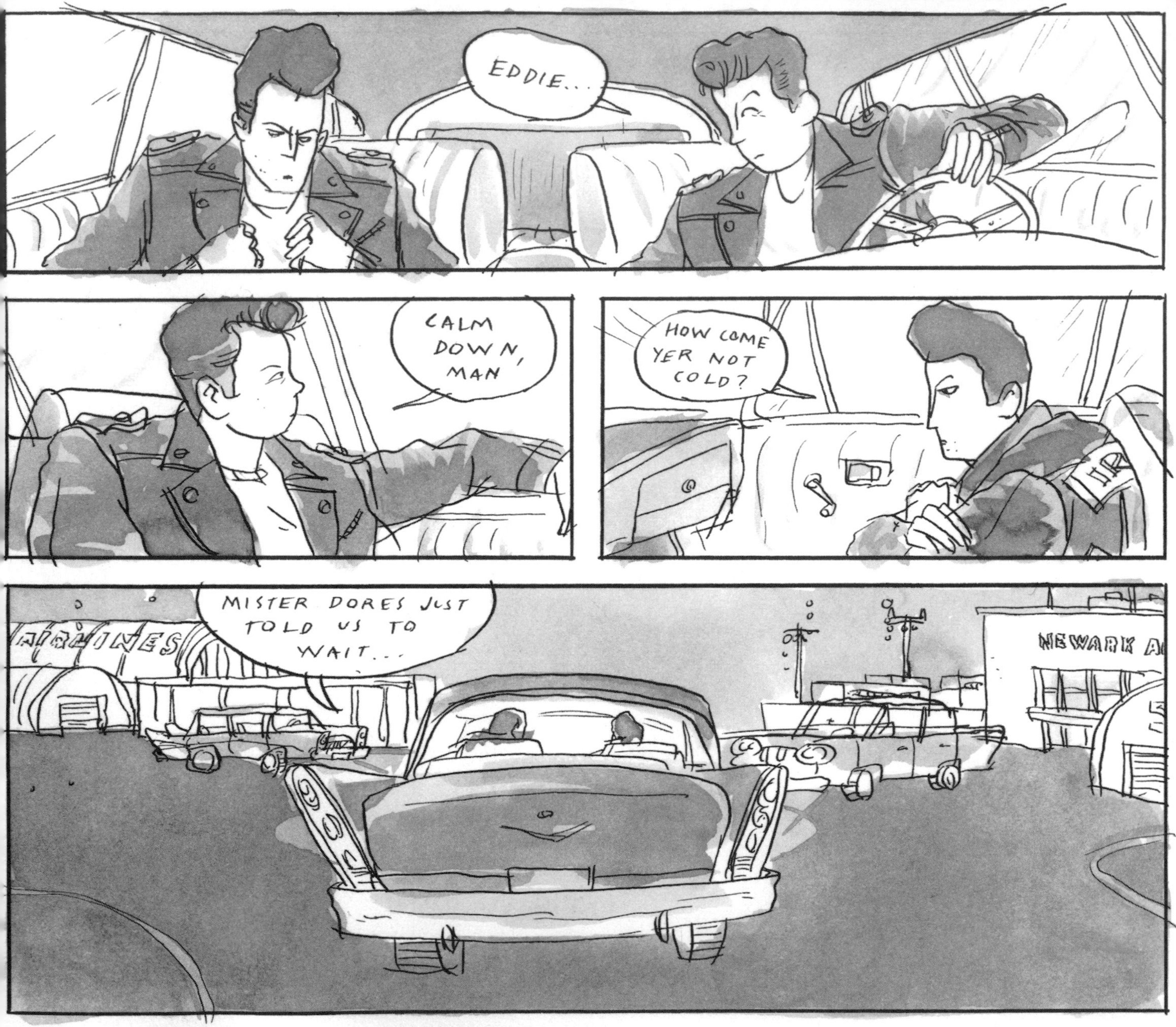
EDDIE...
CALM DOWN, MAN
HOW COME YER NOT COLD?
MISTER DORES JUST TOLD US TO WAIT...
NEWARK A

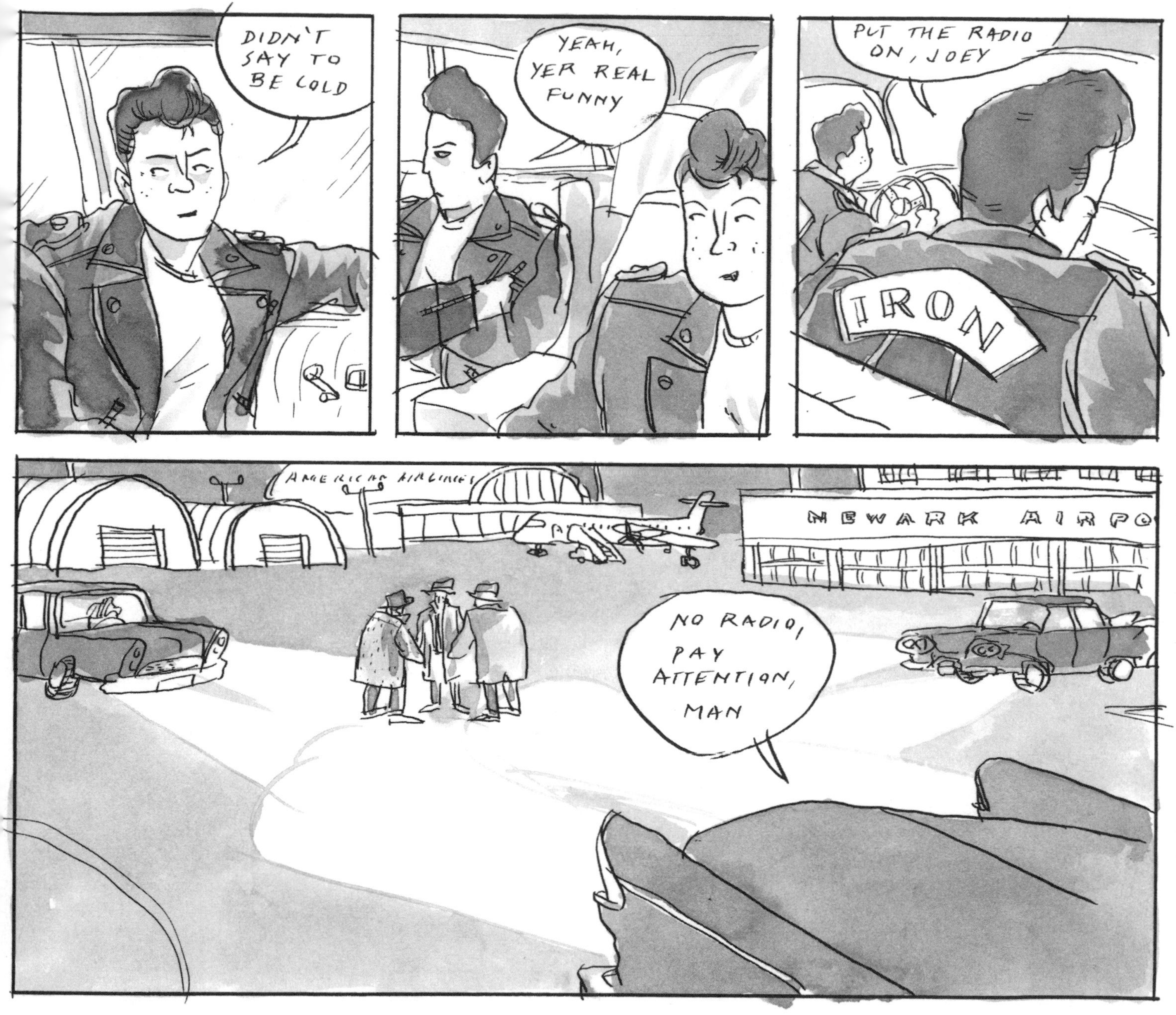
DIDN'T SAY TO BE COLD
YEAH, YER REAL FUNNY
PUT THE RADIO ON, JOEY
IRON
AMERICAN AIRLINES
NEWARK AIRPO
NO RADIO, PAY ATTENTION, MAN

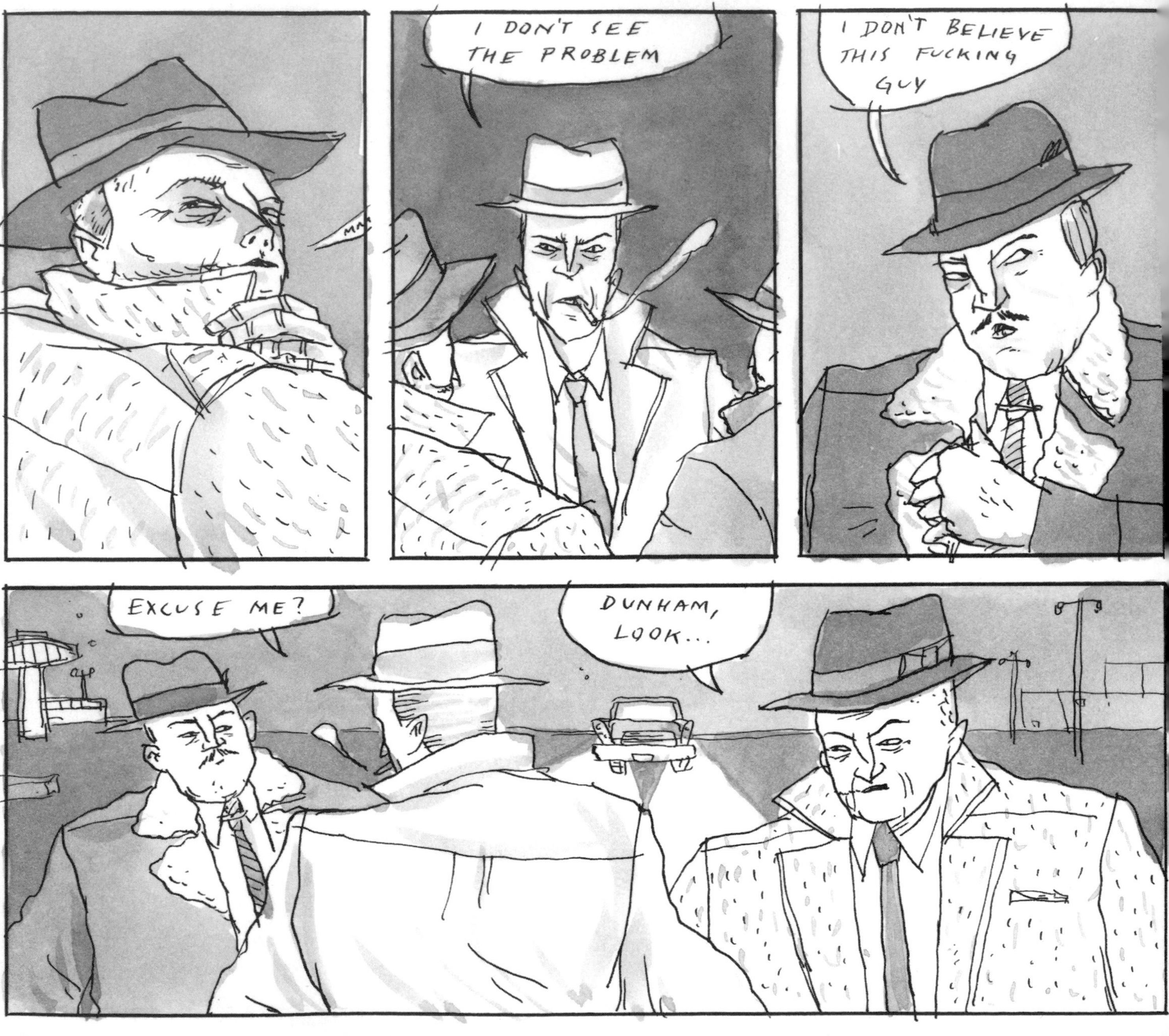
MM
I DON'T SEE THE PROBLEM
I DON'T BELIEVE THIS FUCKING GUY
EXCUSE ME?
DUNHAM, LOOK...

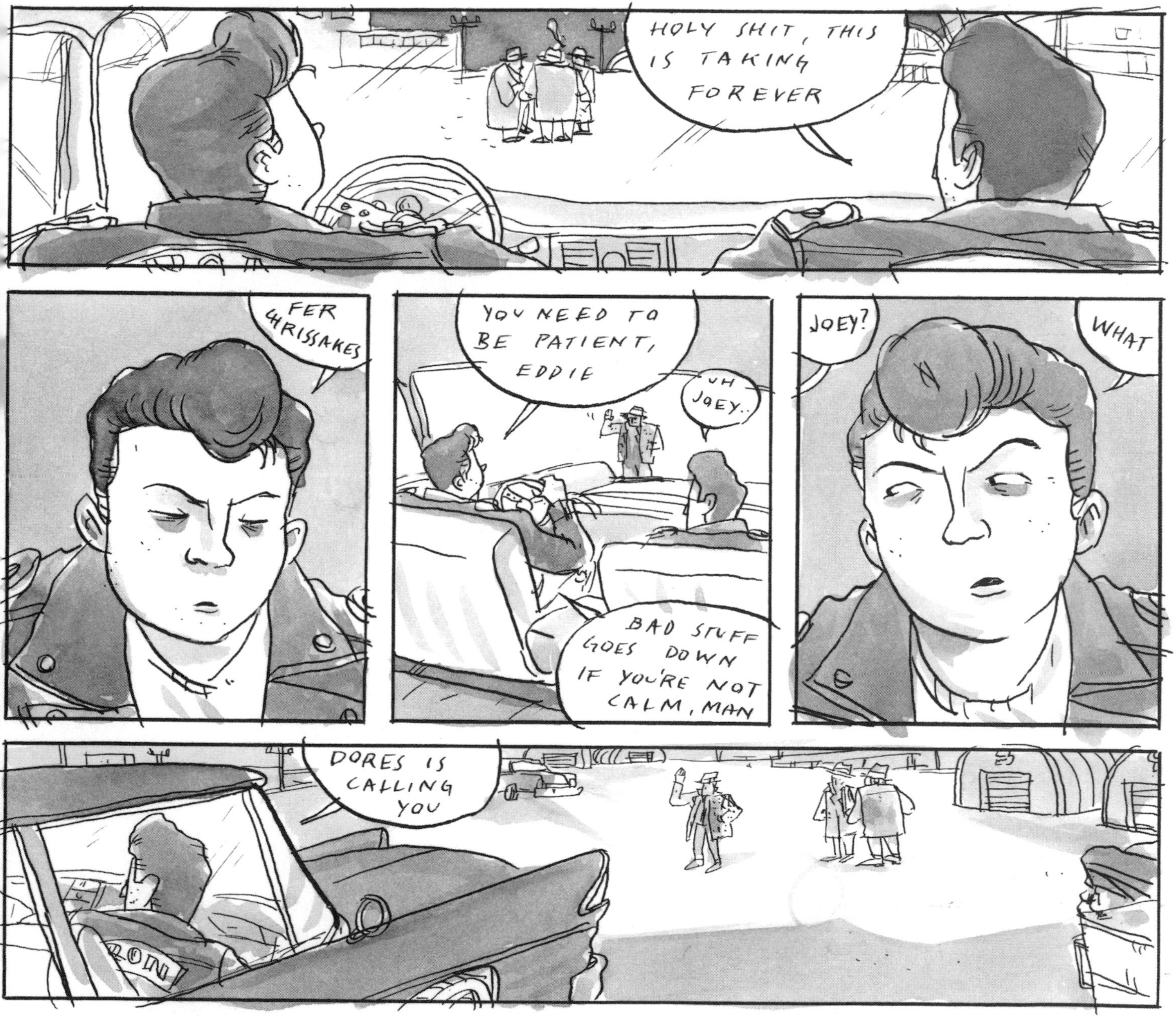
HOLY SHIT, THIS IS TAKING FOREVER
FER CHRISSAKES
YOU NEED TO BE PATIENT, EDDIE
UH JOEY..
BAD STUFF GOES DOWN IF YOU'RE NOT CALM, MAN
JOEY?
WHAT
DORES IS CALLING YOU
RON

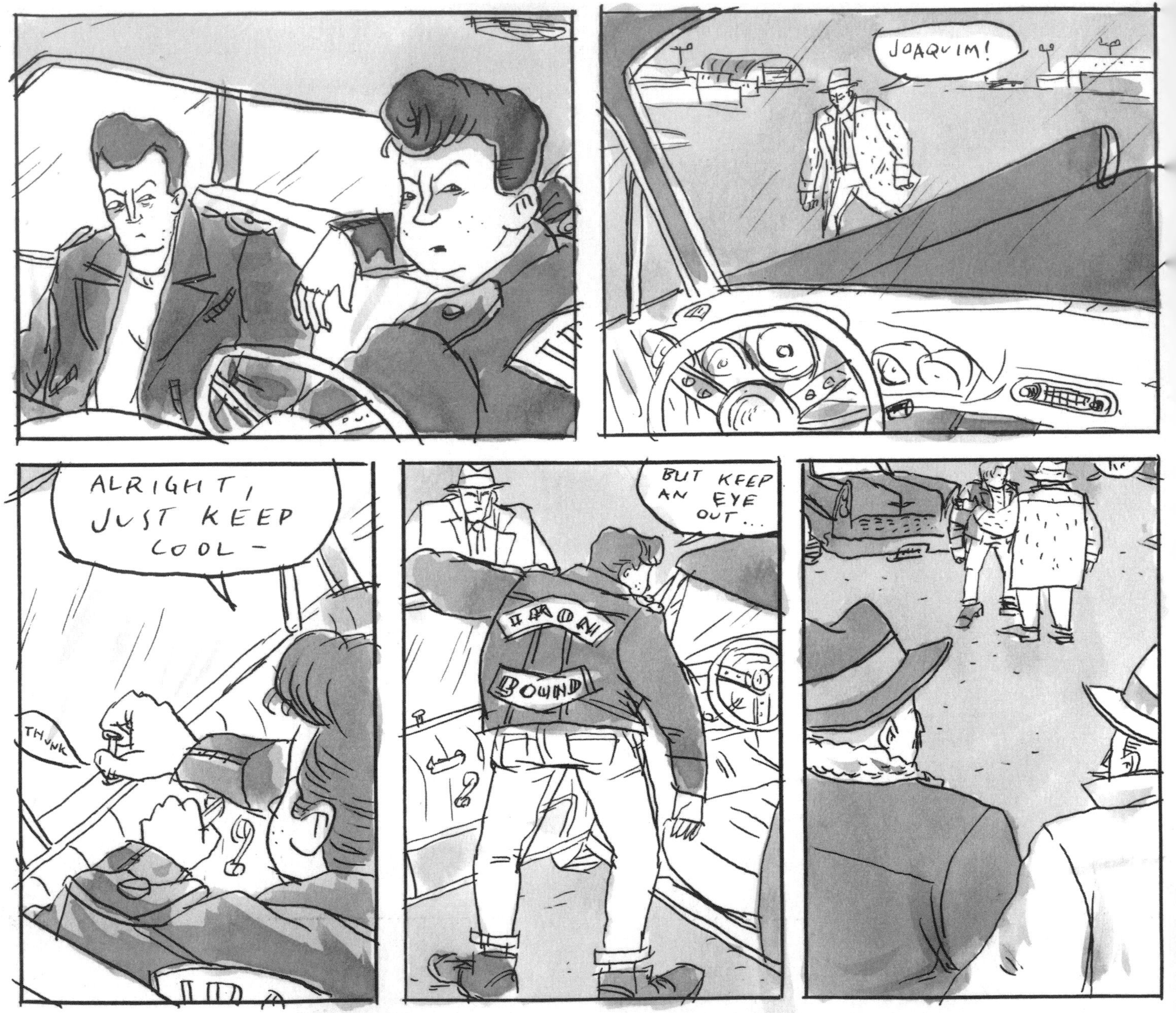
JOAQUIM!
ALRIGHT, JUST KEEP COOL -
THUNK
BUT KEEP AN EYE OUT...
BOUND

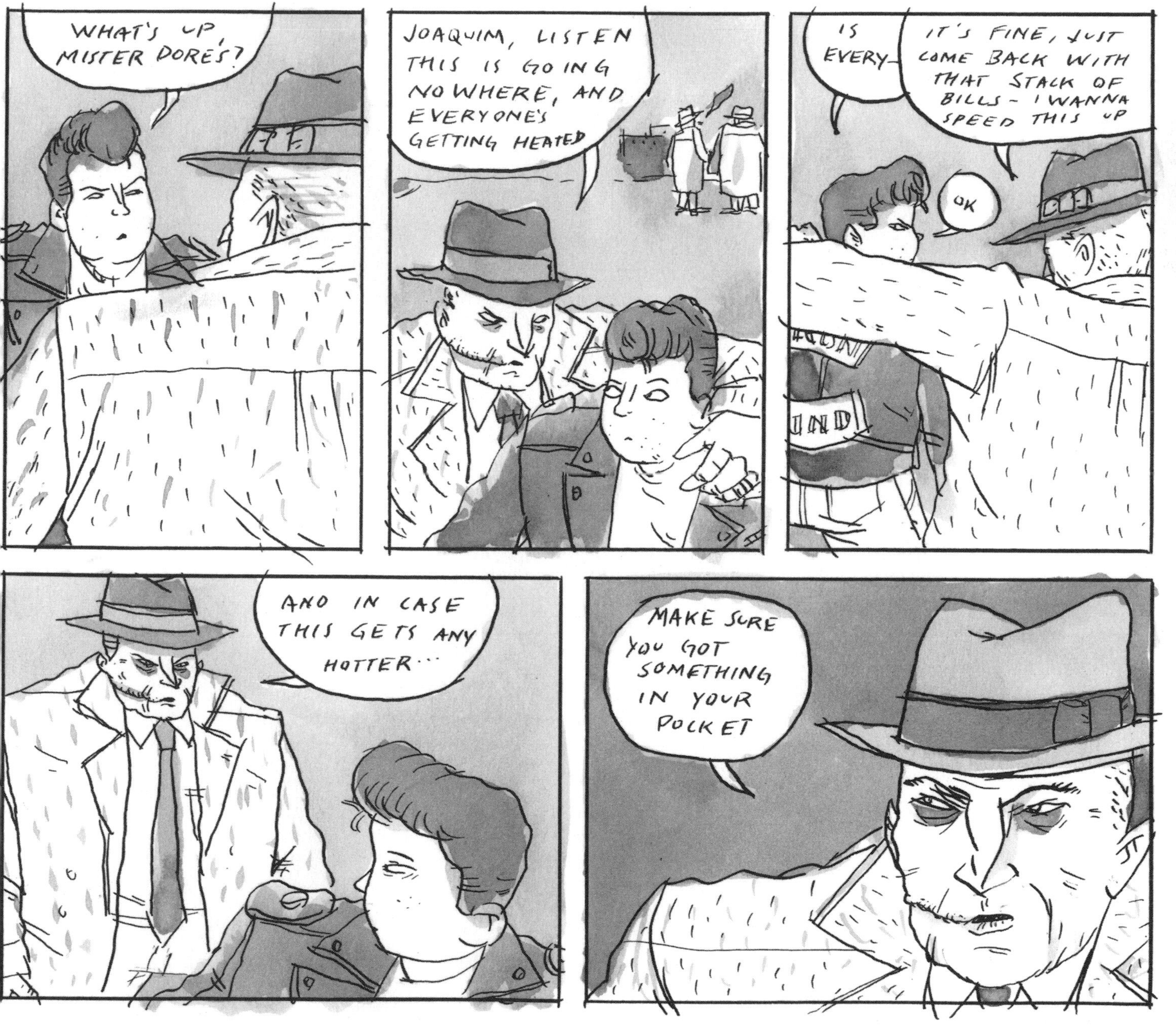
WHAT'S UP, MISTER DORES?
JOAQUIM, LISTEN THIS IS GOING NOWHERE, AND EVERYONE'S GETTING HEATED
IS EVERY—
IT'S FINE, JUST COME BACK WITH THAT STACK OF BILLS - I WANNA SPEED THIS UP
OK
AND IN CASE THIS GETS ANY HOTTER...
MAKE SURE YOU GOT SOMETHING IN YOUR POCKET

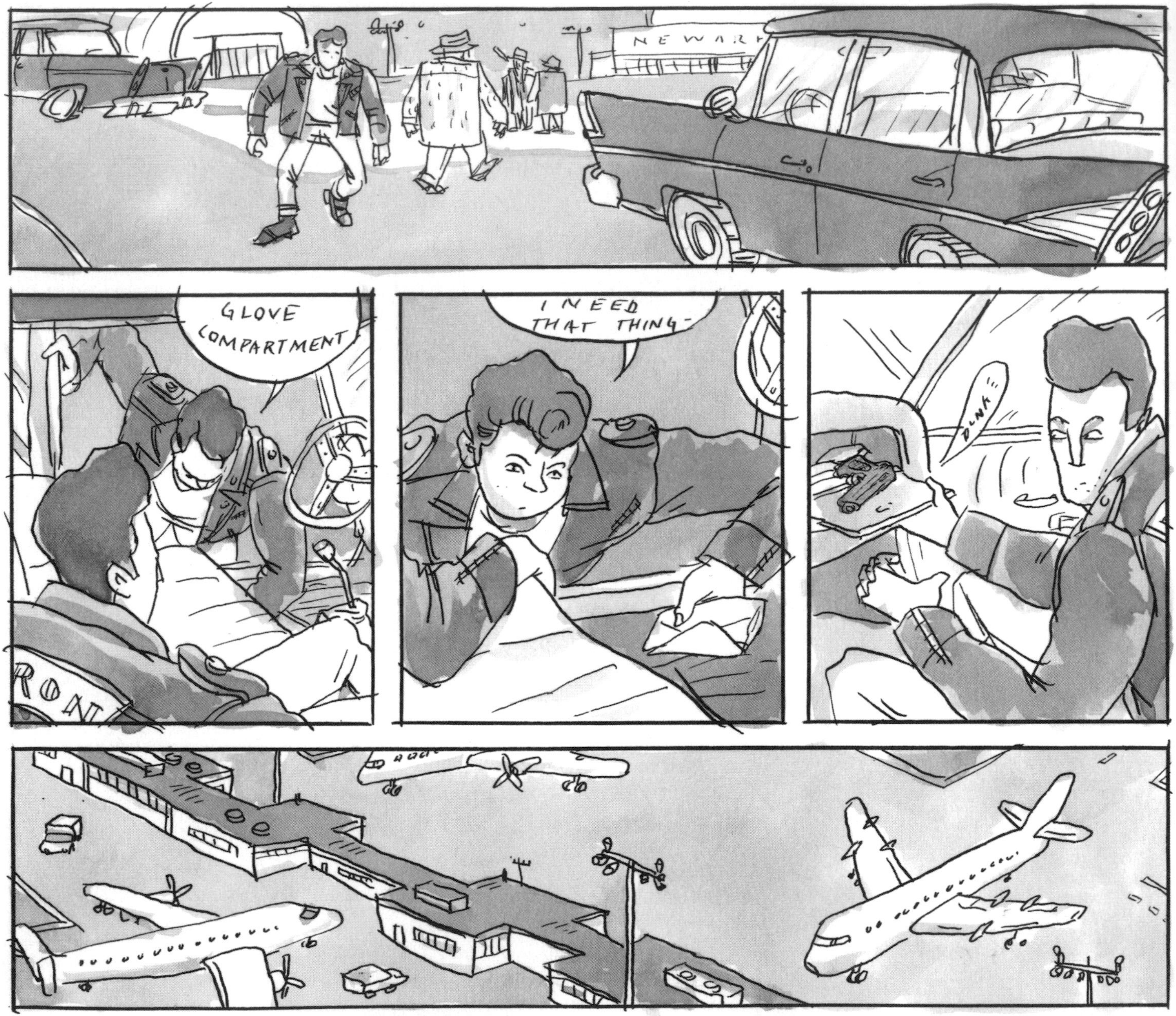
NEWAR
GLOVE COMPARTMENT
RON
I NEED THAT THING-
DUNK!!!

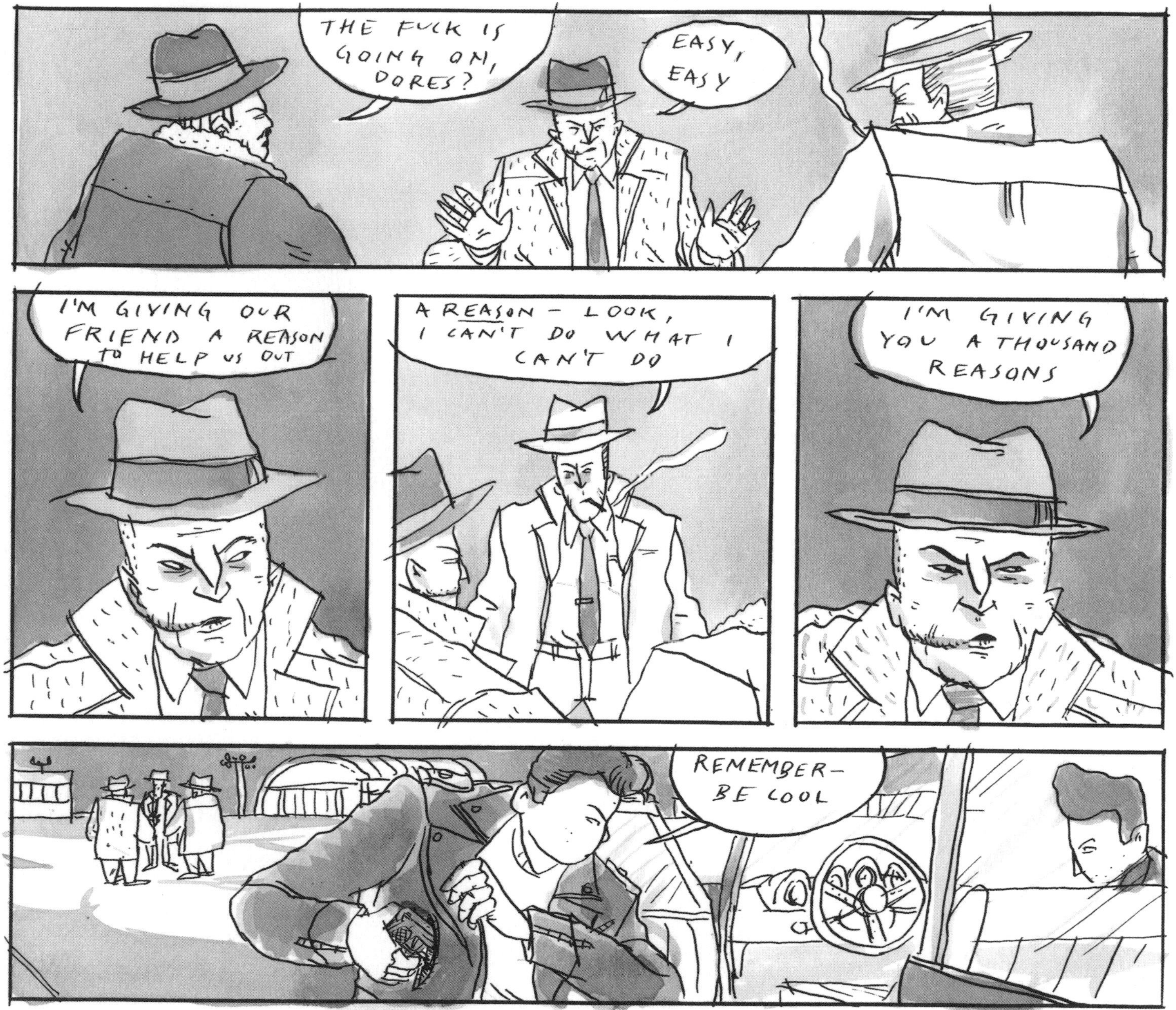
THE FUCK IS GOING ON, DORES?
EASY, EASY
I'M GIVING OUR FRIEND A REASON TO HELP US OUT
A REASON - LOOK, I CAN'T DO WHAT I CAN'T DO
I'M GIVING YOU A THOUSAND REASONS
REMEMBER- BE COOL

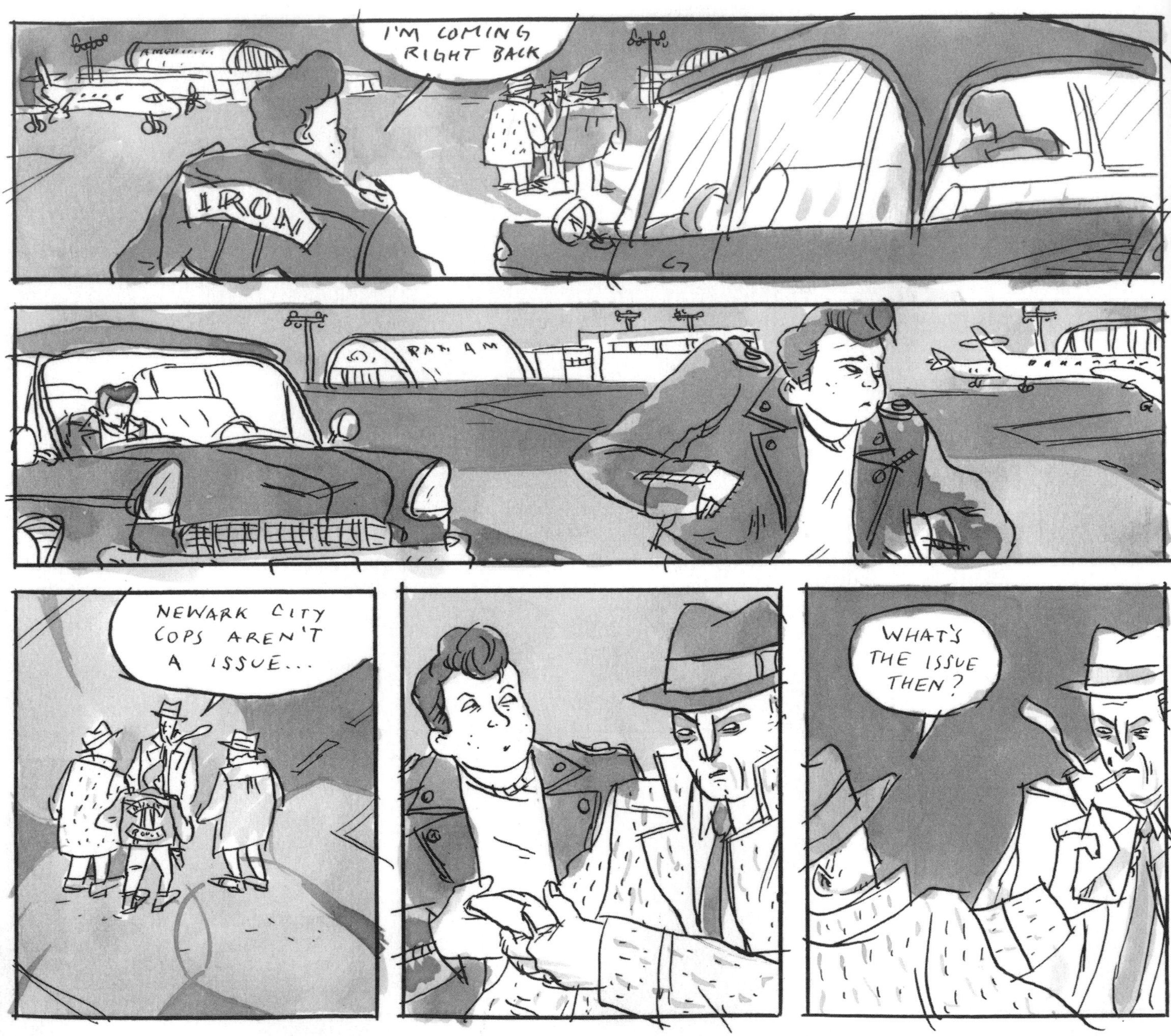
I'M COMING RIGHT BACK
IRON
PAN AM
NEWARK CITY COPS AREN'T A ISSUE...
WHAT'S THE ISSUE THEN?

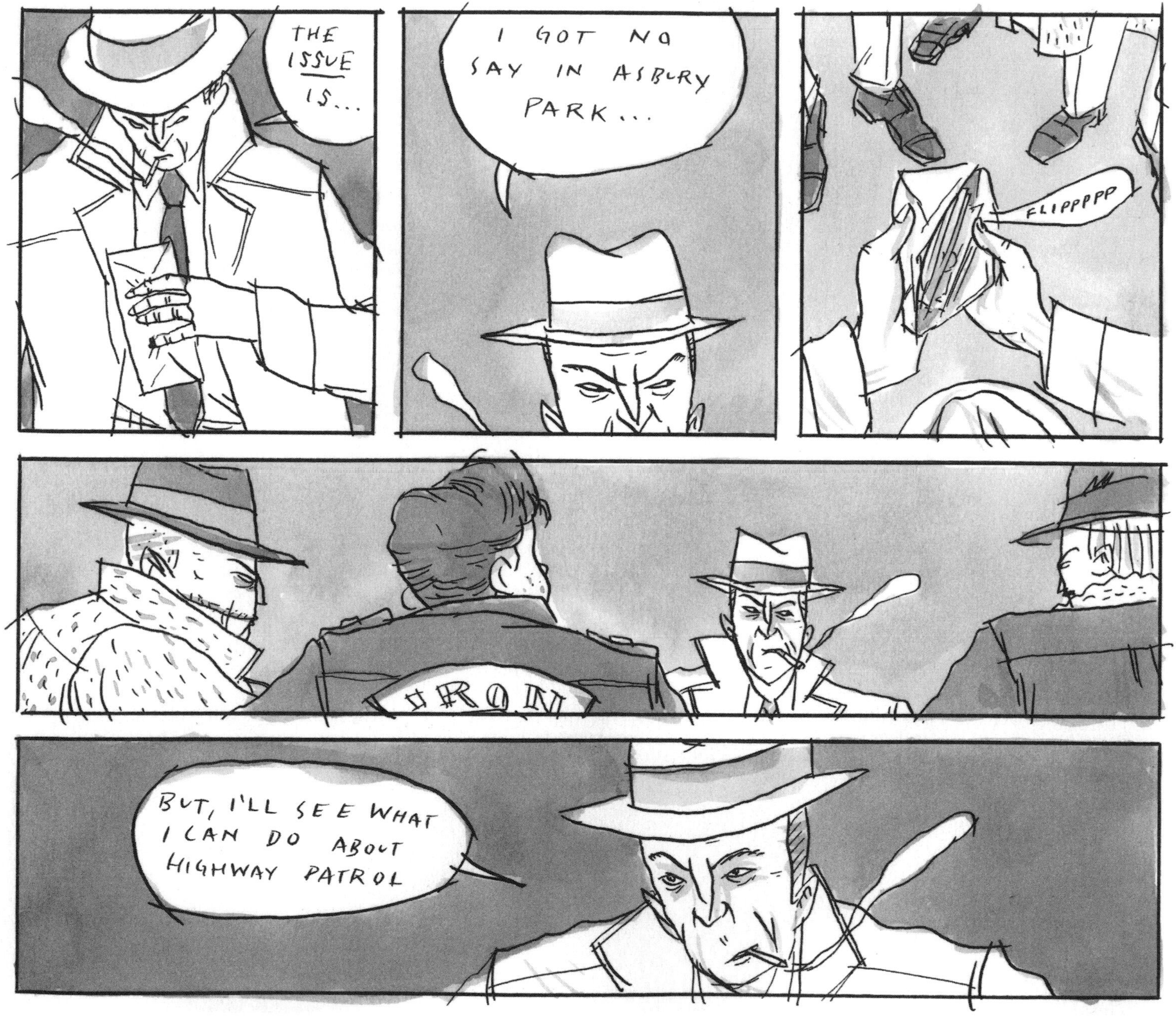
THE ISSUE IS...
I GOT NO SAY IN ASBURY PARK...
FLIPPPPP
IRON
BUT, I'LL SEE WHAT I CAN DO ABOUT HIGHWAY PATROL

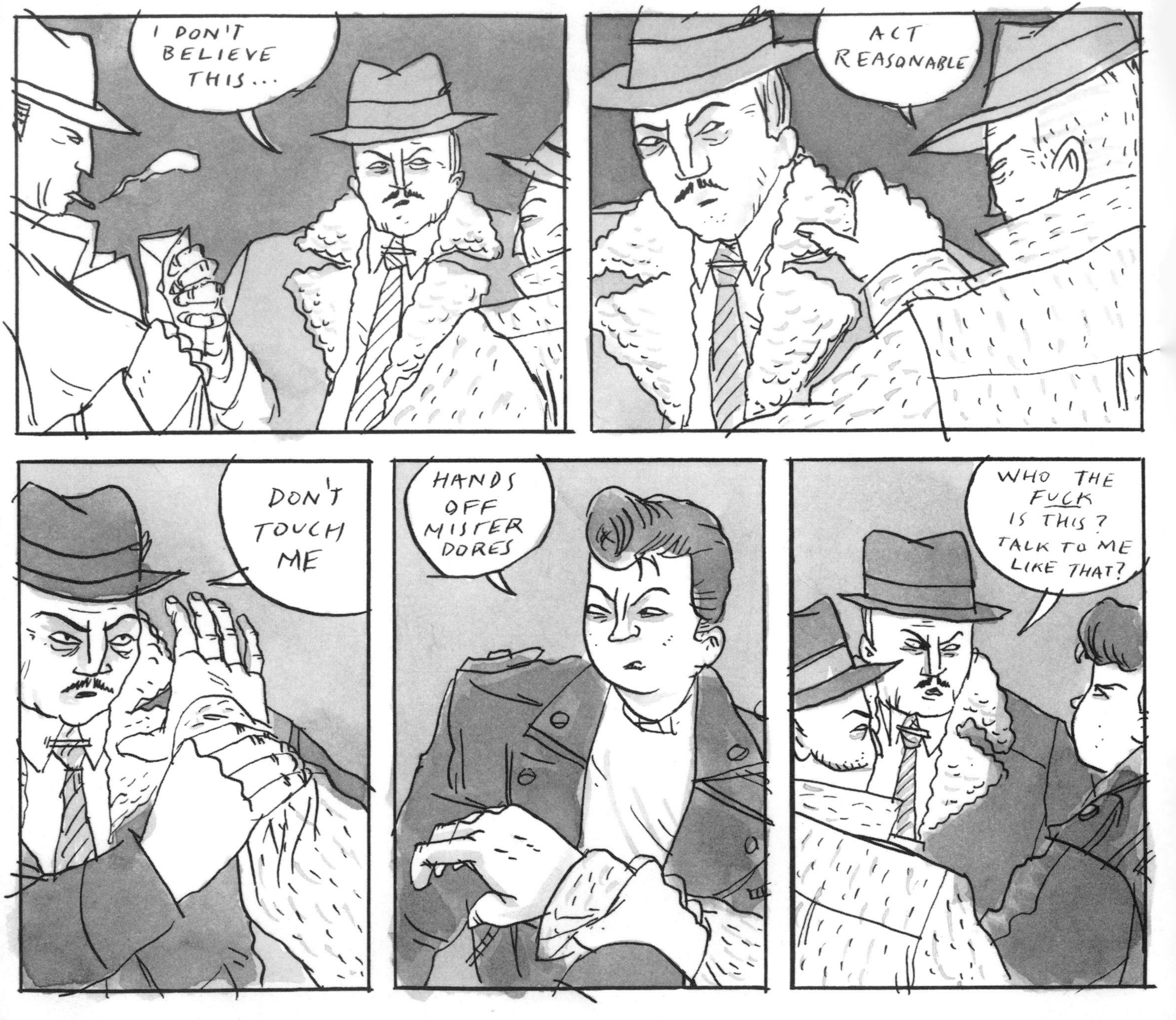
I DON'T BELIEVE THIS...
ACT REASONABLE
DON'T TOUCH ME
HANDS OFF MISTER DORES
WHO THE FUCK IS THIS? TALK TO ME LIKE THAT?

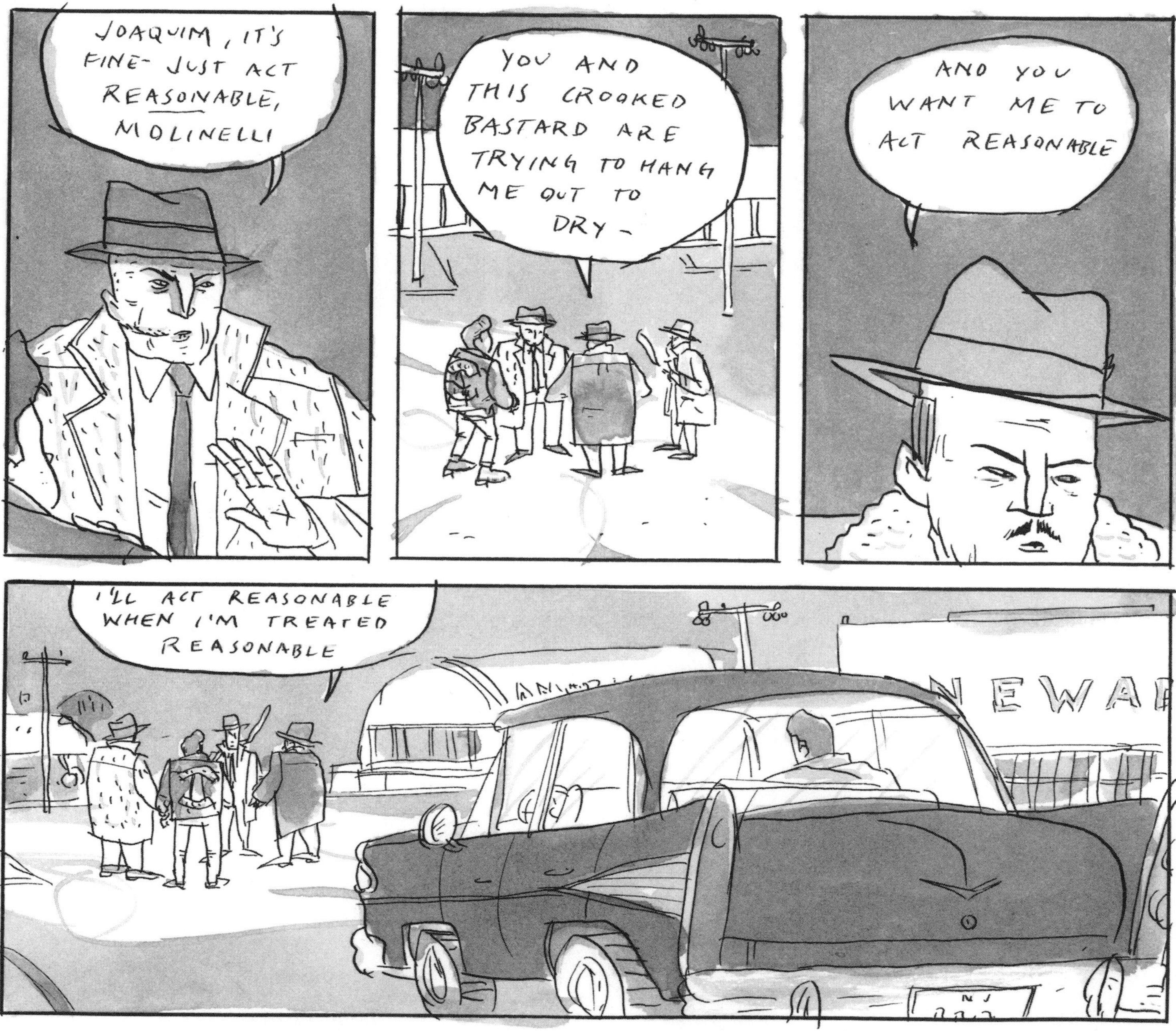
JOAQUIM, IT'S FINE- JUST ACT REASONABLE, MOLINELLI
YOU AND THIS CROOKED BASTARD ARE TRYING TO HANG ME OUT TO DRY-
AND YOU WANT ME TO ACT REASONABLE
I'LL ACT REASONABLE WHEN I'M TREATED REASONABLE

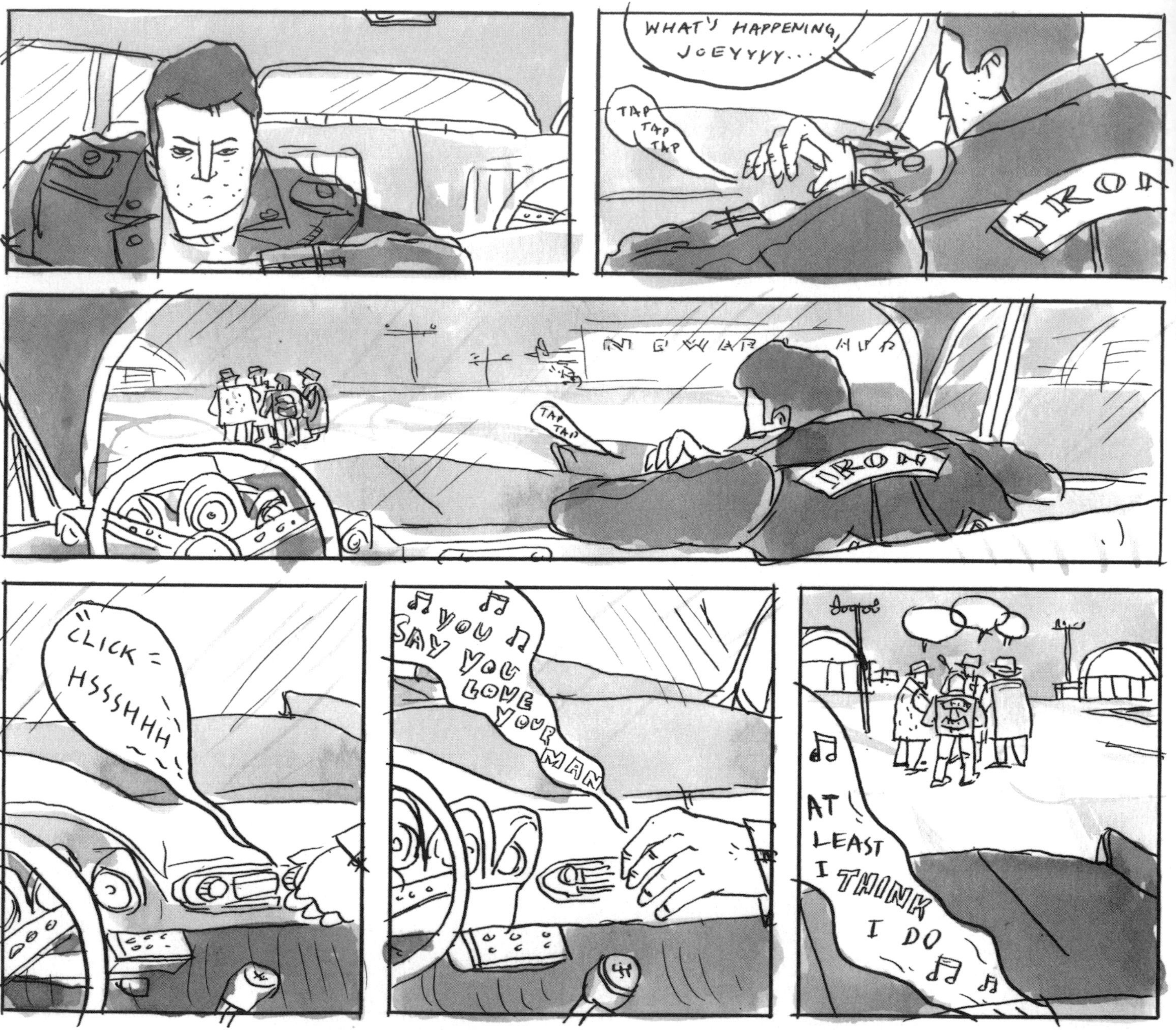
WHAT'S HAPPENING, JOEYYYY...
TAP TAP TAP
IRON
N E W A R
TAP TAP
IRON
CLICK HSSSHHH
♫ YOU ♫ SAY YOU LOVE YOUR MAN
♫ AT LEAST I THINK I DO ♫

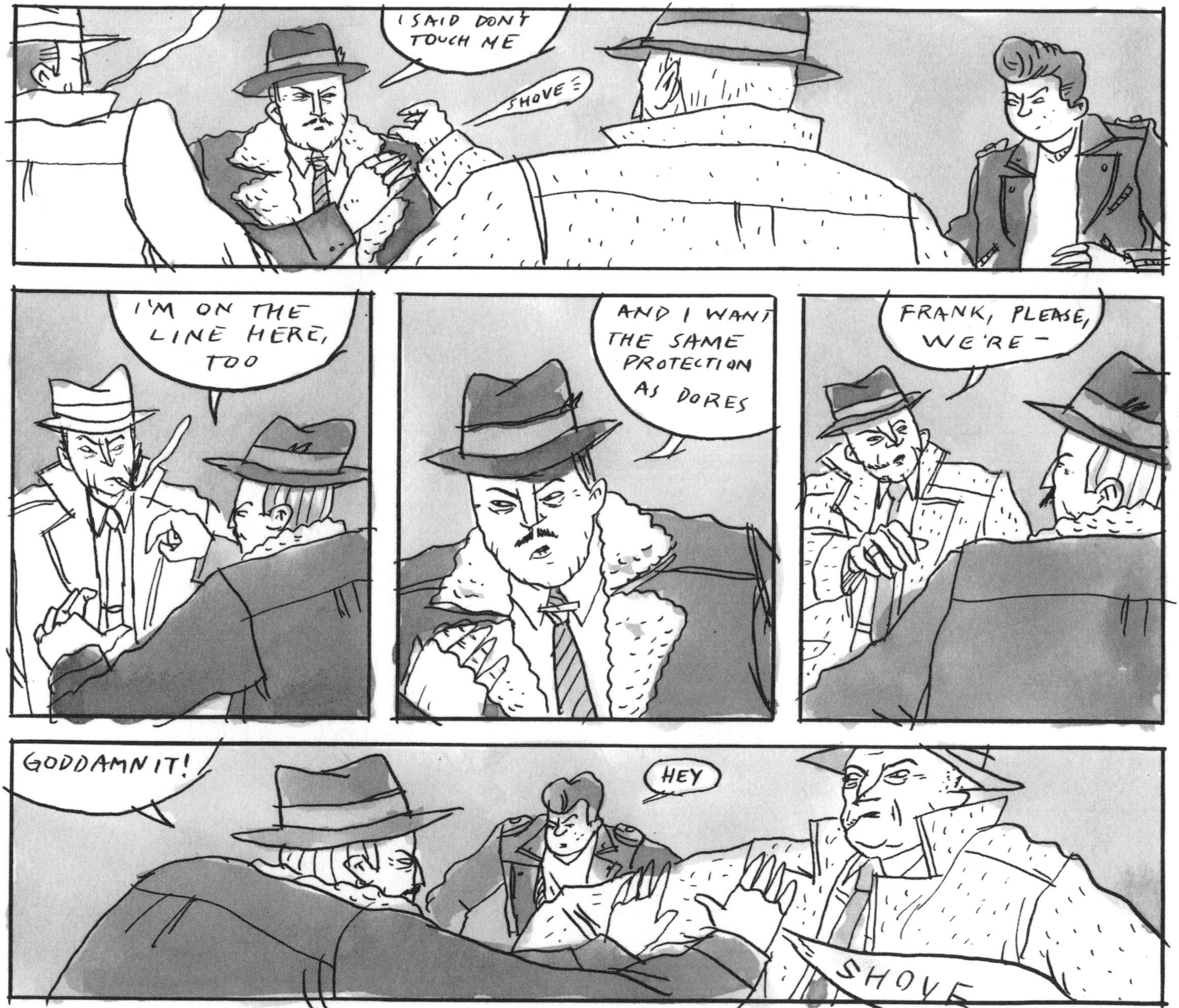
I SAID DON'T TOUCH ME
SHOVE
I'M ON THE LINE HERE, TOO
AND I WANT THE SAME PROTECTION AS DORES
FRANK, PLEASE, WE'RE -
GODDAMNIT!
HEY
SHOVE

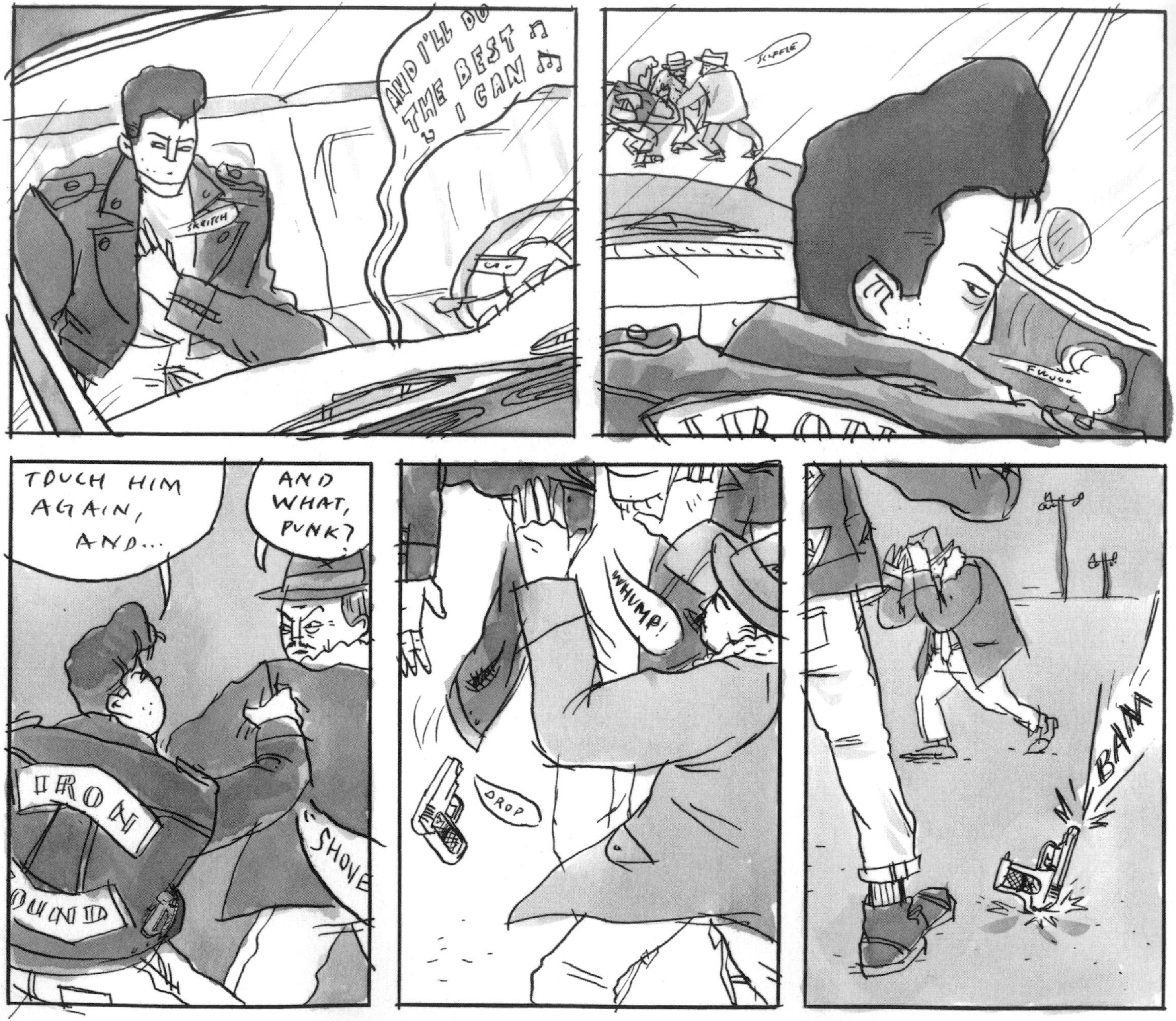
AND I'LL DO THE BEST I CAN
SKRITCH
SCUFFLE
FWUOO
TOUCH HIM AGAIN, AND...
AND WHAT, PUNK?
IRON
SHOVE
WHUMP!
DROP
BAM

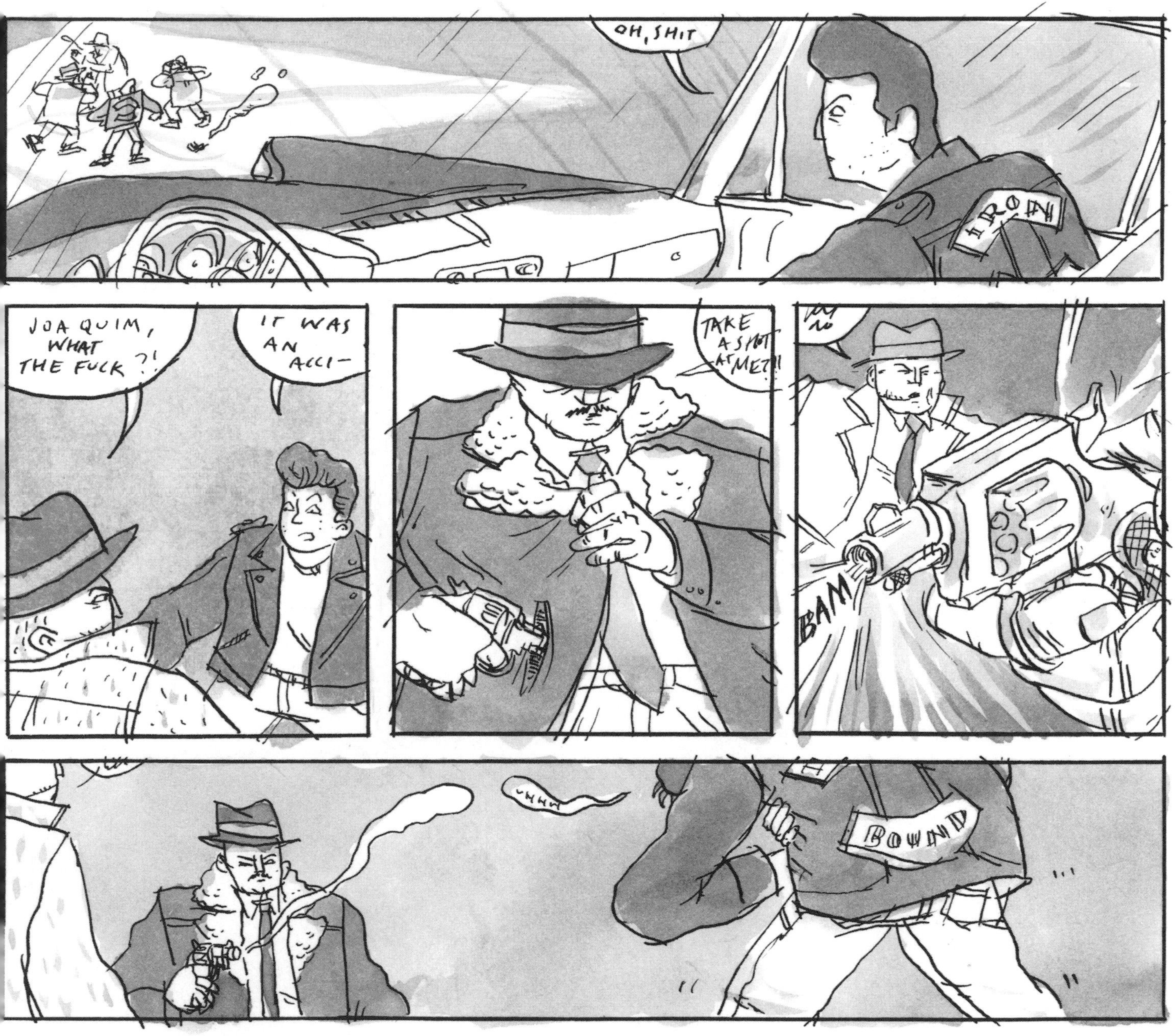
OH, SHIT
IRON
JOAQUIM, WHAT THE FUCK?!
IT WAS AN ACCI-
TAKE A SHOT AT ME?!
BAM
UHHH
BOUND

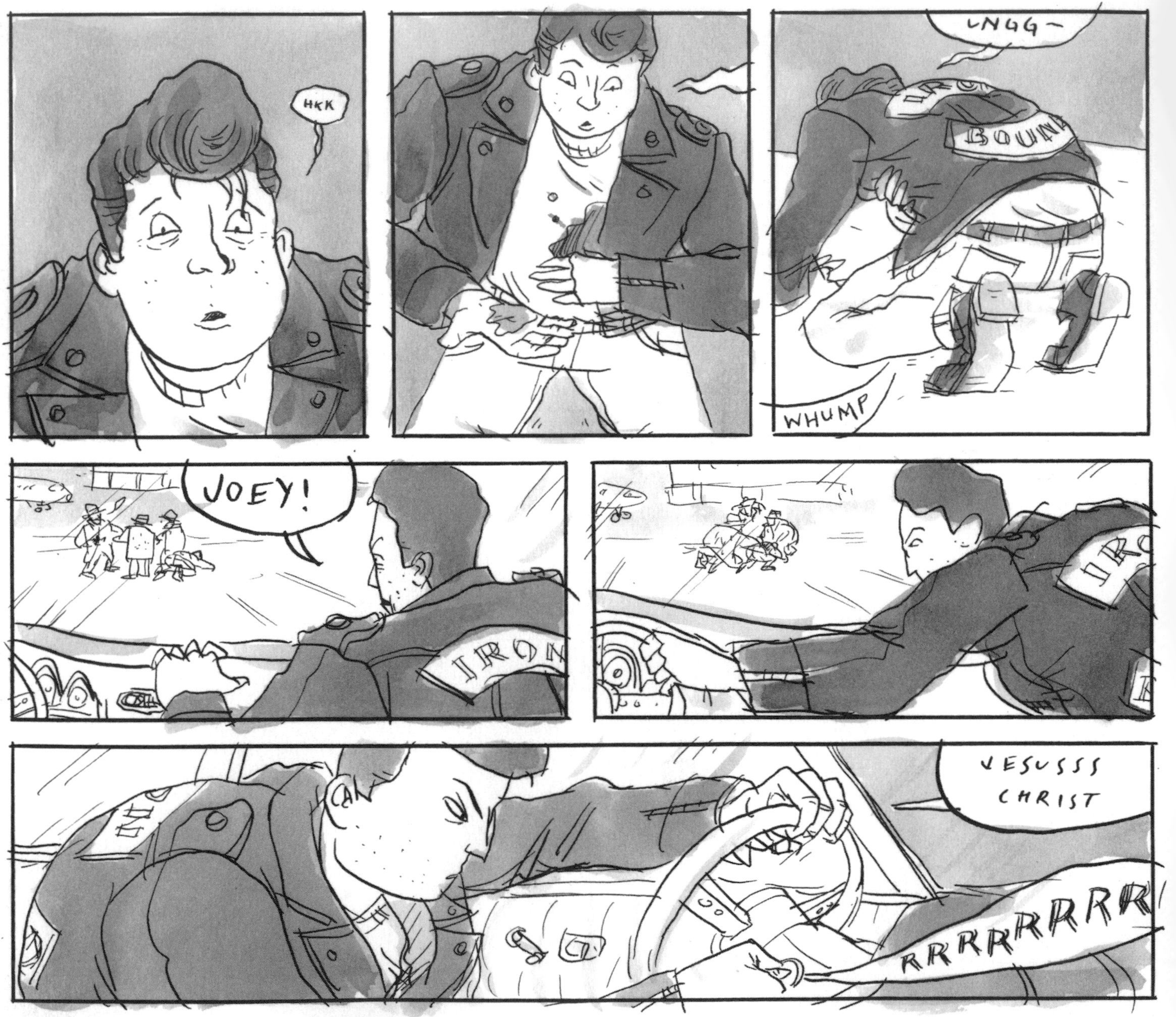
HKK
UNGG—
WHUMP
JOEY!
JESUSSS CHRIST
RRRRRRRRR

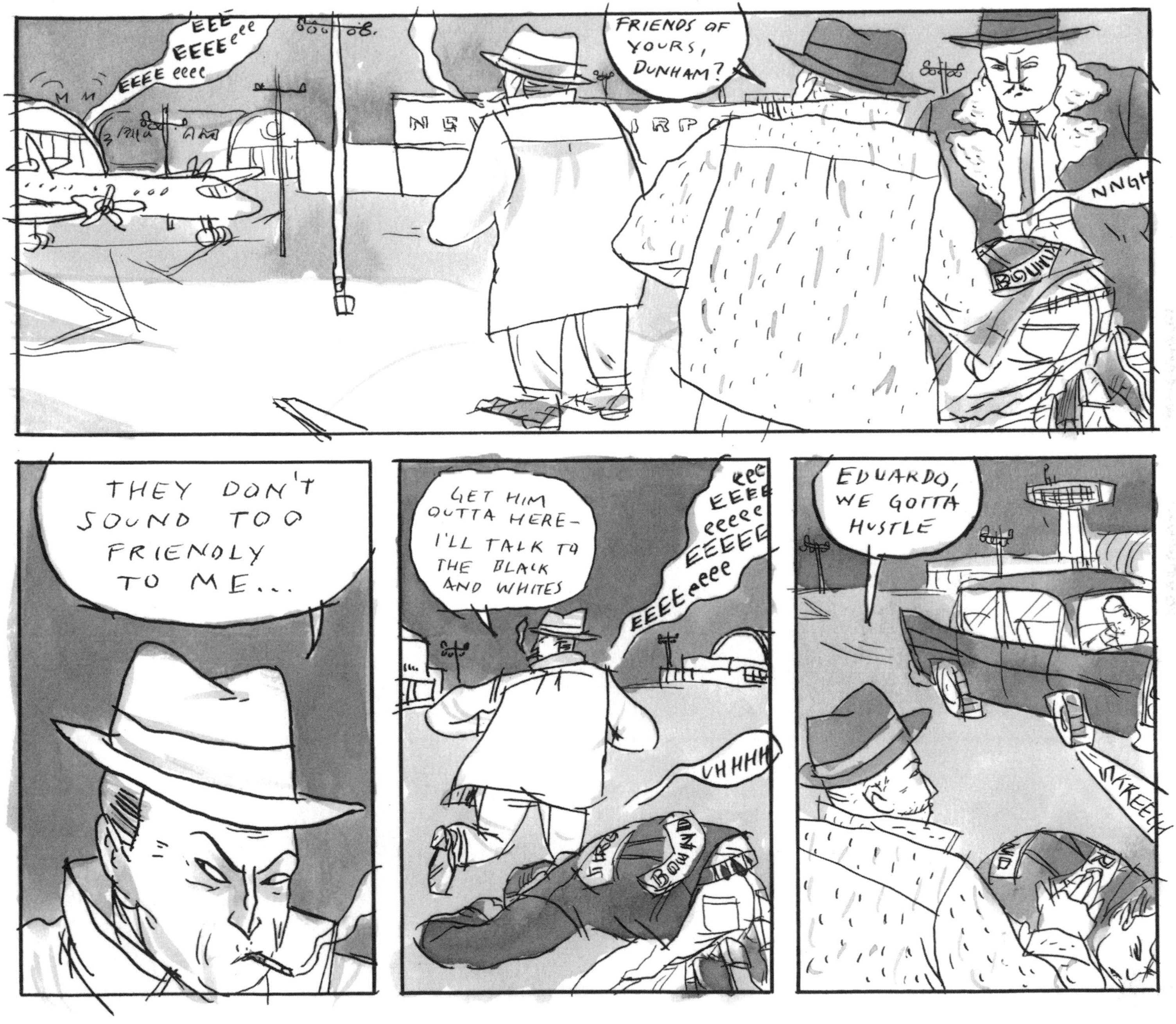
EEE EEEEeee EEEE eeee
FRIENDS OF YOURS, DUNHAM?
NNGH
THEY DON'T SOUND TOO FRIENDLY TO ME...
GET HIM OUTTA HERE- I'LL TALK TO THE BLACK AND WHITES
eee EEEE eeeee EEEEE EEEEeeee
UHHHH
EDUARDO, WE GOTTA HUSTLE

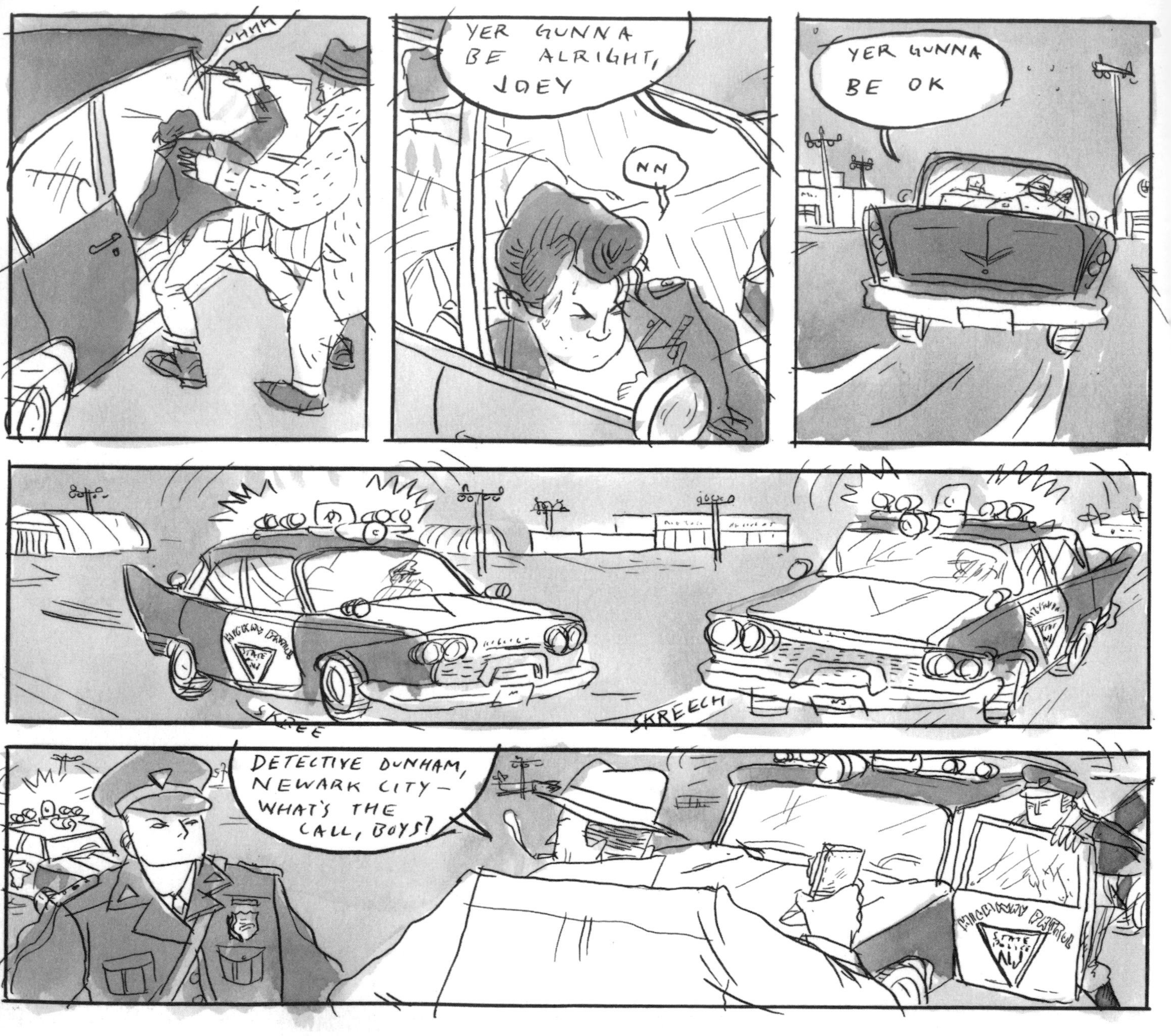
UHMM
YER GUNNA BE ALRIGHT, JOEY
NN
YER GUNNA BE OK
SKREE
SKREECH
DETECTIVE DUNHAM, NEWARK CITY— WHAT'S THE CALL, BOYS?

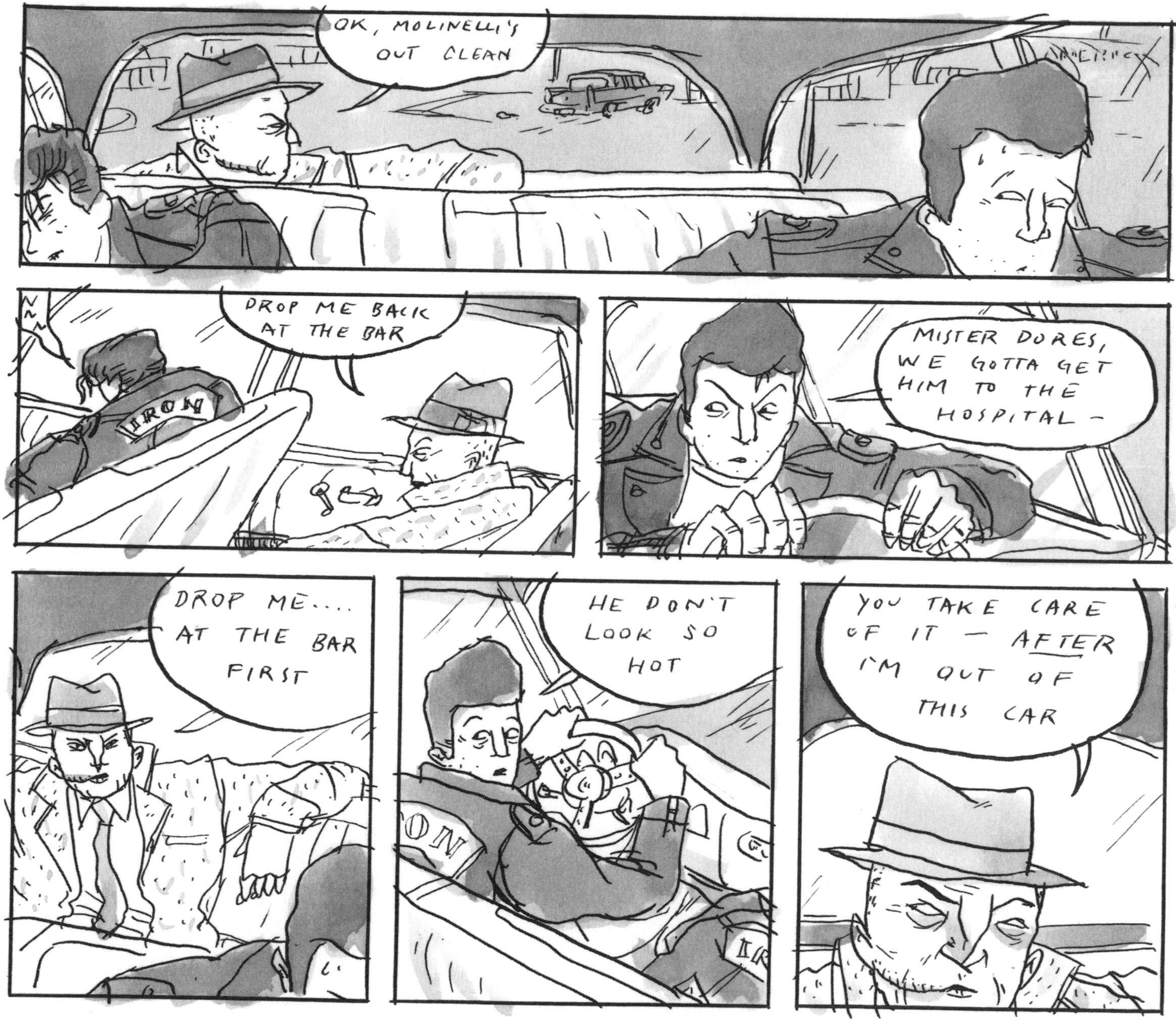
OK, MOLINELLI'S OUT CLEAN
DROP ME BACK AT THE BAR
IRON
MISTER DORES, WE GOTTA GET HIM TO THE HOSPITAL -
DROP ME.... AT THE BAR FIRST
HE DON'T LOOK SO HOT
ON
YOU TAKE CARE OF IT - AFTER I'M OUT OF THIS CAR

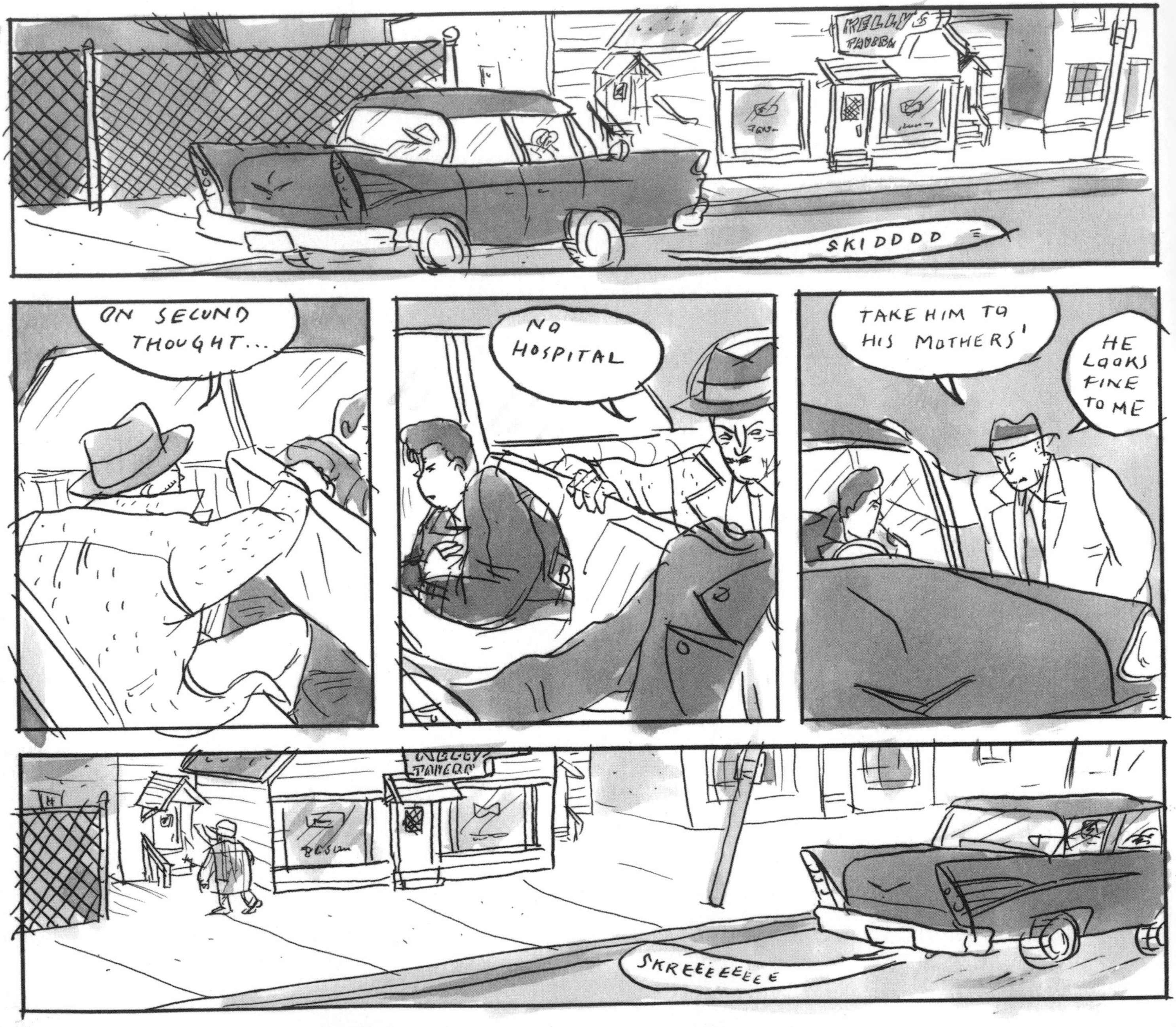
KELLY'S TAVERN
SKIDDDD
ON SECOND THOUGHT...
NO HOSPITAL
TAKE HIM TO HIS MOTHERS'
HE LOOKS FINE TO ME
SKREEEEEEEEE

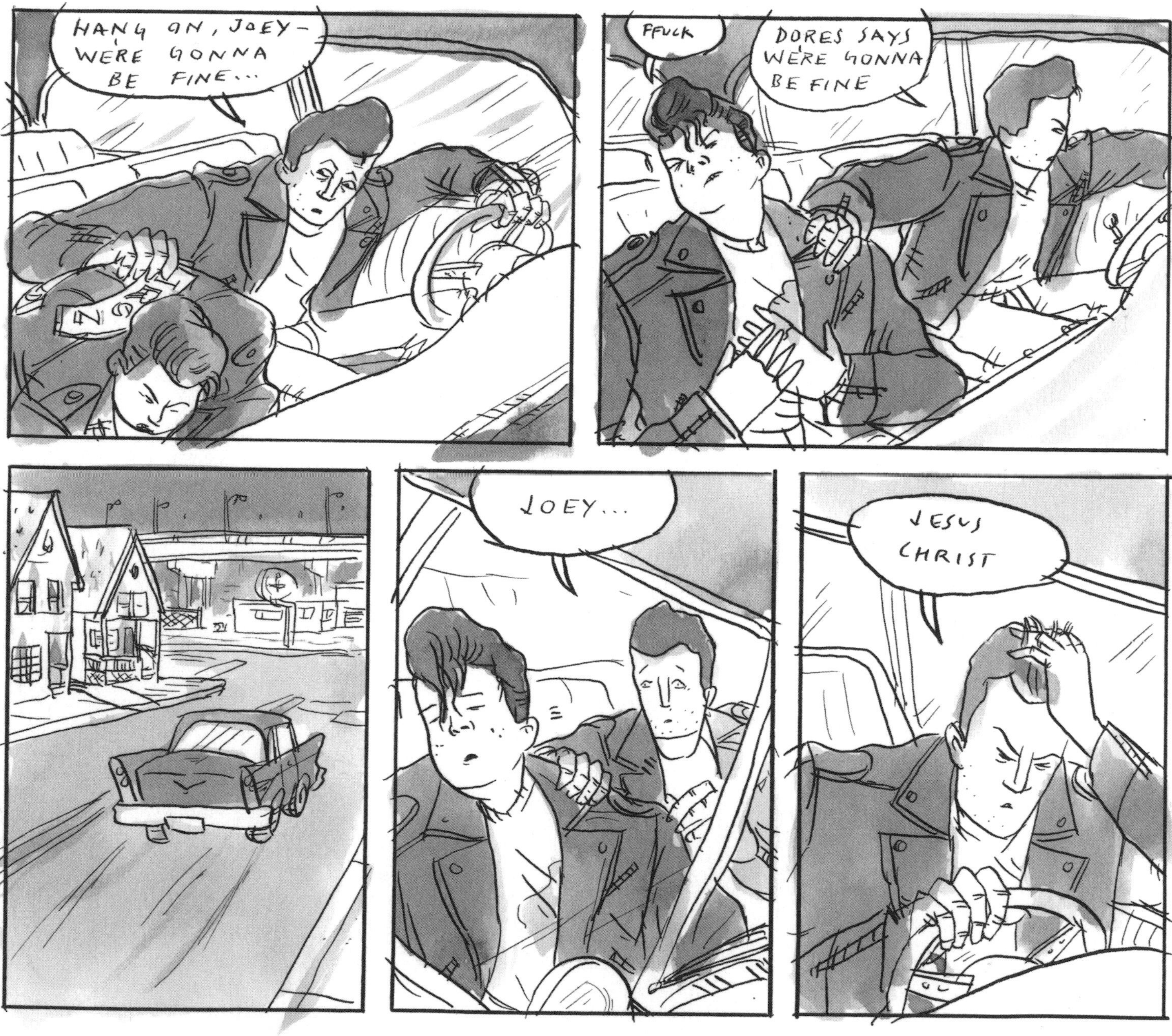
HANG ON, JOEY- WE'RE GONNA BE FINE...
FFUCK
DORES SAYS WE'RE GONNA BE FINE
JOEY...
JESUS CHRIST

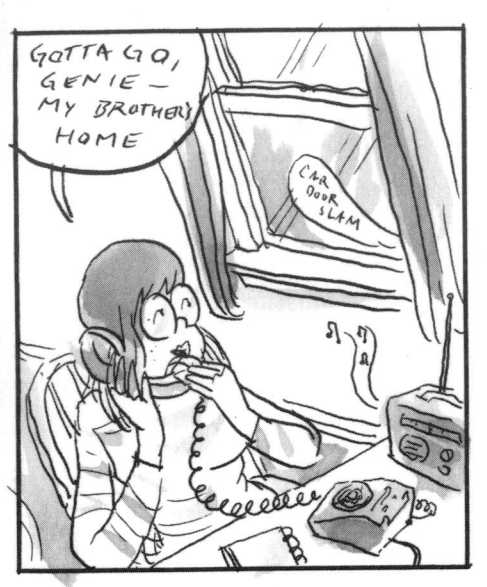

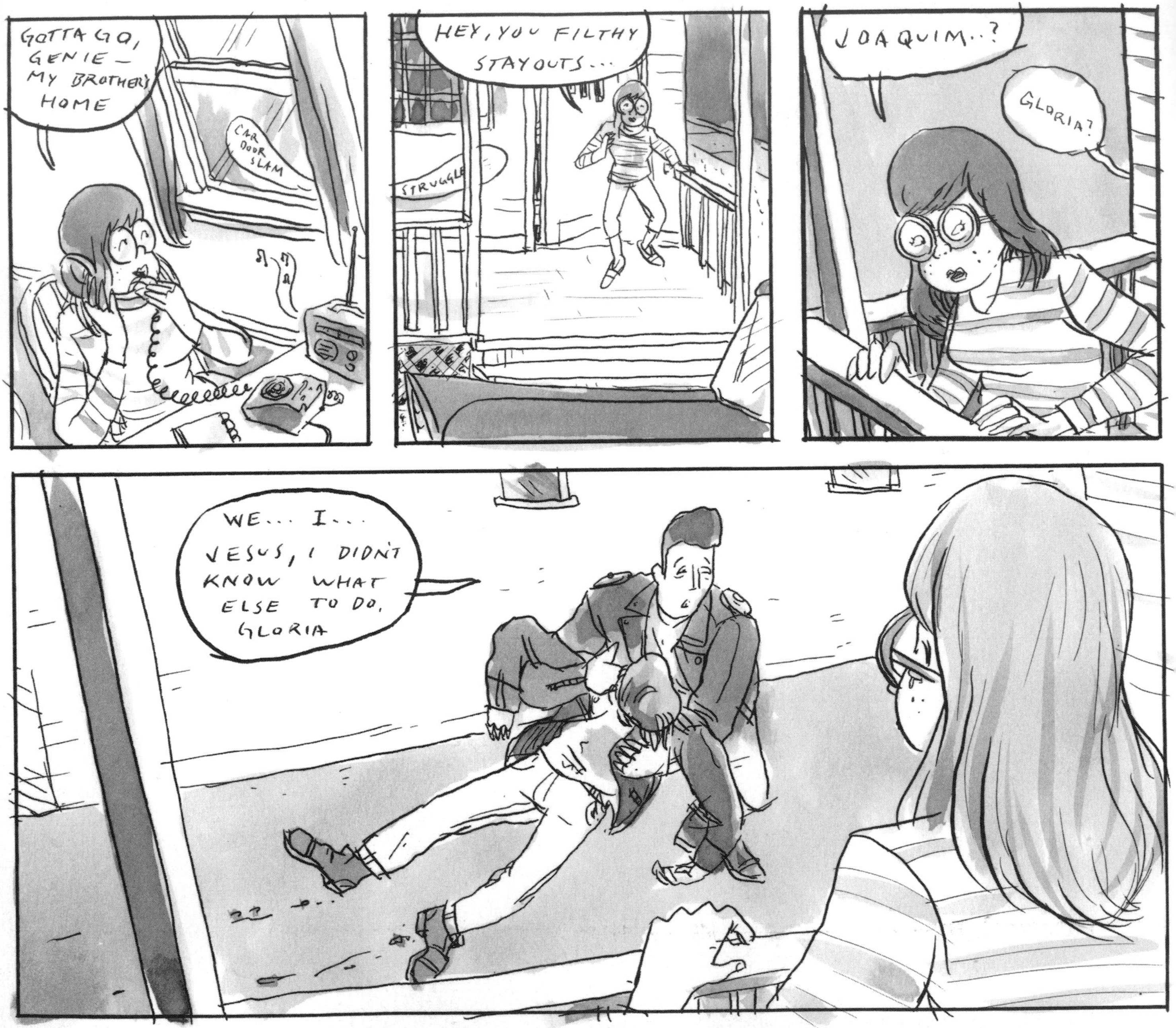
GOTTA GO, GENIE — MY BROTHER'S HOME
CAR DOOR SLAM
HEY, YOU FILTHY STAYOUTS...
STRUGGLE
JOAQUIM..?
GLORIA?
WE... I... JESUS, I DIDN'T KNOW WHAT ELSE TO DO, GLORIA

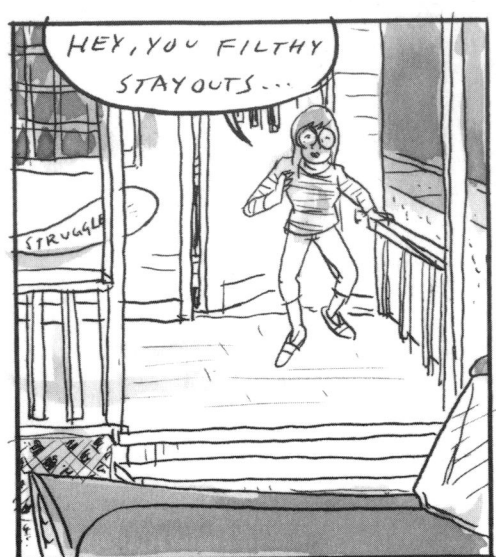

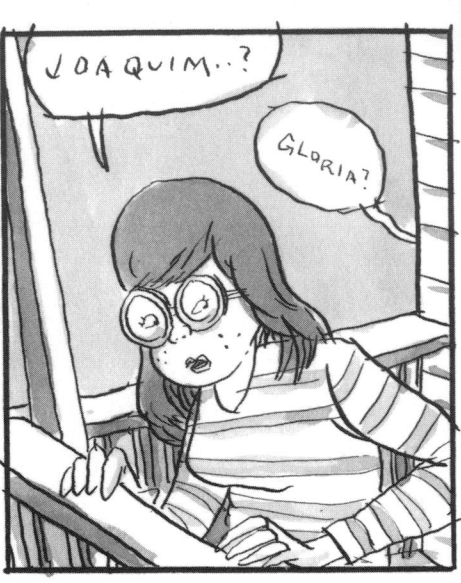

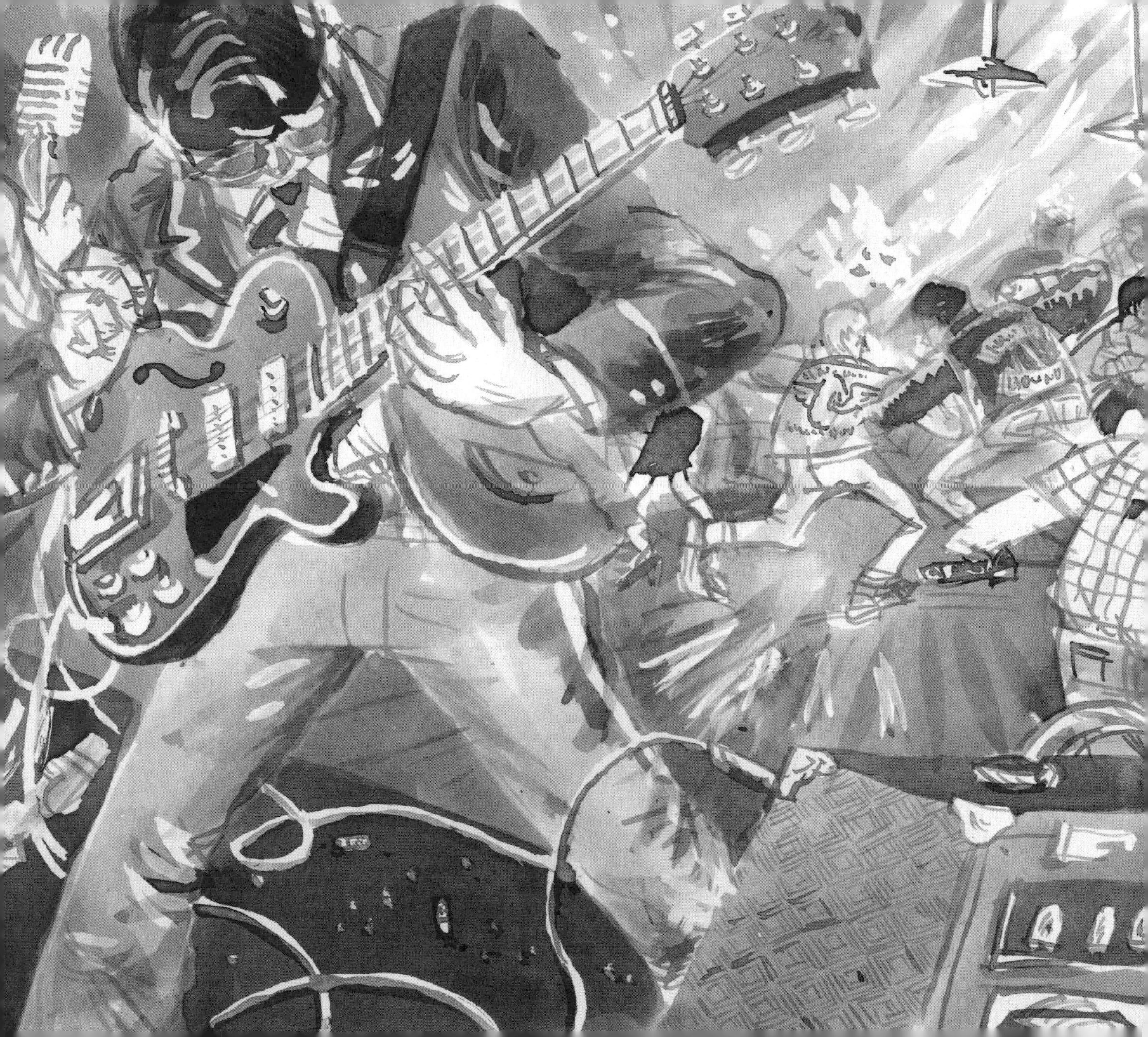

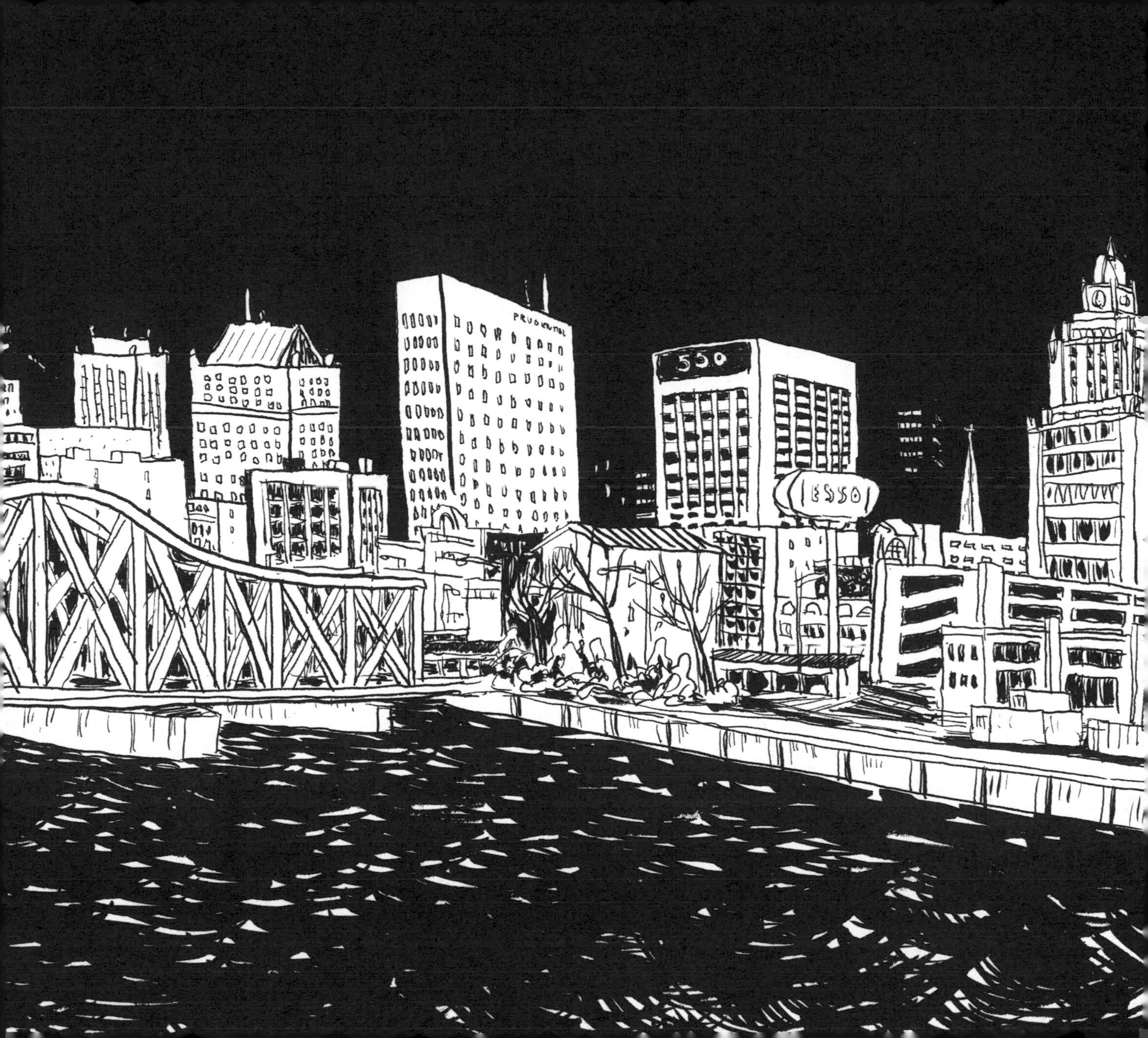
PRUDENTIAL
550
ESSO

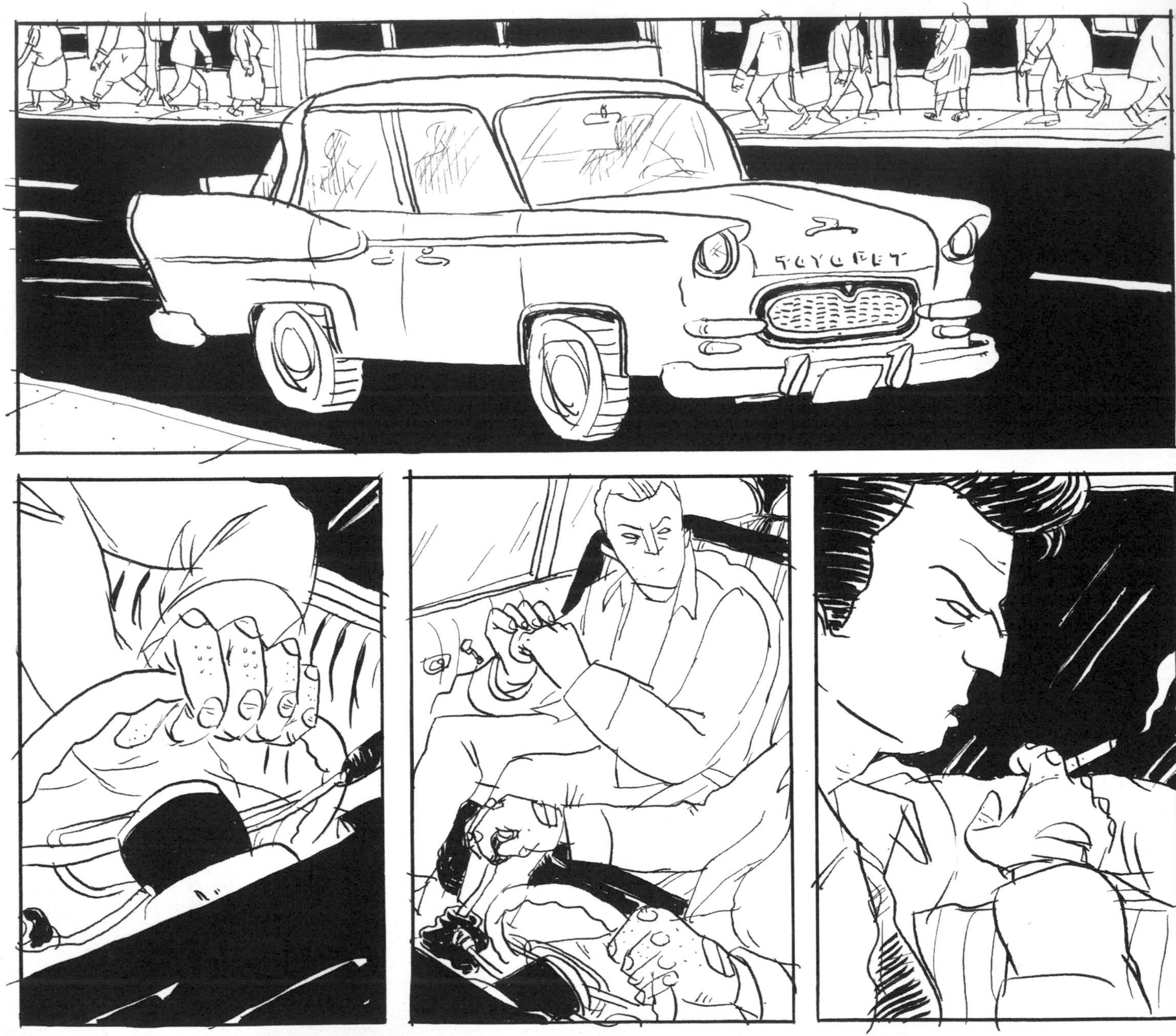
TOYOPET

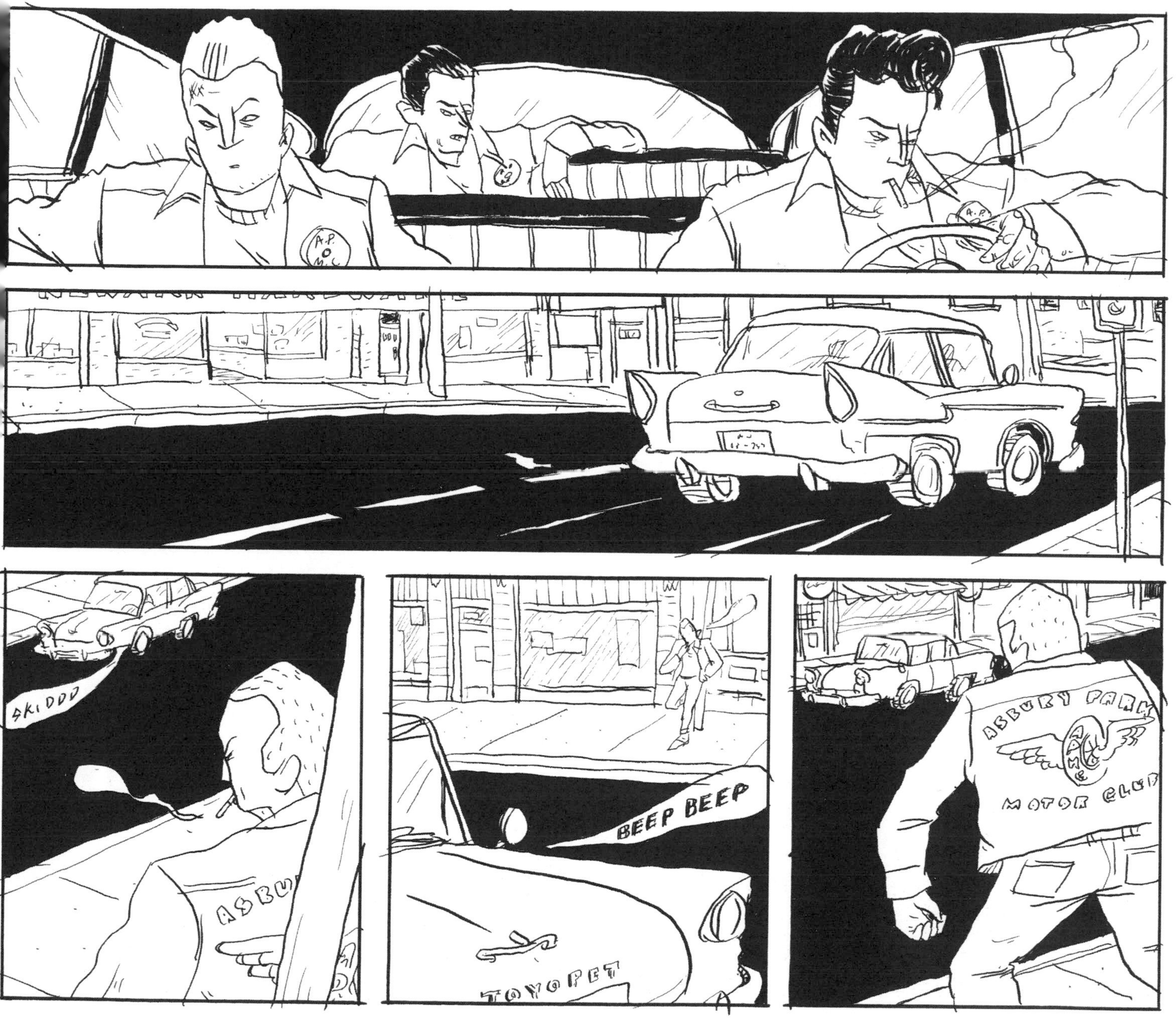

SKIDDD
ASBU
BEEP BEEP
TOYOPET
ASBURY PARK
MOTOR CLUB

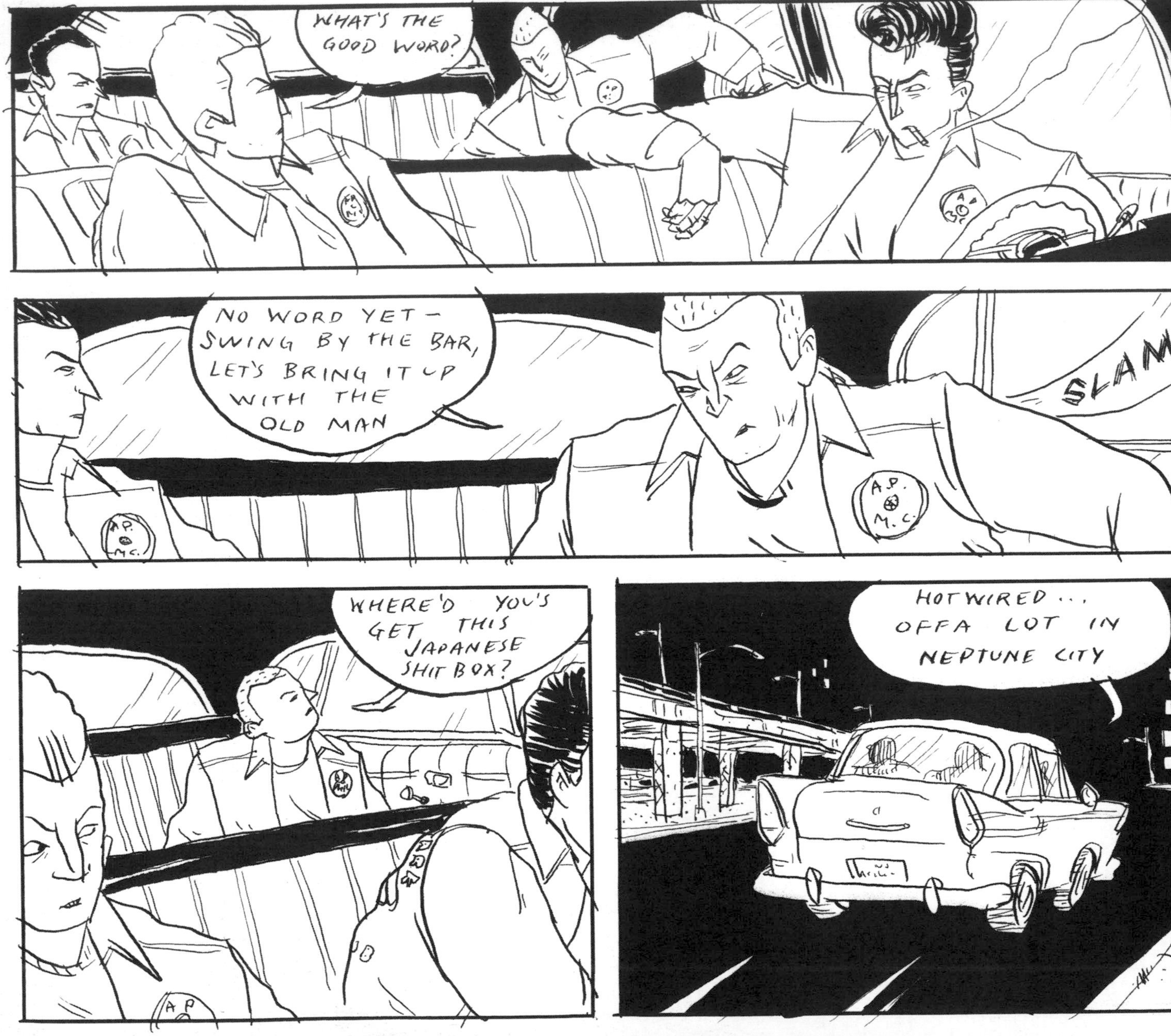
WHAT'S THE GOOD WORD?
NO WORD YET - SWING BY THE BAR, LET'S BRING IT UP WITH THE OLD MAN
SLAM
WHERE'D YOU'S GET THIS JAPANESE SHIT BOX?
HOTWIRED... OFFA LOT IN NEPTUNE CITY

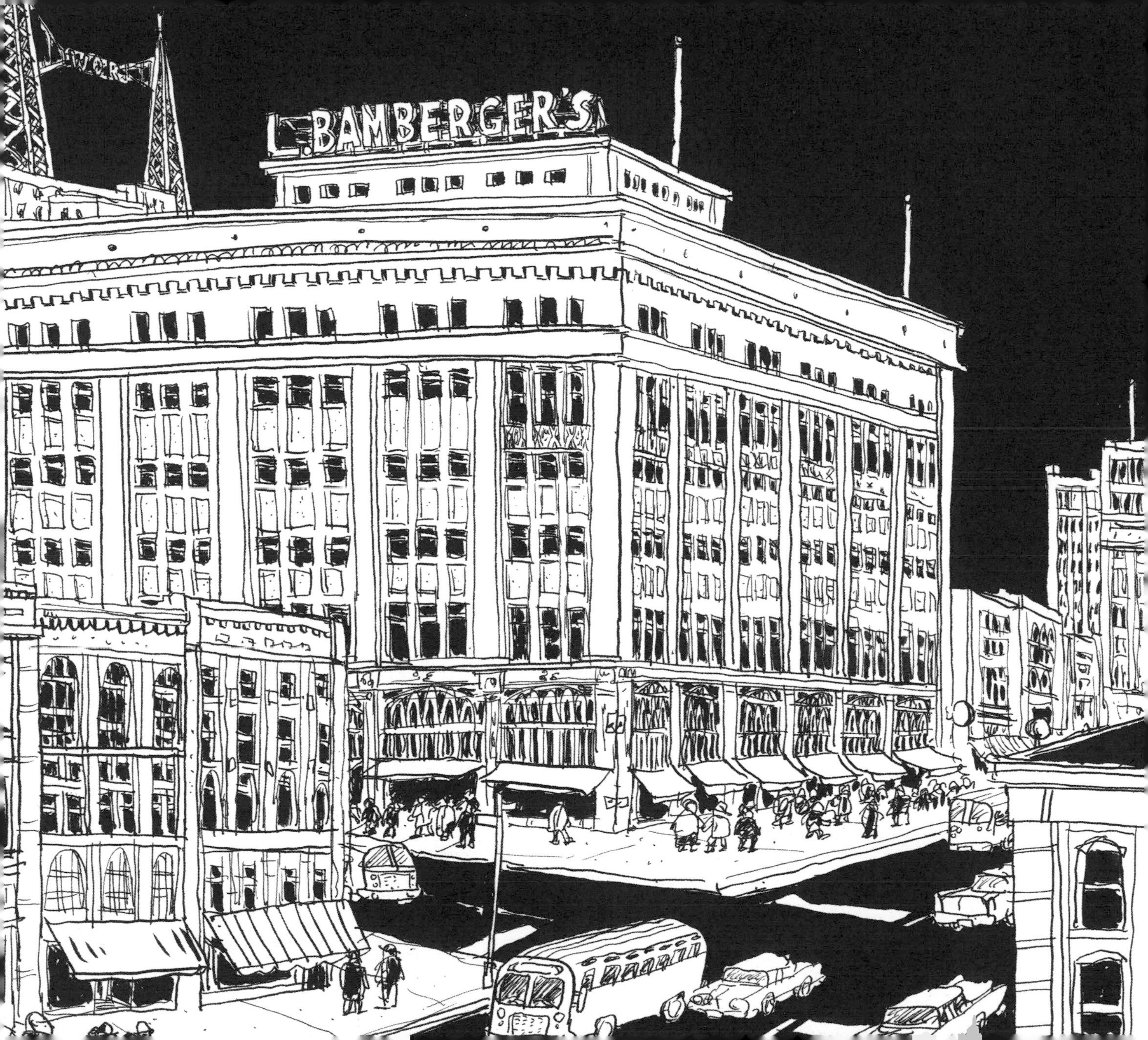
L. BAMBERGER'S
WOR

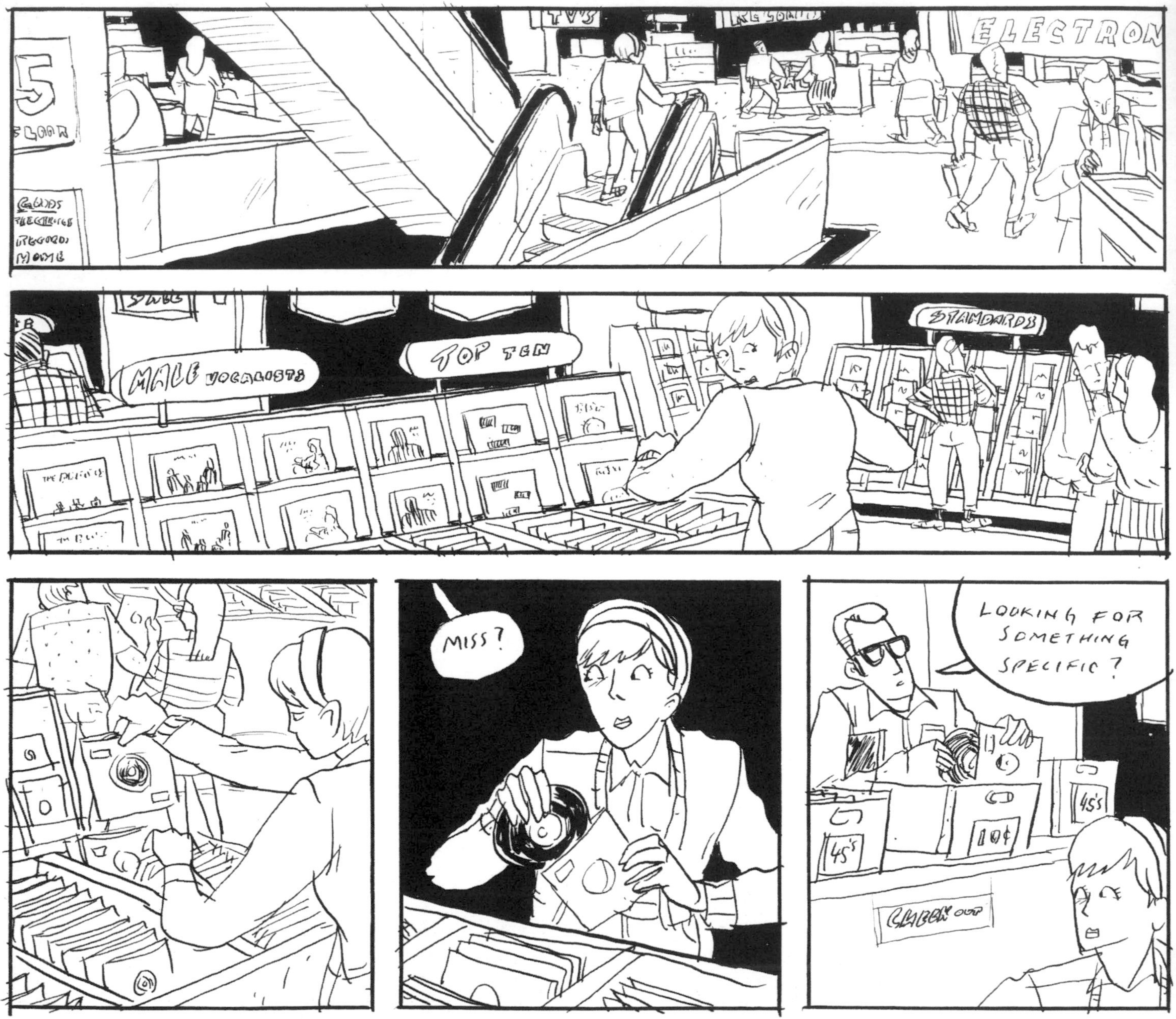
TV'S
ELECTRON
5
MALE VOCALISTS
TOP TEN
STANDARDS
MISS?
LOOKING FOR SOMETHING SPECIFIC?
45's
10¢
45's

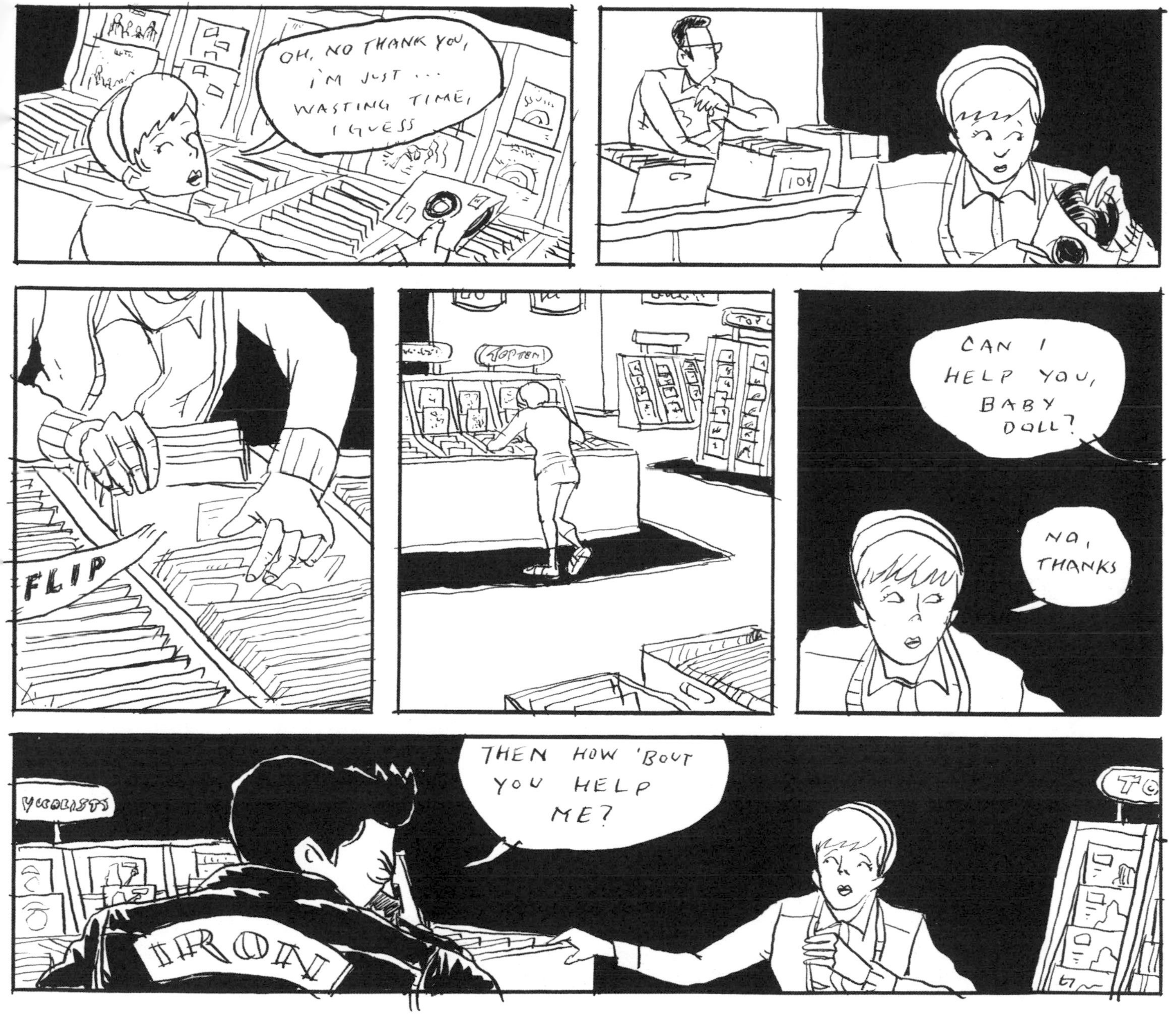
OH, NO THANK YOU, I'M JUST ... WASTING TIME, I GUESS
FLIP
TOP TEN
CAN I HELP YOU, BABY DOLL?
NO, THANKS
THEN HOW 'BOUT YOU HELP ME?
VOCALISTS
RON

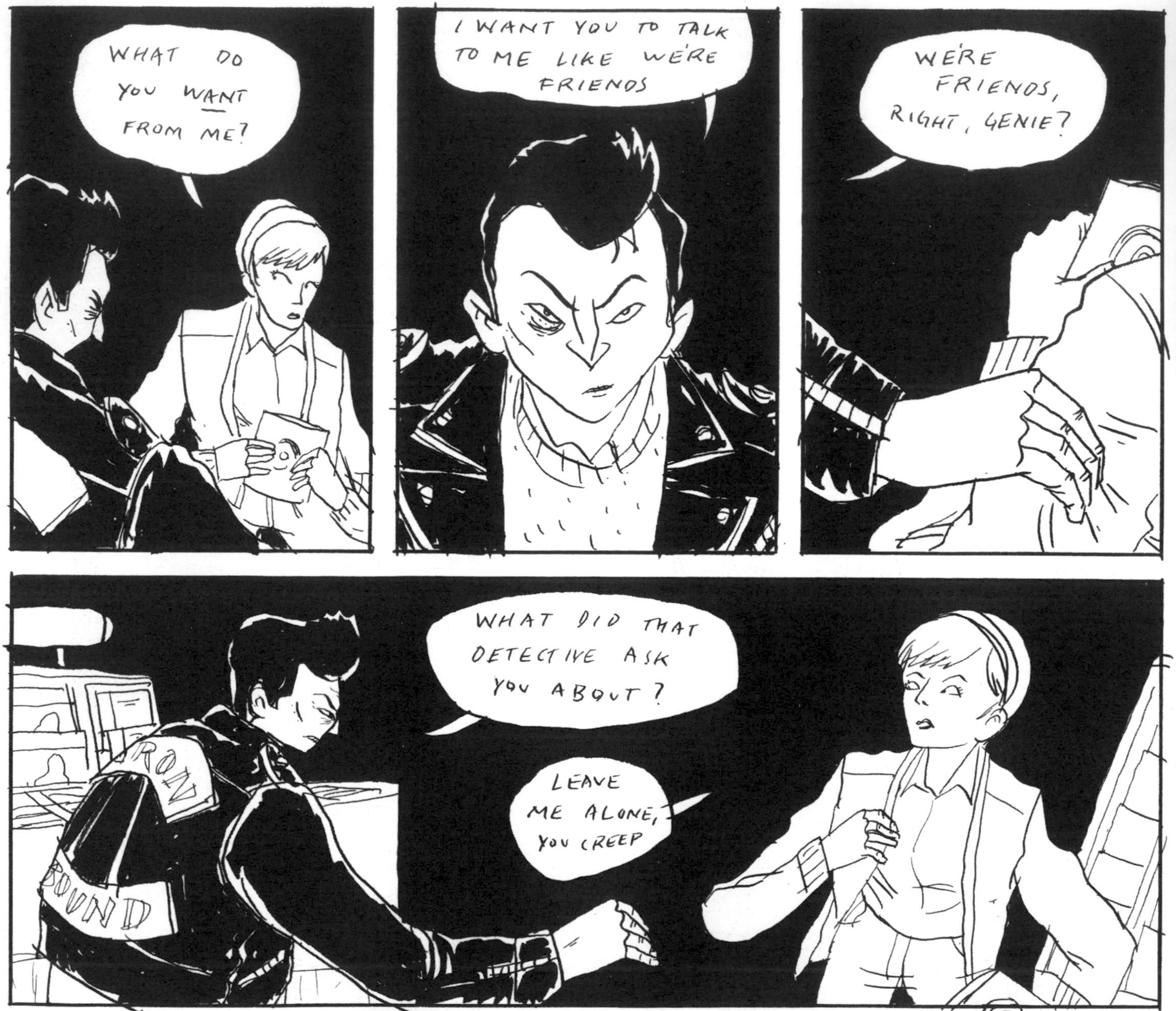
WHAT DO YOU WANT FROM ME?
I WANT YOU TO TALK TO ME LIKE WE'RE FRIENDS
WE'RE FRIENDS, RIGHT, GENIE?
IRON BOUND
WHAT DID THAT DETECTIVE ASK YOU ABOUT?
LEAVE ME ALONE, YOU CREEP

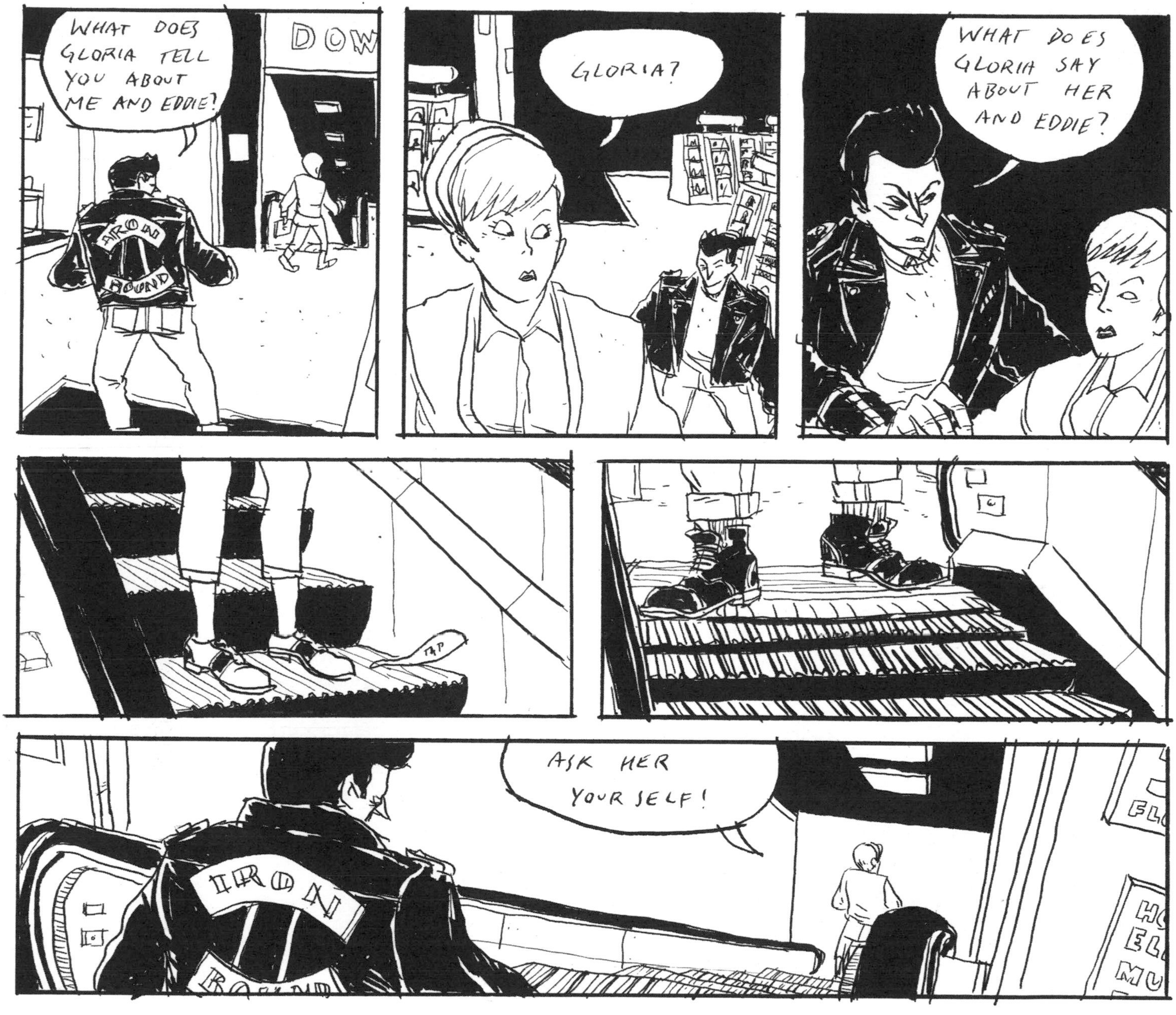
WHAT DOES GLORIA TELL YOU ABOUT ME AND EDDIE?
IRON HOUND
GLORIA?
WHAT DOES GLORIA SAY ABOUT HER AND EDDIE?
TAP
ASK HER YOUR SELF!
IRON

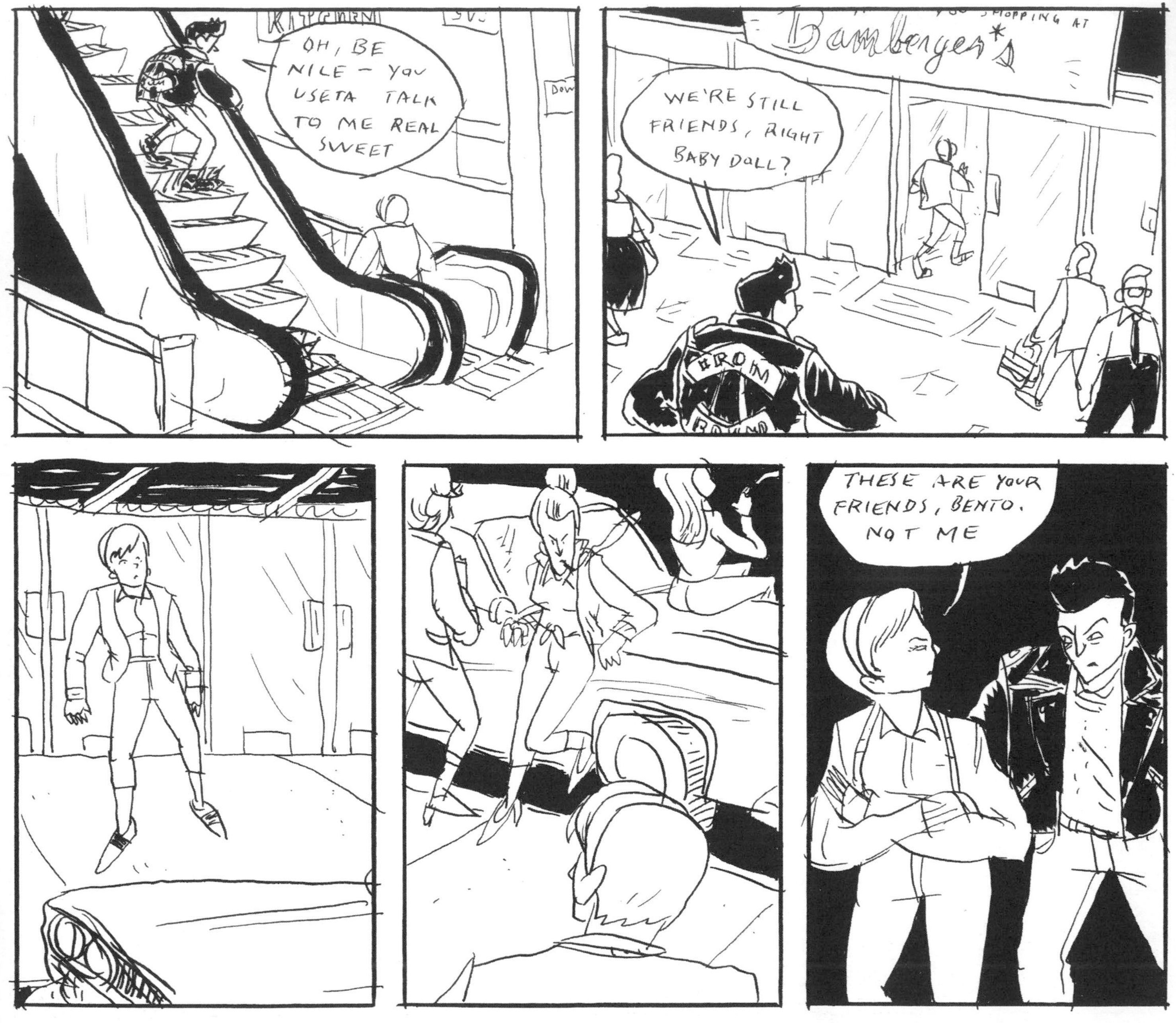
OH, BE NICE - YOU USETA TALK TO ME REAL SWEET
Bamberger's
WE'RE STILL FRIENDS, RIGHT BABY DOLL?
THESE ARE YOUR FRIENDS, BENTO. NOT ME

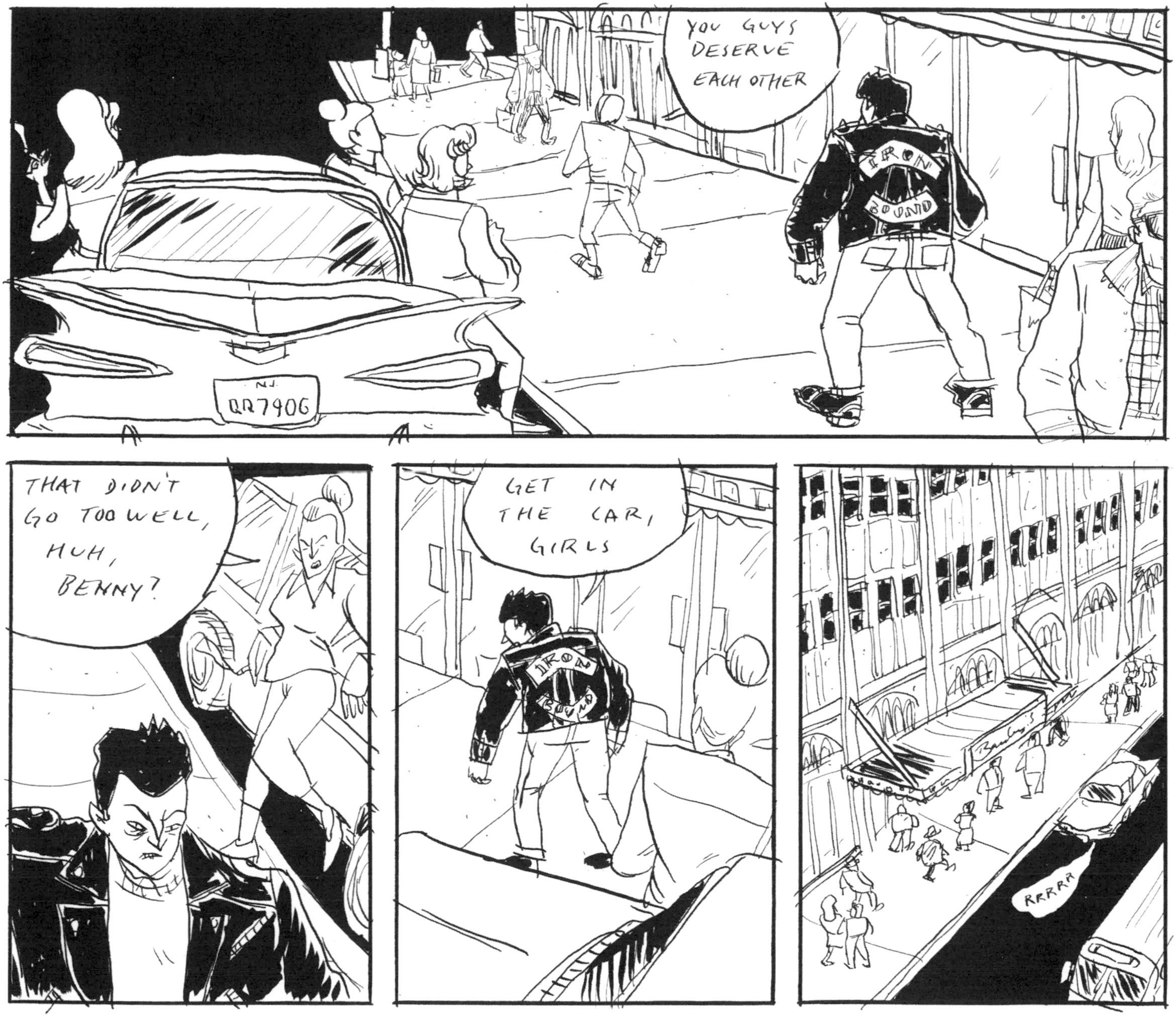
YOU GUYS DESERVE EACH OTHER
THAT DIDN'T GO TOO WELL, HUH, BENNY?
GET IN THE CAR, GIRLS
RRRRR

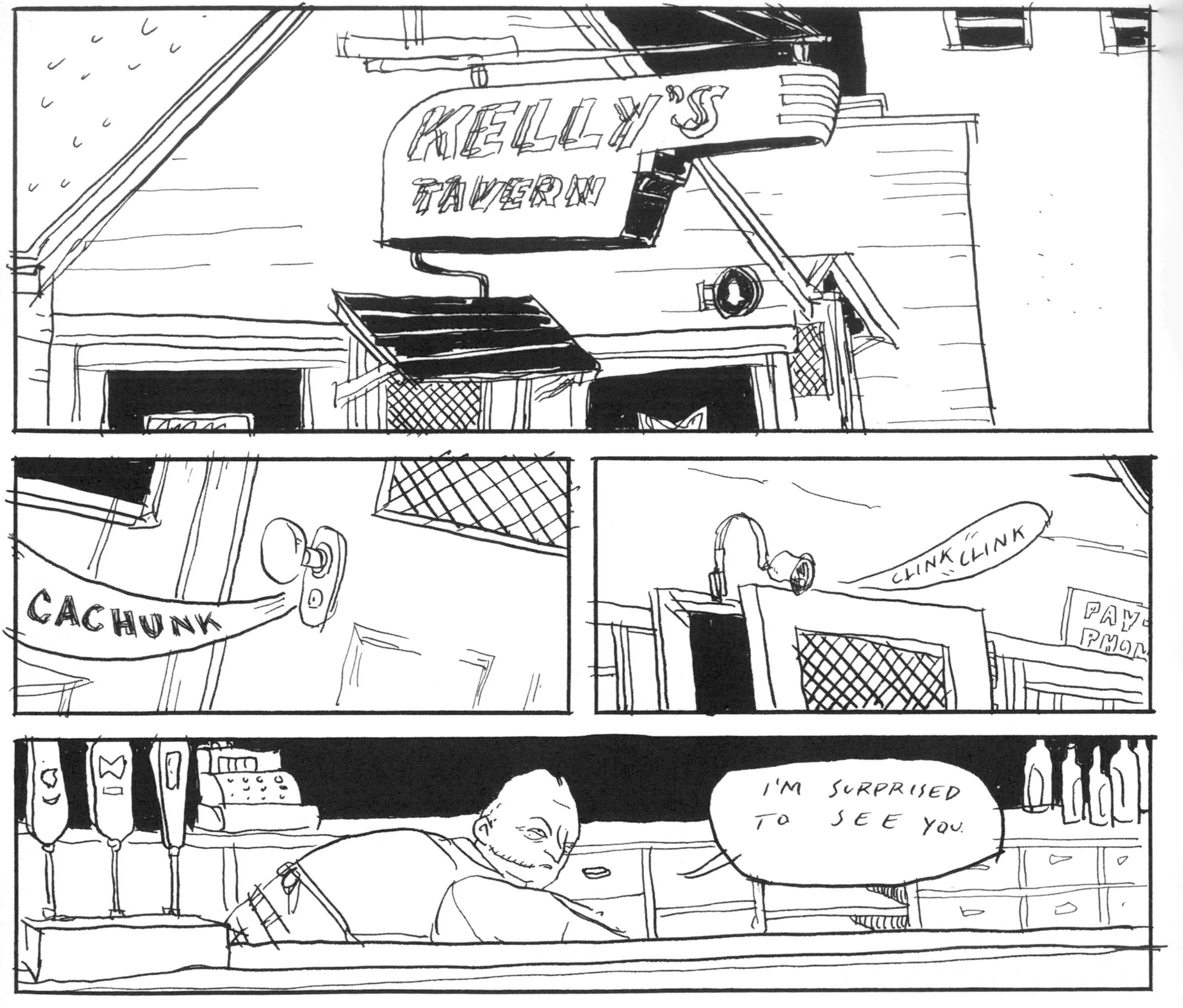
KELLY'S
TAVERN
CACHUNK
CLINK CLINK
PAY-
PHON
I'M SURPRISED TO SEE YOU.

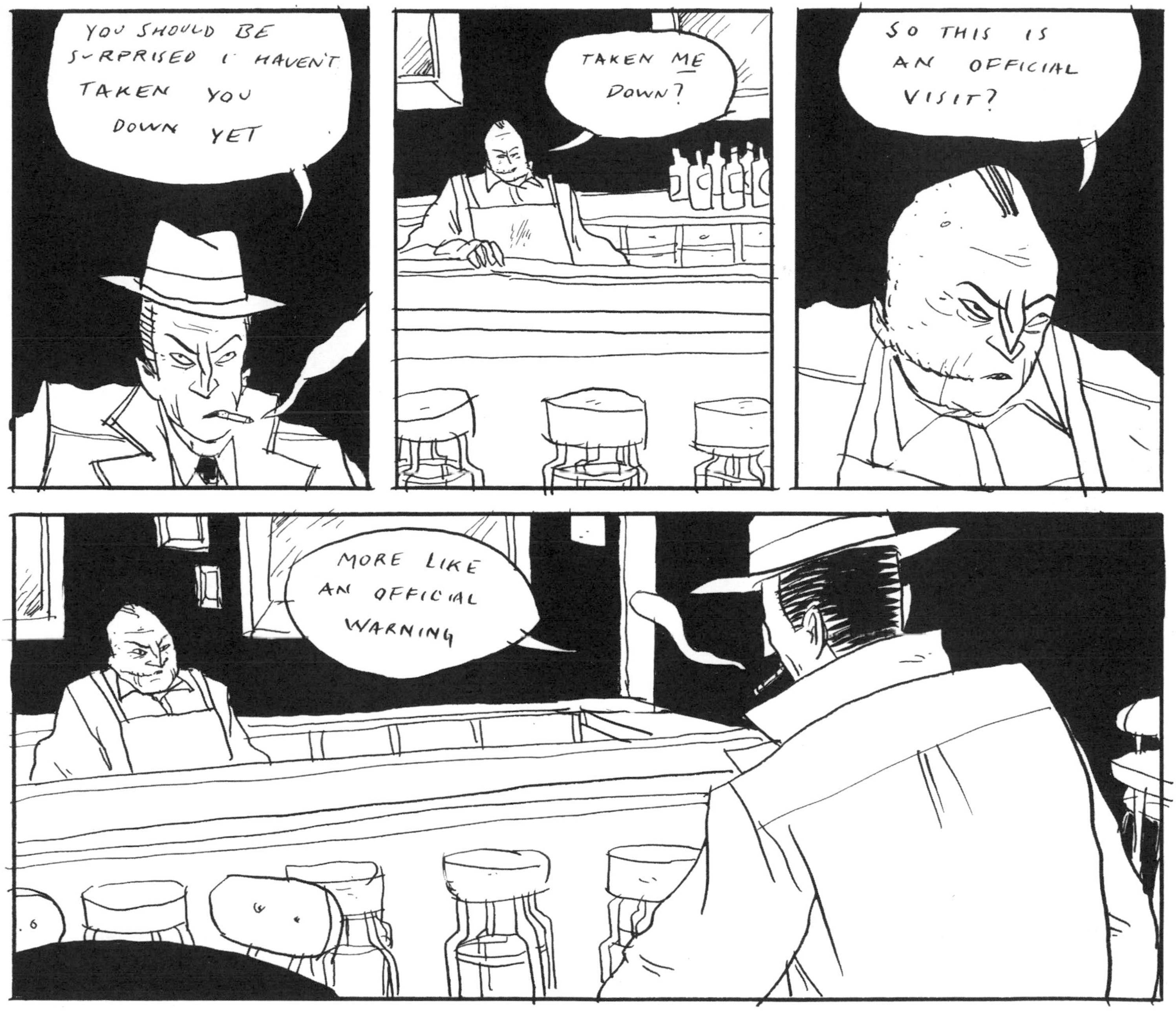
YOU SHOULD BE SURPRISED I HAVEN'T TAKEN YOU DOWN YET
TAKEN ME DOWN?
SO THIS IS AN OFFICIAL VISIT?
MORE LIKE AN OFFICIAL WARNING

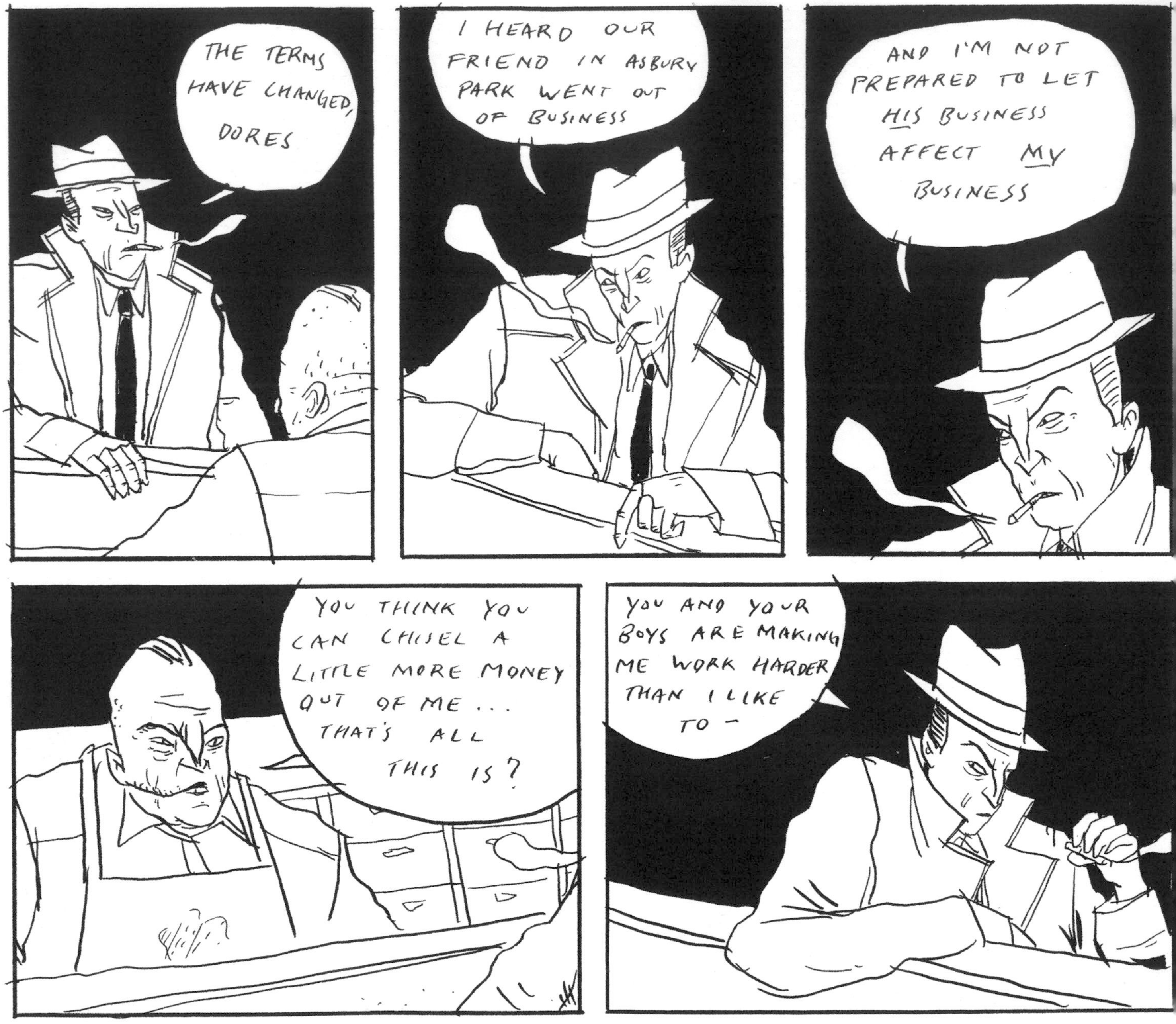
THE TERMS HAVE CHANGED, DORES
I HEARD OUR FRIEND IN ASBURY PARK WENT OUT OF BUSINESS
AND I'M NOT PREPARED TO LET HIS BUSINESS AFFECT MY BUSINESS
YOU THINK YOU CAN CHISEL A LITTLE MORE MONEY OUT OF ME... THAT'S ALL THIS IS?
YOU AND YOUR BOYS ARE MAKING ME WORK HARDER THAN I LIKE TO -

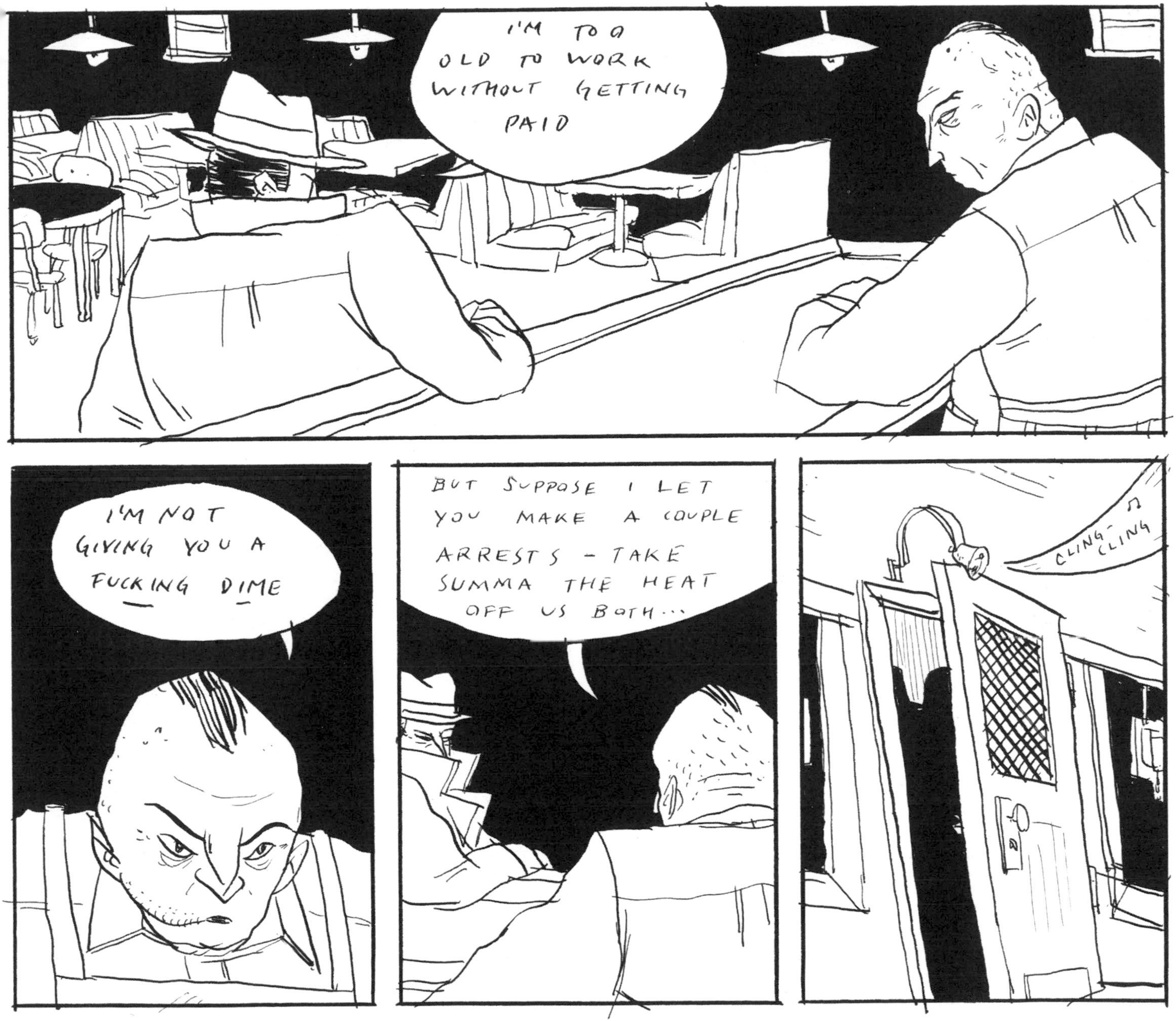
I'M TOO OLD TO WORK WITHOUT GETTING PAID
I'M NOT GIVING YOU A FUCKING DIME
BUT SUPPOSE I LET YOU MAKE A COUPLE ARRESTS - TAKE SUMMA THE HEAT OFF US BOTH...
CLING-CLING

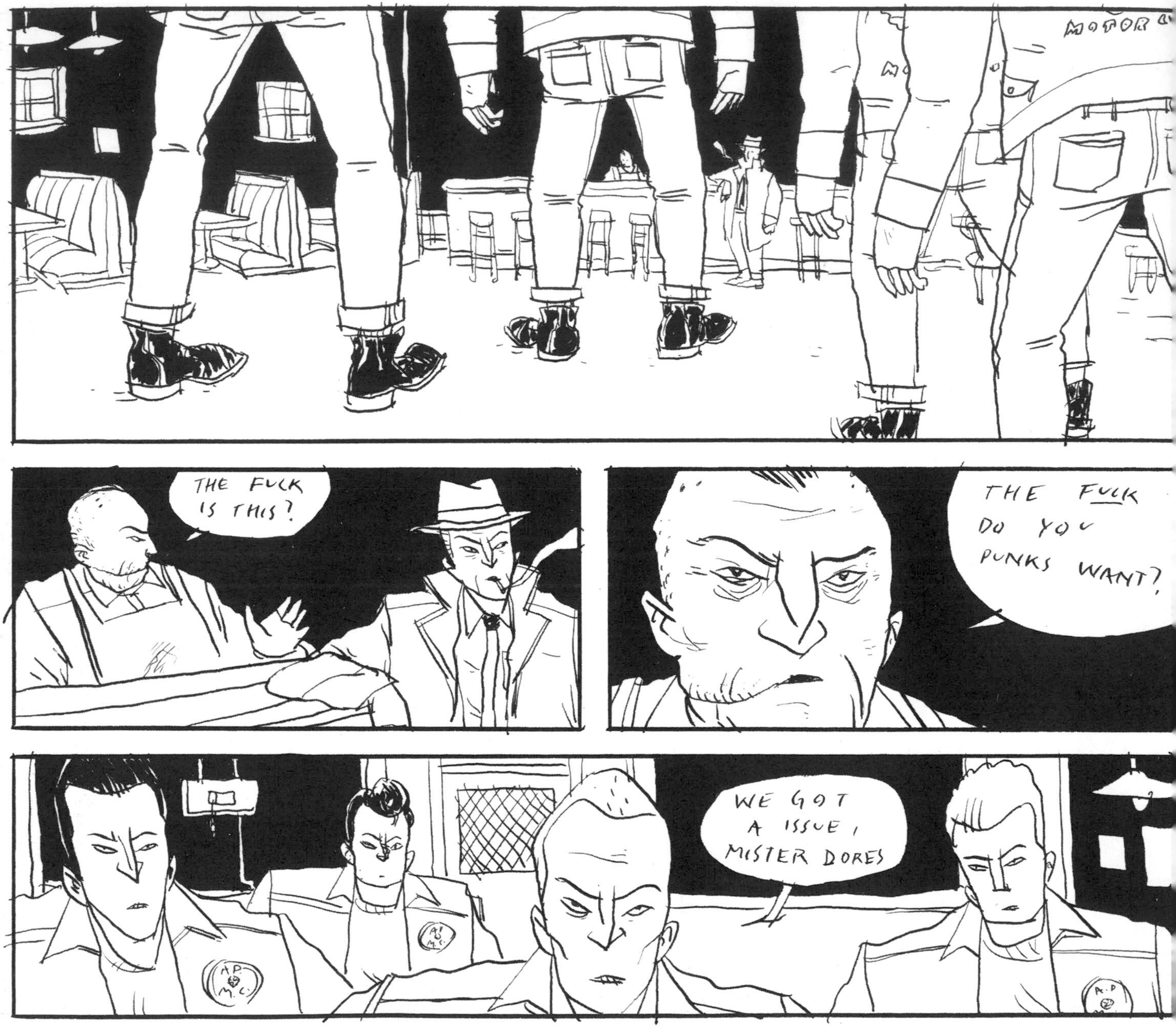
MOTOR
THE FUCK IS THIS?
THE FUCK DO YOU PUNKS WANT?
WE GOT A ISSUE, MISTER DORES

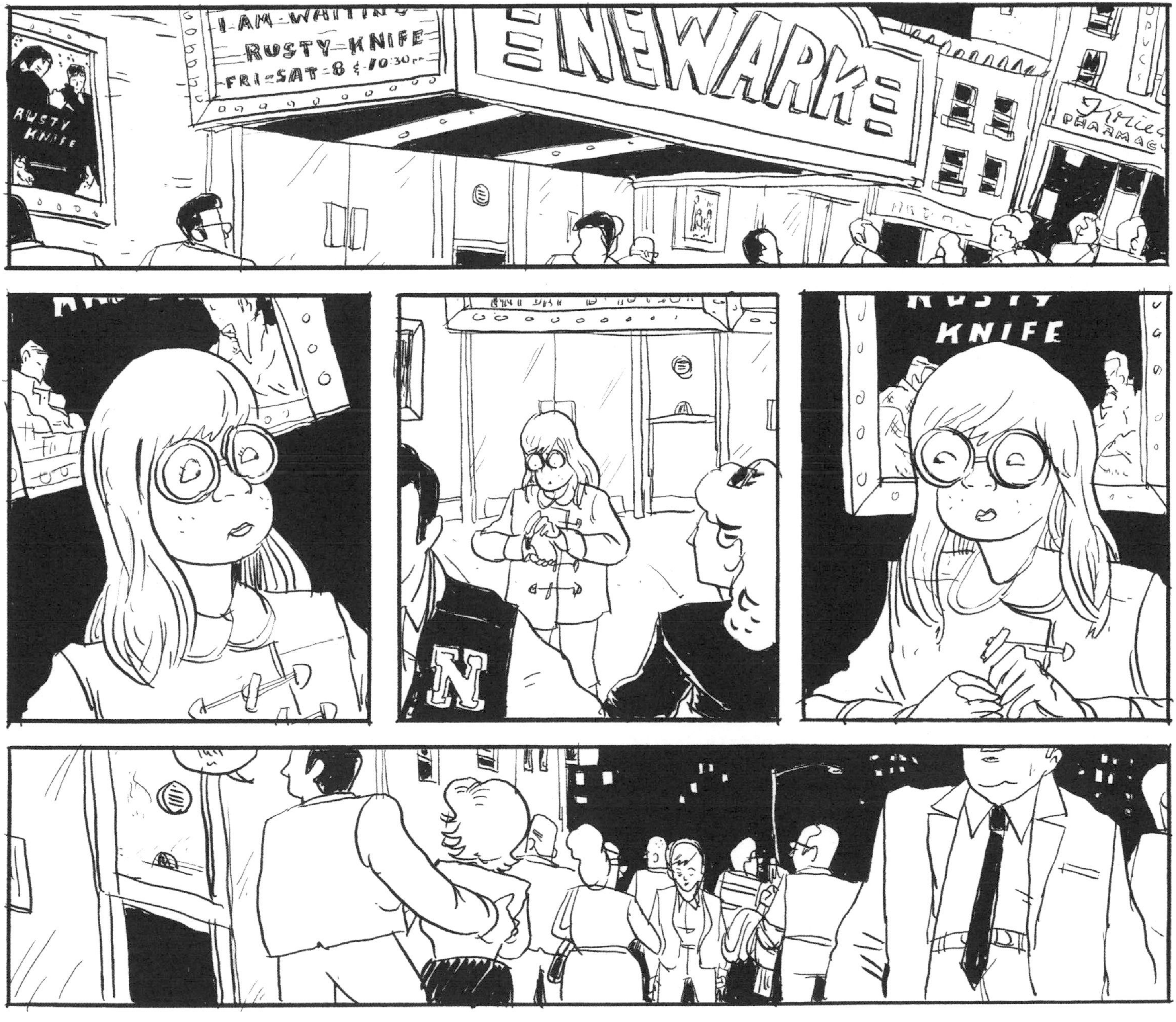
RUSTY KNIFE
FRI-SAT 8 & 10:30
NEWARK
RUSTY KNIFE
KNIFE

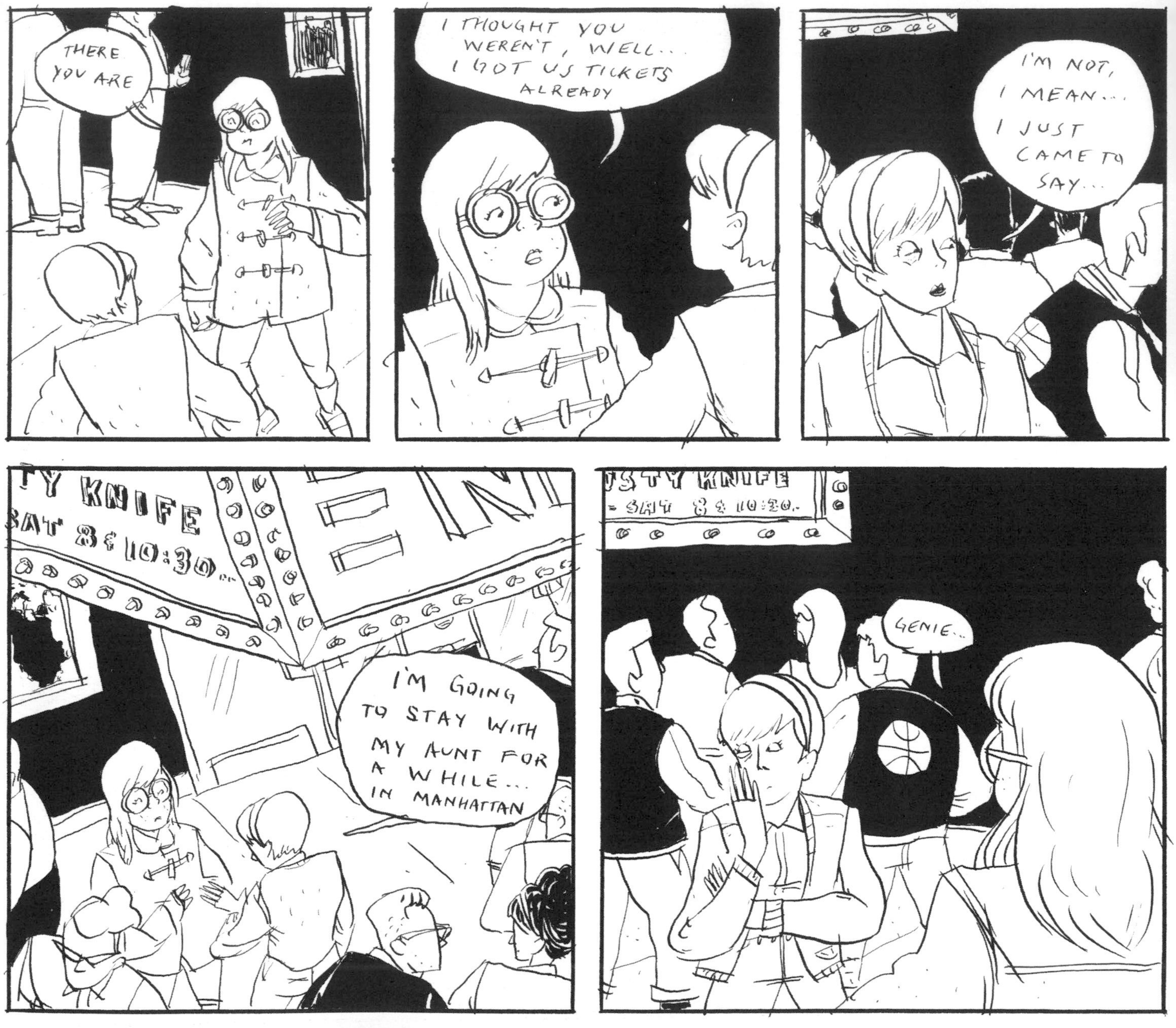
THERE YOU ARE
I THOUGHT YOU WEREN'T, WELL... I GOT US TICKETS ALREADY
I'M NOT, I MEAN... I JUST CAME TO SAY...
TY KNIFE
SAT 8 & 10:30
I'M GOING TO STAY WITH MY AUNT FOR A WHILE... IN MANHATTAN
STY KNIFE
SAT 8 & 10:30.
GENIE...

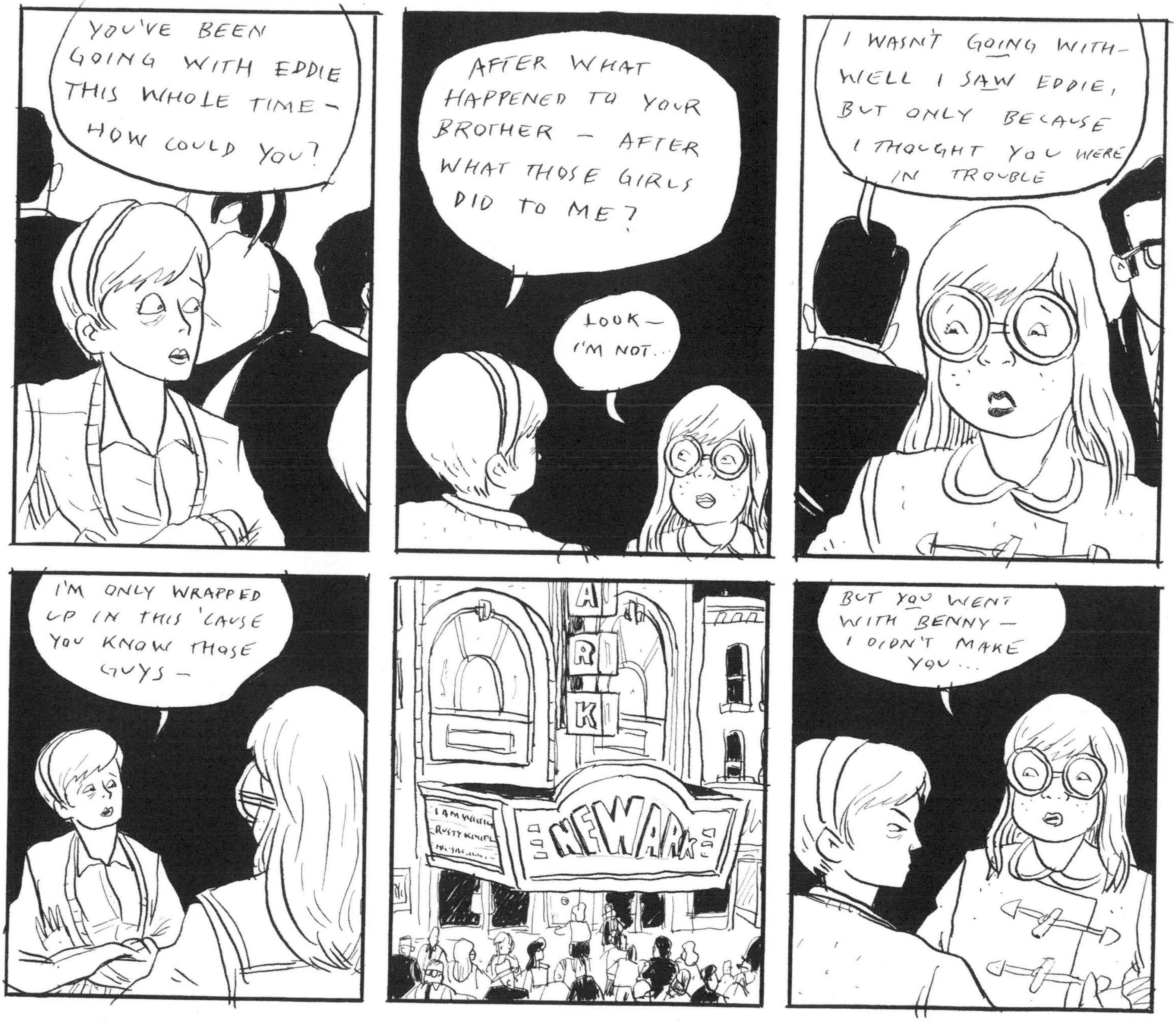
YOU'VE BEEN GOING WITH EDDIE THIS WHOLE TIME- HOW COULD YOU?
AFTER WHAT HAPPENED TO YOUR BROTHER - AFTER WHAT THOSE GIRLS DID TO ME?
LOOK- I'M NOT...
I WASN'T GOING WITH- WELL I SAW EDDIE, BUT ONLY BECAUSE I THOUGHT YOU WERE IN TROUBLE
I'M ONLY WRAPPED UP IN THIS 'CAUSE YOU KNOW THOSE GUYS-
NEWARK
BUT YOU WENT WITH BENNY- I DIDN'T MAKE YOU...

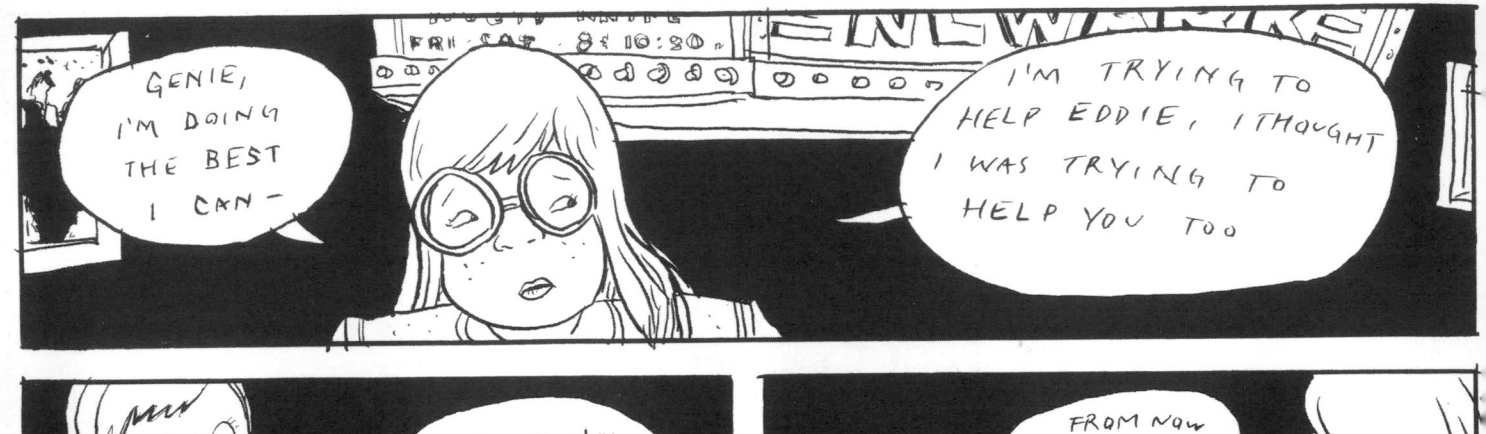

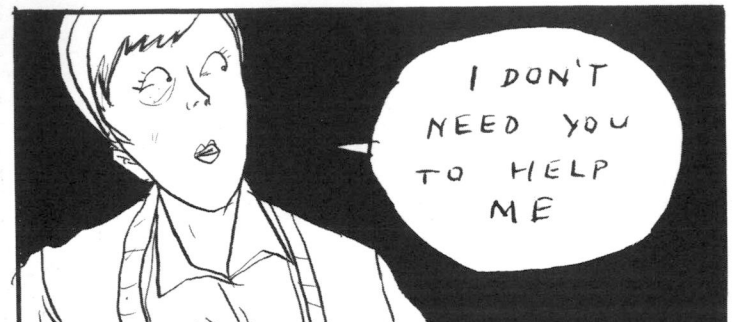

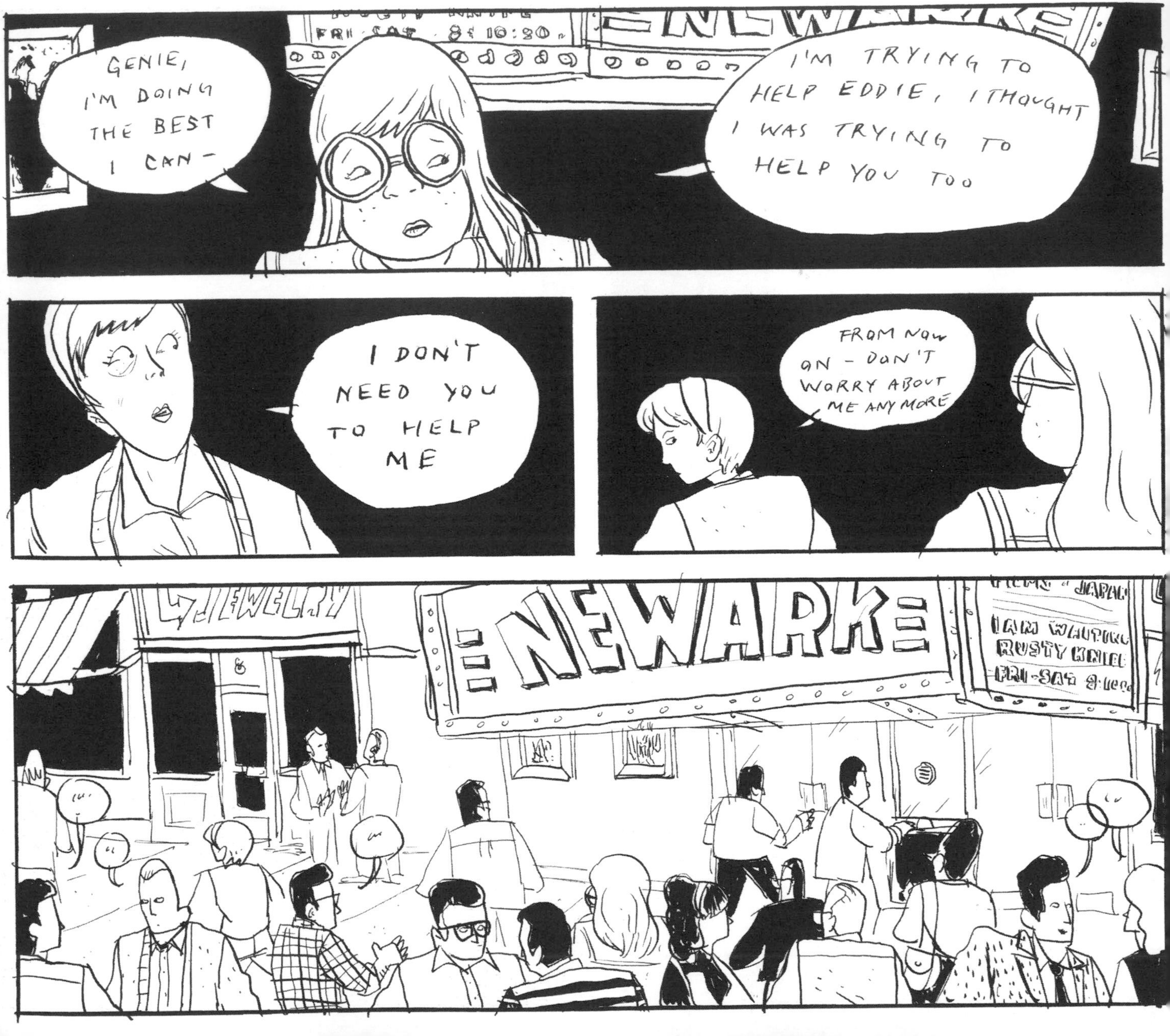
GENIE, I'M DOING THE BEST I CAN-
I'M TRYING TO HELP EDDIE, I THOUGHT I WAS TRYING TO HELP YOU TOO
I DON'T NEED YOU TO HELP ME
FROM NOW ON - DON'T WORRY ABOUT ME ANYMORE
NEWARK

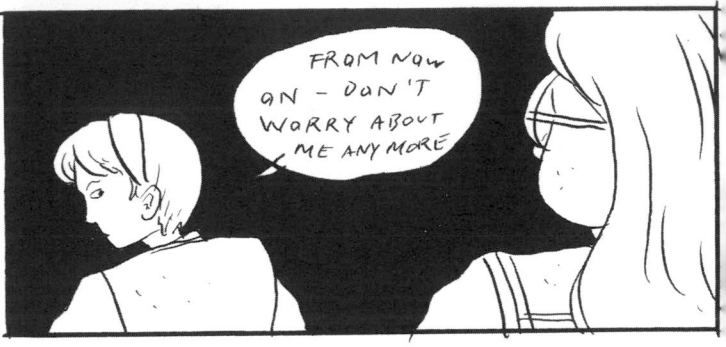

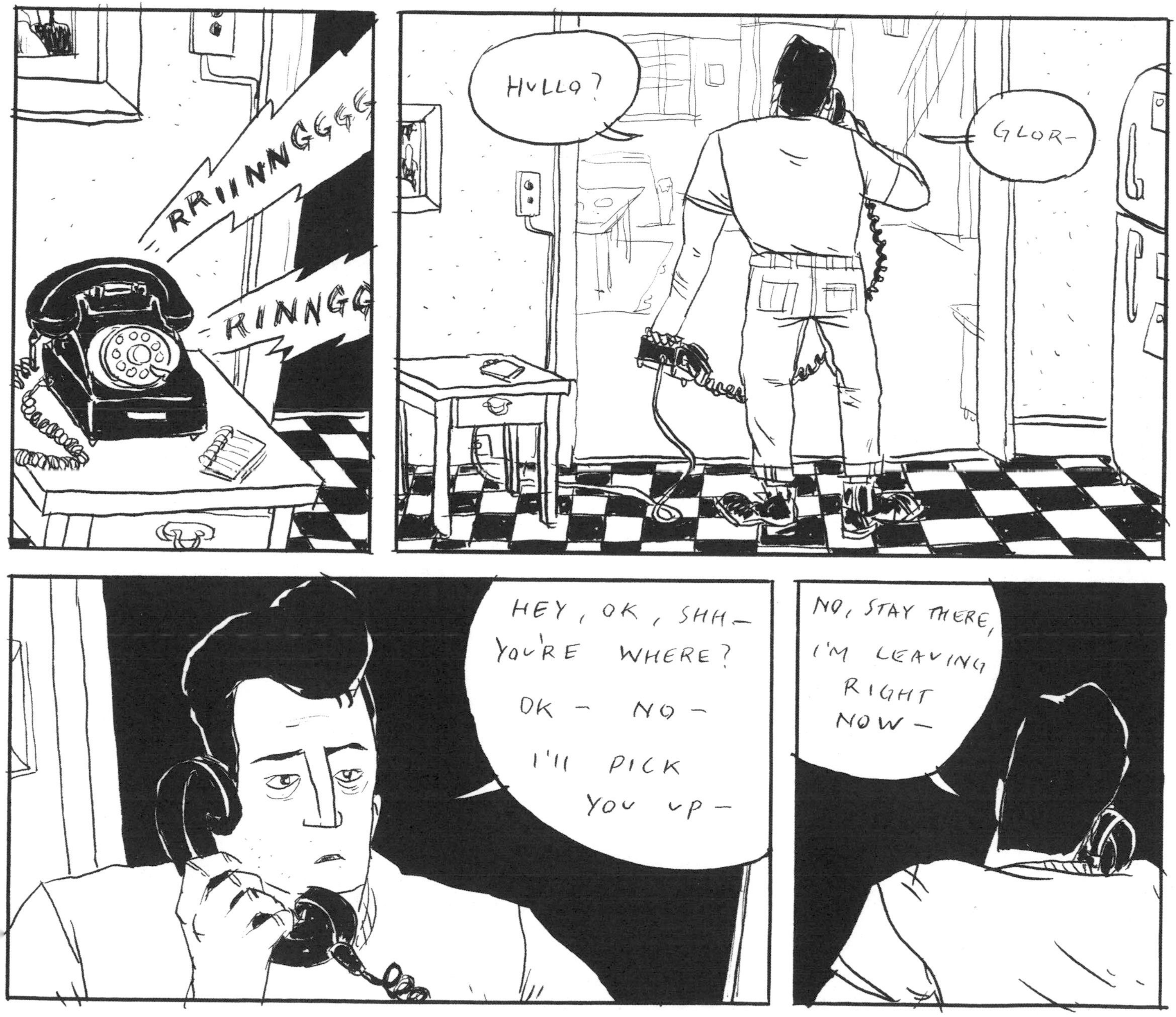
RRIINNGGGG
RINNGG
HULLO?
GLOR-
HEY, OK, SHH-
YOU'RE WHERE?
OK - NO -
I'LL PICK YOU UP-
NO, STAY THERE,
I'M LEAVING RIGHT NOW-

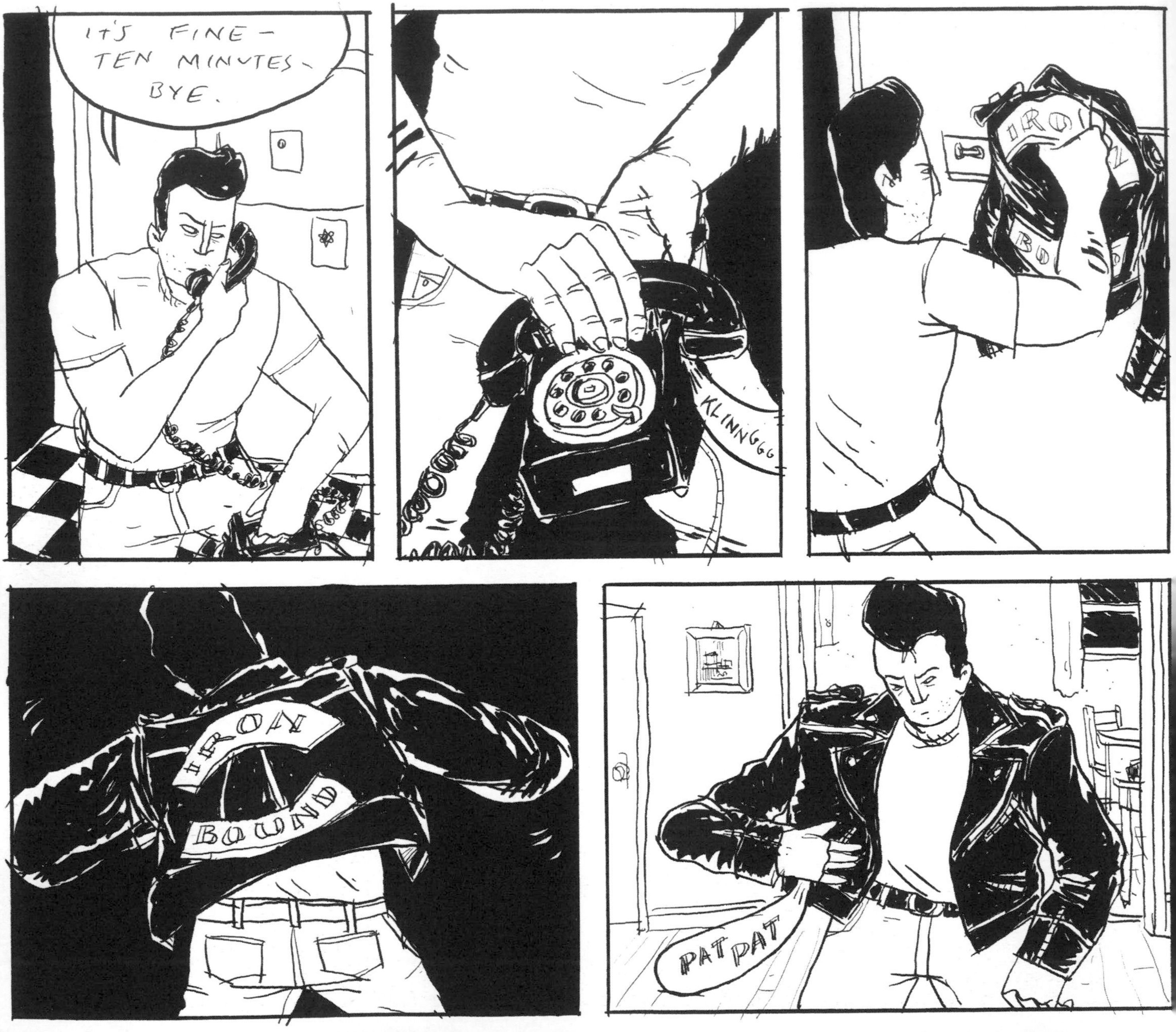
IT'S FINE - TEN MINUTES - BYE.
KLINNGGG
IRON
BOUND
PAT PAT

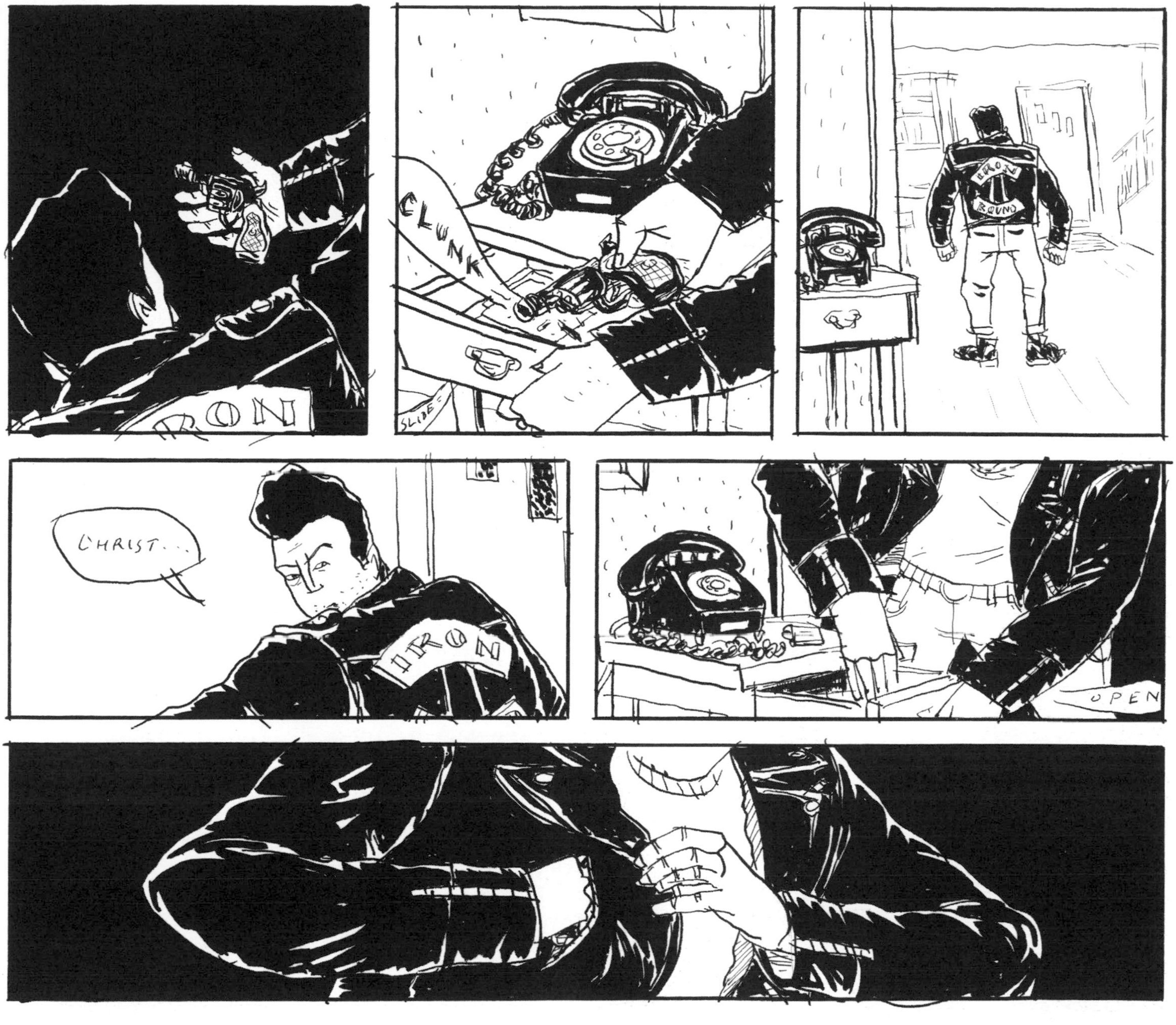
IRON
CLUNK
SLIDE
IRON
BOUND
CHRIST...
IRON
OPEN

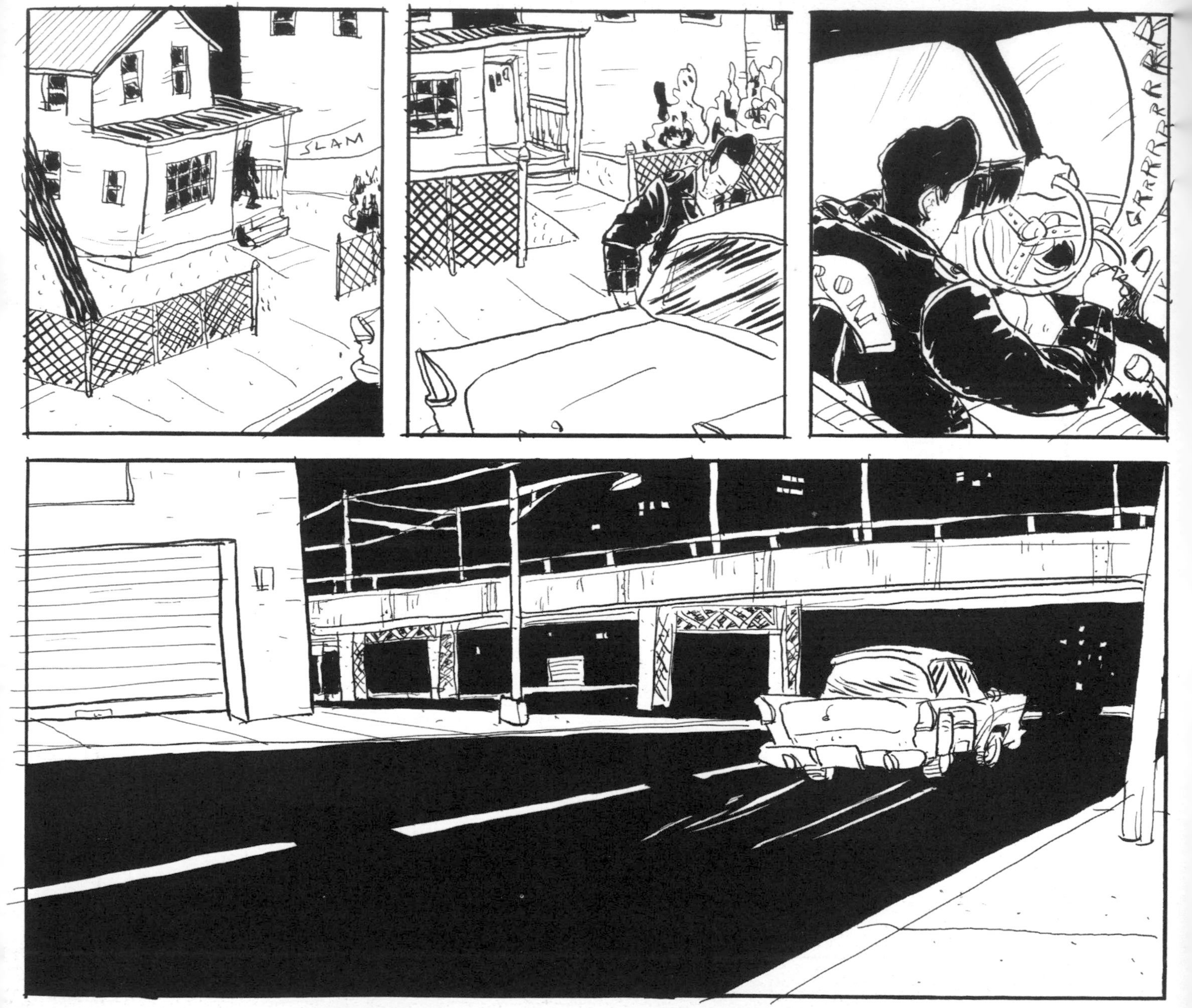
SLAM
GRRRRRRRRR

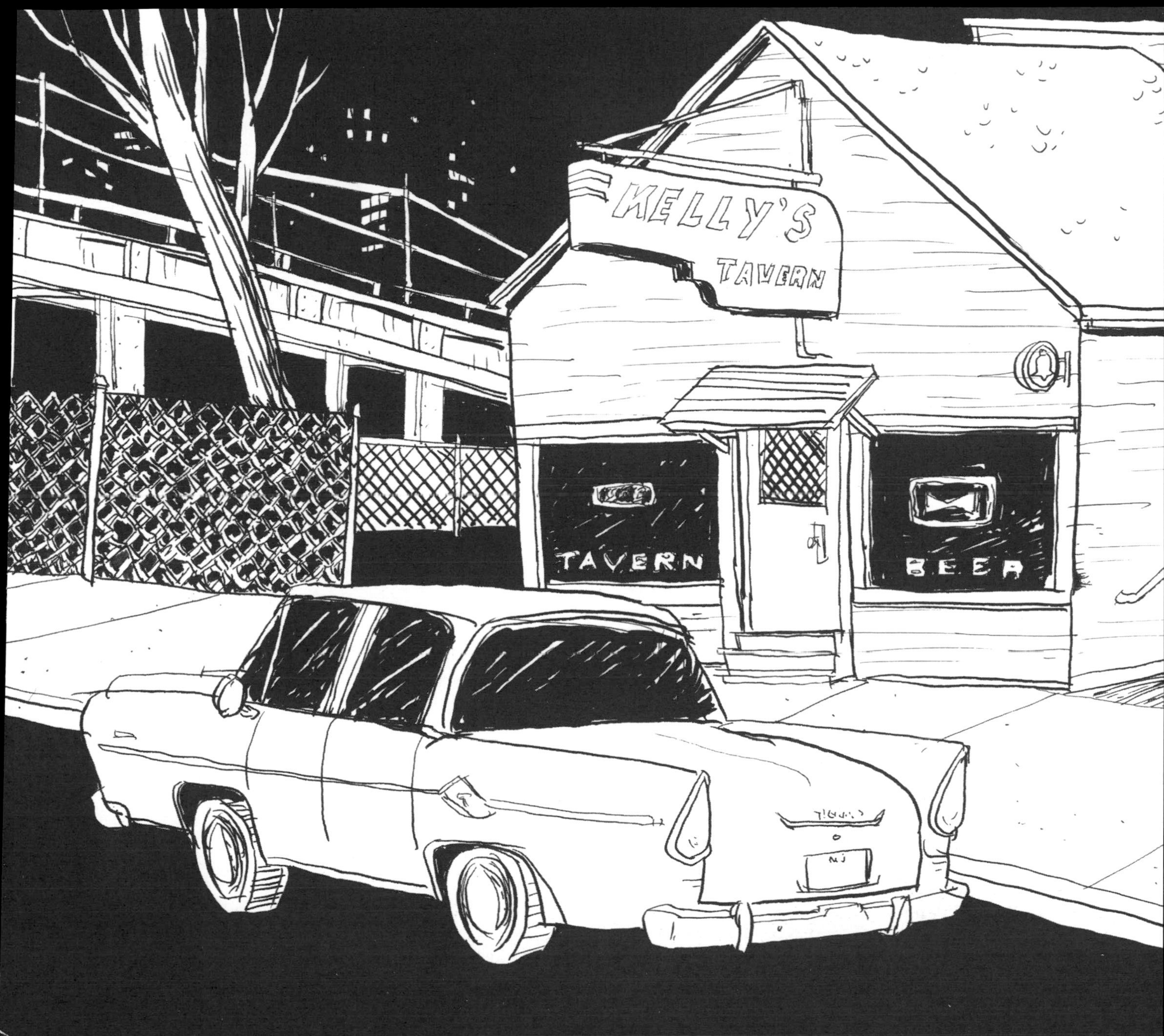
KELLY'S
TAVERN
TAVERN
BEER

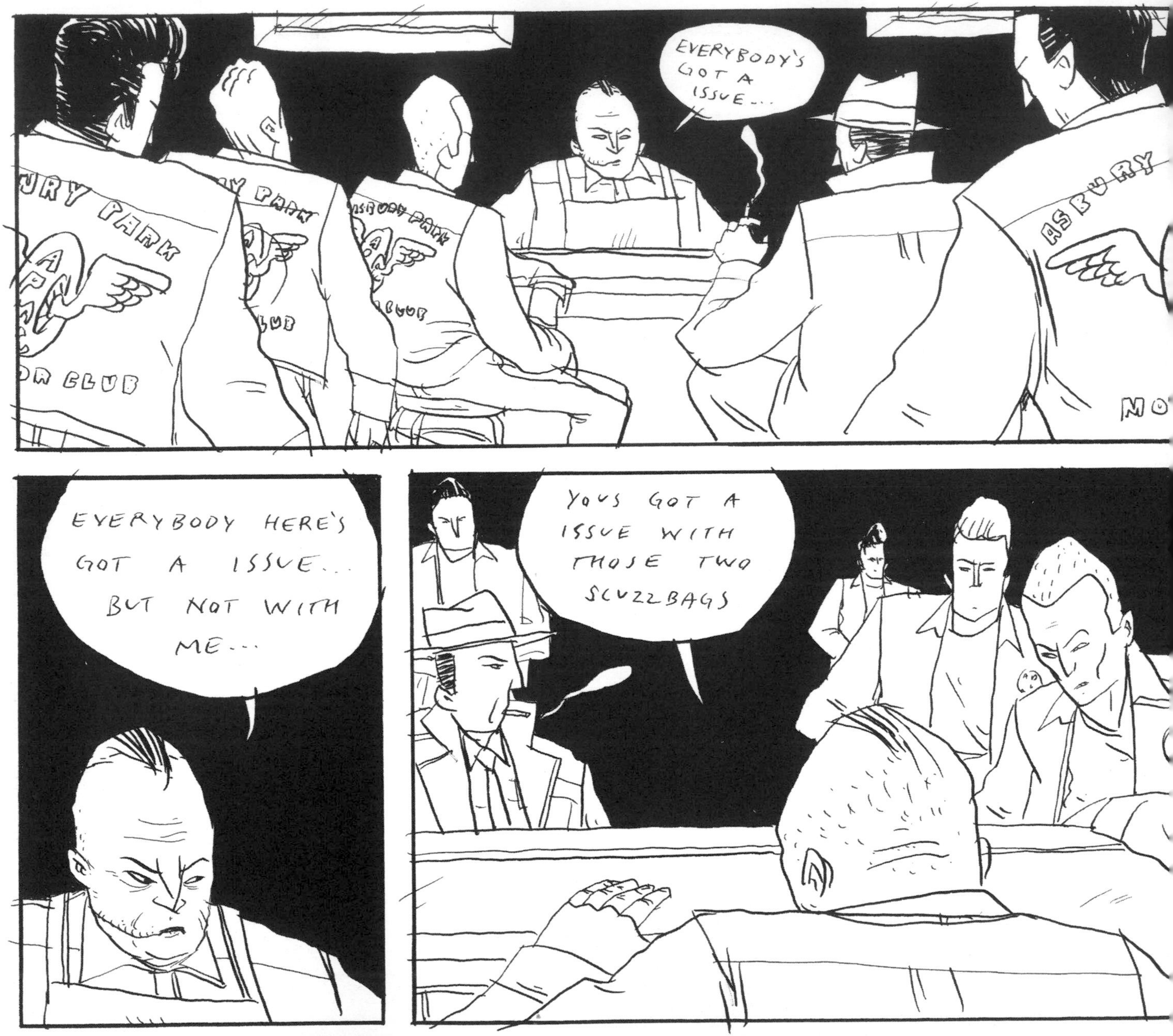
EVERYBODY'S GOT A ISSUE...
ASBURY
EVERYBODY HERE'S GOT A ISSUE... BUT NOT WITH ME...
YOUS GOT A ISSUE WITH THOSE TWO SCUZZBAGS

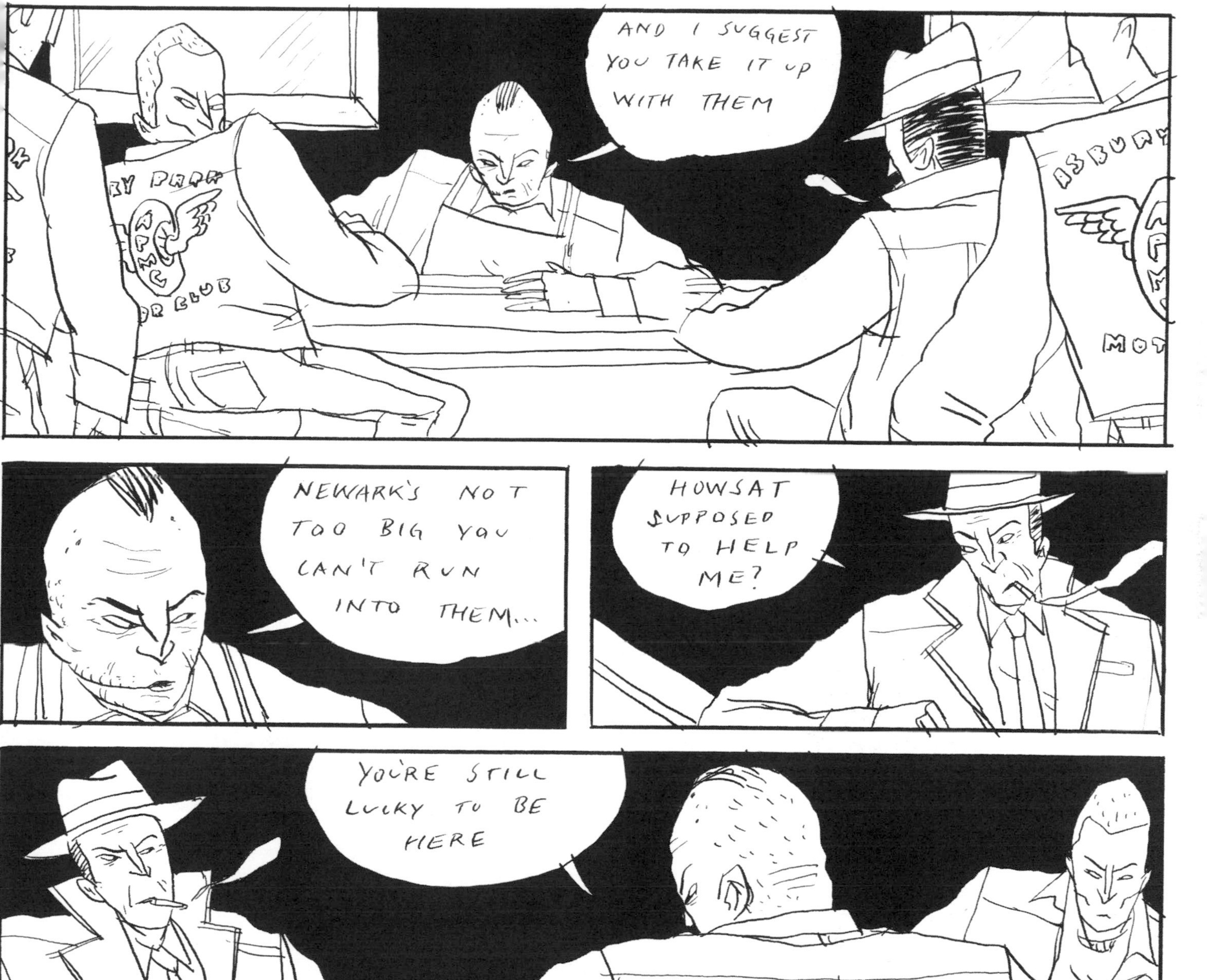

AND I SUGGEST YOU TAKE IT UP WITH THEM
ASBURY
NEWARK'S NOT TOO BIG YOU CAN'T RUN INTO THEM...
HOWSAT SUPPOSED TO HELP ME?
YOU'RE STILL LUCKY TO BE HERE

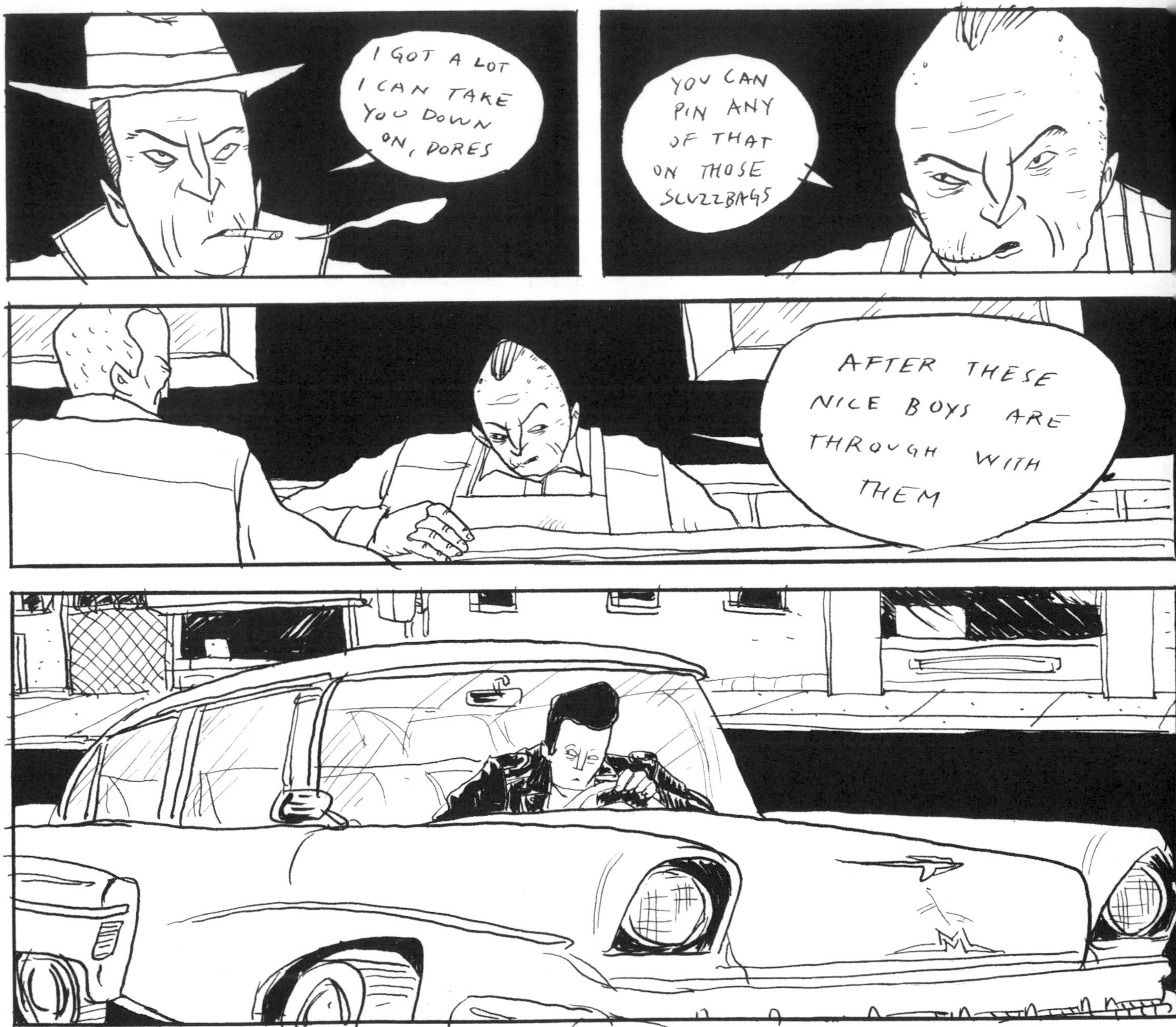
I GOT A LOT I CAN TAKE YOU DOWN ON, DORES
YOU CAN PIN ANY OF THAT ON THOSE SCUZZBAGS
AFTER THESE NICE BOYS ARE THROUGH WITH THEM

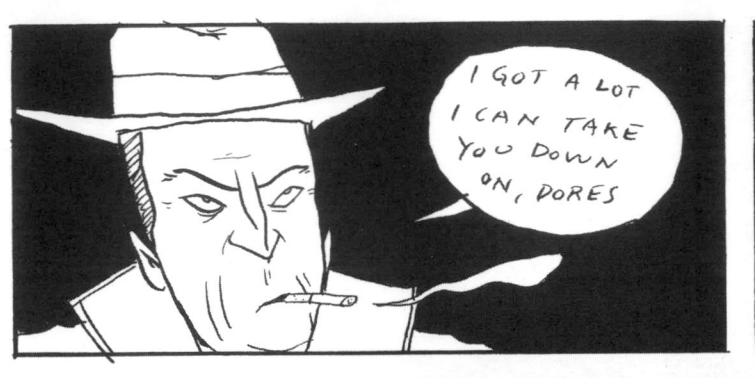

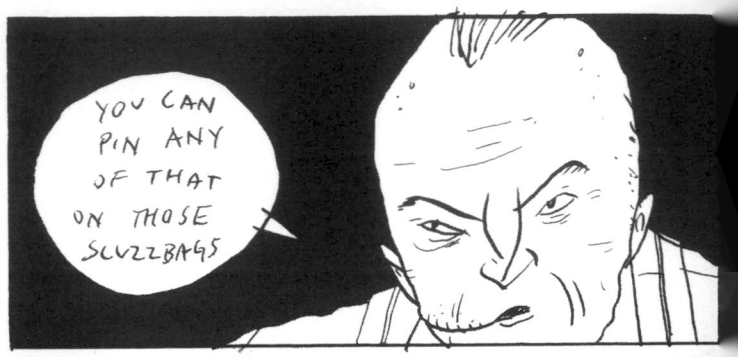

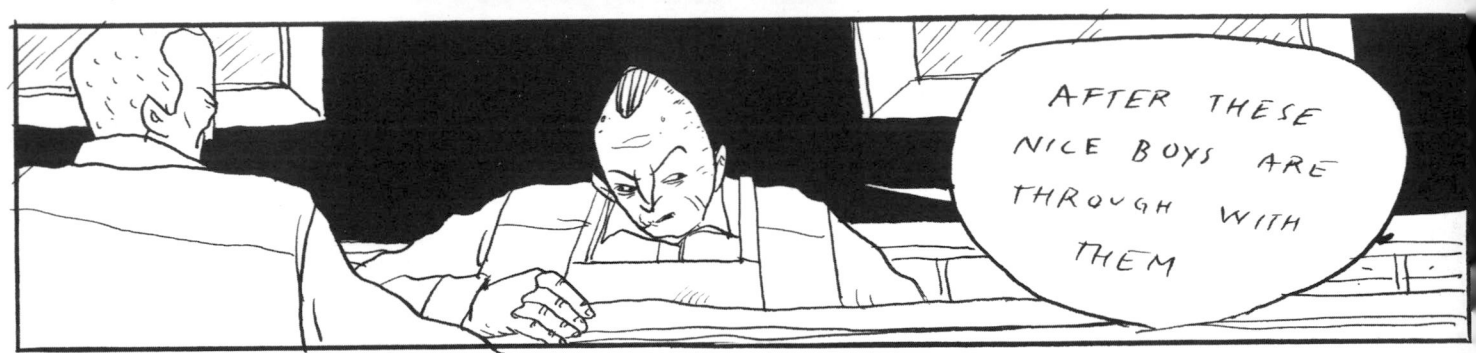

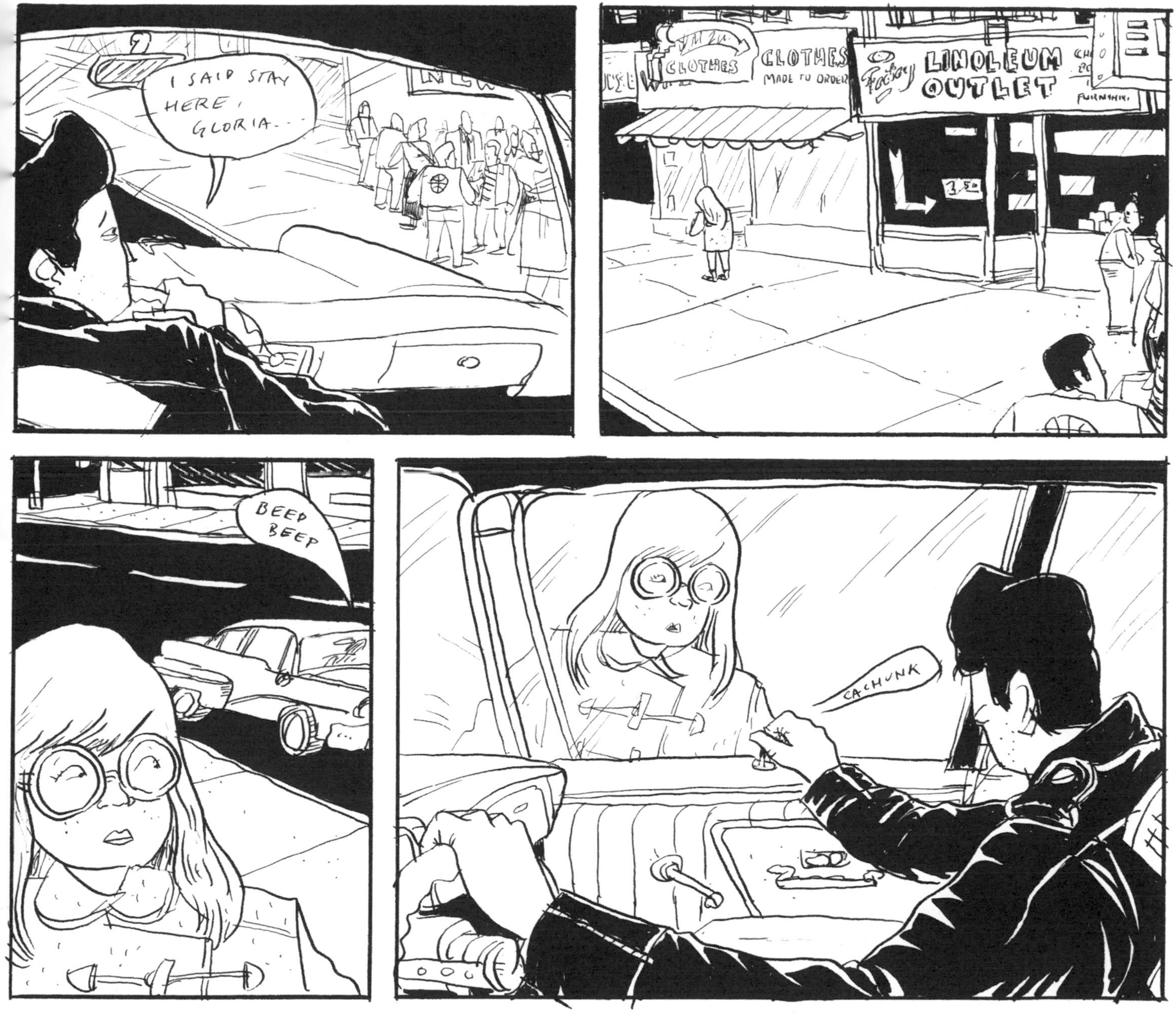
I SAID STAY HERE, GLORIA...
CLOTHES
CLOTHES MADE TO ORDER
Factory LINOLEUM OUTLET
3.50
BEEP BEEP
CACHUNK

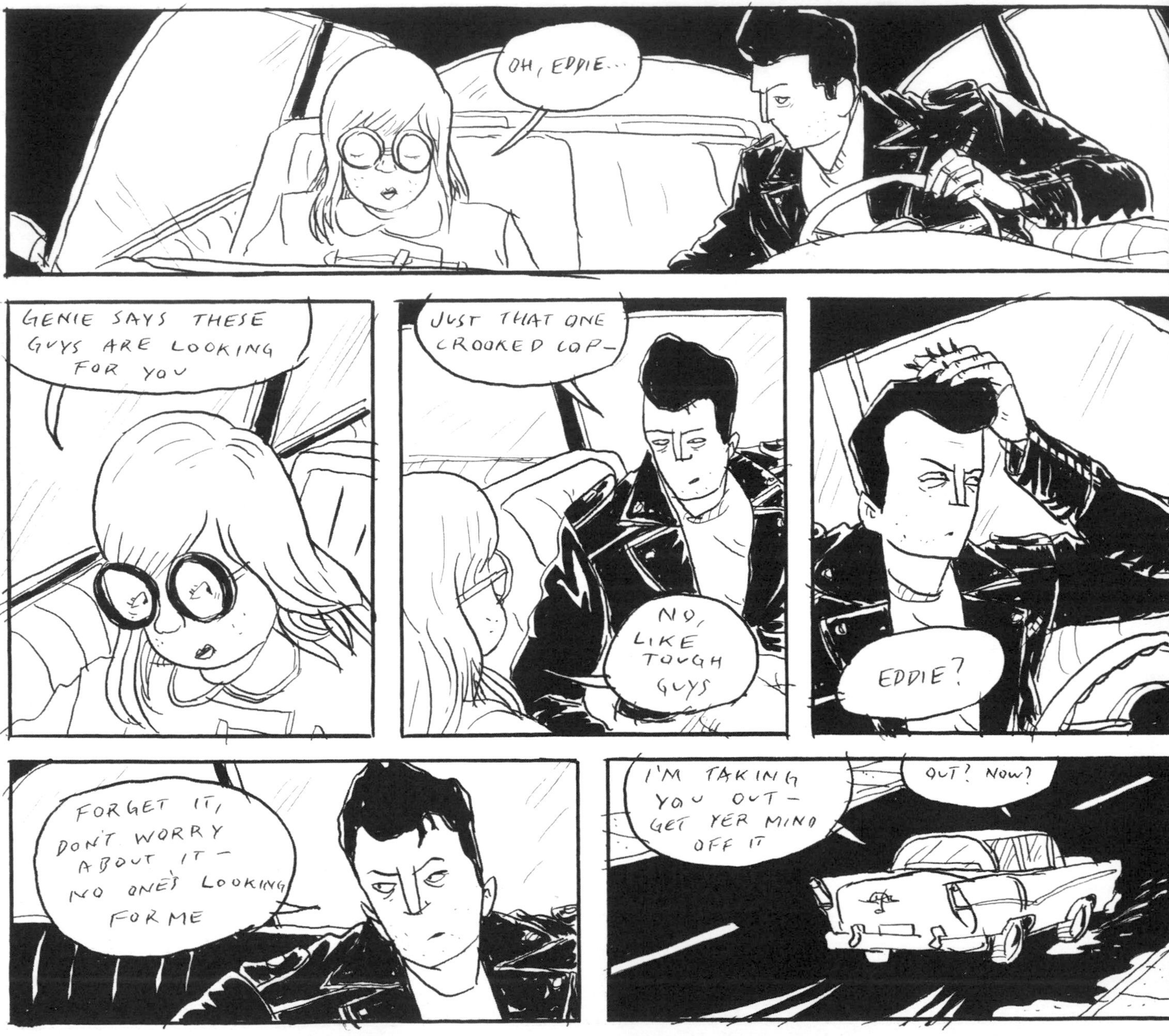
OH, EDDIE...
GENIE SAYS THESE GUYS ARE LOOKING FOR YOU
JUST THAT ONE CROOKED COP—
NO, LIKE TOUGH GUYS
EDDIE?
FORGET IT, DON'T WORRY ABOUT IT— NO ONE'S LOOKING FOR ME
I'M TAKING YOU OUT— GET YER MIND OFF IT
OUT? NOW?

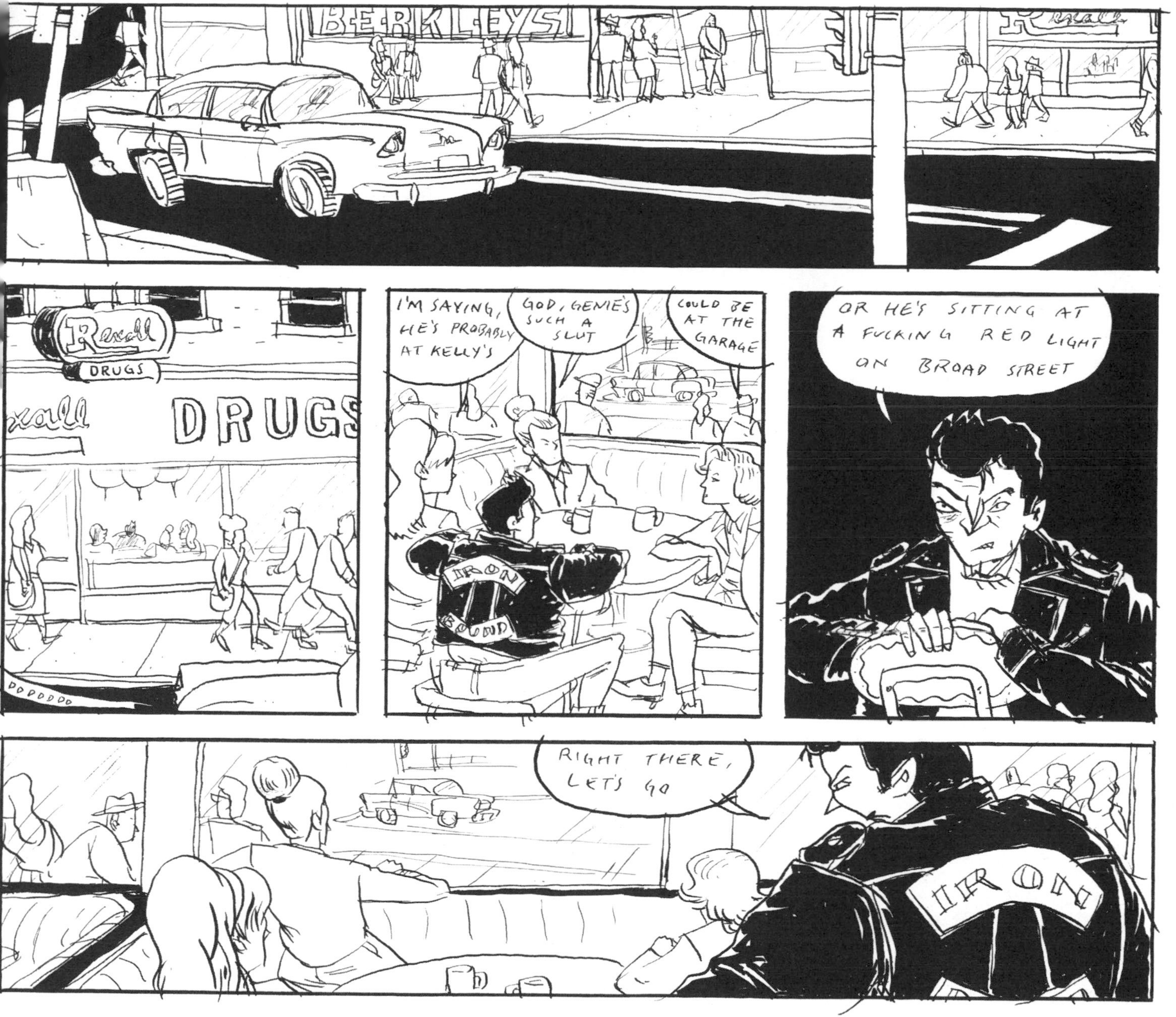
BERKLEYS
Rexall
Rexall
DRUGS
DRUGS
I'M SAYING, HE'S PROBABLY AT KELLY'S
GOD, GENIE'S SUCH A SLUT
COULD BE AT THE GARAGE
IRON
BOUND
OR HE'S SITTING AT A FUCKING RED LIGHT ON BROAD STREET
RIGHT THERE, LET'S GO
IRON

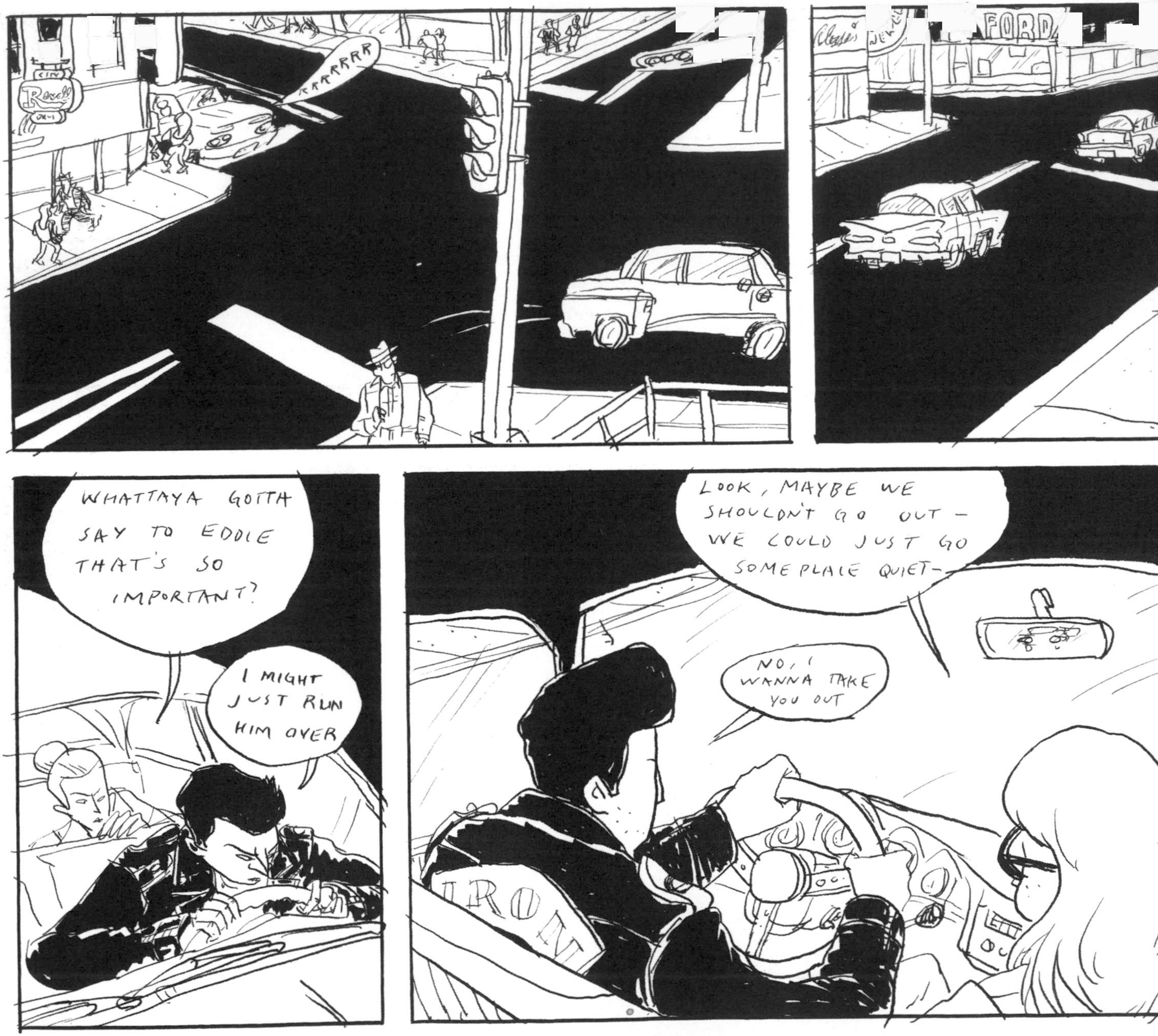
FORD
WHATTAYA GOTTA SAY TO EDDIE THAT'S SO IMPORTANT?
I MIGHT JUST RUN HIM OVER
LOOK, MAYBE WE SHOULDN'T GO OUT – WE COULD JUST GO SOMEPLACE QUIET –
NO, I WANNA TAKE YOU OUT
IRON

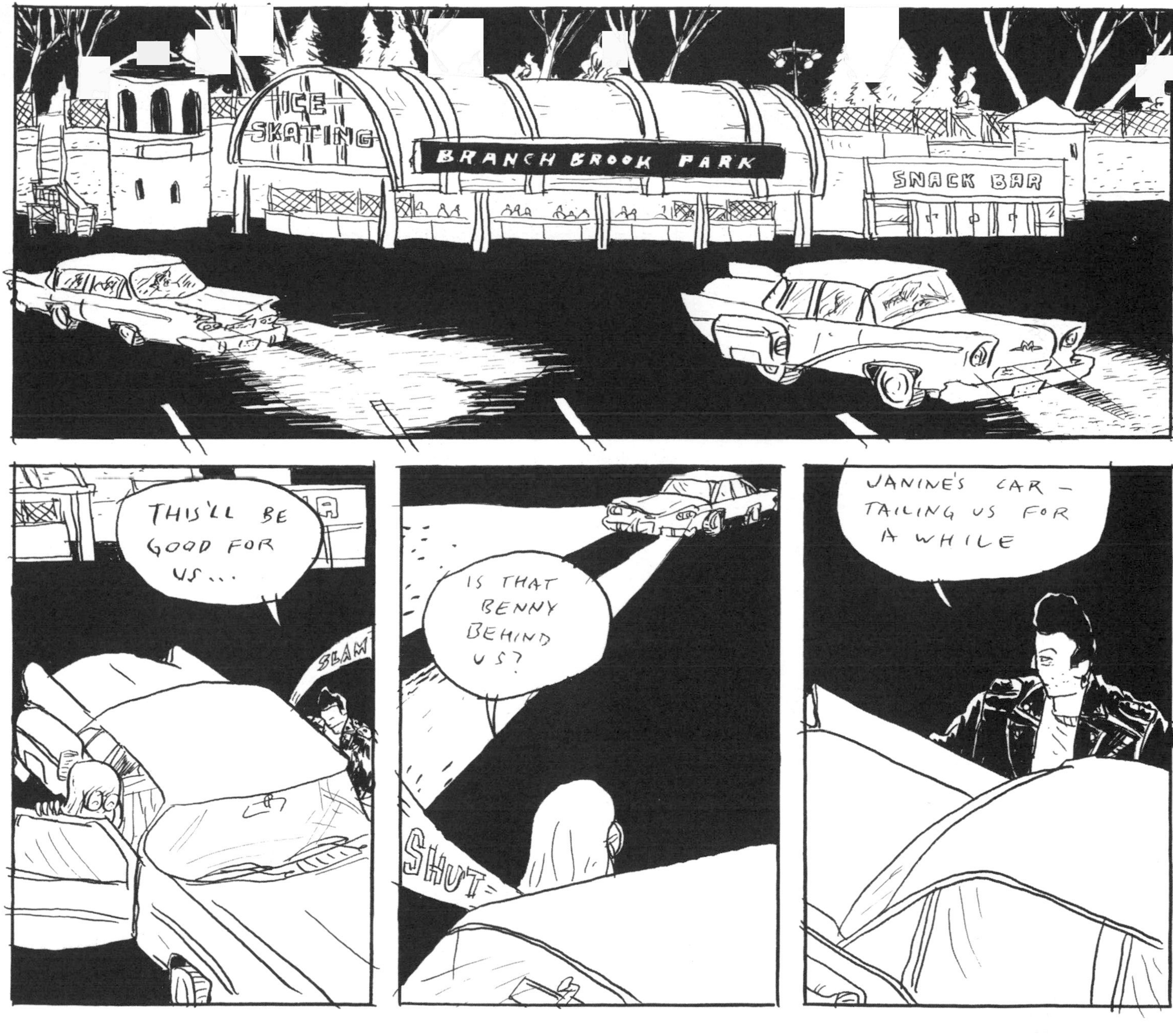
ICE SKATING
BRANCH BROOK PARK
SNACK BAR
THIS'LL BE GOOD FOR US...
SLAM
IS THAT BENNY BEHIND US?
SHUT
JANINE'S CAR — TAILING US FOR A WHILE

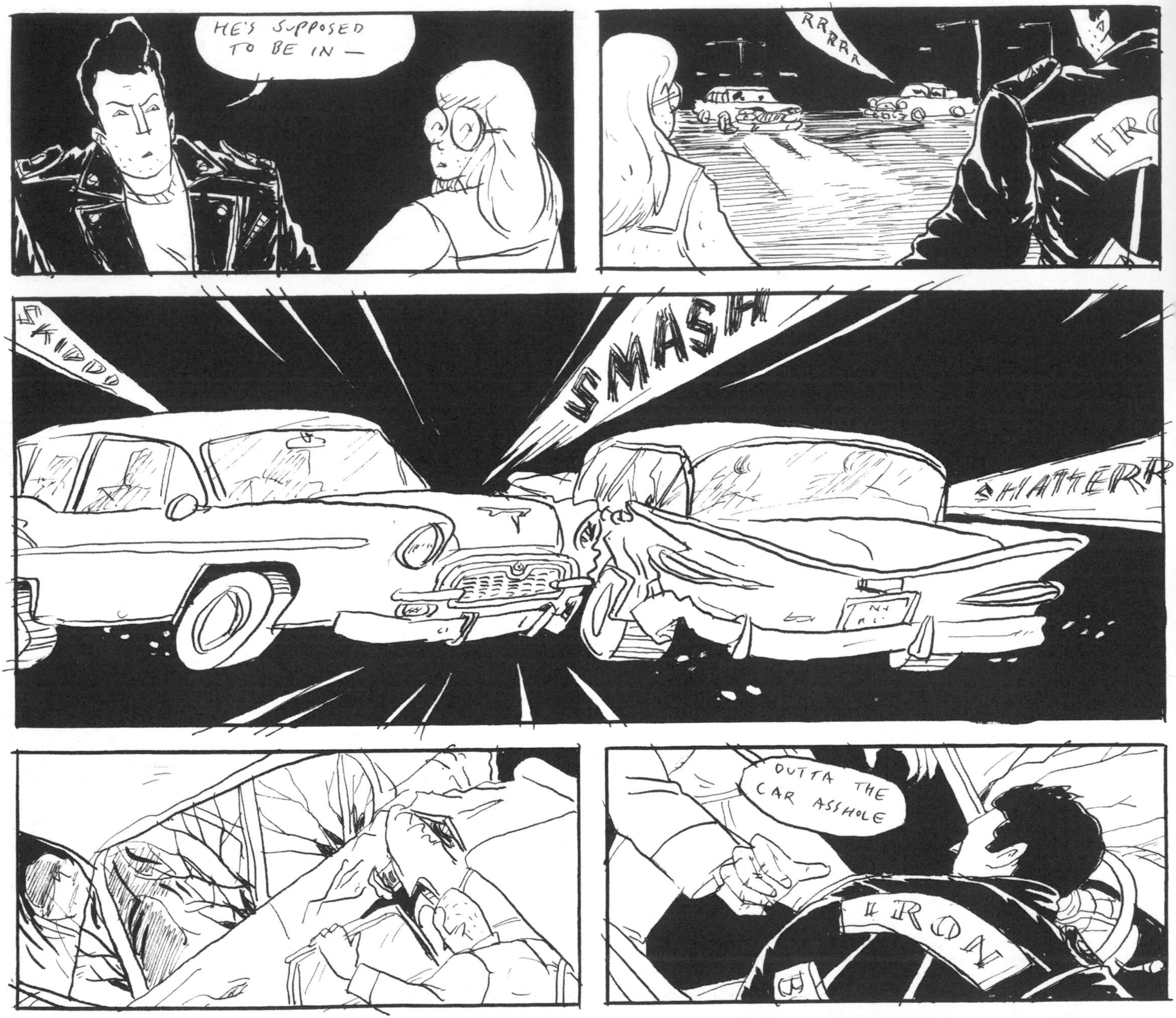
HE'S SUPPOSED TO BE IN—
RRRRRA
IRO
SKIDDD
SMASH
SHATTERR
OUTTA THE CAR ASSHOLE
IRON

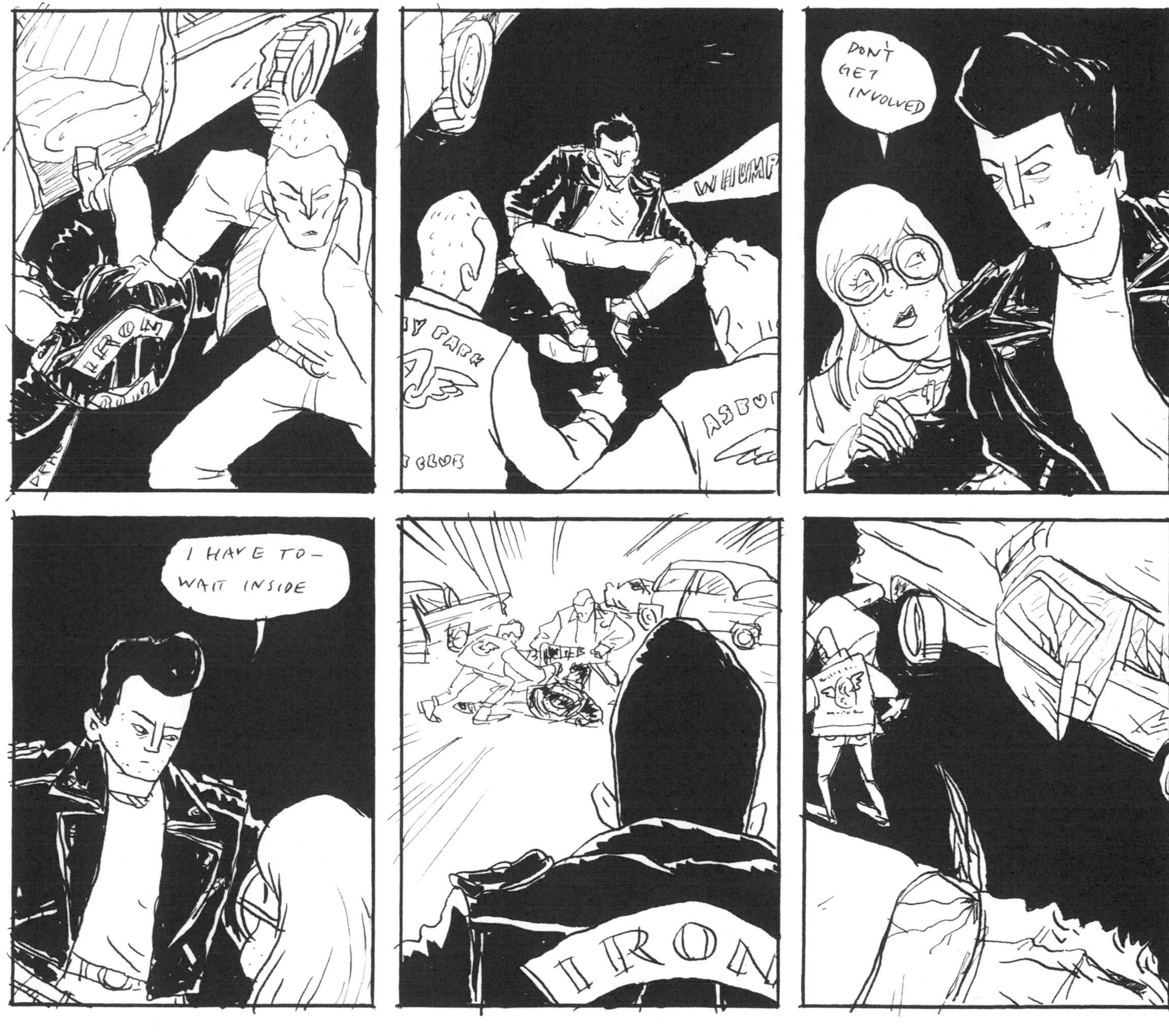

IRON
WHUMP
Y PARK
ASBU
DON'T GET INVOLVED
I HAVE TO-
WAIT INSIDE
IRON

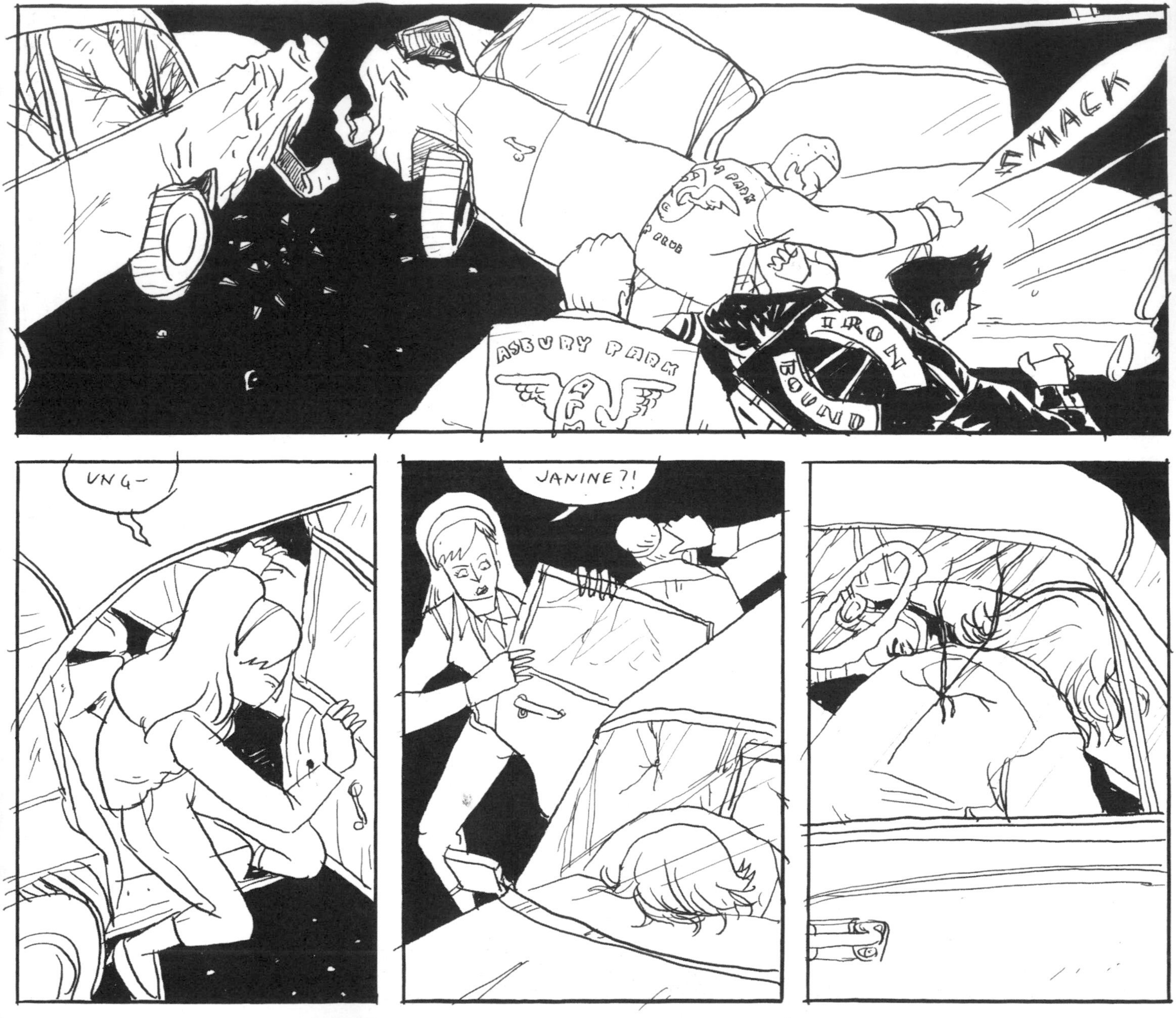
SMACK
ASBURY PARK
IRON BOUND
UNG-
JANINE?!

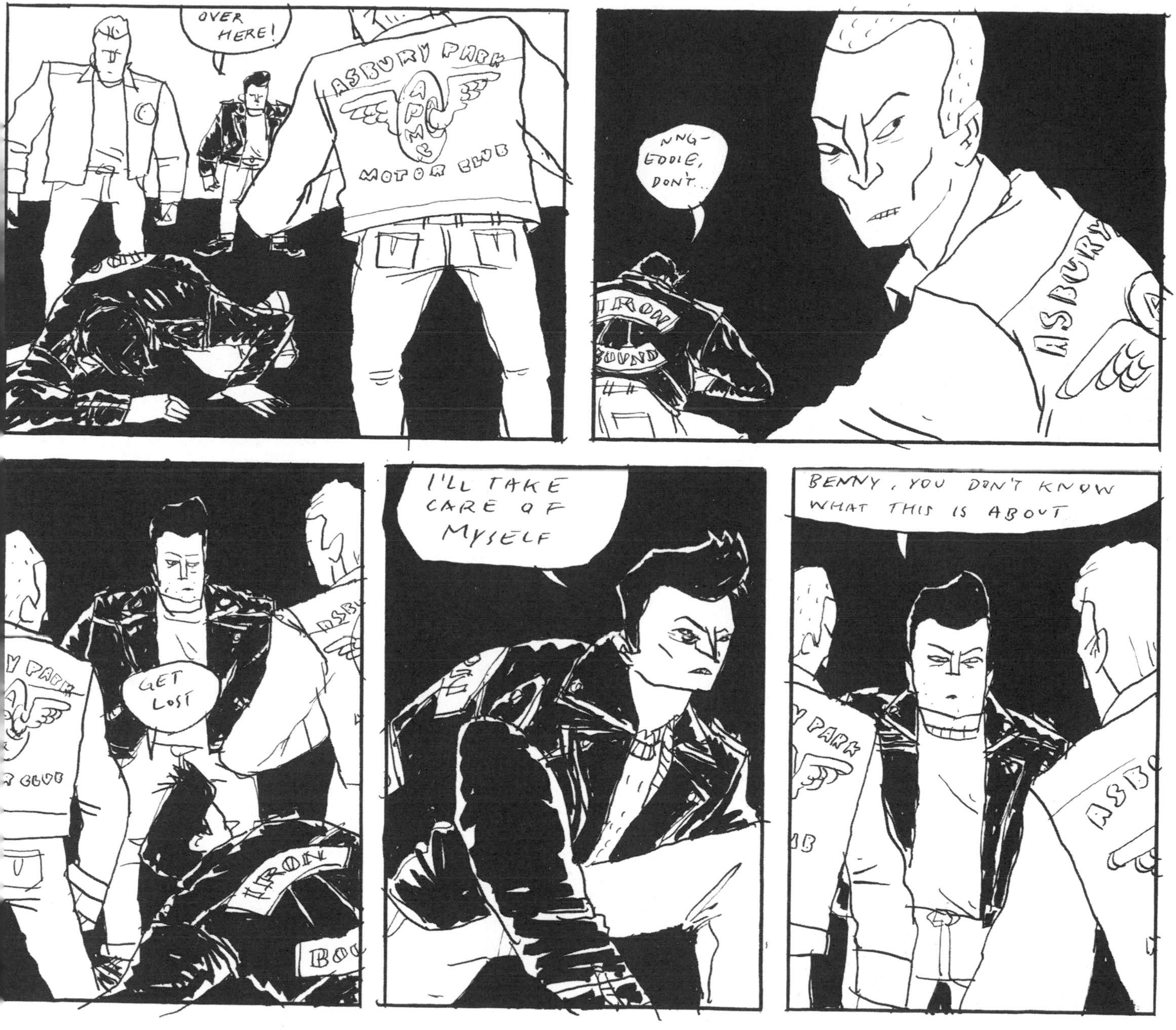
OVER HERE!
ASBURY PARK
APMC
MOTOR CLUB
NNG- EDDIE, DON'T...
ASBURY
IRON
BOUND
GET LOST
I'LL TAKE CARE OF MYSELF
BENNY, YOU DON'T KNOW WHAT THIS IS ABOUT

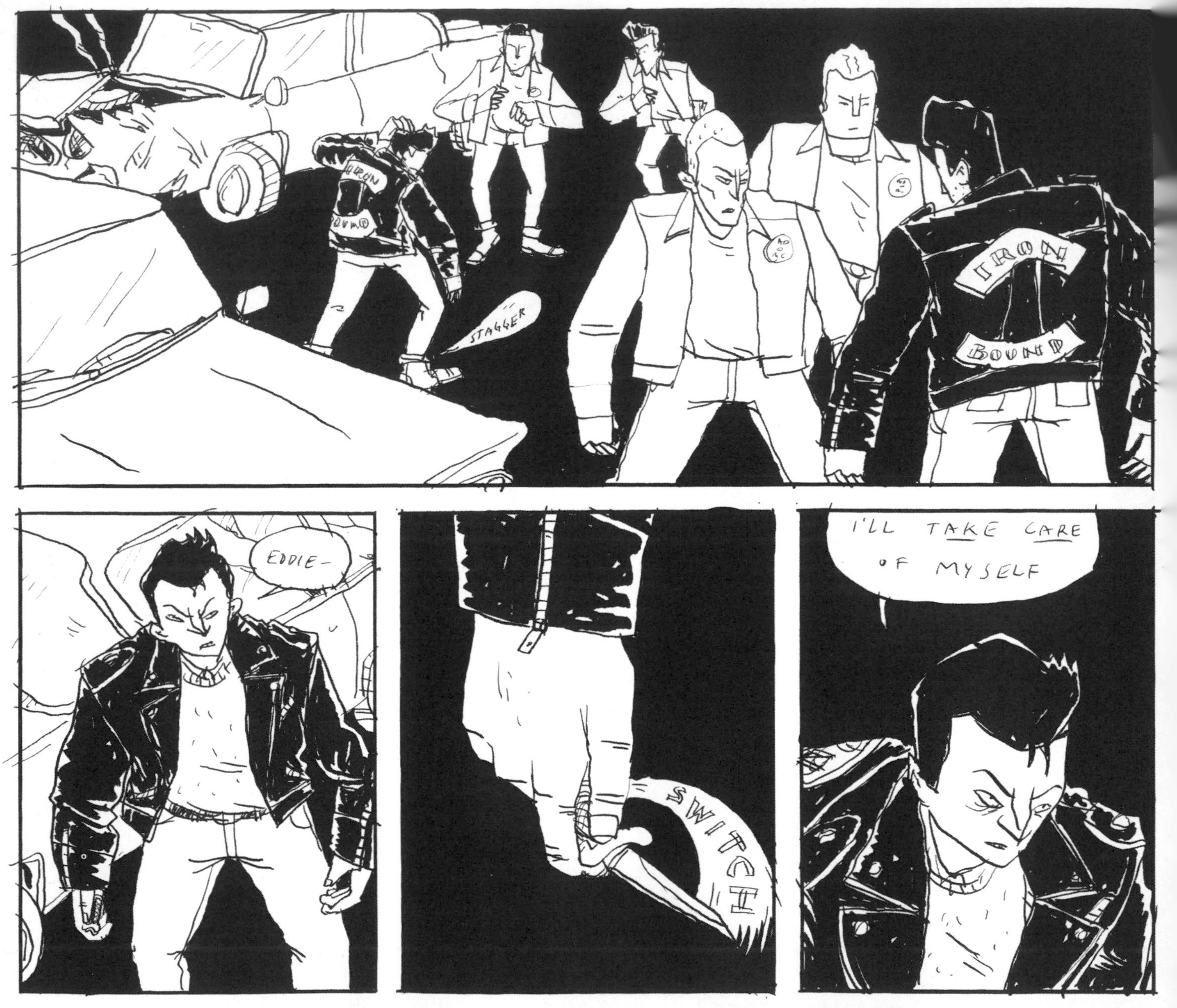
IRON
BOUND
STAGGER
IRON
BOUND
EDDIE-
SWITCH
I'LL TAKE CARE OF MYSELF

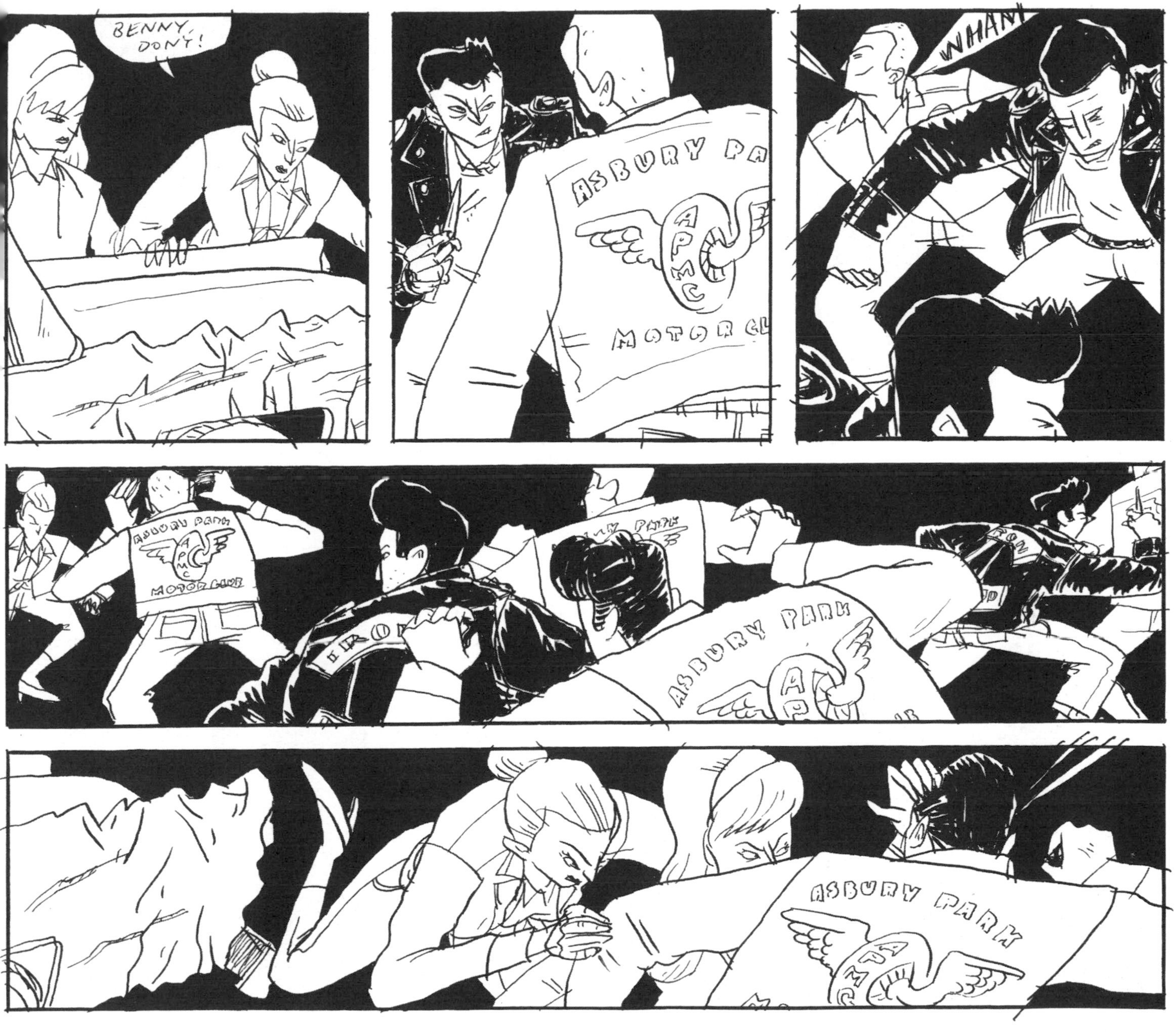
BENNY, DON'T!
WHAM
ASBURY PARK
MOTOR CLUB
ASBURY PARK
ASBURY PARK

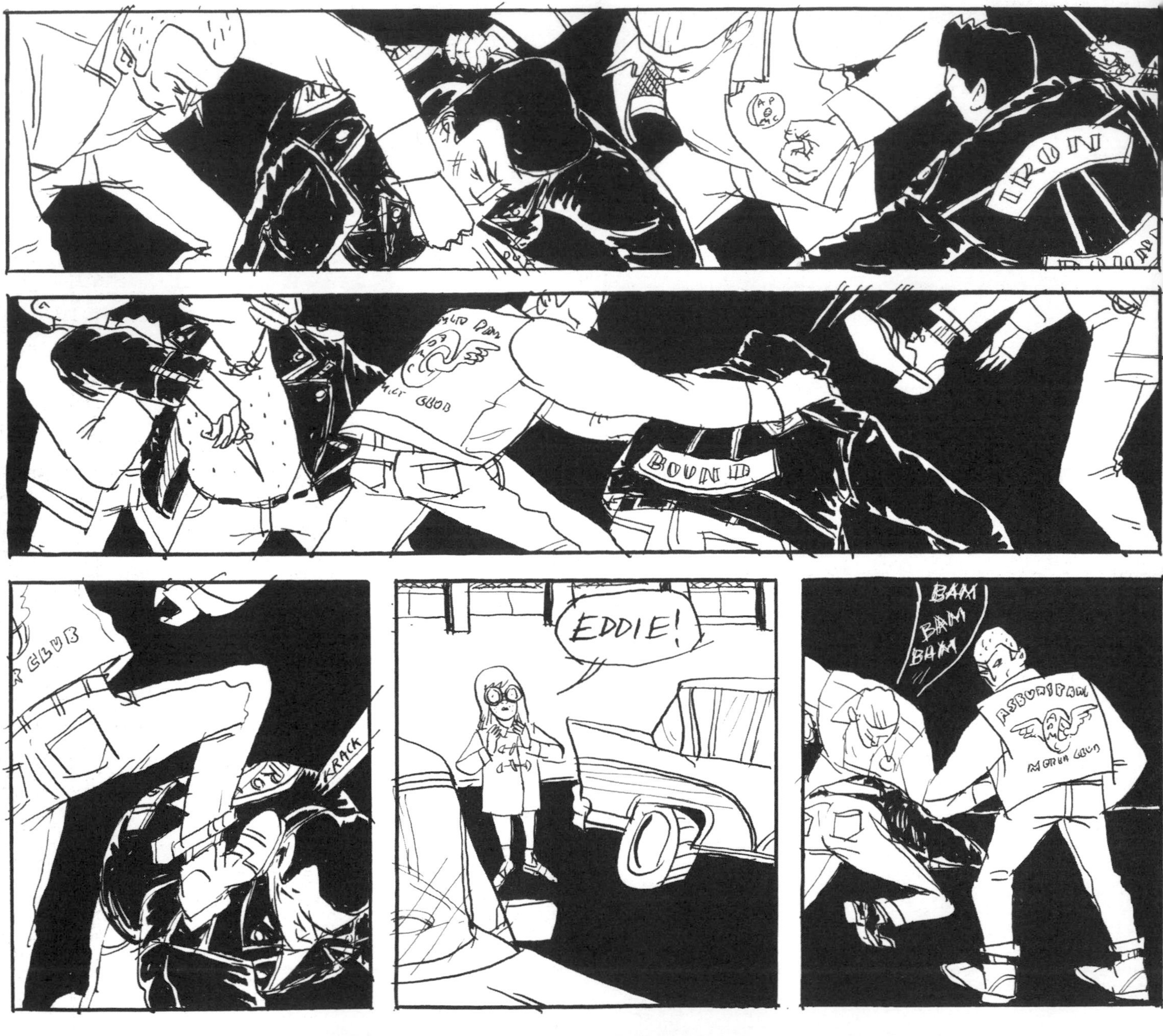

IRON
BOUND
R CLUB
KRACK
EDDIE!
BAM
BAM
BAM

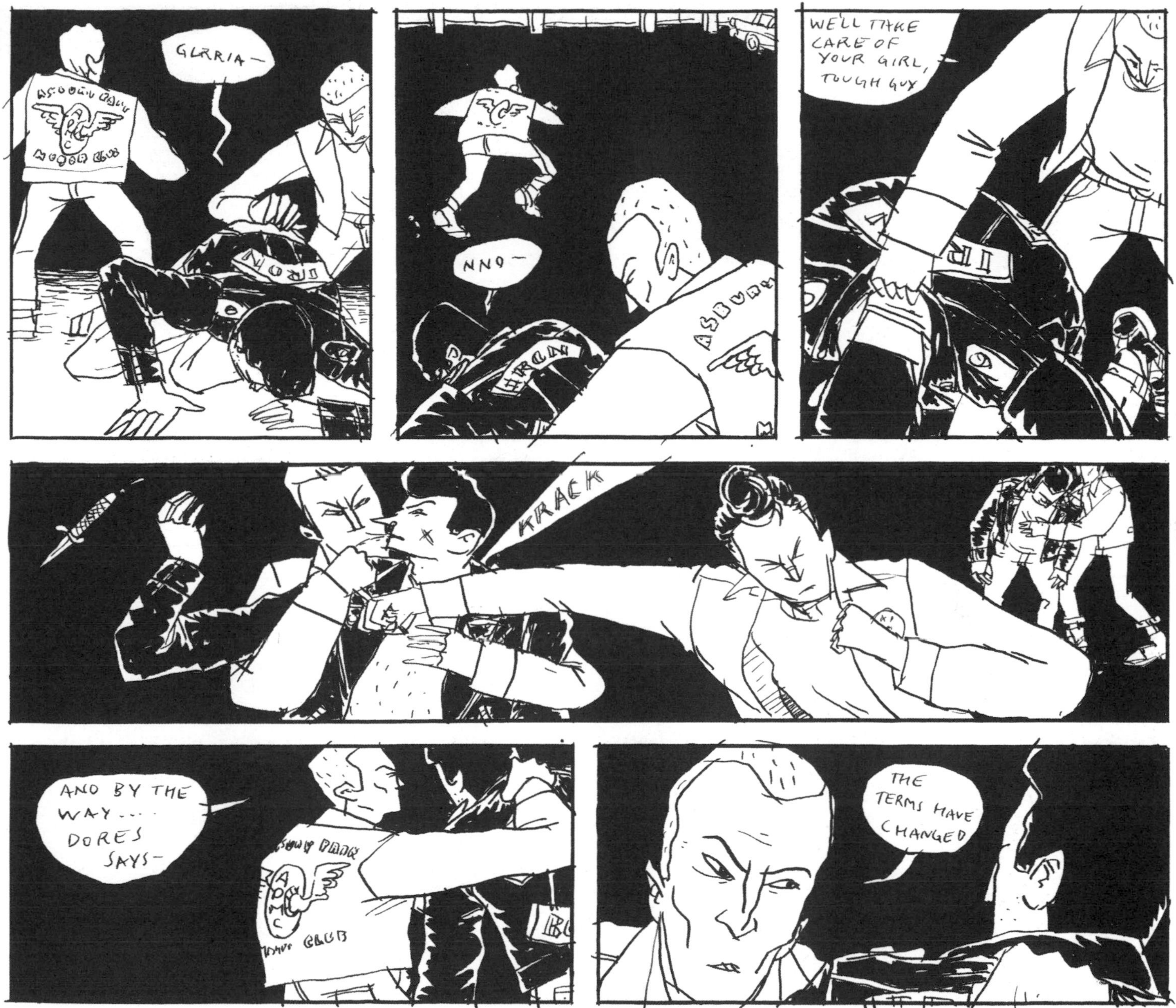
GLRRIA—
NNO—
WELL TAKE CARE OF YOUR GIRL, TOUGH GUY
KRACK
AND BY THE WAY.... DORES SAYS—
THE TERMS HAVE CHANGED

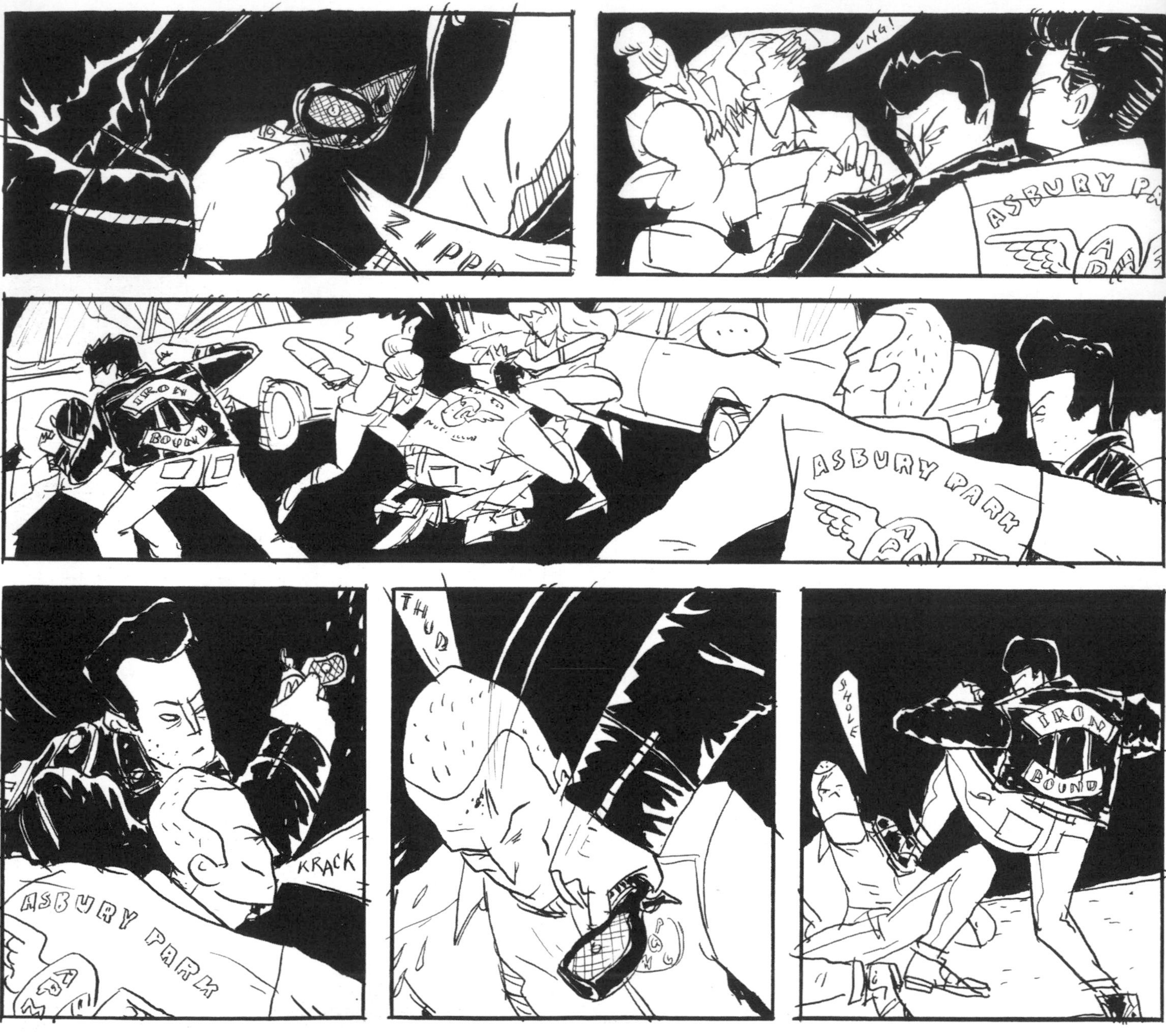
ZIPPP
UNG!
ASBURY PA
...
IRON
BOUND
ASBURY PARK
ASBURY PARK
KRACK
THUD
SHOVE
IRON
BOUND

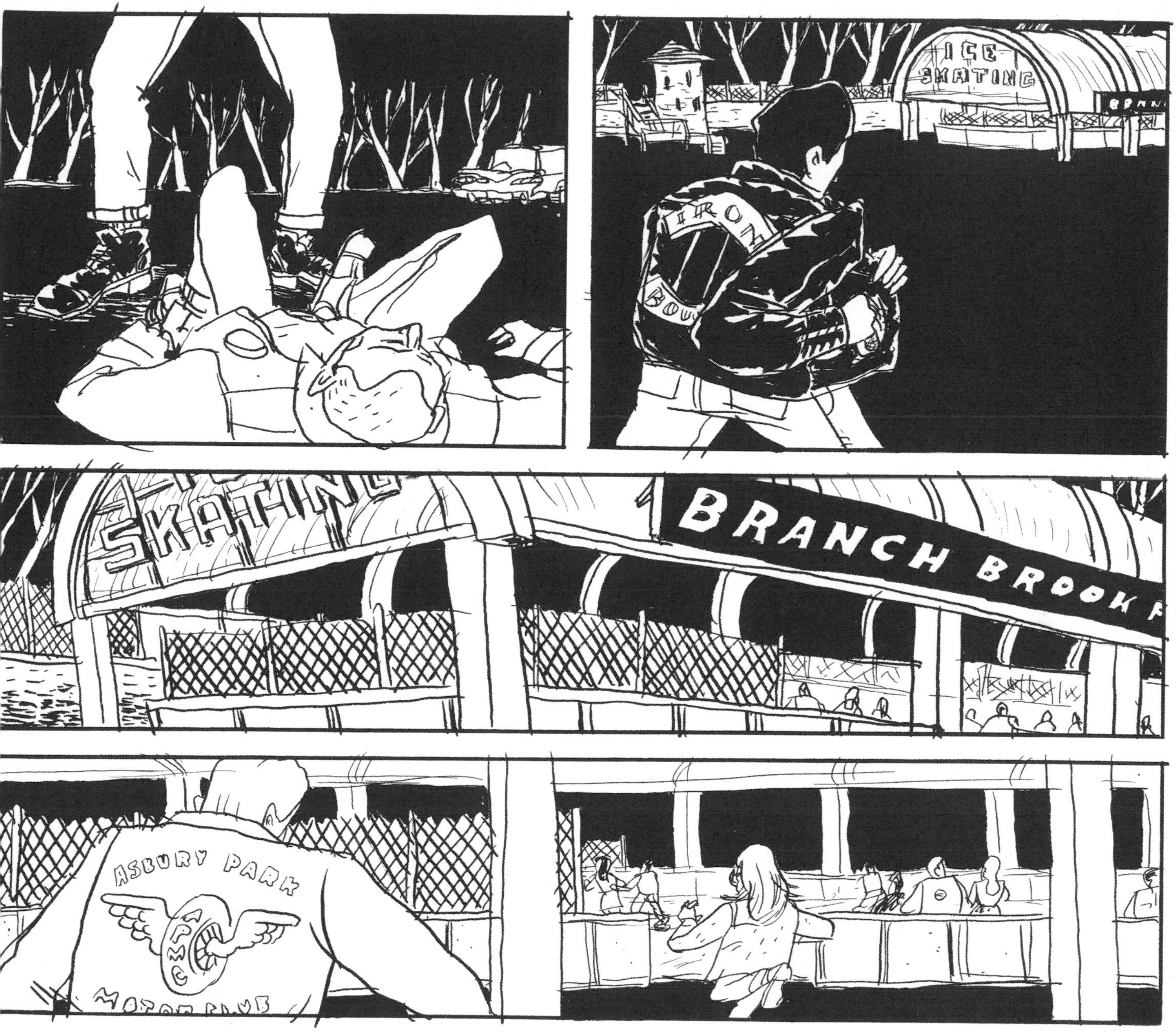

ICE SKATING
IRON
SKATING
BRANCH BROOK
ASBURY PARK

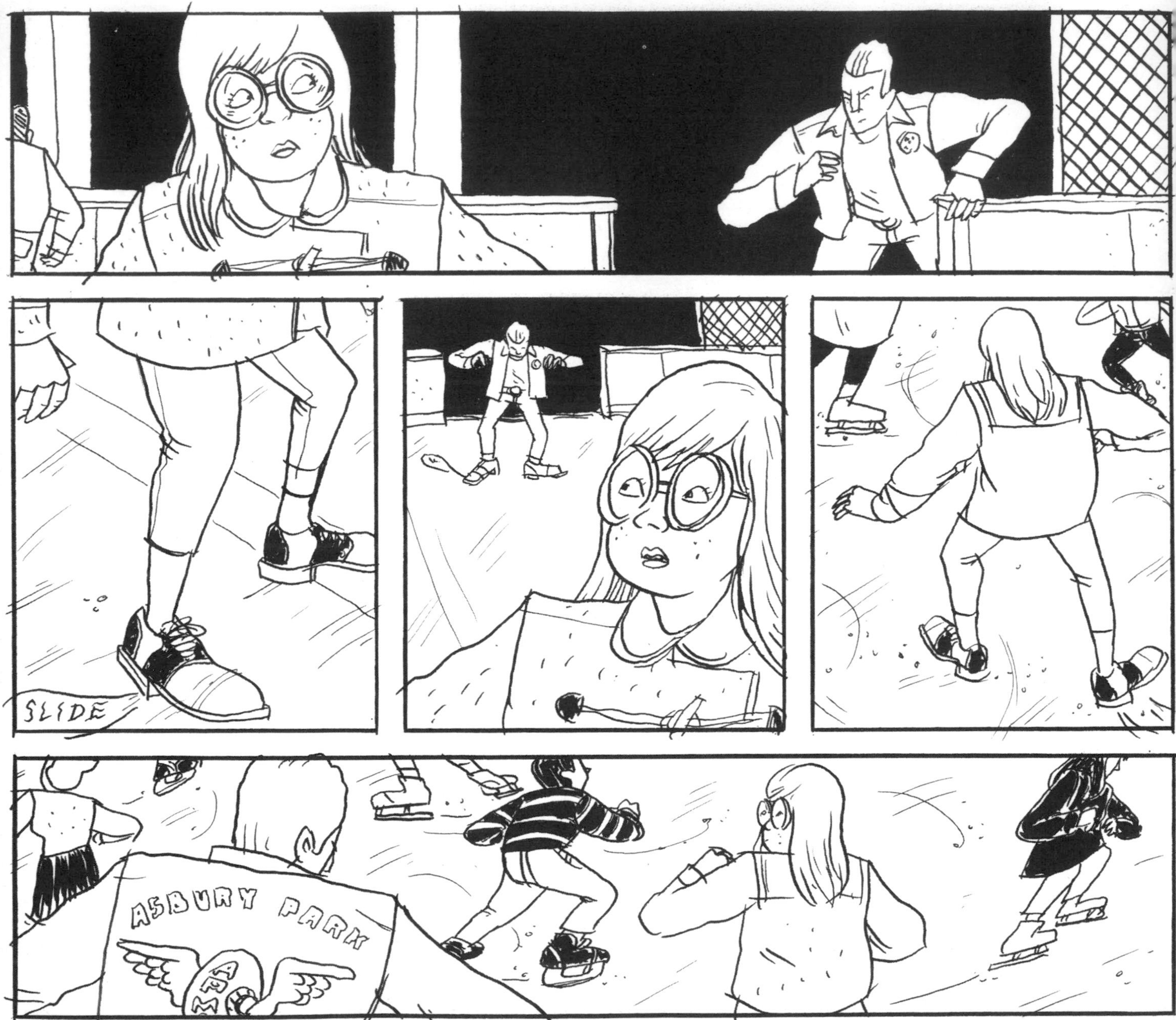
SLIDE
ASBURY PARK

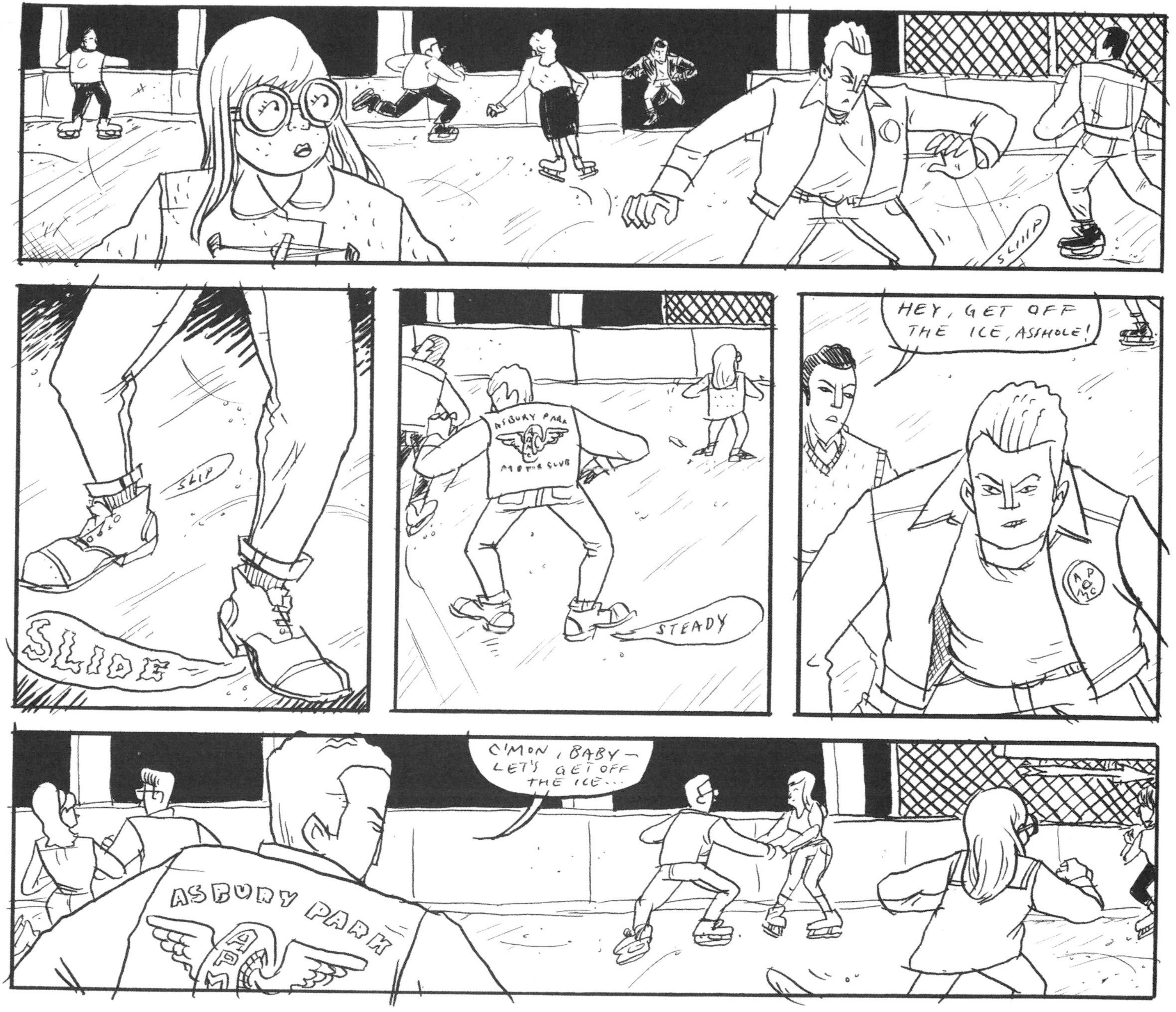
SLIIIP
SLIP
SLIDE
ASBURY PARK MOTOR CLUB
STEADY
HEY, GET OFF THE ICE, ASSHOLE!
C'MON, BABY— LET'S GET OFF THE ICE...
ASBURY PARK

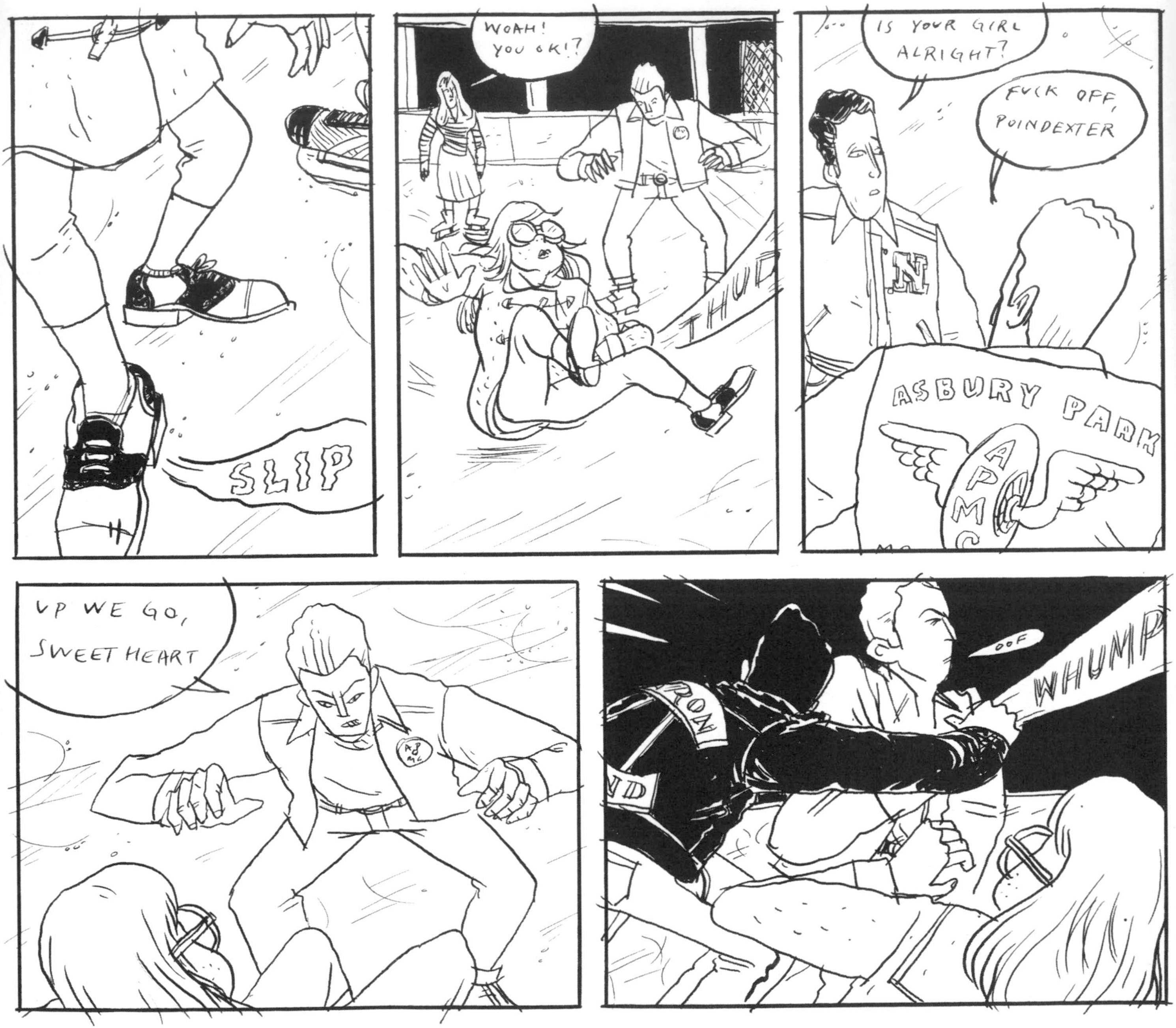
SLIP
WOAH! YOU OK!?
THUD
IS YOUR GIRL ALRIGHT?
FUCK OFF, POINDEXTER
ASBURY PARK
APMC
UP WE GO, SWEETHEART
OOF
WHUMP

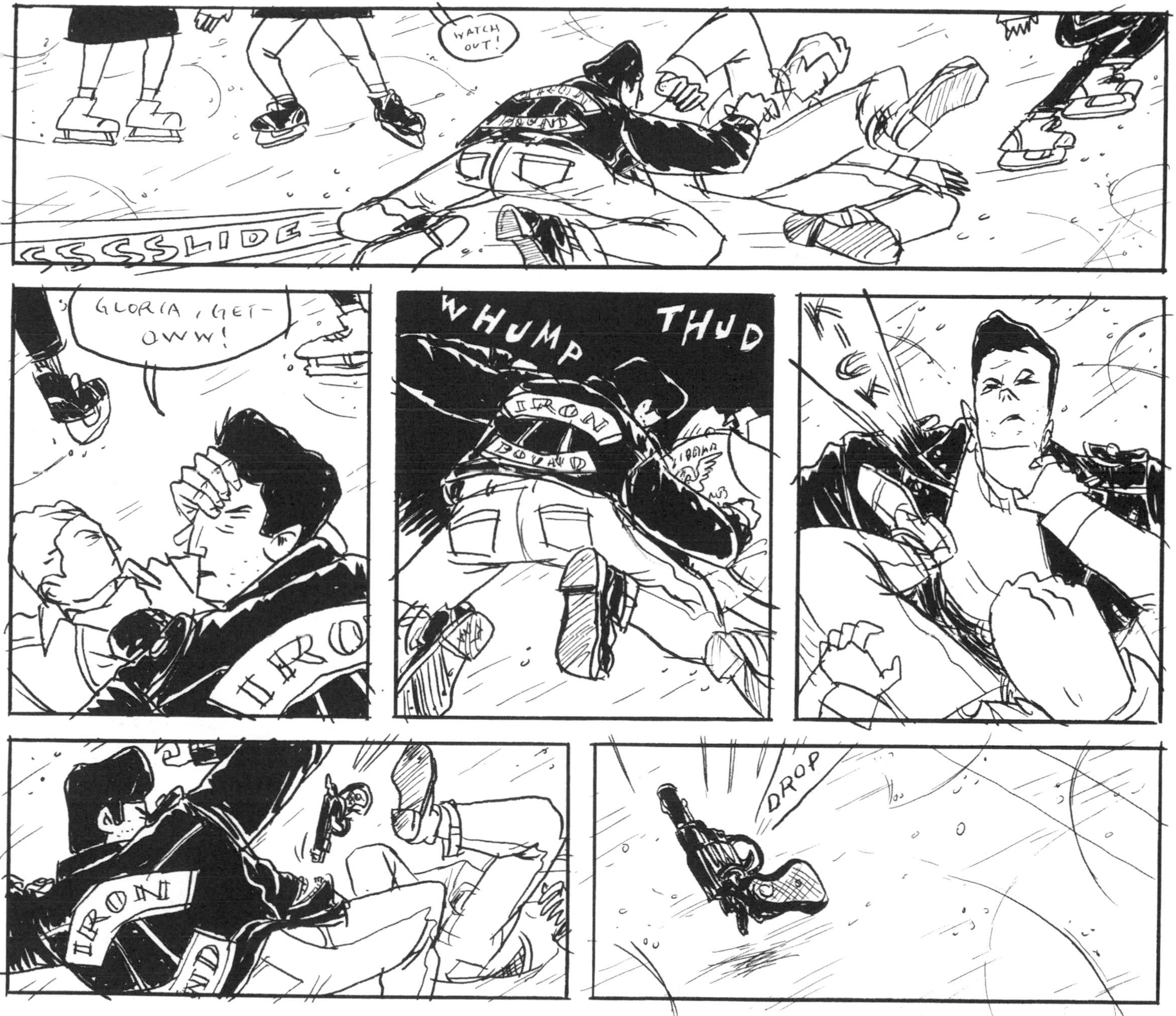
WATCH OUT!
SSSSSLIDE
IRON BOUND
GLORIA, GET-OWW!
IRON
WHUMP
THUD
IRON BOUND
KICK
IRON
DROP

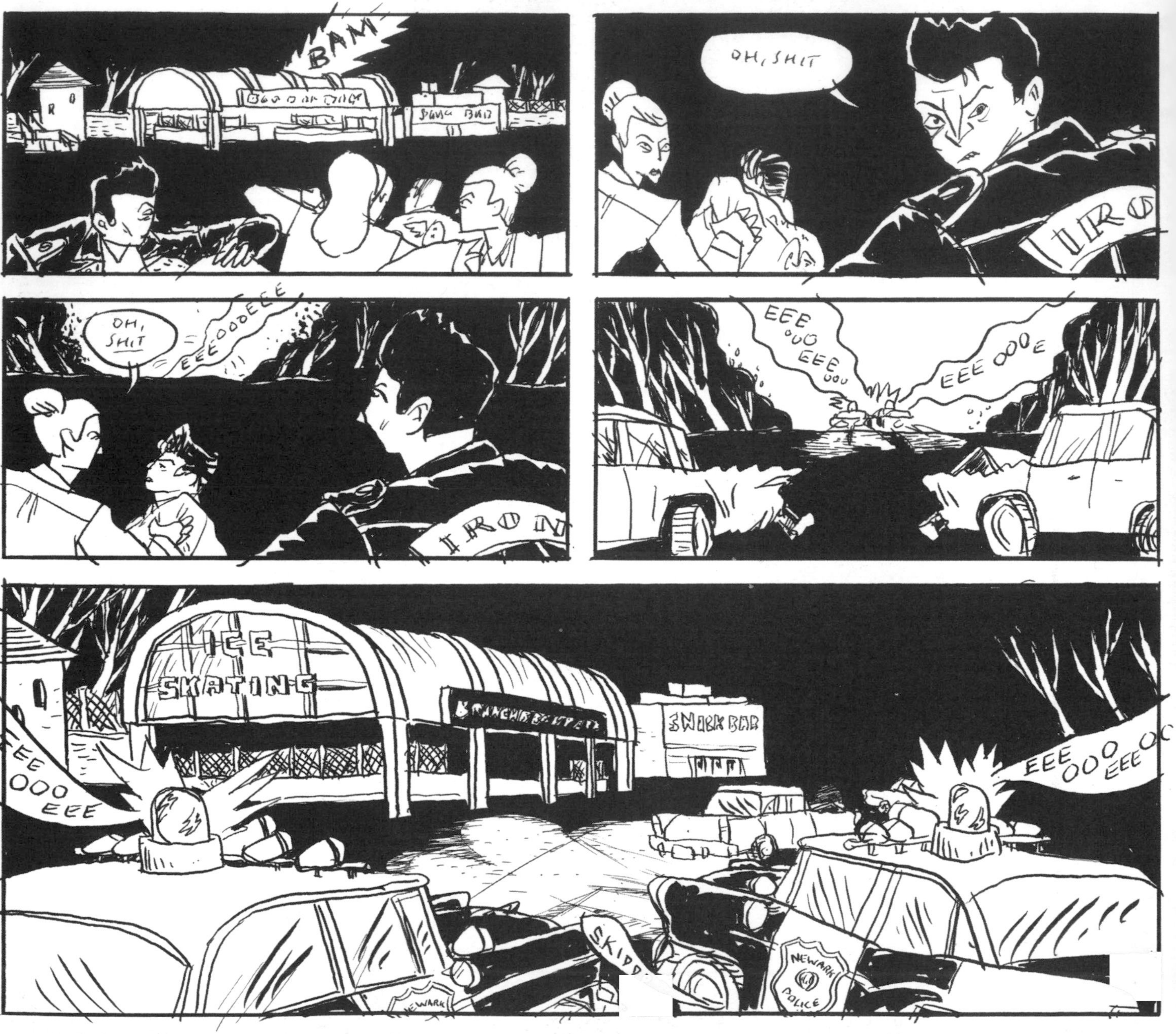
BAM
OH, SHIT
OH, SHIT
EEEOOOEEE
IRON
EEE OOO EEE OOO
EEE OOOE
ICE SKATING
SNACK BAR
EEE OOO EEE
EEE OOO EEE
NEWARK POLICE

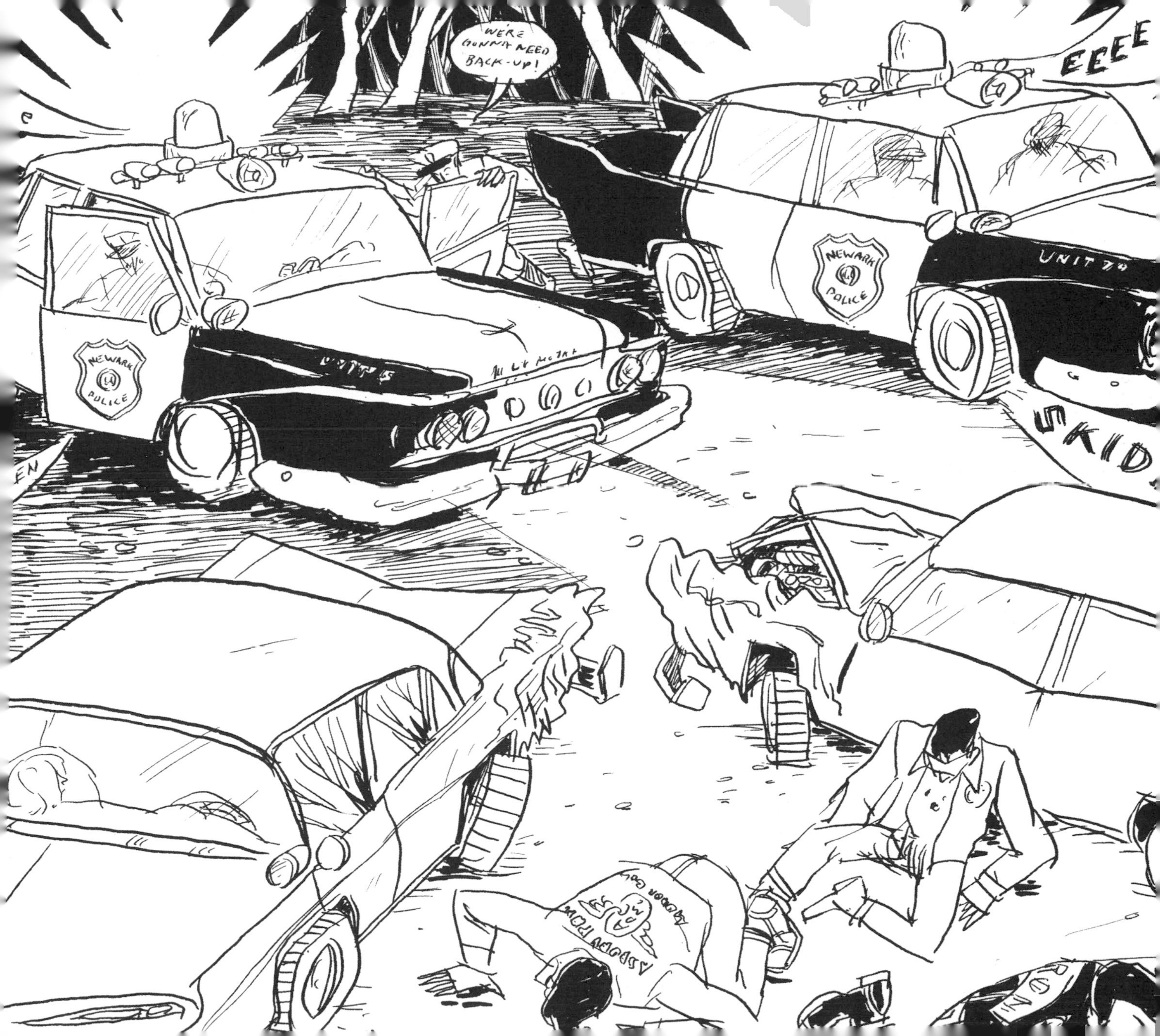
WE'RE GONNA NEED BACK-UP!
EEEE
NEWARK POLICE
UNIT 74
NEWARK POLICE
SKID

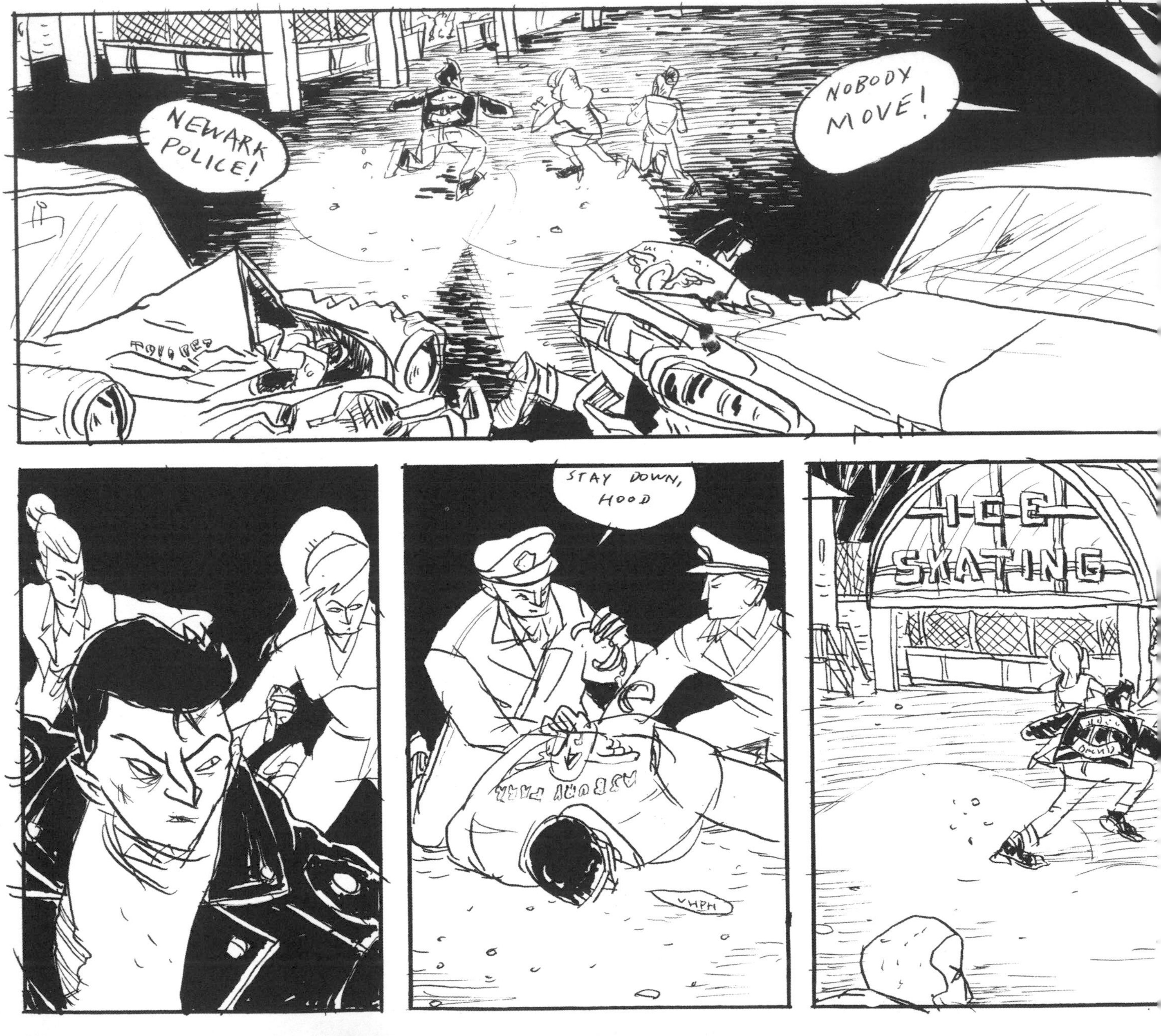
NEWARK POLICE!
NOBODY MOVE!
STAY DOWN, HOOD
UHPH
ICE SKATING

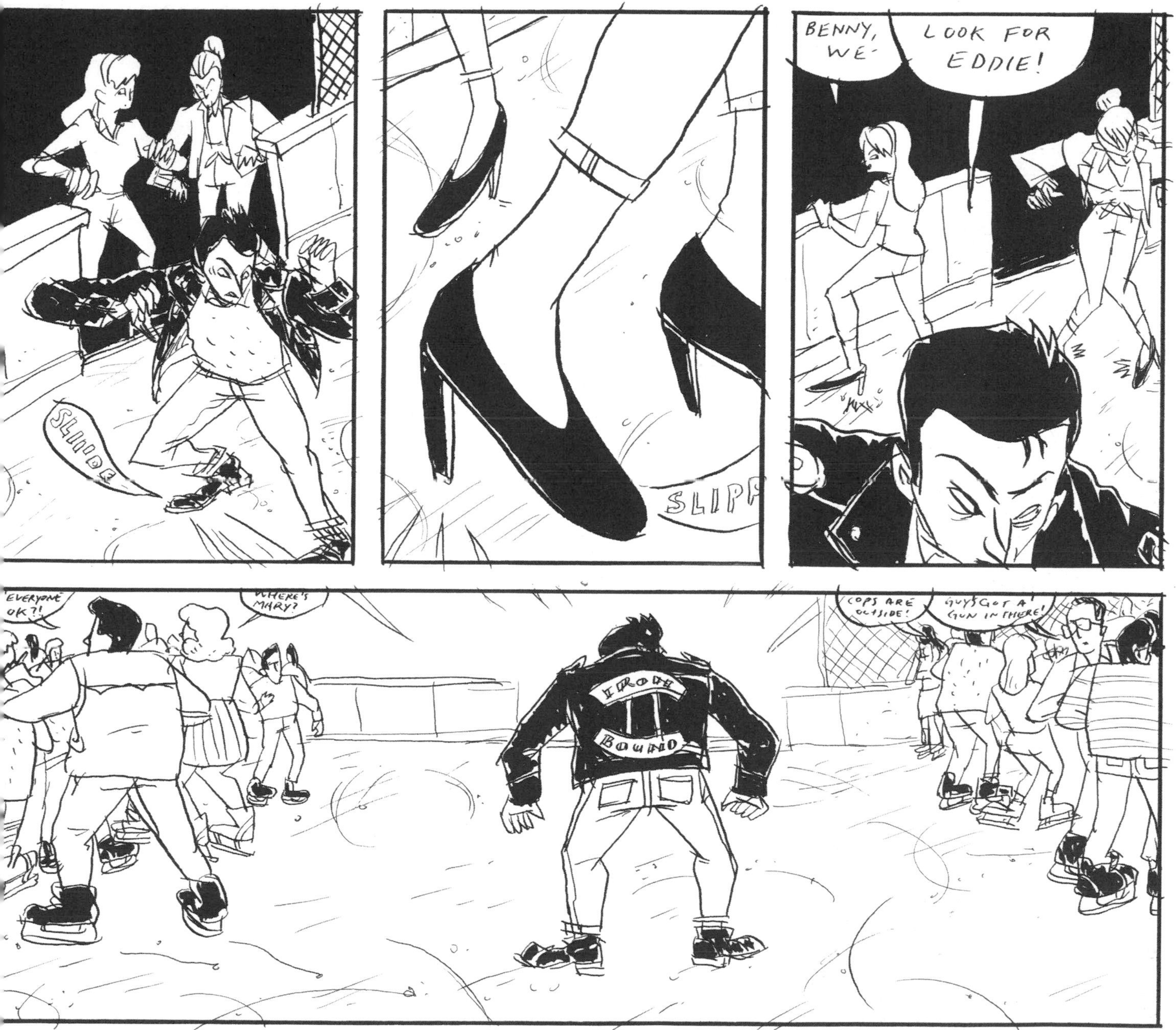
SLIIIDE
SLIPP
BENNY, WE-
LOOK FOR EDDIE!
EVERYONE OK?!
WHERE'S MARY?
IRON
BOUND
COPS ARE OUTSIDE!
GUYS GOT A GUN IN THERE!

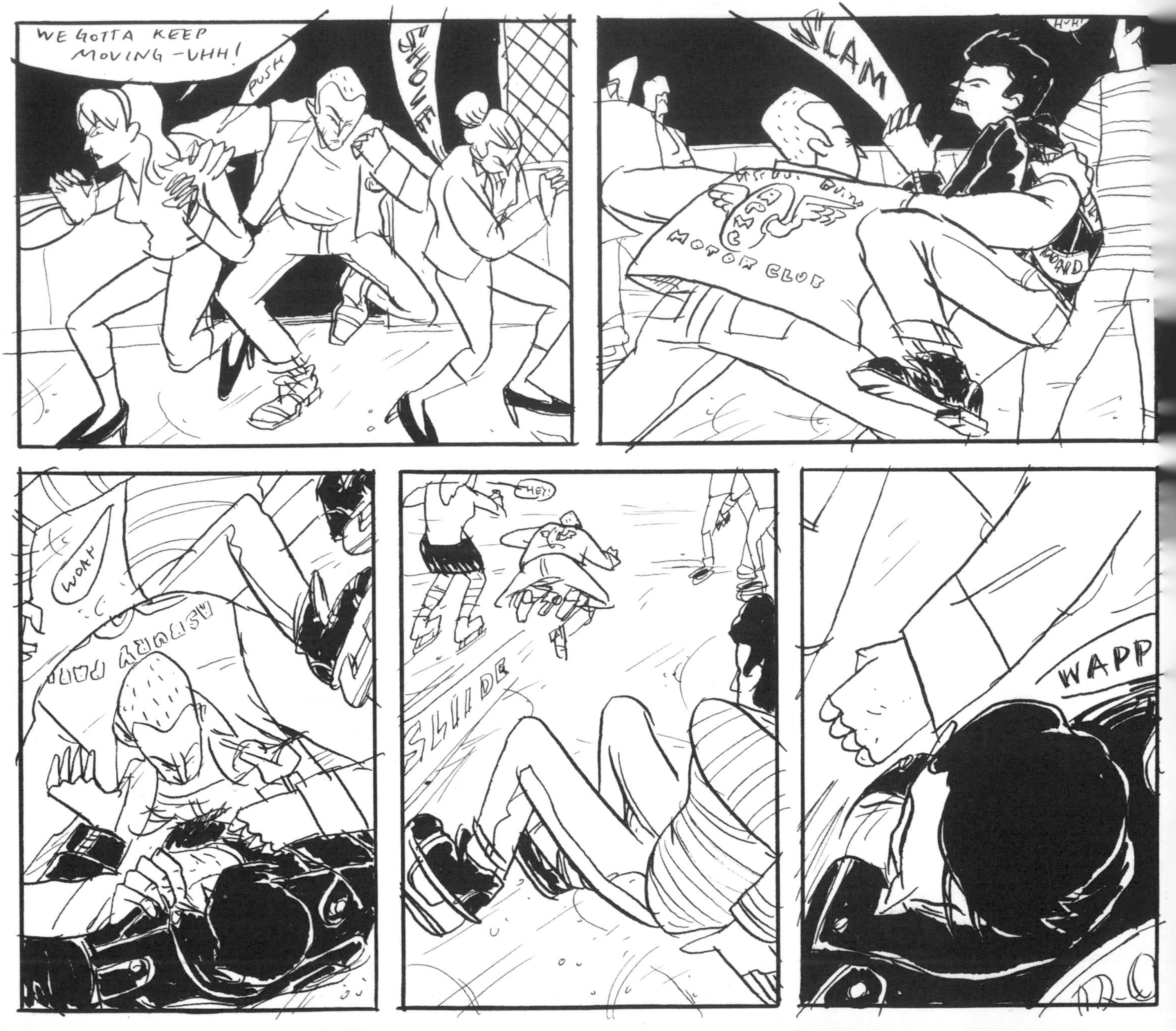
WE GOTTA KEEP MOVING-UHH!
PUSH
SHOVE
SLAM
MOTOR CLUB
WOAH
HEY!
SLIIDE
WAPP

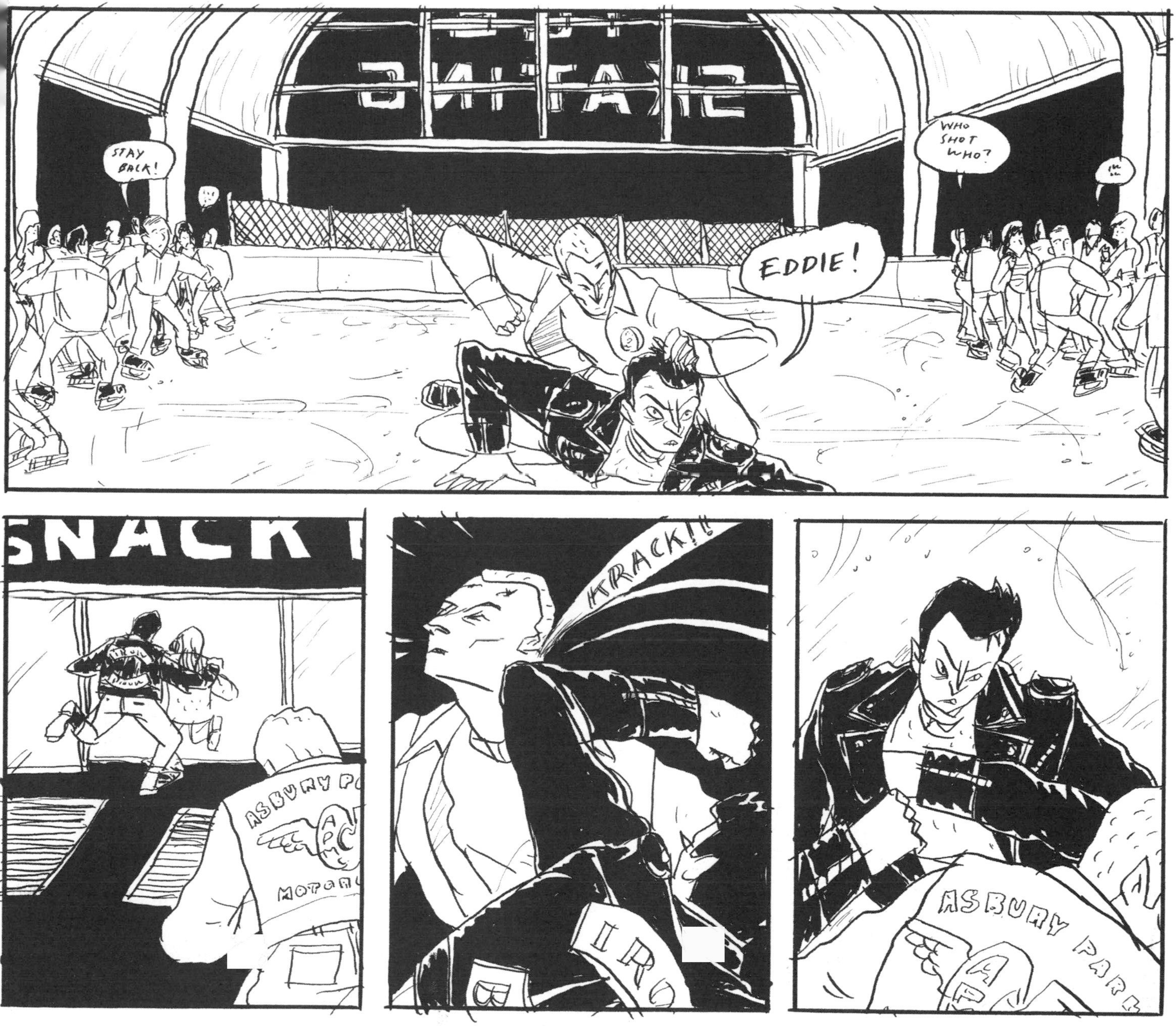
STAY BACK!
WHO SHOT WHO?
EDDIE!
SNACK
KRACK!!
ASBURY PARK

SWITCH
ONE
TWO
ONE, TWO, THREE, FOUR!
HUMMMMM
CLICK
NEWARK
Wanderers

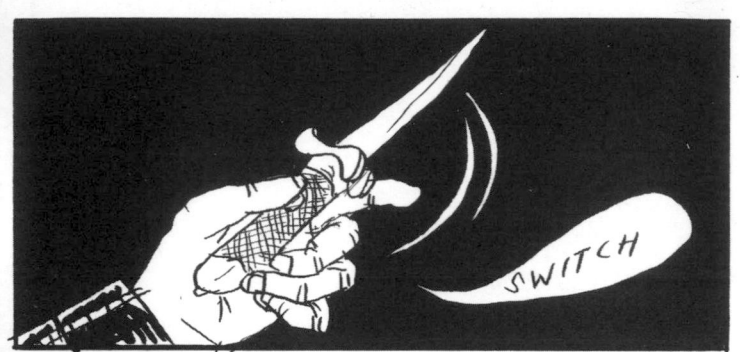

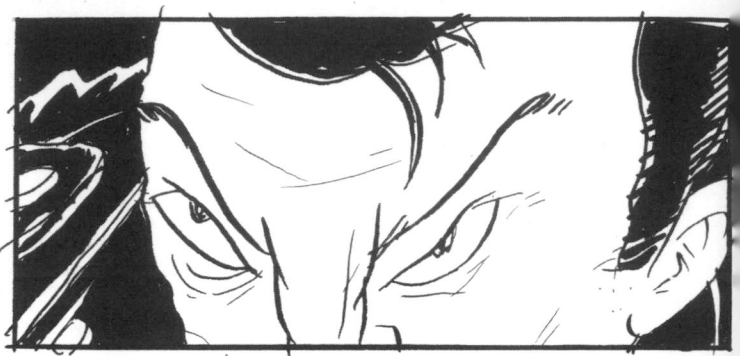

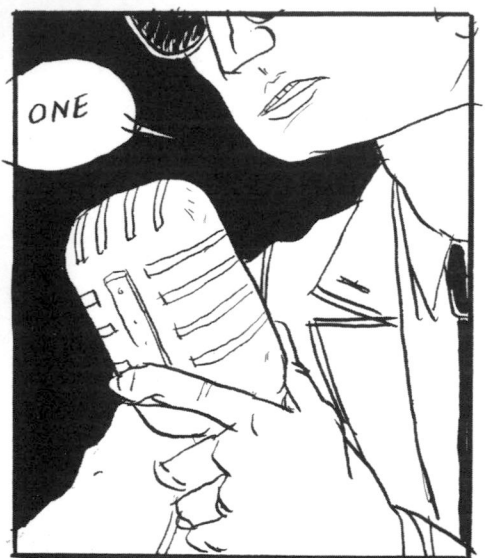

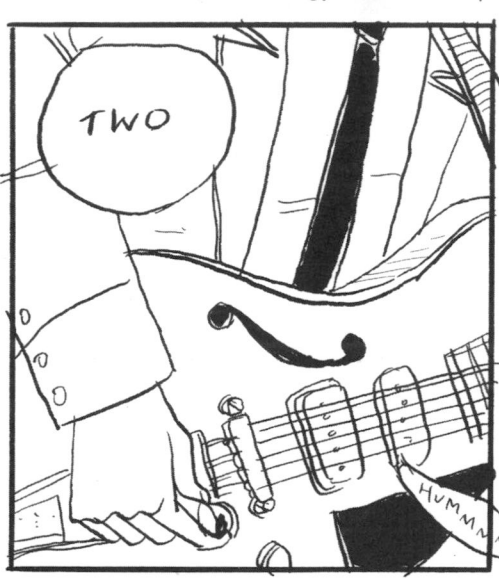

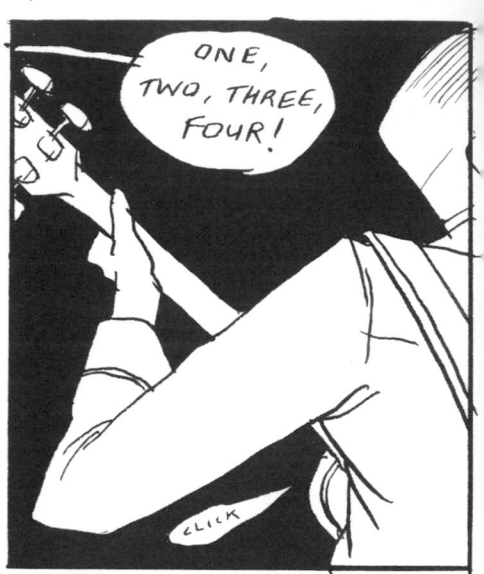

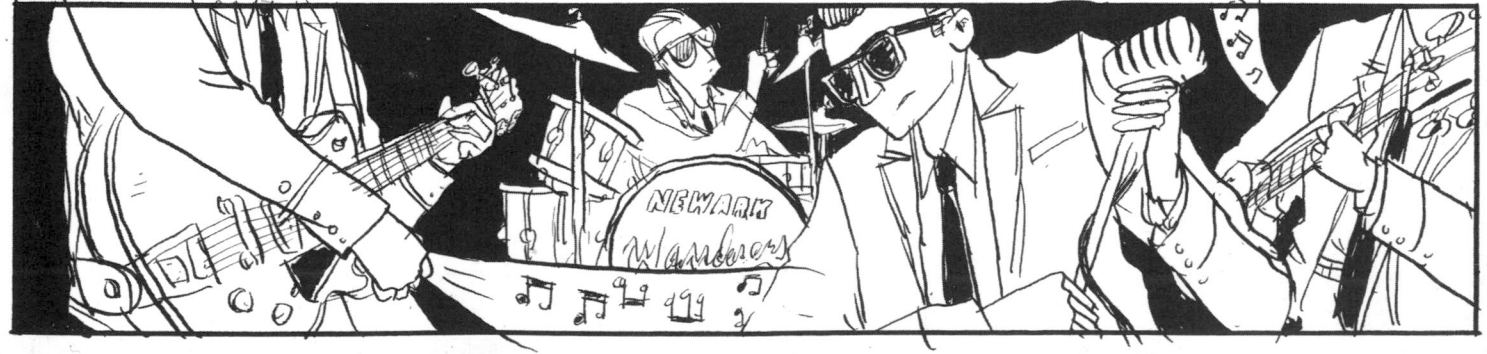

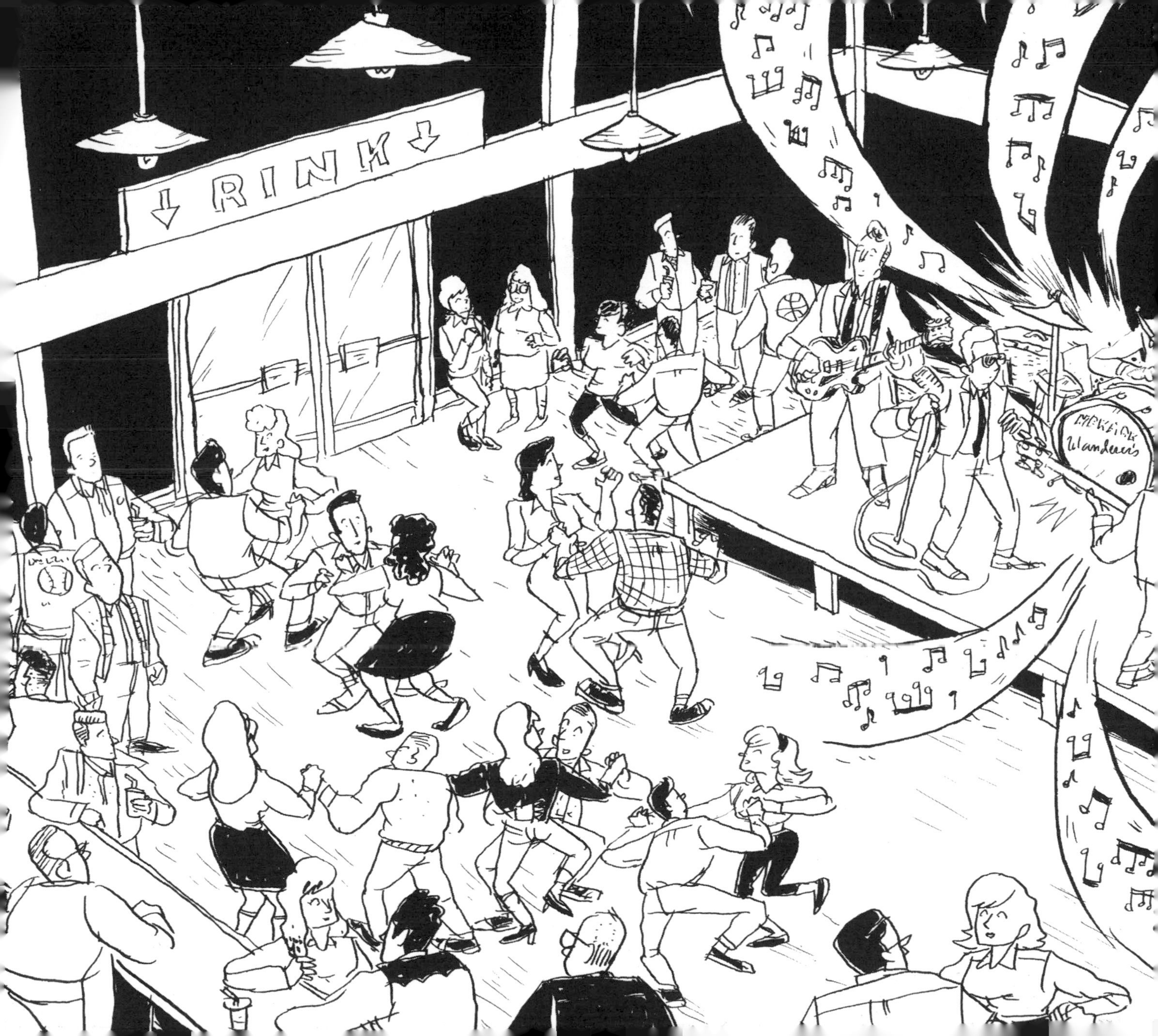
RINK
Wanderers

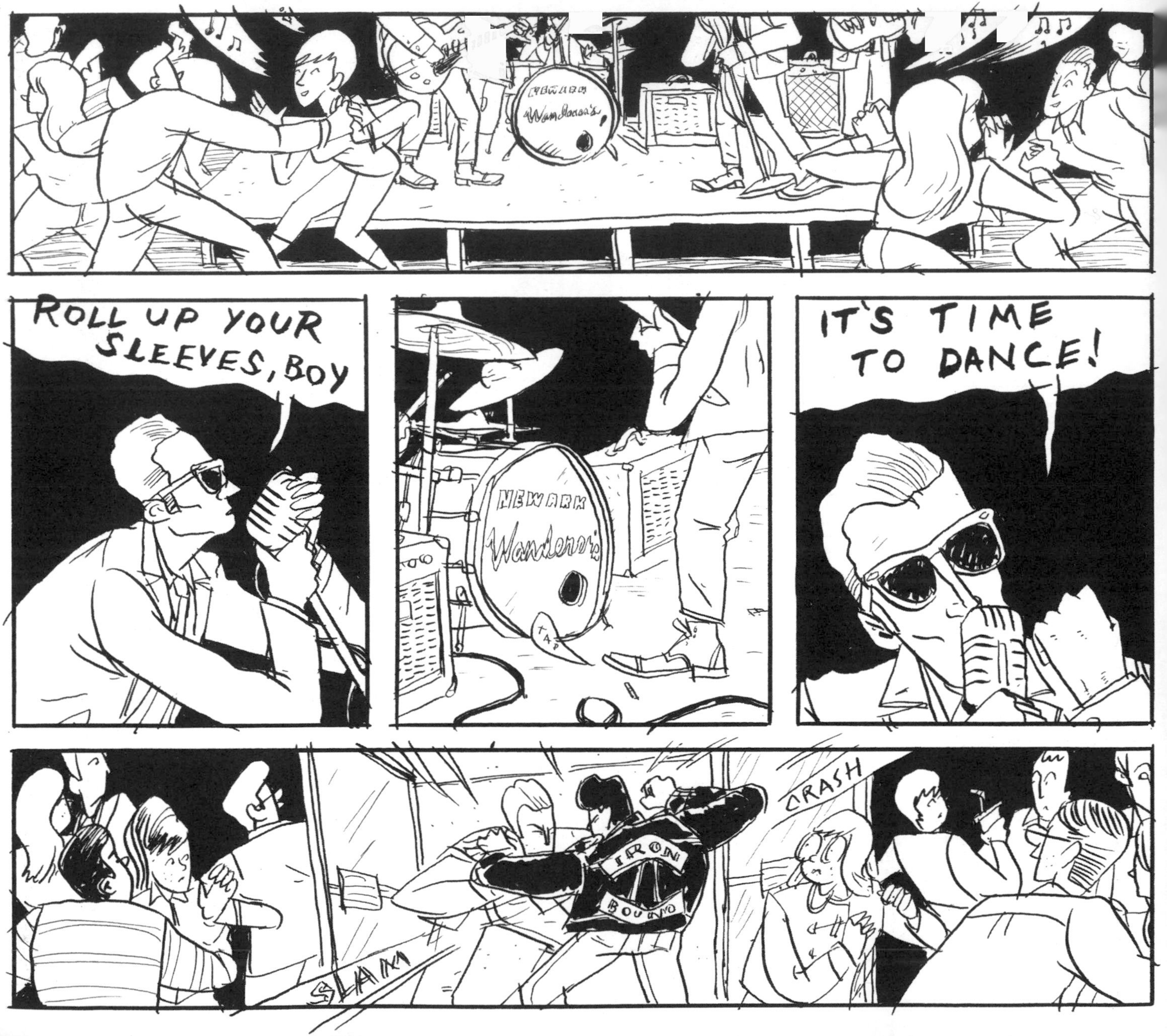
NEWARK
Wanderer's
ROLL UP YOUR SLEEVES, BOY
NEWARK
Wanderer's
TAP
IT'S TIME TO DANCE!
IRON
BOUND
CRASH
SLAM

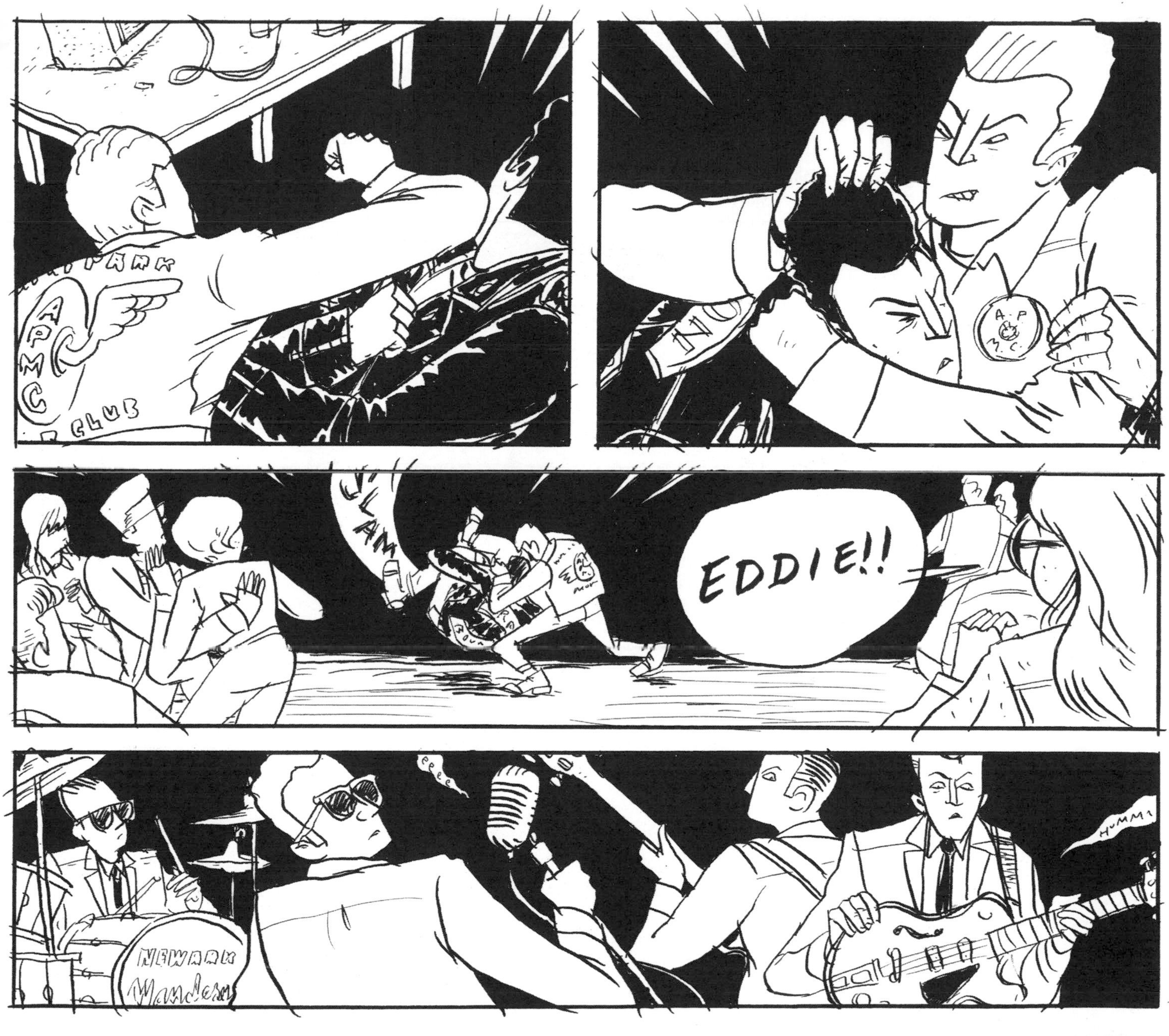

EDDIE!!
NEWARK

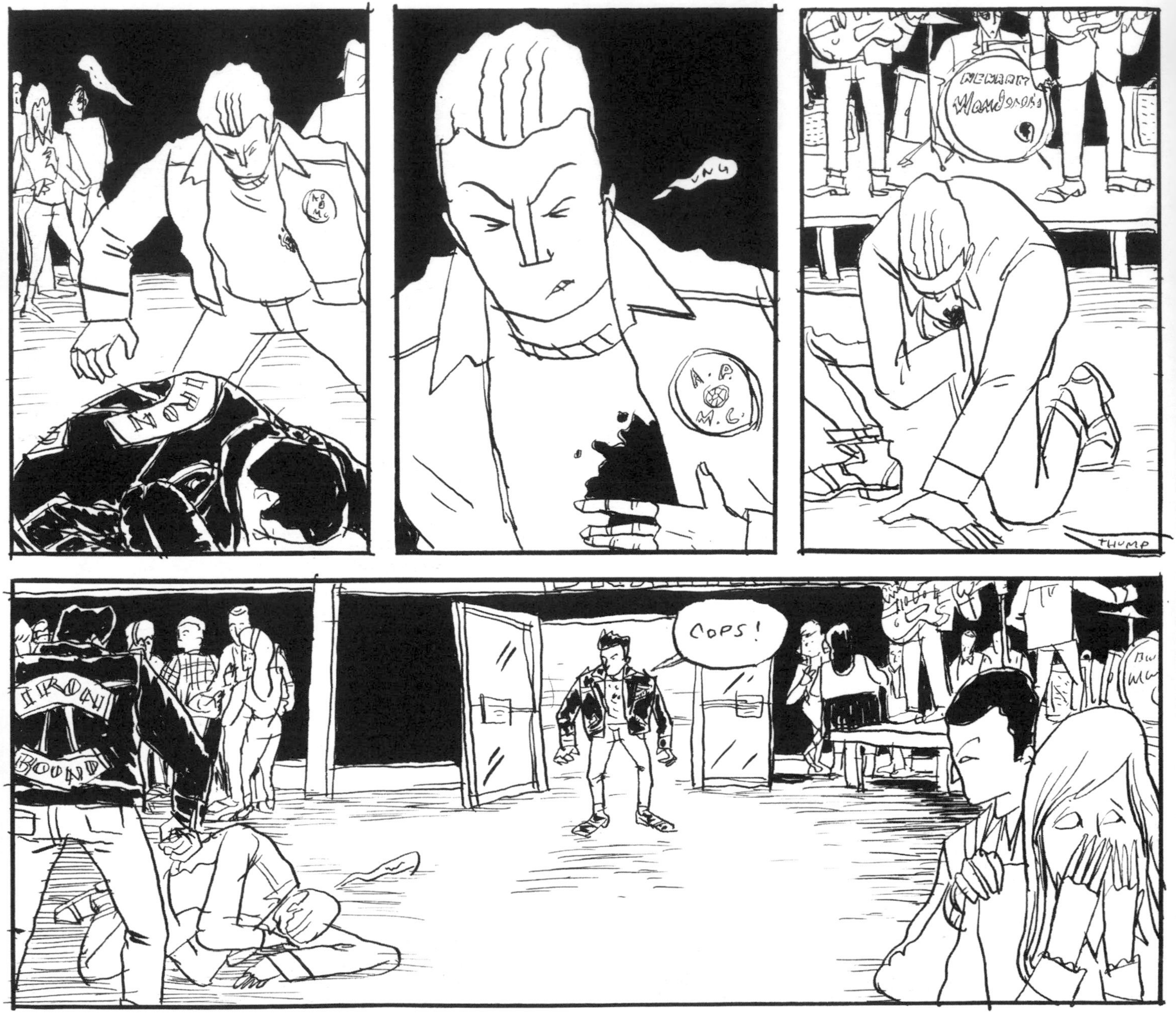
IRON
UNG
A.P.
M.C.
THUMP
IRON
BOUND
COPS!

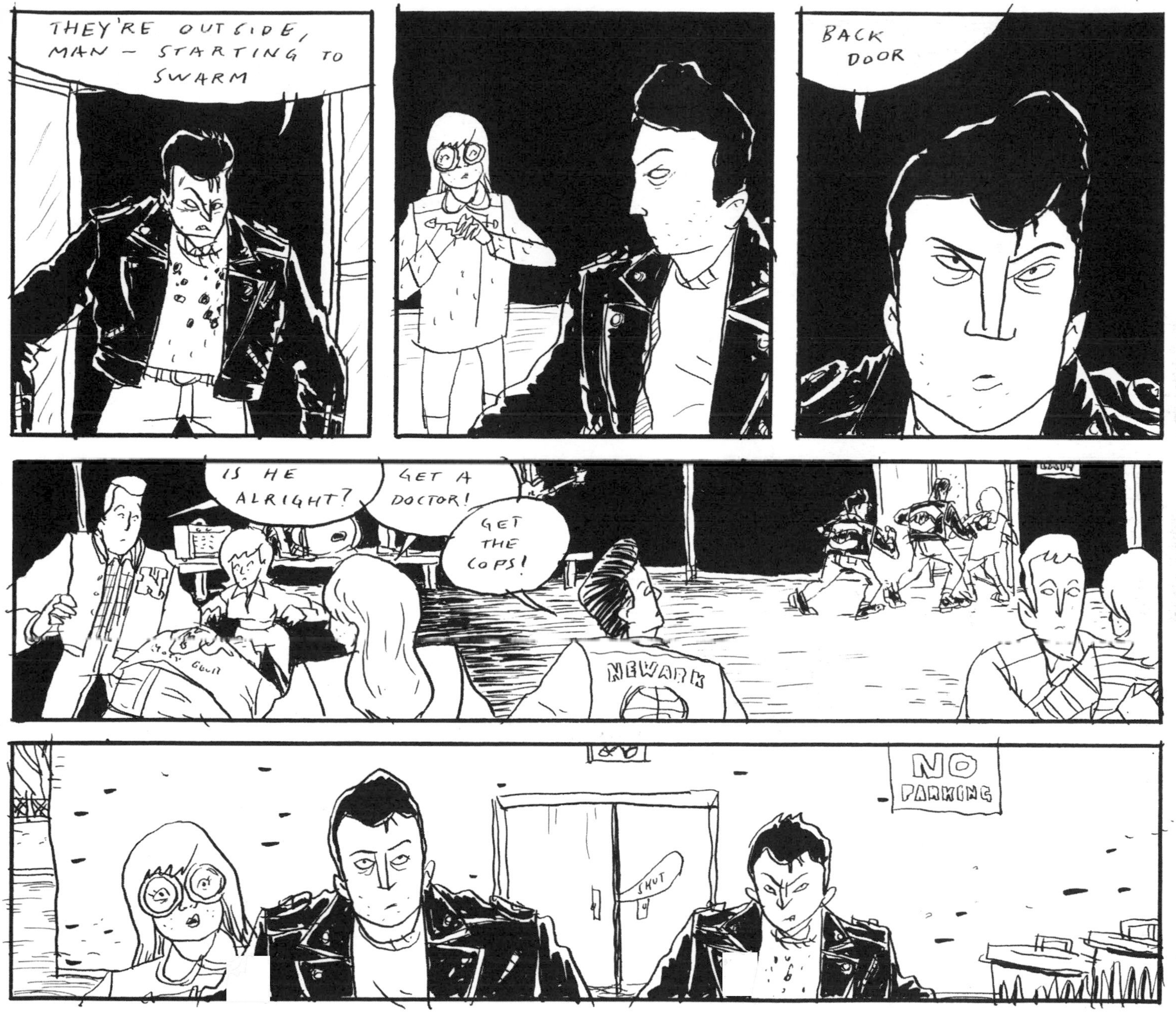
THEY'RE OUTSIDE, MAN — STARTING TO SWARM
BACK DOOR
IS HE ALRIGHT?
GET A DOCTOR!
GET THE COPS!
NEWARK
NO PARKING
SHUT

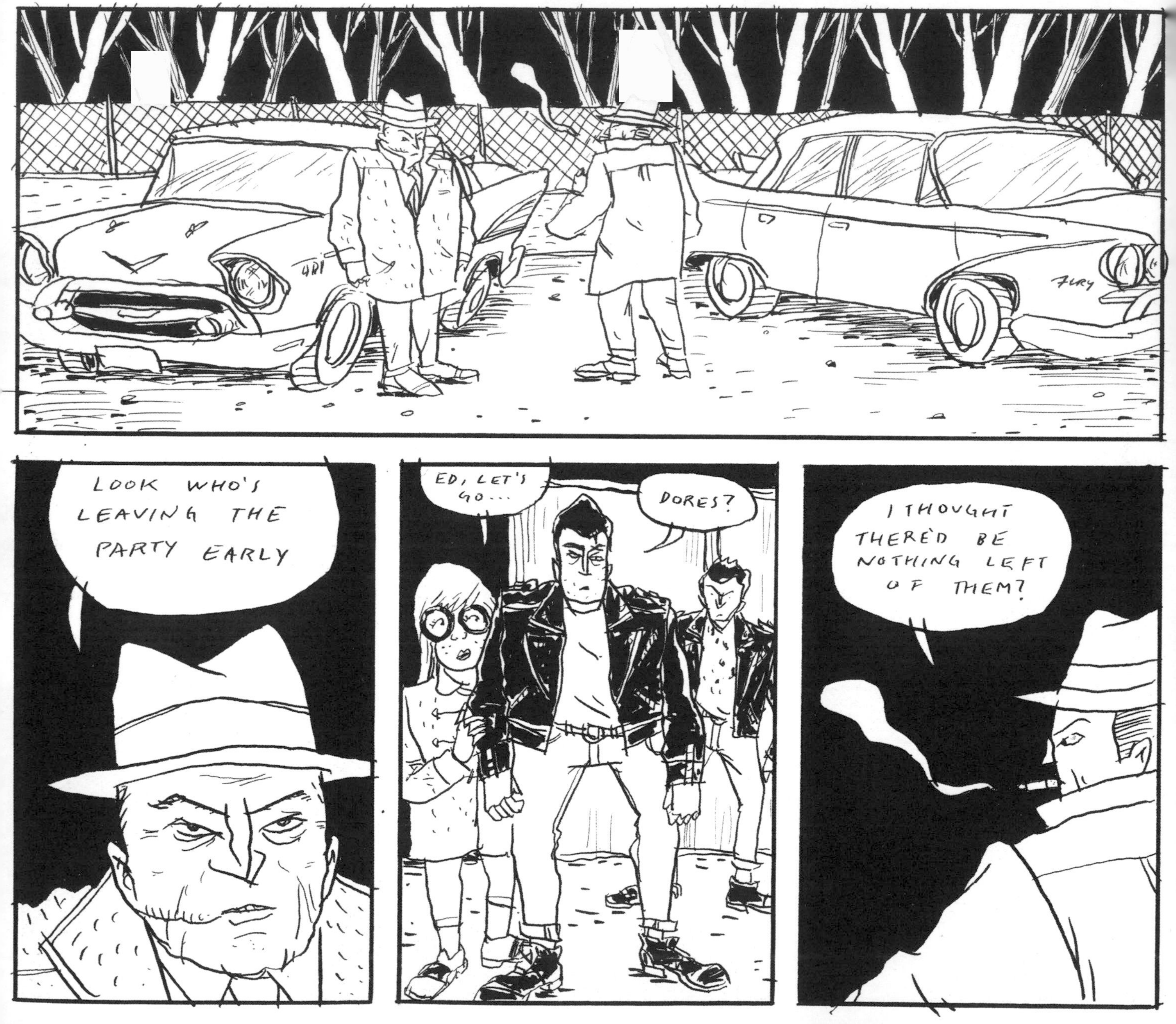
FURY
LOOK WHO'S LEAVING THE PARTY EARLY
ED, LET'S GO...
DORES?
I THOUGHT THERE'D BE NOTHING LEFT OF THEM?

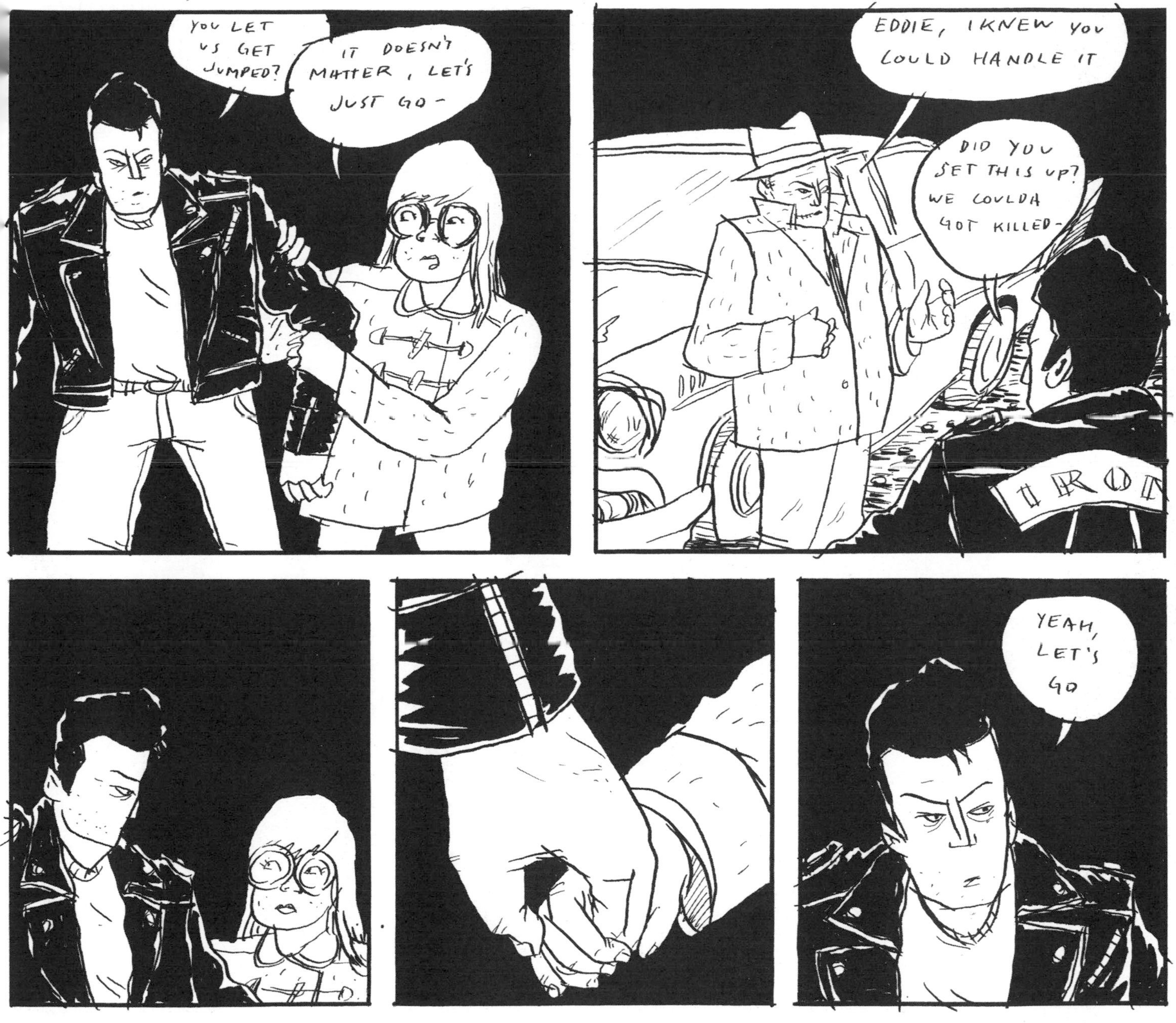
YOU LET US GET JUMPED?
IT DOESN'T MATTER, LET'S JUST GO-
EDDIE, I KNEW YOU COULD HANDLE IT
DID YOU SET THIS UP? WE COULDA GOT KILLED-
YEAH, LET'S GO

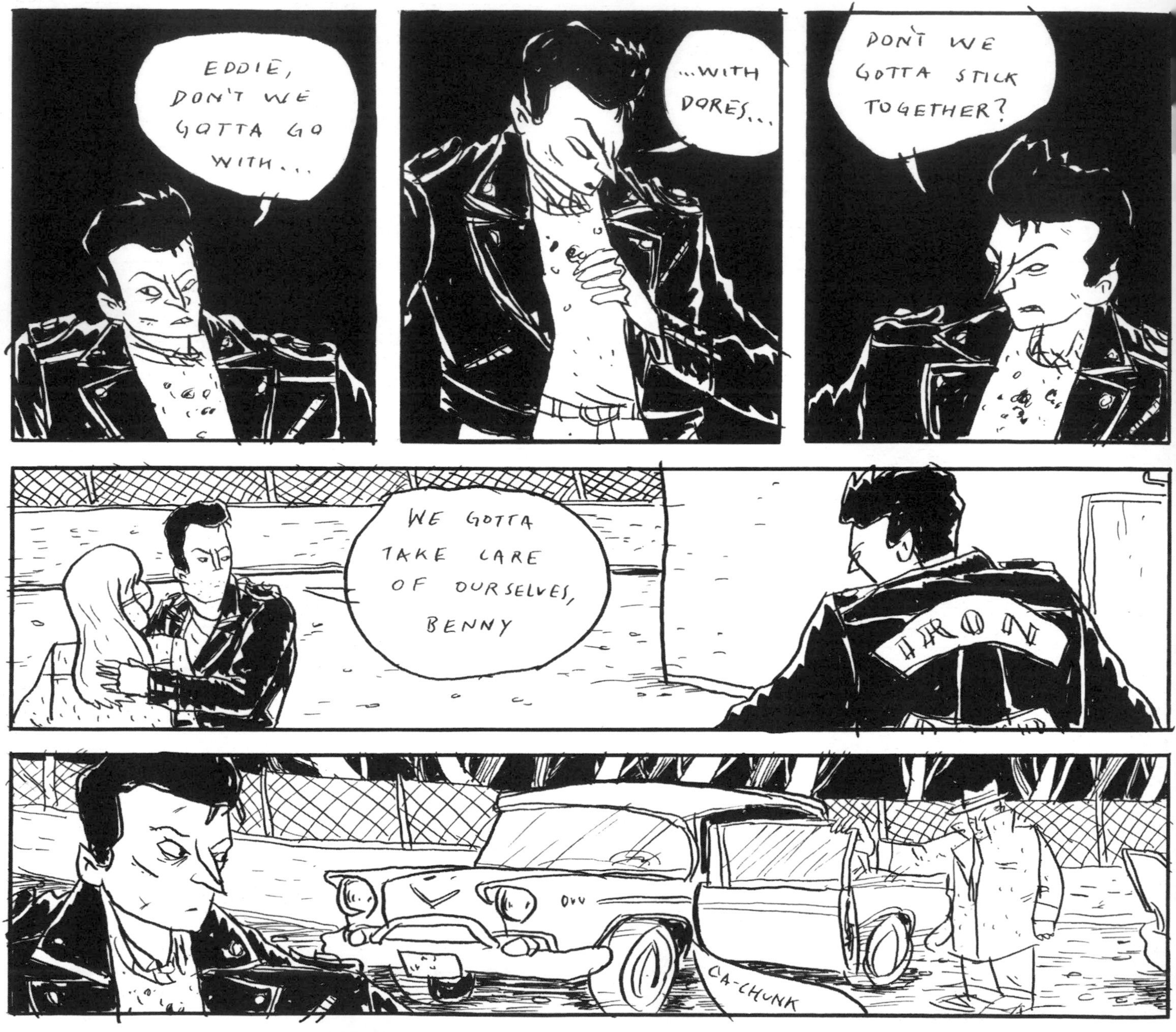
EDDIE, DON'T WE GOTTA GO WITH...
...WITH DORES...
DON'T WE GOTTA STICK TOGETHER?
WE GOTTA TAKE CARE OF OURSELVES, BENNY
IRON
CA-CHUNK

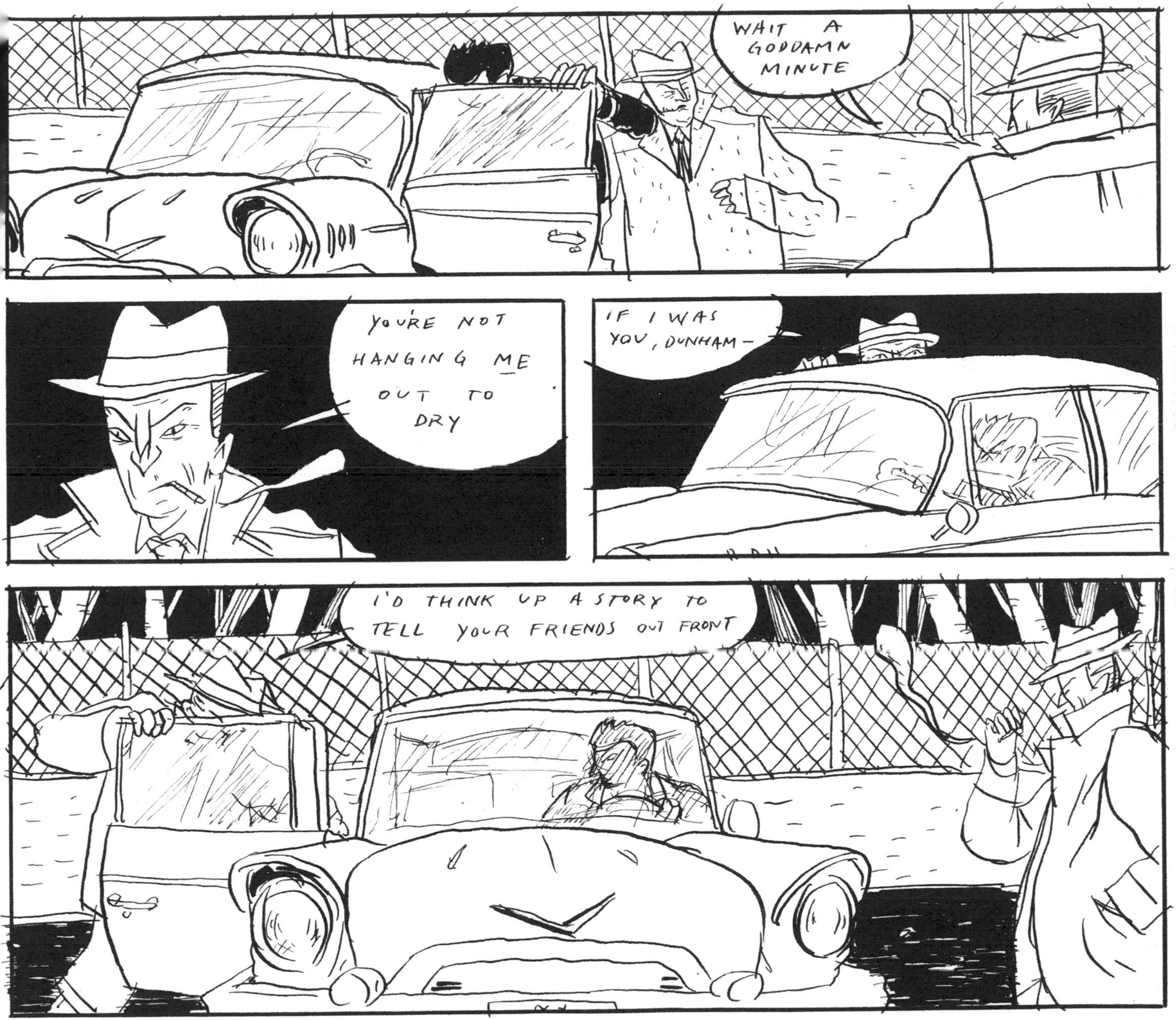
WAIT A GODDAMN MINUTE
YOU'RE NOT HANGING ME OUT TO DRY
IF I WAS YOU, DUNHAM—
I'D THINK UP A STORY TO TELL YOUR FRIENDS OUT FRONT

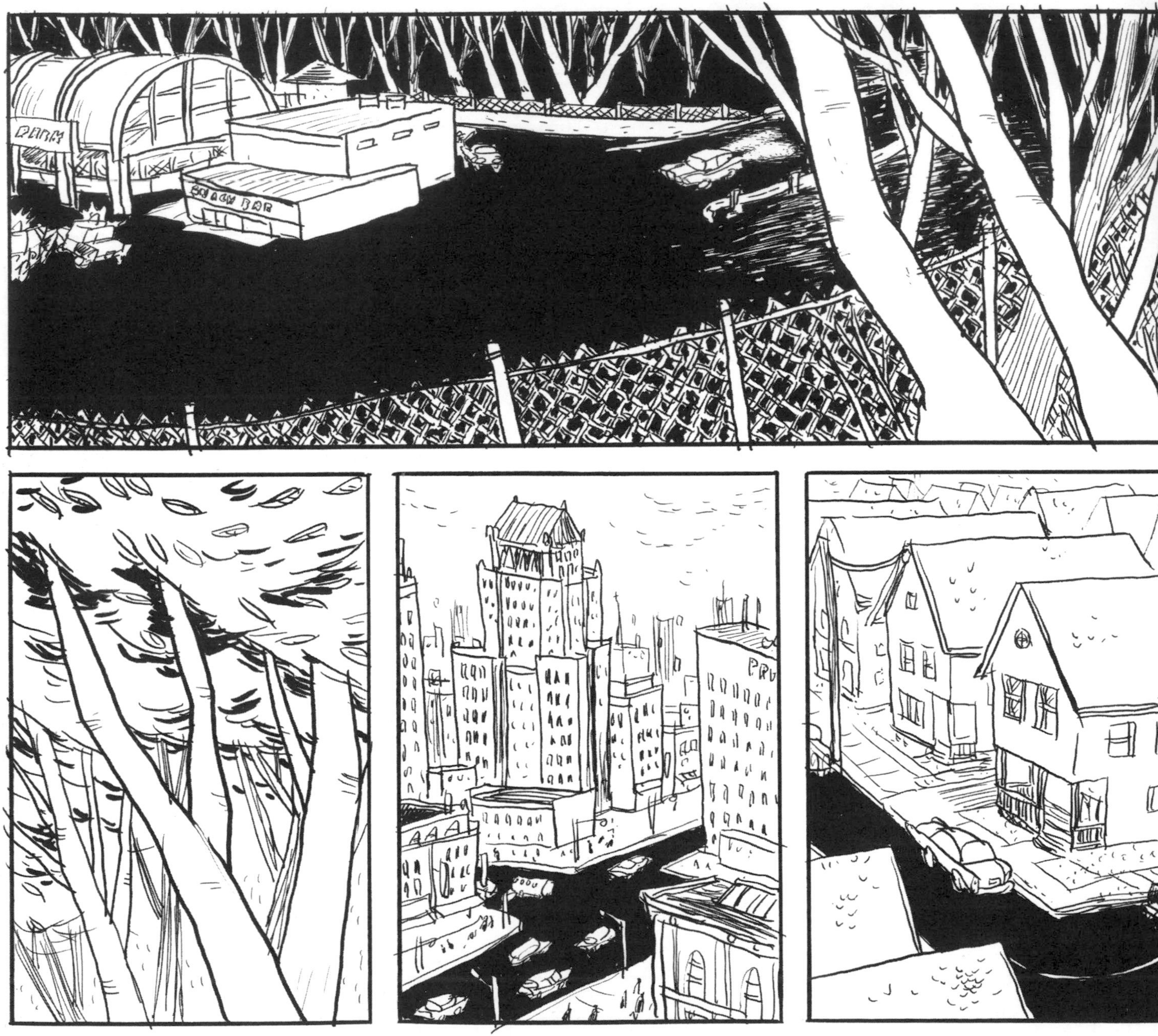

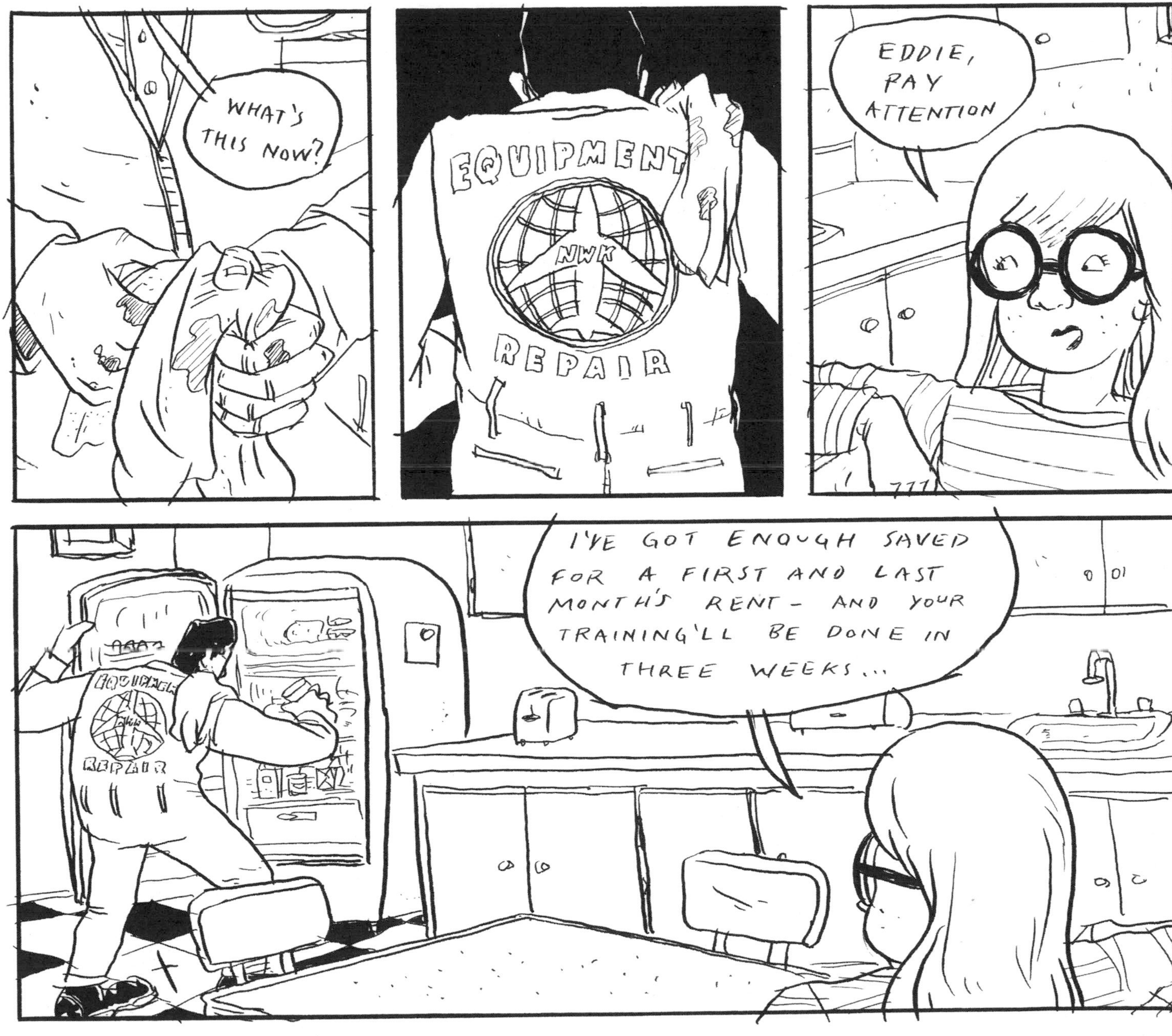
WHAT'S THIS NOW?
EQUIPMENT NWK REPAIR
EDDIE, PAY ATTENTION
I'VE GOT ENOUGH SAVED FOR A FIRST AND LAST MONTH'S RENT - AND YOUR TRAINING'LL BE DONE IN THREE WEEKS...
EQUIPMENT REPAIR

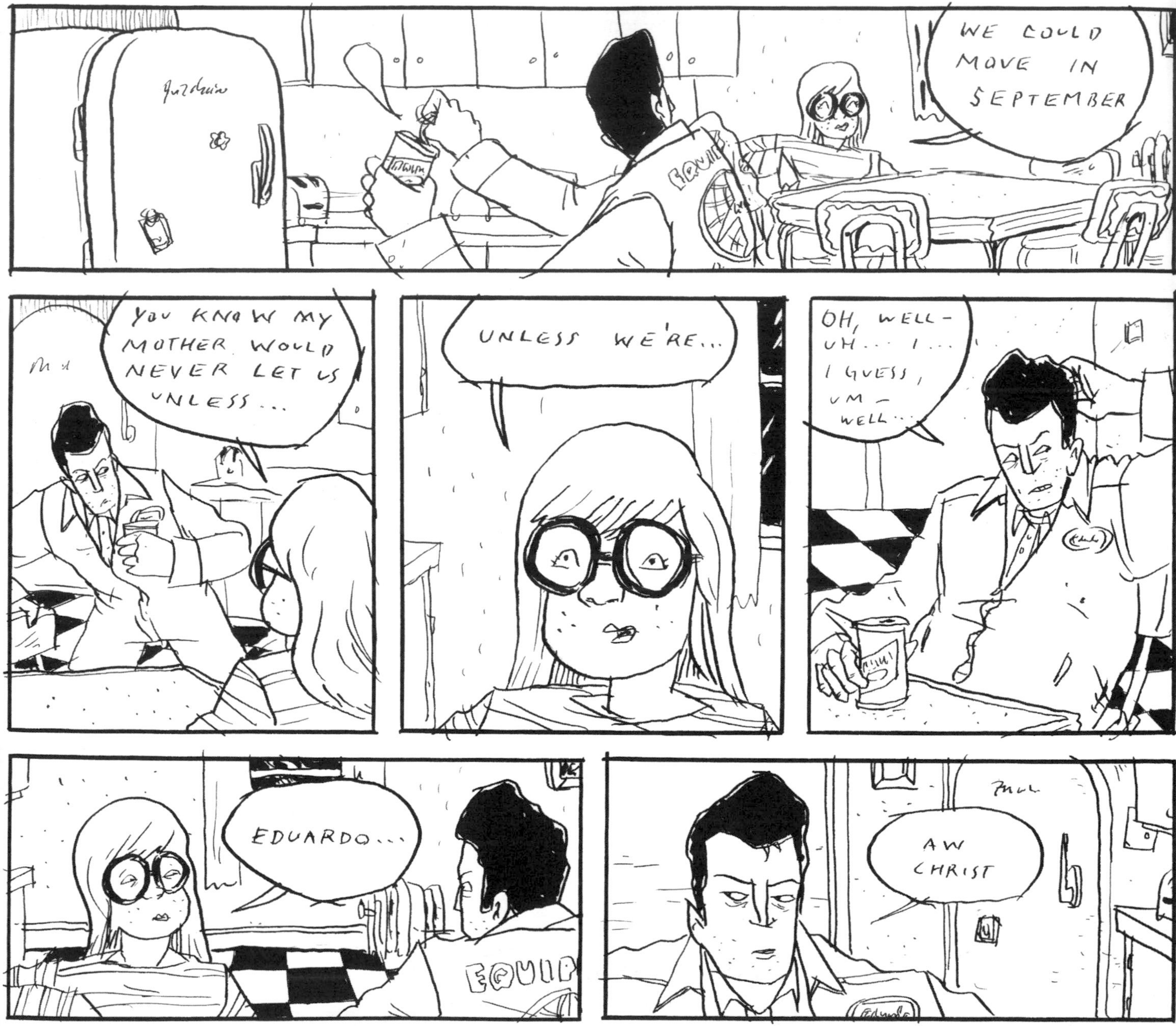
WE COULD MOVE IN SEPTEMBER
YOU KNOW MY MOTHER WOULD NEVER LET US UNLESS...
UNLESS WE'RE...
OH, WELL- UH... I... I GUESS, UM- WELL...
EDUARDO...
AW CHRIST
EQUIP

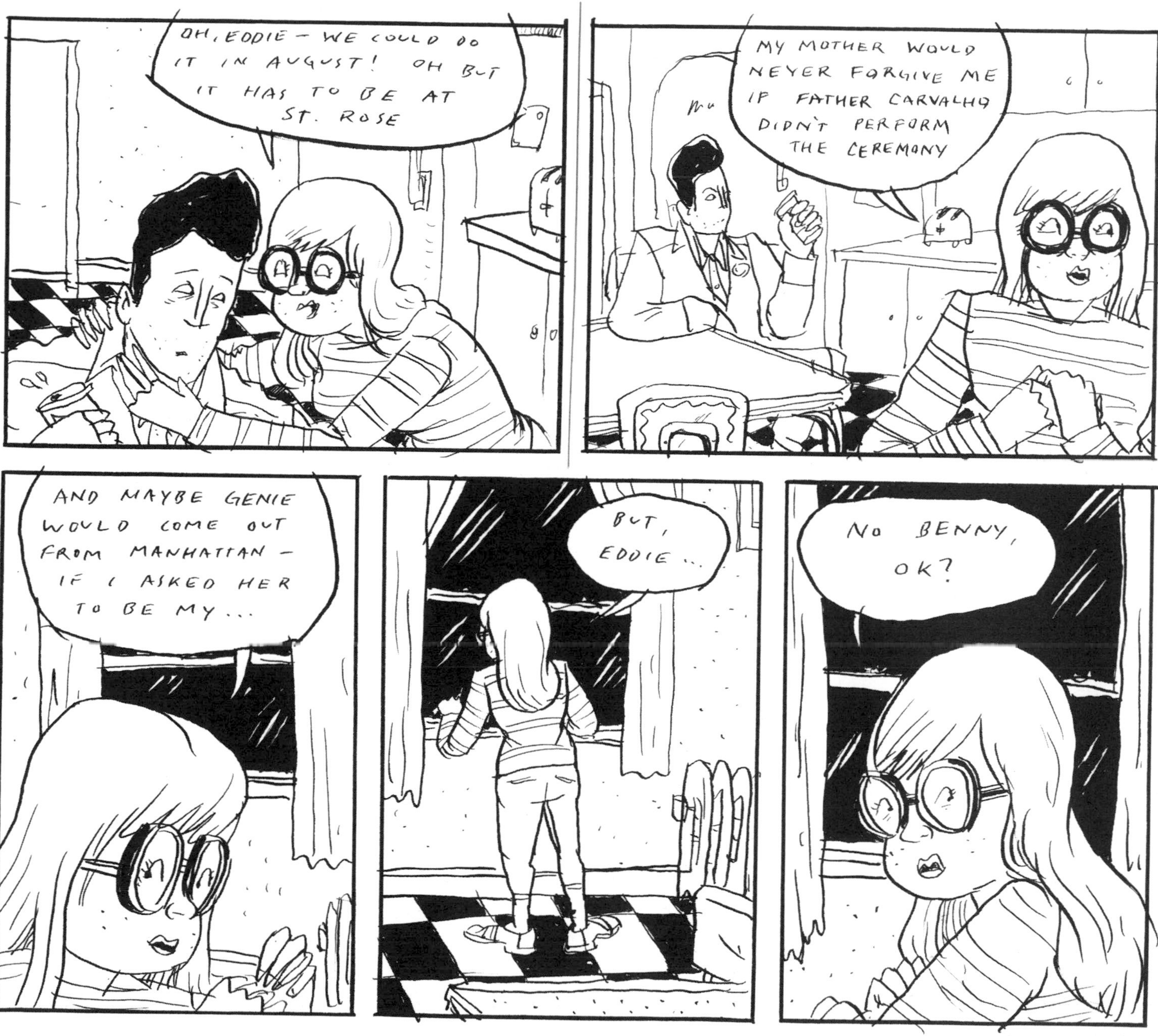
OH, EDDIE – WE COULD DO IT IN AUGUST! OH BUT IT HAS TO BE AT ST. ROSE
MY MOTHER WOULD NEVER FORGIVE ME IF FATHER CARVALHO DIDN'T PERFORM THE CEREMONY
AND MAYBE GENIE WOULD COME OUT FROM MANHATTAN – IF I ASKED HER TO BE MY...
BUT, EDDIE...
NO BENNY, OK?

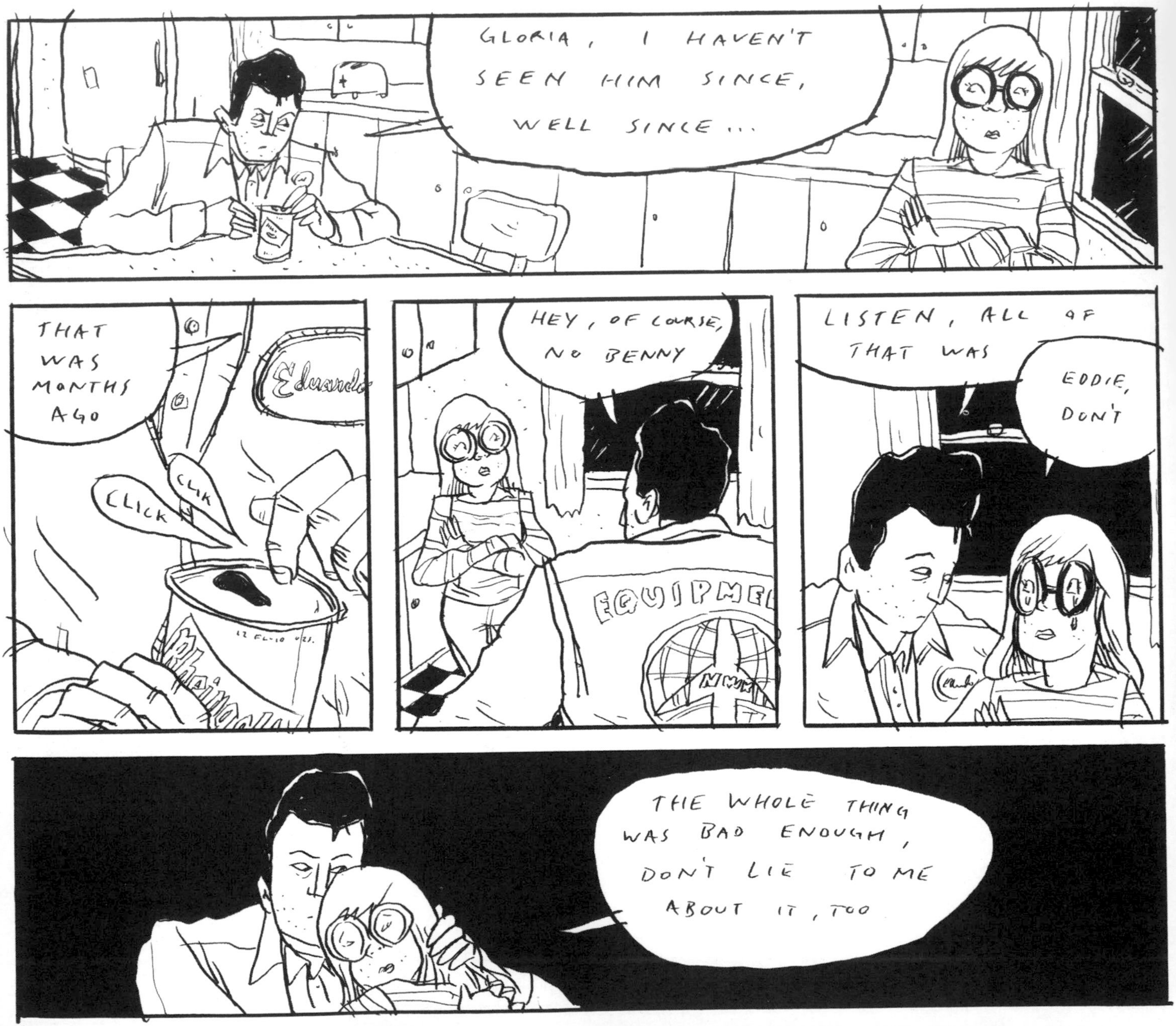
GLORIA, I HAVEN'T SEEN HIM SINCE, WELL SINCE...
THAT WAS MONTHS AGO
CLICK
CLIK
Eduardo
HEY, OF COURSE, NO BENNY
EQUIPME
LISTEN, ALL OF THAT WAS
EDDIE, DON'T
THE WHOLE THING WAS BAD ENOUGH, DON'T LIE TO ME ABOUT IT, TOO

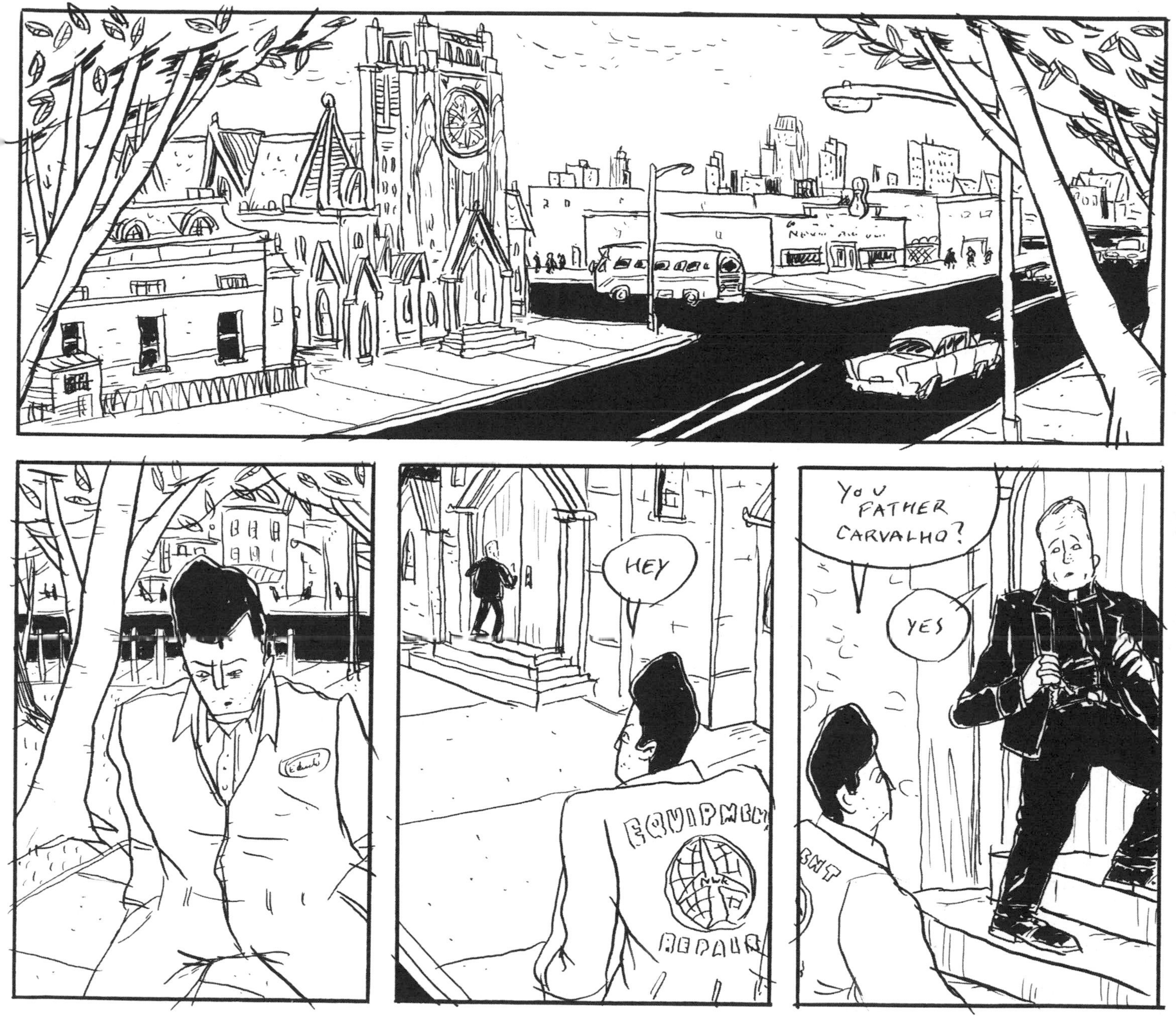
EQUIPMENT
REPAIR
HEY
YOU FATHER CARVALHO?
YES

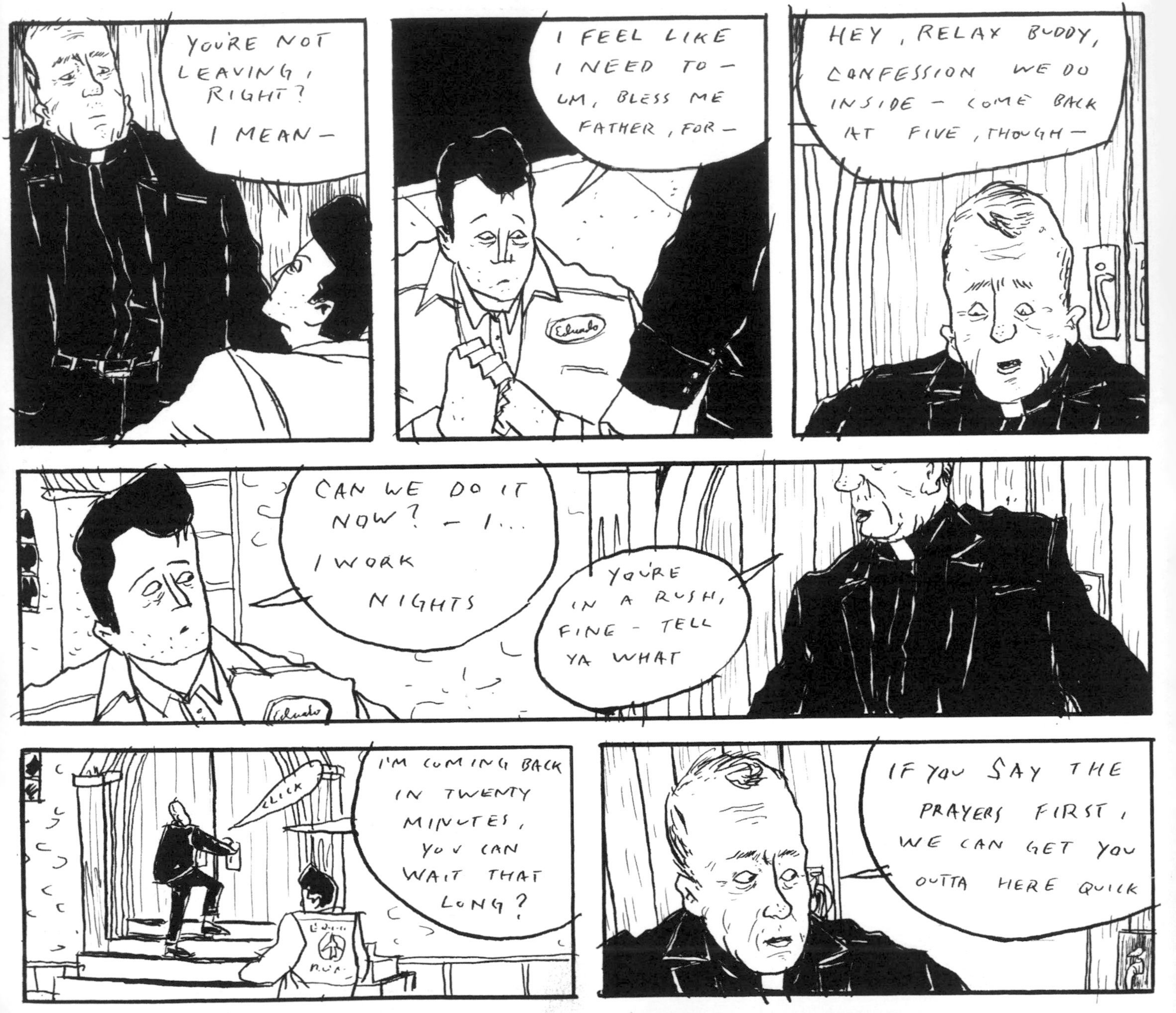
YOU'RE NOT LEAVING, RIGHT? I MEAN—
I FEEL LIKE I NEED TO— UM, BLESS ME FATHER, FOR—
HEY, RELAX BUDDY, CONFESSION WE DO INSIDE — COME BACK AT FIVE, THOUGH—
CAN WE DO IT NOW? — I... I WORK NIGHTS
YOU'RE IN A RUSH, FINE — TELL YA WHAT
CLICK
I'M COMING BACK IN TWENTY MINUTES, YOU CAN WAIT THAT LONG?
IF YOU SAY THE PRAYERS FIRST, WE CAN GET YOU OUTTA HERE QUICK

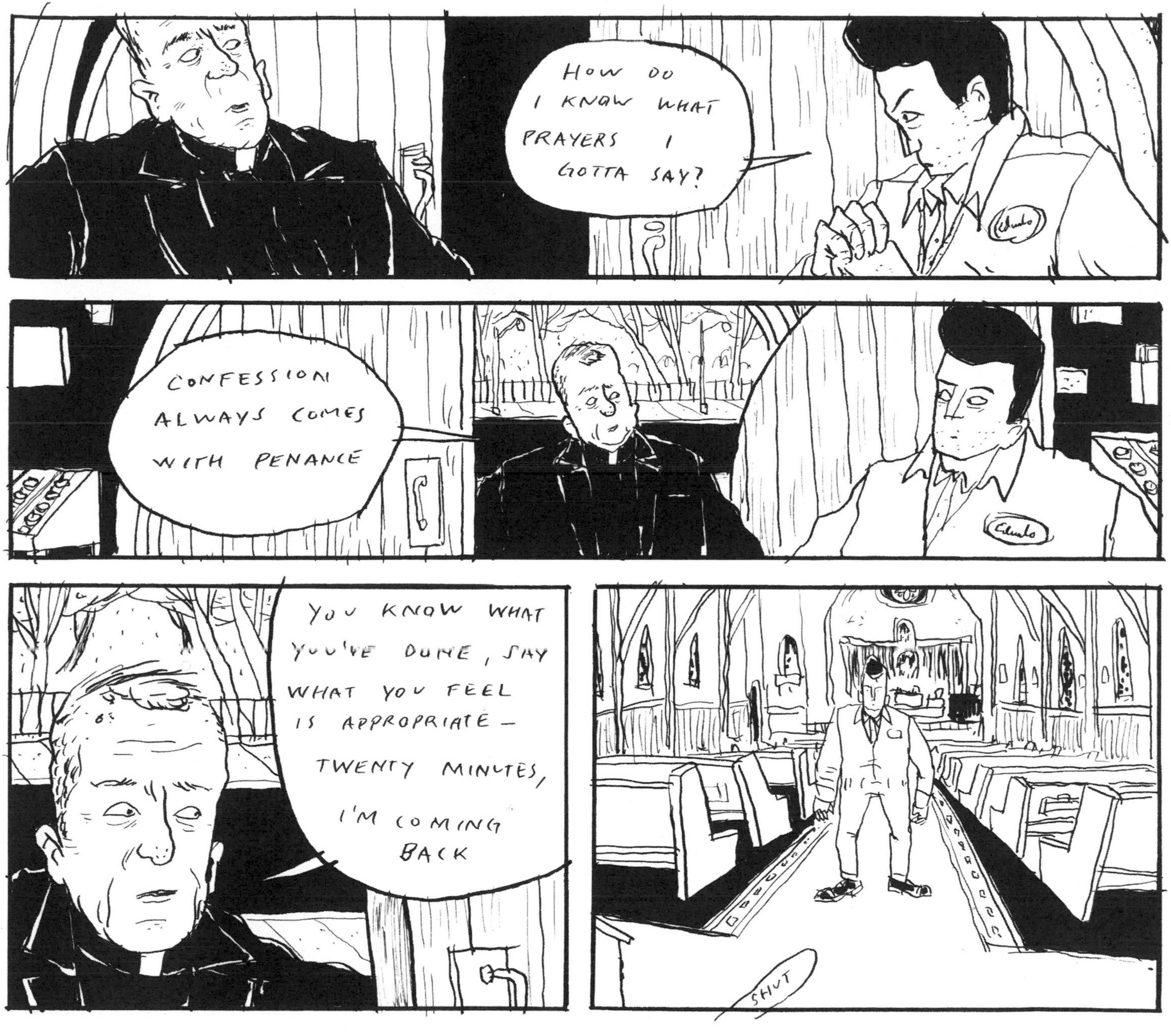
HOW DO I KNOW WHAT PRAYERS I GOTTA SAY?
CONFESSION ALWAYS COMES WITH PENANCE
YOU KNOW WHAT YOU'VE DONE, SAY WHAT YOU FEEL IS APPROPRIATE — TWENTY MINUTES, I'M COMING BACK
SHUT

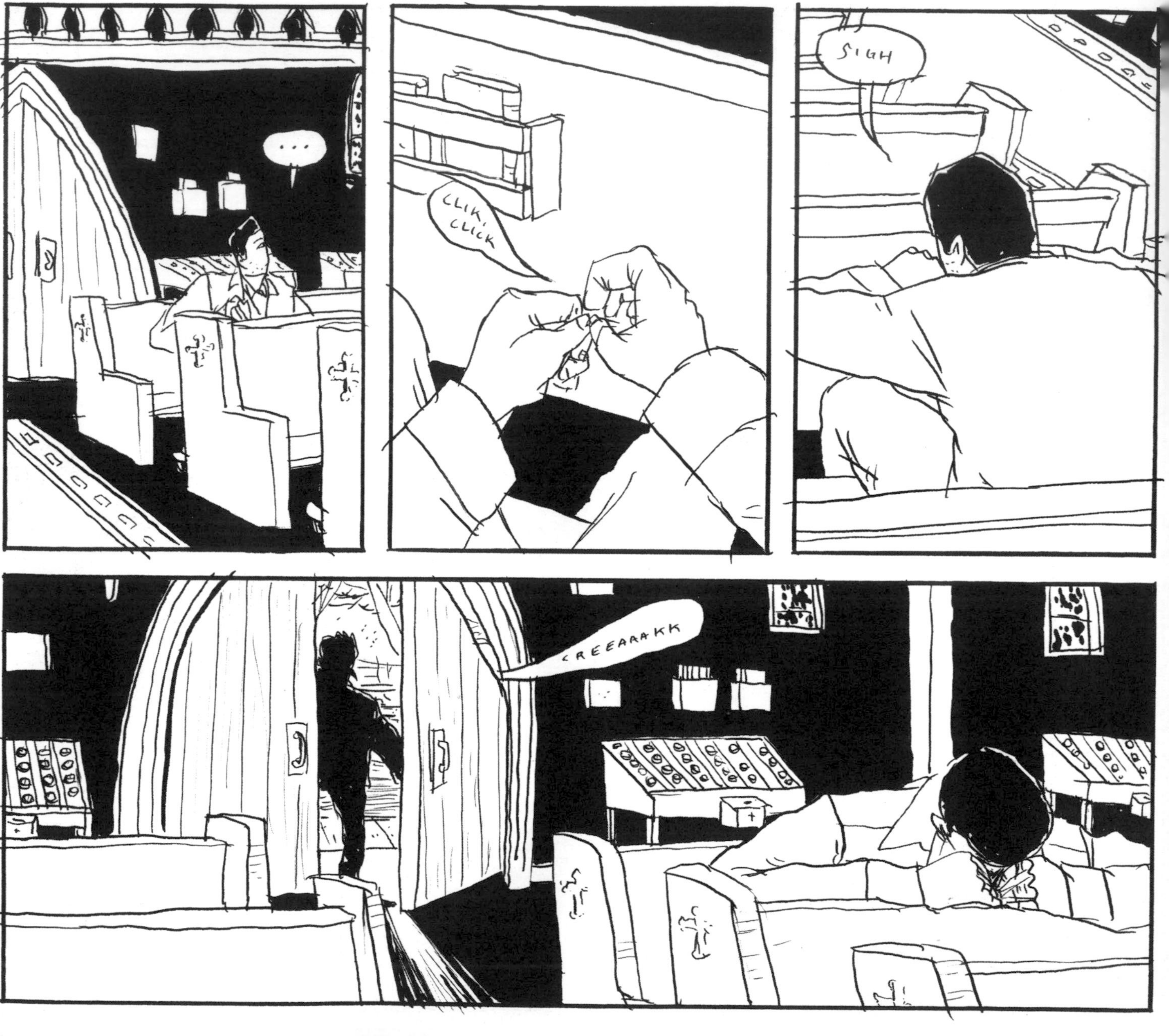
...
CLIK, CLICK
SIGH
CREEAAAKK

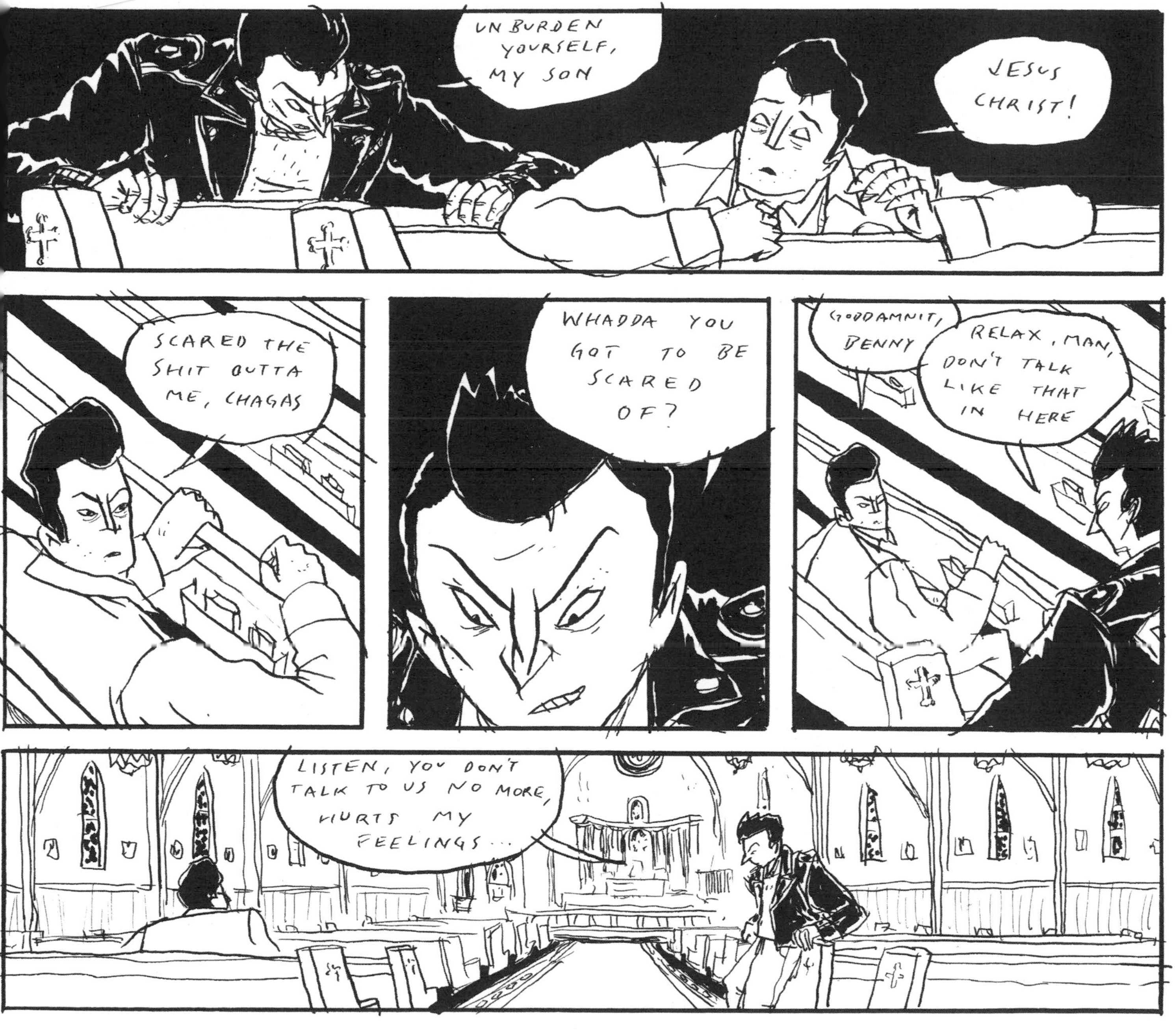
UNBURDEN YOURSELF, MY SON
JESUS CHRIST!
SCARED THE SHIT OUTTA ME, CHAGAS
WHADDA YOU GOT TO BE SCARED OF?
GODDAMNIT, DENNY
RELAX, MAN, DON'T TALK LIKE THAT IN HERE
LISTEN, YOU DON'T TALK TO US NO MORE, HURTS MY FEELINGS...

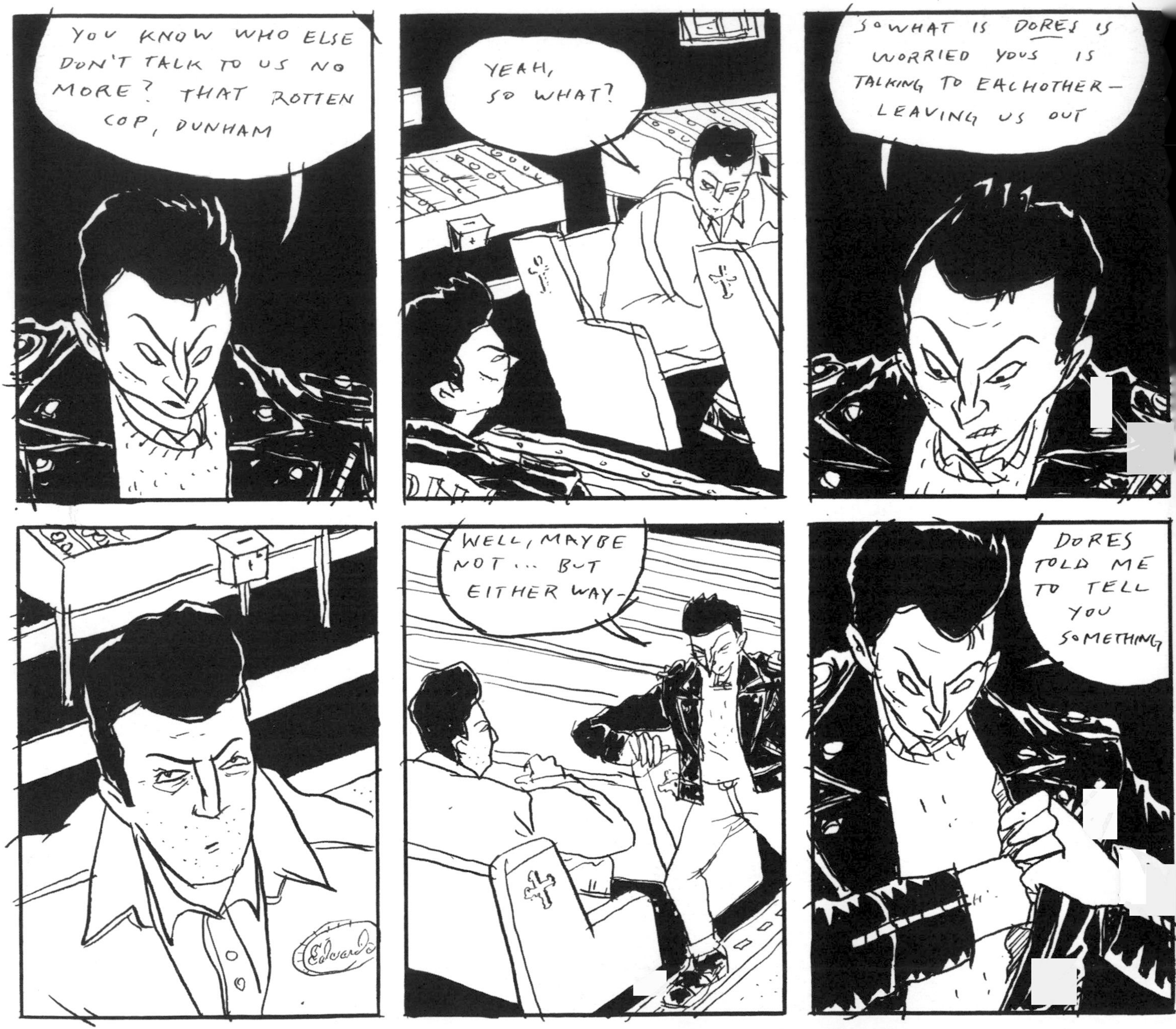
YOU KNOW WHO ELSE DON'T TALK TO US NO MORE? THAT ROTTEN COP, DUNHAM
YEAH, SO WHAT?
SO WHAT IS DORES IS WORRIED YOUS IS TALKING TO EACHOTHER— LEAVING US OUT
WELL, MAYBE NOT... BUT EITHER WAY—
DORES TOLD ME TO TELL YOU SOMETHING

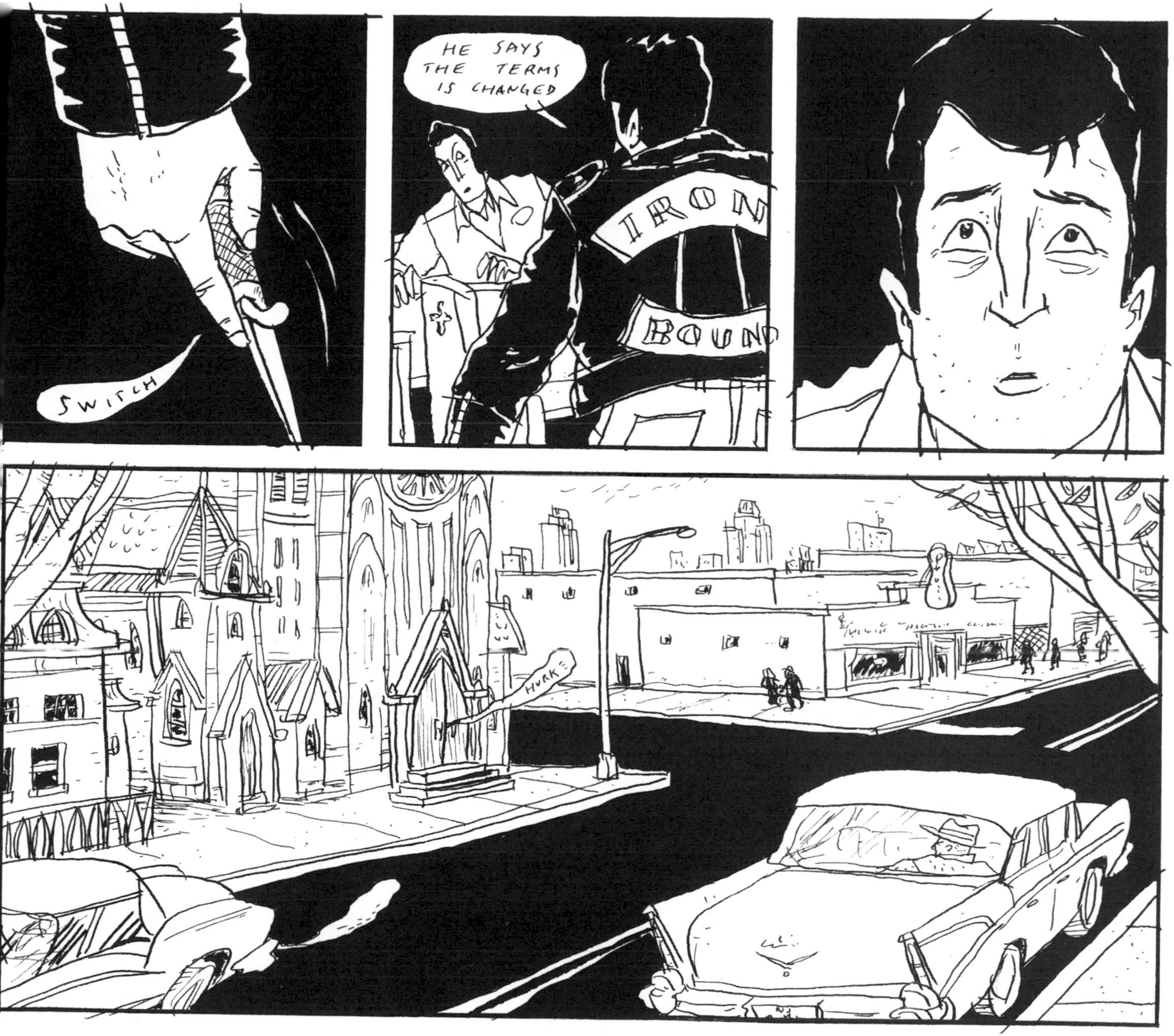
SWITCH
HE SAYS THE TERMS IS CHANGED
IRON
BOUND
HURK

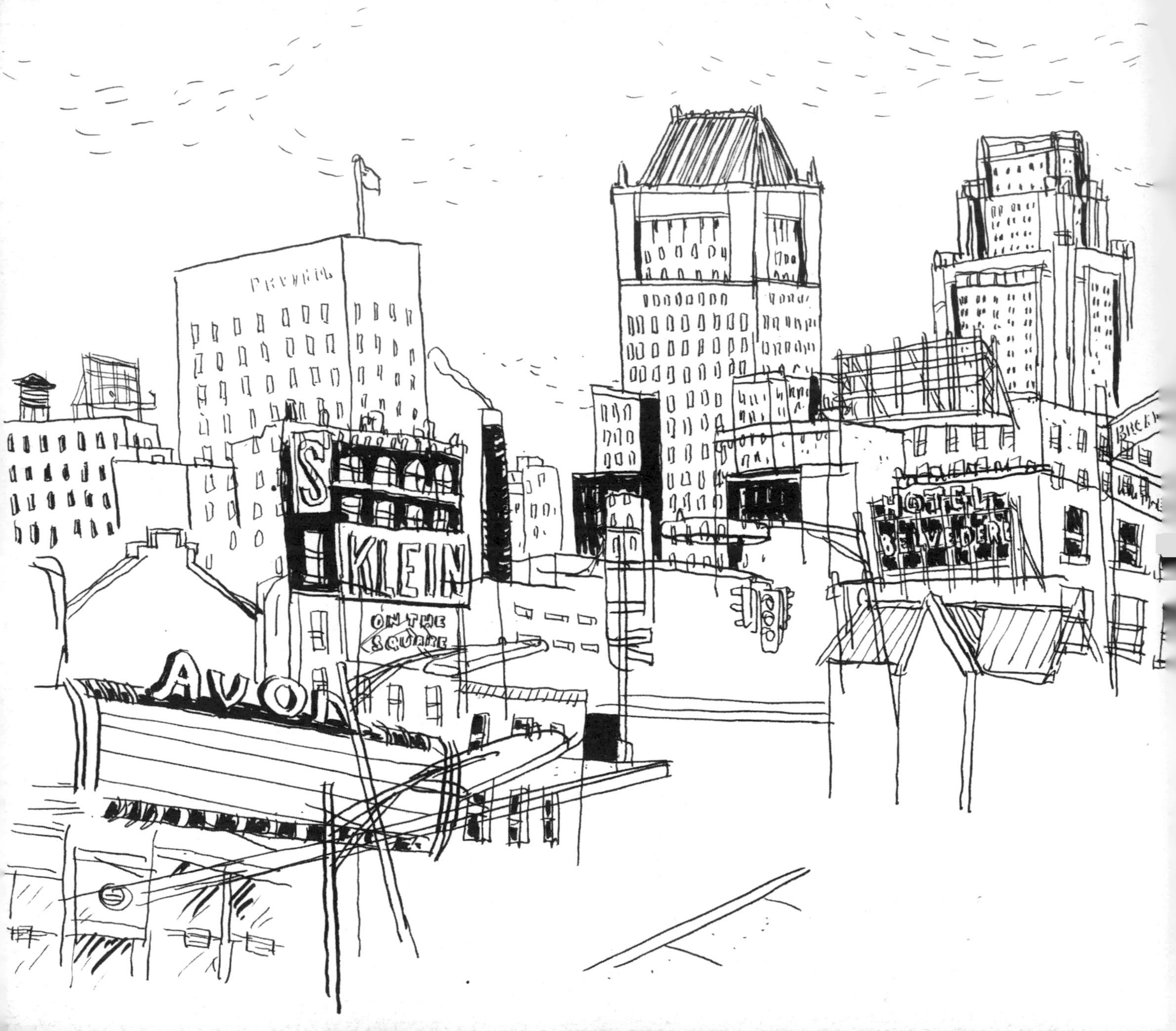
KLEIN
ON THE
SQUARE
HOTEL
BELVEDERE

SINCERE THANKS TO EVERYONE WHO HELPED (OR HAD TO DEAL WITH ME) DURING THE WRITING AND DRAWING OF THIS BOOK.

ESPECIALLY:

LEON, BARRY, LUCAS, JEN, ANDREW, JONATHAN B, ANNE, KELLEY, OMER, NATE, JOSH, JONATHAN FV, MIKE, SEAN, AARON, ROB, PAUL, JONNY, GENE, GLORIA, EUGENIA, DAVE, CAITLIN, MOM, DAD, AND (FOR EVERYTHING, ALWAYS) BARBARA JEAN.

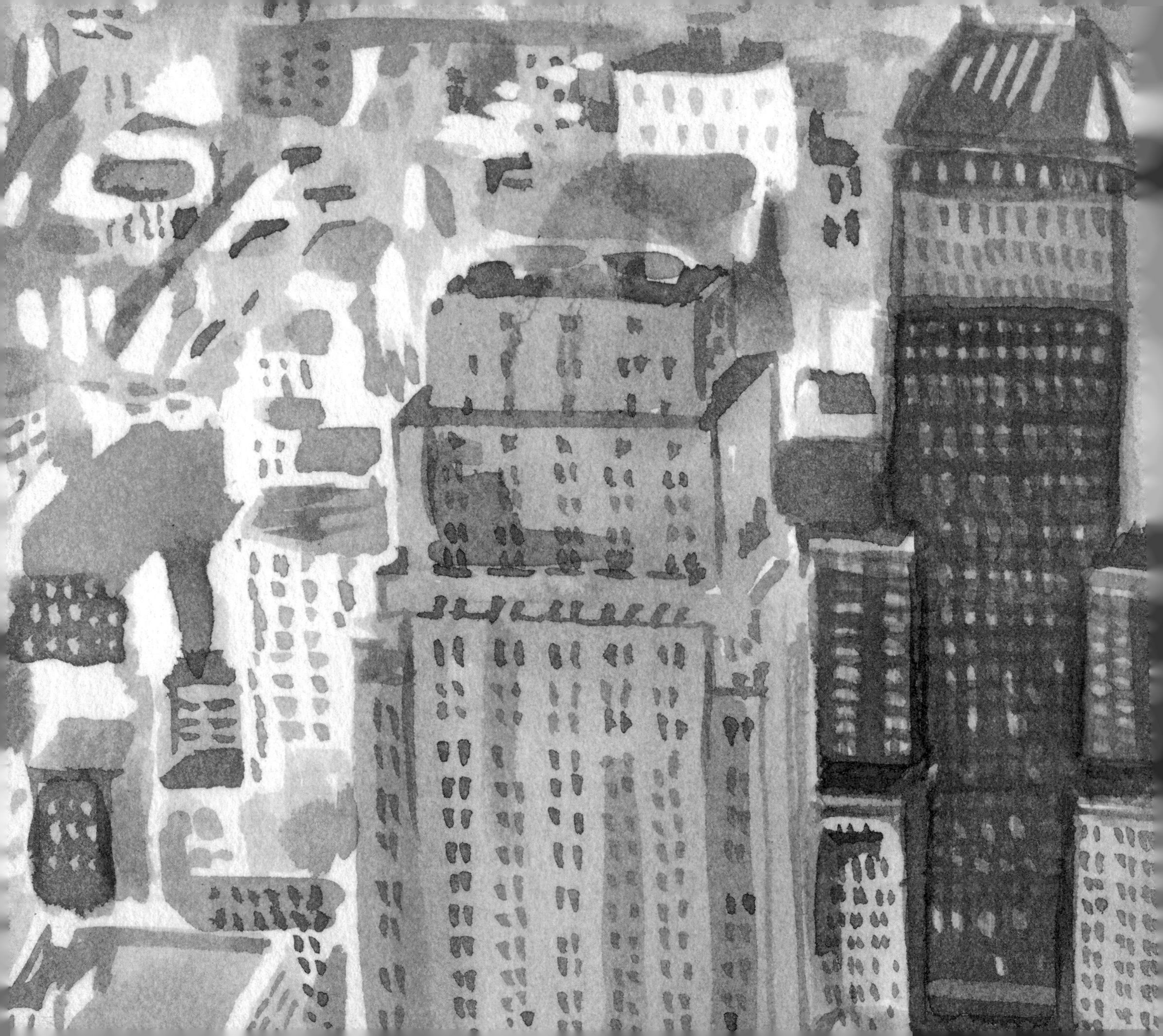